BOOKS BY HARRY TURTLEDOVE
The Guns of the South

THE WORLDWAR SAGA
Worldwar: In the Balance
Worldwar: Tilting the Balance
Worldwar: Upsetting the Balance
Worldwar: Striking the Balance

COLONIZATION
Colonization: Second Contact
Colonization: Down to Earth
Colonization: Aftershocks

Homeward Bound

THE VIDESSOS CYCLE
The Misplaced Legion
An Emperor for the Legion
The Legion of Videssos
Swords of the Legion

THE TALE OF KRISPOS
Krispos Rising
Krispos of Videssos
Krispos the Emperor

THE TIME OF TROUBLES SERIES
The Stolen Throne
Hammer and Anvil
The Thousand Cities
Videssos Besieged

Noninterference
Kaleidoscope
A World of Difference
Earthgrip
Departures

How Few Remain

THE GREAT WAR
The Great War: American Front
The Great War: Walk in Hell
The Great War: Breakthroughs

American Empire: Blood and Iron
American Empire: The Center Cannot Hold
American Empire: The Victorious Opposition

Settling Accounts: Return Engagement
Settling Accounts: Drive to the East

Settling Accounts: Drive to the East

HARRY TURTLEDOVE

SETTLING ACCOUNTS: DRIVE TO THE EAST

DEL REY

BALLANTINE BOOKS

NEW YORK

Copyright © 2005 by Harry Turtledove

Published in the United States by Del Rey Books,
an imprint of The Random House Publishing Group,
a division of Random House, Inc., New York.

DEL REY is a registered trademark and the Del Rey colophon
is a trademark of Random House, Inc.

ISBN 0-345-45724-2

Printed in the United States of America

Settling Accounts: Drive to the East

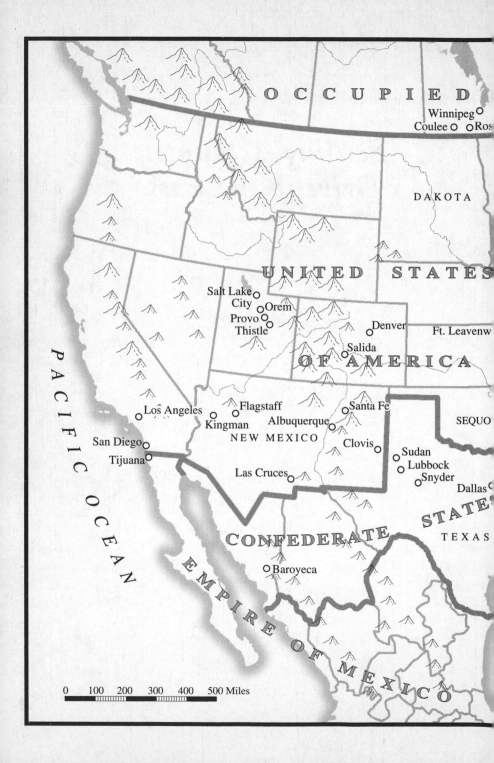

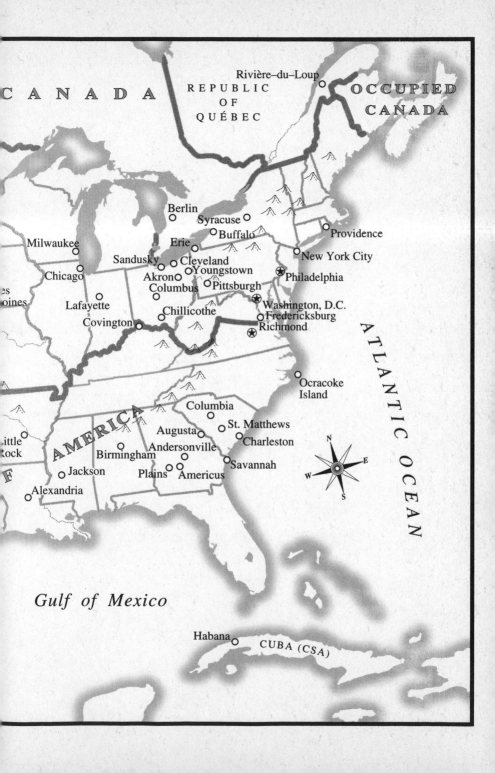

I

Every antiaircraft gun in Richmond seemed to thunder at once. The sky above the capital of the Confederate States filled with black puffs of smoke. Jake Featherston, the President of the CSA, had heard that his aviators called those bursts nigger-baby flak. They did look something like black dolls—and they were as dangerous as blacks in the Confederacy, too.

U.S. airplanes didn't usually come over Richmond by daylight, any more than Confederate aircraft usually raided Washington or Philadelphia or New York City when the sun was in the sky. Antiaircraft fire and aggressive fighter patrols had quickly made daylight bombing more expensive than it was worth. The night was the time when bombers droned overhead.

Today, the United States was making an exception. That they were, surprised Jake very little. Two nights before, Confederate bombers had killed U.S. President Al Smith. They hadn't done it on purpose. Trying to hit one particular man or one particular building in a city like Philadelphia, especially at night, was like going after a needle in a haystack with your eyes closed. Try or not, though, they'd flattened Powel House, the President of the USA's Philadelphia residence, and smashed the bomb shelter beneath it. Vice President La Follette was Vice President no more.

Featherston wasn't sure he would have deliberately killed Al Smith if he'd had the chance. After all, he'd hornswoggled a plebiscite on Kentucky and the part of west Texas the USA had called Houston and

Sequoyah out of Smith, and triumphantly welcomed the first two back into the Confederacy. But he'd expected Smith to go right on yielding to him, and the son of a bitch hadn't done it. Smith hadn't taken the peace proposal Featherston offered him after Confederate armor sliced through Ohio to Lake Erie, either. Even though the USA remained cut in two, the country also remained very much in the war. The struggle wasn't as sharp and short and easy as Jake had hoped.

So maybe Al Smith was better off dead. Maybe. How could you tell? Like any Vice President, Charlie La Follette was the very definition of an unknown quantity.

But it was only natural for the United States to try to take revenge. Kill our President, will you? We'll kill yours!

U.S. Wright-27 fighters, no doubt diverted from shooting up Confederate positions near the Rappahannock, escorted the bombers and danced a dance of death with C.S. Hound Dogs. Level bombers, two- and four-engined, rained explosives down on Richmond.

With them, though, came a squadron of dive bombers, airplanes not usually seen in attacks on cities. To Jake's admittedly biased way of thinking, the CSA had the best dive bomber in the world in the Mule, otherwise known on both sides of the front as the Asskicker. But its U.S. counterparts were also up to the job they had to do.

That job, here, was to pound the crap out of the Confederate Presidential residence up on Shockoe Hill. The building was often called the Gray House, after the U.S. White House. If the flak over Richmond as a whole was heavy, that over the Gray House was heavier still. Half a dozen guns stood on the Gray House grounds alone. If an airplane was hit, it seemed as if a pilot could walk on shell bursts all the way to the ground. He couldn't, of course, but it seemed that way.

A dive bomber took a direct hit and exploded in midair, adding a huge smear of flame and smoke to the already crowded sky. Another, trailing fire from the engine cowling back toward the cockpit, smashed into the ground a few blocks away from the mansion. A greasy pillar of thick black smoke marked the pilot's pyre.

Another bomber was hit, and another. The rest bored in on their target. Back before the Great War started in 1914, lots of Confederates believed the Yankees were not only enemies but cowardly enemies. They'd learned better, to their cost. The pilots in these U.S. machines were as brave and as skilled as the men the CSA put in the air.

Yet another dive bomber blew up, this one only a few hundred feet above the Gray House. Flaming wreckage fell all around, and even on, the Presidential residence. The survivors did what they were supposed to do. One after another, they released their bombs, pulled out of their dives, and scurried back towards U.S.-held territory as fast as they could go.

No antiaircraft defenses could block that kind of attack. The Gray House flew to pieces like an anthill kicked by a giant's boot. Some of the wreckage flew up, not out. The damnyankees must have loaded armor-piercing bombs into some of their bombers. If Jake Featherston took refuge in the shelter under the museum, they aimed to blow him to hell and gone anyway.

But Jake wasn't in the Gray House or in the shelter under it.

Jake wasn't within a mile of the Gray House, in fact. As soon as he heard Al Smith was dead, Jake had ordered the Presidential residence evacuated. He'd done it quietly; making a fuss about it would have tipped off the damnyankees that he wasn't where they wanted him to be. At the moment, he was holed up in a none too fancy hotel about a mile west of Capitol Square. His bodyguards kept screaming at him to get his ass down to the basement, but he wanted to watch the show. It beat the hell out of Fourth of July fireworks.

Saul Goldman didn't scream. The C.S. Director of Communications was both more restrained and smarter than that. He said, "Mr. President, *please* take cover. If a bomb falls on you here, the United States win, just the same as if you'd stayed up on Shockoe Hill. The country needs you. Stay safe."

Jake eyed the pudgy, gray-haired little Jew with something that was for a moment not far from hatred. *He* ran the Confederate States, ran them more nearly absolutely than any previous North American ruler had run his country—and that included all the goddamn useless Maximilians in the Empire of Mexico. Nobody could tell him what to do, nobody at all. Saul hadn't tried, unlike the Freedom Party guards who'd bellowed at him. No, Saul had done far worse than that. He'd talked sense.

"All right, dammit," Featherston said peevishly, and withdrew. He affected not to hear the sighs of relief from everyone around him.

Sitting down in the basement was as bad as he'd known it would be. He despised doing nothing. He despised having to do nothing. He wanted to be up there hitting back at his enemies, or else hitting them first and hitting them so hard, they couldn't hit back at him. He'd tried to do that to the United States. The first blow hadn't quite knocked them out. The next one . . . He vowed the next one would.

Catching his foul mood, Goldman said, "Don't worry about it, Mr. President. When you go on the wireless and let the United States know you're still here, that will hurt them worse than losing a big city."

Again, the Director of Communications made sense. Jake found himself nodding, whether he wanted to or not. "Well, you're right," he said. "They can't afford to come after me like that all the time. They won't have any airplanes or pilots left if they do, on account of we'll blow 'em all to hell and gone." He pointed to Goldman. "Make sure there's a studio waiting for me just as soon as these Yankee bastards let up, Saul."

"I'll see to it, sir," Goldman promised.

He was as good as his word, too. He always was. That by itself made him somebody to cherish. Most people did what they could and gave excuses for the rest. Saul Goldman did what he said he'd do. So did Jake himself. People hadn't believed him. He'd taken more than sixteen years, a lot of them lean and hungry, to get to the top. Now that he'd arrived, he was doing just what he'd told folks he would. Some people had the nerve to act surprised. Hadn't they been listening, dammit?

An armored limousine took him to a studio. Nothing short of a direct hit by a bomb would make this baby blink. Jake had already survived two assassination attempts, not counting this latest one from the USA. Except when his blood was up, the way it had been during the air raid, he didn't believe in taking unnecessary chances.

By now, sitting down in front of a microphone was second nature to him. He'd been a jump ahead of the Whigs and Radical Liberals in figuring out what wireless could do for a politician, and he still used it better than anybody else in the CSA or the USA. Having Saul Goldman on his side helped. He knew that. But he had himself on his side, too, and he was his own best advertisement.

In the room next door, the engineer held up one finger—one minute till airtime. Jake waved back at the glass square set into the wall between the rooms to show he'd got the message. He always acknowledged the competence of people like engineers. They did their jobs so he could do his. He took one last look around. There wasn't much to see. Except for that glass square, the walls and ceiling of the studio were covered in what looked like cardboard egg cartons that helped deaden unwanted noise and echoes.

The engineer pointed to him. The red light above the square of glass came on. He leaned toward the microphone. "I'm Jake Featherston," he said, "and I'm here to tell you the truth." His voice was a harsh rasp. It wasn't the usual broadcaster's voice, any more than his rawboned, craggy face was conventionally handsome. But it grabbed attention and it held attention, and who could ask for more than that? Nobody, not in the wireless business.

"Truth is, I'm still here," he went on after his trademark greeting. "The Yankees dropped bombs on the Gray House, but I'm still here. They threw away God only knows how many airplanes, but I'm still here. They wasted God only knows how much money, but I'm still here. They murdered God only knows how many innocent women and children, but I'm still here. They've thrown God only knows how many soldiers at Richmond, but I'm still here—and they're not. They've had God only knows how many fine young men, who could've gone on and done other things, shot and gassed and blown to pieces, but I'm still here. They've had God only knows how many barrels smashed to scrap metal, but I'm still here. They've given guns to our niggers and taught 'em to rise up against the white man, but I'm still here. And let them try whatever else they want to try. I've taken it all, and I'll take some more, on account of I'm—still—here."

The red light went out. Behind the glass, the engineer applauded. Jake grinned at him. He didn't think he'd ever seen that before. He raised his hands over his head, fingers interlaced, like a victorious prize-fighter. The engineer applauded harder.

When Jake came out of the studio, Saul Goldman stood in the hall with eyes shining behind his glasses. "That . . . that was outstanding, Mr. President," he said. "Outstanding."

"Yeah, I thought it went pretty well," Featherston said. Around most people, he bragged and swaggered. Goldman, by contrast, could make him modest.

"No one in the United States will have any doubts," Goldman said. "No one in the Confederate States will, either."

"That's what it's all about," Jake said. "I don't want anybody to have any doubts about what I've got in mind. I aim to make the Confederate States the grandest country on this continent. I aim to do that, and by God I'm going to do that." Even Saul Goldman, who'd heard it all before, and heard it times uncounted, nodded as if it were fresh and new.

A ship of his own! Sam Carsten had never dreamt of that, not when he joined the Navy in 1909. He'd never dreamt of becoming an officer at all, but he wore a lieutenant's two broad gold stripes on each sleeve of his jacket. The *Josephus Daniels* wasn't a battlewagon or an airplane carrier—nothing of the sort. The U.S. Navy called her a destroyer escort; in the Royal Navy, she would have been a frigate. She could do a little bit of everything: escort convoys of merchantmen and hunt submersibles that menaced them, lay mines if she had to (though she wasn't specialized for that), bombard a coast (though that was asking for trouble if airplanes were anywhere close by), and shoot torpedoes and her pair of four-inch popguns at enemy ships. She was all his—306 feet, 220 men.

Commander Cressy, the *Remembrance*'s executive officer, had been surprised when he got her—surprised, but pleased. Sam's own exec was a lieutenant, junior grade, just over half his age, a redheaded, freckle-faced go-getter named Pat Cooley. Cooley was probably headed for big things—he was almost bound to be if the war and its quick promotions lasted . . . and if he lived, of course. Carsten knew that he himself, as a mustang, had gone about as far as he could go. He could hope for lieutenant commander. He could, he supposed, dream of commander— as long as he remembered he was dreaming. Considering where he'd started, he had had a hell of a career.

Cooley looked around with a smile on his face. "Feels like spring, doesn't it, Captain?"

Captain. Sam knew he couldn't even dream about getting a fourth stripe. But he was, by God, captain of the *Josephus Daniels*. "Always feels like spring in San Diego," he answered. "August, November, March—doesn't make much difference."

"Yes, sir," the exec said. "Another three weeks and we'll have the genuine article."

"Uh-huh." Sam nodded. "We'll think it's summer by then, I expect, cruising off the coast of Baja California."

"Got to let the damn greasers know they picked the wrong side— again," Cooley said.

"Uh-huh," Sam repeated. The Empire of Mexico and the Confederate States had been bosom buddies ever since the Second Mexican War. There was a certain irony in that, since Mexican royalty came from the same line as the Austro-Hungarian Emperors, and Austria-Hungary lined up with Germany and the USA. But Confederate independence and Confederate friendship with the first Maximilian had kept the USA from invoking the Monroe Doctrine—had effectively shot the Doctrine right between the eyes. The Emperors of Mexico remembered that and forgot who their ancestors had been.

Pat Cooley was the one who took the *Josephus Daniels* out of San Diego harbor. Sam knew damn near everything there was to know about gunnery and damage control. His shiphandling skills were, at the moment, as near nonexistent as made no difference. He intended to remedy that. He was and always had been a conscientious man, a plugger. He went forward one step at a time, and it wasn't always a big step, either. But he *did* go forward, never back.

Three other destroyer escorts and a light cruiser made up the flotilla that would pay a call on Baja California. Sam could have wished they had some air support. Hell, he did wish it. He'd heard that a swarm of light carriers—converted from merchantman hulls—were abuilding. He hoped like anything that was true. True or not, though, the light carriers weren't in action yet.

He smeared zinc-oxide ointment on his nose, his cheeks, and the backs of his hands. Freckled Pat Cooley didn't laugh at all. Sam was very blond and very fair. Even this early impression of San Diego spring was plenty to make him burn. He offered Cooley the tinfoil tube.

"No, thank you, sir," the exec said. "I've got my own." He'd start to bake just about as fast as Carsten did.

The long swells of the Pacific, swells all the way down from the Gulf of Alaska, raised the destroyer escort and then lowered her. She rolled a few degrees in the process. Here and there, a sailor ran for the rail and gave back his breakfast. Sam smiled at that. His hide was weak, but he had a strong stomach.

He took the wheel when they were out on the open sea. Feeling the whole ship not just through the soles of his feet but also through his hands was quite something. He frowned in concentration, the tip of his tongue peeping out, as he kept station, zigzagging with his companions.

"You're doing fine, sir," Cooley said encouragingly. "Ask you something?"

"Go ahead." Sam watched the compass as he changed course.

"Ease it back just a little—you don't want to overcorrect," Cooley said, and then, "How bad are things over in the Sandwich Islands?"

"Well, they sure as hell aren't good." Sam did ease it back. "With no carriers over there right now, we're in a bad way." He remembered swimming from the mortally damaged *Remembrance* to the destroyer that plucked him from the warm Pacific, remembered watching the airplane carrier on which he'd served so long slide beneath the waves, and remembered the tears streaming down his face when she did.

Cooley frowned. "We've got plenty of our own airplanes on the main islands. We should be able to make the Japs sorry if they come poking their noses down there, right?"

"As long as we can keep 'em in fuel and such, sure," Carsten answered. "But the islands—Oahu, mostly—just sit there, and the Japs' carriers can go wherever they want. There's a gap about halfway between here and the islands that we can't cover very well from the mainland or from Honolulu. If the Japs start smashing up our supply convoys, we've got big trouble, because the Sandwich Islands get damn near everything from the West Coast."

"We ought to have airplanes with longer range," the exec said.

"Yeah." Sam couldn't say the same thing hadn't occurred to him. It had probably occurred to every Navy man who'd ever thought about the question. "Only trouble is, that's the *one* place where we need 'em. The Confederate States are right next door, so the designers concentrated on guns and bomb load instead. Before the war, I don't think anybody figured we'd lose Midway and give the Japs a base that far east."

Cooley's laugh was anything but amused. "Surprise!" He cocked his head to one side and studied Sam. "You think about this stuff, don't you?"

Commander Cressy had said almost the same thing in almost the same bemused tone of voice. Like Cressy—who was now a captain— Cooley came out of the Naval Academy. Finding a mustang with a working brain seemed to have perplexed both of them. Cooley had to be more careful about how he showed it: Sam outranked him.

Shrugging, Sam said, "If you guess along, you're less likely to get caught with your skivvies down. Oh, you will some of the time—it comes with the territory—but you're less likely to. The more you know, the better off you are."

"Uh-*huh*," Cooley said. It wasn't disagreement. It was more on the order of, *Well*, you're *not what I thought you were going to be.*

The first Mexican town below the border had a name that translated as Aunt Jane. In peacetime, it was a popular liberty port. The handful of Mexican police didn't give a damn what American sailors did—this side of arson or gunplay, anyhow. If you couldn't come back to your ship with a hangover and a dose of the clap, you weren't half trying.

But it wasn't peacetime now. The Mexicans hadn't built a proper coast-defense battery to try to protect poor old Aunt Jane's honor. What point, when overwhelming U.S. firepower from across the border could smash up almost any prepared position? The greasers *had* brought in a few three-inch pieces to tell the U.S. Navy to keep its distance. Some of them opened up on the flotilla.

Sam called the *Josephus Daniels* to general quarters. He laughed to himself as the klaxons hooted. This was the first time he hadn't had to run like hell to take his battle station. Here he was on the bridge, right where he belonged.

The Mexicans' fire fell at least half a mile short. Columns of water leaped into the air as shells splashed into the Pacific. Sailors seeing their first action exclaimed at how big those columns were. That made Sam want to laugh again. He'd seen the great gouts of water near misses from fourteen-inch shells kicked up. Next to those, these might have been mice pissing beside elephants.

"Let's return fire, Mr. Cooley," Sam said.

"Aye aye, sir." The exec relayed the order to the gun turrets. Both four-inchers—nothing even slightly fancy themselves: not even secondary armament on a capital ship—swung toward the shore. They fired almost together. At the recoil, the *Josephus Daniels* heeled slightly to starboard. She recovered almost at once. The guns roared again and again.

Shells began bursting around the places where muzzle flashes revealed the Mexican guns. The other members of the flotilla were firing, too. The bigger cannons on the ships could reach the shore, even if the guns on shore couldn't touch the ships. Through binoculars, Sam could easily tell the difference between bursts from the four-inch guns on the destroyer escorts and the light cruiser's six-inchers.

Plucky if outranged, the Mexicans defiantly shot back. "I wouldn't do that," Cooley said. "It just tells us we haven't knocked 'em out. Now more'll come down on their heads."

"They're making a point, I suppose." Sam peered through the binoculars again. "Our gunnery needs work. I'd say that's true for every ship here. I can't do anything about the others, but by God I can fix things on this one."

"Uh, yes, sir." Cooley looked at him, plainly wondering whether he knew any more about that than he did about conning a ship.

Sam grinned back. "Son, I was handling a five-inch gun on the *Dakota* about the time you were a gleam in your old man's eye."

"Oh." The exec blushed between his freckles. "All right, sir." He grinned, too. "Teach me to keep my mouth shut—and I hardly even opened it."

One of the bursts on shore was conspicuously bigger than the others had been. "There we go!" Sam said. "Some of their ammo just went up. I don't know whether they've got real dumps there or we hit a limber, but we nailed 'em pretty good either way."

"Blew some gunners to hell and gone either way, too," Cooley said.

"That's the point of it," Carsten agreed. "They won't care if we rearrange the landscape. After they bury José and Pedro—if they can find enough of 'em left *to* bury—they'll get the idea that we can hurt them worse than they can hurt us. It's about people, Pat. It's always about people."

"Uh, yes, sir," Pat Cooley said again. This time, it wasn't doubt in his eyes as he looked Sam over: it was bemusement again. Sam laughed inside himself. *No, the mustang isn't quite what you figured on, eh, kid?*

The light cruiser's skipper didn't choose to linger to continue the one-sided gun duel. The flotilla steamed south. Sam hoped the Mexicans didn't have anything more up their sleeves than what they'd already shown.

For *you, the war is over.* The Confederate officer who took Major Jonathan Moss prisoner after his fighter got shot down over Virginia had sounded like an actor mouthing a screenwriter's lines in a bad film about the Great War. The only thing that had kept Moss from telling him so was that the son of a bitch was likely right.

Moss strolled near the barbed-wire perimeter of a prisoner-of-war camp outside the little town of Andersonville, Georgia. He didn't get *too* close to the barbed wire. Inside it was a second perimeter, marked only by two-foot-high stakes with long, flimsy bands supported on top of them. The red dirt between the inner and outer perimeters was always rolled smooth so it would show footprints. The goons in the guard towers outside the barbed wire would open up with machine guns without warning if anybody presumed to set foot on that dead ground without permission.

Other officers—fliers and ground pounders both—also walked along the perimeter or through the camp. The only other thing to do was stay in the barracks, an even more depressing alternative. The Confederates had built them as cheaply and flimsily as the Geneva Convention allowed. No doubt U.S. accommodations for C.S. prisoners were every bit as shabby. Moss didn't care about that; he wasn't in a U.S. camp. What he did care about was that, when it rained here— which it did all too often—it rained almost as hard inside the barracks as it did outside.

Clouds were rolling in out of the northwest, which probably meant yet another storm was on the way. Moss looked down at his wrist to see what time it was. Then he muttered to himself. He'd been relieved of wristwatch and wallet shortly after his capture.

All things considered, it could have been worse. The food was lousy—grits and boiled greens and what the guards called fatback, a name that fit only too well—but there was enough of it. Meals were the high points of the day. Considering how dreary they were, that said nothing good about the rest of the time.

A captain came up to Moss. Nick Cantarella looked like what he was: a tough Italian kid out of New York City. "How ya doin'?" he asked.

Moss shrugged. "All things considered, I'd rather be in Philadelphia." He wasn't above stealing a line from one of the more inspired film comics he'd seen.

Chuckling, Cantarella said, "Yeah, this place makes Philly look good, and that's sayin' somethin'." He looked around. The guard in the closest tower was watching the two of them, but he couldn't hear a quiet conversation. No prisoners were in earshot, either. "It could happen one of these days."

"Could it?" Moss said eagerly.

"Could, I said." Cantarella left it at that, and trudged away with his head down and the collar of his leather jacket turned up.

However much Moss wanted to learn more, he kept quiet. Trying to know too much and learn too fast only made people in the Andersonville camp suspicious. Not all the inmates were prisoners: so Moss had been assured, anyhow. The United States and Confederate States were branches off the same trunk. They'd grown apart, but not that far apart. It wasn't impossible for a clever Confederate to impersonate a U.S. officer. No one here was trusted with anything important—indeed, with anything at all—till someone known to be reliable vouched for him. Till then, he was presumed to be talking to the guards.

That had made it harder for Moss to gain people's confidence. His squadron was fairly new in Maryland, and not many people fighting in the East knew him. Finally, another pilot shot down over Virginia proved to have flown with him in Ohio and Indiana, and also proved to be known to a couple of pilots already in the Andersonville camp. Once they'd assured their friends that Joe was legit, Joe could do the same for Moss.

So now he knew there were plans to stage an escape from the camp. That was all he knew about them. Details would come sooner or later. He had no idea whether he'd be on the list of prisoners chosen to disappear. He did think the breakout had a chance. Following Geneva Convention rules, the Confederates paid prisoners who were commissioned officers the same salary as they gave to men of equal grade in their own service. Escapees would have money, then. They spoke the local language, even if their accent was odd. If they could get outside the barbed wire, get a little start . . .

For you, the war is over. Moss could hope not, anyhow. He didn't know what the hope was worth. In the meantime . . . In the meantime, the rain arrived about half an hour later. It drove Moss back into the barracks. The red dirt outside rapidly turned to a substance resembling nothing so much as tomato soup. Inside, rain dripped between the unpainted pine boards of the roof. Some of the leaks were over bunks. Makeshift cloth awnings channeled away the worst of them.

Moss' mattress and pillow were cheap cotton sacking stuffed with sawdust and wood shavings. Eight wooden slats across the bed frame supported the bedding. The mattress was every bit as comfortable as Moss had thought it would be when he first set eyes on it. He might have had worse nights sleeping on the slats. Then again, he might not have.

A poker game was going on in one corner of the barracks. A poker game was always going on in one corner of the barracks. The prisoners had little on which to spend the brown banknotes—not bills, not down here—the Confederates gave them. They could buy cigarettes at what passed for the camp canteen. They could pay guards a little extra to bring them something besides grits, greens, and fatback. Past that . . . Past that, they could play poker and redistribute the wealth.

Every once in a while, Moss sat in, but only every once in a while. The gods might have designed poker as a way to separate him from his money. In a poker game, you were either a shark or you were bait. In the courtroom, he'd been a shark. In the air, he'd been a shark—till a Confederate took a bite out of his fighter. At the poker table, he was bait.

Other captured officers came in out of the rain. Some of them sat down on their bunks. Some of them lay down. Two or three went to sleep. Some men seemed to go into hibernation here, sleeping fourteen or sixteen or eighteen hours a day. Geneva Convention rules said officers didn't have to work. The sleepy ones took not working to an extreme. Moss didn't know whether to envy them or to give them a good swift kick in the ass to get their motors started.

As it happened, he didn't have to boot them today. Confederate guards took care of that. They burst into the barracks, submachine guns at the ready. "Everybody up!" they shouted. "Out of the sack, you lazy fuckers!" Even the yelling didn't roust one POW. He could have slept through the Trump of Doom, but not through getting thrown out of bed onto the floor.

"What the hell?" he said plaintively, picking himself up.

No one paid any attention to him. The guards didn't pay attention to any of the prisoners once they were out of the bunks. They paid attention to the bunks themselves, and to the number of slats that held each one up. They were not top-quality human material, to put it mildly—if they had been, they would have been up at the front. Some of them seemed to have trouble counting to eight. *Good thing there aren't eleven slats,* Moss thought. *They'd have to take off their shoes.*

"How come this here one's only got seven?" one of them demanded.

"Because one of 'em damn well broke, because you damn well used cheap-shit wood when you made it," answered the lieutenant whose bunk that was. His accent was identical to Cantarella's, though he looked Irish rather than Italian. He also had the New Yorker's way of challenging anything he didn't like.

Moss didn't give the guards a hard time. It struck him as cruising for a bruising. He'd seen the guards rough people up. That violated the Geneva Convention, but you couldn't call them on it. They would say the roughee had it coming, and the camp commandant would back them right down the line.

Here, though, the guards didn't push things. They grumbled and they fumed and then tramped out of the barracks. "What the hell was that all about?" asked a captain who'd been in Andersonville only a few days.

"Beats me," somebody else answered—an officer who'd been a prisoner longer than Moss had.

It beat Moss, too. When he got the chance to ask Nick Cantarella, he did. Cantarella started laughing. "I'll bite. What's funny?" Moss asked.

"The Confederates know what they're doing, that's all," Cantarella answered. He was still laughing, and didn't care who heard him. He thought it was funny as hell. "If we're digging a tunnel, those slats are about the best thing we could use to shore it up."

"Oh." A light dawned. "And if they're not missing, then we're not digging a tunnel?"

"I didn't say that." Cantarella was nothing if not coy. "You said that. With a little luck, the guards think that."

"Then we *are* digging a tunnel?" Moss persisted.

"I didn't say that, either. I didn't say anything. It's the waddayacallit—the Fifth Amendment, that's it."

Moss hadn't had much to do with the Fifth Amendment while practicing law in occupied Ontario; it hadn't crossed the border with the U.S. Army. It wasn't as strong as it might have been in the USA, either. From the 1880s until the Great War, the United States had geared up for a rematch against the Confederacy. Nothing had got in the way of gearing up—and, thanks to a pliant Supreme Court, that nothing included big chunks of the U.S. Constitution.

When he expressed his detailed opinion of the Fifth Amendment and of the horse it rode in on, he just made Cantarella laugh some more. "Dammit, you know I'm legit now," Moss groused. "The least you could do is tell me what's going on."

"Who says I know?" Cantarella answered. "I just work here." Had he put a pot full of cold water on Moss' head, it would have boiled in about thirty seconds. Moss' face must have told him as much. When he laughed again, it was in some embarrassment. "Don't ask for what I shouldn't give you, buddy."

"Why shouldn't you?" Moss went on steaming. "Only reason I can see is that you still think I might *not* be the goods."

"Then you aren't looking hard enough." The New Yorker's voice took on a hard edge. "I don't give a shit if you're as legitimate as Teddy Roosevelt. The more people who know more stuff than they ought to, the better chance Featherston's fuckers have of tearing it out of them. Have you got that through your goddamn thick head now, or shall I draw you a picture?"

"Oh." Jonathan Moss' temperature abruptly lowered. He didn't like security concerns, but he understood them. "Sorry, Captain. I was out of line there."

"Don't worry about it." Like most people, Cantarella was more inclined to be magnanimous after he'd got his way. "When the time comes—if the time comes—you'll find out whatever you need to know. Till then, just relax. Let Jake Featherston pay your room and board—and your salary, too."

"He needs to learn something about the hotel business. You're not supposed to have to lock up your customers to get 'em to stay," Moss said. Nick Cantarella thought that was funny as hell. Moss would have, too, if he'd been on the other side of the barbed wire.

For quite a while after rejoining the Confederate Army, Brigadier General Clarence Potter had worked underground, in War Department offices that officially didn't exist. Intelligence tended to get quartered in places like that. For one thing, it was supposed to be secret. For another, if you didn't have to look at spies, you could use what they gave you and still pretend to yourself that your hands were clean.

When he got the wreath around his three stars that meant promotion to general's rank, he also got his unfortunate predecessor's upstairs office. Being able to look out at Richmond instead of just walls was very nice. That is, it had been very nice till U.S. bombers started coming over Richmond in large numbers.

These days, only the foolhardy and those who had no choice worked above ground in the heart of the city. A lot of War Department operations had moved to the suburbs. Those that couldn't had gone underground. Potter's new office was only a few doors down from the one he'd had as a colonel. Returning to the subbasement, he'd displaced a captain, not the colonel who had the old room. As long as the electricity kept working, he could get the job done.

He stared at the papers on his desk through the bottoms of his bifocals. He was an erect, soldierly-looking man, nearer sixty than fifty, with iron-gray hair, a stern expression, and the same style of steel-rimmed glasses he'd worn as a major in Intelligence in the Army of Northern Virginia during the Great War (they hadn't been bifocals then). The spectacles softened what would otherwise have been some of the coldest gray eyes anyone ever owned.

One of the reasons he glowered at those papers was that they should have got to him weeks before they did. Before the shooting started, he'd run Confederate espionage operations in the USA. Two countries hardly separated by language made spying here easier in many ways than it was in Europe. Some Confederate operatives had been in place in Washington and Philadelphia and elsewhere since before the Great War.

There were two problems with that. Shooting and moving armies and closed ordinary channels of mail and telegraphy made it harder for information to get across the border—which was why these papers were so late. The other problem was, what were the damnyankees doing in the CSA? Ease of spying cut both ways, worse luck.

Formally, counterintelligence was on Brigadier General Cummins' football field, not his. He wasn't sorry about that, or most of him wasn't. Even guzzling coffee as if they'd outlaw it day after tomorrow, he did have to sleep every once in a while. He didn't see how he could conjure up enough extra hours in the day to do a proper job if more responsibility landed on his head.

Jake Featherston and Nathan Bedford Forrest III, the head of the Confederate General Staff, thought he could handle it if he had to. He had a hard time quarreling with either of them, because they both had more in their laps than he did. But he was a relentless perfectionist in ways they weren't, and couldn't let go of things till they were exactly as he wanted them. He had enough insight to understand that that wasn't always a desirable character trait. Understanding it and being able to do anything about it were two different things.

Someone knocked on the door. Down here, the rule was that you didn't walk in till you were invited. Potter checked to make sure nothing sensitive was out in the open before he said, "Come in."

"Thank you." It was Nathan Bedford Forrest III. Potter started to come to attention; Forrest waved him back into his chair before the motion was well begun, saying, "Don't bother with that silly nonsense." The great-grandson of the cavalry raider in the War of Secession had a fleshier face than his famous ancestor, but his eyes, hooded under strong dark brows, proclaimed the relationship.

"Good morning, sir, or afternoon, or whatever time of day it is out there," Potter said. "What can I do for you?"

Instead of answering right away, Forrest cocked his head to one side, an odd sort of smile on his face. "I purely love to listen to you talk, General—you know that?"

"You may be the only person in the Confederate States who does," Potter answered. He'd gone to college up at Yale before the Great War. U.S. speech patterns and accent had rubbed off on him, not least because even then the Yankees had made things hard for Confederates in their midst. He'd wanted to fit in there, and he had—and he'd had a certain amount of trouble fitting into his own country ever since.

"But I know how useful it is to be able to talk like that," Forrest said.

Quite a few of the C.S. spies Potter ran in the USA were Confederates who'd been raised or educated on the other side of the border. Sounding like a damnyankee helped a lot. It made real Yankees believe you were what you said you were, and was often more convincing than the proper papers. If you sounded right, you might never have to show your papers.

With a sour chuckle, Potter said, "It's almost got me shot for a spy here a few times."

"Well, that's some of what I want to talk to you about." Nathan Bedford Forrest III sank into the chair in front of Potter's desk. He pulled a pack of cigarettes from the breast pocket of his butternut tunic, stuck one in his mouth, and offered Potter the pack. After Potter took one, Forrest lit them both.

They smoked for a couple of drags apiece. Potter knocked ash into a brass astray on the desk. He said, "If you think you've intrigued me . . . you're right, dammit."

The chief of the General Staff grinned at him, unabashed. "I hoped I might, to tell you the truth. I'm getting up a volunteer battalion I'm going to want you to help me vet."

"Are you? A battalion of our people who can sound like damn-yankees?" Potter asked. Forrest nodded. Potter sucked in smoke till the coal at the end of his cigarette glowed a furious red. After he let it out, he aimed another question at his superior: "Are you putting them in U.S. uniforms, too?"

Nathan Bedford Forrest III didn't jump. Instead, he froze into immobility. He clicked his tongue between his teeth after fifteen seconds or so of silence. "Well, General," he said at last, "you didn't get the job you've got on account of you're a damn fool. If I didn't know that already, you just rubbed my nose in it like I'm a puppy getting house-trained."

"If they're captured in enemy uniform, the United States will shoot *them* for spies," Potter said. "We won't be able to say boo about it, either. Under the laws of war, they'll have the right."

"I understand that. Everybody who goes forward with this will understand it, too," Forrest answered. "You have my word on that, General. I already told you once, this is a project for volunteers."

"All right," Potter said. "But I did want to remind you. As a matter of fact, for something like that I was obliged to remind you. So where exactly do I fit in?"

"You're the fellow who's been running people who can sound like damnyankees and act like damnyankees." Forrest stubbed out his smoke and reached for the pack to have another one. When he offered it to Potter this time, Potter shook his head. The chief of the General Staff lit up again. He sucked in smoke, then continued, "If they can be half-way convincing to you, they'll be good enough to convince the enemy, too."

"It's not just accent." Potter scratched his chin as he thought. "You can get away with flattening out the vowels some. Even swallowing *r*'s might make the Yankees think you're from Boston or somewhere up there—what even the Yankees call a Yankee. But some things will kill you if the USA hears 'em coming out of your mouth."

"*Banknote* is one," Forrest said. "I know they say *bill* instead."

"Just about everybody knows that one—just about everybody

thinks about money a good deal," Potter agreed. Nathan Bedford Forrest III laughed, though Potter hadn't been kidding, or not very much. He went on, "They don't say *tote* up there, either—it's *carry.* And they mostly say *bucket* instead of *pail,* though you might get by with that one. You won't ever get away with *windscreen;* they always say *windshield.* They might think somebody who says *windscreen* is an Englishman, but that won't help anybody in a U.S. uniform much, either."

"No, not hardly." Forrest laughed once more: a grim laugh.

"What will you be using them for?" Potter quickly held up his right hand. "No, don't tell me. Let me figure it out." He thought for a little while, then nodded—at least as much to himself as to his superior. "Infiltrators. They have to be infiltrators. Get them behind the lines, giving false directions, sabotaging vehicles, putting explosives in ammunition dumps, and they'll be worth a lot more than a battalion of ordinary men."

Again, Forrest gave him a careful once-over before speaking. When he did, he said, "Shall I put you in an operational slot, Potter? If you want your own division, it's yours for the asking."

"I think I can do the damnyankees more harm right where I am, sir," Potter replied. Nathan Bedford Forrest III didn't argue with him. He thought a bit more. "Do you know what the really elegant part of the scheme is? As soon as the damnyankees realize we've got men behind their lines like that, nobody in a green-gray uniform will trust anybody he doesn't know. And that'll last for the rest of the goddamn war."

Forrest slowly nodded. He looked like a man trying to show nothing on his face at a poker table. Did that mean he or whoever'd come up with the notion hadn't thought so far ahead? Potter would have bet it did. He almost asked, but checked himself. That might have looked like showing off.

One other thing did occur to him, though: "You know they'll do the same thing to us? They just about have to, if for no other reason than to make us as scared of our own shadows as they will be."

"I'll . . . take that up with the President," Forrest said. Were the raiders in Yankee uniform Jake Featherston's idea? Potter wouldn't have been surprised; Featherston had a genius for making trouble in nasty ways. He also had the gifted amateur's problem of not seeing all the consequences of his troublemaking.

This long war, for instance. He really thought Al Smith would make peace. Potter muttered unhappily. If only the Yankees would have quit. Jake Featherston would have gone down in history then, no doubt about it. Things wouldn't be so easy now. He asked Forrest, "What do you think of Charlie La Follette?"

"We'll just have to see," the chief of the General Staff replied. "So far, he sounds like Smith. But who knows what he'll be like once he gets out from under the other fellow's shadow? How about you? You probably know more about him than I do."

"I doubt it. Who pays attention to the Vice President?" Potter said, and Forrest laughed, again for all the world as if he'd been joking. He went on, "I think you've got it about right. Doesn't look like he's going to pack in the war."

"No, it sure doesn't. Too bad. It'd make our lives easier if he did, that's for damn sure," Forrest said—one more thing Potter thought he had about right.

They'd pulled Armstrong Grimes' regiment, or what was left of it, out of the lines in Utah for a while. The corporal and his buddies had to march away. The powers that be saved most of their trucks to haul men to and from fights they thought more important than the one against the Mormon rebels.

Marching out meant he and his fellow survivors tramped past the men coming up to take their places in Provo. Telling who was who couldn't have been easier. The new fish had fresh uniforms, and carried very full packs on their backs. They were clean-shaven. They looked bright and eager.

Armstrong and the rest of the veterans stank. He couldn't remember when he'd last bathed or changed his underwear. He was as whiskery as any of the others. His uniform had seen better days, too. He carried nothing he couldn't do without. And his eyes went every which way at once. They were the eyes of a man who never knew which way trouble was coming from, only that it was coming.

Most of the soldiers pulling out had eyes like that. The rest just stared straight ahead as they trudged along. The thousand-yard stare belonged to men who'd seen and done too much. Maybe rest would turn them back into soldiers again. Maybe nothing would. The way war was these days, it had no trouble overwhelming a man.

Some of the veterans jeered at the rookies: "Aren't you pretty?"

"Aren't you sweet?" "Do your mothers know you're here?" "Where do you want your body sent?"

The men going into the line didn't say much in return. They eyed the troops they were replacing like people in a zoo eyeing tigers and wolves. But no bars stood between them and the veterans. They plainly feared they'd get bitten if they teased the animals. They were right, too.

"Got a cigarette, Sarge?" Grimes asked. He was a big man—he'd been a second-string lineman on his high-school football team what seemed a million years ago and was actually just over one. Under the whiskers, his face was long and oval like his mother's, but he had his old man's dark hair and eyes.

"Here you go." Rex Stowe pulled one out of a pack.

"Thanks." Armstrong lit up and sucked in smoke. He was named for George Armstrong Custer; his father had been born in the same little Ohio town as the hero of the Second Mexican War and the Great War. Armstrong was born in Washington, D.C., where Merle Grimes settled down and married after a war wound from which he still limped. He'd had a comfortable postwar career as a minor government functionary. He and the rest of the family probably weren't comfortable now. Washington was too close to the border with the CSA to be safe, though as far as Armstrong knew his father and mother and younger sister were well.

A middle-aged woman and a couple of little kids stood in the rubble by the side of the track and watched the U.S. soldiers go by. Silent hatred burned in their eyes. Of itself, Armstrong's Springfield swung a couple of inches toward them. Plenty of Mormon women fought alongside their husbands and brothers and sons. Plenty of kids threw homemade grenades and firebombs—Featherston Fizzes, people called them. You never could tell, even with people behind the lines.

"They don't like it that you're smoking," Stowe said.

No mere cigarette could have made them look like that. They wished him straight to hell. If they'd had weapons, they would have done their best to send him there.

Every civilian he saw looked at him like that. He knew there were people in Utah who weren't Mormons. The Mormon majority called anybody who wasn't one of them a gentile. Even Jews were gentiles here. One of Armstrong's buddies was a New York City guy named Yossel Reisen. He thought that was funny as the devil.

But a lot of the so-called gentiles had joined their Mormon neighbors in rising up against the USA. Armstrong had trouble figuring that out. What had the U.S. government ever done to *them*? Had they hated the way Utah was treated so much that they wanted to leave the USA? Weren't they a little crazy, or more than a little, if they had? Yeah, the rebels were brave, no doubt about it. But bravery had only so much to do with anything when it ran up against superior firepower.

The rebels were taking a while to lose, because the United States had other things to worry about and weren't giving them anything like their full attention. But the Mormons and their pals had to be chewing locoweed if they thought they had a Chinaman's chance of bailing out of the USA.

Rex Stowe said, "The way things are around here, I don't even know if I want to come out of the line. Aren't they likelier to jump us when our guard is down than when we're looking for it?"

"Who says our guard's going to be down? I don't know about you, but I'm still watching all the goddamn time," Armstrong answered.

Stowe considered, shrugged, and nodded. "You've got something there."

On they slogged, past buildings pulverized in the slow, brutal U.S. advance. Armstrong wondered if there'd be enough Mormons left alive to keep their faith going after this rebellion finally got smashed. There had been the last time around, which struck him as a damn shame.

He marched for a solid day to get back to the recuperation center that had sprung up in Thistle, southeast of Provo. That put it out of range of Mormon guns—unless the rebels got sneaky, which they might well do. Barbed wire and machine-gun nests around the center made the place seem like a prisoner-of-war camp, but the guns faced out, not in.

Once inside the perimeter, Armstrong followed signs to a bank of showers and then to a delousing station. The showers were cold. His father had talked about hot water as part of the delousing process, but times had changed. They sprayed him with something that smelled like poison gas instead of boiling him or soaking him or whatever they'd done in his old man's day.

"What is this shit?" he asked the guy doing the spraying.

"It's like Flit, only more so. It *really* kills bugs," the other soldier answered, and sprayed the naked man in line behind him.

They didn't bother trying to get his uniform clean. That would have defeated Job's patience. They issued him fresh clothes instead, from long johns on out. He felt like a new man.

The new man got a feed of bacon and real eggs and hash browns and toast and jam. Most of what he'd eaten lately had come out of cans or cartons. This felt like heaven, especially since he could pile as much as he wanted on his mess tray. After about three breakfasts' worth, he said, "That's a little better."

Rex Stowe had eaten at least as much. "Yeah, a little," he agreed. "I expect I'll be able to handle lunch, though."

"Oh, fuck, yes." Armstrong took that for granted.

Yossel Reisen sat on Armstrong's other side. He'd also put away a hell of a lot, though he skipped the bacon. He often swapped ration cans, too, so he wouldn't have to eat pork. He gulped down a big white china mug full of coffee pale with fresh cream. "Damn good," he said—he was at least as foul-mouthed as anybody else.

"Ask you something?" Armstrong said to him, and waited for him to nod. "You already did your conscript time, right? And then they sucked you back in?"

"Yeah, that's true. You know it is," Yossel answered. "So what?"

"So how come I'm a corporal when I've been in less than a year and you just made PFC?" Armstrong asked. "They should've given you two stripes the minute you came back, and you ought to be at least a sergeant by now."

Reisen shrugged. "You know who my aunt is." It wasn't a question.

"Well, sure," Armstrong said. Everybody knew Yossel's aunt had been married to the President and was a Congresswoman herself. "You don't make a big deal out of it, the way a lot of guys would. But that ought to get you promoted faster, right, not slower?"

"I don't want it to." Yossel Reisen spoke with quiet emphasis. "I don't want anybody giving me anything on account of Aunt Flora. I just want to be a regular guy and get what regular guys get. I know damn well I earned the stripe I've got. If somebody handed it to me, what would it be worth?"

Armstrong was chewing a big mouthful of bacon, so he couldn't answer right away. If he were related to somebody famous, he would have milked it for all it was worth. A cushy job counting brass buttons five hundred miles away from guns going off sounded great to him.

Yossel went on, "When my Uncle David got conscripted in the last war, my aunt was already in Congress. She could have pulled strings for him. He wouldn't let her. He lost a leg. He's proud of what he did. He wouldn't have it any different."

He's out of his fucking mind, Armstrong thought. And yet his own father was unmistakably proud of his war wound, too. No doubt he'd screamed his head off when he got it, just like anybody else when a bullet bit him. Memory did strange things, no doubt about it.

"Have it your way," Armstrong said when at last he swallowed. "You pull your weight. Anybody tells you anything else, kick his ass for him."

"Thanks," Reisen said. "You, too." Armstrong followed the bacon with a swig of coffee. Till he got in the Army, he'd always been half-assed about things, doing enough to get by and not another nickel's worth. You couldn't do that once you put on the uniform, though. It might get you killed. Even if it didn't, it would make your buddies hate you. If you let your buddies down, they'd let you down, too—and that *would* get you killed. Having somebody he cared about tell him he was all right felt damn good.

After they ate, they went over to a barracks hall. It was cheap plywood, and probably better suited to prisoners on the U.S. side. Armstrong wasn't inclined to be critical. He threw his few chattels into a footlocker at the end of a real cot with a real mattress and real bedding. Then he took off his shoes and threw himself down on the mattress. "Oh, Jesus Christ!" he said ecstatically. A real bed. The first real bed since . . . He'd tried to remember not so long before. He tried again, harder. He still couldn't.

Nobody told him he had to get out of it. He was full. He was clean, in a clean uniform. Nobody was shooting at him or even near him. He allowed himself the luxury of taking off his shoes. Then, blissfully, he fell asleep.

As far as he could tell, he hadn't changed position when reveille sounded the next morning. He yawned and stretched. He was *still* tired. But he wasn't weary unto death anymore. He was also starved—he'd slept through the lunch that had sounded so inviting and dinner, too, damn near slept the clock around.

By the way the rest of the men in the hall rose, they'd done nothing much in the nighttime, either. Some of them had had the energy to strip to their shorts and get under the covers instead of lying on top of them. *Maybe tonight,* Armstrong told himself.

He made an enormous pig of himself again at breakfast. Then he went back to the barracks and flopped down again. He didn't fall asleep right away this time. He just lay there, marveling. He didn't have to go anywhere. He didn't have to do anything. He didn't have to have eyes in the back of his head—though having them doubtless was still a good thing. He could just ease back and relax. He wondered if he still remembered how. He aimed to find out, for as long as he had in this wonderful place.

Jefferson Pinkard hadn't been in Texas since he headed home to Birmingham after the Great War ended. He'd fought north of where he was now, but the country around Snyder wasn't a whole lot different from what he'd known half a lifetime earlier: plains cut by washes, with low rises here and there. The sky went on forever, and the landscape seemed to do the same.

Bulldozers were kicking dust up into that endless sky right now. Along with their diesel snorting, the sounds of saws and hammers filled the air. Camp Determination would seem to go on forever when it got finished, too. Jeff had run Camp Dependable near Alexandria, Louisiana, for years. Once Determination got done, you'd be able to drop Dependable into it and not even know the older camp was there.

The barbed-wire perimeter stretched and stretched and stretched. A lot of people would go through Camp Determination. It had to be able to hold them all. And Pinkard had to make sure nobody got out who wasn't supposed to. Guard towers outside the walls had gone up before the barracks inside. Machine guns were already in place inside the towers. Anybody who tried to escape would be real sorry real fast—but probably not for long.

Stalking along outside the perimeter, Jeff looked up at each tower he passed. He'd climbed up into all of them, checking their fields of fire. If you wanted something like that done right—hell, if you wanted anything done right—you were better off doing it yourself.

His black, shiny boots scuffed still more dust into the air. He wore three stars on each collar tab, the equivalent of a colonel's rank. But he was called Standard Leader, not Colonel. He had a Freedom Party rank, not one from the Army. His uniform was of the same cut as a colonel's, but gray rather than butternut.

Tunic and trousers both had some extra room for his belly. He still carried muscle under the fat, though; he'd been a steelworker till he got conscripted and for a while after the war, and no weakling ever went into the Sloss Works. If he scowled more often than he smiled, that was true of most people who bossed other people around.

After he got done prowling the perimeter, he went inside the camp. He carried a submachine gun with a full magazine when he did. So did all the whites who went inside. He had another man with him, too. The rule was that no white man went in alone. He'd made the rule. He lived up to it.

The construction-gang bosses were white. Negroes did most of the actual work, building the barracks where they would later live . . . for a while. If they did a lousy job, they had only themselves to blame.

Pinkard checked with the straw bosses. He could tell by looking that things were pretty close to being on schedule. The bosses blamed the rain that had come through a few days earlier for what delays there were. "Make it up," Jeff told them. "We'll open on time, or I'll know the reason why. And if we don't, I won't be the only one who's sorry. Have you got that?"

He was bigger than most of the gang bosses, and he had a loud, rasping voice, and everybody knew he was in good odor in Richmond. People might grumble about him behind his back, but nobody had the nerve to get mouthy to his face.

There was also another reason for that. Jeff Pinkard didn't just talk to the construction-gang bosses. He poked his nose in everywhere, as had been his habit ever since he started taking care of prisoners during the civil war between the Emperor of Mexico and the U.S.-backed republican rebels after the Great War ended.

He went up to a colored man nailing boards to the side of a barracks unit. "You got everything you need to do your job?" he demanded.

"Yes, suh. Sure do," the Negro answered. "Got me a hammer an' plenty o' nails." He looked Pinkard in the eye. "You give me a rifle an' plenty o' bullets, I do a job on *you*."

"I bet you would," Pinkard said. "But you tried that, and they caught you." Most of the laborers were men taken in rebellion against the CSA. "If you try and you lose, this is what you get."

"I ain't got my population reduced yet," the black man said, and went back nailing up boards.

Population reduction and its variants had been Confederate slang for a little while now. *I'll reduce your population, you bastard!* an angry man might shout, when he meant no more than, *I'll fix you!* Used that way, the phrase wasn't so heavily freighted with meaning. But, like a lot of slang, it sprang from something that was literally true. More Negroes, many more, were going into camps all over the CSA than were coming out—coming out alive, anyhow.

Jeff Pinkard eyed the colored man with the hammer in his hand. How did he mean what he'd just said? Was it only slang in his mouth, or had he seen enough to understand exactly where the slang came from? Jeff wondered, but he didn't ask. As long as it was possible for Negroes to stay optimistic, they made more docile, more cooperative prisoners. Men who were sure they were doomed anyhow had nothing to lose. They caused trouble no matter what it cost them. Better to keep them as happy as you could.

That wasn't real happy. Several Negroes asked Jeff if they could have bigger rations. He just shook his head and kept walking. They didn't complain too much. The grits and occasional beans or biscuits they got didn't quite amount to a starvation diet. The ration was just small enough to remind people it should have been larger.

The workers had no shortage of building supplies. Ferdinand Koenig, the C.S. Attorney General, had promised Pinkard a railroad spur would run to Camp Determination, and he'd kept his word. Everything Jeff needed came right to his front door. As soon as the camp was finished, trainloads of prisoners would come right to his front door, too. It wouldn't be very long.

More colored prisoners were paving the road that led into Camp Determination and the big parking area at the end of it. Along with the railroad spur, there'd be plenty of truck traffic going in and out of the camp. Jeff smiled to himself. That had been his idea, back at Camp Dependable. But there he hadn't had the room to do things right. Here, he did. And if anybody came up with something better than trucks, he'd have room for that, too, whatever it turned out to be. Nobody'd improved on trucks yet, but you never could tell what someone might think up.

"You make sure you get that concrete nice and smooth," Jeff barked to a Negro working on the lot.

"Oh, yes, suh, I do dat. You don't gots to worry none. Everything be fust-rate. We takes care of it." As any Negro would when a white boss bore down on him, this one was quick and ready to promise the moon. Whether he'd deliver was liable to be a different question.

Pinkard didn't care so much about the barracks halls. But the parking lot and the road—they really counted. The trucks were important and expensive. They had to be well taken care of. "I'll have my eye on you," Pinkard growled. "You think I'm kidding, you'll be sorry."

"Yes, suh." The Negro didn't get up from his hands and knees. He probably wanted to show Jeff how diligent he was. "Don't you fret none."

As things advanced here, more barbed wire with gates in it would separate the road and the lot from the rest of the camp. He had everything planned. The blueprints for Camp Determination had come out of Richmond, but he had permission from Ferd Koenig to modify them as he thought best. This was going to be *his* camp, and by God it would work the way he wanted it to.

Guards saluted as he and his silent gun-toting companion left the perimeter. He'd need more manpower when the camp got going, but he didn't expect that to be a problem. The Confederate Veterans' Brigades had a guard-training center not far outside of Fort Worth. The way Jeff saw things, the men who came out of it would probably do better than the cops and tough guys who made up most of the guard force now. They'd really know what they were supposed to do.

He had his own office by the growing camp. Telephone and telegraph lines connected it to the outside world. That was more so Richmond could send him instructions than so he could reach other places, but the powers that be back in the capital didn't mind if he did.

When he walked up to the telegrapher, the young man didn't quite sit at attention, but he came close. Jeff said, "Billy Ray, I want you to send a wire to Edith Blades in Alexandria, Louisiana. You've got the address, right?"

"Yes, sir, Standard Leader!" Billy Ray said. If he didn't have the address of his boss's fiancée handy, he'd be in trouble. He grabbed a message pad and poised a pencil over it. "Go ahead, sir."

"Right." Jeff paused a moment to work out what he wanted to say before he said it. He always felt like a damn fool when he had to mumble and stumble and backtrack. "Here we go. . . . 'Dear Edith, All well here. Progress on schedule. Will be back to visit in about two weeks.

Expect things to start up in less than two months. Miss you and the boys. See you all soon. Love, Jeff.'" He tried to keep things short, even if he wasn't paying for the wire out of his own pocket.

"Let me read that back for you, sir." Billy Ray did. He had it right. *The boys* had surprised him the first time he heard it; he hadn't known Edith was a widow. Now he took them for granted.

"Send it off," Jeff told him. The telegraph key started clicking.

Jeff went into his inner office. He'd been careful about more than keeping things short. Suppose the damnyankees got their hands on this wire. He hadn't given his last name or his rank. He hadn't said anything specifically about the camp, either. Anybody who didn't already know what he was talking about wouldn't be able to make much sense of it. He sounded like a drummer or an efficiency expert, not a camp commandant.

I damn well am an efficiency expert, he thought. A lot of the changes he'd made to the blueprints involved smoothing things out, clearing up bottlenecks, avoiding trouble wherever he could. The parking area was bigger than it had been in the original drawings, and the road leading to and from it better laid out. A lot of trucks would go in and out of Camp Determination. A hell of a lot of Negroes would come in and go out.

He knew where the road out of camp led. At the end of it, there was another barbed-wire enclosure. That one kept people out, not in. Texas had a hell of a lot of prairie. If you put some dozer crews on the job, they could dig a lot of trenches without drawing much notice. Fill those trenches full of bodies, bulldoze the dirt back over them, and dig some new ones . . .

Jeff nodded to himself. The Negroes who got into trucks would think they were on their way to some other camp. So would the ones who stayed behind. They wouldn't know the exhaust fumes were routed into the airtight passenger box, not till too late they wouldn't.

Camp Determination was big. The burial ground was even bigger. The Freedom Party was—was *determined,* by God!—to solve the Negro problem in the CSA once and for all. It would take a lot of work, but Jeff figured they could do it.

II

Brigadier General Irving Morrell wished to God he could get out of the hospital. His shattered shoulder was improving, but there was an unfortunate difference between *improving* and *improved*. Morrell, a rawboned, weathered man of fifty, had found out all about that when he was wounded in the Great War. An infection after he got shot in the leg had kept him on the shelf for months, and kept the doctors darkly muttering about amputation. In the end, they didn't have to go in there with a hacksaw, for which he'd never stopped being grateful.

No wound infection this time, or none to speak of. They had drugs now they hadn't dreamt of a generation earlier. But he still needed to heal, and that took time, however much he wished it didn't. He could use his right hand again, though he feared the arm would never regain all its strength and dexterity.

"When can I go back to work, Doc?" he asked the Army physician who was tending his wound. He might have been a roofer who'd taken a fall—most wounds in war weren't that different from industrial accidents. Most—but not his. The sniper who'd wounded him hadn't been aiming at anybody else. Two more bullets had cracked past him as the gunner on the barrel he commanded hustled him out of harm's way.

Like any Army doctor, Conrad Rohde held officer's rank so he could tell enlisted men what to do. He had a major's gold oak leaves on the green-gray tunic he wore under his white hospital coat. He was big and blond and slow-moving—slow-talking, too. After his usual careful consideration, he answered, "Well, sir, it shouldn't be too long now."

"Gee, thanks a lot. Thanks a hell of a lot," Morrell said. Rohde'd been telling him the same thing for a while now. Before that, he'd said *a few weeks . . .* for a few weeks.

"I'm sorry I can't be more exact." As usual, the sawbones sounded not the least bit sorry. "You aren't ready yet, not unless you don't intend to do anything more strenuous than stay behind the line—far behind the line—and move pins on a map."

Since Morrell intended no such thing, he swore under his breath. A barrel commander who didn't lead from the front wasn't worth much. So he told himself, anyhow. It was true enough. The other half of the truth was that he'd always been a man who liked to mix it up with the enemy.

Rohde knew what that muttering meant. He didn't even smirk and look superior; he had a deadpan that probably won him money in poker games. He did say, "You see?"

"The arm's not *too* bad," Morrell insisted. "Honest to God, it's not."

Dr. Rohde didn't come right out and tell him he was a liar. He thought for a moment, then said, "You're in a barrel. It gets hit. It starts to burn. You have to bail out—right now. Can you open a hatch with that arm?"

Morrell thought about it. He raised the injured member. It hurt. That didn't bother him so much. He'd learned to live with pain. What bothered him was how weak the arm was. Savagely, he said, "I wish I were lefthanded."

"I can't do anything about that. You should have talked to God, or to your parents." Rohde was maddeningly unhelpful. "Since you aren't lefthanded, do I take it you've answered my question?"

"Yes, dammit." Morrell couldn't have been more disgusted. He was even willing to make what was, for him, not far from the ultimate sacrifice: "If they need me on light duty behind the lines for a while, I'll do that. Anything to get out of here."

Rohde looked at him. "You don't like it in beautiful, romantic Syracuse?"

"Now that you mention it, no."

"And if I turn you loose, how do I know you won't head straight for the front? That's the reputation you've got."

The reputation was well deserved. Morrell knew as much. He said, "I could sign a pledge, but you probably wouldn't believe me. Or you could take your chances and let me take mine. I'm a big boy, Doc. I *can* take my own chances if I think I ought to and if I think the country needs me."

"Part of my job, General, is to see that you don't endanger yourself without good reason," Dr. Rohde replied. "And do you really think you're as indispensable to the United States as all that?"

"As a matter of fact, yes," Morrell said. "Go call Philadelphia and find out what the War Department thinks. They wouldn't have given me stars if they didn't think I was good for something. Call them. If they say I can sit on the shelf a while longer, I'll sit. I'll even stop bitching about it. But if they say they need me . . ."

He was rolling the dice. Not everybody in the War Department loved him. He also had a reputation for being right in spite of people. High-ranking officers were supposed to be right. They weren't supposed to rub their superiors' noses in it, as Morrell had done. But if even the Confederates thought him worth killing, his own side ought to be able to figure out he was worth a little something. That was how he'd got promoted to general's rank.

"I'll take you up on that—sir." Dr. Rohde lumbered out of the room.

He didn't say anything to Morrell about the War Department for the next several days. With some men, that would have made Morrell suspect he hadn't got on the horn to Philadelphia at all. The barrel officer didn't believe that of Rohde. The doctor struck him as honest, if stuck in a rut. And the War Department never had been, wasn't, and probably never would be an outfit that could make up its mind in a hurry—which was part of the reason the United States were in the current mess.

I'll give him a week. Then I'll ask him, Morrell thought. Nobody could get huffy about his asking after a week. And if Rohde hadn't made the call or if the War Department was still twiddling its thumbs, well, at least he would know what was what.

Come the day, he got ready to beard Rohde. But the doctor forestalled him. Wearing an uncommonly sour expression, the big blond man said, "Pack your bags—sir. Philadelphia is dying to have you, and I don't suppose you'll die if you go there."

"Thanks, Doc!" Morrell grinned as if he'd just stuck in his thumb and pulled out a plum. "Uh—what bags? All I came here with was the uniform I got shot in, and that's never going to be the same."

"A point," Dr. Rohde said. "Nothing to flabble about, though. I'm sure we can fix you up. This sort of thing happens now and again."

The hospital proved to have a good selection of uniforms for both officers and enlisted men. Some of them bore signs of being repaired; others seemed as fresh as the day they were made. Morrell didn't care to think about how they'd been obtained, or about what had happened to the men who'd formerly worn them. He chose an officer's tunic and trousers that fit well enough, and pinned his stars on his shoulder straps and the Purple Heart with oak-leaf cluster above his left breast pocket. He got his own shoes back. The hospital had cleaned off whatever blood he'd got on them, and polished them to a higher gloss than he usually achieved himself.

Getting dressed was tougher and more painful than he'd thought it would be. It left him feeling worn as a kitten, and without the kitten's sharp claws and teeth. He did his best not to show Dr. Rohde weakness. The doctor didn't say a word, but Morrell doubted he was fooling him.

A driver took him to the train station in an ordinary auto. He'd wondered if Rohde would stick him in an ambulance and gain a measure of revenge for getting overruled by Philadelphia. Maybe the doctor was too nice a man to do something like that. On the other hand, maybe it just hadn't occurred to him.

Coming down from upstate New York brought Morrell back to the war a little at a time. It hadn't touched Syracuse. The farther east and south the train went, the more bomb damage he saw. Before long, the train started sitting on sidings or just on the tracks when it should have been moving. He wondered whether that was bomb damage or sabotage. Whatever it was, it slowed him to a crawl.

A sergeant waited for him on the platform when he finally pulled into Philadelphia in the middle of the night. The man wasn't standing there in plain sight. He dozed on a bench near the far wall. Morrell shook him awake.

Horror spread over the noncom's face when he saw a general looming over him. "I'm sorry, sir!" he cried, and sprang to his feet.

"It's all right. Don't blow a gasket." Morrell returned a rather frantic salute. "You weren't on sentry duty. Nobody's going to shoot you for sacking out. How late was I, anyway?"

Before answering, the sergeant looked at his watch. "Uh—just over three and a half hours, sir."

"That's about what I thought," Morrell said. "Are things always that bad around here?"

"Well . . ." The sergeant didn't want to admit it. "They're not what you'd call real good." Whether he wanted to admit it or not, he didn't seem to have much choice. Reality spoke for itself.

"Take me to the War Department," Morrell said.

"Yes, sir." The sergeant did. The short journey was slow and round-about. Philadelphia had a battered look. Months of bombing hadn't knocked it out of action, though. Traffic still moved, even if it had to detour around craters in the street. Repairmen swarmed over damaged buildings, even if the next raid might hit them again. Men and women filled the sidewalks and the shops: Philadelphia ran around the clock. They didn't seem beaten or intimidated, just determined to get on with the job no matter what.

Antiaircraft guns were everywhere, their snouts poking up from vacant lots and street corners and roofs. Searchlight batteries would do what they could to find the guns' targets. Signs pointed the way to air-raid shelters.

The War Department was one of the buildings under repair. That didn't surprise Morrell. It was a big target, and the Confederates knew where it was. Even bombing by night, they were bound to score some hits.

"Here we go, sir." The sergeant jumped out of the auto and held the heavy bronze doors that led inside for Morrell. The barrel officer was gladder of that than he cared to admit. He wasn't sure he could have opened them with his right hand, though his left would have done the job.

Even in the War Department, brigadier generals were uncommon birds. Morrell got whisked to the offices of the assistant to the chief of the General Staff, a much more senior one-star general named Edward McCleave. "How are you feeling?" McCleave asked.

"Sir, I'll do," Morrell answered. "That's why I wanted to get out of the damn hospital. I wasn't doing anybody any good there."

"Except yourself," McCleave pointed out.

Morrell shrugged. It didn't hurt—too much. "Sitting on the shelf was worse than getting shot. Can you send me to Virginia, sir? If we're going to make a real run at Richmond, I want to be part of it."

"Your attitude does you credit," the older man said. "Although General MacArthur has forced a crossing of the Rappahannock, he does not anticipate an immediate armored assault on the Confederates. The terrain is not conducive to such movements."

"You're telling me he's stuck," Morrell said.

"That's not what I said." Brigadier General McCleave sounded prim.

"It's what you meant, though," Morrell said, and McCleave didn't deny it. Morrell went on, "Do you want me to take over the barrels down there and see what I can shake loose?"

"MacArthur has not requested your presence," McCleave said. "If, however, the War Department were to order you to the Virginia front . . ." He waited. Morrell nodded. The two men exchanged smiles that were downright conspiratorial. *And so much for staying behind the lines,* Morrell thought.

Lieutenant-Colonel Tom Colleton knew his regiment helped hold an important position. His soldiers defended Confederate positions east of Sandusky, Ohio, on the southern shore of Lake Erie. As long as the Confederate States held a corridor from the Ohio River to the lake, they cut the United States in half. The damnyankees couldn't ship anything or anybody by rail or road from east to west or west to east within their own territory. They had to take the long way around, through occupied Canada—and Canada didn't have nearly so many lines or roads as the USA did.

No matter how true that was, though, Tom Colleton wasn't happy. He didn't like standing on the defensive. He'd reveled in the push north from the border. That was what war was supposed to be about. He'd fought in Virginia the last time, and hated stalemates with the grim and bitter passion of a man who'd seen too many of them. Barrels meant soldiers didn't have to huddle in trenches this time around. They didn't have to, no—but too often they did anyway.

Fortunately, the Yankees were as preoccupied with Virginia these days as the Confederates had been with Ohio and Indiana at the start of the war. Even more fortunately, U.S. forces weren't doing as well in Virginia as the Confederates had here farther west. In Sandusky, Tom couldn't help hearing both C.S. and U.S. wireless reports. When both sides told the same story, it was probably true. When they diverged, he had to try to figure out who was lying and who wasn't.

No matter what his sister had thought about Jake Featherston,

Tom had no great love or admiration for him. His mouth tightened. Anne had died in the opening days of the war. If she hadn't been down in Charleston when that damnyankee carrier raid hit the town . . . But she had, and nobody could do anything about it now.

His own wife and boys were safe in St. Matthews, not far from Columbia, the capital of South Carolina. *The last of the Colletons,* he thought. He'd never felt that way while Anne was alive, even though she'd been childless. She'd bossed the family ever since their parents died. Now everything rode on his shoulders.

He laughed as he looked east toward the damnyankees' lines. The Colletons were a family with a fine future behind them. Before the Great War, Marshlands was one of the leading plantations in South Carolina, with hundreds of colored hands working in the cotton fields. The mansion went up in flames in the Negro uprising in 1915, and not even Anne could make a go of cotton after the war.

Up ahead, the Yankees and some of Tom's men started banging away at one another. Telling which side was which by ear was easy. The U.S. soldiers used bolt-action Springfields, rifles much like the Tredegars C.S. troops had carried in the last war. In this fight, soldiers in butternut had either automatic rifles or submachine guns. The damnyankees were always going to outnumber them, so each Confederate soldier needed to have more firepower than his U.S. counterpart.

The only trouble was, rifles and submachine guns weren't the sole weapons involved. U.S. and C.S. machine guns were as near identical as made no difference. So were the two sides' artillery, barrels, and aircraft. Add all that in and what had been a good-sized edge for the Confederate foot soldier shrank considerably.

Sure as hell, machine guns from both sides joined the conversation within a couple of minutes. Mortar rounds didn't make much noise leaving their tubes—soldiers on both sides called them stove pipes—but the harsh, flat *crump!* of the bursting bombs was unmistakable.

Colleton shouted for his wireless man. When the small soldier with the large pack on his back came up, Tom said, "What the hell's going on there? This was a pretty quiet sector up until a few minutes ago. Get me one of the forward company command posts."

"Yes, sir." The wireless man did his job without fuss or feathers. "Here's Captain Dinwiddie, sir—A Company, First Battalion."

"Dinwiddie!" Tom called into the mouthpiece. "Who went and pulled on the damnyankees' tails?"

"Other way round, sir," the captain answered. "Yankee sniper potted Lieutenant Jenks. He's not dead, but he's hurt pretty bad. Some of our boys spotted the muzzle flash up in a tree. They started shooting at him, and some of those green-gray fuckers shot back, and now it's hell's half acre up here."

"You want artillery? You want gas?" Tom asked. He hated gas, as every Great War veteran did, which didn't mean he wouldn't use it in a red-hot minute. God only knew the damnyankees weren't shy about throwing it around.

"Not right now, sir," Dinwiddie said. "They're just shooting. There's no real attack coming in. If we stir 'em up, though, Lord only knows what they might try."

"All right." Colleton wasn't particularly sorry about the response. His job now was to keep the USA out of Sandusky, no matter what. If that meant not stirring up the enemy, he didn't mind. He didn't much feel like getting stirred up himself. It was a cold, miserable day, and he would sooner have stayed inside by a nice, hot fire.

The firefight lasted about half an hour. Well before then, Confederate medics with Red Cross armbands and Red Crosses on their helmets went up to the front to bring back the wounded. A couple of medics came back on stretchers themselves. Tom swore, but without particular fury. He'd never yet seen the Yankees make a habit of picking off medics, any more than the Confederates did. But neither machine-gun bursts nor mortar bombs were fussy about whom they maimed.

After the shooting eased, a U.S. captain came across the line under flag of truce. An officer at the front sent him back to Tom. The Yankee gave him a stiff little nod. "I'd like to ask you for a two-hour truce, Lieutenant-Colonel, so the corpsmen on both sides can bring in the dead and wounded."

"Do you think they'll need that long?" Tom asked.

"Been a lot of shooting going on up there," the U.S. captain answered. He had a flat, harsh Midwestern accent, far removed from Colleton's South Carolina drawl. They spoke the same language—they had no trouble understanding each other—but they plainly weren't from the same country.

Tom considered, then nodded. "All right, Captain. Two hours, commencing at"—he looked at his watch—"at 0945. That gives you half an hour to get back to your own line and pass the word that we've agreed. Suit you all right?"

"Down to the ground. Two hours, starting at 0945. Thank you, Lieutenant-Colonel. You're a gentleman." The captain stuck out his hand. Tom hesitated, but shook it. The man was an enemy, but he was playing by the rules—was, in fact, making a point of playing by the rules.

As the U.S. officer left, Tom had his wireless man tell the forward positions that the truce was coming. He sent runners up to the front, too, to make sure no platoon with a busted wireless set failed to get the word. Once the truce started, his men would probably swap cigarettes with the damnyankees for some of the ration cans the U.S. Army issued. Tom didn't intend to issue an order forbidding it: less than no point in issuing an order bound to be ignored. Like everybody on both sides of the front, he knew the USA made horseshit cigarettes but had rations better than their C.S. counterparts.

It won't make a dime's worth of difference who wins the war, he consoled himself. That same sort of illicit trading had gone on in the Great War and in the War of Secession, too. Then it was tobacco for coffee. That wasn't a problem these days, not with the Caribbean a Confederate lake.

At 0945, the guns on both sides fell silent. The sudden quiet made Tom jumpy. He didn't feel he could trust it. But the truce held. Confederate medics brought back more bodies and pieces of bodies than wounded men, though they did save a couple of soldiers who might have died if they'd been stuck where they were. Graves Registration— usually called the ghouls—took charge of the remains. Colleton was damned if he knew how they would figure out just whose leg came back in a stretcher, especially since it had no foot attached. That, thank God, wasn't his worry.

Sure as hell, he saw men in butternut chowing down on corned-beef hash and creamed beef and something tomatoey called goulash, all from cans labeled with the U.S. eagle in front of crossed swords. The only thing he wished was that he had some of those cans for himself.

At 1130, both sides started shouting warnings to their opposite numbers. At 1145, firing picked up again. Neither side shot as ferociously as it had earlier in the morning, though. Tom thought the gunfire was as much an announcement that the truce was over as anything else.

That didn't turn out to be quite right. At about 1205, the Yankees started shelling his front—not just with the mortars they'd been using before but with real artillery, too. Shouts of, "Gas!" rang out through the chilly air. Dismayed wireless calls came in from the front and from his reserves. The U.S. guns seemed to know just where to hit.

Tom started swearing horribly enough to startle his wireless man, who asked, "What's the matter, sir?"

"I'll tell you what's the matter, goddammit," Colleton ground out, furious at himself. "I'm an idiot, that's what. That Yankee son of a bitch who came back here to dicker the truce—to hell with me if the bastard didn't spy out our dispositions on the way here and back. Nothing in the rules against it, of course, but fuck me if I like getting played for a sucker."

U.S. forces followed the bombardment with an infantry push, and drove Tom's regiment from several of the positions it had been holding. He got on the field telephone with division HQ in Sandusky, warning them what had happened and how.

"Sneaky bastards," was the comment he got from the major to whom he talked. "How much ground have they gained?"

"Looks like about a mile," Tom said ruefully. He'd be kicking himself for weeks over this one. He hadn't thought he was a trusting soul, but that Yankee captain had sure made a monkey out of him.

The major back in Sandusky didn't seem all that upset. "Don't get your balls in an uproar, Lieutenant-Colonel," he said. "We'll see what we can do about it."

Later that afternoon, eight or ten butternut-painted barrels came rumbling up the road and across the fields to either side of it. Confederate foot soldiers loped along with them. The armored fighting vehicles started shelling the ground the U.S. forces had gained. Just seeing and hearing them was enough to make soldiers who'd been huddling in foxholes ready to get out and fight some more. The Confederates still sometimes called their battle cry the Rebel yell, though they'd been their own country, not rebels at all, for eighty years. The shrill ululation resounded now, way up here in Yankeeland. The surge that had gone west reversed course once more.

But nothing came cheap today. The Yankees had brought a couple of antibarrel cannons to the front. The sound of an armor-piercing round smashing into steel plate reminded Tom of an accident in a smithy. The stricken barrel burst into flames. A couple of men managed to get out. The other three didn't. The blazing barrel sent up a plume of greasy black smoke. Some of what burned in there had been alive moments before.

Colleton cursed softly. "See if I give those sons of bitches another truce," he muttered. "Just see if I do, ever."

Mary Pomeroy always liked driving out from Rosenfeld and visiting the farm where she'd grown up. Her mother was all alone on the Manitoba prairie these days. Maude McGregor still had her health, but she wasn't getting any younger. Mary felt good checking up on her every so often.

The visits did remind her how much time had passed by. Mary's mother had had hair as red as her own. No more; it was almost all gray now. As Mary neared thirty-five, the first silver threads were running through her copper, too.

She and her mother sat in the kitchen, drinking coffee and eating sweet rolls her mother had baked. "Oh, Ma," Mary said, "the smells in here take me back to when I was a little girl. The oilcloth on the table, the coal fire, the kerosene lamps, all the cooking . . ." She shook her head, lost in a world that would never come back again, a world where her father and older brother were alive, a world where the Yanks hadn't occupied Canada for a generation.

"It does smell different in your apartment," her mother agreed. Quickly, she added, "Not bad—not bad at all—but not the same, either."

"No, not the same," Mary said. She had a gas stove and electricity; the one didn't smell like coal, while the other didn't smell like anything. And what she cooked just wasn't the same as what her mother made. She couldn't put her finger on the difference, but she knew it was there.

"How are the Frenchies?" Maude McGregor asked.

"They're there." Mary made a sour face. These days, the United States needed all the soldiers they could scrape up to fight the Confederate States. The men now occupying Rosenfeld and a lot of other Canadian towns came from the Republic of Quebec. They wore blue-gray uniforms, not U.S. green-gray. Mary couldn't stand them. They should have been Canadians, too, but instead they helped the Yanks oppress their countrymen. Most of them—almost all of the young ones who'd grown up in the so-called Republic—spoke nothing but French, and jibber-jabbered in it all the time. As far as she was concerned, that added insult to injury.

"Any trouble with them?" her mother asked.

"No," Mary said tonelessly. "No trouble at all."

She wondered where her mother would go with that, but Maude McGregor didn't go anywhere at all. She only nodded and got the teapot and filled her own cup. She held the pot out to Mary, who nodded. Her mother refilled it. The milk Mary added came from one of the cows in the barn.

"How's Alec?" her mother asked.

Mary smiled. She didn't have to consider her answers and watch every word about her son. "He's fine, Ma. He's growing like a weed, he raises trouble every chance he gets, and he's doing good in kindergarten. Of course, he already pretty much knew how to read and write before he started."

"I should hope so," her mother said. "You and Julia and Alexander did, too."

Alec was named for Mary's dead older brother. Remembering him took the smile off her face. She said, "You know what the bad thing is about school these days?"

"Of course I do," Maude McGregor said. "The Yanks pound their lies into the heads of children who aren't old enough to know malarkey when they hear it."

"That's it. That's just it." Mary didn't know what to do about it, either. Her mother and father had pulled her out of school when the Americans started throwing propaganda around instead of teaching about what had really happened—that was how Canadians saw it, anyhow. No one had raised a fuss back then, but rules were stricter now. And Mary didn't want the Yanks paying attention to her for any reason.

Her mother said, "And Mort? How's the diner doing?"

"Pretty well," Mary answered. "One of the cooks burned his hand, so he'll be out a few days. Mort's filling in behind the stove."

"Must be strange, having a man who knows how to cook," her mother remarked.

"It is. It keeps me on my toes all the time," Mary said. "But it's all right. I'm glad I found anybody, and Mort and I get along real good."

She'd had a young man courting her when her father was killed by his own bomb trying to blow up General Custer as he passed through Rosenfeld. Afterwards, the young man dropped her as if she were explosive herself. Nobody looked at her for years after that, not till Mort Pomeroy did. Was it any wonder she'd promptly fallen in love?

Her mother said, "I'm glad you do. It's nice. Your father and I, we hardly had a harsh word between us."

"I know, Ma." Mary also knew why. Her mother noticed everything and said nothing. If she didn't complain, how could Pa have found fault with her? Mary wasn't like that. She'd never believed in suffering in silence. If something was wrong, she let the world know about it. She didn't always restrict herself to words, either, any more than her father had. She asked, "How are things here?"

"Oh, I get along," Maude McGregor answered. "I've been getting along for years and years now. I expect I'm good for a little while longer."

The farm lacked not only electricity but also running water and indoor plumbing. Mary had never noticed what was missing when she was growing up. She'd taken the pungency of the outhouse as much for granted as the different pungency of the barn. Kerosene lamps had always seemed good enough. So had the pot-bellied coal-burning stove. Now the stinks and the inconveniences, though still familiar, jolted her when she visited. Little by little, she'd got used to an easier life in town.

Even so, she said, "I'm going out to the barn for some chores."

"Oh, you don't need to do that," her mother said quickly.

"It's all right. I don't mind." Mary did intend to gather eggs and feed the animals while she was out there; she wasn't dressed for mucking out the place. That wasn't all she would do, though. Her mother knew as much, knew and worried. But, being who and what she was, she couldn't bring herself to say much.

A motorcar rolled along the dirt track that ran in front of the McGregor farm as Mary went from the farmhouse to the barn. The dirt road didn't see much traffic these days, though Mary remembered endless columns of soldiers in green-gray marching along it when she was a little girl: U.S. soldiers heading for the front that had stalled between Rosenfeld and Winnipeg. Then the front wasn't stalled anymore, the Yanks got what they'd always wanted, and hard times descended on Canada. They weren't gone yet.

The barnyard stink wasn't as sharp and oppressive as the one from the privy. It made Mary smile instead of wrinkling her nose. Her shoes scrunched on straw as she walked back toward the chickens. She proved to herself that she still knew how to get eggs out of nests without ruffling feathers and without getting pecked. A few hens clucked complaints, but that was all. Smiling a self-satisfied smile, she put the eggs in a basket.

That done, she fed all the livestock. She could still handle a pitchfork, too. She didn't have much need to do that in the apartment in Rosenfeld. Come to think of it, though, sometimes a pitchfork would come in handy for prodding Alec along in the right direction.

Off in one corner of the front of the barn lay an old wagon wheel. Its iron tire was red with rust. It had been lying there for at least twenty years, probably longer. Anyone who saw it would figure it was just a piece of junk nobody'd bothered getting rid of. Mary had thought the same thing for years.

Now, grunting, she shoved it off to one side and scraped away at the straw and dirt under it. Before long, her fingernails rasped against a board. She got the board free and looked down into the neat, rectangular hole in the ground it and the wagon wheel concealed.

Her father had dug out that hole to hide his bomb-making tools. The U.S. occupiers had long suspected him. They'd searched the farmhouse and the barn again and again. Despite their suspicions, they'd never found a thing. Arthur McGregor had known what he was doing, in explosives as in everything else.

These days, the bomb-making tools belonged to Mary. She hadn't used them as often as her father had. But she'd bombed the general store in town (owned by a Yank), killed a traitor in Ontario (she thought of it that way, not as blowing up a woman and a little girl), and derailed a train not far from Coulee, the next town west of Rosenfeld. With Ohio lost, the United States depended on rail traffic through Canada. Doing the train had proved easier than she'd expected. She thought she would go in some other direction when she planted her next bomb.

She was so intent on her work, she didn't hear the running feet till they were just outside the barn. She looked up in horror as half a dozen men in green-gray, some with pistols in their hands, others with rifles, burst in shouting, "Hold it right there! You're under arrest, in the name of the United States of America!"

It was over. After all these years, it was over. Mary lifted one of the sticks of dynamite that had sat in her lap. "If you want to take the chance of shooting this instead of me—" she began. If the dynamite went up, the Yanks would go up with it—a good enough last exchange, as far as she was concerned.

But one of the riflemen said, "Ma'am, I've been on the national rifle team at ranges a lot longer than this—they didn't know if they'd need a sharpshooter to take you. If I shoot, I won't miss, and I won't hit the explosives."

He sounded coldly confident, confident enough to make Mary believe him. She set down the dynamite and slowly got to her feet. "Raise your hands!" two Americans shouted at the same time. She obeyed. Why not? Nothing mattered anymore. One of the Yanks said, "Out of the barn now. Slow and easy. Don't do anything cute, or you won't last long enough to stand trial."

"Oh, yes. I'm sure you're worried about that," Mary said. They didn't answer her. Why should they? They'd won.

When she got outside, she saw two more Yanks holding her mother back. They'd slapped a gag on her so she couldn't scream and warn Mary. Two motorcars were parked by the side of the house. She thought one was the auto she'd seen driving along the dirt road. They must have been keeping an eye on her all along, then.

"Leave my mother alone," she said dully. "She never had anything to do with this. It was all me."

"We'll see about that," one of the Yanks said. But he turned to the men holding Maude McGregor. "Take the gag off her, Jack. She can yell her head off now. It won't make any difference."

As soon as Jack removed the gag, Mary's mother said, "She's lying to save me. I was the one who set the bombs."

"That isn't so!" Mary exclaimed. "How about that one the other side of Coulee, Ma? You don't even drive."

"I took the wagon," her mother said with stubborn, hopeless defiance.

"And that's how come we caught your daughter in there with dynamite in her lap, right?" said the Yank who seemed to be in charge of things. He waved to his men. "Get her into the auto. We'll take her up to Winnipeg and tend to business there."

As the other Americans obeyed, one of them asked, "How about the old broad?" Both Mary and her mother squawked irately. The Yanks ignored them.

"Leave her alone for now," their boss said. "Looks to me like we've got the one we want." They shoved Mary into a Chevrolet. As it sped off down the dirt road, she knew how right he was.

Chester Martin had known rejoining the U.S. Army would make his wife furious. He hadn't known *how* furious. Rita had lost her first husband in the Great War, and seemed sure she would lose her second in this one. When Chester reupped, he'd asked for a month to get his affairs in order before he went in. The Army gave it to him; they weren't conscripting middle-aged retreads, even if they were glad to have them, and so they'd acted accommodating as all get-out.

Now he wished he hadn't asked for so long. It was the longest month of his life. "You said they'd shot you last time, and that was plenty for you!" Rita said over and over again. "You lied!" She might have accused him of falling off the wagon—or maybe falling into the arms of an old girlfriend came closer to the mark.

And maybe he was. He had no romantic illusions about war. Nobody who'd been a noncom in the trenches all the way through the Great War could possibly have any illusions about it. But he kept saying, "The country needs me," and that was no illusion. The United States needed all the help they could get from anywhere.

"Have you looked at yourself in the mirror lately?" Rita would ask. That stung, not least because he had. His hair, once sandy-brown, was graying and thinning at the temples. There were lines on his forehead, and more beside his pointed nose. He had a double chin and something of a belly. He still had muscles, though; nobody could hold a construction job without them.

His son, Carl, who was six, didn't know whether to be proud of him or worried about him. Carl knew people could get shot. "You won't let that happen to you, will you, Dad?" he would ask.

"Not me," Chester would answer gravely. "That kind of stuff always happens to the other guy." Carl accepted that. Chester knew better, but didn't want to burden the boy with worries he couldn't do anything about. Rita knew better, too, and wasted no time pointing out to Chester what a liar he was.

With all that going on, then, he wasn't altogether unhappy escaping the little rented house in East Los Angeles and heading to the recruiting station a few blocks away when the time finally came. He took the oath there, which officially put him back in uniform. They gave him just enough of a physical to make sure he had a pulse and could see out of both eyes. If he'd flunked the second half, he suspected they would have worked something out.

They gave him a uniform, too. The tunic was too tight and the trousers were baggy; the tailoring hadn't changed a bit since the Great War. They gave him a first sergeant's stripes on his left sleeve. He knew what that meant. "You're going to have me nursemaid some officer who was still spitting up sour milk when the Confederates tossed in the sponge the last time."

He got exactly no sympathy, which was exactly what he'd expected. The sergeant who'd talked him into rejoining said, "Well, Martin? What about it? Are you going to tell me you're not qualified for the job? I'll say bullshit to your face if you've got the brass to try it."

Martin didn't have that kind of brass. Maybe he could keep a kid from getting some good men killed. He might even save the kid's neck—and, with luck, his own in the process.

His orders were to report to a replacement depot in Virginia. Accompanying them was a travel voucher for rail transportation from Los Angeles to Milwaukee. He asked the noncom who gave him the voucher, "How the devil do I get from Milwaukee to where I'm supposed to go? Stick out my thumb?"

"Beats me," that worthy said cheerfully. "For all I know, hitching's faster than any other way. Once you get to Milwaukee, I promise they'll tell you what to do next."

"I hope so." Martin didn't trust Army bureaucracy. While the people in Wisconsin were figuring out how to get him past the Confederate corridor that split the USA in two, the people in Virginia were liable to decide he was AWOL if he didn't show up on time and throw him in the guardhouse when he finally did. He knew that was unreasonable. He also knew the Army had some strange notions about what was reasonable and what wasn't.

He had a brand-new green-gray duffel bag slung over his shoulder when he went to Remembrance Station, the big new railroad depot in downtown Los Angeles. Rita and Carl came along to say good-bye. If Rita cried, she wasn't the only wife with a husband in uniform who did. He squeezed her and kissed her one last time, kissed Carl on the forehead, and climbed into a second-class car. Maybe officers got Pullman berths. Sergeants, or at least one sergeant in particular, didn't.

More than half the men in the car were soldiers, either coming back from leave or reporting to duty for the first time. Chester listened. The chatter sounded much like what he remembered from the last go-round. Nobody seemed to want to talk to him. That didn't surprise him. He had a lot of stripes on his sleeve, and he was at least twice the age of most of the men in green-gray.

When night came, the train slowed down to a crawl. He hadn't thought about how the blackout applied to trains. He realized he should have. If locomotives went tearing along at full speed behind the beam of a big, bright light, they shouted, *Hey, come shoot me up!* at whatever enemy airplanes happened to be in the neighborhood. That made perfect sense—once you worked it out.

Conductors went through the cars making sure blackout curtains were in place on every window. Light leaking out the sides was as bad as any other kind. Chester wondered how likely an attack was. He shrugged. If it could happen at all, you didn't want to take needless chances.

About half an hour after the blackout curtains came down, Chester went back to the dining car. The featured entrée was something called Swiss steak. It struck him as a good reason for emigrating from Switzerland. He looked at the private at the table next to his and said, "I'm not back on duty yet, but now I feel like I'm back in the Army, by God."

"Yeah." The kid was pushing the gravy-smeared meat around with a noticeable lack of enthusiasm. "This is pretty lousy, isn't it?" He eyed Martin's heavily striped sleeve. "Have you, uh, been in the Army all along?"

By the way he said it, he might have meant since the War of Secession, or possibly since the War of the Roses. Chester laughed and shook his head. "Nope. I got out in 1917"—undoubtedly before the private was born—"and went on with my life."

"Oh." The youngster digested that, which had to be easier than digesting the Swiss steak. He risked another question: "How come you came back? They conscripted me. I had to go. But you must've had it made."

"Well, not quite," Martin said. "I was doing all right, but I wasn't rich or anything. But I didn't want to see Jake Featherston kicking us in the slats, and so here I am."

"Uh-huh." The private seemed surprised anybody who didn't have to would put on the uniform. Maybe he was what was wrong with the

USA, part of the reason the country was having so much trouble with the CSA. On the other hand, maybe he just had a good deal of common sense.

Chester wondered how the Chicago-bound train would go to avoid both the Mormon uprising and the chance of bumping into Confederate raiders. It headed east through Kingman and Flagstaff, New Mexico, and on to Santa Fe, where it turned north for a run through the mountains to Denver. It got hung up there for two days, though, at a little Colorado town called Salida. Somebody said *Salida* meant *exit* in Spanish, but there was no exit from the place till damaged track up ahead was repaired. Avalanche? Sabotage? No one seemed to want to say, which left Chester suspecting the worst.

He dug a greatcoat out of his duffel and used it to stay warm. Sleeping in his seat was anything but delightful. Everybody grumbled. Nobody could do anything but grumble. Misery might not have loved company, but had a lot of it.

Once they got going again, they made pretty good time till they came to Chicago. The Confederates had done what they could to bomb the railroad yards. Given the accuracy of night bombing, that meant the whole city had caught hell. But the crawl at which the train proceeded showed the enemy had hurt the tracks and the stations to which they led.

Following signs that said MILITARY PASSENGERS for the transfer to Milwaukee, Chester stood in line for twenty minutes and then presented his voucher to a bored-looking corporal who eyed it and said, "You're late."

"My whole goddamn train is late. So sue me," Chester said. The corporal looked up, wondering who could be so cavalier about this business. Seeing a man with a lot more stripes than he owned instead of a scared young private, he kept his mouth shut. Chester went on, "I knew I was late before I got here. Now I want to know how to get where I'm going."

"I'll fix it, Sergeant," the corporal promised, and he did. If he took it out on some luckless kid later on, Chester didn't find out about that.

From Chicago to Milwaukee was a short hop, like the one from Toledo to Cleveland. Naturally, whatever eastbound transport they'd planned from Milwaukee was also obsolete. Another noncom did some more fixing. An hour and a half later, Martin found himself taking off in a twenty-two-seat Boeing transport, bound for Buffalo: the first airplane ride of his life.

He didn't like it. It was bumpy—worse than bumpy, in fact. Several people were airsick, and not all of them got all of it in their sacks. There was a snowstorm over Buffalo. The pilot talked about going on to Syracuse or Rochester. He also talked about how much—or rather, how little—fuel he had. The kid next to Chester worked his rosary beads hard.

They did put down in Buffalo, snowstorm or not. The transport almost skidded off the end of the runway, but it didn't quite. The rosary beads got another workout during and after that. "Give 'em some for me, too," Chester said when the airplane finally decided it *did* intend to stop. The only thing that could have made the landing more fun would have been Hound Dogs shooting up the transport while it came in.

He wondered if the Army would try to fly him down to Virginia. If they did, he might have found out more about Confederate fighters than he ever wanted to know. But he got on another train again instead. And he got delayed again, twice: once from bombed-out rails and once from what they actually admitted was sabotage.

Somebody in the car said, "Christ, I hope we're doing the same thing to the Confederates."

"If we weren't, we would've lost the goddamn war by now, I expect," somebody else replied. Chester suspected that was true. He also suspected the United States were using Negro rebels to do a lot of their dirty work down there. He knew they'd done that in the last war; he'd led a Negro Red through U.S. lines to get whatever he needed in the way of arms and ammunition. Blacks now had even less reason to love the CSA than they'd had then.

"You're late," a sergeant growled at him when he finally got where he was going.

"That's right," Chester said. "I'm damn lucky I'm here at all." The other sergeant stared at him. He stared back. He'd had three years of guff the last war. Enough, by God, was enough.

Cincinnatus Driver sat in the Brass Monkey soaking up a bottle of beer. The Brass Monkey wasn't the best saloon in Covington, Kentucky. It wasn't even the best saloon in the colored part of Covington.

But it was the closest one to the house where he lived with his father and his senile mother. He walked with a cane and had a permanent limp. Close counted.

A couple of old black men sat in a corner playing checkers. They were regulars, and then some. As far as Cincinnatus could tell, they damn near—*damn* near—lived at the Brass Monkey. They'd nurse a beer all day long as they shoved black and red wooden disks back and forth. Every so often, they would stick their heads up and join in some conversation or other. More often, though, they stayed in their own little world. Maybe they were smart. The one outside looked none too appetizing to any Negro in the Confederate States of America.

Talk in the saloon reflected that. A middle-aged man named Diogenes blew cigarette smoke up at the ceiling, smiled, and said, "Shoulda got outa here when the gettin' was good. Too damn late now."

"Do Jesus, yes!" another man said, and knocked back his shot. He set a quarter on the bar for another one. "We is nothin' but the remnants—the stupid remnants, I should oughta say. Remnants." He repeated the fancy word with an odd, somber relish.

He wasn't wrong. After Kentucky voted to return to the CSA in early 1941, a lot of blacks voted with their feet, heading across the Ohio to states that remained in the USA. Cincinnatus had intended to do that with his father and mother. He'd been sure ahead of time how the plebiscite would go. If he hadn't stepped in front of a car searching for his mother after she wandered off . . .

Diogenes savagely stubbed out his cigarette. "God damn Al Smith to hell and gone. Reckon he fryin' down there now, lousy, stinkin' son of a bitch."

Several men nodded, Cincinnatus among them. Al Smith hadn't had to give Jake Featherston that plebiscite. He hadn't had to, but he'd done it. Cincinnatus wasn't sorry he was dead, not even a little bit.

The bartender ran a rag over the smooth top of the bar. The rag was none too clean, but neither was the bar. Cincinnatus couldn't tell what, if anything, went on behind that expressionless face. Nodding while somebody else cursed Al Smith had probably been safe enough. He wouldn't have cursed Smith himself, not where people he didn't know could hear. Even if everybody here was black, that was asking for trouble. Anybody—anybody at all—could be an agent or a provocateur.

And sometimes trouble came without asking. The doors to the

Brass Monkey flew open. In stormed half a dozen Freedom Party guards, all in what looked like C.S. Army uniforms, but in gray cloth rather than butternut. They all had submachine guns and mean looks on their faces. When the one with a sergeant's stripes on his sleeve said, "Don't nobody move!" the saloon suddenly became a still life.

The white men fanned out. They weren't quite soldiers, but they knew how to take charge of a situation. The three-striper (he wasn't officially a sergeant; the Freedom Party guards had their own silly-sounding names for ranks) barked, "Let's see your passbooks, niggers!"

No black in the CSA could go anywhere or do anything without showing the book first. It proved he was who he was and that he had the government's permission to be where he was and do what he was doing. Cincinnatus dug his out of the back pocket of his dungarees. He handed it to the gray-uniformed white man who held out his hand. The guard checked to make sure his photo matched his face, then checked his name against a list.

"Hey, Clint!" he exclaimed. "Here's one we're looking for!"

Clint was the noncom in charge of the squad. He pointed his submachine gun at Cincinnatus, then gestured with the weapon. "Over here, nigger! Move nice and slow and easy, or that spook back of the bar's gonna have to clean you off the floor."

Cincinnatus couldn't move any way but slowly. The noncom was careful not to let him get close enough to lash out with his cane. He hadn't planned to anyhow. He might knock the gun out of the man's hand, but then what? He wasn't likely to shoot all the Freedom Party guards before one of them filled him full of holes. He couldn't run, either, not with his ruined leg. He was stuck.

They hauled him away in a paddy wagon. He felt some small relief when they took him to a police station, not a Freedom Party meeting hall. The police still stood for law, no matter how twisted. The Party was a law unto itself, and beyond anyone else's reach.

And a police captain rather than a Freedom Party guard questioned him. "You know a man named Luther Bliss?" the cop demanded.

That told Cincinnatus which way the wind was blowing. "I sure do, an' I wish to Jesus I didn't," he answered.

"Oh, yeah? How come?" The policeman exuded skepticism.

"On account of he lured me down here and threw me in jail back in the Twenties," Cincinnatus said, which was nothing but the truth. He didn't like and didn't trust Luther Bliss. He never had and never would. The U.S. secret policeman and secret agent with the hunting-hound eyes was too singlemindedly devoted to what he did.

His reply seemed to take the policeman by surprise. "How come?" the cop repeated. "He reckon you was a Red nigger?"

"Hell, no." Cincinnatus sounded as scornful as a black man in a Confederate police station dared. Before his interrogator could get angry, he explained why: "Reds didn't bother Luther Bliss none back then. They weren't out to overthrow the USA. Bliss was afraid I was too cozy with Confederate diehards."

"Nigger, we can look all this shit up. If you're lyin', you're dyin'," the cop growled.

"Why you reckon I'm telling you this stuff? I *want* you to look it up," Cincinnatus said. "Then you see I ain't done nothin' to hurt the CSA." The one didn't follow from the other, but he hoped with all his heart that the policeman wouldn't see that.

His attitude did confuse the white man, anyhow. He sounded a little less hostile when he asked, "You seen Bliss since?"

That was a dangerous question, because the answer was yes. Since Luther Bliss was one of the worst enemies the Confederates had in Kentucky, Cincinnatus would be suspected for not reporting that he'd spotted him. Cautiously, he said, "I done heard tell he was in town, but I ain't set eyes on him. Don't want to set eyes on him, neither." The last sentence, at least, was true.

If the Confederates asked the right questions of the right people, they could show the rest was a lie. The cop pointed a warning finger at Cincinnatus. "Don't you go nowhere. I'm gonna check up on what you just told me. What happens next depends on whether you were tryin' to blow smoke up my ass. You got me?"

"Oh, yes, suh. I surely do," Cincinnatus said. "An' I ain't goin' nowhere." He almost laughed at the policeman. If the fellow thought he could just waltz out of the station, that didn't say much for how alert the Covington police usually were.

He sat there in the little interrogation room and worried. After a while, he needed to use the toilet—the Jax he'd drunk was taking his revenge. He stuck his head out the door and asked another cop if he could. He was afraid the white man would say no, if only to pile more discomfort and indignity on him. But the cop took him down the hall, let him do his business, and then led him back.

Cincinnatus had almost started to doze when his interrogator came back. "Well, looks like you weren't lying about your run-in with Bliss," he said grudgingly. He pointed an accusing finger at Cincinnatus. "Why didn't you tell me you'd been living in Iowa? Why the hell didn't you get your black ass back there when you had the chance? What have you been doin' here since you came back?" He seemed sure Cincinnatus' answer would have to be something incriminating.

"Suh, I been takin' care o' my mama, an' my pa's been taking care o' me." Cincinnatus explained how he'd returned to Kentucky to get his parents out, and what had gone wrong. He finished, "You don't believe that, go check the hospital."

"I seen you walk. I know you're screwed up some kind of way," the cop said.

"Do Jesus! That is the truth!" Cincinnatus said.

"I know what we ought to do with you," the policeman told him. "We ought to send you over the damn border. If the Yankees want you, they're welcome to you. Sounds like all you want to do is get the hell out, and take your ma and pa with you. The longer you stay here, the more likely you are to get in trouble."

Hope flowered in Cincinnatus. He needed a moment to recognize it; he hadn't felt it for a long time. He said, "Suh, you do that for me, I get down on my knees to thank you. You want me to kiss your foot to thank you, I do that. I was laid up when I could have taken my folks out of here. By the time I could get around even a little bit, the border with the USA was closed."

"I'll see what we can cook up," the policeman said. "We deal with the damnyankees every now and then under flag of truce. If they want to let you cross the border, we'll let you go."

"Suh, when them guards grabbed me, I reckoned I was a dead man," Cincinnatus said, which was also nothing but the truth. "But you are a Christian gentleman, an' I thank you from the bottom of my heart."

"Don't get yourself all hot and bothered yet," the police captain said. "These things don't move fast. When we've got to talk to the Yankees or they've got to talk to us, though, you're on the list. For now, go on home and stay out of trouble."

"Yes, suh. God bless you, suh!" Cincinnatus had dished out a lot of insincere flattery to white men in his time. He didn't know any Negroes in the CSA—or, for that matter, in the USA—who hadn't. It was part of life for blacks in both countries. Here, though, he meant every word of what he said. This Confederate cop hadn't had to do anything for him. Cincinnatus had expected the man to do things to him. Maybe the policeman thought he *would* turn subversive if he stayed in the CSA. (Fortunately, the man didn't know he'd already turned subversive.) Whatever his reasons, he wanted Cincinnatus out of the CSA and back in the USA. Since Cincinnatus wanted the same thing . . .

Since he wanted the same thing, he didn't even complain about the long walk home. It didn't hurt as much as it might have, either. When he got there, he found his father almost frantic. "What you doin' here?" Seneca Driver exclaimed, eyes almost bugging out of his head in disbelief. "Some damnfool nigger done tol' me them Freedom Party goons grab you."

"They did, Pa," Cincinnatus answered, and his father's eyes got bigger yet. He went on, "An' then they let me go." He told what had happened at the station.

"You believe this here *p*oliceman?" His father didn't sound as if *he* did.

But Cincinnatus nodded. "Uh-huh. I believe him, on account of he didn't have no reason to lie to me. I was *there*. He had me. He coulda done whatever he pleased. Who's gonna say boo if a cop roughs up a nigger? Who's gonna say boo if a cop kills a nigger, even? Nobody, an' you know it as well as I do."

The older man thought it over. He screwed up his face in what was almost a parody of cogitation. "He don't mean nothin' good by it," he said at last. He wouldn't believe a Confederate cop could be decent, and Cincinnatus had a hard time blaming him.

Cincinnatus had a trump card, though. "I'm here," he said, and his father couldn't very well quarrel with that.

Congresswoman Flora Blackford clicked on the wireless set in her Philadelphia office. She usually left it off, turning it on at the hour and half hour to get what news she could. She had little—no, she had no—use for the music and advertising drivel that came out of the speaker most of the time.

Some people were saying television—wireless with moving pictures—was the next big thing. The war had put it on hold, and might have derailed it altogether. Flora wasn't sure she was sorry. The idea of having to watch advertisements as well as listen to them turned her stomach.

She wasn't listening to news now, though, or not directly. She looked at the clock on the wall. It was a quarter to five. What were they waiting for? The announcer said, "Ladies and gentlemen, live from New York City and newly escaped from the Confederate States of America, we are proud to present . . . Satchmo and the Rhythm Aces!"

Out of the wireless poured music the likes of which was almost unknown in the United States. Negroes in the Confederate States had been oppressed for hundreds of years, and had no hope of anything else, anything better. They poured their wish for a different life—and a jaunty defiance of the life they were forced to live—into their music. Those sly rhythms and strange syncopations had no parallel in the USA. Satchmo might almost have been playing his trumpet in Portuguese rather than English.

And yet, a great singer could make an audience feel what he felt even in a foreign language—would opera have been so popular if that weren't true? Satchmo had the same gift. Nobody in the United States played his kind of music. But joy and despair and anger came through just the same.

When the Rhythm Aces finished their number, the announcer said, "You know folks will hear this program in the CSA as well as the USA. What do you have to say to the people of the country you chose to leave?"

"Ain't got nothin' much to say to the white folks there," Satchmo answered, sounding like a gravelly bullfrog. "White folks down there don't listen to the niggers anyways. If you is colored an' you is in the Confederate States, I gots one thing to tell you—git out if you can. You stays dere, you gwine end up dead. I hates to say it, but it's de Lawd's truth."

His English was almost as foreign to Flora's ear as his music. White Confederates had their own accent, or group of accents; she was used to those. People from the USA, though, seldom got to hear how uneducated Confederate Negroes spoke.

"How did *you* get out of the CSA?" the announcer asked.

Flora already knew that story; she'd met Satchmo after he and his fellow musicians came to Philadelphia. Knowing what he was going to say helped her follow his account: "We was up in Ohio, playin' fo' de sojers dere. We done decided we better run, on account of we never gits no better chance. So we steals a command car—you know, one o' dem wid a machine gun on it." His accent got even thicker as excitement filled his voice. "We drives till we comes to de front. It's de nighttime, so de Confederate pickets, dey reckons we's ossifers—"

"Till we commences to shootin' an' drives on by," one of the other Rhythm Aces broke in. They all laughed at the memory.

"Good for you. *Good* for you," the announcer said. Flora didn't like his fulsome tones; she thought he was laying it on with a trowel. The idea wasn't to patronize the Negroes. It was to show the world they were human beings, too, human beings abused by their white Confederate masters. She couldn't think of a better word than that, even though the Confederates had formally manumitted their slaves in the 1880s. Neither side's propaganda was subtle these days. The announcer asked, "What will you play for us next?"

As usual, Satchmo spoke for the band: "This here is a song dat show we is glad to be where we's at."

They broke into "The Star-Spangled Banner." It was not the National Anthem as Francis Scott Key had written it. It was not the National Anthem as Flora had ever imagined it, either. They did things with and to the rhythm for which she had no names. But what they did worked. It made the staid old tune seem new and fresh to her again. Most of the time, she listened to "The Star-Spangled Banner" with half an ear, if that. She knew it too well to pay much attention to it. Not here, not now. She had to listen closely, because she couldn't be sure just what was coming next. She didn't think even the Rhythm Aces knew before the notes flowed from their instruments.

After the last proud wail of Satchmo's trumpet, even the bland announcer seemed moved when he murmured, "Thank you very much."

"You is mighty welcome, suh," Satchmo said. "You is mighty welcome, an' we is mighty glad to be in 'de land o' de free an' de home o' de brave.' If we was still in de CSA, maybe they fixin' to kill us."

The announcer still didn't seem to know what to make of that. Getting people in the USA to believe that whites in the CSA were systematically killing blacks wasn't easy. Getting people in the USA to care even if they did believe was harder yet. People in this country wanted as little to do with blacks as they could, and wanted as few blacks here as possible.

Flora wondered if Satchmo and his fellow musicians had bumped up against that yet. They weren't valued for themselves; they were valued because their escape gave the Confederates a black eye.

"What will you do now that you're in our great country?" the wireless man asked at last.

"Play music." By the way Satchmo said it, he could conceive of no other life. "Wherever folks wants us to play music, we do dat."

How many people would want them to play music as alien to the U.S. tradition as that National Anthem had been? Flora couldn't know. One way or another, Satchmo and his band would find out. They wouldn't starve; the government wouldn't let them. And they wouldn't have to worry about pogroms and worse. People might not like them, but their lives weren't in danger anymore.

After farewells and commercials, the news did come on. It wasn't good. The big U.S. push in Virginia remained bogged down. U.S. counterattacks in Ohio hadn't come to much. The fight to grind down the Mormon uprising remained stalled in Provo. If the United States could have thrown their full might at Utah, the revolt would have been crushed in short order. The Mormons, of course, had the sense not to rebel when the USA could do that. Flora hoped Yossel stayed safe.

Other fronts were sideshows. Confederate-sponsored Indian uprisings in Sequoyah kept the occupied territory in an uproar. That wouldn't have mattered much if Sequoyah didn't have more oil than you could shake a stick at. As things were, the United States had trouble using what they could get, and sabotage ensured that they didn't get much.

Sequoyah was one more piece of trouble left over from the Great War and the harsh peace that followed. If the peace had been milder, maybe someone like Jake Featherston never would have arisen in the Confederate States. The smoldering resentments and hatreds that fueled the Freedom Party's growth wouldn't have existed. On the other hand, if the peace had been more draconian—more on the order of what the United States had visited on Canada—any sign of trouble would have been ruthlessly suppressed before it could turn dangerous.

Which would have been better? Flora didn't know. All she knew for sure, all anyone in the battered USA knew for sure, was that what they'd tried hadn't worked. That was particularly bitter to her because so much of what they'd tried had been under Socialist administrations, including her own late husband's.

The Democrats had ruled the USA almost continuously between

the disaster of the War of Secession and the bigger disaster of the Great War. Teddy Roosevelt hadn't seen the Great War as a disaster; he'd seen it as a vindication, a revenge toward which the country had worked for two generations. Maybe he'd even been right. But the voters thought otherwise. They'd elected Socialists ever since, except for one four-year stretch.

And what had that got them? The economic collapse while Hosea Blackford was in the White House, and the rebirth of Confederate military power while Al Smith was. If only he hadn't agreed to the plebiscites in Kentucky and Houston and Sequoyah . . . But he had, and he'd won reelection on the strength of it, and none of Jake Featherston's solemn promises turned out to be worth the paper it was written on.

We aren't immune from mistakes, either, Flora thought, and laughed bitterly. There were times when the Socialists seemed to go out of their way—a long way out of their way—to prove that.

The telephone rang, dropping a bomb on her train of thought. Not sorry to see it go, she picked up the handset and said, "Yes? What is it, Bertha?"

"Mr. Roosevelt is on the line, Congresswoman," her secretary answered.

"Is he?" Flora could hear the pleasure in her voice. "Put him through, of course."

"Hello, Flora! How are you today?" the Assistant Secretary of War said. Franklin Roosevelt always sounded jaunty, even though poliomyelitis left him paralyzed from the waist down. He was only a distant cousin to Theodore, and had always been a solid Socialist.

"I'm fine, Franklin. How are you? What can I do for you today?" Flora said.

"I'm about as well as can be expected," he replied. "I'd be better if the war were better, but I expect that's true of the whole country. Reason I called is, I wondered whether you'd listened to Satchmo and his pals on the wireless just now."

"I certainly did," Flora told him. "I don't think I ever heard the National Anthem sound like *that* before."

Roosevelt had a big, booming laugh, a laugh that invited everyone who heard it to share the joke. "Neither did I, by God!" he said. "But it didn't sound *bad,* you know—just different."

Had he been a Democrat like his late cousin, the two words would have meant the same thing to him. Flora said, "I liked the way he and the Rhythm Aces talked between numbers. They'll make some people think—here and in the CSA."

"That's the idea," Roosevelt said. "We made sure this broadcast went out over a big web. Featherston's boys could try till they were blue in the face, but they couldn't jam all our stations. People on the other side of the border *will* have got the message."

"Good. Excellent, in fact," Flora said. "Featherston says he tells the truth. His people—white and black—need to know better." She knew white Confederates wouldn't pay much attention to anything Negroes said. But plenty of blacks in the Confederate States had wireless sets, too.

"They sure do." Franklin Roosevelt paused. It seemed very casual. Then he went on, "President La Follette wanted me to pass on to you that, as far as he's concerned, the bargain you had with Al Smith still holds. He'll meet his end of it. He wants me to check and see that you will, too."

"If he does, I will." Flora hoped she hid her bemusement. Two presidents, now, had agreed to speak out against Confederate atrocities on Negroes if she *didn't* speak out on a strange budget item she'd found. Stranger still, she didn't even know what the item was for.

When Scipio was Anne Colleton's butler, back in the days before and at the start of the Great War, he'd got an education less formal but more thorough than he would have had at most colleges. He knew the name for a group of people forced to live in a walled-off part of a town. They formed a *ghetto*.

The Terry had been Augusta, Georgia's colored district for God only knew how long. Blacks lived there and nowhere else. Whites didn't live there, no matter what. But it hadn't been a ghetto. Negroes had worked all over Augusta, waiting tables, cleaning houses, cutting hair, and doing all sorts of backbreaking, low-paying jobs that were beneath whites' dignity.

But the Terry was a ghetto now. Barbed wire surrounded it. Armed guards—police and Freedom Party stalwarts—patrolled the perimeter. The only people who got out were the ones who showed their passbooks at the gates and were approved. Reentering was controlled just as rigidly.

Even before the barbed wire went up, the authorities swept out—emptied—one big chunk of the Terry. Word was that the people removed had been resettled somewhere else. Scipio didn't know of anybody who'd heard from any of them, though. His guess was that they'd gone to a camp. Negroes went into camps. He didn't know of anybody who'd come out of one, either.

All he could do was live his life one day at a time, try to get through, try to get by. Every afternoon, he put on the tuxedo he wore to his job at the Huntsman's Lodge and headed for the nearest gate.

He'd been waiting tables there for a long time. The cops and the stalwarts knew him. They'd known him long enough that most of them had even stopped teasing him about the penguin suit he wore—and for a white man, or even a black, to abandon that particular joke required a forbearance not far from the superhuman. Better still, they'd even known him long enough to let him back into the Terry when he got off work after the usual curfew hour for Negroes.

That he worked at the Huntsman's Lodge in particular undoubtedly helped him and his fellow waiters and cooks and busboys acquire their immunity from the curfew. The place was the finest and fanciest restaurant in Augusta. It was where the town's most important whites gathered—and of course they had to be well served. Of course.

As usual, Scipio arrived for his shift about twenty minutes early. Showing up early and showing up all the time no matter what were two of a restaurant worker's chief virtues. Reliability counted for more than anything else he could think of.

He ducked into the staff entrance—customers had a much fancier one—and hung his ratty overcoat on a hook. He didn't think he'd need it much longer. Spring came early to Augusta, and summer followed hard on its heels. In the subtropical heat and humidity of a Georgia summer, his wing collar and tailcoat became a torture and a torment.

"Hello, Xerxes." That was Jerry Dover, the manager at the Huntsman's Lodge. The sharp-faced white man made a pretty good boss.

"Good day to you, suh." Scipio responded to his alias more readily than he would have to his own name. As Scipio, he was still a wanted man in South Carolina. He hadn't thought the Red uprising during the Great War had a prayer of success, which hadn't kept him from becoming a prominent and visible part of the short-lived Congaree Socialist Republic. As far as he knew, the others who could say that were long dead; his son Cassius was named for one of them.

He expected Jerry Dover to go on his way after the greeting. The manager ran himself ragged making sure the Huntsman's Lodge stayed the best place in town. However much Dover's bosses paid him, it wasn't enough.

Instead, though, Dover said, "Grab yourself some grub and then come see me in my office. I've got something I want to talk to you about."

"I do dat, suh. What you need?"

"It'll keep till then." Jerry Dover did hurry off after that. Scipio scratched his head. Something was on Dover's mind. The manager hadn't seemed anxious or upset, so it probably wasn't anything too dreadful.

You couldn't get rich waiting tables. (If you were a Negro in the CSA, you were most unlikely to get rich any which way, but you sure wouldn't by waiting tables.) The job had its perquisites, though. The meals the cooks fixed for themselves and the rest of the help weren't so fancy as the ones they made for the paying customers, but they weren't bad, and they were free. Scipio ate fried chicken and string beans and buttery mashed potatoes smothered in gravy, and washed them down with coffee with plenty of cream and sugar.

Thus fortified, he went to Jerry Dover's office, tapped on the open door, and said, "What kin I do fo' you, suh?"

"Come on in," Dover told him. "Close that thing, will you?"

"Yes, suh." As Scipio did, he began—oh, not to worry, but to wonder. What didn't Jerry Dover want anybody else hearing? The restaurant business had few secrets—fewer, most of the time, than the people who believed they were keeping them imagined.

Jerry Dover pointed to the battered chair in front of his battered desk. "Sit down, sit down," he said impatiently. "You don't need to stand there looking down at my bald spot. I've got something I want you to take care of for me."

"I do dat," Scipio said, assuming it was something that had to do with the restaurant. "Ask you one mo' time—what you need?"

"Something a little special," Dover answered. Scipio still didn't worry. Later, he realized he should have started right then. But he just sat there politely and waited. His mama had raised him to be polite, going on seventy years ago now, and Anne Colleton's relentless training reinforced those early lessons. Dover went on, "I need you to take something to somebody down in Savannah for me."

"Savannah, suh?" Automatic deference tempered even the horror Scipio felt. "Do Jesus, suh! How I gonna git to Savannah, things like they is now? I is lucky I kin git outa de Terry."

"I'll get you authorized to leave town. Don't you fret about that," Jerry Dover said, which only made Scipio more alarmed than ever.

"What is this thing?" he demanded. "You can't go your ownself? You can't put it in de mail, let de postman bring it?"

"No and no," the manager answered. "If I go out of town, people will notice. Right now, I can't afford to have anybody notice me leaving town. And the mail's not as safe as it used to be. A lot of people are mighty snoopy these days." He doubtless meant people who worked for the Freedom Party. He doubtless meant that, but he didn't say it.

"You reckon nobody care about some raggedy-ass nigger?" Scipio said. Quite calmly, Jerry Dover nodded. His very coolness infuriated the black man. "Suh, this here ass o' mine may be raggedy, but it be the onliest one I got."

"Then you'll be careful of it, won't you . . . Scipio?"

There it was. He'd feared it was coming. Anne Colleton had known who he was, had known what his right name was. She'd eaten at the Huntsman's Lodge—was it really less than a year earlier?—and recognized him. Naturally, she'd wanted him arrested, brought back to South Carolina, and shot. Jerry Dover had forestalled her. He'd shown her that a colored waiter named Xerxes had worked at the Lodge before the Great War. It was, of course, a different Xerxes, but she couldn't prove that. Anne Colleton had always been a woman who got her own way. She couldn't have liked being thwarted here.

Maybe she would have done something about it had she lived. Thanks to the U.S. raid on Charleston, she hadn't. Scipio was free of her forever. But . . . She'd told Jerry Dover his right name. It was a gun in Dover's hands no less than it had been in hers.

Dover opened a desk drawer and reached inside. What did he have in there? A pistol? Probably. What had Scipio's face shown? What he was really thinking? A Negro in the CSA could do nothing more dangerous. Dover said, "You know what I'm talking about, don't you?"

"I know what you talkin' 'bout, yes, suh," Scipio said. Then he let the accent he'd used only once or twice since the downfall of the Congaree Socialist Republic, the educated white man's accent Anne Colleton had made him learn, come out: "I know exactly what you are talking about, and I wish to heaven that I didn't."

Jerry Dover's eyes widened. "You *are* a sandbagging son of a bitch. How many times did you tell me you could only talk like a swamp nigger?"

"As many times as I needed to, to keep myself safe," Scipio answered. Bitterly, he added, "But I see there is no safety anywhere. Now—suppose you eliminate the nonsense. What must I deliver, and to whom, and why?"

Accent was almost as important in the CSA as color. Scipio remained black. He couldn't do anything about that. But his skin said he was one thing. Now, suddenly, his voice said he was something else. His voice proclaimed that he was not just a white man, but someone to be reckoned with: a lawyer, a judge, a Senator. Jerry Dover shook his head, trying to drive out the illusion. Plainly, he wasn't having an easy time of it.

He had to gather himself before he answered, "You don't need to know that. You don't need to know why. The less you know, the better for everybody."

"So you say," Scipio replied.

"Yeah. I do. And I say something else, too: you don't want to mess with me. Anything happens to me, I got stuff written down. You'll wish you was dead by the time they get through with you—and with your family, too."

Bathsheba, whom he'd loved since they met at a boarding house in the Terry. Cassius, who had reached the age when every boy—almost a man—was as much a rebel as the Red he'd been named for. Cassius's older sister, Antoinette, old enough for a husband now—but in these mad times, how much sense did marrying make?

Scipio wasn't the only one whose life Jerry Dover held in the hollow of his hand. Everything in the world that mattered to him—and if Dover made a fist . . .

"All right, Mr. Dover," he said, still with those white men's tones. They helped him mask his feelings, and his feelings needed masking just then. "I shall do what you require of me."

"Figured you would," the restaurant manager said complacently. "Talkin' fancy like that may help you, too."

But Scipio held up a hand. "I had not finished. I shall do what you require—but you will pay my wife my usual wages and tips while I am away, and—"

"Wait a minute," Dover broke in. "You think you can dicker with me?"

"Yes," Scipio answered. "I can bargain with you because I can read and write, too. You have a way to protect yourself against me. That knife cuts both ways, Mr. Dover. I shall do what you require, and I shall carefully note everything I have done, and I shall leave my notes in a safe place. I have those, and they have nothing to do with this restaurant."

Dover glared at him. "I ought to turn you in now."

"That is your privilege." Scipio masked terror with a butler's impenetrable calm. "But if you do, you will have to find someone else to do your service, someone on whom you do not have such a strong hold." He waited. Jerry Dover went on scowling, scowling fearsomely. But Dover nodded in the end. He hadn't intended to end up with a bargain— he'd intended just to impose his will, as whites usually intended and usually did with blacks—but he'd ended up with one after all.

Dr. Leonard O'Doull was a tall, thin man with a long jaw and a face as Irish as his name. He worked in a U.S. Army aid station a few hundred yards behind the line in Virginia. A few hundred yards, in this case, was enough to put him on the north side of the Rapidan when the front was on the south side, in the almost impenetrable second-growth country called the Wilderness. He didn't like that. Getting wounded men back over the river meant delay, and delay, sometimes, meant a death that faster treatment could have stopped.

But there was no help for it. The U.S. bridgehead over the Rapidan was small and under constant assault by air, armor, and artillery. The Confederates were no worse about respecting the Red Cross than their counterparts in green-gray, but there was nowhere in the bridgehead itself that an aid station could hope to escape the evil chances of war.

First Sergeant Granville McDougald waxed philosophical when O'Doull complained: "We do what we can do, Doc, not what we want to do."

"Yeah, Granny, I know." O'Doull had an M.D. He'd had a civilian practice up in Rivière-du-Loup, in the Republic of Quebec, where he'd settled after a stint as an army surgeon there in the Great War. McDougald had been a medic in the last go-round, and ever since. O'Doull wasn't at all sure which of them knew more about medicine. He went on, "Just 'cause I know it doesn't mean I have to like it."

"Well, no," McDougald allowed. "But there's not a hell of a lot of point to flabbling about things you can't help."

O'Doull grunted. Like any doctor, he was an officer—he had a major's oak leaves on his shoulder straps. Like any long-service noncom, McDougald had ways of subverting the privileges rank gave to officers. Being right most of the time was not the least of them.

Before O'Doull could do anything more than grunt, a flight of northbound shells roared by overhead. The sound put him in mind of a freight train rumbling down the track. Confederate artillery constantly tried to disrupt U.S. supply lines.

Disrupt supply lines. That was a nice, bloodless phrase. What the Confederates were really trying to do was blow up trucks and motorcars and trains, to turn the vehicles into fireballs and the men inside them into burnt, mangled, screaming lumps of flesh. That was what it boiled down to.

Granville McDougald also listened to the shells flying north. "Didn't hear any gurgles that time," he said.

"Happy day," O'Doull answered. And it was a happy day . . . of sorts. Rounds filled with poison gas made a distinctive glugging noise on their way through the air. Mustard gas hardly ever killed quickly. But the blisters it raised on the skin could keep a man out of action for weeks. And the blisters it raised on the lungs could keep him an invalid for years, strangling him half an inch at a time and making all his remaining days a hell on earth.

Nerve agents, on the other hand . . . Get a whiff of those, or get even a little drop on your skin, and the world would go dark because your pupils contracted to tiny dots. Your lungs would lock up, and so would your heart, and so would your other muscles, too—but when your lungs and heart stopped working the rest of your muscles didn't matter a whole hell of a lot.

Soldiers on both sides carried syringes full of atropine. Anyone who thought he was poisoned with a nerve agent was supposed to stab himself in the thigh and ram the plunger home. If he was right, the atropine would block the effects of the poison gas. If he was wrong, the antidote that would have saved him would poison him instead. That wasn't usually fatal, they claimed.

All the same, it made for one hell of a war.

"You know," O'Doull said meditatively, "twenty-five years ago I thought we'd hit bottom. I thought we were doing the worst things to each other that human beings could think of to do." He laughed— in lieu of sobbing or screaming. "Only goes to show what I know, doesn't it?"

"Well, I don't suppose you were the only one with that idea," McDougald said. "Kind of makes you wonder where we go from here, doesn't it?"

"*Tabernac!*" O'Doull said, and Granny McDougald laughed at him. When he didn't watch himself, he swore in Quebecois French. Why not? He'd spoken it every day for a quarter of a century. English was the rusty language for him. He was surprised it had come back as well as it had. He'd read it all through his time in Rivière-du-Loup, to keep up with medical literature. That had probably helped.

U.S. counterbattery fire answered the C.S. artillery. By the sound of things, the U.S. bombardment had plenty of poison gas in it. Intellectually, O'Doull understood why. The gas would either deny Confederate guns to their gunners or force the men to don masks and heavy, rubberized outfits that covered every inch of them. Those were unpleasant in cool weather. In the summer, there was some question whether gas or protection from it was more lethal.

As far as O'Doull was concerned, though, the intellect had little to do with gas. He loathed it, pure and simple. He'd never known a doctor or a medic who didn't. How could anyone not loathe stuff made to incapacitate and torment?

People on both sides of the front seemed to have no trouble at all.

Savagely, O'Doull said, "I wish to God they'd test that shit"—he could swear in English, too—"on the people who invent it and the people who improve it and the people who make it. Then they'd be sure they've got it just right."

"Works for me," McDougald said. "Write up a memo and send it on to the Ordnance Bureau. See what they have to say about it."

"I'll be damned if I'm not tempted to," O'Doull said. "What can they do? Court-martial me and throw me out of the Army? I'd thank 'em and go home, and they'd never see my ass again."

"Do it," McDougald urged. "I'll sign it. They want to bust me down to private, I don't care. I'd be doing the same thing with a lot of stripes or without any, and I won't get rich on Army pay no matter what grade I'm in."

Before O'Doull could say anything to that, a shout from outside the aid station brought him back to the real and immediate world of war: "Doc! Hey, Doc! You there? We got a casualty for you!"

"No, I'm not here, Eddie," O'Doull yelled back. "I went to Los Angeles for the sun."

"Funny, Doc. Funny like a crutch." Eddie and another corpsman, a big, burly, taciturn fellow named Sam, carried a stretcher into the tent. Both medics wore smocks with Red Crosses fore and aft, Red Cross armbands, and Red Crosses painted on the fronts and backs of their helmets. Corpsmen on both sides sometimes got shot anyway.

The corporal on the stretcher wasn't at death's door. He was, in fact, swearing a blue streak. He had most of one trouser leg cut away, and a blood-soaked bandage on that thigh. His opinion of the Confederate who'd shot him wasn't far from Sophocles' of Oedipus.

"Round tore out a big old chunk of meat," Eddie said. "Missed the femoral artery, though."

"I guess it did," Granville McDougald said. "He'd be holding up a lily if the artery got cut."

O'Doull nodded. A man could bleed out in a hurry if anything happened to his femoral artery. "Let's get him on the table," O'Doull said. "I'll do what I can to patch him up, but he's going to be on the shelf for a while." He spoke to the noncom: "You've got yourself a hometowner, buddy."

"Oh, yeah, just what I fuckin' need," the corporal said as Eddie and Sam lifted him off the stretcher and onto the operating table. "Got a letter from my sis last week—my wife's fuckin' around with the fuckin' milkman. I go back to fuckin' St. Paul, I'll beat the fuck out of her."

A man of strong opinions but limited vocabulary, O'Doull thought. He nodded to McDougald: "Pass gas for me, Granny." Before the corporal could editorialize about that, McDougald stuck an ether cone over his face. He got out another couple of blurry four-letter words, then went limp.

"Watch what the fuck you're doin' with the fuckin' scalpel, Doc," Eddie said.

"Everybody's a funny man," O'Doull said mournfully. Eddie wasn't half so impassioned as the corporal. Of course, he hadn't just stopped a bullet, either. O'Doull cut away still more of the trouser leg and the wound dressing, too. *Had* the corporal stopped the bullet, or had it just taken a bite out of him and kept on going? O'Doull would have bet the round was long gone, but he did some probing all the same. You never could tell.

"Anything?" McDougald asked.

"Doesn't look like it," O'Doull answered. "They can X-ray him when they get him back to the division hospital, but it sure as hell looks like a hometowner to me. I'm going to try to spread his skin over as much of the wound as it'll cover, tie off some of the bigger bleeders, dust him with sulfa and bandage him up, and then send him on his merry way."

"Make sure you don't tie off the artery when you're fooling around in there," McDougald warned.

"I'll be careful." O'Doull knew some doctors would have got their noses out of joint at a warning from a mere medic. You wouldn't make a mistake like that if you were paying attention to what you were doing. But you could if you got careless. Granny helped make sure O'Doull didn't.

The wound wasn't pretty after he got done with it, but he thought the corporal had a good prognosis. Whether the noncom's wife had a good prognosis might be a different story. When O'Doull said as much, McDougald said, "This guy won't enter the hundred-yard dash in the Olympics any time soon. Maybe she can outrun him."

"Olympics. Right." O'Doull turned to Eddie and Sam. "Take him back to division. Tell 'em to keep an eye on his blood pressure, give him plasma if it falls. I don't think it will—he looks pretty good—but they should monitor it."

"Right, Doc," Eddie said. Sam nodded—a paragraph from him.

O'Doull let out a sigh after they carried the wounded corporal away. "Another miracle of modern medicine," he said.

McDougald clucked at his sarcastic tone. "Hey, you did good, Doc. I think that guy'll be fine, and he lost a lot of meat off the bone."

"Only thing I did that a surgeon in the War of Secession couldn't have was put sulfa powder on the wound," O'Doull said. "That doesn't make me feel special, believe me."

"Leg wounds are what they are," McDougald answered with a shrug. "Nobody in the War of Secession knew anything about X-rays or plasma, I'll tell you that. And the old-timers couldn't do anything about chest or belly wounds—they had to watch people die of shock and blood poisoning. We've got a real chance against them—well, some, anyhow."

"Hot damn." But O'Doull shook his head. "Sorry, Granny. I'm tired as hell." He didn't see that changing any time soon, either.

Honolulu was a nervous town these days. With the Japanese holding Midway and with their airplane carrier probing down from the northwest, all of the main Sandwich Islands were nervous these days. The United States had taken them from Britain at the start of the Great War, and it looked altogether too possible that they might change hands again in the not very indefinite future.

George Enos, Jr., understood exactly why the Sandwich Islands were nervous. His destroyer, the USS *Townsend,* was in dry dock at Pearl Harbor. Japanese carrier aircraft had pummeled her when she poked her nose up too close to Midway. There were no U.S. airplane carriers in the Pacific right now. Sending ships around the Horn wasn't easy, fast, or efficient—and the fight in the North Atlantic was right at the USA's front door. U.S. warships and what chunks of the German High Seas Fleet that could get out of the North Sea squared off there against the British, Confederate, and French Navies. The Sandwich Islands? The Sandwich Islands were a long way from anywhere.

The chief of George's twin 40mm antiaircraft gun owned the rock-ribbed Republican name of Fremont Blaine Dalby. His politics matched his name, which made him a queer bird. The Republicans, to the left of the Democrats and the right of the Socialists, had won few elections since the 1880s.

"You coming into town with us, George?" he asked. The gun crew had got a twenty-four-hour liberty. The whole ship's crew was getting liberty in rotation while repair teams set the destroyer to rights again.

"I dunno," George said uncomfortably.

"I dunno." Dalby mocked not only his indecision but his flat Boston accent, which sounded especially absurd in the petty officer's falsetto. "Well, you better make up your mind pretty damn quick."

"Yeah." George didn't mind going into Honolulu with his buddies. He didn't mind drinking with them, even if he got blind drunk. Part of him, though, did mind the idea of standing in line at one of Honolulu's countless brothels for a quick piece of ass. He was married and had a couple of boys, and he'd never fooled around on Connie. Of course, he'd never been so far from her, either, or had so little chance of seeing her any time soon. When he was out on a fishing run, he made up for lost time as soon as his boat got back to T Wharf. He wasn't coming back to T Wharf, or even to Boston, maybe for years.

And Fremont Dalby knew exactly what ailed him. The gun-crew chief gave him an elbow in the ribs. "What she don't know won't hurt her," he said.

"Yeah," George said again. Connie was a long way away. His pals, the men he ate and slept with, the men he fought beside, were right here. He didn't want them to think he was a wet blanket. *And I don't have to stand in line at a whorehouse,* he told himself. That helped salve his conscience. He nodded. "Sure, I'll come."

"Oh, boy." Dalby made as if to bow. "Thank you so much. Well, come on, then, if you're coming."

Along with the other ratings given liberty, the gun crew showed their paperwork before leaving the barracks and then headed for the nearest trolley stop. From the Pearl City stop, they rode east past Custer Field, one of the many airstrips on Oahu. Even as they passed, Wright fighters were landing and taking off. An air umbrella floated over Oahu at all times.

"I wish we'd had some of those guys up over our heads when the Japs jumped us," George said.

"Would've been nice," agreed Fritz Gustafson, the loader on the twin 40mm cannon. The rest of the men from the gun crew nodded.

"Technically, we *were* under air cover," Dalby said. Several people, George Enos, Jr., among them, let out snorts, guffaws, hoots, and other expressions of derision and disbelief. Dalby held up his right hand, as if taking oath in court. "So help me, we were. Fighters could have flown up from here to the ship and got back."

"Big fucking deal," George said. Others expressed similar opinions, some even more colorfully.

"Yeah, I know," Dalby said. "It would've taken 'em most of an hour to get there, the fight would've been over by the time they did, and they couldn't've hung around anyway, not if they *did* want to get back. But we were under air cover, by God. That's how the brass sees it."

The way George saw it, the brass was full of idiots. He would have found formidable support for that view among ratings—and probably more than he would have imagined among officers as well. Flabbling about it would just have ruined the day, so he made himself keep quiet. The Sandwich Islands were too nice a place to waste time getting upset and fussing for no good reason.

It wasn't too hot. It wasn't too cold. From everything he'd heard, it never got too hot or too cold. The air was moist without being oppressively sticky, the way it got in Boston in the summertime. It could rain at any time of the day or night all year around, but it rarely rained hard. The hills north of Honolulu were impossibly green, the sky improbably blue, the Pacific bluer still.

"I don't just want to be stationed here," George said. "I want to live here."

"In a little grass shack?" Dalby jeered.

"Why not?" George said. "You don't need anything more than that."

Civilians started getting on as the trolley stopped here and there. The sailors eyed them suspiciously. Some were Orientals, and how could you tell if the Japs were loyal to the USA? And quite a few of the whites, especially the older ones, spoke with British accents. They probably wouldn't be sorry to see the United States booted out of Honolulu, either.

Well, too bad, George thought. *It's not going to happen.* He hoped it wouldn't, anyway. The place where the islands were vulnerable was their dependence on the mainland for food and fuel. If the Japanese could cut off supplies, holding them might not be easy no matter what the actual battle situation looked like.

Then the trolley got into Honolulu, and he stopped worrying about things like that. The city had a filigreed, before-the-Great-War feeling to it. Not a whole lot had been built during the American occupation. The hotels that had accommodated visitors before the new war shut down tourism were the ones that had accommodated them before 1914.

Even the red-light district had been there a long time. The saloons and tattoo parlors and "hotels" that greeted sailors and soldiers had the look of places that might have greeted their grandfathers. The lurid neon signs a lot of them sported seemed afterthoughts, not essentials.

"We need a few drinks," Fremont Dalby declared, and nobody presumed to disagree with him. He swaggered into a dive called the Swizzle Stick. The rest of the gun crew followed.

Dalby ordered whiskey. Most of the other sailors followed suit. George and Fritz Gustafson got beers instead. "What do you want to go and do that for?" somebody asked. "Haven't you got better things to do with your dick than piss through it?"

"It's good for both," Gustafson said, which quelled that in a hurry.

Some of the barmaids were white, others Oriental. They were all female, and wore low-cut white blouses and short black skirts. Seeing them reminded George how long it had been since he'd set eyes on a woman, let alone touched one. He stared down at his glass of beer. He didn't want to be unfaithful to Connie—but he didn't want to go without loving, either.

The facsimile of loving you could buy for money wasn't as good as the real thing. You didn't need to be an egghead to figure that out. It was a lot better than nothing, though. Was it enough better than nothing to make him decide to do it? *That's the question,* he thought, and chewed on it as hard as Hamlet had grappled with *To be or not to be.*

He didn't have to choose right away. They weren't going anywhere for a while. Some of the sailors had already knocked back their whiskeys. They were waving their glasses for refills. George didn't feel like drinking that fast. If he drank that fast, he'd get drunk. If he got drunk, he'd do something stupid. He could feel that coming like a rash. And if he did something stupid and he wasn't lucky, he'd end up with a goddamn rash, too.

But his glass emptied, as if by magic. "You want another?" a slant-eyed, tawny-skinned barmaid asked. George found himself nodding. The next beer appeared in short order. It vanished in short order, too. So did the one after that, and the one after *that.* About then, George stopped counting them.

Fremont Dalby got to his feet. Considering how much he'd put down, that he could get to his feet proved he was made of stern stuff. "The time has come," he declared, "and we're damn well going to. Drink up, you bastards."

George knew all the reasons he didn't want to go to a brothel. He knew, all right, but he'd stopped caring. Connie was five thousand miles away—a lot farther if he had to sail it. What she didn't know wouldn't hurt her. Dalby's words came back to him, handy as could be. Everybody who went to stand in one of those lines told himself the same thing. If he drank enough beforehand, he might even make himself believe it.

The line moved forward at a good clip. "They hustle guys in and out, don't they?" George said. The rest of the gun crew laughed as if that was the funniest thing they'd ever heard. George had to listen to himself before he realized what kind of joke he'd made. Then he laughed, too.

It cost three dollars, payable in advance. He didn't even get to choose a girl. He got assigned a cubicle. He went to it and there she lay, already naked on the bed. She was plump, and had black hair; she might have been part Oriental. "Hurry up," she said. "You only got five minutes."

He wondered if he'd drunk too much to perform. He quickly discovered he hadn't. And, speaking of quickly, it was over almost before it began. He didn't need to worry about spending too much time in the nasty little room. *That was it?* he thought as he did up his pants. *I got all hot and bothered about* that? He had, too.

Whoever had designed the place knew his business. The exit funneled customers into a pro station. Taking care of prophylaxis against venereal disease—something new for George—proved nastier than the brief coupling had been enjoyable. When he said so to a pharmacist's mate, the fellow shrugged and asked, "Would you rather have VD?"

"Couldn't be worse than this," George said.

"Shows what you know. Shows you never tried pissing through a dose of the clap, too." The pharmacist's mate jerked a thumb toward the door at the far end of the room. "I ain't got time to argue with you. Go on, get the hell out of here."

Out George went. The sordidness of what he'd just been through far outweighed the pleasure. The spasm of drunken guilt he felt didn't help, either. *If Connie ever finds out, she'll murder me. I'll have it coming, too.*

Most of the other men from the gun crew were already out on the sidewalk. Some of them seemed as subdued as George. Not Fremont Dalby, though. "Twice!" he bragged.

Two times nothing is still nothing, George thought. Then he blinked. He'd never been anything special in school. He wouldn't have bet he remembered how multiplying by zero worked, not in a million years. Things came back in the strangest ways.

There were times when Brigadier General Abner Dowling suspected he must have been a fire brigade in some past life. Not a member of a fire brigade, but a whole brigade all by himself. That was the only thing that could explain how many fires he'd put out in his long career in the U.S. Army.

More than ten years as adjutant to General George Armstrong Custer made a good start—or a bad one, depending on how you looked at things. Custer was the hero of the Great War, but no man was a hero to his adjutant, any more than he was to his valet. Dowling knew too well how vain, how stubborn, how petulant the old fool was . . . and how those qualities went a long way toward making him the man who, in spite of everything—including himself—made the decisions that ended up beating the Confederate States.

After the Army finally put Custer out to pasture—over his vehement and profane objections—what had Dowling's reward been? Eagles on his shoulders, eagles and the post of commandant of Salt Lake City. Trying to hold the Mormons down was even more fun than trying to hold Custer down had been. Dowling had been in General Pershing's office when a sniper assassinated Pershing. No one had ever caught the murderer—the Mormons took care of their own. And after that, Utah was Abner Dowling's baby.

He'd kept the lid on. The permanently rebellious state had even seemed quiet enough to persuade President Al Smith, in his infinite wisdom, to lift military occupation and restore full civil rights to the inhabitants. When Dowling left, the War Department gave him stars on his shoulders. He was immodest enough to think he'd bloody well earned them, too.

And his reward for that? He'd been sent to Kentucky to hold down Freedom Party agitation. There'd been times when the Freedom Party maniacs made the Mormons seem a walk in the park by comparison. Then President Smith, infinitely wise again, agreed to Jake Featherston's demands for a plebiscite. Afterwards, Dowling got to preside over the U.S. withdrawal over Kentucky and the Confederate reoccupation.

War, plainly, was right around the corner then. They'd put Dowling in Ohio, which turned out to be the Confederate *Schwerpunkt*. The U.S. War Department had always had trouble seeing west of the Appalachians. Dowling didn't have enough barrels or airplanes to counter Confederate General Patton's armored onslaught. He still thought he'd put up the best campaign he could, given what he had to work with.

Maybe the War Department even agreed with him. They recalled him from Ohio after it fell, but they didn't quite—make him the scapegoat for that fall. After a spell in Philadelphia counting rubber bands and making sure everyone's necktie was on straight, they'd put him back to work. Oh, he wasn't an army commander anymore, but they did give him a corps under Major General Daniel MacArthur for the great U.S. counterstroke, the move against Richmond.

Forward to Richmond! was a rallying cry in the War of Secession. It didn't work then. It didn't work so well this time as the USA hoped, either. It was the obvious U.S. rejoinder to what the Confederates had done—obvious enough for Featherston's men to have anticipated it. They hadn't stopped the U.S. attack, but they'd slowed it to a crawl.

And Abner Dowling, commanding MacArthur's right wing, had had to face a second armored attack from General Patton, this one aimed at his flank. Patton, plainly, had wanted to roll up the whole U.S. force facing him, but he hadn't brought it off. He wouldn't, either.

But was it any wonder Dowling felt the weight of the world on his broad shoulders?

Yes, those shoulders were broad. His belly was thick. He had a series of chins cascading down to his chest. He was, all things considered, built like a barrel. If he took to food to shield himself from the slings and arrows of outrageous fortune, well, it was a wonder he hadn't taken to drink.

He sighed and stretched and yawned. He hated paperwork. He'd earned the right. He'd done too much of it for too many years, first for Custer and then on his own hook. The more rank he got, the more paperwork went with it. He'd got good at the bureaucratic infighting, too, the sort of quiet warfare that measured itself as much by things prevented as by those accomplished.

That thought made him look east toward Warrenton, where Daniel MacArthur had his headquarters. MacArthur had wanted to pull one out of General McClellan's book from the War of Secession, land at the mouth of the James, and go after Richmond from the southeast. It could have been a good plan in 1862 had McClellan pursued it with energy—a word not often associated with his name. In 1942, against aircraft and the C.S. Navy, it would have been an invitation to suicide.

Well, it wouldn't happen now. A quiet coded message from Dowling to the War Department had made sure of that. He'd got good at what he did, all right; MacArthur wasn't sure even yet who'd put paid to the project he thought so wonderful. But Dowling remained convinced he'd prevented Western Union messenger boys from delivering a lot of Deeply Regrets telegrams in a campaign that wouldn't have been worth them.

His own headquarters were in Washington, Virginia, a town with nothing to recommend it that he could see. U.S. soldiers walked through the place in groups of five or six or by squads; even traveling in pairs wasn't enough to keep them from getting knocked over the head and having their throats cut. The locals kept chalking FREEDOM! and CSA! on light walls and painting the slogans on dark ones. There were rumors the local women of easy virtue deliberately didn't get their VD treated so they could pass it on to U.S. soldiers. For once, the brass hadn't started those rumors. The men had.

Dowling went outside. The sentries in front of the house he'd commandeered came to an attention so stiff, he could hear their backs creak. "As you were," he told them, and they relaxed—a little. Relax too much in hostile territory and you'd relax yourself right into the grave. "Anything seem strange?" he asked them.

They looked at one another. At last, with unspoken common consensus, they shook their heads. "No, sir," they chorused.

"All right. Good, in fact," Dowling said. Enlisted men had a feel for such things that all the fancy reports from Intelligence often couldn't match. They listened to what the locals said, and to what they didn't. If they'd been in enemy territory for even a little while, they got good at adding two and two—and sometimes even at multiplying fractions.

Guns boomed off to the south and east. Corps headquarters was supposed to be out of artillery range of the front. So were divisional headquarters. Dowling had noticed, though, that the most effective divisions were the ones whose COs ignored that rule. The closer to actual fighting an officer got, the better the feel for it he came to have. Dowling did his best to apply that rule to himself as well as to the officers who served under him.

The guns boomed again, and then again. Dowling cocked his head to one side, studying the sound. After due consideration, he nodded. That was just the usual exchange between a couple of U.S. batteries and their Confederate counterparts. It was liable to smash up a few unlucky men on each side, but it wouldn't change the way things turned out if it went on for the next million years. It was just part of the small change of war.

Somewhere overhead, airplanes droned by. Dowling wasn't the only one who listened to the sound of their engines with a certain concentrated attention, or who glanced around to see where the nearest trench was in case he had to dash for cover. Not this time. One of the sentries delivered the verdict: "Ours."

"Yeah." Another man nodded. "Sounds like they're going to drop some shit on Featherston's head in Richmond."

"Good," Dowling said.

The sentries nodded again. "We nail him, we win big," one of them said, and then, meditatively, "Asshole."

"Chrissake, Jimmy," hissed the soldier who'd spoken first. "You don't say that in front of a general."

Jimmy looked abashed—or rather, worried that he might get in trouble. "Don't get yourself in an uproar about it, son," Dowling said. "I guarantee you I have seen and worked with and worked for more people of the asshole persuasion than you can shake a stick at."

"Like who, sir?" Jimmy asked eagerly.

Abner Dowling could have named names. The question was, could he stop once he got started? He was tempted to let all the resentment out at once, in a great torrent that would leave the sentries' eyes bugging out of their heads. He wouldn't get in trouble for that; a man with a silver star on each shoulder strap was allowed his little eccentricities. That was what they called them for generals, even if a lot of them would have landed lesser mortals in the stockade. But it took a hell of a lot to make the powers that be decide to jug a general.

So it wasn't fear of consequences that kept Dowling's mouth shut. It was more the fear of seeming like a four-year-old—a fat four-year-old with a white mustache—in the middle of a temper tantrum. Dowling remembered too many times when he'd had to calm General Custer down after one of his snits. What was distasteful in another man might also be distasteful in him.

He wagged a coy finger at Jimmy and the other soldiers. "That would be telling." The men looked disappointed, but not too—he didn't suppose they'd really expected him to spill the beans. He took out a pack of cigarettes and stuck one in his mouth. Then he held out the pack to the sentries. They accepted with quick grins and words of thanks. The Raleighs—spoil from a dead Confederate—bore Sir Walter's face above an enormous, and enormously fancy, ruff.

"Damn, but these are good," Jimmy said after his first drag. "Stuff we call tobacco nowadays tastes like an old cowflop."

"A *real* old cowflop," one of the other sentries added. "One that's been out in the sun for a while and got all dried out."

Dowling thought of burnt weeds and lawn trimmings when he smoked U.S.-made cigarettes. He blew out a cloud of smoke, then said, "You boys want to make me give up the habit."

The sentries laughed. Jimmy said, "Don't do that, sir. Only thing worse than lousy tobacco is no tobacco at all. Besides, when you're smoking you can't smell the goddamn war so much."

You can't smell the goddamn war so much. Dowling wouldn't have put it that way, which didn't mean the kid was wrong. Even here in Washington, well back of the line, you noted whiffs of that smell. Dowling didn't know what all went into it. Among the pieces, though, were unburied corpses, unwashed men, and uncovered latrine trenches. Cordite and smoke were two other constants. The smell had a sharper note in this war, for exhaust fumes had largely ousted the barnyard aroma of horses.

And there was one other stink that never went away. It blew out of the War Department. With luck, it blew out of the War Department on the other side, too. And it usually did, for most wars went on for a long, long time. No, there was no escaping the all-invasive, all-pervasive reek of stupidity.

Hipolito Rodriguez had worn butternut in the Great War. The Confederate Conscription Bureau had pulled him off his farm in the state of Sonora, given him a uniform and a rifle and rather more English than he'd had before, and sent him out to fight. And fight he had, first in Georgia against the black rebels in one of the Socialist Republics they'd proclaimed there and then in west Texas against the damnyankees.

He had a son in butternut in this war, and two more bound to be conscripted before long. And he was back in uniform himself. He'd signed up as a member of the Confederate Veterans' Brigades: men who weren't fit for front-line service anymore but who could still help their country and free fitter men for the fight.

Now he found himself in Texas again, riding a bus across a prairie that seemed to stretch forever. He wore uniform again—of similar cut to the one he'd had before, but of gray rather than butternut cloth. The rest of the new camp guards wore identical clothes. Only two or three of them besides Rodriguez were from Sonora or Chihuahua. The rest came from all over the CSA.

Being in Texas was a mixed blessing for a man of Mexican blood. White Texans often weren't shy about calling their fellow Confederate citizens greasers and dagos, sometimes with unprintable epithets in front of the names. But at least Confederates of Mexican blood *were* citizens.

In an odd way, Rodriguez thanked heaven for the Negroes who would fill the camp where he was to become a guard. If not for them, Mexicans would have been at the bottom of the hill, and everything would have flowed down onto them. As things were, most of the trouble went past them and came down on the *mallates'* heads. That suited him fine.

The bus stopped once, in a dusty little town whose name—if it had a name—Rodriguez didn't notice. The place had a Main Street with a filling station, a saloon that doubled as a diner, and a general store that doubled as a post office. It was even smaller than Baroyeca, the Sonoran town outside of which Rodriguez had a farm. It looked to be even poorer, too. Since Sonora and Chihuahua were and always had been the two poorest states in the CSA, that said frightening things about this place on the road to nowhere.

Along with everybody else, Rodriguez lined up to use the toilet at the filling station. It was dark and nasty and smelly. The proprietor stared at the camp guards as if they'd fallen from another world.

Some of them bought cigarettes and pipe tobacco at the general store. Rodriguez went into the saloon with others. The bartender must have been used to three customers a day. Having a dozen all at once made his eyes bug out of his head. Somebody ordered a ham sandwich. In an instant, all the men in gray uniforms were clamoring for ham sandwiches. The barkeeper worked like a man possessed, slicing bread, slicing ham, slicing pickles, slapping on mustard and mayonnaise. The bus driver leaned on his horn.

"Screw him," one of the camp guards said. "He ain't gonna take off without all of us." As if to contradict him, the driver blew another long blast.

None of the guards paid any attention. They stayed right there, waiting for their sandwiches and slapping down quarters as they got them. When Rodriguez's turn came, the man in the boiled shirt and the black bow tie—as much a uniform as his own gray one—gave him a funny look. His dark skin and black hair said one thing, while the outfit he had on said another. Rodriguez just waited. The man handed him the sandwich.

"*Gracias,*" Rodriguez said as he paid him. He spoke more Spanish than English, but his English was more than good enough for *thank you.* He wanted to make the Texan twitch, and he did.

When they'd all got their food and their tobacco, they deigned to reboard the bus. The driver muttered to himself. He did no more than mutter, though. Considering how badly he was outnumbered, that was smart of him.

Rodriguez sank down into his seat with a grunt of relief. Not long after his farmhouse got electricity, he'd almost electrocuted himself. He hadn't been the same since—otherwise, he might have gone to the front himself, and not into the Confederate Veterans' Brigades.

Away went the bus, rattling west down the imperfectly paved highway. "Reckon I'm gonna pawn my fuckin' kidneys when we finally get where we're goin'," one of the men in gray said.

"You been fuckin' with your kidneys, Jack, there's some shit your pappy never learned you," another one replied. Goatish laughter erupted. The rattletrap bus filled with cigarette smoke.

Towards evening, the bus came into Snyder. It looked like all the other Texas towns through which Rodriguez had passed on the way west: bigger than some, smaller than others. Then the bus rolled on a few miles farther. Somebody sitting up near the front who could see out through the big windscreen said, "Son of a bitch!" It was an expression of awe, not anger.

Other soft oaths, and a few not so soft, followed. Rodriguez, who was sitting somewhere near the middle, tried to peer past the men in front of him to find out what they were getting excited about. He didn't have much luck. They were all shifting and moving, too.

The bus stopped. This was where they were going, whatever *this* was. The driver answered that, saying, "Welcome to Camp Determination. Everybody off."

With a tired wheeze, the bus' front door opened. One by one, the new camp guards filed out. Some of them gathered in front of the luggage bin, waiting for the driver to unlock it so they could get out their duffels. Others, Rodriguez among them, took a look at Camp Determination first. He decided the fellow who said *son of a bitch* had known just what he was talking about.

"I was eighteen years old and in the Army in the last war before I saw a town that size," said one of the gray-haired men in gray uniforms.

"*Sí*, me, too," Rodriguez agreed. You could drop Baroyeca down in the middle of that camp, and it wouldn't even make a splash.

Barbed wire surrounded an enormous square of Texas prairie. Machine guns poked their snouts out of guard towers outside the wire perimeter. Barracks halls built of bright yellow pine as yet unbleached by the sun and unstained by the rain and rusty nails rose in the middle distance. There were a lot of them, but the vast acreage inside the barbed wire had room for at least as many more.

Somebody else pointed in a different direction. "Holy Jesus!" the man said. "Will you look at all them trucks?"

There they sat, on an asphalted lot separated from the barracks by more barbed wire. Along with the rest of the guards, Hipolito Rodriguez had become very familiar with those trucks. They looked like ordinary Army machines, except that the rear compartment was enclosed in an iron box—an airtight iron box. Pipe the exhaust in there and people who got into the trucks didn't come out again . . . not alive, anyhow.

"They're gonna get rid of a hell of a lot o' niggers in this place," the man next to Rodriguez said. "*Hell* of a lot."

"You want to shut your mouth about that, Roy," somebody else told him. "We don't talk about that shit. If we do it amongst ourselves, we're liable to do it where the coons can hear us, and then we'll have trouble." He'd learned his lessons well; the Freedom Party guards who'd trained them at the much smaller camp near Fort Worth had rammed that home again and again. "Far as the niggers know, when they get on those trucks, they're always going somewhere else."

"Yeah, yeah," Roy said impatiently. "Far as *I* know, they're all goin' to hell, and it damn well serves 'em right."

"Come on, come on." The bus driver sounded even more impatient than Roy did. "Y'all get your gear and get moving. I got to get moving myself, get the hell outa here and back towards where I live."

Rodriguez found the gray canvas bag with his last name and first initial stenciled on it in black paint. He slung it over his shoulder and joined the column of guards thumping toward what looked like the main gate, at least on this side of the square. Extra guard towers watched over it. Anyone who tried attacking it without a barrel would get chopped to hamburger.

The camp was already manned. A couple of the men at the gate lowered the muzzles of their submachine guns toward the ground. "New fish," one of them remarked.

"Don't look so new to me." His pal had the heartlessness of a man with all his hair and all his teeth.

"Sonny boy, I learned to mind my own business before you were a hard-on in your old man's dungarees," said a man from the Confederate Veterans' Brigade.

"I believe you, Pops," the guard answered. "Some people need as big a head start as they can get." He didn't smile when he said it.

Guards on duty and new arrivals glared at one another. Before anybody could get around to demanding papers and showing them— and before anybody could get around to tossing out more insults like grenades—a man with a deep voice spoke from inside the gate: "What's going on here? Are these the new guards they've been promising us? About goddamn time, that's all I've got to say."

As soon as the men at the gate heard that voice, they became all business. As soon as Hipolito Rodriguez heard it, he had to look around to remind himself that he wasn't in a trench somewhere even farther west in Texas, with damnyankee machine-gun bullets cracking by overhead and damnyankee shells screaming in.

Out through the gate came Jefferson Pinkard. He was older now, but so was Rodriguez. He had a good-sized belly and two or three chins and harsh lines on his face that hadn't been there in 1917. Back when Rodriguez was training, he'd heard that a man named Pinkard was high in the camp hierarchy. He'd wondered if it was the man he'd known. He didn't wonder anymore.

He took half a step out of line to draw Pinkard's eye to him, then said, "How are you, *Señor* Jeff?"

Pinkard eyed him for a moment without recognition. Then the big man's jaw dropped. "Hip Rodriguez, or I'm a son of a bitch!" he exclaimed, and thundered forward to fold Rodriguez into a bear hug. The two of them pounded each other on the back and cursed each other with the affection a lot of men can show no other way.

"Teacher's pet," said one of the guards who'd ridden on the bus with Rodriguez. But he made sure he sounded as if he was joking. If one of his comrades turned out to be a war buddy of the camp commandant's, he didn't want to seem to resent that, not if he knew which side his bread was buttered on.

When Pinkard let Rodriguez go, he said, "So you're here to help us deal with the damn niggers, are you? Freedom!"

"Freedom!" Rodriguez echoed automatically. He was used to saying it in English now instead of going, *¡Libertad!* the way he had down in Baroyeca. "*Sí, Señor* Jeff. That is why I have come."

"Good," Camp Determination's commandant told him. "We're gonna have us a hell of a lot of work to do, and we're just about ready to do it."

Since coming to Augusta near the end of the Great War, Scipio hadn't gone far from his adopted home. For one thing, he hadn't cared to go anywhere else; he'd made his life there, and hadn't wanted to wander off. And, for another, travel restrictions on Negroes had started tightening up again even before the Freedom Party came to power. They'd got much worse since.

Just how much worse, he discovered in detail when he went to the train station to buy a ticket for Savannah. The line for whites was much longer than the one for blacks, but it moved much, much faster. Whites just bought tickets and went off to the platforms to board their trains. Blacks . . .

"Let me see your passbook, Uncle," said the clerk behind the barred window. Scipio dutifully slid it over to him. The man made sure the picture matched Scipio's face. "Xerxes," he muttered, botching the alias the way most people did when they saw it in print. "What's the purpose of your visit to Savannah, Uncle?"

"See my family there, suh," Scipio said. He had no family in Savannah, but it was the safest reason to give.

The clerk grunted. "You got permission from your employer to be away from work?"

"Yes, suh." Scipio produced a letter from Jerry Dover on Huntsman's Lodge stationery authorizing him to be absent for one week.

Another grunt from the clerk. He jerked a thumb to the left. "Go on over there for search and baggage inspection."

Scipio went "over there": to a storeroom now adapted to another purpose. A railroad worker—a weathered fellow who couldn't have been far from his own age—patted him down with almost obscene thoroughness. Two more white men of similar vintage pawed through his carpetbag.

"How come you do all dis?" Scipio asked the man who was groping him.

"So nobody sneaks a bomb on the train," the white man answered matter-of-factly. "It's happened a couple-three times. We've had to tighten up." He turned to the men checking Scipio's valise. "How's it look?"

"He's clean," one of them said. "Bunch of junk, but it ain't gonna go boom."

Stung by that appraisal of his stuff, Scipio said, "Ask you one mo' thing, suh?"

"Yeah?" The white man who'd searched him spoke with barely contained impatience. *Why are you bothering me, nigger?* lay at the bottom of it. But Scipio had sounded properly deferential, so the fellow let him go on.

"What you do when a lady come in here?"

"Oh." The man laughed and gestured as if grasping a woman's breasts from behind. Scipio nodded; that was what he'd meant. The frisker said, "We got a couple of gals who take care of that. Don't you worry your head about it, Uncle. Just get on down to Platform Eight."

"Thank you, suh." Scipio picked up the carpetbag and headed for the platforms. The Confederate authorities—or maybe it was just the railroad employees—were shrewd. If they had white men groping black women, they would stir up trouble they didn't need. They already stirred up a whole great storm of troubles; at best, life for Negroes in the CSA was one long affront. But it often wasn't the sort of affront that made people flash into fury. Back in the days of slavery—the days into which Scipio had been born—white men did as they pleased with black women . . . and with black men who presumed to object. Resentment still simmered, ready to boil. The railroads didn't turn up the heat under it.

The corridors were designed so that nobody could give Scipio anything while he was on the way from the inspection station to the platform. Some of the barriers were of new, unweathered wood. *We've had to tighten up lately,* the railroad man said. They seemed to have done a good job.

Several whites were already waiting on the platform. A couple of them sent Scipio suspicious glances. *Do you have a bomb? Did you sneak it past the inspectors? Will you blow us up?* For his part, he might have asked them, *If you send colored folks into camps, why don't they come out again?*

He didn't say anything, any more than they did. The questions hung in the air just the same. Despair pressed down heavily on Scipio.

How were you supposed to make a country out of a place where two groups hated and feared each other, and where anybody could tell to which group anyone else belonged just by looking? The Confederate States of America had been working on that question for eighty years now, and hadn't found an answer yet.

The Freedom Party thought it had. It said, *If only one group is left, the problem goes away.* The trouble was, the problem went away for only one group if you tried that solution. For the other, it got worse. No one in the Party seemed to lose any sleep over that.

More whites came onto the platform. So did a few more Negroes. The blacks all grouped themselves with Scipio, well away from the whites. Had they done anything else, they would have fallen into a category: uppity niggers. Nobody in his right mind wanted to fall into that category these days.

A little blond boy pointed up the tracks. "Here comes the train!" He squeaked with excitement.

It rumbled into the station. Departing passengers got off, got their luggage, and left the platform by a route different from the one Scipio had used to get there. He and the other Negroes automatically headed for the last two cars in the train. They wouldn't sit with whites, either: they knew better. And if the cars in which they sat were shabbier than the ones whites got to use, that was unlikely to be a surprise.

Rattles and jolts announced the train's departure. It rolled south and east, the tracks paralleling the Savannah River. When Scipio looked across the river, he saw South Carolina. He shook his head. Even after all these years, he wasn't safe in the state where he'd been born. Then he shook his head again. He wasn't safe in Georgia, either.

Cotton country and pine woods filled the landscape between Augusta and Savannah. Scipio saw several plantation houses falling into ruin. Marshlands had done the same thing. Raising cotton on plantations wasn't nearly so practical when the colored workforce was liable to rise up against you.

People got on and off at the stops between the two cities. Scipio wouldn't have bet that God Himself knew the names of hamlets like McBean Depot, Sardis, and Hershman.

And, when the train was coming out of the pine woods surrounding Savannah, it rolled through a suburb called Yamacraw that seemed to be the more southerly town's Terry. Negroes did what they could to get by in a country that wanted their labor but otherwise wished

they didn't exist. Drugstores in white neighborhoods sold aspirins
and merthiolate and calamine lotion—respectable products that actually worked. Scipio saw a sign in Yamacraw advertising Vang-Vang
Oil, Lucky Mojoe Drops of Love, and Mojoe Incense. He grimaced,
ashamed of his own folk. Here were the ignorant preying on the even
more ignorant.

As soon as he got on the east side of Broad Street, things changed.
The houses, most of them of brick, looked as if they sprang from the
eighteenth century. Live oaks with beards of moss hanging from their
branches grew on expansive lawns. That moss declared that Savannah,
its climate moderated by the Atlantic only fifteen miles away, was a
land that hardly knew what winter was.

"Savannah!" the conductor barked, hurrying through the colored
cars as the train pulled into the station. "This here's Savannah!" He
didn't quite come out and snap, *Now get the hell off my train, you
lousy coons!* He didn't, no, but he might as well have.

Scipio grabbed his carpetbag and descended. As at Augusta, the
exit to the station kept him from having anything to do with boarding
passengers. He gave the system grudging respect. That it should be necessary was a judgment on the Confederate States, but it did what it was
designed to do.

Once he got out of the station, he stopped and looked at the sun,
orienting himself. Forsyth Park was east and south of him. He walked
towards it, wondering if a policeman would demand to see his papers.
Sure enough, he hadn't gone more than a block before it happened. He
displayed his passbook, his train ticket, and the letter from Jerry Dover
authorizing him to be away from the Huntsman's Lodge. The cop
looked them over, frowned, and then grudgingly nodded and gave
them back. "You keep your nose clean, you hear?" he said.

"Yes, suh. I do dat, suh," Scipio said. His Congaree River accent
had marked him as a stranger in Augusta. It did so doubly here; from
what little he'd heard of it, Savannah Negroes used a dialect almost in-
comprehensible to anyone who hadn't grown up speaking it.

Forsyth Park was laid out like a formal French garden, with a
rosette of paths going through it. With spring in the air, squirrels frisked
through the trees. Pigeons plodded the paths, hoping for handouts.
Flowering dogwood, wisteria, and azaleas brightened the greenery.

Scipio had to find the Albert Sidney Johnston monument. The Confederate general, killed at Pittsburg Landing, was something of a mar-

tyr, with statues and plaques commemorating him all over the CSA. In this one, he looked distinctly Christlike. Scipio fought the urge to retch.

He sat down on a wrought-iron bench not far from the statue. One of those importunate pigeons came up and eyed him expectantly. When he ignored it, he half expected it to crap on his shoes in revenge, but it didn't. It just strutted away, head bobbing. *You'll get yours,* it might have said, and it might have been right.

A squirrel overhead chittered at him. He ignored it, too. He had no certain notion how long he'd have to wait here, so he tried to look as if he were comfortable, as if he belonged. Several white women and a few old men passed with no more than casual glances, so he must have succeeded. Very few white men between the ages of twenty and fifty were on the streets. If they weren't at the front, they were in the factories or on the farms.

"How do I get to Broad Street from here?" asked a woman with brown hair going gray.

"Ma'am, you goes west a few blocks, an' there you is," Scipio answered.

"Oh, dear. I was all turned around," the woman said. "I'm afraid I have no sense of direction, no sense of direction at all."

The code phrases were the ones Scipio had been waiting for. He hadn't expected a woman to say them. He wondered why not. Jerry Dover hadn't said anything about that one way or the other. A woman could do this as well as a man—maybe better, if she was less conspicuous. Scipio took a small envelope out of the hip pocket of his trousers. As casually as he could, he set it on the bench and looked in the other direction.

When he turned his head again, the envelope was gone. The woman was on her way toward Broad Street. No one else could have paid any attention to, or even seen, the brief encounter in the park. Scipio wasn't sure what he'd just done. Had he given the Confederate States a boost or a knee in the groin? He had no way of knowing, but he had his hopes.

IV

Jefferson Pinkard was a happy man, happier than he had been since moving out to Texas to start putting up Camp Determination. For one thing, Edith Blades was coming out to Snyder with her boys before too long. That would be nice. She didn't want to marry Jeff till her husband was in the ground for a year, but he'd still be glad to have her close by instead of back in Louisiana.

And, for another, now he had a man he could trust absolutely among the guards. "Hip Rodriguez!" he murmured to himself in glad surprise. He hadn't seen the little greaser for twenty-five years, but that had nothing to do with anything. After what they'd been through together in Georgia and west Texas, he knew he could count on Rodriguez. He didn't know how many times they'd saved each other's bacon, but he knew damn well it was more than a few.

And he knew how important having somebody absolutely trustworthy was. Running prison camps was a political job, though he wouldn't have thought so when he started it. And the higher he rose, the more political it got. When the only man over you was the Attorney General, you found yourself in politics and maneuvering up to your eyebrows, because Ferdinand Koenig was Jake Featherston's right-hand man—and about two fingers' worth of the left as well.

Back by Alexandria, Mercer Scott was heading up Camp Dependable these days. Scott had led the guard force when Jeff commanded the camp. He'd had his own ways to get hold of Richmond. No doubt the guard chief here did, too. The Freedom Party people at the top wanted to make sure they knew what was going on, so they had independent channels to help them keep up with things.

And if the guard chief started telling lies, or if he started scheming, having someone on your side in the guard force was like an insurance policy. Hip Rodriguez couldn't have fit the bill better.

With a grunt, Pinkard got up from his desk and stretched. He pulled a pack of cigarettes out of the top drawer, lit one, started to put the pack back, and then stuck it in his pocket instead. He was about to start his morning prowl through the camp when the telephone rang.

"Who's bothering me now?" he muttered as he picked it up. His voice got louder: "This here's Pinkard."

"Hello, Pinkard. This is Ferd Koenig in Richmond."

"Yes, sir. What can I do for you, sir?" *Speak of the devil and he shows up on your front porch,* Jeff thought.

"I want to know how things are coming," Koenig said, "and whether you can make a few changes in the way the camp's laid out."

"Things *were* coming fine, sir. There's been no problem on shipments out of here," Pinkard answered. *Shipments* was a nice, bloodless way to talk about Negroes sent off to be asphyxiated by the truckload. It kept him from thinking about what went on inside those trucks. He didn't feel bloodless toward Ferd Koenig. If the son of a bitch thought he could run a Texas camp from Richmond . . . he might be right, because he had the authority to do it. Grinding his teeth, Pinkard asked, "What do you need changed?"

"Way you've got the place set up now, it's just for men—isn't that right?" the Attorney General said.

"Yes, sir. That's how all the camps have been, pretty much," Jeff replied. "Not a hell of a lot of women and pickaninnies packing iron against the government." There were some, but not many. He didn't know if there were separate camps for black women, or what. He guessed there were, but asking questions about things that were none of your business was discouraged—strongly discouraged.

"That's going to change." Koenig's voice was hard, flat, and determined. "You can bet your bottom dollar that's going to change, in fact. What's wrong with the CSA is that we've got too many niggers, period. Not troublemaking niggers, but niggers, period—'cause any nigger's liable to be a troublemaker. Am I right or am I wrong?"

"Oh, you're right, sir, no doubt about it," Jeff said. Koenig was just quoting Freedom Party chapter and verse. Jake Featherston had been going on about niggers and what they deserved ever since he got up on the stump for the Party. Now he was keeping his campaign promises.

"All right," Koenig said. "If we're gonna get rid of 'em, we've got to have places to concentrate 'em till we can do the job. That means everybody we clean out of the countryside and the cities. Everybody. So can you separate off a section for the women?"

"I can if I have to," Pinkard replied; you didn't come right out and tell the big boss no, not if you wanted to hold on to your job you didn't. Thinking fast on his feet, he went on, "It'd mess things up here pretty bad, though, the way Determination is laid out now." *Ain't that the truth?* he thought. "What'd be better, I reckon, is building a camp for women right *alongside* the one we've got now. That way, we could start from scratch and do it right the first time. Lord knows we've got the land we need to do it."

He waited for Koenig to tell him all the reasons that wouldn't work. Not enough time was always a good one, and often even true. After perhaps half a minute's silence, the Attorney General said, "Can you have a perimeter up and a place for shipments to go out of ready in ten days' time? They can sleep in tents or on the ground till you get the barracks built."

"Ten days? Oh, hell, yes, sir," Jeff said, trying not to show how pleased he was. He would have agreed to five if he had to. He hadn't expected Koenig to say yes at all.

But Koenig went on, "That's what I like to see—a man who'll show initiative. I told you one thing, but you had a different idea, and it looks to me like a better idea. Make sure you fix up this new camp so it's the same size as the one you've got now. It'll need to be."

"I'll take care of it," Pinkard promised, slightly dazed. "Uh—if you aim to do shipments out of two big camps like that, I'm gonna need more trucks. The ones I've got now won't begin to do the job."

"More trucks," Koenig echoed. Across all those miles, Jeff heard his pen scratching across paper. "You'll have 'em." Another pause. "Instead of building the new camp *right* alongside, why not put it across the railroad spur from the old one? That way, you can separate the niggers out soon as they get off the trains."

"I'd have to run another side of barbed wire that way, 'stead of using what we've got." Pinkard thought for a moment. "I'd need to get some dozers back again, too, to level out the ground over there."

"Can't you use the niggers you've got in the men's camp?" Koenig demanded.

"Well, I could, yeah, but dozers'd be a hell of a lot faster," Jeff replied. "I figured that mattered to you. If I'm wrong, you'll tell me."

Ferdinand Koenig paused once more. "No, you're not wrong. All right—fair enough. You'll have your bulldozers. And I'm going to bump you up a rank to brigade leader. That translates to brigadier general in regular Army ranks. You'll get a wreath around your stars, in other words. Congratulations. When you were in the Army the last time around, did you ever reckon you'd make general?"

"Hell, no. I never even worried about making corporal," Jeff answered, which was the God's truth. "Thank you very much, sir."

"You're welcome. A raise comes with the promotion. I expect you'll earn the money," Koenig said. "More responsibility comes with the promotion, too. You're going to be in charge of a really big operation out there, and a really important one, too. I wouldn't do this if I didn't think you could swing it."

"I'll do my damnedest, sir," Pinkard said. "It's for the Party and it's for the country. You can count on me."

"I do. So does the President. You've shown you've got what it takes," Koenig said, which made Jeff button-popping proud. The Attorney General went on, "Those bulldozers and their crews'll show up in the next few days. You tell 'em what needs doing, and they'll do it. Anything else you need—barbed wire, lumber, whatever it is—you holler, and you'll have it. If you don't, somebody's head'll roll, and it won't be yours. Freedom!"

"Freedom!" Jeff echoed the Party slogan, but he was talking to a dead line.

He got up from his desk, stretched, and went to the window. Out beyond the barbed wire, and out beyond the railroad spur and the road that ran alongside it, what was there to see? Nothing but more prairie—sagebrush and tumbleweed and jackrabbits and little gullies that turned into torrents when it rained. Leveling them out would be the dozers' main job. They could do it, and it wouldn't take long.

"Son of a bitch," he said softly. "A women's camp." They were serious back there in Richmond. He'd known they were serious—he wouldn't have been a Freedom Party man if they weren't—but he hadn't known they were *that* serious. If they kept on the way they were going, there wouldn't be a Negro left in the CSA before too long.

Pinkard shrugged as he headed out the door. He wouldn't shed a whole lot of tears if that happened. If there weren't any Negroes, white men wouldn't have to worry about them taking away their jobs. They wouldn't have to worry about Negroes eyeing white women. And they wouldn't have to worry about Red uprisings. He'd got his baptism of fire in 1916 against Red Negro rebels in Georgia. They'd fought harder than the damnyankees had. Of course, the USA and CSA took prisoners. Neither side in the black uprisings had bothered with that very often. So . . . good riddance to bad rubbish.

Out into the sunshine he went. Spring was in the air, but the sun wasn't biting down with full force yet. He'd grown up in Alabama and spent time in Louisiana. Texas summer was no fun for anybody, but it wouldn't be any worse than what he was used to.

With several submachine-gun-toting guards at his back, he did his usual prowl through Camp Determination. That he did it was normal. How he did it wasn't. He tried not to make his rounds the same two days running. He'd stick his head into barracks halls, or he'd go through the kitchens, or he'd go around just inside the perimeter checking for signs of tunneling, or he'd talk with prisoners, or . . . He never knew ahead of time. He just followed whatever gut feeling he had.

The Negroes had found they could complain to him if they stayed respectful. "Suh, we needs mo' food," a skinny black man said. He didn't ask for better food; that was obviously a lost cause.

"You're getting what I can give you," Jeff said, which was more or less true. "If I get more in, you'll get more, too." That was also true, although he didn't expect to see the camp's supply increased. To drive the point home, he added, "I can't make you any promises, mind."

"Do what you can, suh, please," the black man said. Pinkard nodded and went on to the next barracks hall. The Negroes there grumbled about the food, too. Jeff listened and nodded and again said he'd do something if he got the chance. As long as they were grumbling about the food and not about the trucks that transported them to other camps, everything was fine. The trucks were what really mattered— and the Negroes didn't seem to know it.

For once, Cincinnatus Driver felt as if he were leading a charmed life. The Confederates had arrested him—and they'd let him go. To him, that went a long way toward proving white men weren't as smart as they thought they were. He might even find himself on the U.S. border one of these days before too long. He dared hope, anyhow.

Meanwhile . . . Meanwhile, life went on in Covington's colored quarter. It wasn't much of a life. Even compared to what he remembered of times before the Great War, it wasn't much of a life. He shrugged. He couldn't do much about that. He couldn't do anything about it, in fact. All he could do was try to get through from day to day.

He thought about staying away from Lucullus Wood's barbecue place. He thought about it, but found he couldn't do it. His showing up there wouldn't make alarm bells go off at the police station. The only Negroes who didn't show up there were the unlucky ones too poor to afford any of Lucullus' barbecue.

He hoped—he prayed—he wouldn't see Luther Bliss at the barbecue place anymore. He hated, despised, and feared the former head of the Kentucky State Police. Of course, he also hated, despised, and feared the Confederate States of America. Bliss was one of the CSA's sincerest and ablest enemies—and gave Cincinnatus the cold horrors just the same.

If the Confederate police didn't have informers posted in the barbecue joint, they were missing an obvious trick. Despite the risk, talk there was freer than anywhere else in Covington that Cincinnatus knew about.

By now, everybody who worked in the place recognized him when he came in. More than a few people also recognized that he had a special connection with Lucullus. They would always find a seat for him, even when the ramshackle restaurant was packed. He got extra barbecue when he ordered, and some of the time they didn't bother charging him. He'd always been a man who paid his own way, but he appreciated that now, because he didn't have a whole lot of money.

Policemen and Freedom Party stalwarts came into Lucullus' place, too. They also recognized Cincinnatus—recognized him and left him alone. They'd caught him once, and it hadn't stuck. Not all of them understood why it hadn't stuck, but they knew it hadn't. They were no more energetic than most mere mortals. They didn't feel like doing anything they didn't have to.

Lucullus came up to Cincinnatus while he was eating a big plate of beef ribs. The barbecue cook was a massive man, muscle more overlain by fat with each passing year. Who could blame him for liking his own cooking? Everyone else did, too. His father, Apicius, had been even wider and thicker.

Cincinnatus set down a rib. "Afternoon," he said.

"Afternoon." Lucullus had a big, deep voice that went with his bulk. "Mind if I join you?"

"You throw me out on my ear if I'm dumb enough to tell you yes in your own place," Cincinnatus said. "I done plenty o' dumb things in my time, but nothin' dumb as that."

"Glad to hear it." Lucullus squeezed into the booth, across the table from him. He waved to one of the waitresses. "Bring me a cup of coffee, would you, Aspasia honey, when you git the chance?" Nodding, the woman waved back.

The coffee arrived faster than *when you git the chance*. Cincinnatus hadn't expected anything different. When the boss asked for something, only a fool kept him waiting—and Lucullus wasn't the sort to put up with fools. Casually, Cincinnatus asked, "So what do you hear from Luther Bliss?"

He'd timed it well; Lucullus was just taking a sip. The cook choked, but the coffee didn't—quite—go up his nose. After managing to swallow, Lucullus sent him a reproachful stare. "Damn you, you done that on purpose."

"Who, me?" Cincinnatus was innocence personified—not easy for a black man on the wrong side of fifty with a ruined leg. But he'd been only partly malicious. "What *do* you hear from him?" he asked again.

Lucullus didn't bother pretending he hadn't had anything to do with the white man with the mahogany eyes of a hunting hound. "Says he owes you one on account of you done that truck for him."

The truck had held mines that went into the Licking River. At least one of them had blown a Confederate gunboat sky-high. The news should have gladdened Cincinnatus' heart. And so it did, in fact. All the same, he said, "Reckon I owe Luther Bliss more'n one."

"Mebbe." Lucullus calmly filched one of the ribs off Cincinnatus' plate and took a bite out of it. Fiery barbecue sauce ran down his chin—an occupational hazard. "How come you didn't spill your guts to the Confederates when they done grabbed you, you feel that way?"

Cincinnatus couldn't squawk at Lucullus' scrounging, not after all the free food the other man let him have. As for the other . . . "Well, I didn't know where the bastard was at, or I might have."

"Better be more to it than that," Lucullus said severely.

There was, no matter how little Cincinnatus wanted to admit it. Scowling, he said, "Don't reckon I'd tell the Confederates where a *dog* was at, let alone a son of a bitch like that one."

Laughing, Lucullus said, "That's better." He lit a cigarette.

"Gimme one o' them things," Cincinnatus said. Lucullus did, and leaned across the table so Cincinnatus could take a light from his. After a long, satisfying drag, Cincinnatus added, "You don't know you're playin' with a rattlesnake there, on account of I ain't told you."

"He is one, sure enough." Lucullus sounded more pleased than otherwise. He explained why: "Dat man be a serpent, sure enough, but he be *our* serpent. He don't bite niggers. He bites Confederates, an' they shrivels up an' dies."

That wasn't quite literally true, but it made a telling metaphor. Cincinnatus wanted no part of it, or of Luther Bliss. "He done bit me," he said angrily.

"Well, but he reckon mebbe you got somethin' to do with them Confederate diehards back then." Lucullus cocked his head to one side and studied Cincinnatus. "Plenty other folks reckon the same thing. My pa, he was one of 'em."

And Cincinnatus *had* had something to do with them, not that he intended to admit it now. "That man steal two years outa my life," he growled. "You reckon I gonna trust him far as I can throw him after that?"

"Trust him to give the Freedom Party a boot in the balls," Lucullus said. "He do dat every chance he git."

Before Cincinnatus could answer, a gray-haired, stooped, weary-looking black man came into the barbecue place. One of the small hells of Cincinnatus' injuries was that he couldn't jump to his feet. He had to make do with waving. "Pa! I'm over here! What is it?"

But he knew what it was, what it had to be. Seneca Driver didn't only look weary. He looked as if he'd just staggered out of a traffic accident. "She gone, son," he said as Cincinnatus did fight his way upright. "Your mama gone." Tears ran unnoticed down his face.

Lucullus had risen, too. He set a hand on Cincinnatus' shoulder. "Sorry to hear the news," he said in a low voice. "Why don't you set your pa down, he tell you what happened."

Numbly, Cincinnatus obeyed. As numbly, his father accepted the cup of coffee Aspasia brought him. His hands added cream and sugar. Cincinnatus didn't think he knew they were doing it. He said, "She done laid down for her nap—"

"I know," Cincinnatus broke in, wanting to say something. "She was asleep when I went out."

"Uh-huh." His father nodded. He sipped from the coffee, then stared at it in surprise, as if wondering how it had got there. "Sometimes I'm glad when she go to sleep, on account of I don't got to worry none fo' the nex' little while."

"I understand that," Cincinnatus said. "Feel the same way my ownself."

"But she don't usually sleep this long," Seneca said. "I go in to see how she is, an'—" He wrinkled his nose. "I don't think nothin' special of it, on account of she makin' messes a while now."

"Yeah." Cincinnatus looked down at the gnawed ribs on the plate in front of him. His mother had cleaned him when he was a baby. He'd found cleaning her one of the cruelest parts of her slide into senility.

"I put my hand on her shoulder, an' she gettin' cold," his father said. "Jus' like somebody blowed out a candle. She go easy. I bless the good Lord fo' dat. Pray to Jesus I go so easy when my time come."

Cincinnatus made himself nod. Grief and relief warred inside him, along with shame that he should feel relief. "It's over now," he said, and choked on his own tears.

Aspasia brought Seneca a plate of ribs. "Why, thank you, child," he said in mild surprise. "You didn't have to do nothin' like that."

"On the house," she said softly. "You need anything else, you jus' sing out, you hear?" She hurried away.

As automatically as he'd fixed the coffee to suit him, Seneca started to eat. He said, "What am I gonna do without your mother?"

"Got to let the undertaker know," Cincinnatus said.

"I do *dat.*" His father sounded impatient, almost irritable. "Yeah, I do *dat.* But so what? Your mama an' me, we been together close to sixty years. Now she ain't there no more." He waved before Cincinnatus could speak, so Cincinnatus didn't. "I know she ain't hardly been here this las' couple years, but it ain't the same. It just ain't." He started crying again, as unknowingly as he had before.

"Maybe we get you up into Iowa," Cincinnatus said. "Start everything all over up there. You got great-grandchildren you never seen."

"I don't believe no ofays. I especially don't believe no Confederate ofay *po*liceman," Seneca Driver replied with a shrug.

"Even if he lied, maybe we get there on our own." Cincinnatus knew it would be easier—not easy, but easier—with his mother gone. He didn't say that; even thinking it gave his relief and shame fresh ammunition.

"We see." His father sounded altogether indifferent. "Got other things to fret about right now."

With Cincinnatus at his side, he arranged them. The funeral was four days later, on a bright spring day. Cincinnatus wore a suit he'd brought down from Des Moines. It wasn't funereally dark, but it was the only one he had. None of the neighbors and friends who'd come presumed to say anything about it.

"Ashes to ashes, dust to dust," the preacher intoned. "God bless and keep Livia Driver, who is free of the evils of this world and free to enjoy a kinder one beyond. We pray for her in Jesus' name. Amen."

"Amen," Cincinnatus echoed. Preachers always said such things. He knew that. But for a Negro in the CSA, the evils of this world were altogether too real.

Part of Clarence Potter wished he hadn't gone to school in the USA. It wasn't that he begrudged the education; he didn't. Yale was a first-rate school. Back before the Great War, quite a few Confederates and Yankees had studied in each other's homelands. Some people had thought that would bring the CSA and USA closer together. It hadn't. It never would. They were as different as chalk and Friday.

So it seemed to a patriot from either one, anyhow. Potter, despite his own differences with the government he served, certainly qualified. But not even the most ardent patriot from either country could deny that they were similar in some important ways, too, language high on the list.

Potter listened to a sergeant talking. "Where did you learn to sound like a damnyankee?" he asked.

"Sir, I grew up in Pittsburgh," the noncom answered. "My father was in the tobacco business, and he lived up there. Wasn't much fun when I came down here, because I already had the accent, and people got on me for it."

"I believe that," Potter said. Somebody else would have to check the man's story. If it was true, it accounted for the accent. If it wasn't, it was outstanding cover for the Yankees to sneak one of their own into a secret Confederate operation.

But that wasn't Potter's worry, or not directly. All he could do was note the possibility. Somebody else *would* have to deal with it. His job was checking the way the sergeant sounded. And the man sounded pretty good to him. He scribbled notes in a loose-leaf binder, then nodded to the sergeant.

"I think you may well hear back from us," he said.

"I hope so, sir," the man said, still sounding much too much like a damnyankee for comfort. "This sounds like a good way to give the United States a good, stiff kick in the nuts."

Potter hadn't said much about the operation. The sergeant, however, plainly had the brains to add two and two and get something close to four. "If you do hear from us, you'll get the details then," Potter told him.

He also had the brains not to ask too many questions. He said, "I hope I do, sir," saluted, and left the underground room in the War Department.

Instead of calling in another candidate, Potter telephoned Nathan Bedford Forrest III. The chief of the Confederate General Staff said, "Forrest here. What can I do for you, General?"

"You've already done it, sir," Potter said. "You've got me playing God for these fellows you're recruiting."

"And so?" Forrest said. "This isn't the first time you've had to select people for a dangerous mission. That's part of your job."

"Oh, yes, sir," Potter agreed. "Usually, though, the men I pick and choose from aren't so eager as these kids. They're going to get killed. Some of them will get a blindfold and a cigarette if they're lucky, or a bullet in the back of the head if they aren't. But they don't care. I could give you a division if willingness were all it took."

"Well, willingness damn well isn't," Forrest said. "These man have got to be *good*. They'll have to convince Yankees that they're Yankees. We don't want just anybody here. We want men who can get well behind enemy lines and raise hell."

"I understand that. There was a fellow a couple of days ago who'd played a Yankee two or three times in amateur theatricals down in Mississippi." Potter sighed. "He was every bit as bad as that would make you think, but he didn't believe it. He got mad as hops when I told him he'd have to fight the war the regular way."

Forrest laughed, not that it was really funny. "Amateur theatricals, eh? I believe you—you couldn't make that up. He must have convinced *somebody* he could sound like he came from the USA, or he never would have got as far as you."

"I suppose he did." Potter drummed his fingers on the binder. "Have to see who he did convince, and weed that man out—whoever he is, he's got a tin ear." He wrote himself another note.

"You think of everything, don't you?" Forrest said admiringly.

"Don't I wish I did? If I'm so smart, how come I'm not rich?" Potter said. Forrest laughed, though again he wasn't joking. He went on, "I'm just trying to stay one step ahead of the damnyankees."

"We'll be farther ahead of them than that if things go the way I hope they do," Lieutenant General Forrest said.

Potter almost asked what kind of things the chief of the General Staff had in mind. He refrained at the last moment, at least as much because he feared Forrest would tell him as because he feared Forrest wouldn't. He didn't have a need to know, no matter how badly he wanted to know. He didn't want to make Forrest responsible for breaching security. *I really have spent too much time in Intelligence,* he thought.

Instead of prodding at things that weren't his proper concern, he asked something that was relevant: "Any sign the United States are training infiltrators who wear butternut?"

He got silence on the line for about half a minute. Then Forrest said, "Thank you for reminding me that anything we can do to the USA, the USA can do to us. No, General, I haven't had any reports like that. But just because I haven't had them doesn't mean the damnyankees aren't doing something like that. They could, couldn't they?"

"Oh, yes—maybe more easily than we could," Potter answered. Kentuckians loyal to the USA had no trouble sounding as if they came from Confederate Tennessee. Men from the less mountainous parts of West Virginia sounded like their Virginia neighbors. And the United States had their share of people who'd grown up in the Confederate States or gone to school here.

"One more thing we'll have to watch out for," Forrest said mournfully. "The President won't be jumping up and down when he hears about it."

"No, he won't," Potter agreed. "But I'll tell you one thing: he'll be a lot angrier if you don't tell him about it till it ups and bites you, if it does."

"You're likely right," Forrest said.

"Yes, I think so," Potter said. He'd known Jake Featherston longer than even the President's oldest Freedom Party buddies. He didn't know Featherston so deeply, but he'd spent a lot of time brooding over what the head of the Freedom Party was likely to do next, and he'd been right more often than he'd been wrong.

"All right, then. I will pass it along," Forrest said. "And I'll try to make sure no more ham actors get as far as you. So long." He didn't quite suppress a snort before hanging up.

It *was* funny. Potter couldn't deny that, though he'd been annoyed at the inept Mississippian and even more annoyed at the officer who'd passed the man. That officer would soon find himself in a new assignment. Potter didn't know whether it would be defusing mines with his teeth or just counting thumbtacks in Georgia or Alabama or somewhere else far away from the real war. Wherever it was, the fellow wouldn't have anything to do with this project.

At the moment, Clarence Potter didn't want to have anything more to do with this project, either. He suddenly seemed to feel the weight of the whole War Department pressing down on him. If he didn't get out, he thought he'd suffocate. That set of symptoms had afflicted other men who worked in the subbasement, but never him, not till now.

Rank had its privileges. If he felt like getting out, he could, and he didn't have to ask anyone's permission. He blinked a little when he came out into Richmond in broad daylight. He might have been a suddenly unearthed mole. When *was* the last time he'd been out and about with the sun in the sky? He couldn't remember, which wasn't a good sign.

Propaganda posters sprouted everywhere: on walls, on fences, on doors. They cursed the enemy and exhorted people to work hard and keep their mouths shut. One of them, an idealized portrait of Jake Featherston (and Potter, who saw Featherston fairly often, knew how idealized it was), simply said, THE PRESIDENT KNOWS. That gave Potter something to think about; he suspected it would have given anybody something to think about. Another one showed two bestial-looking Negroes with knives sneaking up on a house where a blond woman slept. LOOK OUT! it warned. The Intelligence officer nodded to himself—there was a good piece of propaganda.

The city of Richmond, now that he was actually looking around, seemed to have taken a worse beating already in this war than it had all through the Great War. Clarence Potter didn't know why that surprised him, but it did. Bombers could rain far more death down onto the ground than they'd been able to a generation earlier. They carried bigger bombs farther, faster, and higher, so they were harder to shoot down. And there were more of them than there had been. It showed.

Buildings that still had glass in their windows were the lucky ones. Some people had replaced the glass with sheets of plywood. Others made do with cardboard, which was fine till it got wet. Quite a few hadn't patched the wounds with anything. *Those* buildings, even when otherwise undamaged, seemed to look out on the world with dead eyes.

A lot of motorcars were missing glass from their windows, too. Patching them with plywood wasn't practical. People made do, not that they had much choice.

Bomb damage beyond broken windows was scattered almost at random throughout Richmond. Here a building would have a chunk bitten out of it or a street would be cordoned off with sawhorses to keep automobiles from diving into a hole in the pavement eight feet deep and thirty feet across. Gangs of Negroes directed by whites with submachine guns worked with picks and shovels to clear rubble and repair roads.

Every now and then, most of a city block of buildings was gone, smashed to matchsticks and bricks and rubbish. Men and women sifted through the rubbish, trying to find fragments of the lives they'd just had blown to smithereens. A girl of about six clutched in her arms a rag doll she'd just picked up and did a triumphant, defiant dance. *Take that,* Potter thought, looking north. The damnyankees might have wrecked her home, but she'd found her best friend again.

Despite the wreckage, morale seemed good. Men and women on the street often greeted Potter with calls of, "Freedom!" He had to return the same answer, too, which made his sense of irony twinge. His rank drew notice. "We'll get 'em, General," one man said. "Don't you worry about it."

"Yankees can't lick us," a woman declared. "We're tougher'n they are."

Potter made himself nod and agree whenever someone said something like that. He also thought any one Confederate was likely to be tougher than any one Yankee. Did that mean the USA couldn't lick the CSA? He wished he thought so. There were a lot more Yankees than Confederates. Jake Featherston had hoped to knock the United States out of the fight in a hurry. It hadn't quite worked.

Now it was a grapple. The Confederates still had an edge, but it wasn't so big as Potter would have liked. *The United States* can *lick us,* he thought. *They'd just better not, is all.*

Mary Pomeroy sat in a jail cell in Winnipeg, waiting for the other shoe to drop. That it would, she had no doubt. They'd caught her red-handed this time. And, of course, now that they had caught her red-handed, Wilf Rokeby's charges looked a lot different. They hadn't believed the retired postmaster when he said she'd sent a bomb through the mail. They hadn't—but they sure did now.

A rugged matron in a green-gray blouse and skirt—a woman's U.S. uniform—led two male guards up the corridor toward her. "Your lawyer is here," she announced. "You have half an hour to talk with him."

"Thanks a lot," Mary said. Sarcasm rolled off the matron like rain off a goose. She opened the door. Mary came out through it; if she hadn't, the matron would have slammed it shut again. Anything was better than just sitting on the rickety cot in there.

The guards pointed the rifles at Mary as she went up the hall. They looked ready to start shooting at any excuse or none. They no doubt were, too. She almost wished they would. If she went up before a real firing squad, she'd have to try to be as brave as Alexander was. *Maybe I'll see him up in heaven,* she thought.

Heavy wire mesh kept her from doing anything but talking with the lawyer. His name was Clarence Smoot; the military judge in charge of her case had appointed him. He was plump and bald and looked prosperous. Maybe that meant he got clients off every once in a while. Mary didn't expect he'd be able to do much for her. She knew she was guilty, and so did the Yanks.

"Half an hour," the matron barked again. "From now. Clock's ticking."

"Oh, shut up, you miserable dyke," Clarence Smoot muttered, loud enough for Mary but not for the matron to hear. The lawyer raised his voice then: "Shall we talk about your chances, Mrs. Pomeroy?"

"Have I got any?" Mary asked bleakly.

"Well . . . you may," Smoot said, fiddling with the knot on his gaudy necktie. "They can't *prove* you blew up Laura Moss and her little girl. They may think so"—*and they may be right, too,* Mary thought—"but they can't prove it. All they can prove is that you had explosives when they caught you, and that those explosives were well hidden. You won't get away with saying you were going to blow up stumps or anything like that."

"They won't listen to me no matter what I say." Mary was more nearly resigned than bitter. "I'm Arthur McGregor's daughter and I'm Alexander McGregor's sister. And now they've got me."

"They may not apply the maximum penalty—"

"Shoot me, you mean."

Clarence Smoot looked pained. "Well, yes." *But you don't have to come right out and say it,* his attitude suggested. "Colonel Colby is a fairly reasonable man, for a military judge."

"Oh, boy!" Mary put in.

"He is," Smoot insisted. "Compared to some of the Tartars they've got . . ." His shudder made his jowls wobble. "If you throw yourself on the mercy of the court, I think he'd be glad enough to let you live."

"In jail for the rest of my life?" Mary said. Reluctantly, Smoot nodded. She shook her head. "No, thanks. I'd sooner they gave me a blindfold and got it over with."

"Are you sure?" Smoot asked. "Do you want your husband to have to bury you? Do you want your mother and your husband and your sister and your son to have to go to the funeral? If you do, you'll be able to get what you want. I don't think there's any doubt of that."

Mary winced. He was hitting below the belt. Alec was too little to understand what all this meant. His mother was in a wooden box and they were putting her in the ground forever? That would have to be a bad dream, except it wouldn't be. It would be real, and when he grew up he would hardly remember her.

But some things were more important. If she'd thought they would let her out one day before too long, she might have weakened. With nothing but endless years in a cell as an alternative, though . . . "My brother didn't beg. My father didn't beg. I'll be damned if I'm going to."

Clarence Smoot exhaled heavily and lit a cigarette. "You don't give me much to work with, Mrs. Pomeroy."

"I'm sorry," she said. Then she shook her head again. "I'm sorry they caught me. That's the only thing I'm sorry for. They've got no business being here. *You've* got no business being here. You're a Yank, eh? You talk like one."

"I'm from Wisconsin. Up till now, I didn't know that made me a bad person." Smoot's voice was dry. He eyed her. "Would you rather have a Canadian lawyer bumping up against an American military judge? I don't think that would do you an awful lot of good, but you can probably find one."

"What I want . . ." Mary took a deep breath. "What I *want* is for all you Yanks to get out of Canada and leave us alone to mind our own business. That's what I've wanted since 1914."

"I'm sorry, Mrs. Pomeroy, but that's not going to happen. It's way too late to even worry about it," Clarence Smoot said. "We're not going to go away. And the reason we won't is that you wouldn't mind your own business if we did. You'd start playing footsie with the Confederates or England or Japan, and you'd make all kinds of trouble for us. We don't aim to let that happen."

"Can you blame us?" Mary exclaimed. "After everything the United States have done to my country, can you blame us?"

Smoot spread his pudgy hands. He wore a wedding ring; Mary hoped he wasn't married to a Canadian woman. "Whether I can blame you doesn't matter," he said. "Whether the United States are going to take that kind of chance . . . well, they won't, so there's no point even thinking about it."

That was how a Yank *would* think. Before Mary could tell him so, the matron stuck her formidable face into the room and said, "Time's up."

Mary's time nearly *was* up. She felt it very strongly. Smoot said, "We'll do the best we can at your hearing. The less you say, the better your chances. I can see that plain as day."

In tramped the guards. They didn't point their rifles at Mary this time, but they looked as if they were just about to. "When I say that's it, that's it," the matron barked, her voice almost as deep as Smoot's.

"Take it easy, Ilse," the lawyer said soothingly. But the matron wasn't inclined to take it easy. She jerked a muscular thumb toward the door. Mary got up and went. If she hadn't, the matron would have made her pay for it—oh, not right there where Smoot could see, but later on. The food would be worse, or Mary wouldn't get to bathe, or maybe the matron would just come in and thump her. She didn't know what would happen, only that it wouldn't be good.

They took her to the hearing in an armored personnel carrier, a snorting monster of a vehicle only one step this side of a barrel. If they had to use it here, they weren't using it against their foreign enemies. That consoled her a little—as much as anything could.

Colonel Colby was a Yank in a uniform. That was all that registered on her at first. Another, younger, Yank, a captain named Fitzwilliams, prosecuted her. He laid out what her family connections were. Clarence Smoot objected. "Irrelevant and immaterial," he said.

"Overruled," the military judge said. "This establishes motive." The worst of it was, Mary knew he wasn't wrong. She hated the Yanks for what they'd done to her country and what they'd done to her family.

Captain Fitzwilliams set out the case linking her to the bombing at Karamanlides' general store (she thought they'd forgotten all about that one) and to the one that killed Laura and Dorothy Moss. Smoot objected to that, too. "The only kind of evidence you've got is the testimony of a man who is obviously biased," he insisted.

"Why obviously?" Fitzwilliams asked. "Because he doesn't agree with you? It doesn't matter much anyhow. She was caught with explosives in the barn on the farm where her mother lived. Bomb-making is—and should be—a capital crime all by itself. The other charges are icing on the cake." By the pained way Smoot grunted, he knew that only too well.

"Does the defendant have anything to say in mitigation or extenuation?" the judge asked. He sounded as if he hoped she did. That surprised her. As Clarence Smoot had said, he wasn't a monster, only a man doing his job.

Smoot nudged Mary. "This is your chance," he whispered. "Think of your little boy."

She hated him then, for trying to deflect her from what she intended to do. She had to steel herself to tell the judge, "No. I did what I did, and you'll do what you do. If you think I love my country any less than you love yours, you're wrong."

Colonel Colby looked at her. "A plea for mercy might affect the verdict this court hands down." It wasn't that he wanted her to beg. He wanted her to live.

"You can give me the same mercy you showed Alexander," she said.

The military judge sighed. "Why do you want to martyr yourself? It won't change anything one way or the other."

"You have no right to be here. You have no right to try me," Mary said.

"We have the best right of all: we won," Colby said. "If your side had, would you have been gentle to the United States? I doubt it." Mary hadn't even thought about that. It didn't worry her, either. Colby let out a long, sad sigh. "I have no choice but to pronounce you guilty, Mrs. Pomeroy. The punishment for the infraction is death by firing squad."

"We will appeal, your Honor," Smoot said quickly.

"No." Mary overruled him, or tried to.

"An appeal in a capital case is automatic," Colby told her. "Part of me hopes I will be overruled. I must say, though, I don't expect to be."

They took Mary back to her cell. They allowed her no visitors. That was more a relief than a torment. She didn't want to see Mort, and she especially didn't want to see Alec. He might have made her weaken. She didn't think she could stand that, not when she'd come so far.

Colonel Colby knew what he was talking about. The appeal was denied. The panel that heard it ordered the sentence carried out, and so it was, on a sunny day with spring in the air. Mary knew she should have been afraid when they tied her to the pole, but she wasn't.

They offered her a blindfold. She shook her head, saying, "This is for Canada. I'll take it with my eyes open."

A minister prayed. She wondered why the Yanks had him here when they were doing something so ungodly. An officer commanded the men in the squad: "Ready! . . . Aim! . . . Fire!" The noise was shattering. So was the impact. And then it was over.

Guards at the Andersonville prison camp often let U.S. POWs see Confederate papers. Sometimes they would offer their own editorial comments, too. They jeered whenever the CSA did something good. If the USA scored a success, it never showed up in the news in the Confederate States.

The guards also jeered at what they called U.S. atrocities. "Look at this here," one of them said, waving a newspaper at Major Jonathan Moss. "Now you people are shooting women up in Canada."

Moss glared at him. "Are you going to let me see it, or are you just going to flap it in my face?" The guard blinked, then handed him the paper, which came from Atlanta. Where Confederate newspapers came from hardly mattered. They all had the same stories in them: whatever the Freedom Party wanted the Confederate people to hear.

Moss read the story. The way the reporter told it, Mary Pomeroy was a martyr whose like the world hadn't seen since St. Sebastian. That the damnyankees alleged she'd blown up a woman and a little girl in Berlin, Ontario, only proved what a pack of liars and murderers came out of the United States.

So the reporter said, anyhow. It proved something different to Jonathan Moss. He thrust the paper under his arm without a word. "Well?" the Confederate asked him. "What have you got to say about that there?"

"She had it coming." Moss' voice was hard and flat.

The guard gaped at him. "How can even a damnyankee say such a heartless thing as that?"

"Because she murdered my wife and my daughter, you cracker son of a bitch." Moss braced himself. If the guard wanted to mop the floor with him, he could. The fellow was bigger than he was and only half his age—and carried a submachine gun besides.

But the guard's gape only got wider. "She killed—*your* kinfolk?" He sounded as if he couldn't believe his ears.

"That's what I told you," Moss answered. "It's the God's truth, too. If she hadn't done that, I'd probably still be up in Canada. I'd be a damn sight happier than I am now, too. I wish I'd been up there even now. I'd have stood in that firing squad. I'd have pulled that trigger. You bet your life I would have."

He wondered if the guard would call him heartless again. The man didn't. He just went off shaking his head. *That'll teach you to wave a newspaper in somebody's face, you know-nothing bastard,* Moss thought savagely.

He was avenged. After a couple of years without any movement, he'd doubted he ever would be. *And so?* he wondered. Was he any happier because this woman was dead? He would gladly have killed her, yes, but was he happier? Slowly, he shook his head. That wasn't the right word. He'd never be happy, not thinking of Laura and Dorothy dead. But he had a sense of satisfaction he hadn't known before. It would have to do.

Of course it will, you fool. It's all you'll ever get. His wife and his daughter wouldn't come back. And neither would the woman who'd sent them the bomb. From what the Confederate newspaper said, she had a husband and a little boy. They'd miss her the way he missed his wife and daughter. There was no end to this. Try as you would to find one, there wasn't any.

He read the story over and over. Rosenfeld, Manitoba . . . That rang a bell. He nodded to himself. Wasn't that where that fellow tried to blow up General Custer and ended up blowing himself up instead? Moss was pretty sure it was, though it had happened almost twenty years earlier. Was this gal any relation to that bomber? He didn't remember the fellow's name, but he was pretty sure it wasn't Pomeroy. But then, the woman was married, and the paper didn't say anything about her maiden name.

It wouldn't. If she was related to the other Rosenfeld bomber, that would make her a murderer from a family of murderers. Somebody like that wouldn't draw sympathy even from the Confederates. And so, if it was true, the C.S. propaganda machine just ignored it.

Here came that guard again. He had another one in tow. The second man, as Jonathan saw when he got closer, was an officer. He strode up to Moss. "What's this I hear?" he demanded.

"I don't know," Moss answered. "What do you hear?"

"Conley here tells me you're related to the people this woman the Yankees shot is alleged to have blown up."

"Alleged?" The word made Moss furious. "I heard the explosion. I saw the building—and some of the other people she hurt while they were getting out. I buried what was left of my wife and little girl. Don't you talk to me about alleged, goddammit."

The guard officer gave back a pace. He hadn't expected such vehemence. *Well, too bad for him,* Moss thought. Weakly, he said, "How do you know she really did it?"

"I don't know for sure." Now Moss did some paper-waving of his own. "But I'm a lawyer. It sure looks beyond a reasonable doubt to me."

"A lawyer? How'd you get captured? Couldn't run away fast enough?" The officer laughed at his own wit.

"I'm a fighter pilot. I fought at the front line or on your side of it," Moss answered coldly. "I wasn't making like a hero in a prison camp hundreds of miles away." The guard officer retreated in disorder.

Moss started to throw the Atlanta paper to the ground, then checked himself. It might not be anything he'd wanted to keep—he had his vengeance, and now he knew it, but the price he'd paid!—but that didn't mean the paper was useless. Torn into strips, it would come in handy at the latrine trenches.

He didn't intend to say anything about the story to his fellow POWs. It was none of their business. But either the guard who'd given him the paper or the officer he'd routed must have blabbed, for the other prisoners found out about it even though he kept his mouth shut.

Every so often, one of them would come up to him, clap him on the back, and say something like, "You got your own back. That's good."

They meant well. He knew as much. That didn't keep him from losing patience. Finally, after about the fourth time it happened, he snapped. "What do you mean, got my own back?" he growled at a luckless first lieutenant. "If I had my own back, I'd still be married. I'd still have my little girl. And I'd probably still be up in Canada."

"Sorry, sir," the lieutenant said stiffly, and he retreated as fast as the Confederate guard officer had. After that, fewer prisoners sounded sympathetic, which suited Moss fine.

In fact, fewer prisoners wanted anything to do with him. That also suited him fine—till he got a summons from the senior U.S. officer, a colonel named Monty Summers. "See here, Moss," he said, "no man is an island."

"Sir, isn't it a little early in the morning for John Donne?" Moss asked.

"It's never too early for the truth," Summers said, which proved he'd never been a lawyer. "We don't want you solitary. It's not good for you, and it's not good for the camp, either."

"I'll worry about me, sir," Moss said, "and the camp can take care of itself, as far as I'm concerned."

Summers snorted in exasperation. He was a corn-fed Midwesterner who'd been captured in Ohio when the war was new. He had sandy hair going gray, ruddy cheeks, blue eyes, and a rock of a chin that he stuck out whenever he wanted to make a point. He stuck it out now. "You haven't got the right attitude," he said.

"Sorry, sir," said Moss, who wasn't. "It's the only one I've got."

"Well, you'd damn well better change it." Summers sounded as if that were as easy as changing a flat tire. He aimed his chin at Moss again. "We're still in the war. We're still fighting the Confederates. We're all in this together. We're a team, dammit. And you let the team down if you don't play along. Don't you want to help drive these fucking goons nuts?"

"Well . . ." Moss nodded. "All right, Colonel. Maybe you've got a point."

"You'd better believe I have," Summer said. "If we weren't all on the ball, for instance, we'd have Confederate spies raising all kinds of trouble."

"How do you know we don't?" Moss asked.

"There are ways." The senior U.S. officer spoke with assurance. "There are ways, but they don't work unless everybody's on the ball. Have you got that?"

"Yes, sir," Moss said.

"All right, then." Monty Summers' nod seemed amiable enough. "I won't say anything more about it, then. A word to the wise, you know." He seemed to like other people's distilled wisdom.

Moss went on much as he had before—but not quite. He'd never been a back-slapping gladhander. He never would be, either. But he did try to stop making his fellow captives actively dislike him. They seemed willing enough to meet him halfway. He started hearing more camp gossip, which gave him something to chew on, if nothing else.

Nick Cantarella sidled up to him one warm spring morning. "How you doing, Major?" he asked.

"Not too bad," Moss answered. "How's yourself?"

"I've been worse. Of course, I've been better, too. This isn't exactly my favorite place," Cantarella said.

"I wouldn't come here on vacation, either," Moss said, and Cantarella laughed. Moss added, "The only people who like it here are the guards. They're too dumb not to—and they get to carry guns, but nobody's going to shoot back at them." He was thinking of the officer he'd routed. Cantarella laughed again, even more appreciatively this time. Moss started to laugh, too, but swallowed the noise in a hurry.

Captain Cantarella was somehow involved in escape plans—if there were any escape plans to be involved in. As casually as Moss could, he asked, "What is your favorite place?"

"New York City," Cantarella replied at once.

With his accent, that didn't surprise Moss at all. Still casually, the fighter pilot asked, "How soon do you expect to see it again?"

Cantarella didn't answer right away. He scratched his cheek. Whiskers rasped against his fingernails; he was a man who got five o'clock shadow at half past one. Then he said, "Well, sir, I hope I don't have to sit out the whole goddamn war here."

"Who doesn't?" Moss agreed. "Let me know if you have any other thoughts along those lines."

"I'll do that, Major," Cantarella said. "You can count on it." Off he went. He gave the impression of still being very much in the war even though he was hundreds of miles behind the lines and on the wrong side of the barbed wire and machine-gun towers. Moss looked after him. How long did he intend to stay on the wrong side of the barbed wire? *Will he take me with him when he goes?* That was the question that mattered most to Moss.

"Hello, General," Brigadier General Irving Morrell said, walking up toward the frame house that held Brigadier General Abner Dowling's headquarters.

"Hello, General," Dowling replied. "Good to see you again, and it's high time you had stars on your shoulders, if anybody wants to know what I think."

"Thanks. Thanks very much," Morrell said. "They do make me think I haven't wasted the past thirty years, anyway."

"I know what you mean," Dowling said, and no doubt he did: he'd been in the Army even longer than Morrell had before trading his eagles for stars. He went on, "How are you feeling?"

"Sir, I'll do," Morrell answered. His shoulder chose that moment to twinge. He did his best not to show how much it hurt. It would sting him if he tried to move it too far—to move it as if he weren't wounded, in other words—or sometimes for no reason at all: certainly none he could find. With a wry chuckle, he continued, "One of the so-called advantages of my new exalted status is that they don't expect me to push back the Confederates singlehanded."

Dowling snorted—a rude noise to come from a general. "You can't fool me. I've known you too long. First chance you get, you're going to climb back into a barrel. Five minutes later, you'll stick your head out of the cupola, because you can't see a damn thing through the periscopes."

"Who, me?" Morrell said, as innocently as he could. Both men laughed. Dowling had him pegged, all right. Morrell added, "I don't know that I like being so predictable."

He'd thought Dowling would go on laughing, but the fat officer sobered instead. "You probably shouldn't be that predictable, as a matter of fact. If you are, the Confederates are liable to take another shot at you."

Morrell grunted. The other general might well be right. Morrell said, "It's an honor I could do without. I never minded getting shot at because I was a U.S. soldier. I minded getting shot, that time in Sonora—it hurt like blazes, and it left me flat on my back for a hell of a long time. But it was one of those things that happen, you know what I mean? But if they're shooting at me *because* I'm me . . . That's assassination. It isn't war."

"They're doing it," Dowling said.

"I know they are," Morrell answered. "We've lost some good people because they're doing it, too—lost them for good, I mean, not just had them wounded the way I was."

"Unofficially—and you haven't heard this from me—we're doing it, too," Dowling said.

That made Morrell grunt again. "Well, I can't even tell you I'm very surprised," he said at last. "It's the only thing we can do, pretty much. If they hit us like that, we have to hit back the same way, or else they get an edge. But I'll be damned if I like it. It makes this business even filthier than it has to be."

"Personally, I agree with you. You'll find those who don't, though." Dowling paused, ruminating on that. After a bit, he went on, "When you were in Ohio, you met Captain Litvinoff, didn't you?"

"The skinny fellow with the little mustache that looked like it was penciled on? The poison-gas specialist? Oh, yes. I met him. He gave me the cold chills." Now it was Morrell's turn to pause. He let out a long, sorrowful sigh. "All right, General. You made your point."

"Over in Richmond or wherever they keep them, the Confederates have men just like dear Captain Litvinoff," Dowling said. Morrell realized the other general liked the poison-gas expert even less than he did. He hadn't imagined such a thing was possible. Dowling went on, "Now we're finding assassins under flat rocks. And things are liable to get worse before they get better."

"How could they?" Morrell asked in honest perplexity.

"Well, I don't exactly know. But I can tell you something I heard from somebody I believe," Dowling said.

"I'm all ears." Morrell liked gossip no less than anyone else.

"You ever hear of that German scientist named Einstein? You know—the Jew with the hair that looks like steel wool in a hurricane?"

Morrell nodded. "Sure. Who hasn't heard of him? He's the one they always make absentminded professor jokes about. What's he got to do with the price of beer, though?"

"He's a hell of a sharp man, no matter how absentminded he is."

"I never said he wasn't. You don't get to be famous like that if you haven't got a lot on the ball. But what about him?"

"He's disappeared," Dowling said portentously. "Not disappeared as in his apartment building got hit by a bomb while he was in the bathtub. Disappeared as in fallen off the map. Quite a few of the other high-forehead fellows in Germany and Austria-Hungary have quietly dropped out of sight, too."

"They're working on something." Morrell didn't phrase it as a question. He'd been in the Army a long time. He recognized the signs. When a lot of people who did the same kind of work quietly dropped out of sight, something—probably something big—was going on behind the scenes. He pointed a finger at Dowling. "Do you know what it is?"

"Not me," Dowling said. "When I need to count past ten, I take off my shoes."

He was sandbagging; he was nobody's fool. Morrell paused one more time. Then he asked, "Whatever the Kaiser's boys are working on, are we working on it, too?"

Dowling had started to light a smoke—a Confederate brand, no doubt captured or confiscated here in Virginia. He froze with the cigarette in his mouth and the match, still unstruck, in his hand. "You know, General, I asked my . . . friend the very same question."

"And? What did he tell you?"

"He told me to mind my own goddamn business and get the hell out of his office." Dowling did light the cigarette then. He took a long, deep drag, as if he wanted to escape the memory of his friend's reply. "So you can take that any way you want to. Either we aren't or we are and we don't want to talk about it—*really* don't want to. You pays your money and you takes your choice."

"You sound like that colored band that got away from the Confederates," Morrell said. "They put them on the wireless enough, don't they?"

"Oh, you might say so." Dowling's voice was dry. "Yes, you just might. But propaganda is where you find it."

"And isn't that the sad and sorry truth?" Morrell looked west from Culpeper, the town where Dowling presently made his headquarters. The Blue Ridge Mountains sawtoothed the horizon. The mountains didn't worry Morrell so much. What the Confederates might have lurking in them did. "Is Patton going to try to hit us from the flank again?"

"He's welcome to, by God. He'll have even less fun than he did the last time," Abner Dowling growled. "But things seem pretty quiet off to the west. If what the spies say is true, the enemy's pulled some forces away from there."

"Where have they gone, then?" Morrell asked the immediately obvious question—not only was it obvious, it was important.

"Best guess is, to attack our salient on the other side of the Rapidan."

"The Wilderness." Morrell made a discontented—almost a disgusted—noise. "I've been down there. I've looked it over. You couldn't come up with worse country for barrels if you tried for a year. What on earth possessed General MacArthur to get a foothold *there*?"

Dowling considered before answering, "Well, General, you'll have to understand that he and I are not on the most intimate terms." By the pained expression he bore, that was an understatement. "My guess is only a guess, then. I suppose that's where we have the foothold because it's the only place we could get one."

"I see," Morrell said—two words that covered a lot of Deeply Regrets telegrams from the War Department. After a meditative pause of his own, he added, "Do you suppose that salient does us more good than it does the Confederates?"

"I *hope* so," Dowling answered, which wasn't quite what Morrell had asked. "If we can ever get out of that nasty second growth, the terrain gets better. But the Confederates know that as well as we do, and they don't want to turn us loose."

"How many casualties are we taking down there?" Morrell asked. "They can hit us from three sides at once."

"It's . . . bothersome," Dowling admitted, which meant it was probably a lot worse than that. "What we need to do is get barrels over onto the other side of the Rapidan in country where we can really use them. I'm glad you're here—if anyone can arrange that, you're the man."

"Thanks," Morrell said. "I'm just glad I'm anywhere right now." As if to underscore that, his shoulder twinged again. "I've been thinking about that particular problem myself, and I've got a few ideas."

"You'll want to talk with a map in front of you," Dowling said, proving he'd done a good deal of planning in his time, too. He waved back toward the frame house. "Shall we?"

"In a minute," Morrell said. "Let me scrounge another one of those nice cigarettes off you, if you don't mind."

"Not a bit." Dowling stuck another one in his mouth, too. "Really taste like tobacco, don't they? Not like . . ." He paused, searching for a simile.

Morrell supplied one: "Horseshit."

Dowling laughed. "Well, now that you mention it, yes." He lit it; his cheeks hollowed as he inhaled. "Damn things are supposed to be hell on the wind. You couldn't prove it by me—I never had any wind to begin with." He patted his belly as if it were an old friend—and so, no doubt, it was.

"I don't think they've hurt mine much," Morrell said. Unlike Dowling, he was usually in good, hard shape, though his stay in the hospital had set him back. He took another drag.

Planes buzzed by overhead. Morrell automatically looked around for the closest trench, and spotted one less than ten feet away. He could jump into it in a hurry if they dove on him. But they kept going: they were U.S. fighters heading south to strafe the Confederates and shoot up C.S. dive bombers and whatever else they could find.

"Good luck, boys," he called to the pilots once he was sure they wouldn't come after him.

"Amen," Abner Dowling agreed, adding, "We could use the Lord on our side. Considering what Featherston's people are up to, He'd better be."

"Well, yes," Morrell said, "but you know what they say about the Lord helping people who help themselves. We'd better do some of that, too, or we're in real trouble." He almost wished Dowling would have told him he was wrong, but Dowling didn't.

V

Second Lieutenant Thayer Monroe wasn't even a bulge in his pappy's pants when the Great War ended. He was just out of West Point, and so new an officer, he squeaked. He really *did* squeak; he had a thin tenor voice that often didn't seem to have finished breaking. He went tomato-red whenever something he was saying came out especially shrill.

First Sergeant Chester Martin hadn't expected anything different, so he wasn't disappointed. The recruiters back in California had as much as told him this was what he'd be doing. Veteran noncoms held pipsqueak officers' hands till the pipsqueaks either figured out what they were doing or got wounded or killed. In the first case, the blooded officers commonly won promotion. In the second, they left the platoon for less pleasant reasons. Either way, the platoon got a new, green CO, and the first sergeant's job started all over again.

At the moment, Lieutenant Monroe's platoon sprawled on the ground under some oaks not far outside of Falmouth, Virginia. On the other side of the Rappahannock, the Confederates held Fredericksburg. Scuttlebutt said General MacArthur's next try at dislodging the enemy from his defenses in front of Richmond would go through the C.S. forces here.

"What do you think, Sarge?" asked Charlie Baumgartner, a corporal who led one of the squads in the platoon. "They gonna send us over the river?"

"Beats me," Martin answered. "I hope to God they don't. I don't like getting shot at any better than the next guy."

"Yeah, well, that's on account of you've got your head screwed on tight," Baumgartner said. He was more than twenty years younger than Chester, but he'd been in the Army for a while. "Some people . . ." He didn't go on.

He didn't need to, either. Lieutenant Monroe was telling anybody who'd listen what a howling waste they were going to make out of Fredericksburg and its Confederate defenders. Since he outranked everyone close by, people had to listen. Whether they believed him was liable to be a different story.

"Our bombardment will stun them. It will paralyze them," Monroe burbled. "They'll never know what hit them. We'll get over the river without the least little bit of trouble."

Baumgartner's grunt was redolent of skepticism. So was Chester Martin's. He'd seen lots of bombardments, which Thayer Monroe plainly hadn't. Not even the fiercest one knocked an enemy out altogether. As soon as the bombing and the shelling let up, the survivors ran for their machine guns and popped up out of their holes with rifles in their hands.

The noncoms in the platoon all plainly knew as much. But rank had its privileges: no one told Monroe to shut up. Chester thought about it. He would have been more diplomatic than that if he'd decided to do it. In the end, he kept quiet with the rest. The young lieutenant was heartening new men who hadn't been through the mill yet. That counted for something.

But when Thayer Monroe said, "We ought to be in Richmond a week after we break through at Fredericksburg," Chester cleared his throat. For a wonder, the lieutenant noticed. "You said something, Sergeant?"

"Well, no, sir. Not exactly, sir." Chester knew he had to be polite to the snotnose with the gold bar on each shoulder strap. He wasn't convinced Monroe deserved such courtesy, but the military insisted on it. "Only, sir, it might be better if you don't make promises we can't keep."

Monroe stared at him. Failure had plainly never crossed the shave-tail's mind. He said, "Sergeant, once we cross the river, we *will* go forward." He might have been propounding a law of nature.

He might have been, but he wasn't. Chester knew it too well. "Yes, sir," he said, meaning, *No, sir.*

Maybe Monroe wasn't altogether an idiot. He heard what Martin wasn't saying. Stiffly, he said, "When the order comes, Sergeant, we *will* go forward."

"Oh, yes, sir," Martin agreed—he couldn't quarrel with that, not without ending up in big trouble himself. But he did want to persuade the lieutenant not to take on faith everything his superiors told him. "Sir, when you were at West Point, did you study the battles on the Roanoke front?"

"Sure." Monroe chuckled. "All twelve or fourteen of them, or however many there were."

To him, those fights were just things he'd studied in school. He could laugh about them. Chester couldn't. His memories were too dark. "Sir, I was there for the first six or eight—till I got wounded. I was lucky. It was just a hometowner. But before every attack, they told us this would be the one that did the trick. Do you wonder that after a while we had trouble jumping up and down when they told us to go over the top?"

"I hope we've got better at what we're doing since then." By the way Thayer Monroe said it, it was a forgone conclusion that the Army had.

"So do I." By the way Chester Martin said it, it was anything but.

The bombardment started on schedule, regardless of Martin's opinion. It didn't go on for days, the way it would have during the Great War. The men in charge of the guns *had* learned something. Long bombardments did more to tell the enemy where the attack was going in than they did to smash him flat. Make him keep his head down, then strike hard—that was the prevailing wisdom these days.

Martin would have liked it better if they hadn't had to throw bridges across the Rappahannock before they could cross. He and the rest of the platoon—the rest of the regiment—waited by the river for the engineers to do their job. Martin liked and admired military engineers. They were good at their specialized trade, and when they had to they made pretty fair combat soldiers, too.

They did their damnedest on the Rappahannock, but they never had a chance. Even though U.S. artillery kept pounding Fredericksburg, Confederate machine guns and mortars started pounding the engineers right back. Guns up in the hills behind the town, guns that had stayed quiet so the U.S. cannon wouldn't spot them and knock them out ahead of time, added their weight of metal to the countershelling.

And they added more than metal. The U.S. engineers had to try to do strenuous work in gas masks. U.S. guns had thrown poison gas at Fredericksburg along with everything else, and the C.S. artillery replied in kind. Martin was wearing his mask well before the order went out to put them on. He'd seen mustard gas the last time around. He hadn't seen what they called nerve agents—those were new. But he didn't want to make their acquaintance the hard way.

Confederate Mules—U.S. soldiers more often called them Asskickers—swooped down on the bridges. These days, the gull-winged dive bombers weren't the symbol of terror they had been when the war was new. They were slow and ungainly; U.S. fighters hacked them out of the sky with ease when they ventured into airspace where the CSA didn't have superiority. But they still had a role to play. They screamed down, put bombs on three bridges, and zoomed away at just above treetop level.

"I hate those bastards, but they've got balls." Because of Corporal Baumgartner's mask, his voice sounded distant and otherworldly.

"You want to know what I think, I think we have to be nuts to try to cross here at all," Martin said. Baumgartner didn't argue with him. He wished the other noncom would have.

U.S. raiders in rubber boats tried crossing the Rappahannock to quiet the mortar crews and machine gunners and riflemen on the other side. Despite smoke screens and heavy U.S. fire, a lot of the boats got sunk before they made it to the south bank of the river. The raiders who managed to cross no doubt did their best, but Chester couldn't see that Confederate fire diminished even a little.

About every half hour, Lieutenant Monroe would say, "We'll get the order to cross any minute now, men," or, "It won't be long!" or, "Be ready!" Knowing how stubborn the high brass could be, Chester feared the platoon leader was right, but kept hoping he was wrong.

The order never came. Towards evening, the units that had been pushed forward drew back out of enemy artillery range. Martin wondered how many casualties they'd taken, and how many they'd inflicted on the Confederates. He would have bet the first number was a lot bigger than the second one.

"Don't worry, men," Thayer Monroe said, invincibly optimistic. "We'll get them soon, even if we didn't get them today."

Chester had never known a common soldier who worried about *not* going into battle. No doubt such men existed. You heard stories about them, stories often prefaced, *There was this crazy bastard who* . . . But he'd never run into one himself.

Like other lower forms of life, second lieutenants were too dumb to know better. Martin thought some more about telling this particular lieutenant to put a sock in it, but refrained. Monroe had a job, too. He was supposed to make soldiers enthusiastic about going out there and getting maimed. Having led that company in the Great War, Chester knew what a nasty job it could be.

At the moment, he worried more about whether the regiment would get its field kitchens set up after all the marching and counter-marching it had done. He wasn't especially surprised when it didn't. "Canned rations," he told the men in his platoon. (Thayer Monroe had a different opinion about whose it was, but what did second lieutenants know?)

"That shit again?" somebody said. It wasn't the only grumble sullying the sweetness of the evening air. Canned rations ranged from boring to actively nasty. The labels usually peeled off, too, so you didn't know ahead of time whether you were getting spaghetti and meatballs—tolerable—or chicken with stewed prunes—disgusting. As with men who liked combat, there were a few who liked the chicken concoction and would trade for it, but Chester didn't think any were in his platoon.

Charlie Baumgartner plopped down beside him. "How's that gonna look in the newspapers, Sarge? 'U.S. Army Pulls Back from Fredericksburg! Does Not Cross!'" He made the headline very convincing.

Chester opened his can. It was hash—not very good, not very bad. He dug in. After the first mouthful, he said, "They can print that if they want to. I don't care. As long as they don't say, 'U.S. Army Massacred at Fredericksburg!' I'm not going to worry about it."

"You got a good way of looking at things," Baumgartner said. "Better'n some people I could name—that's for damn sure."

"He's nothing but a puppy," Martin said, identifying one of those unnamed people without undue difficulty.

"You know what a puppy is?" the corporal said. He waited for Chester to shake his head, then answered the rhetorical question: "Just a little son of a bitch."

"Ouch," Martin said. To his own surprise, he found himself defending Lieutenant Monroe: "He's not so bad. He just needs experience."

"He needs a good, swift kick in the ass," Baumgartner said.

"Odds are he'll get one. Let's just hope he lives through it," Chester said.

"Yeah." Baumgartner nodded. "Let's hope we do, too."

Armstrong Grimes didn't know where the Mormons got all their machine guns. He supposed the Confederates had sneaked some to them and they'd taken others from U.S. arsenals when they started their latest uprising. Or, for all he knew, maybe they had secret machine shops out in the desert somewhere, and men with green eyeshades working lathes to turn out their own.

Wherever the machine guns came from, they had a hell of a lot of them.

The one in front of Armstrong and his companions now was firing from the window of a house in Orem, Utah; U.S. forces had finally managed to drive the Mormons out of Provo. An enormous canning plant dominated Orem. The rebels were holed up inside the factory, too, but the Americans were going to have to clear them out of the buildings in front of the place before they could even think about attacking it.

Clearing them wouldn't be easy. Nothing that had to do with Mormons ever was. The machine gun spitting death in front of Armstrong, for instance, hadn't just been set in that window. As soon as it started up, Sergeant Stowe called artillery fire in on it. The guns had turned the house to rubble. They hadn't bothered the machine gun or its crew one bit.

Crouched in a hole that didn't feel nearly deep enough with bullets cracking past just overhead, Armstrong turned to Yossel Reisen and said, "Bastards have that thing all sandbagged."

"Either that or there's a real cement bunker inside the place," Reisen answered. "Wouldn't surprise me a bit."

"Me, neither," Armstrong agreed with a sour sigh. "They were probably getting ready here while they were still fighting down in Provo."

"I bet you're right," Reisen said. They both swore: part of the automatic obscenity that made up the small change of any conversation between military men. To Armstrong, the idea of preparing a position long before you fell back into it felt like cheating.

A runner scrambled into the hole with the two of them. "When the whistle blows, pop up and start shooting at that machine gun as hard as you can," he said, and then climbed out to pass the word to the next few U.S. soldiers.

"What's going on?" Armstrong called after him. The runner didn't answer. Armstrong did some more swearing, this time in earnest. He didn't like orders he didn't understand, especially when they were liable to get him killed.

Like them or not, he had them. About fifteen minutes later, an officer's whistle shrilled. He popped up and fired a shot, then ducked down again to work the Springfield's bolt. He felt like a jack-in-the-box after a while, or maybe like a jackass. But everybody else in front of the machine gun was doing the same thing, so the Mormons manning the piece didn't aim all their attention—to say nothing of all their fire—at him.

"Ha!" Yossel Reisen spoke with a certain somber satisfaction. "I see what's going on."

"Yeah?" said Armstrong, who didn't. "What?"

"Guy with a flamethrower sneaking up on that house," Reisen answered.

"Is that what it is?" Armstrong said. "Well, no wonder we're supposed to keep 'em busy, then."

The only drawback to a flamethrower was that the fellow who used it had to get close to his target before opening up—and had to get close while he was lugging a tank of jellied gasoline on his back. Armstrong's opinion was that the men who carried flamethrowers had to be nuts. If, say a tracer round hit that tank of fuel . . .

And one did, just when Armstrong was squeezing off a round. The fireball made him blink. "Oh, fuck," he said softly. Nobody would ever bury that soldier, because there wouldn't be much left of him. Armstrong hoped it was over in a hurry. He'd got hardened to a lot of war, but that was a nasty way to go. The poor bastard hadn't had time to scream, anyhow. Maybe his silence meant something.

After the flamethrower man's untimely demise, firing at the Mormon strongpoint eased off. That made perfect sense, as far as Armstrong was concerned. Why take a chance on getting killed when you wouldn't accomplish anything doing it?

Yossel Reisen summed it up in four words: "So much for that."

"Yeah. You said it." Armstrong sagged back down into the hole they shared. "You got a cigarette?" As Reisen gave him one, the enemy machine gun cut loose with a defiant burst to tell the world its crew was alive, well, and sassy.

That machine-gun position had to go if U.S. troops were to advance. Armstrong hoped a barrel would waddle up and blast the nest to kingdom come. But barrels, even the old-fashioned waddling kind, were in short supply in Utah these days. A lot of them had gone up in flames in the house-to-house fighting in Provo. Without them, the soldiers still might have been stuck down there. But none seemed to be close by right now.

"What would you do if you were a general?" Yossel Reisen asked.

"Me? Find another line of work," Armstrong answered. Reisen laughed but waved to show he'd really meant the question. Armstrong thought about it, then said, "Probably another guy with a flame-thrower. Cheapest way there is to make those fuckers say uncle if we don't have a barrel ready, and it doesn't look like we do."

He guessed wrong, which didn't much surprise him—he'd never wanted to be a general. The powers that be decided to try shelling the machine-gun nest out of existence again. As soon as Armstrong heard the first couple of shells gurgle by overhead, he knew they weren't just counting on explosive power to do the job this time. "Gas!" he shouted. "Gas!" He jammed the mask over his head as fast as he could. Some of those shells were bound to fall short, the artillery being what it was. And even if they didn't, the breeze, what there was of it, came from the north, and would blow some of the poison back towards U.S. lines.

A big stretch of the world disappeared with the pig-snouted mask over his face. What was left he saw through two portholes of none too clean glass. The air tasted of rubber. He didn't feel as if he could get quite enough of it. That was an illusion; he'd proved as much plenty of times. But he did have to work harder to suck breaths through the activated-charcoal filter cartridge, so the illusion persisted.

Sure as hell, a couple of rounds were short, which meant they came down among the soldiers stuck in front of the machine gun. Armstrong hoped they weren't carrying what people called nerve agents. That crap could kill you if it got on your skin. Everybody had rubberized cover-alls. Nobody wanted to wear them. They were unbearably hot.

With infinite caution, Armstrong stuck up his head. The machine-gun nest was catching hell, no doubt about it. With a little luck . . .

That officer's whistle squealed again. "Forward!" he shouted.

"Aw, shit," Armstrong muttered. They were going to find out if they'd got rid of the Mormons, all right. Armstrong thought of spraying Flit all over an ants' nest. Mormons stung even harder than red ants, though.

They were harder to kill, too. The U.S. soldiers ran toward the machine-gun nest in little scuttles from one bit of cover to the next. The gun that had held them up stayed silent. Some of them, the green ones, whooped and got a little less cautious, figuring the rebel gunners were dead.

Armstrong kept his belly on the dirt and the snout of his gas mask banging the ground. He trusted Mormons no farther than he could throw them. They were as sneaky a bunch of bastards as you could imagine. He tried not to show himself as he scooted up toward that battered house.

Beside him, Yossel Reisen took no chances, either. He snaked ahead. He didn't walk. He didn't even crawl. He snaked on his belly, pulling himself along with his elbows.

And their wariness and distrust paid off, for the Mormons inside the machine-gun nest must have had masks and must have got them on in time. The gunners waited till they found good targets, then opened up with a savage burst that cut down half a dozen American soldiers. After that, the advance congealed. Everybody knew you couldn't charge a well-served machine-gun nest. If armor or artillery didn't take it out, infantry would just keep piling up corpses in front of it.

Quite suddenly, the Mormon machine gunners ceased fire. Armstrong didn't even twitch; he suspected another nasty trick. Then somebody behind him shouted, "Flag of truce! Flag of truce coming forward!"

That didn't make Armstrong move, either. Mormons sounded just like anybody else. They looked just like anybody else, too. And they had no trouble getting green-gray uniforms from dead or captured U.S. soldiers. They often pretended to be ordinary Americans, and they caused a lot of trouble when they did.

But a flag of truce *was* coming forward. The U.S. captain who carried it shouted to the men in the machine-gun nest: "I have a message for your leaders." He had trouble being as loud as he wanted through his mask, but he managed.

"Come ahead." The Mormon who answered was also yelling through a gas mask. "We won't shoot as long as nobody in front of us tries moving forward."

"Agreed," the captain said. Waving the white flag so the rebels could see who he was, he picked his way through the wreckage, towards and then past the machine-gun nest. Other Mormons emerged from concealment that didn't look big enough to hide a cat. One of them blindfolded the U.S. officer, which struck Armstrong as a sensible precaution. Then they led him north.

"Wonder what that's all about," Yossel Reisen said. "Are they flabbling so much about this one strongpoint? They wouldn't call a truce just on account of it . . . would they?"

"Christ, I hope not," Armstrong said. "Wish I had a cigarette." No matter how much he wished he did, he didn't take off his mask and light up. There was bound to be gas still floating in the air. If he saw somebody else smoking and getting away with it, he'd try. Till then, no. He went on, "Most of the damn Mormons don't smoke. Makes 'em harder to spot."

He didn't stick his head up or expose himself unduly. The rebels were good about honoring cease-fires, but they weren't perfect—and they'd said they would open up if anybody on the American side got frisky.

After the truce had stretched for a couple of hours, Americans got up and stretched and began to move around. The Mormons let them. When someone was dumb enough to start to go toward the machine-gun nest, the gunners fired a warning burst well over his head. He got the message and drew back in a hurry.

A little before sunset, the captain returned. This time, he waved the flag of truce so his own side wouldn't shoot him. With him came a little old man in a somber black suit. He looked like a grandfather who was having a tough day. Nimble as a mountain goat, he followed the captain through the rubble of what had been Orem.

"What the hell's going on here?" Armstrong asked. Neither Yossel Reisen nor anybody else had a good answer for him.

* * *

"**W**hat the hell's going on here?" Senator Robert Taft demanded. He was a thoroughly reactionary Democrat who'd run against Al Smith in 1940. Flora Blackford didn't think along with him very often when they met together with the rest of the Joint Committee on the Conduct of the War. She didn't very often, but she did now.

The chairman rapped loudly for order. "You were not recognized, Senator," he said in tones of bureaucratic severity.

"I'm very sorry, Mr. Chairman." Taft sounded anything but. "I must say that I have trouble recognizing what the present administration is up to."

Bang! The chairman rapped again. "You are out of order, sir. Your remarks will be stricken from the record." He pointed to Flora. "Congresswoman Blackford!"

"Thank you, Mr. Chairman," Flora said. George Norris smiled in relief. Like her, the Senator from Nebraska was a Socialist; he judged she was likely to go easy on President La Follette and his henchmen. Not today, though; she continued, "Mr. Chairman, I would also like to know what the hell is going on here."

Several people exclaimed in surprise in the Philadelphia meeting room. "*Thank* you, Mrs. Blackford!" Senator Taft said in glad surprise. Senator Norris looked as if he'd stepped on a land mine.

"I didn't do it for you, Senator. I did it for me," Flora replied. That made the chairman no happier. She'd hoped it would—Norris was an old man, and a Party warhorse—but hadn't really expected it to. Turning to him, she went on, "What *is* the administration doing by negotiating with the Mormons? What have they done that makes them deserve negotiation?"

"I couldn't have put that better myself," Taft said.

"Congresswoman, I am not the right person to answer your question, as I trust you are aware," the chairman said.

"Certainly," Flora said. "That is why I move that we call the Secretary of the Interior to come before the committee and explain this extraordinary action."

"Second!" Robert Taft wasn't the only one to call out the word; it came from half a dozen throats. Some were Democrats, some Socialists; here, people were breaking party lines.

Seeing as much, Senator Norris looked even more pained than he had before. "With talks in progress, I am not sure the Secretary would respond to such a summons," he replied. "I am not sure he *should* respond to such a summons."

"There, Mr. Chairman, I must respectfully disagree," Flora said. The language of Congress was marvelously polite. Anywhere else, she would have said something like, *My God, you're an idiot!* Polite language or no, the message came through. Norris turned a dull red. Flora went on, "If the Secretary does not respond to an invitation to come before us, I will move that we subpoena him. We need to know why the administration thinks it can offer concessions to a group now rebelling against the U.S. government not for the first, not for the second, but for the third time."

"You will not need to look far to find a second for that motion, either, Congresswoman," Senator Taft said. Flora nodded back to him. He was only half the man his father had been; he was on the lean side, where William Howard Taft had been as round as the golf balls he'd loved to whack. William Howard Taft had also had the fat man's gift of being, or at least seeming, good-natured most of the time. His son was far more acerbic—which had probably helped him lose the last election.

George Norris coughed. "You do realize that publicizing disagreements over policy may give aid and comfort to the Confederate States?"

"Oh, no, you don't!" Flora said sharply. "I'm sorry, sir, but no one is going to get away with that. You can't say I'm not a proper patriot if I don't agree with everything this administration does. That's Jake Featherston's way of doing things, and he's welcome to it. Why have we got a Joint Committee on the Conduct of the War if we can't ask questions that have to do with the way we're conducting the war?"

Several Senators and Representatives clapped their hands. The chairman licked his papery lips. He spoke carefully: "We are at war with the Confederate States, Congresswoman, and with the Empire of Mexico, and with Britain, France, Japan, and Russia. We are not at war with the state of Utah."

Flora curtsied. "Thank you for informing me of that, Mr. Chairman. You might do better to inform the state of Utah, which seems unaware of the fact." She got a laugh loud enough to make Norris ply his gavel with might and main. She continued, "By all precedent, it is a war. Congress established a Joint Committee on the Conduct of the

War during the War of Secession, long before we had to recognize the CSA as an independent nation. Will you tell me I'm wrong, sir?"

By his expression, George Norris would have liked nothing better, but knew he couldn't. "Call the question on the motion!" someone yelled. Looking even more unhappy, the chairman did. It passed with only a couple of dissenting votes.

When Flora walked into to her office, her secretary said, "Mr. Roosevelt called a little while ago, Congresswoman. He'd like you to call him back."

"Thanks, Bertha. I'll bet he would," Flora said. How angry would the Assistant Secretary of War be? Only one way to find out. She went into the inner office and made the call.

"This is Franklin Roosevelt." As always, his voice conceded nothing to the illness that left him in a wheelchair. When Flora gave her name, Roosevelt started to laugh. "You've been naughty today, haven't you?" he said.

"I don't think so. I think the administration has," Flora said. "Talking with the Mormons? It's madness."

"Is it? President La Follette doesn't think so. Neither do I," Roosevelt said. *If he did, you would, too,* Flora thought. But a lot of politics worked that way. Roosevelt went on, "Don't you think the Confederate States would be better off if Jake Featherston tried talking with his colored rebels instead of doing his best to put them all six feet under?"

"I don't want the Confederate States better off," Flora said.

Roosevelt's laugh invited everyone who heard it to share the joke. "You can't duck me like that and expect me not to quack," he said. "You're too smart not to know what I'm talking about."

"We can talk to the Mormons till we're blue in the face," Flora said. "What good will it do if they don't want to listen?"

"That's what Ferdinand Koenig would say, all right." Roosevelt was being as exasperating as he could.

"What can we possibly give the Mormons that would satisfy them and us?" Flora asked.

"I don't know," Roosevelt admitted. "But the President thinks we ought to find out and not go on till everyone who could fight us is dead." Pointedly, he added, "And he thinks his own party ought to back him while he's doing it."

"I will happily back the President when I think he's right, or even when I'm not sure—I haven't said a word about whatever is going on in western Washington, and I don't intend to," Flora said. "But when I think he's wrong . . . I'm sorry, Franklin, but party loyalty doesn't go that far."

A lot of people thought it did. Presidents were usually of that opinion. Roosevelt just sighed. "I might have known you'd say that. As a matter of fact, I did know you'd say that. It doesn't make things any easier for me, you know."

I'm the one who's in charge of keeping you from running wild, Flora translated mentally. "Tell me what sort of terms we're offering the Mormons. Then maybe I'll change my mind and believe this is worth doing," she said.

"Not my bailiwick," Roosevelt told her. "But I'd hope you'd trust Charlie La Follette far enough to believe he wouldn't make terms that are bad for the country."

"I trusted Al Smith not to make a deal that was bad for the country," Flora said. "Look how that turned out." *Good God!* she thought. *I sound just like my reactionary brother David.* But that didn't mean she thought she was wrong now, however much she wished it did.

"Low blow," Franklin Roosevelt said.

"Is it? We'll see what the Secretary of the Interior has to say," Flora answered.

"Some people are disappointed in the stand you're taking."

Though Roosevelt couldn't see her, Flora shrugged. "They can put up another Socialist candidate when my district nominates this summer. Or they can back the Democrat against me this fall."

"No one would do anything like that," Roosevelt said hastily. Flora also knew nobody would do anything like that. She'd represented her district for most of the past twenty-six years, and she was a President's widow. They'd need better reasons than this to oppose her: treason, say.

A few days later, the Secretary of the Interior *did* appear before the Joint Committee on the Conduct of the War. Harry Hopkins came from Iowa and still spoke with a flat Midwestern accent, but he'd gone to New York as a young lawyer. He'd got to know Al Smith there, and had risen with him. Now he had to defend the policies of another President.

"What terms has the administration offered the Mormon insurgents in Utah?" Senator Norris asked the question reluctantly. He knew the other members would be sharper than he if he faltered.

"No more than a return to the *status quo ante bellum* if they lay down their arms," Hopkins answered. "If they want peace, we will give them peace: no treason trials, no persecutions. But that is absolutely as far as we will go. Demands for autonomy and independence for the so-called State of Deseret have been and will continue to be rejected out of hand."

"And what is the response of the Mormon representative to this proposal?" the chairman asked. "Uh—what is the gentleman's name?" He plainly wanted to call the Mormon representative something else, something less polite, but refrained.

"Rush. Hyrum Rush." Hopkins spelled the Mormon's first name. Having done so, he let out a resigned sigh. "Mr. Rush does not feel our proposal goes far enough, and fears it leaves his people vulnerable to further U.S. aggression. Those are his words, not mine."

Flora raised her hand. With a certain amount of trepidation, Norris recognized her. She said, "Mr. Hopkins, why does Mr. Rush think Utah would be any safer as an independent country surrounded by the United States than as one state among many? This makes little sense to me."

"He said, 'You gave Kentucky and Houston and Sequoyah plebiscites, but you wouldn't give us one. You thought we were a bunch of perverts, and we didn't deserve one,'" Hopkins replied.

Hyrum Rush wasn't so far wrong. Flora said, "Don't you think we ought to get rid of an abscess like that instead of putting a bandage on it?"

"Normally, Congresswoman, I'd say yes. Right now, we've got bigger things to worry about than an abscess."

Flora winced. With the country cut in half, she couldn't very well disagree with the Secretary of the Interior. "The rebels show no sign of agreeing to these terms?" she asked.

"That's correct, ma'am," Harry Hopkins said.

Good, Flora thought, but she kept it to herself. She nodded to the chairman. "No further questions."

Brigadier General Abner Dowling studied Confederate dispositions on a large map pinned to a wall of the house in Culpeper he used as a headquarters. If the U.S. Army ever moved deeper into Virginia, the house's owner would get it back, and would probably be unhappy about the holes in his plaster. Dowling, whose own disposition was none too good, intended to miss not a moment of sleep worrying about that.

He called Captain Toricelli in to look at the latest dispositions. His adjutant was a sharp young officer. "Tell me what you make of this," Dowling said, as neutrally as he could. He left it there. He wanted to see if the junior officer noticed the same thing he had—and if it was truly there to notice.

Angelo Toricelli eyed the map with unusual care. He knew Dowling wouldn't have asked him for no reason. After a thoughtful pause, he said, "They really are thinning out their positions a bit, aren't they?"

"It looks that way to me," Dowling answered. "It's got to the point where we can't ignore it, hasn't it?"

His adjutant nodded. "I'd say so. But the bastards in butternut don't want us to spot it. Just by the way they're doing it, I'd bet money on that."

"Does seem so, doesn't it?" Dowling said. "And why not? For fear we'll pour through? They aren't weakening themselves *that* much."

"Where are those men going?" Toricelli asked.

"If I knew, I would tell you." Dowling scratched his head. His hair was thinning—one more indignity of age. He sighed. "We ought to send out raiders, bring back some prisoners. They may know where their pals are headed. It doesn't seem to be down toward the Wilderness. That was what I guessed when I conferred with General Morrell. If it turns out to be over toward Fredericksburg instead, we'll have to alert General MacArthur, assuming such a thing is possible."

"Er—yes, sir," Captain Toricelli said. These days, Dowling didn't bother hiding his scorn for his superior. MacArthur didn't like him, either, and manifested it by withholding men and matériel from his corps. That was how things looked to Dowling's jaundiced eye, anyhow.

"Draft the orders," Dowling said. "Send them by runner, not by telegraph or telephone or wireless, not even in code. I don't want the Confederates getting wind of what we're up to and priming some men to lie like Ananias." Maybe he had what the smart alienists these days were calling a persecution complex. He didn't intend to worry about it. An Army officer who didn't worry that the enemy was out to diddle him didn't deserve his shoulder straps.

And Toricelli didn't think his orders were anything out of the ordinary—or, if he did, he had the sense to keep his mouth shut about it. "I'll have them on your desk in twenty minutes, sir," he promised.

"That sounds good," Dowling said.

As if further to disguise whatever they were up to, the Confederates in front of Dowling's corps suddenly turned aggressive—not in any big way, but with lots of raids and artillery barrages and all the other things that made it look as if a major offensive might be brewing. Several regimental commanders sent panicky messages back to Culpeper.

One thing Dowling was good at was not getting excited at every little thing. Had he got excited at every little thing while serving under General Custer, he would have jumped out a window early in his career. He managed to calm down his subordinates, too. Had he been wrong, had the Confederates been planning a big push, he might have ended up with egg on his face for calming them down too well. But no big push came.

In due course, the interrogation reports did. Dowling's eyebrows rose toward his retreating hairline when he read them. He looked up to Captain Toricelli, who'd given him the transcripts. "The questioners think this is reliable and accurate?" he asked.

"Yes, sir. I talked to one of them. They're pretty certain," Toricelli replied.

"All right. We'll relay it to General MacArthur's headquarters, and we'll also relay it to the War Department," Dowling said. "In code, mind you."

"Oh, yes, sir," his adjutant agreed. "This is too hot to go out in clear." For once, he showed none of the quiet scorn with which adjutants often greeted their superiors' ideas. *I hope my notions aren't as bad as a lot of Custer's were,* Dowling thought. And yet one of Custer's ideas—as foolish at first sight and as stubbornly maintained as any of the others—had gone a long way toward winning the Great War. You never could tell.

A few hours later, Dowling's telephone jangled. He picked it up. "First Corps Headquarters, Dowling speaking."

"Hello, sir. This is John Abell." The General Staff officer didn't give his rank or affiliation. That was no doubt wise. A lot of telephone wire lay between Philadelphia and Culpeper. If the Confederates weren't tapping it somewhere, Dowling would have been amazed. Abell went on, "You have confidence in the information you sent us?"

"Would I have sent it if I didn't?" Dowling returned.

"You'd be amazed," Abell said, and that was probably true. He continued, "We still have to confirm it at the other end."

"I don't know anything about that," Dowling said. "But I do know what I've seen, and I know—or I think I know—I wasn't imagining it."

"You weren't, not if these reports are even close to accurate," Abell said. "Have you heard anything from General MacArthur yet?"

"No, not a word," Dowling said.

The General Staff officer sniffed disdainfully. "Why am I not surprised?"

"I've alerted him to the possibility. That's all I can do," Dowling said. *That's all I want to do,* he added to himself. *If I could have found any way to keep from doing even that much, I would have grabbed it like you wouldn't believe.*

"I hope something good comes of it." Abell's tone suggested he didn't think that was likely. "So long, sir. Take care of yourself." He hung up.

So did Dowling, muttering to himself. Daniel MacArthur didn't want to talk to him any more than he wanted to talk to MacArthur. So he thought, anyhow. But when the telephone rang again and he picked it up, what he heard was an abrupt rasp: "This is MacArthur."

"Yes, sir." Dowling unconsciously came to attention in his chair. "What can I do for you, sir?"

"It's really true that the Confederates are draining men away from this entire front?" MacArthur demanded.

"Sir, that's the way it looks from here." Dowling didn't intend to commit himself any further than that. Assert that something was really true and it was only too likely to come back and haunt you.

What he did say seemed to satisfy MacArthur. "In that case, I'm going to take one of the divisions out of your corps and bring it east."

"What?" The word burst from Dowling's throat as a pained yelp. "What do you want to do that for?"

"We mounted an attack at Fredericksburg that could have succeeded—that should have succeeded, in fact," MacArthur answered. "I intend to send more men in this time—send them in and have them break through."

From everything Dowling had heard, the attack on Fredericksburg hadn't come anywhere near as close to succeeding as MacArthur claimed. From everything Dowling had heard, U.S. forces hadn't even got over the Rappahannock and into Fredericksburg itself. Would throwing in more men help? Dowling didn't know. Custer had always liked to smother fires by burying them in bodies. He'd had his share of bloody fiascoes, but he'd also finally had his breakthrough. Maybe Daniel MacArthur would, too. Maybe.

One thing was certain: if MacArthur wanted one of Dowling's divisions, he had the right to take it. Dowling did what he could, saying, "We'll be spread thin here if you do shift it east."

"So are the Confederates you're facing. You found that out yourself. Since they are, why worry? It seems to me that you spend too much time carping and complaining and not enough figuring out how to strike the foe."

It seemed to Dowling that MacArthur spent too much time figuring out stupid ways to strike the foe. He didn't say so. What point to it? He'd just get MacArthur angry at him again. He wouldn't change his superior's mind. No one except MacArthur could do that, and he wasn't in the habit of doing so.

Suppressing a sigh, Dowling said, "Sir, I'll do my best with whatever men you leave me. You can rely on that."

"There. You see?" Daniel MacArthur actually sounded pleased. "You can be cooperative when you set your mind to it."

By *be cooperative,* he meant *do exactly what I tell you without asking any inconvenient questions no matter what.* Dowling knew that only too well. Again, though, what could he do about it? Not much, as he knew all too well. He tried his best to keep resignation out of his voice as he answered, "Yes, sir."

"Good," MacArthur said. Dowling wondered if it was. MacArthur went on, "You'll have your orders soon. Thin their lines against *me,* will they? I am going to bury those Confederates—bury them, I tell you. There's no doubt in my mind."

"Yes, sir," Dowling said. Maybe he would. But how many U.S. soldiers would they bury, too? No way to know, not till it happened. Dowling had long since abandoned optimism along with the other illusions of his youth. He had thought before that MacArthur had more in common with George Custer than either of the two generals would ever have admitted: a complete lack of doubt and a strong belief in their own brilliance running neck and neck.

As if to underscore that, MacArthur said, "See you in Richmond, then," and slammed down the telephone. Dowling slowly replaced his own handset in its cradle. *See you in Richmond?* MacArthur would either make good on the boast or an awful lot of young men would die trying.

Dowling knew which way he would bet. He couldn't say anything about that, not to anybody, not without being accused of deliberately damaging morale. He couldn't even get on the telephone to Philadelphia, the way he had when MacArthur proposed the amphibious operation aimed at the mouth of the James. That had been madness. This might work. Dowling didn't think it would, but he had to give his superior the benefit of the doubt.

He said something filthy. However much he'd longed for combat posts, he'd spent much of his career either as Custer's adjutant or on occupation duty in Utah—his main job there, in fact, had been to keep that from turning into a combat post, and he'd done it. Now he had what he'd always wanted. He had it, and he hadn't covered himself with glory in it. Maybe he wasn't cut out to be a hero. Or maybe he should have been more careful about what he wished for, lest he get it.

Jake Featherston peered down from Marye's Heights over the town of Fredericksburg toward the Rappahannock and the damnyankees on the other side. He turned to Nathan Bedford Forrest III, who stood by his side. "I was right about here when the last war ended," the President of the CSA said.

"Yes, sir," replied the chief of the Confederate General Staff, who'd been too young to fight in the Great War.

"Well, I was, goddammit," Featherston said. "When the order to cease fire came, I waited till the very last minute. Then I took the breech block out of my piece and chucked it in that creek over yonder." He pointed. "I was damned if the United States were gonna get anything they could use from me."

"Yes, sir," Forrest repeated, adding, "That sounds like you."

"Good. It ought to," Jake said, more than a little smugly. "Maybe what pissed me off most about having to quit, though, was that I could have killed every damnyankee in the world from right here, if the bastards kept coming at me and my ammo held out."

"It's a good position," Forrest allowed. "Not as good as it would have been in the Great War—artillery's better now than it was then, and barrels and bombers are a hell of a lot better. But it's still mighty good."

"I know it is," Jake said. "That's how come I was more than half disappointed we didn't let the enemy get into Fredericksburg and then try to storm these heights. We'd have been shooting 'em till they got sick of trying."

Nathan Bedford Forrest III frowned. "Conventional wisdom says you don't want to let them have a bridgehead if you can help it. You can get around conventional wisdom a lot of the time, but not always. That foothold they've got south of the Rapidan in the Wilderness still worries me."

One of the reasons Forrest headed the General Staff was that he wasn't afraid to speak his mind, even to the President of the Confederate States. Jake asked, "Are you telling me they might break through if they cross the river here? We couldn't hold 'em and drive 'em back?"

Forrest scratched his mustache with his right thumb. "Odds are we could, but it's not a sure thing. Remember, sir, they kept fighting after we thought they wouldn't."

After you thought they wouldn't, he meant. Featherston couldn't even swear at him, not when he wasn't wrong. Because Forrest spoke his mind, Jake handled him more carefully than he would have dealt with some Party yes-man. "What's your judgment, then, General? If you reckon the risk is too high, we won't take it. But if you don't, this looks like a dandy place to bleed the damnyankees white."

"If everything goes well, sir, we ought to be able to do that," Forrest said at last. "If things go wrong, though . . . If things go wrong, we've given ourselves a lot of trouble that we didn't have to. And remember, Mr. President—we'll need more men here to bleed the Yankees than we would if we just kept 'em on the north bank of the Rappahannock. Those are men we wouldn't be able to use for other operations. The one thing the Yankees always have is more men than we do. So which is more important to you?"

Featherston smiled. He almost laughed out loud. He'd put the burden on Forrest's shoulders, and the chief of the General Staff had put it right back on his. And Forrest's question was a serious one. Jake hated nothing worse than being deflected from any purpose of his—indeed, he'd made a hallmark of being impossible to deflect. Here, though, Nathan Bedford Forrest III was speaking plain good sense, much too plain to ignore. "All right, dammit," Jake said grudgingly. "Hold 'em on the other side of the Rappahannock if you can."

He didn't fail to note how relieved Forrest looked. "We'll do that, sir, or we'll do our best to do it, anyhow," the general said. "If they try to force another crossing, they may get over whether we want them to or not. In that case, we'll do our best to give you the killing ground you have in mind."

He's trying to let me down easy. Again, Jake almost laughed. He said, "All right, that's how we'll do it, then. Make your orders out that way. And make sure the other thing, Coal-scuttle, is going forward the way it's supposed to. I want to make the United States feel the pinch, goddammit."

"Things are moving into place on that one, Mr. President," Forrest said. "Keeping a smaller presence here will help that, too. I don't think you'd find anyone who'd disagree there."

"All right. All right. You made your point." No, Jake didn't like being balked. It didn't happen very often, not when he was both President of the Confederate States and head of the Freedom Party. He'd thought he knew just how Al Smith's mind worked, but then the son of a bitch decided to go on with the war. And now this . . .

"Mr. President, we simply aren't big enough to do two big things at once," Forrest said. "That's a nuisance, but it's the truth. If we try to pretend we are, we'll end up in trouble."

"If you try to teach your grandma how to suck eggs, *you'll* end up in trouble," Jake said. Nathan Bedford Forrest III chuckled, though Jake hadn't been joking. The President went on, "Let's get back to Richmond, then." He all but spat out the words. He'd wanted to take off his shirt and serve a gun, the way he had in the Great War. Things were simple then. With the enemy right in front of you, you went ahead and blew him up. You didn't need to worry about anything else.

These days, enemies were everywhere: not just the damnyankees, not just the niggers who tormented the CSA, but fools and bunglers who wouldn't go along and traitors who wanted to see him fail just because that would mean they were right and he was wrong. *I'll settle them all—every last one of them,* Jake thought. *By the time I'm through, this country will look the way it's supposed to, the way I want it to.*

As usual, he went back to Richmond in an ambulance. If U.S. airplanes appeared overhead, the Red Crosses on the vehicle ought to keep the Yankees from shooting it up. Also as usual, he had an ordinary—

although armored—motorcar take him the last leg of the journey so no Yankee reconnaissance aircraft or spies on the ground would spot an ambulance going into the Gray House.

Bomb craters turned the grounds around the Presidential residence into a lunar landscape. And repairmen swarmed over the building itself. "Jesus!" Jake exclaimed. "How come nobody told me it got hit again?"

"Probably didn't want to get you all upset, sir," his driver answered.

Probably didn't want to make you blow a gasket, that meant. The driver was probably right, too. Jake had succeeded in making people afraid of him. Men who would tell him what they thought, men like Nathan Bedford Forrest III and Clarence Potter, were rare. The rest said what they thought he wanted to hear—either that or they hunkered down and didn't tell him anything. That last looked to be what had happened here.

"Is Lulu all right?" he demanded when he got inside. If his secretary wasn't and they'd kept that from him, they'd be sorry, and pretty damn quick, too.

But the flunky he'd asked nodded. "She sure is, Mr. President. Just about everybody got down to the shelter before the bombs started falling."

"Well, that's good, anyway," Featherston said. The bomb shelter below the Gray House was as elaborate as the one under the Confederate War Department. No doubt the shelter under Powel House in Philadelphia was just as fancy, but it hadn't done Al Smith one damn bit of good. Jake preferred not to dwell on that.

When he got to his office, Lulu greeted him with a nod. "Hello, Mr. President," she said, as calmly as if nothing had happened while he was away.

"Hello, sweetie," he said, and gave her a hug. She was one of the tiny handful of people he cared about as people and not as things to order around or otherwise manipulate. If he'd lost her . . . He didn't know what he would have done.

Her sallow cheeks turned pink. "You worry about running the country, sir," she said. "You don't need to worry about me." In such things, she could give him orders, or thought she could.

"I'll worry about whatever I . . . darn well want to," he said. He swore like the old soldier he was around everyone else, but tried not to around her. Her disapproving sniffs were too much for him to take. He went on, "Can I still work at my desk, or did it get blown to, uh, smithereens?"

"I'm afraid it did, sir," Lulu answered. "But everything down below came through just fine."

Jake made a discontented noise, down deep in his throat. He didn't want to run the war from down in the bomb shelter, even if its air conditioning made it a comfortable place in the hot weather that lay ahead. It felt like being cooped up inside a submarine. Actually, Jake had never been inside a sub, so he couldn't prove that, but it felt like what he thought being cooped up in one *would* feel like. And what he wanted to do wasn't always the same as what he needed to do. The shelter bristled with telephone and wireless links. He *could* run the war from it. If he didn't like it—well, too bad. This was war, and people all over the continent were putting up with things they didn't like.

A young man in a State Department uniform came up to him, waited to be noticed, and then said, "Sir, may I speak to you for a moment?"

"You're doing it," Jake told him.

"Er—yes." For some reason, that flustered the State Department fellow. He needed a moment to gather himself. Then he said, "Sir, we've heard from the Emperor of Mexico. His Majesty will provide the three divisions you requested."

"Good. That's good." Featherston tried to make his smile benign instead of tigerish. Maximilian hadn't wanted to cough up the men. Jake had been blunt about what would happen to his miserable gimcrack country—and to him—if he didn't. Evidently the message had got through. The President went on, "We've saved the greasers' bacon a few times. Only fitting and proper they pay us back."

"Yes, sir," the State Department man said. He looked as if he would have been more comfortable in striped trousers and cutaway coat. Too damn bad for him.

"Anything else, sonny?" Jake asked. The puppy shook his head. Featherston jerked a thumb toward the front door, which hadn't been damaged. "All right, then. Get lost."

The kid from the State Department disappeared. Jake stared after him. Either they really were making them younger than they had once upon a time or he himself was starting to get some serious mileage on him. He suspected the problem did not lie with the State Department.

Whether he was getting old or not, he still had a war to run. He could do that better than anybody else in the CSA. *Better than anybody else in the USA, too, by God,* he thought. And those three Mexican divisions would help, especially since, now that Maximilian had agreed once, he'd have a harder time saying no if Jake asked again. And Jake intended to do just that.

Dr. Leonard O'Doull wondered what was going on when he and his aid station got pulled out of their position across the Rapidan from the Wilderness and shifted east. Now he knew: they'd left the frying pan and gone straight into the fire.

Most of the frying was getting done on the other side of the Rappahannock, in and just beyond Fredericksburg. The U.S. Army had battered out a foothold there, as it had in the Wilderness. It was trying to feed in enough men and machines to make the foothold mean something. Whether it could was very much up in the air.

Whether the kid on the table in front of O'Doull would make it was also up in the air. A piece of shrapnel had torn the hell out of his chest. He was bleeding faster than O'Doull could patch him. "Keep pouring in the plasma!" O'Doull barked to Granville McDougald. "Gotta keep his blood pressure up."

"Pretty soon there won't be any blood in the pressure," McDougald said. That exaggerated, but not by much. An awful lot of blood had come out, and an awful lot of plasma had gone in. "Shit!" McDougald exclaimed. "We haven't got any pressure now!"

"Yeah." O'Doull had no trouble figuring out why, either—the kid's heart had stopped. He grabbed it and started cardiac massage. Once in a blue moon, that worked. Most of the time, a heart that stopped would never start again. This was one of those times. After a few minutes, he let it go and shook his head. "We've lost him."

McDougald nodded. "Afraid you're right. That was a nasty wound. We did everything we could." He beckoned to a corpsman. "Get him off the table, Eddie. He's Graves Registrations' business now."

"Right, Granny," Eddie said. "One more Deeply Regrets telegram. One more time when everybody hopes the Western Union delivery boy stops next door."

The corpse was hardly out of the tent before a groaning sergeant with a shattered knee came in on a stretcher. "Granny, you do this one and I'll pass gas," O'Doull said. "You're neater at orthopedic stuff than I am."

"I've had more practice, Doc, that's all." But McDougald sounded pleased. He wasn't an M.D. despite his vast experience; to have a real doctor defer to him had to make him feel good.

"Gas!" the sergeant said when O'Doull pressed the ether cone down over his nose and mouth. O'Doull had seen that before. He and Eddie kept the wounded man from yanking off the cone till the anesthetic took hold.

Eddie shook his head as the sergeant's hands finally went limp. "That's always so much fun," he said.

"Yeah," O'Doull agreed. "How's he look, Granny?"

"It's a mess in there. Kneecap's smashed, medial collateral's cut," McDougald answered. "Can you get him down a little deeper? I want those leg muscles as relaxed as I can get 'em."

"Will do." O'Doull opened the valve on the ether cylinder a little more.

After a minute or so, McDougald gave him a thumbs-up. The medic worked quickly and skillfully, repairing what he could and removing what he couldn't repair. When he was through, he said, "He'll never run the mile, but I think he'll walk . . . pretty well."

"Looked that way to me, too," O'Doull said. "That medial collateral was nicely done. I don't think I could have got it together anywhere near as neat as you did."

"Thanks, Doc." McDougald's gauze mask hid most of his smile, but his eyes glowed. "Had to try it. A knee's not a knee without a working medial collateral. It's not a repair that would do for a halfback, but for just getting around it ought to be strong enough."

"They play football in Quebec, too. Well, sort of football: they've got twelve men on a side, and the end zones are big as all outdoors. But it's pretty much the same game. Guys get hurt the same way, that's for sure," O'Doull said. "I've had to patch up a couple of wrecked knees. I told the men I'd come after 'em with a sledgehammer if I ever caught 'em playing again."

"Did they listen to you?" McDougald asked, amused interest in his voice.

"Are you serious? Quebecois are the stubbornest people on the face of the earth." Leonard O'Doull knew *he* sounded disgusted. "Repairing a knee once isn't easy. Repairing it twice is damn near impossible." He flexed his none too impressive biceps. "I'm getting pretty good with a sledgehammer, though."

"I believe that." McDougald and Eddie eased the wounded sergeant off the table. He would finish recovering farther back of the line. McDougald caught O'Doull's eye. "Want to duck out for a butt before the next poor sorry bastard comes in, Doc?"

"I'd love to. Let's—" But O'Doull stopped in midsentence, because the next poor sorry bastard came in right then.

One look made O'Doull wonder why the hell the corpsmen had bothered hauling him all the way back here. He had a bullet wound— pretty plainly an entry wound—in his forehead, just below the hairline, and what was as obviously an exit wound, horrible with scalp and blood, in back.

Seeing O'Doull's expression, one of the stretcher-bearers said, "His pulse and breathing are still strong, Doc. Maybe you can do *something* for him, anyways."

"Fat chance," O'Doull muttered. Military hospitals still held men who'd got turned into vegetables by head wounds in the Great War. Some of them had a strong pulse and breathed on their own, too. Some of them would die of old age, but none would ever be a functioning human being again.

Then the wounded man sat up on the stretcher and said, "Have any aspirins, buddy? I've got a hell of a headache."

"Jesus Christ!" Everybody in the aid tent except the fellow with the head wound said the same thing at the same time. One of the bearers and Eddie and O'Doull crossed themselves. O'Doull had seen a lot of things in his time, but never a man with a through-and-through head wound who sat up and made conversation.

Granville McDougald strode forward. He bent low and looked not at the soldier's injuries but at the scalp between them. Then he shook his head in slow wonder. "I will be damned," he said. "I've heard of wounds like this, but I didn't think I'd ever run into one myself."

"What is it, Granny?" O'Doull asked. He wanted to latch on to something, anything, but the idea of a dead man talking.

"Look, Doc. You can see for yourself." McDougald's finger traced the injury. "The slug must have gone in, then slid around the top of this guy's skull under the scalp till it exited back here. It didn't do a damn thing more. It couldn't have, or he'd be dead as shoe leather."

"I'm fine," the soldier said. "Except for that headache, anyhow. I asked you guys for aspirins once already."

"Well, I'll be a son of a bitch," O'Doull said, ignoring him. "You're right. You've got to be right. That is the luckiest thing I have ever seen in my life. I thought he was a ghost for a second, I swear to God I did." The rational part of his brain started working again. "We'd better send him back for X-rays once we clean him up. He could have a fracture in there—though his head's so hard, he might not."

"What the hell's that supposed to mean?" the wounded man demanded.

"If you didn't have a thick skull, pal, that bullet might've gone through instead of around," O'Doull told him. "Can you get up on the table by yourself? We're going to want to get some disinfectant on that and stitch you up and bandage you. You've got a story you can tell your grandchildren, that's for sure."

The soldier walked to the table and sat down. "You ain't doin' nothin' to me till I get my aspirins, you hear?"

"Give him a couple, Eddie," O'Doull said wearily. "Hell, give him a slug of the medicinal brandy, too. If anybody ever earned it, he did."

That produced the first thing besides loud indignation he'd got from the wounded man, who exclaimed, "Now you're talkin', Doc! Want a smoke? I got these off a dead Confederate—fuck of a lot better'n what we make."

O'Doull grabbed his hand before he could light a match. "You don't want to do that in here," the doctor said in gentle tones that camouflaged the panic inside. "You're liable to blow us sky high if you do."

After the little white pills and the knock of honey-colored hooch, the wounded man was willing to sit still while O'Doull patched him up. He grumbled about the way the doctor's novocaine burned before it numbed. He grumbled that he could feel the needle even after the novocaine started working. Except for complaining about his headache, he didn't grumble at all about getting shot in the head.

"Don't get the bandages over my eyes, dammit," he said. O'Doull had to coax him back into the stretcher so the corpsmen could take him away—he wanted to walk.

Once he was gone, O'Doull let out a long sigh and said, "Now I *am* going to have that smoke, by God!"

"Me, too," Granville McDougald said. They both left the tent to light up—and they both smoked Confederate tobacco, too.

O'Doull blew out a long plume of smoke. "Great God in the foothills," he said. "Now I really have seen everything."

"Yeah, well, you know what's gonna happen as well as I do, Doc,"

McDougald said. "They'll patch him up and they'll send him home till he finishes healing, and he'll be a nine days' wonder while he's there. And then he'll come back to the front, and he'll stop a shell burst with his nuts, and he won't have to worry about telling his grandchildren stories anymore."

"Christ!" Whatever O'Doull had expected him to say, that wasn't it. "And I thought this war was making *me* cynical."

McDougald shrugged. "You got out after 1917. You found yourself a nice little French gal and you settled down. I've worn the uniform all that time. I've got a long head start on you. The shit I've seen . . ." He shook his head. But then he shook it again in a different way. "I'd never seen anything like that before, though. Talk about beating the odds! I'd heard of it. I knew it was possible. But I'd never seen it, and I never thought I would."

"You sure were one up on me," O'Doull said. "When he rose up on the stretcher there, I figured he was Lazarus."

"Gave me a turn, too, and I won't try to tell you any different." McDougald took a last drag on his cigarette and crushed it out under his boot. "Well, at least we can feel good about things for a while. Lazarus is going to get better. Some of the ones like that help make up for the sorry bastards we lose."

On the other side of the Rappahannock, Confederate guns started pounding. Asskickers screamed down out of the sky. Bombs burst. O'Doull stamped out his cigarette, too. "They'll be bringing more back to us before very long," he predicted. "Either that or they'll move us forward up into Fredericksburg."

"Gotta keep us close to the source of supply," McDougald said.

"The source of supply," O'Doull echoed. "Right." That was cynical, too, which didn't mean it was wrong.

VI

Snyder, Texas, was a long way north of Baroyeca, Sonora. It could get just as hot, though. Hipolito Rodriguez didn't know how or why that was so, but he knew it was. He'd seen as much in the summertime in Texas during the Great War.

It wasn't summer yet, but the hot weather had arrived ahead of the season. Down in Baroyeca, he'd have worn a broad-brimmed straw sombrero, a loose-fitting cotton shirt, baggy trousers, and sandals. He would have been a lot more comfortable than he was in his gray guard uniform, too. The cap he had on didn't keep the sun off him nearly well enough. And he especially hated his shiny black boots. He didn't think he would ever get used to them. They pinched his feet at every step he took.

Nothing he could do about it, though. Guards had to stay in uniform. That was one of the rules, and nobody who didn't stick to the rules had any business being a guard. Along with the rest of his squad, he stood by the train tracks that ran between Camp Determination and the new women's camp alongside it.

Officially, the women's camp was part of Camp Determination. Brigade Leader Pinkard—Rodriguez's old war buddy—was in charge of it, too. Unofficially, the guards called the women's half Camp Undecided. Despite being married to a thoroughly decisive woman, Rodriguez thought that was pretty funny.

All the guards carried submachine guns. Tower-mounted machine guns also bore on the disembarking point. Prisoners who tried anything cute ended up dead in a hurry. The overwhelming firepower on display helped persuade incoming Negroes that acting up wasn't smart.

A big, swag-bellied Alabaman named Jerry pointed east down the track. "Look at the smoke," he said. "Another load of niggers coming in."

The sergeant in charge of the squad said, "Well, what the hell would we be cookin' our brains for out here if there wasn't another goddamn train comin' in?" Tom Porter, like the men he led, was a Freedom Party guard, so his formal rank was troop leader, not sergeant, but he wore three stripes on the sleeve of his gray tunic, and he acted like every senior noncom Rodriguez had ever known.

Up in the towers, the machine guns swung toward the train when it was still a good half a mile off. A couple of the men in Rodriguez's squad hefted their weapons. Other guards along the track also grew alert. Dog handlers patted their coon hounds. The dogs were called that because they were most often used to hunt raccoons. The men who used them here had a different sort of fun with the name.

Wheezing and groaning, the train slowed and then stopped. The locomotive had to date back to the turn of the century, if not further. Even in sleepy Sonora, it would have been an antique. More modern machines served closer to the front. This one would do for hauling *mallates*.

The passenger cars and freight cars it pulled had also seen better decades. Again, they were good enough for this. The passengers cars had shutters hastily nailed up outside their windows. That kept the blacks inside from looking out and people outside from looking in.

All the cars were locked from the outside. Tom Porter pointed to the two closest to his squad. "We'll take 'em one at a time," he said, "the front one first." As he set his beefy hands on the latch, he added, "Be ready for anything. Niggers comin' out, they're liable to be a little crazy, or more than a little."

When he opened the door, the first thing that rolled out was a ripe, rich stench: shit and piss and puke and stale, sour sweat. Rodriguez wrinkled his nose. Far too many people had been packed inside that passenger car for much too long. They came spilling out now, a jumble of misery, blinking and shading their eyes against the sudden harsh sunlight.

If you got the jump on them early, they usually didn't get it back.

"Move!" Porter screamed, and the other guards echoed him. "Men to the left! Women and pickaninnies to the right! Move, God damn you!"

They moved—the ones who could. Some just collapsed by the railroad car. Kicks and punches drove most of those to their feet. The rest were too far gone for even brutality to rouse. "Water!" one of them croaked in a dust-choked voice. "I gots to have water. Ain't had no water since I dunno when."

Rodriguez kicked him—not hard enough to cripple, just hard enough to make sure the *mallate* knew who was boss. "Get up!" he yelled. "No water here. Water inside the camp." Slowly, the Negro struggled upright and stood swaying.

A plump black woman said, "Dey's dead folks inside de car dere, poor souls."

There usually were casualties on a journey like this. The cars carried six or seven times as many people as they were designed to hold. Food was whatever the Negroes managed to smuggle aboard the train. The windows wouldn't open, and the shutters would have kept out most of the air if they had.

And, all things considered, this carload of blacks had it easy. They could have come to Camp Determination in a cattle car, the way a lot of Negroes in this train had. Nobody bothered cleaning cattle cars very well before loading people into them. They had no windows, shuttered or otherwise. They had no toilets, either, only a honey bucket or two. And they were so jammed with men, women, and children that getting to a honey bucket would have taken a small miracle.

A striking young woman with a dancer's walk and high cheekbones that argued for an Indian grandparent sidled up to Rodriguez. "You keep me safe in here, I do anything you want," she purred in a bedroom voice. "Anything at all. My name's Thais. You look for me. I'm *real* friendly."

"Go on. Get moving," he said stonily, and her face fell. Like most of the guards, he heard something like what she'd said at least once whenever a train came in. Women thought it would help. Sometimes they were even right. Not here. Not now.

"Form lines! Bring your luggage! Form lines! Bring your luggage!" Like every squad leader, Tom Porter yelled the same thing over and over. "You gotta be searched! You gotta be deloused! You gotta be searched! You gotta be deloused!"

The searchers would take away all the weapons and all the valuables they found. That stuff was supposed to go back into the war effort. Some of it, maybe even most of it, did. The rest stuck to the searchers' fingers. Searchers were senior men. They'd paid their dues, and now they were getting their reward. Some of them were getting to be wealthy men.

Slowly the lines formed. Even more slowly, they moved forward. Men and women too weak to rise in spite of calculated brutality lay by the railroad cars. "Get the stretcher parties out!" an officer shouted. "We'll move them to the transfer facility!"

None of the guards laughed or winked or nudged one another. They'd got lessons about that. *Never do anything to spook the spooks,* one trainer had put it. *The transfer facility* was a killing truck. The only place they'd be transferred was the mass grave not far away. All the prisoners in Camp Determination were heading that way. The ones too weak to rise got an express ticket—that was the only difference.

Black men carried away the weaklings. The story the bearers got was that the trucks would take them to an infirmary a couple of miles away. The infirmary existed. Every once in a while, a Negro came back from it. That kept the inmates from flabbling about what happened to the ones who didn't. More guards with submachine guns kept an eye on the stretcher bearers. But guards kept an eye on everybody all the time, so that didn't seem out of the ordinary.

Guards went through the cars to bring out the dead, the dying, and anybody who thought he'd get sneaky and try to hide. It was nasty work, but they couldn't trust it to the stretcher bearers, who were too soft on their own kind. Some of the dead ones had money or jewelry worth lifting. You never could tell.

Shouts farther down the train said another squad had caught a lurker. More shouts—these of pain—said he was getting what was coming to him. The guards would beat him to within an inch of his life. Then he'd get thrown on the first available truck "to the transfer facility"—and that would take care of the last inch.

"They're such damn fools," said a guard heaving bodies out of the car with Rodriguez. "They think we're not gonna check the fuckin' cars. Gotta be dumb as rocks if they do."

"That's right," Rodriguez said.

"Damn straight it is," the other guard said. Buchanan Thornton was his name—he told people to call him Buck. He had no doubts about anything, not as far as Rodriguez could see. Few whites in the CSA did, and Buck Thornton was as white as they came: sandy hair with a lot of gray in it, blue eyes, pointy nose, freckles.

If there weren't blacks around to revile, he probably whiled away the time cussing at greasers. Where he was, though, he didn't have the time or energy to worry about anything but Negroes. As a Sonoran, Rodriguez knew he was on the bottom rung of the social ladder. But he was on the ladder; down below lay the ooze and the muck—the blacks on whose back the ladder stood.

He looked down on them all the more because he was closer to them than people higher up the ladder. In an odd way, though, Negroes were an insurance policy for people of Mexican blood. As long as they were there, nobody except a few Texans got excited about his kind.

The first trucks rolled out of Camp Determination. When they came back, the *mallates* aboard them wouldn't be there anymore. Rodriguez wouldn't miss them a bit, either. The first Negroes he'd ever met had had guns in their hands. They'd done their level best to kill him. He'd hated and feared them ever since. If Jake Featherston wanted to get rid of them, more power to him and to the Freedom Party.

As more stretcher bearers hauled away dead and dying blacks, Rodriguez had an odd thought. Suppose Camp Determination and others like it—for there were bound to be others like it—succeeded. Suppose they made the Confederate States Negro-free. What would the country be like then?

It would be a lot safer, was the first answer that sprang into his mind. *Mallates* were nothing but trouble. Even now, they left car bombs in cities and bushwhacked whites in the countryside. Good riddance to them.

But if they were gone—if they were *all* gone—what would that social ladder be like? People always needed someone at whom they could look down their noses. Who would fall into that unenviable role?

People like me, Rodriguez thought—people with brown skin and black hair, people who spoke English with an accent. That might not be so good. He wondered why the question hadn't occurred to him sooner.

He shrugged. That would come later, much later, if it ever happened at all. It wasn't anything he had to lose sleep over, and he didn't intend to. He had a job to do, and he was going to do it the best way he knew how.

And maybe he shouldn't have looked down his nose at that Thais. She wasn't bad, and he hadn't seen Magdalena for a long time now. He shrugged again. It wasn't as if there weren't plenty of fish in that particular sea.

Air-raid sirens howled, tumbling George Enos, Jr., out of bed much too early on a Sunday morning. Either somebody with a sadistic sense of humor had picked the time for a drill—always a possibility in the Navy—or the Japs were feeling friskier than usual.

When antiaircraft guns not far from the barracks started banging away, George got his answer. He also heard several anguished groans— gunfire and hangovers mixed poorly.

He took the time to throw on tunic and trousers and shoes before running for the closest slit trench. Not everybody bothered. Some people dashed out in nothing but skivvies. Nobody ragged them for it, either. In combat, what you had to do came first, with everything else a long way behind.

A fighter swooped low. Machine-gun bullets chewed up the grass and sent dirt jumping. Some of them kicked into the trench, too. Somebody howled like a coyote when a bullet found him. George scrunched himself up as small and as low as he could. His whites got filthy, but that was the least of his worries.

Most of the action, though, was well away from the barracks. The Japs were aiming for the harbor and the nearby airfield. Warships and airplanes could hurt them. Mere men were an afterthought.

Fremont Blaine Dalby jumped into the trench and just missed pulverizing George's kidneys with his big feet. He must have dodged the strafing fighter's bullets like a halfback dodging tacklers. "Bastards are going to pay for this," he panted, crashing down beside George.

Something blew up with force enough to make the ground shake. "Looks like they're dishing it out, not taking it," George pointed out in a bellow that, under those circumstances, did duty for a whisper.

"Yeah, but if they want to yank the lion's tail, they gotta stick their head in his mouth," Dalby said. That wasn't the way George would have gone about pulling a lion's tail, assuming he were mad enough to try such a thing, but he knew better than to criticize a CPO's choice of metaphors. And when Dalby went on, he was as concrete as Boulder Dam: "If their airplanes can reach us, ours can reach their carriers. And we must have known they were coming unless every goddamn Y-range operator in the Sandwich Islands is asleep at the switch. So we oughta be good and ready for 'em."

"Here's hoping," George said.

An airplane smashed to the ground not far enough away. He stuck his head up, hoping to watch a Japanese pilot fry in the wreckage. But the burning fighter was American: he could still make out the eagle and crossed swords painted on the fuselage. He hoped the pilot had bailed out before his machine crashed. Then the warm, tropical breeze brought him the stink of burning meat. His stomach did a flipflop worse than any in the North Atlantic in wintertime.

Dalby stuck his head up, too. He was looking along the trench. "We've got a lot of our crew here," he said. "We ought to find us a gun to man."

The prospect of getting out of the trench did not fill George with delight. He wanted to tell Dalby as much. What came out of his mouth was, "I'll follow you, Chief." The desire not to look bad before one's fellow man is a strange, compelling, and terribly powerful thing.

When Dalby yelled, Fritz Gustafson answered the call right away. George might have known nothing would faze the loader; even if he was scared, he was too damn stubborn to show it, probably even to himself. Dalby looked around again. The rest of the gun crew were either out of earshot or sensibly keeping their heads down and their mouths shut. "Screw it," Dalby said. "We got a shell-heaver, a loader, and I can damn well aim. Come on."

He scrambled out of the trench. George did follow him. If he muttered about how many different kinds of damn fool he was, then he did, that was all. There was still a hell of a lot of racket all around. Dalby either didn't hear him or had a good enough excuse to pretend he didn't.

"Plenty going on," Gustafson said: a novel's worth of words from him.

He wasn't wrong. American and Japanese warplanes tangled overhead. If anybody had an edge, George couldn't tell who it was. Both ground-based antiaircraft guns and those mounted on ships in Pearl Harbor were throwing shells up as fast as they could. Shrapnel was starting to come down, pattering and clattering off roofs and sidewalks and thumping into bare ground. George wished he had a helmet. That stuff would rearrange your brains if it hit you in the head.

"Come on," Fremont Dalby said again. "Let's find us a gun." He trotted off as if he knew exactly where to do it.

And damned if he didn't. Twin 40mm mounts were almost as thick as fleas on land as well as aboard ship. This one had fallen silent because a bomb burst behind it turned the crew to tattered red rags. George gulped. Blood splashed the guns' breech ends and dappled the shells.

Dalby looked at the fallen gunners. "They're dead," he said, which was almost an understatement. "Not a damn thing we can do for 'em—except maybe pay the Japs back. You guys feed and load, I'll aim, and we'll all hope like hell."

George got blood on his hands when he passed shells to Fritz Gustafson. The loader got more on his when he shoved them home. Dalby aimed at a bomber.

The gun roared. Shell casings leaped from the breeches and clanged on the cement sidewalk. With only three men to serve the piece, it couldn't fire as fast as it would have with a whole crew. Nobody cared. They were hitting back, not just taking a pounding the way they had been.

George had no idea whether they hit anything. He didn't have time to look up. He was too busy doing his job, trying to pass as much ammunition as two men would. The loader didn't complain, and neither did Fremont Dalby. He couldn't have done too badly, then.

Only when the gun fell silent did he pause, blinking in surprise. "No more targets," Dalby announced. "They've flown the coop."

When George glanced at his wristwatch, he blinked in amazement. He also took a good, long look to make sure the second hand was going around. "We've only been here fifteen minutes?" he said.

"Time flies when you're having fun," Dalby said. "I think maybe we ran 'em off. Other question is, what did they do to us?"

Whenever George moved, his shoes left bloody footprints. He didn't want to look at what was left of the gun's original crew. But, in a fight like this, men were small change. How many airplanes had the Japs lost? Would they lose any carriers? Measure that against the damage they'd done and you'd get some idea of who'd come out on top. Maybe.

"You men!" That was an unmistakable officer's bark. Along with his shipmates, George turned, came to attention, and saluted. The unmistakable officer—a lieutenant commander, no less—kept on barking:

"I haven't seen you before, and I know damn well this isn't your proper station. Explain yourselves."

"Sir, we're from the *Townsend*," Dalby answered. "We were looking for a way to hit back at the enemy. You can see for yourself what happened to the men who were posted here. We fought this gun as well as we could, sir." He spoke calmly, quietly, respectfully. Only his eyes asked, *What were* you *doing while all this crap was going on?*

The lieutenant commander had some mileage on him. By the fruit salad on his chest, he'd started out during the Great War. He knew what the petty officer wasn't saying. Knowing, he turned red—not so red as George's footprints, but red enough. "Carry on," he said in a choked voice, and got out of there in a hurry.

"You showed him," George said.

"Yeah." Fremont Dalby didn't sound happy. "You shouldn't *have* to show officers, though, especially not the ones who've been around the block. But some of 'em just have to make like they're God."

When stretcher bearers came by, the men from the *Townsend* waved to them. They hurried over, but they didn't stay. "We're supposed to be looking for wounded," one of them said. "Those birds ain't goin' anywhere if we leave 'em where they're at. Sooner or later, the meat wagon will deal with 'em."

"Not right," George said. "These guys were doing everything they could till their number came up. Shouldn't just leave 'em like garbage." Actually, they reminded him of what was all over the decks of the *Sweet Sue* after the men on the fishing boat had been gutting big cod.

But Dalby cut the stretcher bearers more slack than he'd given the officer. "Wounded count for more," he allowed. "You can still save them."

"Thanks, Chief," said the man who'd spoken before. The bearers hurried away.

Dalby looked at his shipmates. "Either one of you notice if we had bombers taking off?"

"Not me," George said at once. "I was too busy trying not to let the Japs blow me to kingdom come, and then trying to shoot 'em down."

"We did," Fritz Gustafson said. "They were already airborne when I hit the trench." Two consecutive sentences from him were a telephone book, an unabridged dictionary, from a noisier man.

Fremont Dalby nodded. "That's pretty good. We ought to be hitting back pretty damn quick, then. Those bastards need to pay."

"Bombers should have taken off the minute we picked up the Japs' airplanes on the Y-range set," George said.

"Yeah," Dalby said thoughtfully, and then, in deeper, gruffer, angrier tones, *"Yeah!"* He kicked at the sidewalk. "Yeah, goddammit. Somebody *was* asleep at the switch again. That would have been the best way to do it, sure as hell. Christ, there are times when I really do think we want to lose this fuckin' war."

"Hey, Dalby, you still in one piece?" The shout came from the direction in which the gunners had come. Only another CPO would have used the gun chief's naked surname with such relish.

"Yeah, we're here, Burnett." Dalby gave back what he'd got. "Leastways we didn't stay in the trench sucking our thumbs and hanging on to our Theodore bears."

Chief Burnett's reply offered an improbable and uncomfortable destination for both thumbs and Theodore bears. Dalby suggested that Burnett's mother already resided there. Burnett gave forth with an opinion on certain habits of Dalby's mother about which he was unlikely to have personal knowledge. Then, in the same unruffled tone of voice, he asked, "You cocksuckers hit anything?"

"Damfino," Dalby answered, also without much heat. "We gave it our best shot, that's all." He slapped Gustafson and George on the back, staggering them both—and George was not a small man, and Fritz Gustafson was a big one. "You already knew the squarehead's solid. And this guy here ain't half bad."

George shuffled his feet on the blood-splashed sidewalk. "Thanks, Chief," he mumbled. A Naval Cross from the hands of an admiral wouldn't have meant nearly so much as that laconic praise from a man who mattered to him.

"Well, well," Tom Colleton said. "What have we here?"

What they had there was a company of Confederate barrels: big, snorting machines painted in butternut with swirls and splotches of dark green and dark brown to make them harder to spot and harder to hit. But they were barrels the likes of which hadn't been seen up in Ohio before.

Lieutenant-Colonel Colleton strolled over for a closer look at the new monsters. They were plainly related to the beasts that had spearheaded the Confederate thrust to Lake Erie the summer before. They were just as plainly bigger and meaner—*Tyrannosaurus rex* next to the earlier *Allosaurus*. They seemed more squat, lower to the ground. As Tom Colleton got up to them, he realized they weren't, but the impression remained. Instead of going straight up and down, most of their armor was cleverly sloped to help deflect shells. And their turret guns were bigger and longer than those of the earlier models.

One of the barrel drivers was head and shoulders out of his machine: no point in buttoning up when the damnyankees weren't close. "That's a two-and-a-half-inch cannon you've got there?" Colleton asked.

"Three inches, sir," the man answered, proud as if he'd said *eight inches* of himself. "Some of those Yankees'll never know what hit 'em. Seventeen-pound shell."

"Sweet Jesus!" Tom exclaimed. "Yeah, that'll make you sit up and take notice, all right. How many of these bastards have we got?"

"Many as we need, I reckon," the driver said.

"Oh, yeah? I'll believe that when I see it," Tom Colleton said. In his experience, nobody ever had as many barrels as he needed. The enemy wrecked a few, some more broke down—and then, just when they would have come in handy to take out some well-sited, well-protected machine-gun nests, there wouldn't be any for miles around.

But the driver nodded. Why not? He could duck down inside all that lovely armor plating. He didn't have to look longingly at it from the outside. He didn't have to worry about machine guns, either, no matter how well protected they were. He said, "Sir, don't you fret. This time, by God, we're going to get the job done."

"Here's hoping," Tom said. The driver—a cocky kid—just grinned at him. He found himself grinning back. It wasn't as if barrel crewmen didn't have worries of their own. When they were in the field, they were cannon magnets. All the enemy's heavy weapons bore on them. The armor that kept out small-arms fire could turn into a roasting pan to cook soldiers if something did get through.

"You'll see." Yeah, the kid was cocky.

He also sounded like somebody who knew more than he was letting on. "What *is* the job we're going to get done?" Tom asked. He commanded a regiment; nobody'd bothered to tell him anything. He should have been miffed that a noncom from another unit knew more about what was going on than he did. He should have been, but he wasn't, or not very. He'd seen enough in both the Great War and this one to know that kind of crap happened all the time.

Before the barrel driver could answer, somebody inside the machine said something to him through the intercom. Tom heard the squawk in the kid's earphones, but he couldn't make out any words. The driver said, "Sorry, sir—gotta go. Orders are to push up a little closer to the front."

"Be careful," Tom warned. "The damnyankees have started sneaking in more and more infiltrators. They like to plant mines, and their snipers try and blow the heads off drivers and commanders who don't stay buttoned up."

"Sir, we've got us this big ol' cannon and two machine guns. I reckon we can make any old infiltrators knuckle under," the driver answered. He ducked down into the barrel, but didn't close the hatch. The engine's note deepened as the machine rattled forward with its companions.

Tom stared after them, coughing a little from the noxious exhaust fumes. He would have bet everything he owned that the kid had never seen combat. Nobody who had was that casual about snipers. If the other guy shot first, how big your gun was or how many rounds per minute you could put out didn't matter.

"Luck," Tom muttered. If that smiling puppy lived through his first couple of brushes with U.S. soldiers, he had a good chance of living quite a while longer. You got experience in a hurry—or, if you didn't, they buried you somewhere up here with a helmet stuck on a stick or on a rifle to mark where you lay.

That fancy barrel the kid was driving couldn't help but improve his odds. *If we'd had these when the war started* . . . Tom shook his head. The CSA hadn't had them, and he couldn't do a thing about it. The damnyankees hadn't had them, either. How long would they need to come up with barrels that matched these? How long before both sides sported land dreadnoughts, behemoths that laughed at danger and squashed antlike mortal men under their tracks without even knowing they were there?

Tom shook his head again. Nothing he could do about it except try to make sure he wasn't one of the poor sorry bastards who got squashed. He had no guarantees of that, either, and he knew it.

The barrels had rolled east out of Sandusky, not west. That said something, anyhow. He'd expected them to go in that direction, but nothing was carved in stone. It did look as if the CSA would have to hit the USA another lick to make the bigger country fall over. Cutting the United States in half hadn't quite done the job.

Why hadn't Al Smith thrown in the sponge, dammit? Everybody could have gone home. Tom would rather have been in St. Matthews than in Sandusky. He didn't know anybody who *wanted* to be here. But needing to be here was a different story.

Not all the reinforcements that came in were armored units. The infantrymen Tom saw made him raise an eyebrow. They weren't raw troops in fresh uniforms. They wore butternut frayed at the cuffs and the elbows and knees, faded by the sun, and deprived of all possibility of holding a crease by hard use. Their weapons were well tended, but a long way from factory-new. They were, in other words, just as much veterans as the men he commanded.

Where had they come from? Virginia seemed the only likely answer. Outside of Ohio, it was the only place that could have produced men like this. Fighting went on here and there in the West, but neither side put full force into that effort. The CSA and the USA both seemed sure the decision would come where they were strongest, not at the periphery. As far as Tom could see, the big brains on both sides were likely right.

But the damnyankees were still pounding away in Virginia. Could the Confederate States pull men out of there and go on holding them off? Tom had to hope so.

A day or two later, he realized that wasn't necessarily the right question. An even more pressing one was, couldn't the Confederate States do anything in Ohio without bleeding Virginia of men? The answer to that one looked to be no, and it wasn't the answer Tom wanted to find. Robbing Peter to pay Paul wasn't a good way to fight a war.

But what choice did the CSA have? None Tom could see. This was the downside of getting into a fight with a country that had a lot more manpower than you did. He called down more curses on Al Smith's head. The whole idea of storming up through Ohio, of cutting the United States in half, had been to knock the USA out of the fight before numbers really mattered. The Confederates had tried it. They'd succeeded as well as they'd hoped to. Everything had been perfect.

Except the United States hadn't quit.

Now the Confederate States faced the same sort of grinding struggle as they'd seen in the Great War. What should have been a one-punch KO was a no-holds-barred wrestling match now.

Airplanes droned by overhead. Tom Colleton cast a wary eye up to the heavens. He knew where he'd jump if they turned out to be U.S. airplanes. He looked for shelter as automatically as he breathed. That he looked for shelter so automatically helped keep him breathing.

But they were C.S. machines. Even when the silhouettes were tiny, he recognized them. He wondered what he'd do when his side—or the damnyankees—brought out new models. He had a pretty good notion, too: the first few times, he'd dive for cover whether he needed to or not. After that, he'd be able to tell friend from foe again.

The day was coming. It was probably coming soon. The Confederate States had new, improved barrels. Before long, they were bound to have new, improved airplanes, too. So were the United States.

Where would it end? Probably with both sides flying to the moon, with guns that could strike from five hundred miles away, and with bombs that could blow up whole counties if not whole states. Tom laughed at himself, but then he wondered why. Back in 1917, he couldn't have imagined the weapons the CSA and the USA were using now. What *would* the state of the art be in 1967, or in 1992?

He shivered, standing there under the warm spring sunshine. Things were much deadlier now than they had been a generation earlier. If that went on for another twenty-five years, wouldn't wars end almost before they started? And if not, why not?

"Sir?"

Tom started. He wondered how long the sergeant standing beside him had been trying to get his attention. By the exaggerated patience on the man's face, he'd done everything but wave wigwag flags. "What is it, Meyers?" Tom asked. "I'm here—I really am."

"That's good, sir," Sergeant Meyers said. "I was going to ask you if you knew when the balloon was going up. Not officially, you understand, but if you knew. It'd help the men get ready."

"I wish to God I did, Sergeant, but whatever we're doing, nobody has bothered to tell me about it yet. You can take that for whatever you think it's worth." Tom's laugh was half rueful, half furious. "One of the drivers for those new barrels had a pretty good notion, or reckoned he did. He had to pull out before he could tell me what it was. Damned impressive barrel, though."

"Oh, yes, sir!" Meyers was not a man given to wild enthusiasms; few sergeants were. That sort of man was much more likely to be a private or a lieutenant. But the sergeant waxed enthusiastic now. "We have enough of those critters, we'll make the damnyankees say uncle for sure."

"I hope you're right, Sergeant." Tom meant it. After what the C.S. Army had been through the year before, though, and after what it had accomplished, he took nothing for granted. That any one weapon, no matter how wonderful, could knock the USA out of the war struck him as unlikely.

He kept his mouth shut. If Sergeant Meyers thought the Yankees would fall over dead as soon as the Confederates kicked them back one more hill, fine. That made him a more cheerful soldier, a *better* soldier, at least until the damnyankees did get pushed back past that last hill, if they ever did. If they got pushed back and didn't fall over dead . . . Well, in that case Meyers and the other men like him would have some rethinking to do. He might not be such a terrific soldier for a while after that.

Wherever we're going, we're going east, Tom thought. *Right into the heart of Yankeeland. We'd better make 'em say uncle, by God.*

"Steady as she goes, Mr. Cooley," Sam Carsten told his executive officer.

"Steady as she goes—aye aye, sir," Pat Cooley replied, his freckled face intent on keeping the *Josephus Daniels* as steady as she could possibly go. The destroyer escort crept through the hot, muggy night towards a shoreline that was. . . .

Carsten didn't like to think about how very ready to receive them that Virginia shoreline probably was. Keeping anything secret in these crowded waters required a miracle beyond the power of any Navy Department functionary to provide. Sam wasn't altogether certain the Holy Ghost could have given him one as big as he needed. Sneaking into Chesapeake Bay without getting either mined or torpedoed hadn't been the smallest of miracles all by itself.

He spoke into the telephone that connected the bridge with the gun turrets: "Everything ready there? You have your targets?"

"Yes, sir!" the gun chiefs answered together.

"All right, then." Sam smiled there in the darkness. Even as a rating, he'd been in charge of bigger pieces than these four-inch popguns. "At my order, and give it everything you've got. . . . *Fire!*"

Twin tongues of flame belched from the turrets, lighting up the night for a heartbeat with a hellish orange glow. Recoil made the ship shudder. Those tongues thrust out again, and then again and again, as each gun crew did its best to prove it was faster than the other. First the bow turret took the lead, then the stern. All told, judging a winner was next to impossible.

Splashes of fire inland told of shell hits. Sam knew where the target was, but not what it was. That evidently wasn't necessary for the mission. He kept an eye on the luminous hands of his watch. When exactly five minutes had gone by, he said, "Cease firing," into the telephone. An aching silence fell. He turned to the exec. "Mr. Cooley, I do believe we may have worn out our welcome. Get us out of here. All ahead full, course 010."

"All ahead full, course 010." Cooley rang the engine room. The *Josephus Daniels* put on as many revolutions and as much speed as she had. Sam was used to ships with a lot more dash. He felt nailed to the surface of the bay despite the phosphorescent wake streaming from the bow. Destroyer escorts were cheap and easy and fast to build. Considering their liabilities, they needed to be.

On the shore, the Confederates were waking up. First one field gun and then a whole battery started firing at where the *Josephus Daniels* had been. Those were 105s—guns of about the same caliber as the destroyer escort carried.

The bridge telephone rang. When Sam picked it up, one of the turret chiefs said, "Sir, permission to return enemy fire?"

"Permission denied," Sam answered, in lieu of screaming, *Are you out of your frigging mind?* He went on, "We've done what we came to do here. Now our job is to get out in one piece so we can come back and do it again one day before long. Shooting back makes us much too visible, and they have more guns than we do. We just scoot. Got that?"

"Yes, sir," the turret chief said sullenly. Carsten found it hard to fault a man who wanted to raise hell with the enemy, but you needed a sense of proportion. *No, I need a sense of proportion. That's why I'm the Old Man.* There were times when he felt like a very old man indeed.

Pat Cooley eyed him from the wheel. Cooley was ten times the ship handler he would ever be. Sam hadn't taken the wheel of any ship till he became the skipper here. "Your thoughts, Mr. Cooley?" Sam asked.

"Sir, I'd like to shoot back at those bastards," the exec answered. Sam stiffened. But after a moment Cooley went on, "You're right, though. Probably a good idea that we don't. They're missing us pretty bad—if I were in charge of that battery, I'd be reaming 'em out right now."

But the man in charge of that C.S. battery—a sergeant or lieutenant tumbled from his blanket when the *Josephus Daniels* opened up—had a better idea. Two of his guns fired star shells that lit up the bay—and the destroyer escort—with a cold, clear, terrible light.

Men at the antiaircraft guns started shooting at the star shells. If they could wreck the parachutes that supported them in the air, the blazing shells would fall into the sea and sizzle out. The bow turret no longer bore on the Confederate battery. The stern turret opened up without orders. Sam only nodded to himself. With the *Josephus Daniels* out there in plain sight, a muzzle flash or three didn't make a rat's ass' worth of difference.

And she *was* out there in plain sight. The Confederate guns on the coast wasted no time correcting their aim. Shells began bursting around and on the destroyer escort. Most of the ships on which Sam had served would have laughed at 105mm shells. But the *Josephus Daniels,* like any destroyer, was thin-skinned. She had no armor to protect her. Screams made Sam grind his teeth. Men serving the antiaircraft guns topside were vulnerable aboard any ship that floated. He knew that. Knowing it left it no easier to take.

"Smoke, Mr. Cooley," he said. "We'll see how much good it does."

"Smoke. Aye aye, sir."

More star shells lit up the night. Smoke blossomed around the *Josephus Daniels*. It helped less than it might have under other circumstances. Sam had feared as much. She was the only thing afloat in this part of Chesapeake Bay. If the smoke screen moved, she had to be at the front end of it. Knowing that, the Confederate gunners didn't lose a whole lot of accuracy from not being able to see their target anymore.

Nothing to do but take the pounding and try to get away. Sam had heard Great War stories about how raiders caught between their trench line and the enemy's hated star shells with a purple passion. Now he understood exactly how they felt. There you were, all lit up, naked as a bug on a plate.

A big boom and a flash of light from the shore said the *Daniels'* gun had hit something worthwhile—probably the ammunition store for one of the guns shooting at the ship. Before Sam could let out a whoop, a Confederate shell burst just forward of the bridge. He watched a machine-gun crew blown to cat's meat. Fragments whistled and screeched past him. After pausing to make sure he was still in one piece, he asked, "You all right, Mr. Cooley?"

"Everything's copacetic here, Skipper," Cooley said, and then, "Well, almost everything." He displayed his left sleeve, which had a brand-new gash in it. An inch farther in and he would have gone down to the sick bay with a wounded arm. Six inches farther in and they would have had to carry him to sick bay with a belly wound. Even with all the fancy drugs they had these days, belly wounds were very bad news.

"Good for you, Pat." That sliced sleeve made Sam less formal than usual. "You don't really want a Purple Heart, no matter how pretty the ribbon would look on your uniform."

"Yes, sir," Cooley said. Another shell screamed in. He and Sam both ducked automatically, not that ducking was likely to do a hell of a lot of good. The shell was a clean miss, bursting a good hundred yards to starboard. A little hesitantly, the exec asked, "Are we going to get out of this, sir?"

Sam thought of talking about the Battle of the Three Navies, when the British and the Japanese hit the *Dakota* with everything but their purse. He thought about the *Remembrance*'s last fight, when Japanese air power finally sank the tough old carrier. In the end, though, he just stuck to business: "Unless we take one in the engine room that leaves us dead in the water, we will. Otherwise, those 105s may hurt us, but they won't be able to kill us before we get out of range."

Cooley considered that, then nodded. He looked at his wristwatch. "At flank speed, we've got to stand the gaff for—what? About another fifteen minutes?"

Carsten checked his watch, too. He laughed ruefully. "Yeah, that's about right. I didn't think it would be so long. Aren't we lucky?"

"Lucky. Right." Cooley managed an answering grin, but one of a distinctly sepulchral sort. A Confederate shell burst just behind the stern. Those near misses were dangerous, because fragments still flew. Screams from that direction said some of these had struck home.

"Can you give us any more down there?" Sam yelled to the engine room through a speaking tube.

"Sir, she's flat out," the chief engineer said. "Shit, we've got the valves tied down the way they did on the old paddle-wheel riverboats."

"All right—thanks." Sam sighed. He shouldn't have expected anything different. He hadn't really, but he'd hoped for something like, *Oh, yes, sir, we'll dreelspayl the paragore and get you two more knots easy as you please.* Two more knots? He snorted. He wanted ten more. *Well, sonny boy, you ain't gonna get 'em.* He turned back to the exec. "Do you think we ought to throw some zigzags into the course?"

"Straight gets us out of range faster," Cooley said doubtfully.

"Yeah, but it lets them lead us, too," Sam answered. "Ever hunt ducks?"

"Once or twice, but I didn't like it. It's not all it's quacked up to be."

"Ouch. Don't do that again. I think I'd rather—" Sam broke off. However bad Cooley's occasional puns were, he didn't prefer being under Confederate gunfire to listening to them.

The exec did start zigzagging at random. That would have been better with another ten knots, too, but you did what you could with what you had. Sam thought it helped. They took another hit and a couple of more near misses, but nothing that slowed them down. And, even though those were some of the longest fifteen minutes of Sam's life, they finally ended.

By then, all the shells were coming in astern of the *Josephus Daniels.* When the Confederates realized as much, they ceased fire.

"Now we're home free, if one of their airplanes doesn't find us," Sam said.

"You're full of cheerful thoughts, aren't you, sir?" Cooley said.

"Like a sardine can is full of sardines, son," Sam answered. "Straighten out and head for home. I'm gong to assess the damage. Keep straight unless we're attacked. If they jump us before I'm back to the bridge—" He broke off again. "Belay that. I'll take the conn. *You* go assess the damage and report back."

"Aye aye, sir." Cooley didn't question him. The *Josephus Daniels* was *his,* Sam Carsten's, no one else's. Responsibility for her was his, too. He couldn't stand the idea of anything happening if he wasn't there when it did. Cooley said, "I'll hustle, sir."

Sam stared at the Y-range screens as the ship sped up toward Maryland. No aircraft heading his way, nothing on the water. He didn't think the Confederates had anything bigger than a torpedo boat operating in the bay, but a torpedo boat could ruin you if you didn't spot it till too late.

Cooley came back. "Sir, looks like four to six dead, a couple of dozen wounded. We've got one wrecked 40mm mount—that's the worst of the damage. The rest is mostly metalwork. All things considered, we got away cheap."

"Thank you, Mr. Cooley," Sam said. *We got away cheap.* The dead and the maimed would not agree with the exec. Sam found that he was inclined to. War measured what you dished out against what you took. By that grim arithmetic, the *Josephus Daniels* had got away cheap.

Hyrum Rush had gone back to Utah and been passed through the lines into Mormon-held territory under flag of truce. As far as Flora Blackford was concerned, even that was better than he deserved. His parting words before getting on the train that would take him west were, "You people will see what this costs you." If he hadn't been under safe-conduct, that would have been plenty to make Flora lock him up and throw away the key.

"The nerve of the man!" she spluttered when his warning—his threat?—got back to the Joint Committee on the Conduct of the War. "We should never have talked with him in the first place!"

"There I agree with you completely," Robert Taft said. "You will have more luck persuading the administration than I'm likely to, though."

Taft was a famously acerbic man, and also one given to understatement. He remained the leading hard-line Democrat in the Senate. Flora worried about agreeing with him. He no doubt also worried about agreeing with her.

"I've never said Socialists can't make mistakes," Flora answered. "I have said they aren't the only ones who can make mistakes. Some people don't recognize the difference."

He gave her a tight smile—the only kind his face had room for. "I can't imagine what you're talking about," he said, and she found herself smiling back.

They had plenty to do, questioning officers and men about the bloody fiasco at Fredericksburg. About the most anybody—including Daniel MacArthur—would say to defend it was, *It seemed like a good idea at the time.* Trying to pin down why it had seemed a good idea was like trying to scoop up water with a sieve. The committee remained very busy and accomplished very little.

Like anyone else these days, Hyrum Rush had to go up through Canada to travel from east to west. Flora kept track of his progress through Franklin Roosevelt. "I hope you're making him cool his heels up there," she told the Assistant Secretary of War.

"We thought about it, Congresswoman," he said. "We thought about it long and hard—believe you me we did. Finally, though, we decided that showing him how bad our bottleneck up there really is would only encourage him. And so we hustled him through instead."

Flora thought about that. Reluctantly, she nodded. "You're inconveniencing him most by inconveniencing him least," she said.

Even over the telephone, his laugh made her want to laugh along with him. "That's just what we're doing, Flora," he said between chortles. "The only thing is, I didn't know it was what we were doing till you told me just now. I'm going to steal your line every chance I get, and most of the time I'm not going to give you any credit."

"Who in politics ever does give anybody else any credit?" Flora said, which only set him laughing again.

She stopped worrying about Hyrum Rush once she heard he'd got back to what his people called Deseret. Sooner or later, the U.S. Army would grind it out of existence—for good this time, she hoped. Utah and the Mormons had been a running sore on the body politic for much too long.

The biggest question facing the Joint Committee was whether it would have the nerve to tell the War Department to put somebody besides Daniel MacArthur in charge in Virginia. Flora was convinced the man didn't deserve his command. But she also saw he had an aura of invulnerability about him—not because of his battlefield talents but because of his personality.

George Custer had had an aura like that during the Great War. Even Teddy Roosevelt had moved carefully around him. Of course,

Custer and Roosevelt—the other Roosevelt—had been rivals for years, ever since the Second Mexican War. But no one in the present administration had anything close to TR's own strength of character. That being so, any decisive steps without prodding from the Joint Committee struck even Flora, a good Socialist, as unlikely.

She was saying so, pointedly enough to dismay Chairman Norris, when an explosion made the building shake. Plaster pattered down from the ceiling. Somebody said, "That was a close one."

Somebody else said, "Damn Confederates haven't sent any day bombers for a while—begging your pardon, Congresswoman."

"Oh, I damn them, too," Flora said. "You don't need to doubt that for even a minute, believe me." She looked down at her notes. "May I continue, Mr. Chairman?"

"You have the floor, Congresswoman." Senator Norris looked as if he wished she didn't.

"Thank you, sir." The florid politeness that had once seemed so unnatural to her was now second nature. "As I was saying—"

But before she could say it, a man in a guard's uniform stuck his head into the meeting room. "We're evacuating the building. That was an auto bomb near the front entrance. We don't know if they've got any more close by." He grimaced. "We don't even know who *they* are, dammit." He didn't apologize for swearing in front of Flora.

They. The enemy within never went away. Who was it this time? Confederate saboteurs? Mormons living up to Hyrum Rush's promise? Rebellious Canadians? British agents? Any combination of those groups working together? Flora didn't know. Somebody was going to have to find out, though.

"Please come with me," the guard said.

"Before we do, let's see your identification," Robert Taft snapped. Flora reluctantly allowed that that made good sense. If the man in the uniform was part of the plot . . . People were going to start looking under beds before they went to sleep if this went on.

The guard showed Senator Taft his identity card without a word of protest. Satisfied, Flora nodded. Flora wondered what Taft would have done if the man had gone for his pistol instead. Probably thrown himself at it—he had the courage of his convictions, as well as plenty of courage of the ordinary sort.

Following the guard, the members of the Joint Committee hurried out of the massive building Congress used in Philadelphia—wags called it the box the Capitol came in. They emerged on the side opposite the one where the auto bomb had gone off. Along with several others, Flora started around the building so she could see the damage for herself. "That isn't safe!" the guard exclaimed.

"And how do you know standing here is?" she answered. "Any one of these motorcars may be full of TNT and ready to blow up." The guard looked very unhappy, which didn't mean she was wrong.

"You told him," Taft said approvingly.

"So I did," she said, and hurried on. A makeshift police and fire line stopped her and the others before they got very close to the site of the explosion. Even what they could see from there was bad enough. Bodies and pieces of bodies lay everywhere. The front of the hall had taken heavy damage. It all seemed worse than the aftermath of an air raid, perhaps because the auto's chassis turned into more, and more lethal, shrapnel than a bomb casing did. One of Flora's colleagues was noisily sick on his shoes.

"Someone will pay for this." Robert Taft sounded grim.

No sooner had he spoken than half the façade of the Congressional hall crashed down to the cratered street. A great gray-brown cloud of dust rose. Soldiers and policemen rushed into it to rescue whoever lay buried under the rubble. Flora covered her face with her hands.

A reporter chose that moment to rush up to her and ask, "Congresswoman, what do you think of this explosion?"

"I hope not too many people got hurt. I hope the ones who did will recover." Flora realized the man had a job to do, but she didn't feel like answering foolish questions right now.

That didn't stop the reporter from asking them. With an air of breathless anticipation, he said, "Who do you think is to blame for this atrocity?"

"I don't know. I'm sure there will be an investigation," Flora said.

"But if you had to guess, who would be responsible?" he persisted.

"If I had to guess right now, *I* would be irresponsible," Flora told him.

The answer should have made him take a hint and go away. No such luck. He was not one of those reporters who recognized anything as subtle as a hint. And that turned out to be just as well, for his next question told Flora something she didn't know: "What do you think of the explosions in Washington and New York and Boston and Pittsburgh and Chicago and—other places, too?"

"What explosions?" Flora and Robert Taft spoke together, in identical sharp tones.

"Whole bunch of auto bombs." The reporter seemed as willing to give information as to try to pry it out of other people. "The Capitol and Wall Street and the State House in Boston and I don't know what all else. Lots of damage, lots of people dead. All about the same time as this one. News was coming over the wire and by wireless when I got the call to get my, uh, fanny over here."

"Jesus Christ!" Taft burst out. Flora didn't echo him, but her thoughts amounted to something similar. He went on, "This has the smell of a conspiracy." Flora wouldn't have argued with that, either.

The reported scribbled in his spiral-bound notebook. "Smell of a conspiracy," he repeated, and dipped his head. "Thank you, Senator—that's a good line." He hurried off.

"A good line," Taft echoed bitterly. "That's all he cared about. But my God—if what he said about those other places is true . . ."

"That would be very bad," Flora said, one of the larger understatements of her own political career. "The Confederates have had a lot of trouble with auto bombs. I wonder if they're paying us back, or if it's someone else."

As she had to the reporter, Taft said, "I don't know."

She nodded. But her conscience niggled at her all the same. She'd applauded when she heard about auto bombs going off in the Confederate States. The Confederates, after all, deserved it for the way they treated their Negroes.

Again, who thought the United States deserved it? The Confederates, because the USA had had the gall to win the Great War? The Mormons, because the United States wouldn't leave their precious Deseret alone? She would have bet one them, but what did she have for proof? Nothing, and she knew it. The Canadians, because the United States still held their land? The British, because the Americans had taken Canada away from them?

All of the above? None of the above?

Sounding both furious and frightened, Robert Taft went on, "We'd better get a handle on this business in a hurry. If we don't, any damn fool with an imaginary grievance will think he can load dynamite into a motorcar and get even with the world."

Flora's thoughts hadn't gone in that direction, which didn't mean the Senator from Ohio was wrong. She said, "We'd better get a handle on this for all kinds of reasons." Two firemen carried a moaning, bloody woman past her on a stretcher. She pointed. "There's one."

"Yes." Taft tipped his fedora to her. "We have our differences, you and I, but we both love this country."

"That's true. Not always in the same way, but we do," Flora said. Cops helped a wounded man stagger by. Flora sighed. "At a time like this, though, what difference does party make?"

Sergeant Michael Pound was not a happy man. His barrel—and, in fact, his whole unit of barrels—had finally escaped from the southern Ohio backwater where they'd been stuck for so long. They were facing the Confederates farther north. That should have done something to improve the gunner's temper. It should have, but it hadn't.

No, Pound remained unhappy, and made only the slightest efforts to hide it. He was a broad-shouldered, burly man: not especially tall, but made for slewing a gun from side to side if the hydraulics went out. He had a deceptively soft voice, and used it to say deceptively mild things. When he thought the men put above him were idiots, as he often did, he had a way of making sure they knew it.

What really irked him was that he'd been the gunner on Irving Morrell's personal barrel. Whatever Morrell found out, Pound had learned shortly thereafter. Morrell hadn't minded his sarcastic comments on the way the brass thought (if the brass thought at all: always an interesting question). And Michael Pound hadn't thought Morrell was an idiot. Oh, no—on the contrary. The only thing wrong with Morrell was that *his* superiors hadn't seen how good he was.

The Confederates had. After their sniper put a bullet in Morrell, Pound was the one who'd carried him out of harm's way and back to the aid tent. Scuttlebutt said Morrell was finally back in action. That was good. The CSA would be sorry.

But Morrell wasn't back in action *here*. That wasn't good, and it especially wasn't good for Michael Pound. He'd declined a commission several times. Now he was paying for it. Because of his reputation as a mouthy troublemaker, he didn't even command his own barrel, though a lot of sergeants did. They'd put him under a young lieutenant instead. Pound didn't know if they'd deliberately intended to humiliate him, but they'd sure done the job.

Bryce Poffenberger might have been born when Pound joined the

Army, but probably hadn't. But he owned a little gold bar on each shoulder strap, and Pound had only stripes on his sleeve. That meant Poffenberger was God—and if you didn't believe it, all you had to do was ask him.

He never asked for Pound's opinion. He didn't seem to think the War Department had issued opinions to enlisted men. If he'd had a better notion of what he was doing himself, Pound wouldn't have minded so much. But he never had been able to suffer fools gladly, and he never had been able to suffer in silence, either.

When Poffenberger ordered the barrel to stop on the forward slope of a hill, Pound said, "Sir, we would have done better to halt on the reverse slope."

"Oh?" The second lieutenant's voice already had a defensive quaver to it, and he'd known Pound for only a few days at that point. "Why, pray tell?"

Pray tell? Pound thought. Had anyone since the Puritans really said that? Bryce Poffenberger just had, by God. Patiently, the sergeant answered, "Because on the reverse slope we're hull-down to the enemy, sir. This way, the whole barrel makes a nice, juicy target."

Lieutenant Poffenberger sniffed. "I don't believe there are any Confederates close by." He stood up in the turret to look out through the cupola. That was something good barrel commanders did. It took a certain nerve. Poffenberger might have been a moron, but he wasn't a cowardly moron.

Not half a minute later, a round from a Confederate antibarrel gun assassinated an oak tree just to the barrel's left. Poffenberger ducked back down with a startled squeak. Sometimes—not often—Sergeant Pound was tempted to believe in God. This was one of those times.

"Reverse!" Poffenberger ordered the driver. "Back up!" The Confederates got off one more shot at the barrel before it put the hill between itself and the gun. Lieutenant Poffenberger eyed Michael Pound. "How did you know that was going to happen, Sergeant?"

"I have more combat experience than you do, sir," Pound answered matter-of-factly. *So does my cat, and I haven't got a cat.*

"They warned me about you," Poffenberger said. "They told me you had a big mouth and were insubordinate."

"They were right, sir." Pound knew he shouldn't sound so cheerful, but he couldn't help it.

The young lieutenant went on as if he hadn't spoken: "They told me you were all puffed up because you'd served with Colonel Morrell for so long, and he used to let you get away with murder. They told me you'd started to think you were a colonel yourself."

That did hold some truth, which Sergeant Pound also knew. He said, "Sir, there was one difference between when I talked to Colonel Morrell and when I talk to you."

"Oh?" What's that?" Poffenberger sounded genuinely intrigued.

"When I said something to the colonel, sometimes he'd believe me before the barrel almost blew up."

Poffenberger was a fair-haired, fair-skinned youngster from somewhere in the upper Midwest. When he turned red, it was easy to see. He turned red as a traffic light now. "Maybe you have a point, Sergeant," he choked out. "Maybe. But I command this barrel. You don't. There's no getting around that."

"I don't want to get around it, sir," Pound answered earnestly. "I don't want to be an officer. I could have been an officer years ago if I wanted to put up with the bother." Watching Lieutenant Poffenberger's jaw drop was amusing, but only for a little while. Pound added, "I don't want to be an officer, but I don't want to get killed, either. Not even sergeants like getting killed . . . sir."

"I didn't think they did." Poffenberger couldn't have sounded any stiffer if he'd been carved out of marble.

Pound pretended not to notice. He said, "Well, in that case, sir, don't you think we ought to scoot to one side or the other? We're hull-down here, but we're not turret-down, and if those butternut bastards get a halfway decent shot at us, they'll remind us the hard way."

He waited. How stubborn was the lieutenant? Stubborn enough not to listen to somebody with a lower rank even if not listening made getting nailed with a high-velocity armor-piercing round much more likely? Some officers—more than a few of them—were like that. They wanted to be right themselves, even if it meant being dead right. Short of knocking them over the head, what could you do?

But Poffenberger spoke to the driver, and the barrel shifted position. Quietly, Pound said, "Thank you, sir."

"I didn't do it for you." The lieutenant was testy. "I did it for the sake of the barrel."

Like a man who'd sweet-talked a girl into bed with him, Sergeant Pound cared little about the whys and wherefores. All he cared about was that it had happened. He didn't point that out to Lieutenant Pof-

fenberger. He didn't want the lieutenant thinking he'd been either se-
duced or screwed. And if Poffenberger hadn't done it for love . . . well,
so what?

No steel dart came hurtling toward them. That was the only thing
that mattered. A little later, a platoon of U.S. foot soldiers went over
the hill and chased away the antibarrel cannon. A tiny triumph, no
doubt, but anything that looked even a little like a victory pleased
Pound.

Lieutenant Poffenberger had an extra circuit on his wireless set,
one that hooked him to division headquarters. When he started saying,
"Yes, sir," and, "I understand, sir," and, "We'll be careful, sir," Pound
started worrying. Something had gone wrong somewhere, and what
was even a tiny triumph worth?

"What's up, sir?" the sergeant prompted when his superior showed
no sign of passing along whatever he'd learned.

Poffenberger gave him a resentful look, but maybe the lesson from
the antibarrel gun was sticking, at least for a little while. "There are reports the Confederates are stirring around," the lieutenant said unwillingly. Even more unwillingly, he added, "There are reports they've got
a new-model barrel, too."

Michael Pound nodded. "Yes, sir, I've heard about that. Did they
give you any details on the beast?"

"What do you mean, you've heard about it?" Poffenberger's eyes
seemed ready to start from his head. "I just this minute got word of it."

"Well, yes, sir." Pound smiled. That only unnerved the lieutenant
more, which was what he had in mind. "Trouble is, you have to wait
for the wireless to tell you things. Enlisted men have their own grape-
vine, you might say. From what I've heard, the new enemy barrel's supposed to be very bad news: bigger gun, better armor, maybe a bigger
engine, too."

"Jesus," Poffenberger muttered, more to himself than to his gunner. "What the hell do we bother with espionage for? Put a few corpo-
rals on the job and they'd have Jake Featherston's telephone number in
nothing flat."

"It's FReedom-1776, sir," Pound answered seriously. Poffenberger
stared at him, convinced for one wild moment that he meant it. That
told Pound everything he needed to know about how much he'd intimidated the lieutenant. In a gentle voice, he said, "I'm only joking, sir."

"Er—yes." Lieutenant Poffenberger gathered himself. The process was very visible, and so funny that Pound had to bite down on the inside of his lower lip to keep from laughing out loud. Carefully, Poffenberger asked, "How did Colonel Morrell ever put up with you?"

"Oh, we didn't have any trouble, sir," Pound answered. "Colonel Morrell wants to go after the bad guys just as much as I do. I hear they've sent him to Virginia. The people over there must be keeping him under wraps, or else we would have heard a lot more out of him."

"I . . . see." Poffenberger eyed Pound the way a man wearing a suit made of pork chops might eye a nearby bear. More than a little plaintively, the lieutenant said, "I want to go after the enemy, too."

"Of course, sir," Pound said in tones meant to be soothing—but not too soothing. "The point is, though, to be as sure as we can that we get them and they don't get us."

Poffenberger started to say something. After what had almost happened on the forward slope of the hill, though, he couldn't say a whole lot, not unless he wanted Pound to blow a hole in it the way the antibarrel cannon had almost blown a hole in the machine he commanded. What he finally did say was, "You are a difficult man, Sergeant."

"Why, thank you, sir!" Pound exclaimed, which only seemed to complete Lieutenant Poffenberger's demoralization.

An officer? Who needs to be an officer? Pound thought, more than a little smugly. *As long as you've got the fellow who's supposed to be in charge of you eating out of the palm of your hand, you have the best of both worlds.*

Bombers rumbled by overhead. Antiaircraft guns started up behind the U.S. lines—they were Confederate airplanes. By the way Poffenberger looked up at them through the cupola, they didn't worry him nearly so much as the man with whom he shared a turret. Michael Pound . . . smiled.

VII

Mail call!"

Like most of his buddies, Armstrong Grimes perked up when he heard that. It wasn't even so much that he expected mail. The only person who regularly wrote to him was his father, and Merle Grimes' letters weren't the most exciting in the world. But being reminded that people back home remembered the soldiers here in Utah were alive counted for a good deal.

"Jackson!" called the corporal with the mail bag.

"He's on sentry duty," somebody said. "I'll take 'em for him."

The soldier with the sack handed him half a dozen letters held together with a rubber band. He pulled out another rubber-banded clump. "Reisen!"

"I'm here," Yossel Reisen answered, and grabbed his mail. He had a lot of family back in New York, and got tons of letters.

"Donovan!" The noncom with the mail held up some more letters and a package.

"He got wounded last Tuesday," one of the gathered soldiers answered. The man with the mail bag started to put back the package. The soldier said, "If that's cake or candy, we'll keep it."

"Depends," the corporal said. "How bad is he?"

Etiquette required an honest answer to that question. After brief consultation, another soldier said, "He can probably eat it. Send it back to the field hospital."

Some more names were called, including Armstrong's. He had a letter from his father and, he was surprised to see, one from Aunt Clara. His aunt, a child of his grandmother's old age, was only a couple of years older than he was. They'd fought like cats and dogs ever since they were tiny. He wondered what the devil she wanted with him now.

Before he could open it, the guy with the sack called, "Appleton!"

Tad Appleton's birth name was something Polish and unpronounceable. That, at the moment, didn't matter. Three men put what did matter into two words: "He's dead." One of them added, "Stopped a .50-caliber round with his face, poor bastard." Armstrong found himself grinding his teeth. When Appleton's body got back to Milwaukee, they'd bury him in a closed casket. No undertaker in the world could fix up what that bullet had done to him.

"Here, then." The soldier with the mail tossed a package to the men gathered around him. That also followed etiquette—such things shouldn't go to waste.

More letters and packages got passed out, till the sack was empty except for mail belonging to the wounded and the dead. The corporal with the sack bummed a cigarette and stood around talking with the men to whom he'd delivered the mail. A few soldiers who hadn't got anything stood there dejectedly. Their buddies consoled them as best they could. That wasn't just for politeness' sake. Armstrong had seen more than one man, forgotten by the folks back home, stop caring whether he lived or died.

He opened the letter from his aunt. It turned out to be a wedding announcement. Clara was marrying somebody named Humphrey Baxter. "Humphrey?" Armstrong said. "Who the hell names their kid Humphrey?"

"There's that actor," Reisen said. "You know, the fellow who was in *The Maltese Elephant*."

"Oh, yeah. Him." Armstrong nodded. "This ain't him, though, I'll tell you that. This guy's probably a bad actor—you know what I mean? He's our age—gotta be—and he's not in the Army. He's pulling some strings somewhere, sure as hell." He eyed the announcement with distaste. "Damn paper's too stiff to wipe my ass with." He scaled it away.

The letter from his father mentioned Clara's upcoming wedding, too. Merle Grimes had little to say about Clara's intended. Armstrong nodded to himself. His old man had seen the elephant, and took pride in it. He wouldn't have much use for somebody who'd managed to wiggle out of conscription.

Yossel Reisen was methodically going through his mail. He held up one letter. "My aunt was in a meeting room when that auto bomb went off in front of Congress." He always played down being the nephew of the former First Lady. If he hadn't downplayed it, Armstrong didn't suppose he would have had to put the uniform back on at all. Unlike this Humphrey Baxter item, Yossel pulled his weight.

"She get out all right?" Armstrong asked.

"Uh-huh. Not a scratch, she says," Reisen answered. "She wasn't near the front of the building, thank God."

"That's good," Armstrong said, and then, "Goddamn Mormons." The Latter-Day Saints hadn't claimed responsibility for the recent wave of auto bombs, but Deseret Wireless didn't go out of its way to deny anything, either. Its tone was, *Take that! Serves you right, too.*

"They look just like anybody else," Yossel said. "That makes them hard to catch, hard to stop."

"Don't it just?" Armstrong's agreement was ungrammatical but heartfelt. He added, "I don't like the way Confederate Connie goes on and on about it."

"Well, who would?" Yossel paused. "Even when you know she's full of crap, though, she's fun to listen to."

"Oh, hell, yes!" Armstrong's agreement there was heartfelt, too. Nobody he knew took Confederate Connie even a quarter of the way seriously. Like every wireless broadcaster from the CSA, she was Jake Featherston's mouthpiece. But a doozie of a mouthpiece she was, and she sounded like a doozie of a piece, period—she had the sexiest voice Armstrong had ever heard.

She spent a lot of time between records gloating about the auto bombs that had U.S. cities so on edge. "Now you-all know how we feel," she would say. "We've been putting up with these contraptions for years. You laughed when it happened to us. Do you-all reckon we're laughing now?" She would pause. She would giggle. "Well, you know what? . . . You're right!"

Yossel Reisen opened another letter. "Who's this one from?" Armstrong asked, having already gone through his meager mail.

"My Uncle David."

"Which one's he again?" Armstrong asked—Yossel had a *lot* of relatives.

"The one who lost a leg in the last war," Reisen answered. "He's a right-wing Democrat now. It drives Aunt Flora nuts."

"Oh, yeah." Armstrong nodded. Yes, his own father was inordinately proud of the wound that made him walk with a cane. Yossel's uncle David overtrumped Dad's wound in a big way. Come to that, Yossel's father had got killed before he was even born. Sure as hell, some people had had a tougher time of it than Merle Grimes, even if he wouldn't admit it this side of the rack. Armstrong asked, "What's he got to say?"

"He's talking about the auto bombs in New York City," Yossel answered, not looking up from the letter. "He says there were four of them—one on Wall Street, one in the Lower East Side where I grew up, and two in Times Square."

"Two?" Armstrong said.

"Two," Yossel repeated, his face grim. "One to make a mess, and then another one that went off fifteen minutes later, after the cops and the firemen showed up."

"Oh." Armstrong grimaced. "That's a dirty trick. Confederate Connie hasn't talked about anything like that."

"Probably doesn't want to give the *shvartzers* in the CSA ideas if they're listening to her," Yossel said. Armstrong nodded; that made pretty good sense. Yossel went on, "Waste of time, I bet. If the Mormons can figure it out, you've got to figure the *shvartzers* can, too."

"Bet you're right. It's a goddamn lousy war, that's all I've got to say. Poison gas and blowing the other guy's cities to hell and gone and both sides with maniacs blowing their *own* cities to hell and gone . . . Some fun," Armstrong said. "And these fucking Mormons won't quit till the last one's dead—and his ghost'll haunt us."

As if on cue, somebody shouted, "Incoming!" Armstrong threw himself flat even before he heard the shriek of the incoming round. It was a terrifying wail. The Mormons had something homemade and nasty. Artillerymen called it a spigot mortar. Most soldiers called the projectiles—each about the size of a wastebasket with fins—screaming meemies.

When they hit, they made a roar like the end of the world. They were stuffed with explosives and scrap iron, to the point where they were almost flying auto bombs themselves. The only drawback they had that Armstrong could see was that, like most of the Mormons' improvised weapons, they couldn't reach very far. But when they did get home . . .

Blast picked him up and slammed him down again, as if a professional wrestler—or possibly God—had thrown him to the canvas. He tasted blood. When he brought a hand up to his face, he found his nose was bleeding, too. He felt his ears, but they seemed all right. After he spat, his mouth seemed better. His nose went on dripping blood down his face and, as he straightened, onto the front of his tunic. That was all right, or not too bad. Anything more and he would have worried about what the screaming meemie had done to his insides.

Instead, he worried about what the horrible thing had done to other people. The corporal who'd brought the mail forward was torn to pieces. If not for the sack, Armstrong wouldn't have recognized him. Poor bastard wasn't even a front-line soldier. Wrong place, wrong time, and he'd make another closed-casket funeral.

Shouts of, "Corpsman!" rose from half a dozen places. There weren't enough medics close by to see to everybody at once. Armstrong bandaged wounds and tied off one tourniquet and gave morphine shots with the syrettes in the soldiers' first-aid kits: all the things he'd learned how to do since he got thrown into battle the summer before.

Yossel Reisen was doing the same sorts of things. He also had a bloody nose, and he'd put a bandage on the back of his own left hand. More blood soaked through it. "There's a Purple Heart for you," Armstrong said.

Reisen told him where he could put the Purple Heart, and suggest that he not close the pin that held it on a uniform.

Armstrong gave back a ghastly grin. "Same to you, buddy, only sideways," he said. They both laughed. It wasn't funny—nothing within some considerable distance of where a screaming meemie went off was funny—but it kept them both going and it kept them from shrieking. Sometimes men who'd been through too much would come to pieces in the field. Armstrong had seen that a few times. It was even less lovely than what shell fragments could do. They only ruined a man's body. When his soul went through the meat grinder . . .

Belatedly, U.S. field guns started shelling the place from which the screaming meemie had come. Odds were neither the men who'd launched it nor the tube from which it started its deadly flight were there anymore.

"Bastards." Even Armstrong wasn't sure whether he was talking about the Mormons on the other side of the line or the gunners on his own. It fit both much too well.

*   *   *

"**N**eed to talk to you for a minute in my office, Xerxes," Jerry Dover said when Scipio walked into the Huntsman's Lodge.

Scipio was already sweating from the walk to work in formalwear under the hot Augusta sun. When his boss told him something like that, he started sweating all over again. But he said the only thing he could: "Be right theah, suh." Maybe—he dared hope—this had to do with restaurant business. Even if it didn't, though, he remained at the white man's beck and call.

Dover's office was as crowded and as filled with lists of things to do as ever. The restaurant manager worked hard. Scipio never would have presumed to think otherwise. The ashtray on the desk was full of butts, a couple of them still smoldering.

Dover paused to light yet another cigarette, sucked in smoke, blew it out, and eyed Scipio. "What's your address, over in the Terry?" he asked.

That wasn't what Scipio had expected. "Same one you got on all my papers, suh," he answered. "I ain't moved or nothin'."

"For true?" Jerry Dover said. "No bullshit? No getting cute and cagey?"

"Cross my heart an' hope to die, Mistuh Dover." Scipio made the gesture. "How come you needs to make sure o' dat?"

His boss didn't answer, not right away. He smoked the cigarette down to a little dog-end in quick, savage puffs, then stubbed it out and lit a new one. When he did speak, he went off on a tangent: "I don't reckon your wife and your young 'uns have ever seen the inside of this place."

"No, suh, they ain't never," Scipio agreed, wondering what the hell Dover was going on about. The restaurant—by which he naturally thought of the part the customers never saw—was crowded enough with the people who had to be there: cooks, waiters, busboys, dishwashers. Others would have fit in as well as feathers on a frog. The manager had to know that better than he did.

No matter what Jerry Dover knew, he said, "Why don't you bring 'em by tomorrow night when you come in for your shift? They get bored, they can spend some time here in the office."

"Suh, my missus, she clean white folks' houses. She already be at work when I comes in here," Scipio said.

Dover frowned. "Maybe you tell her to take the day off tomorrow so she can come in with you."

"People she work fo' ain't gwine like dat," Scipio predicted dolefully. Blacks in the CSA never had been able to risk antagonizing whites. With things the way they were now, even imagining such a thing was suicidal.

The second cigarette disappeared as fast as the first one had. Dover lit a third. He blew a stream of smoke up at the ceiling. "Scipio," he said softly, "this is important."

Scipio froze, there in the rickety chair across the desk from the restaurant manager. Jerry Dover used that name to remind Scipio who had the power here.

By why he would want to use that power for this purpose baffled the Negro. Sending him down to Savannah made sense. This? This seemed mere whim. A man who expended power on a whim was a fool.

In the tones of an educated white man, Scipio said, "Perhaps you will be good enough to tell me *why* you require my family's presence, sir?"

Dover's eyes widened. He laughed out loud. "Goddamn!" he said. "She told me you could do that, but I plumb forgot. That's fucking amazing. You ought to go on the wireless instead of some of those muttonheads they've got."

"As may be, sir," Scipio answered, and Jerry Dover laughed again. The black man added, "You still have not answered my question." He dared hope Dover would. Skin color was the most important thing in the CSA; no doubt about it. But accent ran color a close second. If he sounded like an educated white man, the presumption that he was what he sounded like ran deep.

But not deep enough, not here. Dover set the live cigarette in the ashtray, steepled his fingertips on the desk, and looked at Scipio over them. "It would be a good idea if you got 'em here," was all he said. His own way of speaking didn't come close to matching Scipio's. By his nervous chuckle, he knew it, too.

Scipio wanted to ask, *A good idea how? Why?* He wanted to, but he didn't. He'd pushed the white man as far as Dover was willing to go. Returning to the Congaree dialect that was his natural speech, Scipio said, "Reckon I do it, den."

"Good," Dover said. "I knew you were a smart fellow. If I didn't think so, I wouldn't have wasted my time banging my gums at you in the first place. Now get your ass out there and go to work."

"Yes, suh," Scipio said, relieved to be back on familiar ground.

When his shift ended, policemen let him through the barbed-wire perimeter surrounding the Terry. They knew him. He had a dispensation to be out after curfew. He made it back to his block of flats without getting knocked over the head.

Then he had his next hurdle: persuading Bathsheba not to do what she usually did. "Why for he want us there?" she demanded.

"Dunno," Scipio answered. "But he want it bad enough to use my fo'-true name."

"*Did* he?" That made Bathsheba sit up and take notice. Worry in her voice, she asked, "You reckon he do somethin' nasty if we don't come?"

"Dunno," Scipio said again, more unhappily than ever. "But I reckons y'all better do it."

Bathsheba sighed heavily. "Miz Kent, she ain't gonna be real happy with me. Miz Bagwell neither. But we come."

When his children got up the next morning, they were even more bemused than his wife was. "Somethin' bad liable to happen, Pa," Cassius said. His hands bunched into fists. "Can we fight back?" He was more like the hunter and guerrilla for whom he'd been named than he had any business being.

"Odds is bad," was all Scipio said. That gave his son very little to react against.

"Don't know that I ever wants to go into the ofay part of Augusta no more," Antoinette said. "They hates us there."

"They hates we here, too," Scipio answered. "You should oughta come, though. I don't reckon Mistuh Dover playin' games." That wasn't quite true. But he didn't know what kind of game the manager was playing, and he couldn't afford not to play along.

His wife and children dressed in their Sunday best for the unusual excursion. Since he was in his own formalwear, the family looked as if they were bound for a fancy wedding or a banquet. When they got to the barbed-wire perimeter, the cops and Freedom Party stalwarts and guards stared at them. There seemed to be more whites manning the perimeter than usual. *Or is it just my nerves?* Scipio wondered—nervously.

The policeman who checked passbooks had sent Scipio through any number of times. He raised an eyebrow to see the black man's family accompanying him, but didn't say anything about it. He was, within the limits of his job and his race, a decent fellow. A stalwart came up to talk to him. Scipio wondered if they would yell at him to halt and send Bathsheba and the children back. They didn't, though.

When Scipio got to the Huntsman's Lodge, he found that Aurelius also had his wife—a plump, dignified, gray-haired woman named Delilah—with him. *Something* was going on. He still didn't know what, and wished he did.

They all got suppers of the sorts the cooks turned out for the waiters. Two or three other waiters and cooks—all of them men who'd worked at the Lodge for a while, and all of them also men who lived not far from Scipio and his family—also had family members with them.

Jerry Dover hovered over the Huntsman's Lodge's uncommon customers. He was fox-quick, fox-clever, and also, Scipio judged, fox-wary. "Thank y'all for being here today," he said. "I've worked with your husbands and fathers for years, and I've never met y'all before. Hope I do again before too long."

He was saying something between the lines. But not even Scipio, who knew he was doing it, could make out the words behind the words. He wanted to scratch his head. Instead, he had to go out and work his shift as if everything were normal.

It only seemed to last forever. In fact, it went as smoothly as most of the shifts he put in. He pocketed a few nice tips and got stiffed once, by a lieutenant-colonel with his left arm in a sling. Scipio hoped the next Yankee who shot him took better aim.

When he left the dining room after the Lodge closed, he found his family on the ragged edge of mutiny. "If I was any more bored, I'd be dead," Cassius snarled.

"Thanks for bringin' 'em by, Xerxes," Jerry Dover said—now he used the alias that seemed to fit Scipio better than his real name these days. "Glad you could do it."

"Uh-huh," Scipio said, still puzzled about what was going on. Something, yes—but what? He nodded to Bathsheba, who was yawning. "Let's go."

The streets of the white part of Augusta were quiet and peaceful. When they got back to the fence around the Terry, another cop who knew Scipio let them through without any trouble about being out after curfew. He laughed as he opened a barbed-wire gate much like the one that would keep livestock in a pen. "You ain't hardly gonna know the place," he said. The rest of the goons at the gate thought that was the funniest thing they'd ever heard.

Only little by little did Scipio and his family discover what they meant. At first, he just thought things seemed too quiet. Curfew or no curfew, there was usually a lot of furtive life on the dark streets of the Terry. A lot of it was dangerous life, but it was life. Tonight, no.

Tonight . . . Cassius figured it out first, from the number of doors standing open that shouldn't have. "Do Jesus!" he exclaimed, his voice echoing in the empty street. "They done had another cleanout!"

As soon as he pointed it out, it was obvious he was right. The northern part of the Terry had been scooped up and sent off to camps—or somewhere—months before. As far as Scipio knew, nobody'd come back, either. Now the heart had been ripped out of the colored part of Augusta. *And all in one day,* Scipio thought dazedly. *All in half a day, in fact.* How long had they been planning this, to bring it off with such practiced efficiency? And where had they got the practice?

Bathsheba squeezed his hand, hard. "If it wasn't fo' Jerry Dover, they'd've got us, too," she whispered.

And that was as true as what Cassius had said. Somehow, Dover had known ahead of time. He'd done what he could—or what he'd wanted to do. Now Scipio owed him not just one life but four. He thanked the God he mostly didn't believe in for the debt. And he wondered how Jerry Dover would want it repaid.

For there would be a price. There was always a price. Scipio knew that in his bones, in his belly, in his balls. For a Negro in the CSA, there was *always* a price.

After his mother died, Cincinnatus Driver had watched his father like a hawk. He knew the stories about old, long-married couples where, when one spouse died, the other followed soon after, as if finding life alone not worth living.

But Seneca Driver seemed as well as ever. If anything, he seemed better than he had for some time. His shoulders came up; his back straightened. "I is free of a burden," he said once. "That weren't your mama we laid in the ground. Your mama was gone a long time ago. What we buried, that there was just the husk."

Cincinnatus nodded. "I saw that, Pa. I saw that real plain and clear. Wasn't sure you could."

"Oh, I seen it," his father said. "Couldn't do nothin' about it, but I seen it."

If that last sentence wasn't a summary of Negroes' troubles in the Confederate States, Cincinnatus had never heard one. And the government and the Freedom Party had always moved more carefully in Kentucky than rumor said they did farther south. Kentucky had spent a generation in the USA. Negroes here knew what it meant to be citizens, not just downtrodden residents. Even some whites here were . . . less hostile than they might have been.

That meant the barbed-wire perimeter that went up around Covington's colored district came as a special shock. Cincinnatus had heard that such things had happened elsewhere. He didn't think they could here. Finding he was wrong rocked him. Finding he was wrong also trapped him. The perimeter included the bank of the Licking River, and included motorboats with machine guns on the river to make sure nobody tried cutting the wire there.

The first place Cincinnatus went when he found out what was going on was, inevitably, Lucullus Wood's barbecue shack. He found the plump proprietor in a worse state of shock than he was. "They told me they wasn't gonna do this," Lucullus said. "They *told* me. They fuckin' lied." He sounded as dazed as a man staggering out of a train wreck.

Seeing Lucullus struck all in a heap discomfited Cincinnatus worse than the barbed wire itself. "What you gonna do about it?" he demanded. "What *can* you do about it?"

"Do Jesus! I dunno," Lucullus answered. "They done ruined me when they done this." Odds were he had that right. Almost as many whites as blacks had come to his place. No more. That perimeter would keep people out as well as keeping them in.

"You can still get word through." That was a statement, not a question. Cincinnatus refused to believe anything different.

"What if I kin?" Lucullus didn't deny it. He just spread his hands, pale palms up. "Ain't gonna do me a hell of a lot of good. Who's gonna pay any mind to a nigger all shut up like he was in jail? They gonna haul us off to them camps nobody never comes out of."

That had a chilling feel of probability to Cincinnatus. Even so, he gave Lucullus the best answer he could: "What about Luther Bliss?"

He hated the man, hated and feared him, but Bliss' remained a name to conjure with. He hoped hearing it would at least snap Lucullus out of his funk and make him start thinking straight again.

And it worked. Lucullus very visibly gathered himself. "Mebbe," he said. "But only mebbe, dammit. Freedom Party fellas is hunting Bliss right now like you wouldn't believe."

"Hell I wouldn't," Cincinnatus said. "If they know he's around, they'll want him dead. He's too dangerous for them to leave him breathin'. Ain't that all the more reason for you to git back in touch with him?"

"Mebbe," Lucullus said again. "What kin he do, though? They gots *p*olice an' them damn stalwarts all around. Anytime they wants to come in an' start gettin' rid of us . . ."

"We got guns. *You* got guns. You ain't gonna tell me you ain't got guns, 'cause I know you lie if you do," Cincinnatus said. "They come in like that, they be sorry."

"Oh, yeah." Lucullus' jowls wobbled as he nodded. "They be sorry. But we be sorrier. Any kind o' fight like that, we loses. Guns we got is enough to make them fuckers think twice. Ain't enough to stop 'em. Cain't be, and you got to know that, too. They uses barrels, we ain't got nothin' 'cept Featherston Fizzes against 'em. They sends in Ass-kickers to bomb us flat, we ain't even got that. We kin hurt 'em. They kin fuckin' *kill* us, an' I reckon they is lookin' fo' the excuse to do it."

Cincinnatus grunted. Lucullus had to be right. Against the massed power of the CSA, the local Negroes would lose. And the Confederate authorities might well be looking for an excuse to move in and wipe them out. Which meant . . . "You got to git hold o' Bliss," Cincinnatus said again.

"What good it do me?" Lucullus asked sourly. "I done told you—"

"Yeah, you told me. But so what?" Cincinnatus said, and Lucullus stared at him. The barbecue cook usually dominated between them. Not now. Cincinnatus went on, "We're all shut up in here. Bad things start happenin' out past the wire, how could we have much to do with 'em? But you kin get hold of Luther Bliss, and that son of a bitch got other ofays who'll do what he tell 'em to."

Lucullus kept right on staring, but now in a new way. "Mebbe," he said once more. This time, he didn't seem to mean, *You're crazy.* Even so, he warned, "Luther Bliss don't care nothin' about niggers just 'cause they's niggers."

"Shit, I know that. Luther Bliss hates everybody under the sun," Cincinnatus said, startling a laugh out of Lucullus. "But the people Luther Bliss hates most are Freedom Party men and the Confederates who run things. We hate them people, too, so we's handy for him."

"Well, yeah, but the people he hates next most is Reds," Lucullus said. "You got to remember, that don't help me none."

"You got any better ideas?" Cincinnatus demanded, and then, "You got any ideas at all?"

Lucullus glared at him. If anything, that relieved Cincinnatus, who didn't like seeing the younger man paralyzed. Cincinnatus would have done almost anything to get Lucullus' wits working again; enraging him seemed a small price to pay. Lucullus said, "I kin git hold o' him. He kin do dat shit, no doubt about it. But how much good it gonna do *us*?"

"What do you mean?" Cincinnatus asked.

"They got the wire around us. We is in here. Whatever they wants to do with us—whatever they wants to do *to* us—they got us where they wants us. How we get out? How we get away?"

Cincinnatus laughed at him. "They gonna let us out. They gonna let a lot of us out, anyways." Lucullus' jaw dropped. Cincinnatus drove the point home: "Who's gonna do their nigger work for 'em if they don't? Long as they need that, we ain't cooped up in here all the time."

"You hope we ain't," Lucullus said, but a little spirit came back into his voice.

"Talk to Luther Bliss," Cincinnatus repeated. "Hell, they let me out for anything, *I'll* talk to him."

"Like he listen to you," Lucullus said scornfully. "You ain't got no guns. You ain't got no people who kin do stuff. I tells you somethin'— you git outa the barbed wire, you try an' get your black ass back to the USA. Ain't far—jus' over de river."

"Might as well be over the moon right now," Cincinnatus said with a bitter laugh. "Confederate soldiers holdin' that part of Ohio. By what I hear, they're worse on colored folks than the Freedom Party boys are here. They reckon they're United States colored folks, an' so they got to be the enemy." Cincinnatus thought that was a pretty good bet, too. He added, "'Sides, I ain't leavin' without my pa."

"You is the stubbornest nigger ever hatched," Lucullus said. "Onliest thing that hard head good for nowadays is gittin' you killed." He made shooing motions with his hands. "Go on. Git. I don't want you 'round no mo'."

Cincinnatus didn't want to be in the barbecue place anymore. He didn't want to be in Covington anymore. He didn't want to be in Kentucky at all anymore. The trouble was, nobody else gave a damn what he wanted or didn't want.

Cane tapping the ground ahead of him, he walked out for a better look at what the whites in Covington had done. He'd seen more formidable assemblages of barbed wire when he was driving trucks in the last war, but those had been made to hold out soldiers, not to hold in civilians. For that, what the cops and the stalwarts had run up would do fine.

Normally, making a fence out of barbed wire would have been nigger work. Whites had done it here, though. That worried Cincinnatus. If whites decided they *could* do nigger work, what reason would they have to keep any Negroes around in the CSA?

A swagbellied cop with a submachine gun strolled along outside the fence. He spat a brown stream of tobacco juice onto the sidewalk. The sun sparkled from the enameled Freedom Party pin on his lapel. Hadn't Jake Featherston climbed to power by going on and on about how whites were better than blacks? How could they be better than blacks if they got rid of all the blacks? Then they would have to work things out among themselves. Race wouldn't trump class anymore, the way it always had in the Confederacy.

That fat policeman spat again. His jaw worked as he shifted the chaw from one cheek to the other. Did he care about such details? Did the countless others like him care? Cincinnatus couldn't make himself believe it. They'd get rid of Negroes first and worry about what happened after that later on.

Cincinnatus suddenly felt as trapped as Lucullus did. Up till now, the rumors about what the Confederates were doing to Negroes farther south in the CSA, things he'd heard at Lucullus's place and the Brass Monkey and in other saloons, had seemed too strange, too ridiculous, to worry him. Now he looked out at the rest of Covington through barbed wire. It wasn't even rusty yet; sunshine sparkled off the sharp points of the teeth. He couldn't get out past it, not unless that cop and his pals let him. And they could reach into the colored district whenever they pleased.

He didn't like the combination, not even a little bit. Except for try-ing to escape with his father as soon as he got even a halfway decent chance, though, he didn't know what he could do about it.

I need a rifle, he thought. *Reckon I can get one from Lucullus. They come after me, they gonna pay for everything they get.*

D**ead** night again, and the *Josephus Daniels* creeping along through the darkness. Sam Carsten peered out at the black water ahead as if he could see the mines floating in it. He couldn't, and he knew as much. He had to hope the destroyer escort had a good chart of these waters, and that she could dodge the mines. If she couldn't . . . Some of them were packed with enough TNT to blow a ship high enough out of the water to show her keel to anybody who happened to be watching. Out on the open sea, he didn't worry much about mines. Here in the nar-row waters of Chesapeake Bay, he couldn't help it.

At the wheel, Pat Cooley seemed the picture of calm. "We're just about through the worst of it, sir," he said.

"Glad to hear it," Sam said. "If we go sky-high in the next couple of minutes, I'm going to remind you you said that."

The exec chuckled. "Oh, I expect I'll remember it myself."

Sam set a hand on his shoulder. The kid was all right—not a nerve in his body, or none that showed. And he was a married man, too, which made it harder for him. "Family all right?" Carsten asked.

"Oh, yes, sir," Cooley answered. "Jane's over the chicken pox, and Sally didn't catch 'em." His wife had worried when his daughter came down with the ailment, because she didn't remember having it as a lit-tle girl. If she hadn't got chicken pox by now, though, she must have had them then, because anybody who could catch them damn well would.

Another twenty minutes crawled by in a day or two. The soft throb of the engines came up through Sam's shoes. The sound, the feel, were as important as his own pulse. If they stopped, the ship was in mortal peril. As things were . . . "I think we're out of it now," Sam said.

Cooley nodded. "I do believe you're right—except for the little bastards that came off their chains and started drifting." He paused. "And unless one side or the other laid some mines nobody knows about that aren't on our charts."

"You're full of cheerful thoughts today, aren't you?" Sam said. Pat

Cooley just grinned. Either or both of those things was perfectly possible, and both men knew it too well. Those weren't the only nasty possibilities, either, and Sam also knew that only too well. He spoke into a voice tube: "You there, Bevacqua?"

"Not me, Skip," came the voice from the other end. "I been asleep the last couple weeks." A snore floated out of the tube.

"Yeah, well, keep your ears open while you're snoozing. This is good submarine country," Sam said.

"Will do, Skip," Vince Bevacqua said. The petty officer was the best hydrophone man the *Josephus Daniels* carried, which was why he was on duty now. Back during the Great War, hydrophones had been as near worthless as made no difference. The state of the art had come a long way since then. Now hydrophones shot out bursts of sound waves and listened for echoes—it was almost like Y-ranging underwater. It gave ships like this one a real chance when they went after subs.

"Not the best submarine country," Cooley observed. "Water's pretty shallow."

"Well, sure, Pat, but that's not quite what I meant," Sam said. "It's good sub country because we've just made it past the minefields. When some people get through something like that, they go, 'Whew!' and forget they're not all the way out of the woods. They get careless, let their guard down. And that's when the bastards on the other side drop the hammer on them."

The bridge was dark. Showing a light in crowded, contested waters like these was the fastest way Sam could think of to get the hammer dropped on him. In the gloom, he watched the exec swing toward him, start to say something, and then think twice. After a few seconds, Cooley tried again: "That's . . . pretty sensible, sir."

He sounded amazed, or at least bemused. Carsten chuckled under his breath. "You live and learn," he told the younger man. "You've got an Academy ring. You got your learning all boiled down and served up to you, and that's great. It gives you a hell of a head start. By the time you get to my age, you'll be a four-striper, or more likely an admiral. I've had to soak all this stuff up the hard way—but I've had a lot longer to do it than you have."

Again, Pat Cooley started to answer. Again, he checked himself so he could pick his words with care. Slowly, he said, "Sir, I don't think that's the kind of thing they teach you at Annapolis. I think it's the kind of thing you do learn with experience—if you ever learn it at all. You're—not what I expected when they told me I'd serve under a mustang."

"No, eh?" Instead of chuckling, Sam laughed out loud now. "Sorry to disappoint you. My knuckles don't drag on the deck—not most of the time, anyway. I don't dribble tobacco juice down my front, and I don't spend all my time with CPOs." A lot of mustangs did hang around with ratings as much as they could: those were still the men they found most like themselves. Sam had been warned against that when he got promoted. He suspected every mustang did. A lot of them, though, didn't listen to the warning. He had.

"Sir, you're doing your best to embarrass me," Cooley said after one more longish pause. "Your best is pretty good, too." He laughed as Sam had. Unlike Sam, though, he sounded distinctly uneasy when he did it.

A tinny ghost, Vince Bevacqua's voice floated out of the mouth of the tube: "Skipper, I've got a contact. Something's moving down there—depth about seventy, range half a mile, bearing 085."

"Seventy," Sam echoed thoughtfully. That was below periscope depth. If the hydrophone man had spotted a submersible, the boat didn't know the *Josephus Daniels* was in the neighborhood—unless it had spotted the destroyer escort and submerged before Bevacqua realized it was there. Sam found that unlikely. He knew how good the petty officer was . . . even if he didn't hang around with him. "Change course to 085, Mr. Cooley," he said, switching to business.

"I am changing course to 085, sir—aye aye," the exec replied.

Sam tapped a waiting sailor on the shoulder. "Tell the depth-charge crews to be ready at my order."

"Aye aye, sir." The sailor dashed away. He didn't care whether Sam was a mustang. To a kid like him, the Old Man was the Old Man, regardless of anything. And if the Old Man happened to be well on the way toward being an old man—that still didn't matter much.

"I'll be damned if he thinks we're anywhere around, sir," Bevacqua said, and then, "Whoops—take it back. He's heard us. He's picking up speed and heading for the surface."

"Let's get him," Sam said. "Tell me when, and I'll pass it on to the guys who toss ash cans."

"Will do, Skipper." Bevacqua waited maybe fifteen seconds, then said, "Now!"

"Launch depth charges!" Sam shouted through the PA system—no need to keep quiet anymore.

During the Great War, ash cans had rolled off over the stern. The state of the art was better now. Two projectors flung depth charges well ahead of the ship. The charges arced through the air and splashed into the ocean.

"All engines reverse!" Cooley said. Sam nodded. Depth charges bursting in shallow water could blow the bow off the ship that had launched them. Carsten recalled the pathetic signal he'd heard about from a destroyer escort that had had that misfortune befall her: I HAVE BUSTED MYSELF. If it happened to him, *he'd* be busted, too, probably all the way to seaman second class.

Even though the *Josephus Daniels* had backed engines, the ash cans did their damnedest to lift her out of the water. Sam felt as if somebody'd whacked him on the soles of his feet with a board. Water rose and then splashed back into the sea. More bursts roiled the Atlantic.

Somebody at the bow whooped: "She's coming up!"

"Searchlights!" Sam barked, and the night lit up. He knew the chance he was taking. If C.S. planes spotted him before he settled the sub, he was in a world of trouble. *Have to settle it quick, then,* he thought.

Men spilled out of the damaged submersible's conning tower and ran for the cannon on the deck. It was only a three-inch gun, but Carsten's destroyer escort wasn't exactly a battlewagon. If that gun hit, it could hurt.

"Let 'em have it!" Sam yelled. The forward gun spoke in a voice like an angry god's. The antiaircraft cannon at the bow started barking, too. They were more than good enough to tear up an unarmored target like a sub. The enemy got off one shot, which went wild. Then men on that deck started dropping as if a harvester were rumbling down it.

"White flag!" Three people shouted the same thing at the same time.

"Cease fire!" Sam yelled through the intercom, and then, "If they make a move toward that gun, blow 'em all to hell!" He turned away from the mike and spoke to Cooley: "Approach and take survivors."

"Aye aye, sir," the exec said. He had a different worry: "I hope to hell she's not one of our boats."

"Gurk!" Sam said. That hadn't even crossed his mind. It wasn't impossible in these waters, one more thing he knew too well. They wouldn't just bust him for that. They'd boot him out of the Navy.

As the *Josephus Daniels* drew closer, he breathed again. The shape of the conning tower and the lines of the hull were different from those of U.S. boats. And the sailors tumbling into life rafts wore dark gray tunics and trousers. They were Confederates, all right.

A last couple of men popped out of the hatch atop the conning tower. The submersible startled rapidly settling down into the sea. *They opened the scuttling cocks,* Sam realized. He swore, but half-heartedly. In their place, he would have done the same thing.

"Watching them will be fun," Cooley said. "We haven't got a brig. Even if we did, it wouldn't hold that many."

"We'll keep them up on deck, where the machine guns will bear," Sam answered. "I don't see how we can make our cruise with them along, though. I'll wireless for instructions."

As soon as the prisoners were aboard, he doused the searchlight. The pharmacist's mate did what he could for the wounded. Sam went down to the deck and called for the enemy skipper. "Here I am, sir," a glum-sounding man said. "Lieutenant Reed Talcott, at your service. I don't thank you for wrecking us, but I do for picking us up." He tipped a greasy cap he'd somehow kept on his head.

"Part of the game, Lieutenant," Sam said, and gave his own name. "If it makes you feel any better, I've been sunk, too."

"Not one damn bit," Talcott said promptly.

Sam laughed. "All right. Can't say as I blame you. We'll put you somewhere out of the way, and then we'll get on with the war."

Not for the first time, Clarence Potter thought that Richmond and Philadelphia were both too close to the C.S.–U.S. border for comfort. When war came between the two countries—and it came, and came, and came—the capitals were appallingly vulnerable. They got more so as time went by, too: each side developed new and better—or was worse the right word?—ways to punish the other. For all practical purposes, the damnyankees had abandoned Washington as an administrative center. It just made too handy a target.

At the moment, though, Washington wasn't the first thing on Potter's mind. He stood behind a sawhorse in Capitol Square, one of at least a dozen that had red rope strung from them to form a perimeter. Signs hung from the rope: WARNING! UNEXPLODED BOMB! If that wasn't enough to get the message across, the signs also displayed the skull and crossbones.

Even so, a woman started to duck under the ropes to take a short-cut to the Capitol. "Get the hell out of there, lady!" a sergeant shouted at her. "You want to get your stupid ass blown off?"

"Well!" she sniffed. "Such language!"

The sergeant sighed and turned to Potter. "It ain't like she hasn't got enough ass so she couldn't use some of it blown off," he said. The Intelligence officer chuckled; indeed, the woman hadn't missed any meals. The noncom, a member of the Bomb Disposal Unit, went on, "Jesus God, sir, you wouldn't reckon people could be so stinking stupid, though, would you?"

"Oh, I don't know," Potter said. "That kind of thing rarely surprises me. A lot of people *are* damn fools, and there's not much you can do about it, except maybe try to keep them from killing themselves."

"Ugly bitch wouldn't have been that much of a loss." The sergeant sighed again. "Still and all, I expect you're right. I just wish the Yankees were damn fools."

Potter pointed toward the hole in the ground where the sergeant's colleagues were working. "If they made better ordnance, that would have gone off," he said, though he knew Confederate munitions factories turned out their fair share of duds, too.

But the sergeant shook his head. "It ain't necessarily so, sir. Some of these fuckers—uh, excuse me—"

"I've heard the word before," Potter said dryly. "I've even used the word before."

"Oh." The sergeant eyed the wreathed stars on either side of his collar. "I guess maybe. Anyways, though, like I was saying, some of 'em have time fuses, so they go boom when people aren't expecting 'em. You'll have heard about that, won't you?"

"I sure have," Potter said. "So you have to get them out of there before they go off. I'd be lying if I said I envied you."

"Sometimes we get 'em out. Sometimes we have to defuse 'em where they're at," the BDU sergeant said. "And that's what I meant when I said I wished the damnyankees were fools. Some of their time fuses're just time fuses. Then we race the clock, like. Some of 'em, though, some of 'em are booby-trapped, so they'll go off when we start messing with the time fuse. They'll put those on ordinary bombs, too, so they'll explode if you tinker. Sons of bitches want to kill *us* off, see, so then more of their time bombs'll work."

"That's . . . unpleasant," Potter said. "How do you handle those?"

"Carefully," the sergeant answered.

Potter laughed, not that the younger man was kidding. Here was a glimpse of a cat-and-mouse game he hadn't imagined before. Of course the Yankees wanted to blow up the people who got rid of unexploded bombs. It made perfect military sense—but it was hard on the men of the BDU. He asked, "Do we do the same thing to them?"

"Beats me, sir," the noncom said, "but if we don't, we're missing a hell of a chance."

"All right. That's fair enough—no reason to expect you to know," Potter said. He could find out for himself—or maybe he couldn't, depending on how tight security was. Discovering the answer to that might be interesting all by itself.

"Hey, Cochrane!" somebody bawled from the direction of the hole in the ground. "Give me a hand setting up the clockstopper. We're going to need it on this son of a bitch."

"The clockstopper?" Potter said, intrigued.

"Sir, I can't talk about that," the sergeant—presumably Cochrane—said. "Security—you know how it is. And now, if you'll excuse me . . ." He sketched a salute and hurried away.

No bomb burst shattered the calm of Richmond in the next half hour, so Potter supposed the clockstopper and whatever other arcane tools the Bomb Disposal Unit brought to bear on the bomb did what they were supposed to do. The war spawned every kind of specialist, not all of whom operated with as many eyes upon them as did the men of the BDU.

After Potter went back to the War Department, he remarked on what he'd seen to Nathan Bedford Forrest III. He couldn't very well breach security with the head of the General Staff; if Forrest didn't have the right to know everything there was to know, nobody in the CSA did. (Given the way things were in the Confederacy these days, quite possibly no one but Jake Featherston did. Potter preferred not to dwell on that.)

As things turned out, he didn't have to dwell on it, because General Forrest knew enough to satisfy his curiosity. Nodding, Forrest said, "The BDU men are some of the best we have. Every one of them is a volunteer, too."

Potter couldn't look out on Richmond from Forrest's office, which had plywood in place of window glass. Before long, window glass here in the capital might grow as extinct as the passenger pigeon. Of course, the same was no doubt just as true in Philadelphia. After pausing to light a cigarette, the Intelligence officer said, "I hadn't thought about it, but I'm not surprised. You wouldn't want somebody who didn't want to be there messing with those bombs."

"That's what everybody thinks," Forrest agreed. "Let me steal one of those from you." Potter gave him a smoke. He tapped it on his desk a couple of times to settle the tobacco, then stuck it in his mouth. Potter lit a match for him and held it out. "Thanks," Forrest said. He took a drag, blew out a plume of smoke, and looked up at the ceiling. "A lot of men volunteer for the duty."

"Good," Potter said. "I'd worry if they didn't."

"Yes, yes." Forrest sounded impatient. "When you put it that way, so would I. But do you know how long the average service career of a BDU man is?"

"No, sir," Potter admitted. "I don't have the faintest idea."

"Two and a half months—I saw the number just the other day, so it's fresh in my mind," Forrest said. "We *need* a lot of volunteers. By the way, we don't talk about that number to BDU personnel, not under any circumstances."

"I believe it." Potter also believed that BDU men could probably figure it out for themselves, or at least come close. They all had to be mourning friends and comrades. Two and a half months . . . That was worse than he would have guessed. *"Nos morituri te salutamus,"* he murmured.

Nathan Bedford Forrest III nodded. "The only good thing you can say about the business is that, if something goes wrong, it's all over before the poor bastards know it. The bombs go off faster than the nervous system can react."

"That does matter," Potter said. He hadn't been at the front in the last war, but he'd been close enough to have seen horrors aplenty. Dreadfully wounded men, as far as he was concerned, were worse horrors than the dead. No matter how gruesome a corpse was, it was beyond suffering. For the living, pain went on and on.

The telephone rang. "Forrest here," Forrest said. Potter left. He didn't wait for Forrest to wave him out because he lacked clearance to hear whatever the chief of the General Staff was talking about. Disappearing without being asked in such circumstances was part of the etiquette of the security-conscious.

Potter's own above-ground office, to which he'd defiantly returned, also had plywood in place of glass. Glass, these days, was not only a luxury but a dangerous luxury. In a bomb burst, shards were so many flying knives. They could chop a man into hamburger in the blink of an eye. Potter knew that. He missed being able to see out even so.

One thing—since he couldn't look out the window, he couldn't use looking out the window as an excuse for daydreaming. He had to buckle down and tackle the work on his desk. And so, reluctantly, he did.

On top of the pile was an urgent request from the Mormons of Deseret for whatever the Confederacy could send them. Getting supplies to them was harder than it had been when the rebellion first broke out. The U.S. noose was tightening. Potter had known it would. In a way, encouraging and helping the Mormon uprising seemed dreadfully unfair. Those people had not a chance in the world of winning, but they were eager to try, eager to the point of madness. It was enough to make a man with a conscience feel guilty.

Of course, a man with that kind of conscience had no business getting into Intelligence in the first place. Potter knew as much. He also knew his damnyankee counterparts were doing everything they could to arm the Negro terrorists in the CSA. If turnabout wasn't fair play, what was? The only thing he really felt bad about was that there were so many more Negroes in the Confederate States than Mormons in the United States. Blacks caused more trouble for his side than the religious maniacs did for the enemy.

He wondered whether some Confederate operative had suggested auto bombs to the Mormons or they'd come up with them on their own. Either way, they made a viciously effective weapon for the weak against the strong. Again, Negroes in the CSA had proved that—and continued to prove it whenever they got the chance.

We need to keep this uprising alive as long as we can, he wrote. *Where else can we tie down so many U.S. soldiers at so little cost to ourselves?*

Even though the question was rhetorical as he wrote it, he knew it did have a possible answer. If Canada flared into rebellion, the Yankees would need endless divisions to hold it down. But, despite assiduous efforts, the Confederates hadn't made a lot of friends up there. To

Canadians, they might as well have been Yankees themselves. That infuriated Clarence Potter—and every other Confederate who'd ever run into the problem—but fury didn't do much good.

If any outsiders could make the Canadians rise up, the Confederates weren't the ones. The British were. Potter paused thoughtfully. Winston Churchill was supposed to favor quixotic schemes like that—and keeping the USA busy was as much in Britain's interest as it was in the CSA's.

A memorandum from Potter would never reach the British Prime Minister. A memorandum from Jake Featherston, on the other hand . . . Potter nodded to himself. Churchill might not agree. That was the chance you took. But he wouldn't be able to ignore the request from an allied head of state. And Featherston would look at a memorandum from Potter. The Intelligence officer paused for a moment to gather his thoughts, then began to write.

Jake Featherston often felt busier than a one-legged man in an ass-kicking contest. He sometimes thought he wouldn't have wanted to become President if he'd known ahead of time how much work the job was. That wasn't true—down deep in his heart, he knew as much—but it gave him something to complain about.

Take paperwork. He'd never known what an obscene word that could be till he came to the Gray House. No matter how much he gave to other people, he still had plenty and then some. Paperwork was the price he paid for being boss.

Every once in a while, he ran into something he really needed to see. When he came to a memorandum from Clarence Potter, he knew he had to read it. For one thing, Potter would give him a hard time if he didn't. And, for another, even though he trusted the Intelligence officer about as far as he could throw him, Potter had a lefthanded way of looking at the world that was often valuable. By his own lights, Potter was a patriot. Where his lights and Jake's corresponded, they got on fine.

As Featherston read through this scheme, he found himself nodding. "Yeah," he said when he was done. "About time we got some help from our so-called allies." He knew as well as anybody that Britain was heavily bogged down in western Germany, trying to hold on to the gains she and France had made when the war was shiny and new. He recognized the feeling. He had it himself. The problem with grabbing a tiger by the tail was that letting go could hurt even worse than hanging on.

He picked up a pen and started to write. If Churchill wanted to play along, this wouldn't cost the limeys much—and if it went off well, it could bring the United States untold grief. That wouldn't break Jake's heart. Oh, no—far from it.

His big worry was that Churchill was too obsessed with the Kaiser to care what happened on this side of the Atlantic. But the USA was the country that had taken Canada and Newfoundland away from England after the Great War. Winston was almost as good at remembering offenses done him as Jake was himself.

"Lulu!" he called from his office.

"What is it, Mr. President?" his secretary asked.

"I want Major Hamilton right away."

Major Ira Hamilton hurried into the President's underground office inside of five minutes. "Reporting as ordered, sir," he said. He was tall, thin, and bespectacled; he looked much more like a math teacher than a major.

"Good. Good." Jake thrust the paper at him. "I need you to put this into our fanciest code and send it to London just as fast as you can." There was a reason Hamilton looked like a math teacher: up till the war started, he'd been a professor of mathematics at Washington University.

"I'll do it, sir," he said. "It doesn't look too long—it should go out this afternoon."

"That'll be just fine, Major. Thank you kindly." Featherston was far more polite with people who were useful to him than with the rest of the world. Hamilton gave him a ragged salute and hurried away. Someone would keep a discreet eye on the unmilitary major to make sure he did what he was supposed to do and nothing else. And someone would watch the man who watched Hamilton, and somebody would. . . .

Things had to work that way. If you didn't keep an eye on people, they'd make you wish you had. Jake even kept an eye on Don Partridge. He'd chosen his Vice President because Partridge was the mildest, safest, most inoffensive, and most useless man he could find— and he kept an eye on him anyway. You couldn't be too careful.

Some of the papers Featherston plowed through were damage reports from the western part of the Confederacy. The damnyankees were trying to knock out the dams he'd built on the Tennessee and the Cumberland Rivers. That infuriated him. It alarmed him, too. The Confederate States needed the electricity those dams produced. It kept factories going. And it changed millions of people's lives. He was as proud of those dams and what they did as of almost anything else his administration had accomplished.

Almost was the key word there. Ferd Koenig came in a couple of hours later. "Good to see you, by God," Jake said. "Have a seat." He opened his desk drawer and pulled out a bottle of fine Tennessee sipping whiskey. "Have a snort."

"Don't mind if I do." Koenig took the bottle from him, raised it, swallowed, and passed it back. "Virgin's milk. The corn that went in there died happy."

"You better believe it." Jake swigged, too. Velvet fire ran down his throat. He set the bottle on the desk after one knock. He wanted the taste. He didn't want to get smashed. "So how's relocation coming?"

"Tolerable. Better than tolerable, matter of fact," Koenig answered. "One neighborhood at a time, one town at a time, we clean 'em out. Off they go. They reckon they're going to camps, and they are. What they don't reckon on is, they don't come out again."

"Towns are all very well. Towns are better than all very well, matter of fact," Jake said. "But there's still the core of the cotton country—from South Carolina through Georgia and Alabama and Mississippi into Louisiana. We thinned that out some when we brought in harvesters—got a bunch of niggers off the farms and into towns where we could deal with 'em easier."

"Got a bunch of 'em with rifles in their hands, too," Ferdinand Koenig said dryly. "They didn't have work anymore, so they reckoned they might as well go out and start shooting white folks."

He wasn't wrong, but Featherston said, "We had trouble with 'em before that, too," which was also true. He went on, "That whole goddamn Black Belt's been up in arms ever since the Great War. Damn Whigs never were able to put it down all the way, and we've had our own fun and games with it. Plenty of places down there where it's never been safe for a white man to go around by himself in broad daylight, let alone after the sun goes down."

"That's only part of the problem," Koenig said. "In towns, you can put barbed wire around the nigger district, and after that you can go in and clean it out one chunk at a time, however you want to. The niggers in the countryside, you can't cordon 'em off so easy. They just slip away. It's like trying to scoop up water with a sieve."

"Gotta keep working on it," Jake said.

The Attorney General's jowls wobbled as he nodded. "Oh, hell, I know that," he said. "But the real trouble is, it takes a lot of man-power, and we haven't got a lot of people to spare, not the way things are going."

"I know, I know." Featherston reached for the whiskey bottle again. More heat trickled down his throat. He'd been so certain he could knock the USA out of the war in a hurry. He'd been so certain—and he'd been so wrong. Soldiers at the front were more important than anything else, even people to help round up the niggers. After yet another swig, he added, "Those trucks that Pinkard came up with can't handle all the volume we need for this operation, either."

"They're the best we've got," Koenig said. "And we don't have guards eating their guns all the goddamn time anymore, either, the way we did before we started using them."

"I know that, too, dammit," Jake said impatiently. "We need some-thing better, though—and no, I don't know what it is any more than you do. But something. We've got to get rid of those niggers in great big old lots."

"You can figure out damn near anything if you throw enough money and enough smart people at it," Ferd Koenig observed. "Is this worth throwing 'em at it? Or do we need the people and the money more somewhere else?"

"This is what we spent all that time wandering in the wilderness for," Jake said, as if he were Moses leading the CSA to the Promised Land. That was exactly how he felt, too. "If we don't do this, we're let-ting the country down."

"Well, all right." Koenig nodded again. "I feel the same way, but I needed to make sure you did. We can do that—you know we can. But it'll likely mean pulling those people and that money away from the war effort."

"This *is* the war effort," Jake Featherston declared. "What else would you call it? *This* is what counts." Even as he spoke, he heard the rumble of U.S. artillery fire, not nearly far enough to the north. He nodded anyway. "We clean out the coons, we'll do something for this country that'll last till the end of time."

"All right, then. We'll tend to it." Koenig sighed. "I wish we had as many people as the Yankees do. They can afford to keep more balls in the air at the same time than we can."

"I don't care about their balls in the air. Those aren't the ones I aim to kick," Jake said.

"Heh," Ferd Koenig said. "Well, I hope we can do it, that's all." He was listening to the gunfire from the north, too. He didn't brush it aside the way Jake did. It worried him, and he made no secret about that, not even to Featherston.

Showing what he thought took nerve. Lesser men had ended up in camps for lesser offenses. But regardless of whether Koenig agreed with Jake's policies, his personal loyalty was unshakable. Jake could count the people he fully trusted on his fingers—sometimes, on a bad day, on his thumbs—but Ferd always had been, was, and always would be one of them.

"We will." Featherston retained his conviction in his own destiny. "The show will be starting soon, and we'll squash 'em flat. You'll see."

"Expect I will." Koenig didn't say *one way or the other*. He didn't even leave it hanging in the air. He believed in Jake's destiny, too. He'd gone on believing in it through the black years in the middle twenties, when so many others wrote Jake and the Freedom Party off. He asked, "You need me for anything else?"

"Don't think so," Jake answered. "But we do need some kind of way to get rid of more niggers faster. You put some bright boys on that and see what they can come up with."

"Right." Ferdinand Koenig heaved himself out of his chair and headed for the door. Jake had no idea what he would come up with or even if he would come up with anything, but had no doubt he would look, and look hard. If you looked hard enough, you generally found *something*.

Muttering, Jake went back to looking through his paperwork. He wished he thought he would find anything else important, or even something interesting, in there. "Fat chance," he muttered. "Fat fucking chance." He made sure he kept his voice down; Lulu didn't like to hear him swear. That didn't always stop him, but it did a good part of the time.

And then he turned up a report from an outfit called the Huntsville Rocket Society. He wondered how the hell anything that bizarre had made it onto his desk. Then he saw why. The brigadier general in charge of air defense of Alabama and Mississippi endorsed it, writing, *However startling these claims sound, I believe they can be made real soon enough to prove useful in the present conflict.*

That made Jake read it more carefully than he would have otherwise. "Son of a bitch," he murmured halfway through. "*Son* of a bitch. Wouldn't that be something if they could?"

VIII

As the weather heated up, the POW camp near Andersonville, Georgia, did an increasingly good impression of hell. With the heat came humidity. With the humidity came thunderstorms that awed Jonathan Moss. The red dirt in the camp turned to something not a great deal thicker than tomato soup after one of those downpours.

And the mosquitoes came. Moss had known mosquitoes up in Canada, too. These seemed a larger and more virulent breed. He slapped and swore and itched. He was anything but the only one. Nick Cantarella said, "This one I smashed last night, you could hang machine guns under its wings and go to war in it."

"Who says they don't?" Moss answered. "That would account for the size of some of the bites I've got."

The other officer laughed. "You're a funny guy, Major."

"Funny like a crutch," Moss said, and then, "Colonel Summers ought to do something about it. We could all come down with yellow fever."

"Do what?" Cantarella asked in reasonable tones. "Moses parted the Red Sea, but all he did was plague the Egyptians with bugs. God was the one who had to call 'em off."

Patiently, Moss answered, "Moses couldn't ask for bug repellent and Flit. Come to think of it, Pharaoh couldn't, either. But Summers damn well can."

"Oh." Cantarella looked foolish. "Well, yeah."

Moss didn't ask him how escape efforts were going. He assumed they *were* still going. He also assumed that much rain did tunnels no good. He looked out the window, out beyond the barbed wire. Even if the prisoners did get out of the camp, could they cross several states and get back to the USA? They spoke with an accent very different from the locals'. They would be pursued—he pictured bloodhounds straight out of *Uncle Tom's Cabin*. And the people they met—the white ones, anyhow—would be Freedom Party fanatics. Put that all together and staying in the camp started to seem the better bargain.

But life here was no picnic, either. And prisoners of war had a duty to escape. Moss knew he'd run if and when he found a chance. As for what would happen after that . . . He'd worry about such things when he had to, not before.

In due course, citronella candles appeared in the prisoners' barracks. They filled the air with a spicy, lemony scent as they burned. The odor was alleged to discourage mosquitoes. Maybe Moss got bitten a little less often after that. On the other hand, maybe he didn't. He wasn't convinced, one way or the other.

Guards went through the camp with spray pumps. The mist that came out of them smelled something like mothballs and something like gasoline. Moss had no idea what it did to mosquitoes. It made him want to wear a gas mask. Since he didn't have one, he just had to put up with it.

Again, he wasn't sure how much difference the spraying made. The bugs didn't disappear, however much he wished they would. Of course, nobody was spraying outside the camp. Even if mosquitoes died by the thousands inside the barbed wire, plenty of replacements flew on in to sample the flavor delights of prisoner of war on the hoof.

Colonel Summers, once prodded, kept right on complaining, both to the Confederate authorities and to his fellow prisoners. "What they really need to do is spray a thin film of oil over every pond and puddle they can find," he said. "That would kill the mosquito larvae, and then we really might get some relief."

"Well, why don't they?" Moss said. "It wouldn't just benefit us. Their own health would get better, too." He thought like the attorney he was, weighing advantages and disadvantages.

Summers only shrugged. "They say they haven't got the manpower for it."

"In a way, that's good news," Moss said. "If they're stretched too thin to take care of important things behind the lines, pretty soon they'll be stretched too thin to take care of things at the front." Like a lawyer—and like a prisoner—he bent reality so it looked better than it really was.

"That hasn't happened yet." Colonel Summers brought him back to earth with a dose of the current news.

"Are you sure, sir?" Moss asked. "Anything you see in the papers the guards give us is just so much Freedom Party garbage."

"I'm sure." And Summers sounded very sure indeed. Moss knew there were a couple of clandestine wireless sets in the camp. He knew no more than that, which was a good thing for all concerned. He looked around the barracks. Two or three of the men were new fish, new officers for whom nobody here could vouch. They probably came from the United States. They talked as if they did. But good Confederate spies would sound like Yankees. The less Summers said while they were around, the better.

Machine-gun fire woke Moss in the middle of the night not quite a week later. His first reaction was fury. They'd pulled off an escape attempt, and they hadn't included him. His second reaction was despair. If the guards were shooting, the attempt couldn't have amounted to much. Was this the best his countrymen could do?

He got very little sleep the rest of the night.

At roll call the next morning, the Confederate guards swaggered and strutted like pouter pigeons. "Damn niggers came sniffin' round the camp last night," one of them said. "We drove 'em off, though— you better believe it."

However proud of themselves they were, their posturing only filled Moss with relief. Nothing inside here had gone wrong. If the guards wanted to jump up and down because they'd beaten back a few sorry guerrillas, they were welcome to, as far as he was concerned.

Later that day, he found an excuse to amble around the grounds with Nick Cantarella. As casually as he could, he asked, "Do we have any way of getting in touch with those colored men on the other side of the barbed wire?"

Cantarella took a couple of steps without saying anything. What he did say, at last, was, "I ought to tell you I don't know what you're talking about."

"Why?" Moss asked. "They could do us a lot of good if we ever happened to get on the other side of the wire ourselves."

"Maybe." Cantarella paused to light a cigarette. It was one of the lousy U.S. brands that came in Red Cross packages from the north. Prisoners could sometimes get the much better Confederate tobacco from the guards. Quiet little deals like that happened every now and again. After the first drag, Cantarella made a face. "Tastes like straw and horseshit." A moment later, he added, "Want one?"

"Sure." Moss took one, then leaned close to get a light. The tobacco *was* bad, but bad tobacco beat the hell out of no tobacco. He blew out smoke and then asked, "How come just maybe?"

The other officer looked around before answering. Satisfied nobody else was in earshot, he said, "For one thing, if the Confederates catch us with them, we're dead. No ifs, ands, or buts. Dead."

That was probably true. Moss shook his head—no, that was bound to be true. The Confederate States played by the usual international rules when they fought the United States. They played by no rules at all when they fought their own Negroes. By all the signs, the Negroes returned the favor—if that was the word. Moss said, "But if we've got a better chance of not getting caught at all . . ."

"Maybe," Nick Cantarella said again, even more dubiously than before. "But why should they help us get back to the USA?"

As if to a child, Moss answered, "Because we're fighting Featherston, too."

"Terrific," the younger man said. "Doesn't that make them more likely to give us rifles and enlist us? You want to be a guerrilla yourself? I don't, or not very much. It's not what I was trained for, but I wouldn't have a Chinaman's chance of convincing the smokes of that." He'd been an artilleryman before he got caught.

"Some of the people here would be good at it," Moss said. Infantry officers might make the black guerrillas considerably more effective. They really did have training in what the Negroes were trying to do. Moss himself was in Cantarella's boat. All his military expertise, such as it was, centered on airplanes. He didn't think the guerrillas would be taking to the air anytime soon.

A flight of a dozen biplanes buzzing along at not much above treetop height made him wonder if he was wrong. Those weren't military aircraft, except in the sense that any aircraft could be military when you had them and the other fellows didn't. As if to prove the point, and to show whose side they were on, they dropped bombs on the woods out beyond the prison camp. The explosions set Moss' teeth on edge.

"Think they'll hit anything in there?" he asked Cantarella.

"Oh, they'll hit *something*," the other officer answered with an expressive shrug. "Whether it'll be anything worth hitting . . . That's liable to be a different question."

"Looking like they were just tossing those bombs out of the cockpit," Moss said. "That's how this whole business got started, back when the Great War was new."

"If you say so." Cantarella wasn't old enough to remember the start of the Great War. He sure as hell hadn't been flying then, as Moss had.

A few days later, Moss put the question he'd asked Cantarella to Colonel Summers. The senior officer looked at him as if he'd suddenly started spouting Cherokee. "Trust a bunch of raggedy-ass niggers? You must be kidding, Major." But for his accent, he sounded like a Confederate himself.

With such patience as he could muster, Moss asked, "Do you know anybody who hates Jake Featherston more—or who has better reason to?"

Summers ignored that. "Besides, Major, we've got no way to get in touch with the spooks." He sounded like a man anxious to close off a subject he found distasteful. He might have been a maiden lady forced into talking about the facts of life.

Moss didn't laugh in his face, which proved military discipline still held. He did say, "Sir, we have all kinds of deals cooking that stretch farther than the camp. Spread a few dollars around and you can do damn near anything."

"Not this." Summers spoke as if from On High. "Not this, by God. No Confederate guard is going to go out and get hold of the niggers for us. That'd be like asking them to cut their own throats."

He had a point—of sorts. "There are bound to be ways if we look for them," Moss persisted. "We haven't even tried."

"Once we're outside the barbed wire, Major, you may put your faith in niggers or Christian Science or any other damnfool thing your heart desires," Colonel Summers said. "Until then, I make the decisions, and I have made this one. Is that clear enough for you, or shall I be more explicit?"

"You are very clear . . . sir." Moss turned the title of respect into one of reproach.

Summers heard the reproach and went red. "Will that be all, Major?" he asked in a voice like ice.

"I suppose so," Moss answered bitterly. "After all, we're not going anywhere, are we?"

"Oh, for Christ's sake!" Jefferson Pinkard slammed down the telephone and scowled at it as if it were a rattlesnake. "Son of a bitch!" he added for good measure. He slammed a fist down on his desk. His coffee mug and the gooseneck lamp there jumped. He had to grab the lamp to keep it from toppling over.

He'd hated calls from Richmond ever since he started running camps. He had good reason for hating them, too. Richmond had a habit of wanting miracles, and of wanting them yesterday.

Jeff had already given them one—a more efficient, more secure way of disposing of excess Negroes than they'd ever had before. Now that wasn't good enough for them anymore. He had to come up with something better yet. He hoped the other people who were running camps had got the same call. Let one of them have a brainstorm for a change!

"Fat chance," he muttered. Some of those people could blow their brains out if they sneezed, goddammit.

He knew the question was ridiculous and unfair. That didn't stop him from worrying at it like a dog worrying at a bone that was plumb out of meat. How *could* you get rid of more spooks faster than with this fleet of special trucks?

Oh, you could use more trucks, but that wasn't the answer Richmond wanted to hear. Richmond wanted something different, something spiffy, something where you could wave a hand and all of a sudden a thousand Negroes weren't there anymore.

And Richmond needed something like that, too. Pinkard couldn't very well deny it. All he had to do was look across the railroad tracks at the new women's half of the camp. Towns were getting their colored districts emptied out one after another. The blacks came into places like Camp Determination. They came in, and they didn't come out again—not alive, anyway.

How many niggers were there in the Confederate States? How many could the camps dispose of every day? How long would the CSA need to start really cutting into their numbers?

"Gotta be done," Jeff said heavily, as if someone had denied it. "It's a tough job, but somebody's got to do it." Every now and then, the sheer amount of work he had to do tempted him toward self-pity.

He pushed back his chair and got to his feet. He could look out at the camp from the window—no substitute for prowling through it, but sometimes a fast way to spot trouble before it got out of hand. Barbed wire and machine-gun towers separated the administrative block from the seething misery in the main compound. At the moment, a long line of blacks was snaking forward, the skinny men often eager to board the trucks that would, they thought, take them to another camp. In fact, their journey would be strictly one-way. That they didn't know it, was one of the beauties of the scheme, for their ignorance kept them docile.

Pinkard shook his head. How could you come up with anything better than this? Oh, sure, it used a lot of trucks, but so what? It did the job, didn't it? Some people were just never satisfied, that was all.

He stuck his head into the chief guard's office. Vern Green was second in command here, and needed to know where Jeff was when he wasn't at the camp. "I'm going into town for a little while," Pinkard told him. "Anything goes wrong, send somebody after me."

"Will do, boss." Green knew Jeff wouldn't be anywhere but three or four places in Snyder, one of them far more likely than any of the other. Finding him wouldn't be hard. Green couldn't help adding, "Things are smooth, though."

"Yeah, I know. They're smooth now, anyways," Pinkard said. "But just in case, I mean."

"Sure, sure." Vernon Green nodded. He smiled. He was no less ambitious than Mercer Scott had been back in Louisiana. Like Scott, Green undoubtedly reported back to someone in Richmond about how Jeff did his job. But he wasn't so obnoxious about it. Scott had had a drill sergeant's manner and a face like a boot. Green smiled a lot of the time, whether there was anything to smile about or not. He caught his flies with honey, not vinegar. He caught a lot of them, however he did it, and that was what a second-in-command was for.

As camp commandant, Pinkard had a motorcar laid on. He could have had a driver, too, but he didn't want one. He could drive himself just fine. Guards saluted as he left the camp. He would have to go through all the boring formalities getting back in. He shrugged. He would have had the guards' heads if they were anything but careful about letting people into Camp Determination.

Snyder, Texas, was a nice little town of perhaps three thousand people. Before the camp went up, business there had centered on cattle and on ginning the cotton grown in the surrounding countryside and making cottonseed cake that the cattle ate. The influx of guards had everybody in the four-street central business district smiling. By local standards, they made good money, and they weren't shy about spending it. And new houses were going up, because a lot of the guards were married men, and didn't want to live right by the camp.

Whoever'd named the roads in Snyder had no imagination at all. The ones that ran east-west were numbered streets. The ones that ran north-south were avenues, identified by letter. He pulled up in front of a house on Thirty-first Street near Avenue Q, in the southern part of town. Two boys were wrestling on the threadbare lawn in front of the house. They broke off when he got out of the motorcar.

"Papa Jeff!" they yelled. "It's Papa Jeff!" They ran up to him and tried out a couple of tackles that would have drawn flags on any football field in the CSA or USA. Fortunately, they were still too little to flatten him.

He ruffled their hair. He liked Chick Blades' sons. He liked Chick Blades' widow even more. "Easy, there," he told the kids, trying to pry them loose from his legs without damaging them. It wasn't easy; they clung like limpets. "Is your mama home?" he asked them.

That did the trick better than any wrestling hold. "She sure is," they said together, and dashed toward the house yelling, "Ma! Ma! Papa Jeff's here!" If the racket wasn't enough to wake the dead, it would have made them turn over in their graves a couple of times.

Edith Blades came out on the front porch. She was a nice-looking blond woman in her early thirties. Each time Jeff saw her, she seemed a little less ravaged by her husband's suicide. Time did heal wounds. Jeff had got over the disastrous end of his first marriage to the point where he was game to try it again. And so was Edith, though she wouldn't tie the knot till after the first anniversary of Chick Blades' death. They were getting there.

"Hello, Jeff. Good to see you," she said as he walked up to the porch. "How are things?"

"Things are . . ." He paused. "Well, they could be better."

"Come in and tell me about it," she said, and then, "Boys, go on and play. Papa Jeff will be with you in a little bit."

They made disappointed noises, but they didn't argue too much. They were good boys, well-behaved boys. She'd done a fine job with them, before Chick died and afterwards. Jeff admired that. He also admired the way she listened to him. He'd never known that with another woman—certainly not with his first wife. Animal heat had held him and Emily together—and then broken them apart.

"Set yourself down," Edith said when she and Jeff went back into the living room.

"In a second." He kissed her. She let him do that. In fact, she responded eagerly. Whenever he tried for more than a kiss, though, she told him they had to wait. That didn't make him angry. He thought the more of her for being able to say no. Emily hadn't, with him or with his best friend. But he didn't want to remember Emily. "How you doin' here?" he asked. "You got everything you need?"

"Sure do," Edith answered. "And I'm not sorry to be out of Alexandria, out of that house, and there's the Lord's truth."

"I do believe it." Jeff wouldn't have wanted to live in a house where somebody'd committed suicide. Actually, Chick had done it in his auto, but still. . . . "What do you think of Texas?"

"There's so much of it, and it's so big and flat," Edith answered. "Seemed like we were on the train forever, and that was just getting most of the way across one state. People act nice enough." She held up a hand. "But tell me what's gone wrong at the camp."

Jeff did. The only thing he didn't tell her was that Chick's suicide with auto exhaust had given him the idea for the trucks that used their fumes to kill off Negroes. He would never say a word about that, not even if he was on fire. There was such a thing as talking too damn much.

When he finished, Edith was suitably indignant for him. "They've got their nerve," she said. "After everything you've done cleaning up the colored problem for them, then they expect *more*? They should get down on their knees and thank God they've got a good man like you, Jeff."

"Ha! Those . . . people in Richmond don't notice anybody but their own selves," Jeff said. Only belatedly, after venting his spleen, did he notice the size of the compliment she'd paid him. "Thank you, darlin'. You say sweet things."

"You're my sweetheart," Edith said, her voice dead serious. "If I don't stick up for you, who's going to?"

Instead of answering with words, he kissed her again. She pressed herself against him. But when, ever optimistic, he let his hand fall on her thigh as if by accident, she knocked it away. He didn't get mad—he laughed. "You're somethin'."

"So are you." Edith was laughing, too. Even if she was, he remained sure she'd keep right on holding him at bay till their wedding night. It wasn't as if she were a virgin—or she could have doubled up on Mary—but she was a respectable woman, and she acted like one.

For a moment, Jeff thought the deep thrumming he heard was the pounding of the blood in his veins. Then he realized it was outside himself. No sooner had he realized that than Edith's kids ran in, yelling, "Ma! Papa Jeff! There's a million airplanes up in the sky! Come look! Quick!"

"What the—?" Jeff was off the couch and heading for the door as fast as he could go, Edith right behind him.

They stared up and up and up. Passing high above them, scribing ruler-straight contrails across the sky, were more big airplanes than Jeff had ever seen before. They flew east in what was obviously a strong defensive formation: in staggered echelons where one bomber could easily fire on enemy fighters attacking another. And *enemy fighters,* here, could mean only one thing: Confederate fighters.

"Damnyankees." Jefferson Pinkard made the calculation almost without conscious thought. "I bet they're headin' for Forth Worth and Dallas."

"How could they?" Edith said.

"They've got their nerve, sending 'em out in the daytime." Pinkard had a nasty feeling the bombers would get through. The war west of the Mississippi had been quiet. He doubted the Confederate authorities were ready for an attack on this scale. The damnyankees had pulled a fast one here.

"Will they drop bombs on *us,* Papa Jeff?" Frank Blades asked anxiously.

"Nah." Now Jeff spoke with great assurance. He set a big, meaty hand on the boy's shoulders. "Ain't nothin' here the Yankees would ever want to touch. Don't you worry 'bout a thing, not as far as that goes."

One thing Chester Martin had to give to Lieutenant Thayer Monroe: the kid could read a map. "We want to call down more fire on these emplacements in back of Fredericksburg, eh, Sergeant?" he said. "I make their positions out to be in square Green-6. That sound right to you?" There was something else Martin had to give him: he did ask the older man's opinion, and sometimes even listened to it.

Martin looked out from the ruins of Fredericksburg toward the heights to the south and southwest. They weren't mountains; they were hardly even hills. But they were plenty to let the Confederate field guns and mortars dug in on them make life hell on earth for the U.S. soldiers *in* the Virginia town.

"Yes, sir. I think Green-6 is right," he said. The platoon commander called for the signalman with the field telephone, then shouted into it. U.S. artillery was still on the far side of the river. Chester had the nasty suspicion that the Confederates had let the U.S. Army get foot soldiers over the Rappahannock so they could bleed them white. All attempts to break out from the town had failed. None seemed likely to succeed, at least not to him.

"Goddammit!" Lieutenant Monroe hung up in disgust. "I can't get through. Bastards must have cut the wires again."

"Wouldn't be surprised," Chester agreed. After a moment, he added, "I wonder how much truth there is in the talk you hear."

"You mean about Confederates running around in U.S. uniforms and raising Cain?" the lieutenant asked. Chester nodded. After some thought, Thayer Monroe said, "I don't know for sure, but I wouldn't be surprised. It's the sort of bastardly trick Featherston's people would pull."

Was it? It struck Martin as the sort of trick anybody with half an ounce of brains would pull, especially in a war where both sides spoke what was for all practical purposes the same language. He said, "I hope we're doing the same thing to them, that's all."

Lieutenant Monroe looked astonished. "It goes dead against the Geneva Convention, Sergeant. If you're caught in the enemy's uniform, you get a blindfold and a cigarette. That's too far to go for a good smoke."

Chester dutifully chuckled, though he had Confederate cigarettes in his pocket. Plundering enemy corpses—and, here in Fredericksburg, plundering shops—kept front-line infantrymen supplied with better tobacco than they could get from their own country. Front-line service had few advantages, but that was one of them.

Freight-train noises filled the air. Monroe might not have been able to get through to U.S. artillery, but someone had. High explosives thundered down on the heights behind Fredericksburg. How much good they would do . . .

Through the din, the lieutenant said, "At least we don't have any orders to get out of our holes and attack as soon as the barrage lets up."

"Thank you, Jesus," Chester Martin said, most sincerely.

His platoon commander nodded. Monroe *could* learn. The company, and the regiment of which it was a part, were in the line because so many men had tried to take the high ground in back of Fredericksburg: tried and bloodily failed. The Confederate gunners on those heights could murder every U.S. soldier in the world if the Army chose to come at them there. Machine guns and artillery swept the rising ground. Not even barrels had a chance of forcing their way forward.

Martin drew in a breath and made a face. Most of the time, you could forget about the stench of death on the battlefield—oh, not forget about it, maybe, but shove it down to the back of your mind. He'd thought about it, though, and that brought it up in his mind again. His guts did a slow lurch. Too many unburied bodies lay out there, bloating in the sun.

When the company went back into reserve, he would bring that stench with him—in his clothes, in his hair, on his skin. It took a long time to go away. And he'd smelled it in plenty of nightmares between the wars. Bad as it was here, it had been worse in the trenches on the Roanoke front, where the line went back and forth over the same few miles of ground for a couple of years, and where every square yard of ground was manured with a corpse or two.

Keeping his head down—he didn't know whether the Confederates had any snipers close enough to draw a bead on him, and didn't care to find out the hard way—he lit one of those smooth Confederate cigarettes and held the pack out to Lieutenant Monroe. "Thanks, Sergeant," Monroe said. He leaned close for a light.

The smoke in Chester's mouth and in his nose masked the smell of death. For that, one of the stables-scrapings cigarettes the USA turned out would have done as well. If you were going to go this way, though, why not go first class?

"I pity those poor bastards who don't smoke," Chester said out of the blue.

"Why's that?" The lieutenant, not unreasonably, couldn't follow his train of thought.

"On account of they can't ever get out from under the goddamn smell."

"Oh." Thayer Monroe considered, then nodded. "Hadn't looked at it like that, but you're right." He started to add something else, probably on the same theme, but all of a sudden he ducked down deep in the foxhole instead. "Incoming!"

"Aw, shit!" Martin got right down there with him. The Confederates were doing something sneaky—something gutsy, too. They couldn't huddle in reinforced-concrete gun emplacements to serve their mortars. They had to come out into the firing pits to use them. But the nasty little bombs flew at Fredericksburg almost silently. With all the big stuff roaring by overhead, nobody was going to notice the mortars till they started bursting, which would be too late for some luckless soldiers.

And sometimes even being right on the money didn't do you a damn bit of good. One of the reasons soldiers hated mortars was that the bombs went up at a steep angle and came down at an even steeper one. Plunging fire, the boys with the high foreheads called it. A foxhole didn't protect you from a round that came right down in there with you.

Chester heard the boom. Next thing he knew, he was grabbing at his leg and bawling for a corpsman. Absurdly, the first thing that went through his mind was, *Rita's gonna kill me.* When he could think of anything past his own pain, he got a look at Lieutenant Monroe— and wished he hadn't. The platoon commander was the only reason Chester was still breathing. He'd been between Chester and the mortar round, and he'd taken almost all of it. There wasn't a hell of a lot of him left, and what there was wasn't pretty.

"That you, Sarge?" one of the stretcher bearers called.

"Yeah." Chester forced out the word through clenched teeth.

The corpsman jumped down into the hole. He swore softly when he saw what had happened to Monroe, then turned to Chester. "How much of that blood is yours and how much is the other poor bastard's?"

"Beats me." Chester looked down at himself. He was pretty well drenched in the lieutenant's mortal remains. He didn't want to let go of the leg, though, or more of what soaked him would be his. He was much too sure of that. "Can you stick me and bandage me or put on a tourniquet or whatever the hell you're gonna do? This hurts like a son of a bitch."

"Right." The corpsman jabbed Chester with a morphine syrette, then said, "Lemme see what you caught." Blood flowed faster when Chester took his hand away from his calf, but it didn't spurt. Frowning, the corpsman went on, "I think we can get by without a tourniquet." He bandaged the wound, watched how fast the gauze turned red, and nodded to himself. "Hey, Elmer! Gimme a hand here, will ya? Let's get the sarge outa this hole."

"Sure." The other corpsman hopped down in there, too. "Fuck," he said when he got a look at the platoon commander's ruined corpse. "Who was that, anyways?"

"Lieutenant Monroe," Chester answered, a certain dreamy wonder in his voice. The painkiller hit hard and fast.

"He got it quick, anyhow," Elmer said, about as much of a eulogy as anyone ever gave Thayer Monroe.

Despite the morphine, Martin howled when the grunting corpsmen got him up on flat ground. Mortar rounds were still landing not far away. A few fragments whistled by. Chester didn't want to get hit again. But he didn't want to stay at the front, either. With another grunt, the corpsmen carried the stretcher on which he lay, back toward the Rappahannock.

A white powerboat with big Red Crosses took him and the medics over the river. The Confederates weren't supposed to shoot at such vessels, any more than they were supposed to shoot at ambulances. Accidents did happen, though.

When he got back to the field hospital, the first thing a doctor did was give him a shot. "Tetanus," the man said. By then, Martin wouldn't have cared if it was French dressing; he was feeling very woozy indeed. The doctor cut away his trouser leg and the bandage and looked at the wound. He nodded thoughtfully. "Not too bad, Sergeant. If it heals clean, you'll be back on duty in a few weeks."

"Terrific," Chester said, more or less at random.

He got some more shots, these to numb the leg while the doctor sewed him up. Eyeing him, the man asked, "Did you have a Purple Heart in the last war?"

"Yeah. Oak-leaf cluster. Hot damn," Martin answered.

"Heh." The doctor sounded more tired than amused. He wrote notes on a form, then tied it to Chester's wrist. "Orders for your disposition," he explained.

"Yeah," Chester said again. He'd always known the Army ran as much on paperwork as on bullets and canned rations.

He got stuffed into an ambulance and sent north up roads cratered by shellfire. Despite morphine and local anesthetic, the jolts made him groan and curse. His partner in misery, a PFC with a bandaged shoulder, was still very groggy from whatever he'd been under, and didn't seem to feel a thing. Martin envied him.

The military hospital was up near the Potomac. Like the power-boat, like the ambulance, it was painted a dazzling white and had Red Crosses on the walls and roof. Chester would rather have been farther away, but Confederate bombers reached all the way up to New York City and Boston, just as U.S. warplanes had recently flown from New Mexico to unload hell on Forth Worth and Dallas.

A briskly efficient nurse in starched whites got him into a bed. "We'll have to clean you up," she remarked.

"That'd be nice," he said vaguely. All he knew was that he wasn't going anywhere for a while. And not going anywhere suited him fine.

Abner Dowling could have done without a summons to report to War-renton, Virginia. That Daniel MacArthur wanted to see him did not fill his heart with joy. Instead, the news filled him with apprehension. He feared it meant MacArthur had come up with another scheme for dis-comfiting the Confederates. The only thing wrong with MacArthur's schemes that Abner Dowling could see was that they didn't work.

MacArthur kept coming up with them, though. He had an end-lessly fertile, endlessly inventive mind. If only he'd had a better sense of what was practical . . . Well, in that case he would have been some-one else. Dwelling on it seemed pointless, which didn't always stop Dowling.

The general commanding made his headquarters in a house differ-ent from the one he'd occupied the last time Dowling came to Warren-ton. Then he'd chosen the fanciest place in town for his own. Perhaps knowing his habits, the Confederates had knocked that house flat—not while he was in it. Dowling tried not to think about whose war effort they would have helped more if they'd got MacArthur as well as the building.

Not that MacArthur's current residence was anything to sneeze at. Having lost the most impressive place—and, no doubt, thereby endeared its owner to the USA for ever and ever—the American general had chosen the next grandest for his own: another Classical Revival home from before the War of Secession. Sandbagged machine-gun nests and a thicket of barbed wire around the place detracted from the air of quiet elegance the colonnaded entranceway tried to project.

Sentries gave Dowling a careful once-over before letting him inside the perimeter. Some of them carried Confederate-made submachine guns in place of bolt-action Springfields. "You really like those better?" Dowling asked a corporal who toted one of the ugly little weapons.

"Yes, sir, for what I'm doing here," the noncom told him. "Wouldn't care to take it up to the front. Not enough range, not enough stopping power. But for putting a lot of lead in the air right up close, you can't beat it."

"All right." That struck Dowling as a well-reasoned answer. He did inquire, "What does General MacArthur say about your using a Confederate weapon?"

"Sir, he says he wished we made one as good."

That also struck Dowling as a cogent comment. He wondered how MacArthur had come up with it. But that was neither here nor there. He walked on toward the house: Greek refinement surrounded by modern barbarity. But then, considering some of the things Athens and Sparta did to each other during the Peloponnesian War, the Greeks had surrounded refinement with their own barbarity.

One of MacArthur's staff officers, a captain as lean and probably as swift as a greyhound, met Dowling at the door. "Please come with me, General," the bright young man said after saluting. "General MacArthur is eagerly awaiting your arrival."

Eagerly? Dowling wondered. What could make MacArthur eager to see him after the way they'd quarreled? Was the commanding general going to cashier him? Dowling resolved to fight like hell if MacArthur tried. He hadn't done anything wrong, and he thought he'd done more things right than his superior.

"Here we are—in the map room," the captain murmured. Daniel MacArthur had had a map room in the other house he used for a headquarters, too. If he'd had the sense to read the maps instead of just having them . . .

"Good afternoon, General," MacArthur said. A cigarette— Confederate tobacco, by the smell—burned in the long holder he affected. He also affected an almost monastically plain uniform, one whose only ornaments were the stars on his shoulder straps. Custer, by contrast, had made his clothes more ornate and gaudy than tightly interpreted regulations would have allowed. Both approaches had the same purpose: to call special attention to the man wearing the uniform.

"Reporting as ordered, sir," Dowling said, and waited to see what happened next.

"You were the one who discovered the Confederates were thinning their lines in front of us here in Virginia."

By the way MacArthur said it, he didn't think Dowling's discovery would go down in history with Columbus'. His tone declared that Dowling might have been found picking his nose and wiping his finger on a trouser leg. Ignoring that, Dowling replied, "Yes, sir, I was the one. I'm sorry you discovered we couldn't take advantage of that at Fredericksburg."

He'd told the exact and literal truth there. He *was* sorry the U.S. attacks hadn't succeeded. If they had, MacArthur would have become a hero. That wouldn't have filled Dowling with delight. Custer was already a hero when Dowling got to know him. When the pompous windbag became a bigger hero, that didn't delight Dowling, either. It hadn't broken his heart, though. Custer's success had meant the USA's success. MacArthur's would mean the same thing. Dowling prided himself on his patriotism. *I'd admire a skunk who helped my country.* He eyed MacArthur in a speculative way.

MacArthur was looking back, also in a speculative way. He was, no doubt, trying to tease an insult out of Dowling's remark. But Dowling hadn't said anything like, *Only a blind jackass would have tried to break the Confederates' line at Fredericksburg.* He might have thought something like that, but MacArthur couldn't read minds—and a good thing, too.

Ash almost as long as the first joint of a man's thumb fell from MacArthur's cigarette. The general commanding ground it into the expensive-looking rug. That was bound to make whoever owned the place love him even more than he did already. He lowered his voice to a portentous whisper: "I think I know where they've gone."

"Do you, sir?" Dowling was ready to get news or gossip from anybody, even MacArthur. "Where?"

"To the west." Yes, the general commanding sounded portentous, all right. Half a dozen Old Testament prophets could have taken lessons from him.

Once Dowling had the news, it didn't strike him as improbable. "What are they going to do there?" he asked.

"I doubt they'll dance around the Maypole and strew flowers over the landscape," MacArthur replied.

"Very funny, sir." Dowling lied dutifully. Why not? He'd had practice. "But I did wonder whether they were going to push toward Toledo and Detroit or go east toward Cleveland and Akron and—what's the name of the place?—Youngstown, that's it." He felt proud of visualizing the map.

"Ah." Daniel MacArthur nodded. He took another cigarette from his pack, stuck it in the holder, and lit it. With his prominent nose and his jowls wattling an otherwise thin face, he reminded Dowling of a chain-smoking vulture. "That, I must tell you, I do not know. If the budding Alexanders at the War Department do, they have not seen fit to impart that information to me."

Dowling snorted. He was little more fond of the functionaries at the War Department than MacArthur was. He realized he'd acquired his attitude from George Custer. That realization didn't thrill him, but also didn't change his mind. He said, "In case they do attack in the West, what's the best thing we can do here?"

He could see he'd made MacArthur unhappy again. He needed a moment to figure out why. MacArthur didn't want to be reduced to a sideshow. He wanted to be the main event. But even MacArthur could see he wouldn't be the main event if major fighting erupted in the West once more. Reluctantly, he said, "Keep the enemy as busy as we can, I suppose. If you see a better choice, point it out to me."

"I'm afraid I don't," Dowling said. What was the world coming to when one of Daniel MacArthur's proposals made sound military sense?

"Very well. I may call on your corps to try to break through the Confederate defenses and threaten Richmond," MacArthur said now.

I failed at one end of my line, so I'll try the other. That was what it amounted to. Dowling gave a mental shrug. MacArthur had the right to ask that of him—and the busier the Confederates were in Virginia, the smaller their chance to send even more men west. With a little luck, they might even have to bring some back. Dowling said what needed saying: "Of course I'm at your service, sir. Whatever you require of me, I'll do."

Nothing made Daniel MacArthur happier than unhesitating obedience. He looked quite humanly pleased as he answered, "Thank you, General. That was very handsomely said."

For once, Dowling made his farewells without getting the impression of breaking off an artillery duel. As he headed for his green-gray motorcar, another one—a bright blue civilian Olds—pulled up alongside it. A woman not far from his own age got out. Her hair was the pinkish white peculiar to aging redheads. She moved with a brisk spryness that belied her years.

"Hello, Colonel Dowling. No, excuse me—hello, General Dowling. I didn't expect to see you here," she said. "Got a cigarette?"

A broad smile spread over Dowling's face. "Hello yourself, Miss Clemens. I sure do. Here you are." He pulled the pack from his pocket and handed it to her.

"Thanks." Ophelia Clemens lit one and sucked in smoke. Then she stuck out her hand. When Dowling took it, she gave his a firm pump and let it go. The formalities satisfied, she nodded toward MacArthur's headquarters and asked, "So how's the Great Stone Face?"

One of the reasons Dowling had always liked her, as a reporter and as a person, was that she said what was on her mind. He, of course, did not enjoy the privilege of being outside the chain of command. He answered, "General MacArthur seems well."

"Oh, yeah?" she said. "Then how come he's dumb enough to keep feeding troops into a meat grinder like Fredericksburg?"

"I'm afraid I'm not the one to answer that, since he is my superior and since my corps is stationed at the other end of our line." Having said what any loyal subordinate ought to say, Dowling couldn't resist adding, "If you need to know his views, you'll have to ask him yourself."

"That's what I'm here for," Ophelia Clemens said, and Dowling wanted to hug himself with glee. Unlike a lot of correspondents, she had no patience with bloated egos or double talk. She had cut through Custer's pompous bluster like a regiment of barrels going through Sioux Indians. He didn't think she'd have any trouble doing the same with MacArthur. Then she surprised him by asking, "And how have *you* been?"

"Oh, tolerable. Yes, tolerable's about right." Dowling batted his eyelashes at her. "I didn't know you cared."

She was taking a drag, and choked on it. She went alarmingly red. Dowling had to pound her on the back. When she could talk again, she wheezed, "God damn you, General—you caught me by surprise."

"Sorry, Miss Clemens." Dowling more or less meant it.

"A likely story," she said, sounding more like her herself. "You're just trying to get rid of me so you don't have to answer questions about how things got screwed up this time."

"I thought you already had all the answers," he teased.

She shook her head. "Not yet. But I aim to get 'em." With determined stride, she advanced on Daniel MacArthur.

The *Townsend* slid over the improbably blue waters of the tropical Pacific as smoothly as if Japanese airplanes had never bombed her. As George Enos, Jr., swabbed her deck, he looked over the side every now and again to see if he could spot the feathery wake of a periscope.

When he did it once too often to suit a petty officer, that worthy barked, "Enos, you're goldbricking. You think your eyeballs are gonna spot something our hydrophones miss?"

"Probably not." George knew better than to make a challenge too blatant. "But you never can tell, can you?"

"I can tell when you're goofing off," the petty officer said. After the one growl, though, he went off to harass somebody else. George's answer held enough truth to let him wiggle off the hook.

He swabbed conscientiously for a while, in case the petty officer came sneaking back and caught him doing too close to nothing. He wasn't terrified of the man, the way some ordinary seamen were. For one thing, he was in his thirties himself; the other man didn't put him in mind of an angry father. For another, he'd been yelled at by experts on the *Sweet Sue*. What was one more fellow with a big voice? Getting along was easier, but one more bawling-out wouldn't be the end of the world.

Fighters buzzed overhead. These days, American ships didn't sail out of range of land-based aircraft from the Sandwich Islands. Somebody in Honolulu, or perhaps somebody back in Philadelphia, had finally had a rush of brains to the head. George wished that would have happened sooner. The *Townsend* would have been better off for it.

Or maybe it wasn't such a rush of brains. About fifteen minutes later, the destroyer's klaxons hooted for general quarters. George threw the mop into the bucket and ran for his antiaircraft gun. He didn't know whether the skipper had spotted an enemy submarine or aircraft or just had a case of the galloping jimjams. That wasn't his worry. Being ready to do his little bit to keep the ship safe was.

He got to the twin-40mm mount just ahead of Fremont Dalby. If you were ahead of your gun chief, you were doing all right. "You know what's going on?" Dalby panted.

"Nope. All I know is, I run like hell when I hear the siren," George answered.

Dalby chuckled. "Long as you do know that, what you don't know doesn't matter anywhere near as much."

The rest of the sailors who served the gun took their places within another minute or so. The *Townsend*'s intercom crackled to life: "Now hear this. We have detected aircraft approaching from the northwest. Y-ranging gear says we have about fifteen minutes. Assistance from more land-based airplanes is promised. That is all." A pause. "Do your duty and all will be well."

George laughed a sour laugh. "'All will be well.' Yeah—unless we get blown to kingdom come, anyway."

"I'd like to see those Army assholes get more fighters out here in fifteen minutes, too," Dalby added. "Matter of fact, I *would* like to see it, but I'm not gonna bet the damn farm."

Two other destroyers cruised with the *Townsend*, a reconnaissance in force north of Kauai. The American powers that be wanted to tell the Japs the Sandwich Islands weren't going to be their ham and cheese on rye. That was what the American authorities wanted to say, yeah, but they were liable to be offering the patrol up as an hors d'oeuvre.

Fritz Gustafson kept things short and to the point: "Give me lots of ammo. Can't do much without it." There was a loader's notion of practicality.

As usual, the time between the call to general quarters and the appearance of enemy fighters seemed an eternity and an eyeblink at the same time. One of the 40mm mounts on another destroyer opened up. Tracers tiger-striped the sky. Shells burst here, there, everywhere. The only trouble was, George couldn't spot any airplanes but the U.S. fighters.

"Spring fever," Dalby said scornfully.

"Better too soon than too late," Gustafson said. That was thoroughly practical, too.

And then everybody spotted the Japs. The American fighters zoomed toward them. All three destroyers put up a curtain of antiaircraft fire. Japanese fighters rushed ahead to hold the enemy away from the torpedo-carriers and dive bombers they shepherded. Almost at the same time, two fighters plunged into the Pacific. One carried the Rising Sun, the other the eagle in front of crossed swords.

George pointed. "Torpedo bomber, coming at us!"

He didn't think he'd ever seen anything so ugly in all his life. In fact, the airplane carrying the torpedo under its belly—offset slightly to the left—was smoothly streamlined. The torpedo itself was a straight tube with a bluntly curved nose and with fins at the stern: a splendid piece of industrial design. But it was designed to sink his ship and to kill him. If that didn't make it ugly in his sight, nothing could.

Streams of tracers converged on the Japanese aircraft. George wasn't the only one who'd spotted it. The pilot had to fly straight and low to launch his fish. That left him a perfect, and perfectly vulnerable, target while he did it. He was a brave man; he did what he'd been trained to do. His airplane exploded into fire. But the torpedo was in the water by then.

"HailMaryfullofgracetheLordiswiththee—" George prayed in a rapid gabble. The prayer he chose took him by surprise. He'd turned Catholic because Connie made it plain she wasn't about to marry him if he didn't. He hadn't thought he took it seriously, not till now. Somebody'd said there were no atheists in foxholes. The deck of a ship under torpedo attack evidently counted.

The *Townsend* was a greyhound of the sea, capable of well over thirty knots. Why, then, did she feel as if she were nailed in place? The heeling, surging turn she made might have been filmed in slow motion. It might have been, but it wasn't. It took her out of harm's way, for the torpedo raced past her stern.

"Thank you, Jesus." Fritz Gustafson used words as if he had to pay for them. He packed a lot of meaning into those three.

Meatballs on its wings and fuselage, a Jap fighter shot up the destroyer. Bullets clanged and snarled and whined in wild ricochets. Wounded men screeched. Every antiaircraft gun on the ship tried to knock the pilot into the Pacific. He darted away just above the wavetops, untouched or at least still flying.

Fremont Dalby gave credit where it was due: "He's a motherfucking son of a bitch, but he's a motherfucking son of a bitch with balls. I hope he gets home."

"I don't." George was not inclined to be chivalrous.

Then, suddenly, the sky was full of airplanes—airplanes blazoned with the American eagle and swords. They threw themselves at the Japs. The Army was on the ball after all. Ignoring the enemy fighters where they could, the fighters bored in on the torpedo-carriers and dive bombers—those were the ones that could sink ships. The Americans outnumbered the Japanese aircraft. Before long, the Japanese decided they'd had enough and flew off in the direction from which they'd come.

No dive bombers had attacked the *Townsend*. George was pretty sure of it. Even near misses kicked up great columns of water and threw splinters of bomb casing every which way. He couldn't have ignored anything like that in his singleminded ammunition-passing . . . could he?

One of the other destroyers hadn't been so lucky. Black, greasy smoke poured from her. A bomb had burst near her bow. She wasn't dead in the water, but she couldn't do much more than crawl. Even as he watched, her starboard list got worse.

Sailors bobbed in the water not far from her. The bomb blast had blown them off her deck. Some—corpses—floated face down. Others struggled to stay above the surface. Still others, in life jackets, didn't have that worry.

As the *Townsend* swung toward her stricken comrade, the exec's voice blared from the intercom: "All hands! Lower lines and nets and life rings for rescue!"

Sailors rushed to obey. The other destroyer slumped lower in the water. They weren't going to be able to save her. Men started coming up on her deck from below. Some of them helped wounded buddies. They were going to abandon ship.

"That could be us," George said.

He didn't realize he'd spoken aloud till Dalby nodded. "That damn near was us last year," the gun chief said. "We pick up these sorry bastards and then figure out what to do next."

Pausing to take on survivors carried risks of its own. If a Japanese submersible prowled these waters, the *Townsend* would be a sitting duck for it. George thought of his father. But the senior George Enos thought the war was over when his destroyer went down. George, Jr., knew better. Again, he kept an eye peeled for periscopes. This time, no one reproved him. He was a long way from the only sailor doing the same thing.

"Pull hard, you lazy fuckers! Put your backs into it! Haul that line!" a petty officer screamed. By his orders, he might have been serving aboard a nineteenth-century ship of the line. But the destroyer's men weren't swinging from one tack to the other; they were bringing a sailor up on deck.

He clung to the rope for dear life. His feet thudded against the side of the ship. "God bless you!" he gasped when he came aboard. He got down on hands and knees and puked his guts out. Nobody could possibly have blamed him for that; he was covered from head to foot in heavy fuel oil, so that he looked as if he'd just escaped from a minstrel show. But if you swallowed much of that stuff, it would kill you as surely as a bullet would. Heaving up your guts was one of the best things you could do.

"Ain't this a fuckup?" one of the rescued men said as he stood there dripping. "Ain't this just a grand fuckup? We wanted to see if there was Japs there. We found out, all right. Didn't we just?"

Didn't we just? The mournful words echoed inside George's head. He turned to Fremont Dalby and said, "I wonder if we'll be able to hang on to the Sandwich Islands."

"We wouldn't have any trouble if the Japs were the only thing on our plate," Dalby said. "We could lick 'em easy enough. But this is the ass end of the goddamn war. Whatever they can spare from fighting the CSA and the big mess in the Atlantic and holding Canada down—whatever they can spare, we get that."

"It's not enough," George said.

Dalby shrugged. "They haven't thrown us out yet. They're not fighting anybody else, either. But the Sandwich Islands are even harder for them to get at than they are for us."

"I guess so." George knew he sounded dubious. He felt dubious. He'd seen too much to feel any other way. And if he hadn't, one look at the draggled survivors from the other destroyer would have been plenty to show him.

*   *   *

Hipolito Rodriguez packed his worldly goods into a duffel bag. He didn't know how many times he'd done that when he was in the Army during the last war—enough so that he hadn't lost the knack, anyhow. Shouldering the duffel wasn't as easy as it had been then, though. A lot more years had landed on him since, and almost getting electrocuted hadn't helped.

All the same, he managed. Some of the other guards from the Confederate Veterans' Brigades were in no better shape than he was. They managed, too. If you couldn't manage, you shouldn't have been here at all.

"Well done, men," said Tom Porter, the troop leader—essentially, the top sergeant. "God knows we do need to fumigate these barracks—we've got more bugs in 'em than you can shake a stick at. I'm not telling you one goddamn thing you don't already know."

"Got that right," a guard drawled. He mimed scratching—or maybe he wasn't miming. Rodriguez had found out about delousing stations during the Great War, too. They'd changed a little since then—a little, but not nearly enough.

"It's all them niggers' fault," another guard said. "They's filthy, and we git their vermin."

He was bound to be right about that. The rank smell of Camp Determination was always in a guard's nostrils. Put lots of unwashed men and women together with Texas heat and humidity and it was no wonder you raised a bumper crop of every kind of pest under the sun.

The exterminators were a cheerful crew who'd come west from Abilene. BUGGONE! their trucks said. On the side of each was painted a man walking up to an overgrown cockroach. He had a mallet behind his back; the roach wore an apprehensive expression.

"Y'all got dogs or cats or canaries or snakes or goldfish or whatever the hell still in the building?" one of the men asked, fumbling in the breast pocket of his coveralls for a cheap cigar. "Better get 'em out if you do, on account of this stuff'll kill 'em deader'n shit."

A couple of the guards did have pets, but they'd taken them out. When the exterminator lit that cheroot, one of Rodriguez's comrades asked him, "You gonna kill the bugs with the smoke from that goddamn thing?"

Laughing, the fellow answered, "How'd you guess? Now our secret's out."

He and his crew covered the barracks with an enormous tent of rubberized cloth. They could make it as big as they wanted; squares of the stuff zipped together. Rodriguez admired that—it struck him as good design.

One of the squares had a round hole in it that accepted the tube from the machine that pumped the poison into the tent: again, good design. The exterminators didn't leave anything to chance, any more than the people who'd designed Camp Determination had done. A small gasoline engine powered the machine, which was hooked up to a gas cylinder with a large skull and crossbones painted on it.

Rodriguez had seen poison-gas cylinders during the last war. He asked the fellow with the nasty cigar, "You use chlorine or phosgene? I remember how chlorine kill all the rats in the trenches. More come later, though." The trenches had been heaven on earth for rats and mice.

"Nah, this here is a different mix," the exterminator told him. "It's stronger than any of the stuff they used back then."

"*Bueno,*" Rodriguez said. "This means, maybe, the bugs don't come back for a while once you kill them?"

"Maybe," the man answered. By the way he hesitated before he said it, Rodriguez decided he meant *no.* Sure enough, he continued, "We get paid to kill all the little bastards that're in there now. What happens after that . . . If you leave out ant syrup and spray Flit around and keep the place clean so you don't draw roaches, you'll do pretty good. And you can always call us out again."

"*Bueno,*" Rodriguez repeated, more sourly this time. Like undertakers, exterminators weren't likely to go out of business anytime soon.

The engine came to noisy life. Whatever was in the gas cylinder started going into the tented barracks hall. Rodriguez got a tiny whiff of something that smelled sort of like mothballs but a hell of a lot stronger. That whiff was plenty to convince him he didn't want to breathe any more of it. He moved away from the barracks in a hurry, and noticed the exterminators had already put some distance between themselves and their machinery.

"How soon can we go back in after y'all leave?" a guard asked one of the Buggone people.

"You folks did leave the windows and doors open so the place can air out?" the exterminator asked in return. The guard nodded. The exterminator said, "Well, in that case you oughta be safe goin' in there tonight—say, after ten."

Several guards swore. Rodriguez gave a mental shrug. Some things you just couldn't help. What was the point of getting all excited about those?

"Wish we could fumigate the damn niggers like they was bugs," a guard said.

Unfortunately for him, he said it where Tom Porter could hear him. The underofficer reamed him out for it: "Goddammit, Newcomb, watch your fool mouth. This here is a transit camp. It ain't nothin' else but a transit camp. You let the idea get out that it *is* somethin' else and you turn the devil loose. Do you want that? *Do* you? Answer me when I talk to you, goddammit!"

"No, Troop Leader," Newcomb said hastily.

"Then shut up, you hear me? Just shut up," Porter said, and put his hands on his hips like an angry parent scolding a five-year-old. "You've all heard this shit before. To hell with me if I know what's so hard about keeping your damnfool mouths shut, but y'all leak like a pail with a hole in it. We got to keep the niggers in camp tame, or we buy ourselves all kinds of shit. They go wild on us, we got to watch our backs every second like they did in the camps in Mississippi and Louisiana. Y'all want that? *Do* y'all?" Now he was yelling at every guard in earshot.

"No, Troop Leader," they chorused, Rodriguez loud among them.

"All right, then," the troop leader said, at least partly mollified. "Try and remember. You're makin' your own lives easier if you do."

When Rodriguez patrolled the camp—either the men's or the women's half—he tried to watch his back every minute anyway. He didn't know anybody who came from the Confederate Veterans' Brigade who didn't. Anybody who'd lived through the last war had seen for himself that not having eyes in the back of your head was a good way to end up dead in a hurry. Some of the younger fellows, the men who'd been Party stalwarts or guards but hadn't actually known combat, were the ones who strolled through the compounds without a visible care in the world. Sooner or later, one of them would get knocked over the head. That might teach the others some sense. Rodriguez hoped it would, anyhow.

His shift was on the women's side today. He would have gone up with the window shade if he'd accepted all the favors offered him. The women figured their lives could be easier if they had a guard on their side, and they knew what they had to give to get one. If he wanted favors like that, he could have them. When they got thrown in his face half a dozen times a day, he mostly didn't want them.

"These nigger bitches is all whores," opined his partner, an Alabaman named Alvin Sprinks.

"It could be," Rodriguez said. He didn't think it was, at least under most circumstances, but he didn't feel like arguing. Life was too short.

A couple of guards with submachine guns at his back, Jefferson Pinkard prowled through the women's camp. Rodriguez had seen how his wartime buddy made his own rounds in Camp Determination, going where he wanted to go when he wanted to go there. That was just an extension of the rule of watching your back all the time. To a man of Pinkard's rank, the whole camp was his back.

"You think we get a lot of pussy thrown at us? Man, what about him?" Sprinks sounded jealous. Rodriguez only shrugged. If they tried to give you more than you wanted or could use, who cared how much more than that they tried to give you?

Pinkard spotted him, waved, and made a sudden left turn to head his way. The guards tramped along behind him like a couple of well-trained hounds. "How you doin', Hip?" the camp commandant called.

"Not bad, sir. Thank you." Rodriguez was always careful to show respect for his friend's rank. Nobody'd called him *Hip* since the Great War ended; it was the sort of nickname only an English-speaker would use. From Pinkard, it didn't bother him; it reminded him of the days when they'd been miserable side by side.

"Your barracks got fumigated this morning—ain't that right?" Pinkard asked.

"Yes, *Señor* Jeff." In spite of himself, Rodriguez was impressed by Pinkard's grasp of detail. Nothing went on in Camp Determination that he didn't know about, often before it happened.

"Bet you'll be glad to get rid of the bugs," Jeff said.

"Oh, yes, sir." Rodriguez nodded. "But it is like anything else, *sí*?" He had the brains not to talk directly about the way the camp worked, not where *mallates* could overhear. "One batch goes away, but before long there is another."

"Yeah, well, then we'll call out those Buggone folks one more time and do it all over again. We'll—" Pinkard broke off. He looked around the women's half of Camp Determination. Then he looked back at Hipolito Rodriguez. "Son of a bitch," he said softly. "*Son* of a bitch!"

"What is it?" Rodriguez asked.

"Don't rightly know yet," Jeff answered. "Might be nothin'. But it might be somethin' big, too. You never can tell till you go and find out. If it is, I promise you I'll get you what you deserve for it. Don't want you to be like Chick Blades, who never did find out what he came up with."

Rodriguez scratched his head. "What you mean, *Señor* Jeff?"

"Never mind. Don't worry about it. It happened a long time ago, back in Louisiana." Pinkard shook his head, as if at something he didn't want to remember but couldn't forget. He gathered himself. "You got to go on with your rounds, and so do I. See you later. Freedom!" Off he went, his guards in his wake.

"What the devil was that all about?" Alvin Sprinks asked.

"I don't know," Rodriguez said truthfully. "The commandant, he has an idea, I think."

"Reckon so." Despite agreeing, Sprinks sounded doubtful. The next idea he had would be his first. He could read and write—Rodriguez didn't think there were any guards who couldn't—but he didn't like to.

"When we gonna git outa this place?" a gray-haired colored woman asked as the guards started through the camp again.

"Soon, Auntie, soon," Rodriguez answered. Alvin Sprinks nodded solemnly. Rodriguez thought he would laugh or give the game away in some different fashion, but he didn't. Maybe the troop leader had put the fear of God in him, at least for a while. He might not have his own ideas, but he could get them from someone else.

IX

Waiting for the balloon to go up was the hardest thing a soldier did. Back in 1914, Tom Colleton had waited eagerly, even gaily, confident the war would be won and the damnyankees smashed before the cotton harvest came in. Everything would be glorious. Three years later, he was one of the lucky ones who came home again, glory quite forgotten.

The new war *had* smashed the USA, had split the country in two. That he was up here by Sandusky, Ohio, proved as much. Like Jake Featherston, like everyone else in the CSA, he'd assumed that splitting the United States meant winning the war. There was a lesson there, on what assumptions were worth, but he didn't care to dwell on it.

"This time for sure," he muttered.

"Sir?" asked an improbably young lieutenant commanding one of the companies in his regiment. He should have had a more experienced officer in that slot, but the replacement depot hadn't coughed one up. Reinforcements were coming into Ohio, which was good. Even with them, though, not every hole got filled.

Tom wished the damnyankees had the same problem. He envied them their manpower pool. Confederate soldiers mostly had better weapons. He thought, and was far from alone in thinking, Confederate soldiers were better trained. Every one of them was worth more in combat than his U.S. counterpart. But Jesus God, there were a hell of a lot of Yankees!

He needed to answer the youngster. "This time for sure," he repeated. "When we hit the U.S. forces this time, we've got to knock them out of the war. We've got to, and we damn well will."

"Oh, yes, sir!" said the shavetail—Tom thought his name was Jackson. It was a safe bet, anyway; about one in every three Confederate soldiers seemed to be named Jackson. "Of course we will!"

He hadn't been at the front very long. He could still think about— could still talk about—inevitable victory, the way Confederate wireless broadcasts did. Tom knew better. He thought the Confederates still had a good chance of doing what they wanted, but a good chance wasn't a sure thing. Anyone who'd ever lost a hand with a flush knew all about that.

"We'll see pretty soon," he said.

Lieutenant—Jackson?—said, "How can we lose?"

Colleton put a hand on his shoulder. "I said the same damn thing when I came to the front at the start of the last war. I would have been a little older than you are now, I suppose, and then I spent all the time that came afterwards finding out how we could lose. I just hope like hell that doesn't happen to you."

"It won't." Jackson sounded supremely confident. "We got stabbed in the back last time. Niggers won't have the chance to do that now. The Party's going to take care of 'em, but good."

He really believed that. To a certain extent, Tom did, too, but only to a certain extent. He said, "We would have had a better chance if they hadn't risen up—sure. But there's something you've got to remember, or you'll go home in a box and never find out how the latest serial ends: the damnyankees can fight some, too."

"Yes, sir." Jackson's tones were those of a well-brought-up young man too polite to correct an elder who's said something obviously foolish. "But they're just doing it on account of their government makes 'em."

"Where did you hear that?" Tom asked, sending him a curious stare.

"In school. Everybody knows it."

Is this what they're teaching my children, too? Tom wondered. *God help us if it is.* Gently, he asked, "Haven't you ever noticed that not everything they teach you in school is true, and that a lot of things 'everybody knows' aren't true at all?"

"No, sir, can't say that I have," Jackson answered after serious, earnest, and very visible consideration.

He meant that, too. For the first time, Tom found himself frightened for the younger generation in the CSA. If this was what they learned . . . "Lieutenant, there's something you have to understand, because it's the Lord's truth. The Yankees don't like us any better than we like them. They don't need the government to make them fight. They'd do it anyhow, on account of we jumped them. Next time we interrogate some prisoners, you listen in. You'll see."

"I'll do that," Jackson said. "But they'll just spout the nonsense their higher-ups told them. They're—what's the word? They're indoctrinated, that's it." He looked pleased with himself for remembering.

And you're not? Tom wondered. He couldn't ask, though. Jackson might see other people's indoctrination. His own was to him like the air under its wings to a butterfly. He didn't think about it. He didn't notice it. He just floated on it and let it support him.

Not far behind them, artillery rumbled. Things were starting to pick up. The Confederate gunners fired barrages to east and west, to keep the U.S. soldiers posted in front of them from guessing which way they would move when the time came. Tom wished the men in green-gray didn't know the time was coming. *Wish for a million dollars while you're at it,* he thought. The Yankees weren't blind men. The Confederate buildup had been as subtle as the soldiers with wreathed stars on their collars could make it, but you couldn't hide everything no matter how hard you tried.

The Confederates were doing their best. As Tom walked up toward the front, he passed barrels—both the older model and the new—crouching under camouflage netting with leaves and sod applied to make them as nearly invisible as possible. They'd moved up under cover of darkness; the orders against moving by daylight were explicit to the point of bloodthirstiness. More C.S. artillery fire had masked the sound of their advance. The damnyankees had used that trick in the last war. Imitation was the sincerest form of flattery. With luck, it would be the best revenge, too.

"Get low, you damn fool, before somebody shoots you!" The raucous advice came from a foxhole by the side of the path. Only the two stars on each side of Tom's collar that marked his rank showed he was an officer. He'd deliberately dulled them, so the Yankees' snipers wouldn't single him out. Evidently his own men couldn't single him out, either.

And getting low was good advice almost any time. Tom hit the dirt and crawled toward the foxhole. U.S. artillery started coming in before he got there. The crawl turned into an undignified scramble.

"Jesus!" The private already in it sounded disgusted. "This fucker ain't big enough for two." Then he noticed Tom's rank badges. "Uh, sir."

He wasn't wrong, even if he was rude. Tom took his entrenching tool off his belt and started digging like a mole after forty cups of coffee. "Just have to make it bigger," he said. He added the dirt from his excavation to the breastwork in front of the hole.

"Huh," the soldier said in surprise. "Didn't know officers knew how to handle one o' them things."

"If I didn't, I would have got killed when I was your age," Tom answered, glad to pause and pant. "Ever hear of the Roanoke front?"

"Sure as hell did. Uncle Lucas came back without most of his arm on account of he was there." The soldier paused, taking longer than he should have to make the connection. "You was there, too?"

"That's right. I'm sorry about your uncle. I never got more than a few scratches myself—I was lucky."

"Better believe you was." The private might have said more, but the scream of an incoming shell warned it would come down somewhere close. He and Tom both ducked. The explosion was close enough to make the ground shake. Fragments maliciously whined and screeched overhead. A few clods of dirt pattered down into the hole, but nothing worse.

On the Roanoke front, that one shell would have been the harbinger of many more, and only extraordinary luck and a hole better than this one would have kept a man from getting maimed or killed. Things were quieter here. The damnyankees had shifted a lot of their weight to Virginia. What was left was good enough to hold the Confederates in place and harass them, but not to work the wholesale slaughter that had been so common in the Great War.

The United States didn't seem to have figured out that the Confederate States were shifting men out of Virginia and sliding them back over here. Nothing made Tom happier than their continued ignorance. The more the Yankees fussed and fumed in the East, the less attention they'd pay to anything out here. If they stayed ignorant till morning after next . . .

They did. The real Confederate barrage started an hour before sunrise. It was thunderous enough to wake Tom. After all the gunfire he'd slept through at the front in two wars—and in fighting the Negroes after the first one—that was no mean feat. Freight-train noises traveled the rails of the sky from west to east.

Yankee counterbattery fire started almost at once. The U.S. soldiers weren't fools. He'd said as much to Lieutenant Jackson. (Absently, he wondered whether Jackson still lived. He thought so, but he hadn't had any reports from that company for most of a day.) They knew trouble when they walked into it. One after another, though, their guns fell silent, battered into submission by a heavier weight of metal.

The Confederate barrage let up precisely at sunrise. Its purpose was to stun, not to kill everything on the U.S. side of the line. Three years of bloody experience had taught the CSA and the USA that they couldn't kill all their enemies, or even enough of them, with big guns alone. And a really heavy artillery preparation, one that went on for days, ruined the ground over which attackers would advance and slowed them down. Less gunnery amounted to more.

Confederate barrels rumbled and rattled and clanked forward. Tom scrambled up out of his hole. He had an officer's brass whistle, and blew a long, shrill blast on it. "Come on, you lazy sons of bitches!" he yelled. "We've caught 'em by surprise, and now we'll make 'em pay. Watch your buddies and follow me!"

An officer who told his men to follow him could almost always get them to obey. An officer who told troops to advance but sat tight himself had a lot more trouble. The only thing wrong with officers of the first sort was that they got shot a lot more often than the others.

If you thought about things like that . . . Tom resolutely didn't. If everybody thought about things like that instead of being afraid to act like a coward in front of his buddies or his men, war would become impossible. The machine-gun fire in front of him said this war remained altogether too possible. Not all the damnyankees were stunned—far from it.

Asskickers screamed down out of the sky to bomb strongpoints the C.S. artillery hadn't silenced. For the moment, the dive bombers—and the Confederates—had it all their own way. Dazed U.S. soldiers threw up their hands and hoped the advancing men in butternut would let them surrender instead of just shooting them and moving on. *Just like last year,* Tom thought, and wondered if that was good or bad.

* * *

When Brigadier General Irving Morrell's train pulled into the Broad Street Station in Philadelphia, he couldn't have been in a worse mood if he'd tried for a week. The endless delays on the trip north from Virginia did nothing to improve his temper. Between bomb damage and rail sabotage, the trip took three times as long as it should have. All he missed was getting the train strafed from the air. But he could have flown up in the Army's fastest fighter and still arrived ready to bite nails in half.

Colonel John Abell met him at the station. That didn't make him any happier, even if the colorless General Staff officer was the one who'd let him know he'd finally earned stars on his shoulder straps.

"Goddammit, Colonel, I'm not a Ping-Pong ball, you know!" Morrell exploded. He almost said, *God damn you, Colonel.* He suspected Abell was responsible for getting him pulled out of Virginia, and he intended to raise Cain about it.

For the moment, Abell was imperturbable. "Consider it a compliment, sir," he answered, his voice—an unmemorable baritone—never rising. "We always try to send you where the country needs you most."

That took some of the wind out of Morrell's sails, but only some. "I'm not a fire brigade all by myself," he pointed out. "Where are my fire engines? Where are my firemen? Where's my . . . hook and ladder?" At the last possible instant, he left off the participle.

"Come with me, sir," Abell said, still mildly. "We'll give you our estimate of the situation in Ohio, and then we'll send you West to—"

"Make bricks without straw," Morrell broke in. The General Staff officer looked pained. How he looked wasn't a patch on how Morrell felt. "I've already tried that in Ohio, thank you very much. Are you going to see if history can repeat itself? And are you setting me up to take the fall if it does? It can't be *your* fault, after all."

By *you* he didn't mean Abell's alone, but all the officers in Philadelphia who thought of war as theory and maps and not as cordite and burning barrels and mangled men. They were good at what they did. Because they were, they thought they knew everything there was to know about the business of organized slaughter. Morrell had a different, and lower, opinion.

"We're both on the same side, sir," Abell said. "We've flushed out several traitors—some of them planted long, long ago—and more no doubt remain in place. But no one has ever questioned your loyalty or patriotism."

"That's white of you, by God," Morrell said.

"Making things as difficult as possible is another story," Abell snapped, his iron control rusting a little at last. "Will you come with me to the War Department, please? We can't hash things out here on the platform."

"I'll come," Morrell replied, and he did.

He and Abell had little to say to each other on the short ride through central Philadelphia. The de facto capital looked more battered every time Morrell saw it. The War Department had taken several hits since the last time he was there. Abell remarked, "Much of what we do these days is underground. We dig like moles."

"You've had your heads in the ground for a long time," Morrell observed, and bright patches of red burned on Abell's sallow cheeks. Morrell went on, "Tell me about the new Confederate barrels. How long will we have to wait before we've got anything like that?"

The General Staff officer got redder. *Amazingly lifelike,* Morrell thought. "Production of an improved model is expected to begin within the next few weeks," Abell said stiffly.

That was better than Morrell expected. He'd feared the USA would have to design anything new from scratch. Even so, he asked, "How late will the improved model be if the Confederates take Pittsburgh away from us? How much of our steel production would that cost?"

"We are hoping . . . sir . . . that that will not happen," Abell answered. "We are hoping you will help keep that from happening. That's why we're sending you to Ohio."

"Why you're sending me *back* to Ohio," Morrell corrected, and had the somber satisfaction of seeing John Abell flinch. To rub it in, he murmured, "Youngstown. Akron. Cleveland."

"They haven't taken Cleveland this past year!" Now Abell sounded truly furious. "What makes you think they can take it now?"

"They weren't trying before," Morrell said. "They wanted to split us, and they did. Now they want to cripple us."

"If you're telling me this is hopeless, General, someone else will be appointed. Your resignation will be accepted. You will be permitted to return home to your wife and daughter. Not just permitted— encouraged."

Will be appointed. Will be accepted. Will be permitted. Abell didn't say who would do any of those things. He probably didn't even think about it. In his world, things just happened, without any particular agency. That made him a good bureaucrat. Whether it made him a good soldier was a different question.

Morrell wanted to go home to Agnes and Mildred—but not that way. "Sorry, no. If you want to get rid of me, you'll have to throw me out. I'm telling you it would have been a lot easier if we'd started getting ready when the Confederates did."

"Hindsight . . ." But Abell's voice lacked conviction. Morrell had been saying the same thing when it was foresight. Abell gathered himself. "We're almost to the map room. You'll see what we're up against there."

Except for lacking windows, the map room could have been three stories above ground instead of two stories below it. A haze of tobacco smoke hung in the air. It also smelled of coffee that had been perking for too long and bodies that had gone unwashed for too long. That last odor pervaded the front, too, so Morrell nodded, as at an old friend, when he recognized it here. The stench of death, at least, was mercifully absent.

Officers were poring over large-scale maps of Virginia and Ohio. John Abell led Morrell to one that covered the eastern part of the latter state. Morrell let out a tuneless note of dismay when he saw where the pins with the red heads were. "They've come that far this fast?"

"I'm afraid it looks that way," John Abell answered.

"Jesus," Morrell said. "They're *already* inside Cleveland. I thought you told me they couldn't take it."

"They must have revised this since I went to meet you at the station," Abell said unhappily.

"Are the Confederates moving *that* fast?" Morrell asked.

"They can't be." Abell spoke with less conviction than he might have liked. "It's just signal lag, I'm sure."

"It had better be," Morrell said. "Well, what do you expect me to do about it? Have we got armor here?" He pointed. "If we do, we can thrust toward the lake and try to cut through their advancing column—do to their supply lines what they've done to us."

"I don't believe we have enough equipment in place there to give us much hope of success," Abell replied.

"Why am I not surprised?" Morrell didn't bother to keep his voice down. Several officers studying other maps looked up at him. He scowled back at them, too furious to care. They looked away. Fury wasn't an emotion they were used to seeing here. *Too bad,* Morrell thought savagely. He turned back to John Abell. "Well, if we can't do that, our next best move is pretty obvious."

"Is it?" The General Staff officer raised an almost colorless eyebrow. "It hasn't seemed that way here."

Morrell almost asked why he wasn't surprised again. Then, remembering the old saw about flies and honey and vinegar, he didn't. He pointed again instead, this time along the lakeshore, from Cleveland over to Erie, Pennsylvania. "We'll have to fight like hell here. We'll have to fight like hell in all the built-up places—barrels aren't really made for street fighting in the middle of towns."

"They can do it," Abell said.

"Sure they can," Morrell agreed. "Dogs can walk on their hind legs, too, but it's not what they're *for*, if you know what I mean. Send barrels through a few good-sized towns and you won't see very many come out the other end."

"Suppose they bypass them." Abell might have been back at West Point, trying to solve a tactical problem. "That's what they did last year. They didn't go into Columbus with armor. They got it in a pocket and attacked with infantry and artillery."

"That's why we defend the towns along the lake like mad bastards," Morrell said. "They can't surround them the way they surrounded Columbus. They have to take them instead, and that's more expensive. If they don't, we can resupply and reinforce by water, maybe break out and get into their rear. They'll know that—they can read maps." *Unlike some people I could name.*

John Abell drummed his fingers on the side of his thigh—from him, the equivalent of another man's jumping up and down and waving his arms and yelling his head off. "This would involve cooperation with the Navy," he said at last. By the way he said it, he might have been talking about eating with his fingers. The Army always had the feeling that the Navy didn't quite pull its weight. Here, though . . .

Morrell shrugged. He had that feeling himself. There'd been no great naval coups in this war, nothing like the capture of the Sandwich Islands. Indeed, the Navy seemed to be losing those islands a few at a time. Even so, he said, "This is something they can do," and hoped he told the truth.

Rather than replying, Abell pulled a notebook from a breast pocket and scribbled in it. "You . . . may be right," he said when he put the notebook back. "It's a, ah, more indirect approach to defending the interior regions than we'd had in mind. What happens if you're wrong?"

"I'll probably be too dead to worry about it," Morrell answered. Abell blinked—no, he didn't think about things like leading from the front. Morrell went on, "But whoever takes over for me will have a couple of things going for him. Either the Confederates won't have taken all the lakefront, or they'll have fought their way through it. If they haven't, he can hit them in the flank. If they have, with luck they'll be bled white and they'll have a tougher time getting to Pittsburgh—if that's where they're going."

"That is the current assessment," Abell said primly.

Bully. But, again, Morrell swallowed the old-fashioned slang before it came out. He and the desk warriors of Philadelphia might not agree on means, but they did on ends. If he were Jake Featherston and he wanted to try to knock the USA out of the war, he would have gone after Pittsburgh, too. Pontiac was the other possibility. Engine production, though, was more widely dispersed than steel. And without steel, you couldn't make engines for very long, either.

"We'll do what we can, Colonel," he said.

"We have to do more than *that,*" John Abell exclaimed.

Morrell started to laugh, then checked himself yet again. Abell hadn't been joking. Morrell looked at the map again. Abell had no reason to joke, either.

Dr. Leonard O'Doull had thought that pulling out of Fredericksburg would cut U.S. casualties. And so it would, no doubt, in the long run. In the short run . . . In the short run, the Confederates on the heights gleefully bombarded the withdrawing men in green-gray. They'd knocked out the pontoon bridges over the Rappahannock more than once, knocked them out and then poured shellfire into the men stuck near them waiting to cross.

"I hate artillery," O'Doull remarked as he worked to repair a mangled leg. He'd thought at first that he would have to take it off. Now he hoped this corporal would be able to keep it, and thought he would, too, if he didn't get a wound infection that spread to the bone.

Across the table from him, Granville McDougald nodded. "The wounds are a lot nastier than anything a bullet can do, aren't they?"

"They're more likely to be, anyhow." O'Doull had seen horrors from both. A lot of the very worst horrors, he'd never seen at all. They were reserved for front-line soldiers and stretcher bearers and Graves Registration personnel. No one could hope to repair some wounds. God almighty would have had trouble repairing some men hit by artillery fire for the Resurrection.

"Get that bleeder there, Doc," McDougald said, and O'Doull did. The bald medic went on, "I thought you were crazy when you said you were going to try and patch this leg. I'd've just reached for the bone saw myself. But you may get a good result out of it. My hat's off to you." He doffed an imaginary chapeau.

"I hope so—and thanks." O'Doull yawned behind his surgical mask. Granville McDougald chuckled, recognizing the expression. O'Doull added, "Jesus, but I'm tired."

"I believe it. This just never ends, does it?"

"Doesn't seem to," O'Doull said. "Now they'll probably ship us back to Ohio, eh? That would give us a few days of vacation."

"Oh, boy," McDougald said in a hollow voice. "We're getting plenty of practice going back and forth, anyway."

They were still joking about it when the corpsman brought in another wounded man. They both fell silent at the same time. All O'Doull said was, "Get him under fast, Granny." McDougald nodded and put the ether cone over the soldier's face. Even that wasn't easy; he'd lost part of his nose. He'd also lost a chunk of his upper jaw and a bigger chunk of his lower jaw. He made horrible gobbling noises nothing like words.

"Can you fix him, Doc?" one of the corpsmen asked. The fellow gulped afterwards, and O'Doull had a devil of a time blaming him. This was another artillery horror, and viler than most.

Before answering, O'Doull told MacDougald, "Get a blood-pressure cuff on him, and watch his airway, too—don't want him drowning on us."

"Right." The medic handled his end of the business with quick but unhurried competence. "BP is 110 over 70," he reported a few seconds later. "He's got a strong pulse, the poor bastard."

"He would," O'Doull said morosely. He nodded to the stretcher bearer then. "I don't think he's going to up and die on us, but I'm not sure we're doing him any favor keeping him alive."

"Yeah." The corpsman looked away. With the best will in the

world, with the best plastic surgery in the world—which, odds were, the wounded soldier wouldn't be lucky enough to get—people would be looking away from the man on the table for the rest of his life. Did he have a girlfriend? A wife? Would he still, once she saw him? Did he have a little boy? What would Junior make of Daddy with half a face?

"Gotta try," McDougald said, and O'Doull nodded. Some men were tough enough to come through something like this not only sane but triumphant. Some had people around them who loved them no matter what they looked like.

Most, unfortunately, didn't.

Knowing that made O'Doull more hesitant than he wished he were. He did what he could to clean the wound, trim away smashed tissue and bone, and make repairs where and as he could. Then he shot the man full of morphine and told McDougald, "Put him under as deep as he'll go, Granny. He won't want to be awake once he finally is. Let's put off the evil minute as long as we can."

"No arguments here. Back at a field hospital, they'll get him all bandaged up so he won't have to look at—that—right away. If they know what they're doing, they'll break it to him gently."

"Yeah," O'Doull said tightly, and let it go at that. Field hospitals were almost as frantic as aid stations. Would the people farther back of the line have the time to think of gently breaking the news of this man's mutilation? Even if they did think of it, would they have the time to do it? Or would they treat him as one more body that took up a valuable cot till they could send him somewhere else? O'Doull didn't know, but he knew how he'd bet.

Granville McDougald straightened and stretched. "I'm gonna have me a cigarette," he announced, and headed out of the tent.

"Sounds good to me." Leonard O'Doull didn't want to look at or think about that operating table for a while. The Virginia countryside wasn't much of an improvement, not battered and bludgeoned by war as it was, but mutilated meadows were easier to bear than mutilated men.

McDougald held out a pack of Confederate cigarettes. O'Doull gladly took one. The veteran noncom gave him a light. He drew in smoke. Here, he almost wished it were the harsh stuff that came from U.S. tobacco. Wanting to choke would have done more to distract him than this rich-tasting smoothness.

Off to the south, artillery rumbled. Nothing was coming down close by. He thanked the God he was having ever more trouble believing in. "Bad one," he said.

"Now that you mention it—yes. Don't see ones like that ever day, and a good thing, too." McDougald exhaled a thin gray stream of smoke. "You fixed him up as well as anybody could have, Doc."

"I know. And he'll still look like something they wouldn't put in a horror movie because it would *really* scare people." O'Doull took a flask off his belt and swigged from it, then offered it to McDougald. He didn't usually drink when he might be operating again in another couple of minutes. This time, he made an exception. You *didn't* see ones like that every day.

"You can do things now you couldn't begin to in the last war," McDougald said after a swig of his own. "Thanks, Doc. That hits the spot. Where was I? Yeah—you really can. Get him to where he looks like—"

"A disaster and not a catastrophe," O'Doull finished for him. "Come on, Granny. There's not enough left to fix. I've seen a lot of wounds, but that poor fucker made me want to lose my lunch."

He tried to imagine writing Nicole a letter about what he'd just done. That was cruelly funny. He wouldn't—couldn't—have written it even if the censors would have passed it. He always wrote her in French, but they would have found somebody who could read it. But you couldn't subject anyone you loved to even the shadow of what you went through when you were in combat or where you could see what combat did to men. His letters to his wife and son were bright, cheerful lies. When somebody at the aid station said something funny, he would pass that along, especially if it stayed funny in French. Otherwise, he just said he was well and safe and not working too hard. Lie after lie after lie. He didn't know anyone who tried to tell the truth, not about this kind of thing.

McDougald ground out the cigarette under his heel and lit another one. "Days like this, I wonder why I stayed in the Army," he said.

"I wonder why I came back," O'Doull agreed.

"Oh, no, Doc. Oh, no. You did more for that guy than I ever could have. You're good. I'm not bad—I know I'm not bad—but you're *good.*"

"Thanks, Granny. I'm not good enough, not for that. Nobody's good enough for that." O'Doull muttered something under his breath.

Even he wasn't sure if it was curse or prayer. He went on, "Is there any point to all this?"

"For us? Sure," Granville McDougald answered. "If not for us, a lot of guys would be a lot worse off than they are. What we do is worth doing. For the whole thing? I'm not the one to ask about that, sir. If you want to cross the lines and talk to Jake Featherston . . ."

"If I ever ran into Jake Featherston, I'd smash his head in with a rock, and screw the Hippocratic oath," O'Doull said. McDougald laughed, for all the world as if he'd been kidding. He hadn't, not even a little bit. In plaintive tones, he added, "Featherston went through the last war, every goddamn bit of it. Wasn't that enough for him?"

"When you lose, a war is never enough," McDougald answered. That probably held an unfortunate amount of truth. "You happen to recall what Remembrance Day was like before the Great War?"

O'Doull grunted, because he did. The United States, twice beaten and humiliated by the Confederates and Britain and France, had had a lot to remember. The regimentation, the constant stinting to build up the Army and Navy, the tub-thumping speeches, the parades with the flag flown upside down as a symbol of distress . . . He sighed. "So we finally won. So what did it get us?" He waved. "This."

"What would we have got if we lost?" McDougald asked. "Something better? Something worse? Christ, we might have grown our own Featherston."

"*Tabernac!*" O'Doull said, startled into the Quebecois French he'd used for so long. "That's a really scary thought, Granny."

The medic only shrugged. "When things go good, everybody laughs at people like that and says they belong in the loony bin. But when times get hard, they come out of the woodwork and people start paying attention. You go, 'Well, how could they make things any worse? Let's see what they can do.'"

"Yeah. And then they go and do it," O'Doull said. Featherston wasn't the only one of that breed running around loose these days, either. *Action Française* and King Charles had mobilized France even sooner than the Freedom Party grabbed the reins in the CSA. And in England, Churchill and Mosley were yet another verse of the same sorry song.

"It's a bastard," McDougald said. "Except for bashing in Featherston's brains, to hell with me if I know what to do about it. And it might even be too late for that to do any good. By now, this mess has a life of its own."

"Some life." The aid station was close enough to the front to share in the smell of the battlefield. O'Doull knew what death smelled like. He lived with that odor—not always heavy, but always there. When war was alive, that smell always got loose.

"Doc! Hey, Doc!" Stretcher bearers hauled another wounded man toward the tent with the big Red Crosses on the sides. Leonard O'Doull and Granville McDougald looked at each other. Maybe they could save this one. Maybe he wouldn't be horribly mangled. Maybe . . . They'd find out in a minute. Shaking their heads, they ducked back into the tent.

Appointments, appointments, appointments. Jake Featherston had started to hate them. They chewed up his time and spat it out. When he was talking with people, he couldn't do the things that really needed doing. He even resented Ferdinand Koenig, and if Ferd wasn't a friend he didn't have any.

Today, a smile lightened the Attorney General's heavy features. "That Pinkard fellow's given us a new line on things," he said. "We may be able to dispose of more niggers faster than we ever dreamed we could."

"Oh, yeah?" Sure as hell, that piqued Jake's interest. "Tell me about it." Koenig did. The more Jake listened, the more intrigued he got. "Will this shit work?" he asked. "Do we make it in bulk now, or would we have to run up a new factory to get as much as we need?"

"That's the beauty of it," Koenig answered. "They already use the stuff to fumigate houses and such. There's a company in Little Rock—Cyclone Chemicals, the name of the place is—that makes it by the ton. They aren't the only one, either. They're just the biggest."

"Well, I will be a son of a bitch. Pinkard's chock full of good ideas, isn't he?" Jake said. "Promote him a grade and tell him to see what he can do to try this out as fast as he can. We've got a big job ahead of us, and we're going to need all the help we can get."

"I'll do it." The Attorney General wrote in a notebook he pulled from a breast pocket. Half apologetically, he said, "I've got so much going on, I lose things if I don't write 'em down. Forget my own head if it wasn't nailed on tight."

Jake laughed. "I know what you mean. Boy, don't I just? But stay on that one, Ferd. Taking care of the niggers is just as important as licking the Yankees. Anything else I ought to know about?"

"Reports I get from here and there, grumbling about the war is up a little."

"We'll deal with it." Jake muttered to himself. Things were dragging on longer than he'd told the country they would. That made propaganda harder than it should have been. "New offensive's going well," he said, looking on the bright side. "I'll talk with Saul, too, see if we can't figure out a way to perk up morale. Anything besides that?"

"Don't think so." Big and ponderous, Koenig rose to his feet. "I'll get on the telephone to Pinkard right away."

"Yeah, you do that." Featherston got up, too, and walked to the door with him. As Koenig left, Jake asked, "Who's next on the list, Lulu?"

"A Professor FitzBelmont, Mr. President," his secretary answered. Working underground fazed her not at all. Jake suspected working underwater wouldn't have fazed her, either.

"FitzBelmont . . ." The name was vaguely familiar. And then, with a good politician's near-total recall for people, Jake remembered exactly who Professor Henderson V. FitzBelmont was. He groaned. "Oh, for God's sake! The uranium nut. How did *he* get another appointment?"

"Do you want me to tell him it's been canceled, sir?" Lulu asked.

"No, no," Jake said resignedly. "If he's out there cooling his heels in the waiting room, he'll raise a stink if you send him home now. Fetch him in. I'll get rid of him as quick as I can."

Professor FitzBelmont was as rumpled and tweedy as he had been the year before. "Good to see you, Mr. President," he said.

"Likewise," Jake lied. "What's on your mind today, Professor? Kindly cut to the chase—I've got a lot to do."

"You will remember, sir, that I told you that uranium—uranium-235, that is—has the potential to make an explosive thousands of times as strong as dynamite."

"I do recollect, yeah. But I also recollect it'd cost an arm and a leg, and you weren't sure how long it'd take or whether you could do it at all. Has anything changed since then? Better be something, Professor, or I won't be real happy with you. I haven't got time to waste."

Henderson V. FitzBelmont licked his lips and nervously fiddled with his gold-framed spectacles. "In terms of what we know about uranium itself, not much *has* changed." Jake started to growl angrily, but FitzBelmont plowed ahead anyway: "But I do know, or I can make a good guess, that the United States are probably looking at this same question."

"How do you know that?" Featherston rapped out. Professor Fitz-Belmont had found a way to make him pay attention, all right.

"For one thing, their journals have suddenly stopped mentioning uranium at all. For another, there are large engineering works in the northwestern USA that appear consistent with an effort along these lines."

"And how do you know *that?*"

"I was asked by C.S. Intelligence to identify buildings in photos," the professor replied. "No doubt because of my previous visit to you, those officers knew of my interest in that field. And if I were to build a plant for producing enriched uranium, it would look something like what the United States are building in Washington."

"All right." Featherston surprised himself by how mildly he spoke. Every once in a while, somebody who looked and sounded like a nut turned out not to be one after all. This felt like one of those times. "If the damnyankees are interested in this uranium stuff, too, there must be something to it. That's what you're telling me, isn't it?"

"I don't know, sir, not for sure. I don't know whether we can isolate U-235, how long doing it would take, or how much it would cost. There also seems to be a possibility that U-238 can be transmuted—"

"Can be what?" Jake wished the prof would stop talking like a prof.

"Changed," FitzBelmont said patiently. "Maybe it can be changed into another element that will also explode. Theory seems to suggest the possibility. I know less about this than I do about U-235. There is much more U-238, so the second possibility would be advantageous to us. But I am certain of one thing."

"Oh? And what's that?" Jake asked, as the physics professor surely wanted him to do. Usually, he manipulated. Not today; not right now.

Henderson V. FitzBelmont moved in for the kill, an intellectual tiger on the prowl: "If the enemy succeeds in acquiring this weapon and we do not, I fail to see how our cause can avoid disaster."

Jake thought about it. Twenty thousand times as strong as TNT? One bomb and no more city? The USA with eight or ten of those bombs and the CSA with none? A fleet of Yankee bombers had done horrible things to Fort Worth and Dallas, catching the Texas towns by surprise. That wouldn't happen again. The officer who'd been asleep at the switch now made his reports in hell; those bombers had made him pay for his mistake. But if the USA didn't need a fleet of bombers, if one airplane would do the job . . . Nobody could stop every single goddamn airplane.

"Figure out what you need, Professor," Jake said heavily. "Money, machinery, people—whatever it is, you'll get it. I want the list as fast as you can shoot it to me. No more than two weeks, you hear?"

"Uh, yes, sir." FitzBelmont sounded more than a little dazed. He lost a point in Jake's book on account of that. If he'd really believed in this, he would have pulled that list out of his briefcase now. Maybe he hadn't believed he could persuade the President of the CSA. Featherston hoped that was it.

He accompanied FitzBelmont out of his subterranean sanctum, as he had Ferd Koenig a little while before. After the physics professor left, Jake turned to Lulu and said, "Get on the horn to General Potter. Tell him I want to see him here ten minutes ago."

"Yes, Mr. President." She didn't bat an eye. She never did. "Can I tell him what this is in reference to?"

"Nope. I'll take care of that when he gets here."

"Yes, Mr. President." Lulu knew what was always the right answer.

Featherston endured a delegation of Freedom Party officials from Alabama and Mississippi going on about how they needed more men and more guns to help keep their smoldering Negro rebellions from bursting into flames. Since Jake couldn't possibly give them more men, he promised them more guns, and hoped he wasn't crossing his fingers on the promise. They seemed satisfied as they went away. Whether he could keep them satisfied . . . *I'll do my goddamnedest, that's all.*

Clarence Potter came in next. Somebody in the waiting room down the hall was bound to be madder than hell. *Too bad,* the President thought. Without preamble, he barked, "What do you know about Henderson V. FitzBelmont and uranium?" *Sweet Jesus Christ,* he thought. *Till FitzBelmont came here last year, I'd never even heard of the shit. I wish I still hadn't.*

"Ah," Potter said. "Has he convinced you?"

"He sure as hell has," Jake answered. "How about you?"

"I'm no scientist," Potter warned. Jake made an impatient noise. Potter made an apologetic gesture. "Yes, sir, he's convinced me, too. Sooner or later, somebody's going to be able to make a hell of a bang with that stuff. If it's sooner, and if it's the damnyankees, we've got us some big worries."

"That's how it looks to me, too," Featherston said unhappily. He pointed at Potter. "How the hell did you find out about that place in Washington? That's as far from here as it can be."

"It's in the U.S. budget—a lot of money, and no details at all about what the Yankees are spending it on," the Intelligence officer replied. "Spotting the combination sent up a red flag."

"Good," Jake said. "Nice to know somebody in your outfit wouldn't blow his brains out if he farted, by God. Now the next question is, how did you get the pictures of that place for FitzBelmont to look at? I didn't think our spy airplanes could fly that far, and I reckon the USA'd shoot 'em down most of the time even if they could."

"Yes, Mr. President, I agree with you—that's what would have happened if we'd taken off from Texas or Sonora," Potter said. "And we would have given away our interest in the area, too. So we didn't do that. Our man in western Washington rented a crop duster at a local airstrip. Nobody paid any attention to him, and he got his photos."

Jake Featherston guffawed. "Good. That's goddamn good. But we won't be able to do it again anytime soon, though."

"I wouldn't be surprised," Potter said, nodding.

"We found out what we need to know, so we don't have to worry about putting the damnyankees' backs up by trying it again," Jake said, and Clarence Potter nodded once more. The President aimed his finger like a rifle. "We've got to keep the USA from finding out that we know what they're up to, and from finding out we're up to the very same thing ourselves. Whatever your super-duper top-secret security business is, use everything you've got and then some on whatever has anything to do with uranium."

"I've already given those orders, sir," Potter said. "Minimum possible in writing, and code phrases all through instead of the name of the metal. No telephone discussion at all—never can tell who might be listening. You did that just right when you had your secretary call me."

"Thanks," Jake said. "Uranium! Who would've thunk it?" He would have bet money Henderson V. FitzBelmont was a nut. He would have bet big—and he would have lost his shirt.

* * *

Scipio felt like a ghost, rattling around in a nearly empty part of the Terry. His family wasn't the only one in the area to have survived the cleanout, but there weren't many. A few others had got advance warning, but only a few—the ones that had good connections with white folks one way or another.

Nobody knew where the people who'd been evacuated had gone— or rather, had been taken. They'd just . . . vanished. No cards, no letters, no photographs came back to Augusta. Maybe the deportees who could write didn't have the chance. Maybe the C.S. authorities weren't letting them. Or maybe they were simply dead.

For the handful who remained, life got harder. The authorities shut off electricity and gas in the depopulated areas. The water still ran. Maybe that was only an absentminded mistake, or maybe the people who ran Augusta kept it on so they could put out fires if they had to. Scipio had nobody he could ask.

He did ask Jerry Dover where the deportees went. The white man looked him in the eye and said, "I have no idea."

"Could you find out, suh?" Scipio asked. "It do weigh on my mind."

The manager of the Huntsman's Lodge shook his head. "No, I'm not about to ask. Some answers are dangerous. Hell, some *questions* are dangerous. Do I have to draw you a picture?"

"No, suh," Scipio answered unhappily. "Don't reckon you do."

"All right, then." Dover hesitated before adding, "Sometimes finding out is worse than wondering. You know what I mean?"

Had the white man not told him to bring his family when he came to work that one night, *they* would have found out. Scipio didn't think the answer would have made them happy. They might yet learn from the inside out, and so might he. He didn't want to.

Dover lit a cigarette, then held the pack out to Scipio, who couldn't remember the last time he'd seen a white man do even such a simple favor for a black. "I thanks you kindly," Scipio said. He had matches of his own. He didn't need to lean close to Dover to get a light from his cigarette; his boss might have taken that as an undue familiarity.

"Everything's gonna be . . ." Dover stopped and shook his head. "Shit, I don't know whether everything's gonna be all right. You got to do the best you can, that's all."

"Yeah." Scipio smoked with short, savage puffs. "Don't mean no offense, suh, but you got an easier time sayin' dat than I does doin' it."

"Maybe. But maybe I don't, too," Dover said. Scipio felt a rush of scorn the likes of which he'd never known. What kind of trouble could the restaurant manager have that came within miles of a Negro's? But then Dover went on, "Looks like they may pull me into the Army after all. More and more people are putting on the uniform these days."

"Oh." Scipio didn't find anything to say to that. Horrible things happened to Negroes in the CSA, yes. But horrible things could happen to anybody in the Army, too. The one difference Scipio could see was that Dover's family wasn't in danger if he went into the service. Then a fresh worry surfaced: "You puts on de uniform, suh, who take over here?"

"Well, I don't exactly know." Dover didn't sound comfortable with the answer.

"Whoever he be, he give a damn about colored folks?"

"Well, I don't exactly know that, either."

"Do Jesus!" Scipio stubbed out the butt in the pressed-glass ashtray on the manager's desk. The deceased cigarette had plenty of company. "He one o' *dat* kind o' buckra, we is all dead soon."

"I do know that," Dover said. "Other thing I know is, I can't do thing one about it. If they call me up . . ." He shrugged. "I can talk to my own bosses till I'm blue in the face, but they don't have to listen to me."

Scipio sometimes had trouble remembering that Jerry Dover *had* bosses. But he didn't own the Huntsman's Lodge; he just ran the place. He was good at what he did; if he hadn't been, he wouldn't have kept his job for as long as he had. As long as he stayed in Augusta, he had no place to move up from the Huntsman's Lodge. He would have to go to Atlanta, or maybe even to New Orleans, to do better.

Now he said, "Go on. Go to work. Get your ass in gear."

Not having anything else he could do, Scipio obeyed. Despite his worries, he got through the shift. When he went back to the Terry, he had no trouble passing through the barriers around the colored part of town. Cops and stalwarts knew who he was.

Getting back to work the next day, he found his boss in a terrible temper—not because he'd been called up but because two dishwashers weren't there when they were supposed to be. That was a normal sort of restaurant crisis, and Dover handled it in the normal way: he hired the first two warm bodies off the street that he could.

Neither of them spoke much English. They were Mexicans—not Confederate citizens from Chihuahua or Sonora, but men out of the Empire of Mexico up in the CSA looking for work. Now they'd found some, and they went at it harder than anyone Scipio had seen in a long time. They wanted to keep it.

At first, thinking of the restaurant and nothing more, Scipio was pleased to see their eagerness. He didn't blame Jerry Dover for telling the black men they'd replaced not to bother coming back to work. The look on the Negroes' faces was something to see, but the color of those faces didn't win the men much extra sympathy from Scipio. If you didn't, if you couldn't, show up, you were asking for whatever happened to you. Showing up on time all the damn time counted for more than just about anything else in the restaurant business.

That was at first. Then, coming up to the Huntsman's Lodge a couple of days later, Scipio walked past a barbershop. All the barbers in there had been Negroes; he couldn't imagine a white Confederate demeaning himself by cutting another man's hair. But now the barber at the fourth chair, though he wore a white shirt and black bow tie like the other three—a uniform not far removed from a bartender's—did not look like them. He had straight black hair, red-brown skin, and prominent cheekbones. He was, in short, as Mexican as the two new dishwashers.

Ice ran through Scipio, not when he noticed the new barber but when he realized what the fellow meant, which didn't happen for another half a block. "Do Jesus!" he said, and stopped so abruptly, the white man behind him almost walked up his back.

"Watch what you're doing, Uncle," the ofay said irritably.

"I is powerful sorry, suh," Scipio replied. The white man walked around him. Scipio stayed right where he was, trying to tell himself he was wrong and having no luck at all. He wasn't sorry. He was afraid, and the longer he stood there the more frightened he got.

For twenty years and more, Jake Featherston had been screaming his head off about getting rid of the Negroes in the Confederate States. Scipio had had trouble taking the Freedom Party seriously, not because he didn't think it hated blacks—oh, no, not because of that!—but because he didn't see how the CSA could get along without them. Who would cut hair? Who would wash dishes? Who would do the field labor that still needed doing despite the swarm of new tractors and harvesters and combines that had poured out of Confederate factories?

Whites? Not likely! Being a white in the Confederacy meant being above such labor, and above the people who did it.

But whites felt themselves superior to Mexicans: not to the same degree as they did toward Negroes, but enough. And the work blacks did in the CSA couldn't have looked too bad to people who had no work of their own. Which meant . . .

If workers from the Empire of Mexico came north to do the jobs Negroes had been doing in the CSA, the Freedom Party and Jake Featherston might be able to have their cake and eat it, too.

Scipio wasn't at his best at work that day. He was far enough from his best to make Jerry Dover snap, "What the hell's the matter with you, Xerxes?"

"Jus' thinkin' 'bout José an' Manuel, Mistuh Dover," he answered.

"They aren't your worry. They're mine. If they keep on like they've started, they're no worry at all, and you can take that to the bank. You just keep your mind on what you're supposed to be doing, that's all. Everything will be fine if you do."

"Yes, suh," Scipio said. But *yes, suh* wasn't what he meant. José and Manuel—and that barber in the fourth chair—were the thin end of the wedge. If Jake Featherston banged the other end, what would happen? Nothing good.

The restaurant manager eyed him. "You wondering if we can find some damn greaser to do *your* job? Tell you one thing: the worse you do it, the better the chances are."

That came unpleasantly close to what Scipio *was* thinking. Say what you would about Dover, he was nobody's fool. "Ain't jus' me I is worried about," Scipio muttered.

"What's that supposed to mean?" Dover asked.

"More Mexicans they is, mo' trouble fo' niggers," Scipio answered.

"Oh." Dover thought about it for a little while, then shrugged. "I can't do anything about that, you know. The only thing I care about is keeping this place going, and I'll handle that till they stick a uniform on me and drag me out of here."

He'd done everything a decent man could—more than most decent

men would have. Scipio had to remind himself of that. "Yes, suh," the
black man said dully.

"Hang in there," Dover said. "That's all you can do right this
minute. That's all anybody can do right this minute."

"Yes, suh," Scipio said again, even more dully than before. But
then, in spite of himself, his fear and rage overflowed. He let them all
out in one sarcastic word: "Freedom!"

Jerry Dover's eyes got very wide. He looked around to see if anyone else could have heard the rallying cry that, here, was anything but.
Evidently satisfied no one else had, he wagged a finger at Scipio, for all
the world like a mother scolding a little boy who had just shouted a
dirty word without even knowing what it meant. "You've got to watch
your mouth there, Xerxes."

"Yes, suh. I knows dat." Scipio was genuinely contrite. He knew
what kind of danger he'd put himself in.

Dover went on as if he hadn't spoken: "You've got a nice family. I
saw them. You want to leave them without their pa?"

"No, suh." Again, Scipio meant it. Still clucking, the restaurant
manager let it go and let him alone. He'd told the truth, all right. Here,
though, how much did the truth matter? His family, like any black
family, was all too likely to be torn to bits regardless of what he wanted.

Chester Martin couldn't have been more bored if the Confederates
had shot him. As a matter of fact, they *had* shot him, or rather, ripped
up his leg with a shell fragment. Everybody kept assuring him he would
get better. He believed it. He did feel better than he had right after he
was wounded. Thanks to sulfa powder and pills and shots, the wound
didn't get badly infected. A little redness, a little soreness on top of the
normal pain from getting torn open, and that was it.

Everybody kept telling him he'd get back to duty pretty soon, too.
He also believed that. People kept saying it as if it were good news. For
the life of him, he couldn't understand why. *Hey, Chester! The Confederates'll get another chance to maim you or kill you before too long.
Ain't that great?* Maybe he was prejudiced, but it didn't seem great to
him.

Meanwhile, he lay on a cot with the iron frame painted Army
green-gray. Once a day, he got exercise and physical therapy. The rest

of the time, he just lay there. The Army gave him better rations in the hospital than it had while he was in the field. That struck him as fundamentally unfair, but then, so did a lot of other things about the Army.

He also got his pay here. Money in his pocket let him sit in on a poker game whenever he felt like it. The only trouble was, he didn't feel like it very often. Sometimes he sat in even when he didn't much feel like it. It was something to do, a way to make time go by.

Because he didn't much care whether he won or lost, he had a terrific poker face. "Nobody can tell what you're thinking," one of the other guys in the game grumbled.

"Me? I gave up thinking for Lent," Chester said. Everybody sitting around the table laughed. And he had been joking . . . up to a point.

He'd just come back from his exercise one day when a ward orderly stuck his head into the room and said, "You've got a visitor, Martin."

"Yeah, now tell me another one," Chester said. "I'm not bad enough off to need the padre for last rites or anything, and who else is gonna want to have anything to do with me?"

The orderly didn't answer. He just ducked back out of sight. Rita walked into the room. "You idiot," she told him, and burst into tears.

Chester gaped at his wife. "What are you doing here?" he squeaked.

She pulled a tiny linen handkerchief out of her purse and dabbed at her eyes. "When I found out you got wounded, I asked the War Department where you were," she answered. "They told me, and so I got on a train—got on a bunch of trains, really—and here I am. Carl's with Sue and Otis till I get back."

"All right," Chester said dazedly. His sister and brother-in-law would do fine with his son. "Jesus, sweetie, it's good to see you."

Rita gave him a look laced with vitriol. "If you like seeing me, why did you go put that stupid uniform on again? You could have stayed in L.A. and seen me every day."

He sighed. "It seemed like a good idea when I did it." How many follies got perpetrated because they seemed a good idea at the time? Was there any way to count them? Chester didn't think so.

By the way Rita drummed her fingers against the painted iron of the bedstead, she didn't, either. "They told me you weren't hurt bad enough for them to discharge you from the Army," she said. "That means the Confederates will have to shoot you at least one more time before I get you back, doesn't it?"

"I . . . hadn't thought of it like that," Chester said, which was true.

"No? Maybe you should have." Rita could be devastating when she felt like it. "How many pieces of you will be missing when you finally do come home?"

"For all either one of us knows, I won't get another scratch the rest of the way," Chester said.

She didn't laugh in his face. She didn't say anything at all. Her silence made his remark sound even more foolish than it would have anyway. He grimaced. He knew that as well as she did.

At last, she unbent enough to ask, "How are you?"

"I'm getting better," he answered. "As soon as the leg is strong enough, they'll send me back."

"Swell," Rita said. "I thought I was going to die when I got the wire that said you'd been hurt."

"Chance I took," Chester said. "It's not that bad." That was true. He would recover, as he had when he got hit in the arm during the Great War. He'd seen plenty of men crippled for life, plenty of others torn to pieces or blown to bits.

Rita's first husband hadn't come out of the Great War alive, so she knew about that, too. "What will it be like the next time?" she demanded pointedly. "I love you. I couldn't stand getting another 'The War Department deeply regrets to inform you . . .' telegram. I'd die."

No, I would. Chester swallowed the words long before they passed his lips. Rita wouldn't find them funny. He did, but only in the blackly humorous way that didn't make sense to anyone who hadn't been through the things front-line soldiers had.

Rita came over, bent down, and laid her head on his shoulder. She really started to bawl then. "I don't want to lose you, Chester!"

"Hey, babe." Awkwardly, he put his arms around her. "Hey," he repeated. "I'm not going anywhere." He did laugh then, because that was literally true.

Almost to Chester's relief, the orderly came in then and said, "You've got to go, ma'am. Doctors don't want him tired out."

The look she gave the man should have put *him* in a hospital bed. She kissed Chester. His eyes crossed; nobody'd done that since he reenlisted. Then, reluctantly, she let the orderly lead her away.

When she'd left the ward, the guy in the next bed said, "Must be nice, getting a visit from your wife." He wasn't even half Chester's age. By pure coincidence, the two of them had almost the same wound.

"Yeah, it was," Chester said, more or less truthfully. "She sure caught me by surprise, though." That was also true.

"Too bad you don't have a private room." The kid—his name was Gary—leered at him.

"Yeah, well . . ." Chester didn't know why he was embarrassed; the same thought had crossed his mind. He went on, "If I wasn't just a noncom, if I was an officer like the snotnose whose hand I was holding, maybe I would have one. Life's a bitch sometimes."

"Would we be here if it wasn't?" Gary was a buck private. To him, a top sergeant was as exalted a personage as any officer, at least this side of a general.

"You've got a point," Chester said. Of course, instead of ending up in a military hospital, they could have ended up dead. Or they could have been maimed, not just wounded.

Or we might not have got hurt at all, Chester thought resentfully. But he knew too well how unlikely that was. If you stayed in the meat grinder long enough, odds were you'd brush up against the blades.

Gary was looking at him. "You're not a lifer, are you?"

"Me? Hell, no," Chester said. "Do I look crazy?"

"Never can tell." Gary wouldn't get in Dutch for sassing a sergeant here; the rules were relaxed for wounded men. "It's like your wife said—if you're so smart, how come you signed up for round two when you'd already been through round one?"

"We licked those Confederate bastards once, but then we let 'em up, and look what we got," Chester answered. "Millions of maniacs screaming, 'Freedom!' and out to take anything they can grab. If we don't beat 'em again, they'll damn well beat us, and then we have to start all over."

"Yeah, but why *you*?" Gary persisted. "You paid your dues the last time. You didn't have to take a chance on getting your ass shot off twice."

"You're too young to know what Remembrance Day was like before the last war," Chester said slowly. "It really was a day of remembrance and a day of mourning. Things shut down *tight* except for the parades and the speeches. Nobody who saw it could ever forget the flag going by upside down. The Confederates and the limeys and the frogs

beat us twice. We had to get tough. We had to build up if we were
going to pay them back—and we did. I don't ever want to see the country go through anything like that again."

"That talks about the country. That doesn't talk about you," Gary
said. "Me, I'm here on account of I got conscripted. But they weren't
going to conscript you." *You old fart.* He didn't say it, but he might as
well have. "So how come you volunteered to let 'em take another shot
at you? You're not Custer—you aren't going to win the war all by
yourself."

That would have been insulting if it hadn't been true. "Yeah, I
know," Chester said with a sigh. "But if everybody sat on his hands,
we'd lose. That's the long and short of it. So I put the uniform back
on."

"And look what it got you," Gary said.

"I think I did some good before I got hurt," Chester said. "I commanded a company for a while the last time around, so—"

"Wait a second," Gary broke in. "You were an officer then?"

Chester snorted. "Hell, no. Just an ordinary three-striper. But when
everybody above me got killed or wounded, I filled the slot for a while.
Did all right, if I say so myself. After a while, they found a lieutenant to
run it. If I could do that then, I didn't have any trouble helping a shavetail run a platoon this time. I'll probably do the same thing somewhere
else when they turn me loose here."

"You're like a football coach," Gary said.

"Sort of, I guess. I never even thought about coaching football,
though. I used to play it—not for money, but on a steel-mill team. We
weren't bad. We sure had some big guys—you better believe that."
Chester's eye went to the clock on the wall. It was a few minutes before
eleven. "Hey, Greek. you've got two good legs. Turn on the wireless,
why don't you? News coming up."

"Sure." The guy called Greek had one arm in a cast, but nothing
was wrong with the other.

The knob clicked. The set started to hum. Everybody waited for
the tubes to warm up. What came out of the wireless when the sound
started reminded Chester of a polka played by a set of drunken madmen. When it mercifully ended, the announcer said, "That was the Engels Brothers' new recording, 'Featherston's Follies.'" Everyone snorted;
the Engels Brothers *were* madmen. The announcer went on, "And now
the news."

"Heavy fighting is reported in and around Cleveland," a different announcer said. "The fierce U.S. defense is costing the Confederates dearly." Chester knew what that meant—the United States were getting hammered. The newsman continued, "Occupation authorities have also declared that the situation in Canada *is* under control, despite enemy propaganda." He went on to another story in a hurry. Chester didn't think *that* sounded good, either.

X

Too many things were happening all at once for Flora Blackford's comfort. None of them seemed to be good things, either. The U.S. offensive in Virginia, on which so many hopes had been pinned, was heading nowhere. The new Confederate assault in Ohio, by contrast, was going much better than she wished it were. The Mormons still tied down far too many soldiers in Utah. And the Canadian uprising, from everything she could gather, was a lot more serious than the authorities were willing to admit in the papers or on the wireless.

All in all, the Joint Committee on the Conduct of the War had plenty to do. She would rather it didn't.

And there were other distractions. Her secretary stuck her head into the inner office and said, "Miss Clemens is here to speak with you, Congresswoman."

"Thank you." Flora meant anything but. Some things couldn't be helped, though. "Send her in."

In marched the reporter. Ophelia Clemens had to be fifteen years older than Flora, but still looked like someone who took no guff from anybody. There, at least, the two women had something in common. "Hello, Congresswoman. Mind if I smoke?" she said, and had a cigarette going before Flora could say yes or no. That done, she held out the pack. "Care for a coffin nail yourself?"

"No, thanks. I never got the habit," Flora said, and then, "That's a Confederate brand, though, isn't it?"

"You betcha. If you're gonna go, go first class," Ophelia Clemens said. Flora didn't know how to answer that, so she didn't try. The reporter came straight to the point: "How many soldiers are we going to have to send up to Canada to help the Frenchies keep the lid on?"

"I don't have a number for that," Flora said cautiously. "You might do better asking at the War Department."

"Yeah, and I might *not*," Ophelia Clemens said with a scornful toss of the head. "Those people were born lying, and you know it as well as I do."

Since Flora did, she didn't bother contradicting the correspondent. "I'm afraid I still don't have the answer. Even if it's just one, it'll be more than we can afford."

Scritch, scritch. Clemens' pencil raced across a notebook page. "That's the truth—and it's a good quote. How come the Confederates can advance whenever they want to, but we keep dropping the ball?"

"If I knew that, I'd belong on the General Staff, not here," Flora said. Ophelia Clemens laughed, though she hadn't been joking. She continued, "The Joint Committee is doing its best to find out."

"Do you think keeping our generals on a red-hot grill will make them perform better?" the reporter asked.

"I hope we don't do that," Flora said.

"*I* hope you do," Ophelia Clemens said. "They'd better be more afraid of us than they are of the enemy." She waited to see if Flora would rise to the barb. When Flora didn't, she tried another question: "Is our publicity making the Confederates treat their Negroes any different—any better, I should say?"

That, Flora was ready to comment on. "Not one bit," she said angrily. "They're as disgraceful as ever, and as proud of it as ever, too."

The pencil flew over the page. "Too bad," the correspondent said. "I've heard the same thing from other people, but it's still too damn bad."

"Nice to know *someone* thinks so." Flora held up a hand. "This is off the record." She waited. Ophelia Clemens nodded. Flora went on, "Too many people on *this* side of the border just don't care, or else they say, 'The damn niggers have it coming to them.'"

"Yes, I've seen that, too," Clemens said. "All depends on whose ox is being gored. If the Freedom Party were going after Irishmen or Jews, they'd be squealing like a pig stuck in a fence." She threw back her head and let out a sudden, startling noise. She knew what a stuck pig sounded like, all right. And then, raising an eyebrow, she added, "No offense."

Flora had wondered if the older woman remembered she was Jewish. That answered that. She said what she had to say: "None taken."

"Good. Some people can get stuffy about the strangest things. Where was I?" That last seemed aimed more at herself than at Flora. Flipping pages in the notebook, Ophelia Clemens found what she was looking for. "Oh, yeah. That." She looked up at Flora. "Have you noticed there's something funny in the budget?"

"There's always something funny in the budget," Flora answered. "We're in a war. That just makes it funnier than usual."

Ophelia Clemens sent her an impatient look. "This has to do with funny business in . . ." She checked her notes again. "In Washington, that's where. Washington State, I mean. The government is spending money hand over fist out there, and I'll be damned if I can figure out why."

"Oh. That." With those two words, Flora realized she'd admitted to knowing what *that* was. She hadn't wanted to, but didn't see that she had much choice. Sighing, she said, "Miss Clemens, I don't know all the details about that, but I have been persuaded that keeping it secret is in the best interests of the United States. The less said about it, especially in the newspapers, the better."

"*You've* been persuaded?" The correspondent raised a gingery eyebrow. "I thought you were hard to persuade about such things."

"I am. I hope I am, anyway," Flora said. "This is one of those times, though. Have you spoken with Mr. Roosevelt about this business?"

"No. Should I? Would he tell me anything?" Ophelia Clemens wasn't writing now.

Flora took that for an encouraging sign. "I don't know whether he would or not. I'm inclined to doubt it," she said. "But I think he might have more to say than I would about why you shouldn't publish."

"Well, I'll try him." Clemens got to her feet. "I'll try him right now, as a matter of fact." She sent Flora a wry grin. "But you'll be on the telephone before I can get over there, won't you?"

"Yes." Flora didn't waste time with denials. "He needs to know. I told you—I do think this is that important."

"All right. Fair enough, I suppose. Nice chatting with you—turned out more interesting than I figured it would." With no more farewell than that, Ophelia Clemens swept out of the office.

No sooner had the door closed behind her than Flora was on the telephone to the War Department. Before long, she had the Assistant Secretary of War on the line. "Hello, Flora. To what do I owe the pleasure of this call?" Franklin Roosevelt inquired, jaunty as usual.

"Ophelia Clemens is on her way to see you," Flora answered without preamble. "Somehow or other, she's got wind of what's going on in Washington."

"Oh, dear. That doesn't sound so good," Roosevelt said. "I wonder how it happened."

"I don't know. I doubt she'd tell you," Flora said. "But I thought you ought to know."

"Thank you. She's a chip off the old block, all right," Roosevelt said. Flora made a questioning noise. Roosevelt explained: "Her father was a reporter out in San Francisco for a million years. He had a nasty sense of humor—funny, but nasty—and he spent most of it on the Democrats. If I remember straight, he died not long before the Great War started. Stan Clemens, his name was, or maybe Sam. Stan, I think."

"You could ask Ophelia when she gets there," Flora said. "She's on her way now, and she's not the kind of person who wastes a lot of time."

Franklin Roosevelt laughed. "Well, I'm sure you're right about that. I wonder what sort of cock-and-bull story I'll have to tell her."

"She knows at least some of the truth," Flora warned, remembering how little of the truth she really knew herself. "If what she hears from you doesn't match what she already knows, that will be worse than if you didn't tell her anything at all. Think of the headlines."

"'Boondoggle to end all boondoggles!'" Roosevelt seemed to be quoting one. He also seemed to be enjoying himself while he did it. He went on, "Where *did* that word come from, anyway? It sounds like it ought to be something a Confederate would say."

"It does, doesn't it?" Flora said. "I don't know where it's from, not for sure. I've certainly heard it. I don't think you can live in Philadelphia without hearing it."

"That's because so many boondoggles live here," Roosevelt said cheerfully.

"No doubt." Flora didn't sound cheerful, or anything close to it. "Is this project out in Washington another one?"

"If it works, no one will ever say a word about what we spent on it," the Assistant Secretary of War answered. "And if it doesn't, nobody will ever stop investigating us. I can't do anything about it either way except hope it works and do everything I can to help the people who know more about it than I do."

That sounded less encouraging than Flora wished it did, but was perhaps more honest than the usual glowing promises. She said, "I think you ought to tell Ophelia Clemens as much as you've told me"—*however much that is*—"and swear her to secrecy."

"If she'll swear *to* instead of swearing *at*." Roosevelt sounded dubious.

"She may not like the administration. She may not even like the government, no matter who's in charge," Flora said. "But I'll tell you one thing, Franklin: I promise she likes it better than she likes Jake Featherston."

"Mm, you've probably got something there," Roosevelt admitted. "No—you've definitely got something there. I think I'm going to have to call the President before I talk to her, but that's what I'll put to him. Before I go, though, I've got a question for you."

"Go ahead. What is it?" Flora said.

"Midterm elections coming up this November. Has the Joint Committee talked about how we're going to handle the House districts the Confederates are occupying? Thank God neither Senator from Ohio is up for reelection this year."

"Senator Taft"—who was from Ohio—"has said the same thing," Flora answered.

Roosevelt laughed. "I'll bet he has!"

"Right now, the plan is to let the Congressmen in occupied districts hold their seats," Flora added. "That seems only fair. And it doesn't hurt that they're pretty evenly split between Socialists and Democrats. There's even a Republican."

"Republicans." Franklin Roosevelt laughed again, this time on a sour note. "The lukewarm, the politicians who can't make up their minds one way or the other. No wonder the American people spewed that party out of their mouths."

The language was from the New Testament, but Flora understood it. She was a Jew, but she was also an American, and the USA, for better or worse—no, for better *and* worse—was a Christian country. If you lived here, you had to accommodate yourself to that reality.

Of course, the Confederacy was also a Christian country . . . and what did that say about Christianity? Nothing good, she was sure.

Clarence Potter did not care for Professor Henderson V. FitzBelmont. The dislike was plainly mutual. Potter thought FitzBelmont was a pompous stuffed shirt. Not being a mind reader, he didn't know just what the physics professor thought of him. Probably that he was a military oaf who couldn't add two and two without counting on his fingers.

That stung, since Potter reckoned himself a cultured man. He'd known a lot of military oafs in his time. To be thought one himself rankled.

His surroundings conspired against him. Instead of bringing Professor FitzBelmont back to Richmond, he, like Mohammed, had gone to the mountain—in his case, to the edge of the Blue Ridge Mountains. Washington University was in Lexington, Virginia, not far from the Virginia Military Institute—what the damnyankees called the Confederate West Point.

War hadn't come home here. It was something people read about in the newspapers and heard about on the wireless. Every once in a while, airplanes would drone by overhead. But the locals were still talking about a U.S. air raid on VMI the year before. After that calling card, the Yankees hadn't come back. For Clarence Potter, who'd watched men work on unexploded bombs and who'd spent enough time underground to get little beady eyes like a mole, this was the next best thing to paradise. The streets weren't full of rubble and broken glass. Artillery didn't rumble in the distance. The air didn't stink of smoke—and of death.

The university sat at the top of a sloping meadow at the northwest edge of Lexington. Professor FitzBelmont's office, in one of the red brick buildings with white porticoes at the heart of the campus, had a fine view of the forested mountains to the west. The professor's tweeds seemed far more appropriate here than Potter's butternut uniform.

With such patience as Potter could muster, he said, "I have to understand this business as well as I can, Professor, to be able to give my people in the United States the best possible idea of what to look for."

"Indeed." Professor FitzBelmont looked like a maiden aunt called upon to discuss the facts of life with the madam of the local bawdy-house. He looked *just* like that, in fact. He might not approve of Clarence Potter the soldier, but he definitely didn't approve of Clarence Potter the spy.

Potter nodded to himself. He'd seen that before. "Professor, there isn't a country in the world that can get along without an intelligence service. We spy on the damnyankees, yes, and you can bet your bottom dollar they spy on us, too. If they're ahead of us in this uranium business, we need to do everything we can to catch up, don't we?"

"Indeed," FitzBelmont repeated, even more distaste in his voice than he'd shown the time before.

"Sir, you were the one who brought this to the President's attention. You must have done that because you're a patriotic citizen," Potter said.

"I don't want *those people* to beat my country again." Henderson FitzBelmont packed more scorn into that than most Confederates did into *damnyankees*. He went on, "If that makes me a patriot, so be it. But if you expect me to jump up on my hind legs and shout, 'Freedom!' every other sentence, I fear you will be disappointed in me."

He was either braver or more naive than Potter had thought— maybe both. The Intelligence officer said, "I don't do that, either." Fitz-Belmont's eyebrow was eloquently skeptical. Potter continued, "By God, sir, I don't. My politics have always been Whig, and I did everything I could to keep Jake Featherston from getting elected." That was not only true, it was a spectacular understatement. He could talk about it, too, because it was common knowledge. Talking about going up to Richmond in 1936 with a pistol in his pocket was a different story. He finished, "I'm also a Confederate patriot, though. For better or worse"—*for better and worse*—"this is my country."

Professor FitzBelmont studied him, perhaps seeing the man instead of the uniform this time. "Maybe," he said at last.

"*Maybe* isn't the right answer, Professor," Clarence Potter said gently. "You can talk to me now, or you can have some less pleasant conversations with some much less pleasant people later on. Your call, either way."

FitzBelmont didn't try to misunderstand him. The physics professor did try to get huffy. "This is not the right way to get my cooperation, General. And if I don't work with you wholeheartedly, how will you go forward?"

Potter's smile, all sharp teeth, might have been borrowed from a gator. He named four physics profs at universities scattered across the CSA. Henderson V. FitzBelmont looked appalled. Still smiling carnivorously, Potter said, "Give me credit for doing my homework, please. If you were the only fellow in the country who could do this work, we couldn't compete with the Yankees anyhow, because they have so much more manpower than we do—and that includes trained manpower along with every other kind. You may be important, Professor—you *are* important—but you're not indispensable, and you'd better get used to it."

Plainly, FitzBelmont wanted to be indispensable. How many years had he been the next thing to invisible? A lot, no doubt—who paid attention to a bespectacled physics professor? Well, important would damn well have to do. With a sigh, FitzBelmont said, "Tell me what you already know."

"There are two kinds of uranium. U-235 will go boom. U-238 won't, but maybe, if you do things to it, it will turn into something else that will go boom. I don't quite follow that part. It seems like magic. But anyway, most of the uranium is 238, and it's going to be harder than hell to separate the 235 out of it." Potter paused. "How am I doing?"

"You'll never make a physicist," Professor FitzBelmont said.

"I don't want to be a physicist. That's your job," Potter said. "I want to know enough to be able to do *my* job. Tell me what my people need to look for to tell whether the damnyankees are separating 235 from 238, or if they're doing this other stuff with 238 to make it go boom."

He'd asked FitzBelmont the same thing when he first walked into the professor's office. If FitzBelmont had started talking then, he could have saved both of them some time. Potter approved of saving time wherever he could. Some people, though, had to work up to things by easy stages.

Potter had done more homework than he'd shown the physics professor; he believed in keeping a couple of hole cards hidden. All the same, once FitzBelmont did start talking he had a hard time keeping up. Gaseous diffusion, thermal diffusion, centrifuges . . .

Those were complicated enough, but what FitzBelmont called an atomic engine was worse. "Wait a minute," Potter protested. "You really change the U-238 into another element?"

"That's right." FitzBelmont nodded.

"When I went to Yale back before the last war, my chemistry professor told us transmutation was impossible," Potter said.

"So *that's* why you talk the way you do," Henderson FitzBelmont murmured. He shrugged narrow shoulders and went on, "Your chemistry professor was right, in a way. You can't transmute elements chemically. Chemistry only has to do with the electrons around the nucleus. Change the nucleus, though, and you change the atom. And nuclear processes are much more energetic than chemical ones."

"Do you have any idea how long it will take us or the Yankees to get the 235 for a bomb or to get one of your atomic engines going?" Potter asked. "Can we do it in this war? Can they?"

"Turning theory into engineering is never simple," FitzBelmont said. "The researchers in the USA must think they can do it fast, or they wouldn't be putting so much effort into it. And who knows where the Germans are? They were the ones who discovered uranium fission in the first place, after all."

"Are England and France working on this stuff, too?" Potter asked.

"I'd be amazed if they weren't. They have some talented people— more than we do, probably." The parenthetical phrase, while true, plainly made Professor FitzBelmont unhappy. It made Clarence Potter unhappy, too. It was true in more areas than nuclear physics. The Confederacy's biggest problem had always been doing all the things it needed to do with the number of white men it had to do them. Doing all of them had proved beyond its ability in the Great War. Potter had to hope it wouldn't this time around.

That one of the things the CSA's whites had to do was hold down the country's blacks made things no easier. The Freedom Party's determination to settle that mess once and for all helped justify its rule in Potter's eyes. If whites didn't have to worry about niggers, they could get on with the serious business of building the country they should have had from the beginning.

Incorporating blacks into the pool of trained manpower would also have reduced the drain on whites and on the CSA generally, but it never once crossed Clarence Potter's mind—or those of any other whites in the Confederate States. They'd experimented with colored soldiers in the Great War . . . and some of those men, who'd learned what fighting was about, remained in arms against the CSA even now. No one in authority would make that mistake again.

Potter pulled his thoughts back to the business at hand. "You don't know for a fact what the British and French are up to?"

"I'm afraid not." FitzBelmont shook his head. "Whatever it is, they'll be keeping it secret, too."

"I suppose so." Potter hesitated, then asked, "Are they likely to be ahead of us? If we get hold of them about it, will they be able to give us information that would help us move faster?"

"It's possible, certainly. I don't know how probable it is."

"Have to find out." Potter wrote himself a note. He wondered whether the British and French *would* help the Confederacy. They'd always looked on the CSA as a poor relation, a tool to keep the United States weak but never more than a local power. But if the Confederate States had this superbomb, they wouldn't be a local power anymore. "One more question, Professor: do you think the Germans are helping the United States?"

Henderson V. FitzBelmont looked at him over the tops of those gold-framed spectacles. "You are the Intelligence officer, General. Surely you would know better than I."

So there, Potter thought. The truth was, he had no idea. He didn't think anyone in the CSA did. You couldn't find an answer if you didn't know you should be asking the question.

Glancing at his watch, FitzBelmont said, "Is there anything else? I have to go to class in a few minutes. Some of the people I'm teaching will probably be working with me when we start real work on this—if we do."

"Oh, I don't think you need to worry about that, Professor," Potter said. "If the damnyankees are going full speed ahead on this, we will be, too. We can't afford not to, can we?" He imagined superbombs blowing Richmond and Atlanta and New Orleans off the map. Then he imagined them coming down on Philadelphia and New York City and Boston instead. He liked that *much* better.

Cleveland was a mess. Tom Colleton had been sure it would be a mess before his regiment got into the city. Built-up terrain was bad for barrels—too many places to ambush them. Machine-gun nests cut into the firepower edge his men had over their U.S. opponents. This was

Great War fighting: block to block and house to house. It wasn't the way the Confederates had wanted to fight this war.

Sometimes, though, you had no choice. Leaving Cleveland and its harbor untaken would have asked for worse trouble than slugging it out in the wreckage. A U.S. landing and a thrust south from the city would have played merry hell with supply lines. Meanwhile, though, a lot of good men were dying.

The only good news was that the damnyankees didn't have as many men in the city as they might have. They'd weakened their defenses to put as much as they could into Virginia, and not all the men who'd gone were back. That let the Confederates keep pushing forward despite casualties. A lot of the big steel mills and refineries on the Flats by the lake, structures that could have turned into formidable fortresses, had already fallen. The Confederate advance had touched the Cuyahoga in a couple of places, but the men in butternut didn't yet own bridgeheads on the east bank of the river.

Above the city, Confederate Hound Dogs and U.S. Wright fighters wrestled in the sky. When the Hound Dogs had the edge, Mule dive bombers screamed down to pound U.S. ground positions. When the Wrights gained the upper hand, they shot down the Asskickers before the bombers could deliver the goods.

Right now, the Confederates were on top in the air war. Maybe C.S. bombers had hit airstrips farther east, so U.S. fighters had trouble getting off the ground. Whatever the reason, Asskickers smashed U.S. positions that even barrels couldn't take out. Antiaircraft fire was heavy, but antiaircraft fire was only a nuisance. Fighters were a Mule pilot's great fear.

All the bridges over the Cuyahoga were down. Tom Colleton wondered if any bridges in the USA and the CSA *didn't* have demolition charges, ready to go up at a moment's notice. He wouldn't have bet on it.

"Sir!" A runner came back from the line, a couple of hundred yards ahead. "Sir, looks like the damnyankees are pulling back. That machine gun that was givin' us hell—it ain't there no more."

"No?" Tom's suspicions roused before his eagerness. That was natural in anyone who'd seen more than a little war. "All right," he said at last. "Send a patrol forward. *Only* a patrol, you hear me? They're liable to be setting up to bushwhack us if we get too happy."

"Yes, sir. Send a patrol forward." The soldier started forward himself. He ran hunched over, dodging from cover to cover. Any runner who lasted more than twenty minutes learned that gait. Odds were it just put off the inevitable. Few runners were likely to last out the war.

Tom waited. He ordered the regimental reserve up closer to the front. If the U.S. soldiers truly had retreated, he wanted to be in position to take advantage of it. If they hadn't . . . Well, the patrol would find out if they hadn't.

The runner came back again. "Sir, they're really gone," he reported. "We're moving up till we bump into 'em again."

"Good. That's good," Tom said. His company commanders were up to snuff. They could see what needed doing without his telling them. He would have been angry if they'd waited for orders before advancing. He turned to his wireless man. "Get back to Division—let 'em know we're up in square Blue-7."

"Blue-7. Yes, sir," the wireless man answered. When the next artillery duel started, Tom didn't want his own side's shells coming down on his men's heads. Some would anyway—some always did. But there wouldn't be so many if the gunners knew where his soldiers were.

Corpsmen wearing white smocks with the Red Cross on chest and back and helmets with the emblem painted in a white circle carried the wounded back to aid stations. "You'll be fine," Tom said more than once, and always hoped he wasn't lying.

One of the injured men wore green-gray, not butternut. The corpsmen had no doubt risked their lives to bring in the Yankee. Nobody was supposed to shoot at them, but accidents—and artillery, which didn't discriminate—happened. To be fair, U.S. medics did the same for wounded Confederates. The Geneva Convention was worth something, anyhow.

Geneva Convention or not, the smell of death filled Tom Colleton's nostrils. So did the other stenches of war: cordite and shit and blood and fear. Just getting a whiff of that sharp, sour tang made him want to be afraid, too. It struck at an animal level, far below conscious thought.

Confederate artillery might have spared his men, but gunners in green-gray didn't. Some of the shells gurgled as they flew through the air. Some of the bursts sounded . . . odd. Colleton swore. He knew what that meant. He'd known since 1915. "Gas!" he shouted, and yanked his mask out of the pouch on his belt. He pulled it on and made sure it fit snugly. "Gas!" he yelled again. This time, the mask muffled the word.

Others, though, were also taking up the cry. Somebody was beating on an empty shell casing with a wrench. The clatter penetrated the din of combat better than most other noises.

It was a hot, sticky summer day in Cleveland. It was, in fact, as hot and sticky as it ever got down in St. Matthews, South Carolina. The damnyankees had nastier winters than the Confederacy ever got, but their summers were no milder. As far as he could see, that meant they got the worst of both worlds.

Even without the mask, he didn't feel as if he were getting enough air. With it, he might as well have been trying to breathe underwater. One of the gases the Yankees used could kill if a drop of it got on your skin. People were issued rubberized suits to protect them from the menace. Tom had never ordered his men to wear those suits. He didn't know anybody who had. Especially in this weather, moving around in them steamed you in your own juices. Soldiers preferred risking the gas to dying of heat exhaustion, which more than a few of them had done.

He swore. The mask muffled the curses, too. Trust the high foreheads to come up with protection that made danger seem welcome by comparison. If that wasn't a metaphor for the futility of war in general . . .

But this war in particular had better not be futile, not for the CSA. "Tell Division we need counterbattery fire, and we need it ten minutes ago!" he shouted to the wireless operator.

For a wonder, the Confederate guns woke up in short order. Some of what they threw at the Yankees was gas, too. Even when the shells flew by far overhead, you could hear the stuff sloshing inside them. Tom laughed. If anything was worse than being an infantryman under gas attack, it was trying to jerk shells with a gas mask on. *Serves you right, you bastards,* he thought savagely. *See how you like it.*

The U.S. bombardment slackened but didn't stop. Then a flight of Mules swooped down on the Yankee gun positions. One of the Asskickers crashed in flames. Maybe it got hit; maybe the pilot didn't pull out of his dive soon enough. What difference did it make, one way or the other? But the dive bombers did a better job of silencing the artillery than counterbattery fire had.

Some Confederate barrels clattered and crunched up to the front. Fighting inside one of them was no picnic in weather like this, either, especially when they needed to stay buttoned up tight against gas. But their guns blasted the U.S. soldiers out of the positions to which they'd withdrawn.

"Come on!" Tom shouted, running forward. "We can get to the river. Maybe we can even get over the river." Before long, he caught up with the barrels, and then ran past them. Soldiers turned to stare at him. In their pig-snouted, portholed masks, they looked like the Martians in that Yankee film that had scared the pants off everybody a few years before the war. But he knew the magic words that would get them moving: "Follow me!"

That spell never failed. Men might balk at going forward alone, but they would go after an officer. Tom's heart thudded in his chest. He hoped he didn't fall over dead leading from the front. Middle-aged officers took that chance when they tried to lead young men.

To his relief, the barrels also rumbled forward. Armor and infantry working together were hard to stop. The damnyankees didn't stop them. Tom whooped. "The river!" he yelled. There was the muddy Cuyahoga, winding its way north and west toward Lake Erie. The tail of a crashed fighter stuck up from the water near the far bank.

On that far bank, U.S. troops didn't seem to know they had trouble. Tom ordered his men not to shoot across the river. He sent an urgent request back to Division for engineers with rubber boats. If they could cross in a hurry, set up a bridgehead on the far bank . . . Maybe they'd get slaughtered. Troops that tried to do too much too fast sometimes did. But maybe they'd shake the Yankees loose from the river line, too.

For a wonder, the engineers showed up in less than an hour. Soldiers piled into the boats as fast as the engineers could inflate them. The Confederates paddled like men possessed. But their foes didn't stay bemused long enough. Heavy machine-gun fire from the east bank of the river turned them back with heavy losses.

C.S. barrels waddled forward and shelled the machine-gun nests. "Let's try it again!" Tom shouted. This time, he scrambled into one of the black rubber boats himself. He'd get over the Cuyahoga or he'd probably die in it. He grabbed a paddle and thrust it into the muddy water.

The machine guns stayed quiet. The barrels had done their job, then. Rifle fire from the far bank was galling, but no worse than galling. Confederate machine guns, some on the barrels and others served by infantrymen, made the damnyankee riflemen keep their heads down.

A bullet cracked past Tom. When you heard that crack, the round came too damn close. He automatically ducked, not that it would have done him any good. Nobody thought anything less of him for ducking. Only a handful of nerveless people lacked that reflex.

Here came the far bank. "Let's go!" Tom yelled, and paddled harder than ever. As soon as the rubber boat grounded on the mud, he leaped out and ran for the closest wreckage. He threw a grenade into what looked like the mouth of a cave in case any U.S. soldiers lurked there, then dove behind a burned-out truck carcass. "Stay down!" he called to his men. "If they want you, make 'em pay for you!"

More Confederates got over the Cuyahoga. U.S. soldiers rushed up to try to wipe out the bridgehead before it got established. A mortar bomb whispered down much closer to Tom than he would have liked. Fragments of hot, jagged steel snarled through the air. Not far away, somebody shrieked—some of those fragments had snarled through flesh instead.

Asskickers that stooped on the attacking men in green-gray might have been angels in camouflage paint. Tom Colleton yelled exultantly at the chance to get killed farther east in Ohio than other Confederates had before him.

Sergeant Michael Pound approved of the way Lieutenant Bryce Poffenberger's combat education was coming. Lieutenant Poffenberger hadn't gone and killed himself yet. Even more to the point, the barrel commander hadn't yet gone and killed Sergeant Pound. Pound strongly approved of that.

What he didn't approve of were the new Confederate barrels. No, that wasn't quite true. He highly approved of them—as machines. What he didn't approve of was that the long-snouted monsters had Confederates inside them and not U.S. barrelmen.

"We could have had barrels like that," he told Lieutenant Poffenberger as they camped somewhere between Akron and Canton. "We could have had them more than ten years ago, but we didn't want to spend the money."

Incautiously, Poffenberger said, "And I suppose you were there at the creation."

"Yes, sir," Pound said—if the puppy forgot, he had to have his nose rubbed in it. "I was at the Barrel Works at Fort Leavenworth when

General Morrell—of course, he wasn't a general then, just a colonel—designed the prototype for the model we're using now. If we'd had that then, we would have upgraded long since. I'm sure of it."

Poffenberger stared at him. Firelight shone from the junior officer's wide eyes. Not for the first time, he asked the question a lot of people had asked before him: "Why the devil aren't you an officer, Sergeant?" What he meant by it was, *Why the devil aren't you out of my hair?*

"I like what I'm doing, sir," Pound replied in his best innocent tones. "Things are—looser this way."

"Hrmp," Poffenberger said, a noise that might have meant anything at all.

"If you'll excuse me, sir . . ." Pound waited to be sure the lieutenant wouldn't hold him, then walked over to the barrel. The driver, a blond from Dakota named Tor Svenson, was fiddling with the engine, wrench in one hand, flashlight in the other. Any good barrel crew did a lot of its own maintenance; the big, heavy machines operated at—or often past—the limits of engine, transmission, and suspension, and they broke down a lot even when coddled and cosseted. "What's up, Svenson?"

The driver had been so engaged in what he was doing, he needed a moment to realize somebody was talking to him. When he looked up, a smear of grease darkened one Viking cheekbone. "Oh, it's you, Sarge," he said, relief in his voice. Relief that it wasn't Second Lieutenant Bryce Poffenberger? Pound wouldn't have been surprised. Svenson went on, "You notice how the beast doesn't quite pick up fast enough when I goose it?"

"Uh-huh." Pound nodded. "Figure it's the carb?"

"Yah, but I can't find anything wrong with the son of a bitch."

"Let me have a look." With a grunt, Pound heaved himself up onto the machine so he could look down on the engine. As a matter of fact, he *did* look down on it; it wasn't powerful enough to let the barrel do everything he wished it could. He had a variety of wrenches and other tools in his coverall pockets. Some of them helped him adjust his beloved gun. The others clanked there because any barrelman who'd been at his trade for a while turned into a pretty fair mechanic.

Svenson had already partly disassembled the carburetor. Pound continued the attack with his own wrenches and, soon, a needle-nosed pliers and a jeweler's screwdriver. Svenson watched with interest, occasionally offering a suggestion. He wasn't a bad mechanic himself, but recognized Pound was a better one.

"What do you think?" the driver asked in due course.

"Looks to me like the metering rod's not quite in synch with the throttle valve, so you get that delay when you want high power," Pound answered. "I like a power jet better—less to go wrong. But we've got what we've got. Clean everything out there real well and it should be all right." He crossed his fingers.

"Yah, I'll do it, Sarge." Some of the flat vowels of Scandinavia lingered in Svenson's speech. "Thanks. I'm not sure I would've picked that up myself."

"I expect you would have." Pound didn't know whether the driver would have or not, but Svenson worked hard. He was also a man whom a pat on the back helped more than a boot in the backside. He grinned a dirty-faced grin at Pound as he started setting the delicate mechanism to rights.

When they moved out the next morning, the engine was noticeably smoother. Pound reminded himself to say something nice to Svenson when they stopped somewhere. There wasn't a lot of really open ground as they moved northwest towards Akron. Ohio was densely settled; suburbs spread from towns like tentacles. That meant a barrel commander had to have eyes in the back of his head to keep from walking into trouble.

Lieutenant Poffenberger did his best. He rode head and shoulders out of the cupola so he could look around in all directions. Staying buttoned up and using the periscopes was safer for the commander but much more dangerous for the barrel as a whole.

The open cupola also let a little fresh air into the machine. That was good; it felt hot enough in there to cook meat. At least the engine had a compartment of its own, which it hadn't in Great War barrels. Pound wiped sweat off his forehead with a coverall sleeve and thought longingly of blizzards.

Foot soldiers trotted alongside the barrels. If they started yelling about gas—or if they started putting on masks, for they might not be heard no matter how they yelled—the machine would have to button up. That would be . . . even less pleasant than it was already.

For all of Lieutenant Poffenberger's good intentions, he never saw the C.S. barrel that wrecked the one he commanded. The shot came from the side. *Wham! Clang!* It was like getting kicked by a mule the size of a *Brontosaurus*. The barrel stopped at once. The steel bulkhead between the engine compartment and the crew would hold fire at bay—for a little while.

"Holy Jesus!" Poffenberger yipped, his voice high and shrill.

"Sir, we've got to get out of here right now," Michael Pound said urgently.

"Yes," Poffenberger said. Had he said no, Pound would have clipped him and then got out anyway. Poffenberger started up through the cupola. A burst of machine-gun fire from that same Confederate barrel—or so Pound thought—made his body jerk and twitch. The lieutenant let out a thin, startled bleat and slumped back down into the turret.

He blocked Pound's escape and the loader's. Swearing, Pound heaved his body up again so he himself could get at the escape hatch on the far side of the turret. His hands left blood on the steel as he un-dogged the hatch. "Come on!" he shouted to the man who sat below him and to his left.

"What about the lieutenant?" asked the loader—his name was Jerry Fields.

"He's gone. Get moving, goddammit! Next one hits right here." Pound hauled himself out of the turret with his muscular arms. He crouched on the stricken barrel's chassis, then dropped to the ground. The loader was right behind him. They used the barrel as cover against enemy fire from the flank. Flame and black smoke boiled up from the engine compartment. That would help hide them from Confederates trying to do them in.

A hatch opened at the front of the barrel. Tor Svenson and the bow gunner tumbled out one after the other. Pound shouted and waved to them. That enemy machine gun blew off the top of the bow gunner's head. Svenson's dash turned into a limp, and then a crawl.

As Pound crouched to bandage the driver's leg, another armor-piercing round slammed into the barrel, just as he'd known it would. Ammunition started cooking off inside, the cheerful *pop-pop-pop* of machine-gun cartridges—like a string of firecrackers on the Fourth of July—mingling with the deeper roars of the shells for the main armament. The explosions blew what was left of Lieutenant Poffenberger's body off the turret. More flames and smoke burst from the cupola—including a perfect smoke ring, as if Satan were puffing on a stogie.

"How is it, Svenson?" Pound asked.

"Hurts like a bastard," the driver answered with the eerie matter-of-factness of a just-wounded man.

Pound nodded. The bullet had taken a nasty bite out of Svenson's calf. Pound gave him a shot of morphine, then yelled for a corpsman.

"Feel naked outside the machine," the loader said.

"No kidding," Pound replied with feeling. He felt worse than naked—he felt like a snail yanked out of its shell. The infantrymen around him knew how to be soft-skinned slugs, but he had no idea. The .45 on his belt, a reasonable self-defense weapon for a barrel crewman, suddenly seemed a kid's water pistol.

The war went on without him. Nobody cared that his barrel had been smashed, or that Lieutenant Poffenberger was nothing but torn, burnt, bleeding meat and the bow gunner'd had his brains blown out. Other U.S. barrels kept grinding towards Akron. For all he knew, some of them were hunting the C.S. machine that had put him out of action. Foot soldiers loped past. None of them stopped for the deshelled snails; as proper slugs, they had worries of their own.

A couple of corpsmen did come up. "All right—we'll take charge of him," one of them said. "Looks like you done pretty good."

"Thanks," Pound said. He turned to Jerry Fields. "Come on. Let's get moving."

"Where to?" the loader asked reasonably.

"Wherever we can find somebody who'll put us back in another barrel, or at least give us something to do," Pound answered. "We can't stay here, that's for damn sure."

He couldn't have been righter about that. The Confederates on the U.S. flank ripped into the advancing men in green-gray. A shell from a C.S. barrel slammed into the turret of a U.S. machine, letting him see what he'd been afraid of a couple of minutes earlier. The high-velocity round almost tore the turret right off the barrel. The men inside never had a chance. They had to be hamburger even before their ammo started cooking off.

"Jesus," Fields said beside him. "That could've been us."

"Really? That never occurred to me," Pound said. The loader, for whom sarcasm was a foreign language, gave him a peculiar look.

In the face of concentrated automatic-weapons fire, U.S. foot soldiers went down as if to a reaper. *A reaper is right—a grim one,* Pound thought. All he knew about infantry combat was to stay low. That didn't seem to be enough. He pulled out the .45, in case any Confederate soldiers got close enough to make it dangerous. It didn't seem to be enough, either.

The attack unraveled. It quickly grew obvious the U.S. soldiers weren't going to make it to Portage Lake, let alone into Akron. Instead of going northwest, they started going southeast as fast as they could. The question became whether they would be able to hang on to Canton, and the answer looked more and more like no.

Pound hated retreats. He wanted to do things to the enemy, not have those nasty bastards on the other side do things to him. But one of the things he didn't want them to do was kill him. He fired several rounds from the .45. He had no idea whether he hit anybody. With luck, he made some Confederates keep their heads down. Without luck . . . No, luck was with him, for he got back to Canton—still in U.S. hands— alive and unhurt. And as for what the powers that be came up with next—he'd worry about that later.

Although the newspapers the Confederates let into the Andersonville prison camp boasted of C.S. victories and U.S. disasters, Major Jonathan Moss didn't throw them away. That was not to say he believed them. Confederates in Cleveland? Ridiculous. Confederates in Canton? Preposterous. Confederates in Youngstown? Absurd.

And the news from more distant lands struck him as even less likely. The Japs threatening to take away the Sandwich Islands? The Russians driving toward Warsaw? He shook his head. Whoever came up with those headlines had a warped sense of humor. Only on the Western Front in Europe, where the papers admitted that Germany still had soldiers fighting, did even the tiniest hint of reality emerge.

Like the rest of the U.S. officers in the camp, though, Moss did hold on to the newspapers he got. Since the Confederates didn't issue toilet paper and Red Cross packages held only a little, the product of Jake Featherston's propaganda mills made the best available substitute.

He wasn't the only one dubious about what sort of leaves Confederate headline writers loaded into their pipes. An indignant-looking captain named Ralph Lahrheim came up to him one breathlessly hot and muggy afternoon and waved a copy of a rag called the *Augusta Constitutionalist* in his face. "What do you think of this, Major?" Lahrheim demanded in irate tones. "What do you *think*?"

"That one? I don't much like it," Moss answered gravely. "It's scratchier than most of the Atlanta papers."

"No, no, no—that isn't what I meant," Lahrheim said. "I was talking about the *story.*"

"Oh, the story. Haven't seen this one yet," Moss said. The younger man—there weren't a lot of older men in the camp—handed him the newspaper. He read the story Lahrheim pointed out, then made a reluctant clucking noise. "Well, Captain, a lot of Canucks don't much like the USA."

"Yeah, I know what. But could they throw us out of Winnipeg? Could they cut the east-west railroads?"

"I'm sure they could cut some of them," Moss answered. "All? I don't know about that. I don't know how strong the rebels are in Winnipeg. I suppose they could drive us out for a while."

"We're busy a lot of other places," Captain Lahrheim said, as if to declare that the Canadians couldn't hope to cause the USA trouble if that weren't so. That was true. It was also rather aggressively irrelevant.

It was, in fact, irrelevant enough that Moss couldn't resist mocking it: "Really? I hadn't noticed."

Lahrheim turned red. "You're making fun of me." He had a rubbery face that conveyed indignation even better than his voice.

"Not of you, Captain, not personally," Moss said. The Andersonville camp was crowded; you had to be able to get along with people if you possibly could. Again, though, lawyer's instinct or perhaps plain cussedness made him add, "You did say something silly."

After a moment, Captain Lahrheim managed a laugh of sorts. "Well, maybe I did," he allowed. But he remained indignant, even if he aimed his ire in a different direction. "Did you see how the damn Frenchies performed? *Did* you? They just cut and run, sounds like."

"I did notice that, yes." Moss was disappointed, if less surprised than the other officer. Men from the Republic of Quebec were tolerable occupation troops. Their mere presence had made English-speaking Canadians think twice about rising against the forces that had beaten them in the Great War. Once the Canucks had thought twice and rose anyway, the men from Quebec proved less then enthusiastic about putting them down. There weren't enough Frenchies to go around, and they weren't really trained for serious combat anyway.

"We have to do everything ourselves," Lahrheim grumbled, a constant complaint in the USA. Maybe there weren't enough Americans to go around, either. Jonathan Moss hoped there were, but how could you tell ahead of time?

Moss looked north. He didn't know how much Lahrheim knew about the tunnel ever so quietly working its way out past the stockade. Since he didn't know, he pretended the tunnel didn't exist. But escape still filled his thoughts. If a good many men could break out, if they could cross Georgia and South Carolina and North Carolina and Virginia or maybe go up through Tennessee and Kentucky . . . If all that could happen, the United States would gain a few reinforcements.

All of which would matter—how much? On the big scale of things, probably not much. If the fate of the United States depended on a handful of escaping POWs, the country was in worse shape than anyone could imagine. But by escaping the prisoners would help the USA and hurt the CSA, which seemed worth doing. They would also embarrass the Confederates. The longer Moss stayed in Andersonville, the more appealing that looked.

Ralph Lahrheim also looked north, or rather northwest. "Storm coming," he remarked.

Since Moss couldn't argue with him, he nodded. Big thunderheads were building and rolling toward the prison camp. "Wouldn't want to fly through those," he said, which was the Lord's truth. The clouds towered higher than a fighter's ceiling, and were full of turbulence that could damn near tear the wings off an airplane.

"I don't much fancy being under them when they get here, either." Captain Lahrheim retreated toward the prisoner barracks.

He wasn't a particularly clever man, which didn't mean he was wrong here. Moss didn't fancy staying out in the open once the storm broke, either. The rain would be bad enough. If you were unlucky, lightning would be worse.

The first raindrops started kicking up puffs of dust from the red dirt just as Moss ducked into his barracks. The inevitable nonstop card game paused for a moment as people made sure he was someone to be trusted. Then the players got back to the serious business at hand: "I'll see that, and I'll raise you five clams."

More rain fell, drumming on the roof. That roof would start leaking any minute. Men who weren't playing cards set buckets and pots where they'd do the most good. Lightning flashed. God's artillery followed close on its heels.

"Well, this is fun," somebody said. The crack got a laugh, but a laugh distinctly nervous around the edges.

Having grown up in Chicago and spent a lot of time in Ontario, Moss had seen his share of several different flavors of bad weather. What Georgia got, though, was different from anything he was used to. It was more . . . *energetic* was the first word that came to mind, and it fit pretty well.

Rain came down as if Noah were somewhere just over the next rise. Moss didn't know about forty days and forty nights, but the next forty minutes marked as ferocious a cloudburst as he'd ever imagined. Lightning crackled again and again, a couple of times close enough to make all his hair stand on end. The thunder that followed sounded like a dress rehearsal for the end of the world.

"Liable to be tornadoes on the edge of a storm like this," a POW observed.

"We're safe, then. We're not on the edge. We're in the goddamn middle," another prisoner said.

"Besides, who'd notice anything as small as a tornado in the middle of this?" a would-be wit added. He got a laugh, but all he did was prove he didn't know the first thing about tornadoes, as several POWs from the Midwest loudly explained to him. Moss agreed, even if he didn't fuss and fume about it. Wherever tornadoes went, they made themselves noticed.

Colonel Summers looked less and less happy with each minute the downpour went on. Moss had a pretty good notion why, too. He sidled up to the senior officer and murmured, "How well is the tunnel shored up?"

"We'll find out, won't we?" was all Monty Summers said. Moss nodded. If something went wrong, there was damn-all he or any other prisoner could do about it right this minute.

Before too long, he stopped worrying about the tunnel. He started worrying about whether they would have to be rescued by rowboat instead. That seemed a much more immediate problem. He also wondered whether the Confederates had any rowboats handy. Had they anticipated storms this big?

Looking out the windows helped very little. Except when lightning tore across the sky, it was almost night-dark. And what the lightning illuminated was mostly a bumper crop of raindrops.

But after something less than an hour, the storm eased. The thunderheads glided off to the east with ponderous dignity. The subtropical sun of Georgia summer came out again. The ground started to steam— not just the puddles and ponds the rain had left behind but the ground itself.

Colonel Summers strode to the north-facing window. The starch came out of his shoulders; he might have aged ten years in ten seconds. "There's a hole in the ground not far from the deadline inside the fence," he said, his tone that of a man in the room with a deathbed. And so he might have been, for that hole meant the passing of many men's hopes.

No one had ever accused the Confederate guards of brilliance. If they'd had any brains at all, they would have been at the front doing something more useful for their country than this. But they didn't have to be Sir Isaac Newton to figure out that holes in the ground, especially long, straight ones like this, didn't happen by themselves.

One of the guards who'd squelched through the mud to the subsidence sighted along it as if down the barrel of a rifle. What he saw when he did was the barracks where Moss stood waiting for the other shoe to drop.

He didn't have to wait long. The Confederates advanced on the building. One of them fell on his can in the slick red mud. Normally, the U.S. captives would have laughed and jeered at his clumsiness. No one made a peep now. The guards were unlikely to find much funny about an escape attempt, especially one they hadn't noticed till the storm betrayed it.

"Y'all come out right now!" one of them shouted. "Y'all come out or else."

The prisoners *did* come out; Moss, for one, didn't think the guards were kidding about that *or else*. Crashing sounds from inside the barracks declared that the Confederates were taking the place apart, looking for where the tunnel started. Along with everybody else in green-gray, Moss stood glumly in the mud, waiting for them to find it.

And they did. He'd known they would. They were stupid, but not stupid enough to miss it. Their leader came out with his face even hotter than the weather. "You sons of bitches!" he screamed. "How dare you try and escape from this here prison? How *dare* you?"

"We have the right." Moss spoke up, the lawyer in him touched by that peculiar brainless fury. "The Geneva Convention says so."

That rocked the Confederate guard officer back on his heels. But he rallied, barking, "It also says I got the right to punish the bastards who try an' break out. 'Fess up, y'all. Who worked on that there tunnel? Rest of you'll have an easier time if we can punish the real criminals."

Every single U.S. prisoner raised his hand at the same time. Most of them hadn't had anything to do with the tunnel. Some, the new fish, hadn't even known it was there. They raised their hands anyway, without hesitation. Moss was proud of them.

What the guard officer felt was something else again. "All right. *All right*," he said heavily, and snorted like a boar hog. "Y'all reckon you're so goddamn smart. Well, you'll all catch it together, then, and see how you like *that*." He stormed away. Moss hoped he would take a pratfall in the mud, but no such luck. The rain was on the Confederate side every which way today.

Dr. Leonard O'Doull was about to get on a train that would take him back from Virginia to Ohio (or perhaps, given the way things were going, only to western Pennsylvania) when a clerk bounced out of a command car with a canvas sack slung over his shoulder. "Hang on, Doc!" he called. "I got mail for youse guys."

Youse guys was as far outside the bounds of ordinary English as the Confederate *y'all*. A lot of languages had separate forms for second-person singular and plural. English didn't, but kept trying to invent them. The thought flashed through O'Doull's mind and flew away in a split second, replaced by simple joy. "Give it here," he told the clerk. "I thought it would be weeks catching up with us."

Red Crosses adorned the tops of the cars and the sides of the locomotive. Locomotive and cars alike were painted white. With luck, that would keep the Confederates from dropping bombs on the train or machine-gunning it from the air. There had been a few horrible incidents, but only a few. There had also been a few south of the Mason-Dixon line. O'Doull wondered if Jake Featherston's propaganda machine had manufactured those, but wouldn't have been surprised if they proved real. War was full of things like that.

He stopped worrying about the war when he saw his wife's handwriting on a letter with a stamp from the Republic of Quebec. Sorting through the pile, he found several of those, and one from his brother-in-law, Georges Galtier. Seeing that one made him smile in a different way. Among his wife's relatives, Georges was the zany, the cuckoo, the odd man out—sometimes very odd indeed.

"Gotta go, Doc. Good luck to you." Without waiting for a reply, the Army mail clerk hopped back into the command car and drove away.

O'Doull carried the stack of envelopes and magazines and newspapers and small packages up into the train. "Mail call!" he shouted, and for the next couple of minutes he was the most popular guy around.

Once the mail was all doled out, that popularity naturally faded. Only Granville McDougald hung around. He looked glum. To show why, he held up an envelope. It had a big handstamp on it: RETURN TO SENDER. ADDRESSEE DECEASED.

"I'm sorry, Granny," O'Doull said. "Who is it?"

"Fellow I've known since the Great War. He lost a hand then, so they wouldn't let him stay in the Army, not even as a medic. Dammit, Don was a good guy—one of the best. Now I've got to see if I can come up with his sister's address, find out what happened to him."

The letter had gone to Trenton, New Jersey. Confederate bombers certainly reached that far. But other things could happen to a middle-aged man, too. As a middle-aged man himself, O'Doull knew that much too well. "I'm sorry he's gone," he repeated. "Whatever it was, I hope it was quick."

"Yeah. Amen," McDougald said. They'd both seen too many men who lingered in agony and would not let go of life, even if some of them wanted to. A fast end—*dead before he knew what hit him*—was far from the smallest mercy the world had to offer, and the world didn't offer it often enough.

"Here." O'Doull reached into his bag and pulled out a bottle of brandy. "Have a knock of this. Medicinal, you know."

"Sure. Thanks, Doc. You're a medical genius." McDougald took the bottle and raised it in salute. "Here's to you, Don." He took one long swig, then handed it back. O'Doull put it away and closed the bag.

As an officer, O'Doull had a Pullman berth. He took his letters there to read them in curtained-off privacy. He opened the one from Georges first. It was the usual nonsense from his brother-in-law: the usual nonsense with the usual ironic sting. *Aren't you glad I am not an*

English-speaking Canadian? Georges wrote—in English, not the French that was his usual language and that he used for almost all of the letter. He went on in English for one more sentence: *If I were, you might have to shoot me.* After that, he returned to his own tongue and the usual doings in and around Rivière-du-Loup.

O'Doull wondered whether Georges had had someone else compose that English for him. He would have studied the language in school before the Great War, when Quebec was still part of Canada, but when would he have needed it since? Of course, being Georges, he might have remembered it just so he could make a sarcastic nuisance of himself thirty years later. The uprising in anglophone Canada worried O'Doull, too, and not because he might be called on to pick up a rifle himself.

He went through his wife's letters one by one, starting with the earliest. He got more gossip from Rivière-du-Loup, and a different view of a small scandal involving a greengrocer and the butcher's wife. Georges had treated the whole thing as a joke. To Nicole, the butcher was a brute and his wife looking for happiness wherever she could find it. O'Doull himself knew all the people involved, but not well. He wouldn't have cared to judge where, if anywhere, the rights and wrongs lay.

Nicole didn't talk about the Canadian uprising till her next to last letter. Then she wrote, *There is a bill in the House of Deputies to extend military service. I am lighting candles and praying it does not pass.*

"So am I, sweetheart," O'Doull muttered, and then, *"Moi aussi."* He'd seen news about that bill, too. The United States were doing everything they could to get the Republic of Quebec to contribute more men to quelling the revolt north of the forty-ninth parallel. That way, the United States wouldn't have to pull so many of their own men off the fighting front against the Confederates, or even out of rebellion-wracked Utah.

But if the Republic of Quebec did contribute more soldiers, one of them was much too likely to be a young man named Lucien O'Doull. One of the great advantages of living in Quebec was that the country was technically neutral, even if it inclined toward the USA. Leonard O'Doull hadn't had to worry about his boy's becoming a soldier. He hadn't had to—but now he did.

Nicole, naturally, kept a close eye on the bill's progress. Her latest letter reported that it had come out of committee. *I do not know any-*

one who favors this bill, not a single soul, she wrote bitterly. *It moves forward anyway. It moves forward because the politicians are afraid of what the United States will do to us if it fails.*

She was bound to be right about that. Without the United States, there wouldn't have been a Republic of Quebec. The Republic's economy had very strong ties to the USA, as strong as the Americans could make them. If Quebec made the United States unhappy, the USA could make the Republic unhappier.

O'Doull swore under his breath. He understood both sides, but, because of Lucien, hoped the Republic's politicians would show some backbone. *All politics is personal,* he thought.

After getting everything off her chest, his wife went back to family chatter and the nine-days' wonders of Rivière-du-Loup. It was as if she didn't want to look at what she'd written about the bill, either. Only one more sentence at the end of the letter betrayed her worry: *I wish you were home.*

"I wish I was home, too, dammit," O'Doull muttered. But he damn well wasn't, and whose fault was that? No one's but his own. The United States were his country, and he'd volunteered to help them in a way that best matched his skills and talents. And so here he was in a white-painted train, rumbling along toward more trouble. "Happy day."

He wondered how the United States could find more trouble than they already had. With Japan bearing down on the Sandwich Islands, with the Confederates raising hell in Ohio and heading for Pennsylvania, with the Mormons still kicking up their heels in Utah and the Canucks north of the border, that looked as if all the troubles in the world, or at least on the continent, had come home to roost.

Back before the Great War, people had talked about how encircled the United States were, with the CSA, Canada, Britain, and France all keeping a wary eye on the giant they'd tied down. The country had burst its bounds in the war, and dominated North America for a generation. Now everybody else was trying to get the ropes back on again.

If Canada broke away from U.S. occupation, if British influence returned to the northern part of the continent, how long could the Republic of Quebec stay independent? That had to be on the minds of the politicians in Quebec City. It was on Leonard O'Doull's mind, too. But so was his son, and his son counted for infinitely more.

Engine puffing, iron wheels screeching against the track and throwing up sun-colored sparks, the train stopped. O'Doull opened the curtains in front of the window and looked out. They were, as far as he could tell, in the middle of nowhere. Something had gone wrong up ahead, but he couldn't make out what.

The conductor was a Medical Service corporal. O'Doull hoped he made a better corpsman than conductor, because he wasn't very good at his secondary role. But he did have an answer when the doctor asked him what had happened farther west: "Sabotage." He seemed to take a certain somber pleasure in the word.

"*'Osti!*" O'Doull burst out, which made the noncom give him a curious look. O'Doull looked back in plain warning. The other man decided walking down the corridor would be a good idea.

O'Doull shook his head. It wasn't that he didn't believe the corporal. No, the trouble was just the opposite. As long as Confederate operatives sounded reasonably Yankeelike, they could hide in plain sight till they went off to work mischief in the middle of the night.

No doubt U.S. operatives were doing the same thing on the other side of the border, and helping C.S. Negroes in their sputtering civil war against Jake Featherston's government. O'Doull hoped they were, anyhow. But that didn't do him, or this train, any good at all.

Three hours later, after a repair crew filled in a crater and laid new track across it, the train got rolling again. By then, the sun was going down in the west and O'Doull was going up in smoke. If he was going to be useful, he wanted to be *useful*. He couldn't do a damn thing stuck here on a train track.

Unlike most trains, this one rolled through the night all lit up. Trains full of soldiers and weapons and raw materials sneaked along, trusting to darkness to hide them from Confederate aircraft. This one showed its true colors, and the enemy left it alone.

There were whispers that the Confederates sometimes used the Red Cross to disguise troop movements. O'Doull hoped that wasn't so. It would make C.S. raiders want to disregard the symbol when the USA used it, and it would make the United States distrust even legitimate Confederate uses. Things were hard enough as they were. Did they have to—could they—get even worse?

XI

Back when Cincinnatus Driver lived in Confederate Covington before the Great War, he hadn't liked going to the zoo. Animals in cages had reminded him too strongly of the black man's plight. Then when he moved up to Des Moines after the war, he'd been able to take his kids to the zoo there and enjoy it himself. He'd felt freer there—and, to be fair, Des Moines had a much fancier zoo than Covington's.

Now things had come full circle. Here he was, back in Covington. Here he was, back in the CSA. And here he was, caged.

When the barbed-wire perimeter around the colored quarter went up, a few blacks figured it was just for show, to let colored people know who was boss without really intending to imprison them. Cincinnatus could have told them they were fools. The Freedom Party lied about plenty of things, but not about what it thought of Negroes. Some of the optimists tried to slip between the strands or attacked them with wire cutters, right there where the guards could see them.

Cincinnatus had known for years what automatic-weapons fire sounded like. Hearing it again saddened him without greatly surprising him. The guards' callousness afterwards *did* surprise him. They left the bodies they'd shot where they fell, so the sight and, after a day or two, the stench would intimidate the Negroes inside the perimeter.

He didn't talk to Lucullus about the odious and odorous events. For one thing, visiting Lucullus probably put him on some kind of list. The powers that be in Covington already had too many reasons to put him on a list. And, for another, Lucullus remained in a state of shock at being closed off from the outside world. Cincinnatus had never dreamt the barbecue cook could stay downcast for so long, but that seemed to be what was going on.

With Lucullus . . . disabled, Cincinnatus took his troubles to the Brass Monkey instead. He didn't talk about them in the saloon, but that didn't mean they didn't go away. A lot of things dissolved in beer, and there was whiskey for what beer wouldn't melt.

Covington's colored quarter had always had a lot of saloons. People there had always had a lot of trouble that needed dissolving. Saloons were the one kind of business in the colored part of town that was doing better now than before the wire went up. Even more sorrows than usual needed drowning. And the Confederate authorities no doubt learned all sorts of things from saloon talk. Some of what they learned might even have been true.

Cincinnatus perched on a stool under one of the two lazily spinning ceiling fans. He slid a dime across the bar. "Let me have a Jax," he said.

"Comin' up." The bartender took one out of the cooler, popped the cap with a church key, and handed Cincinnatus the beer.

Resting his can against one knee, Cincinnatus closed both palms around the cold, wet bottle. "Feels good," he said, and held it for a little while before lifting it to his lips and taking a long pull. "Ah! That feels even better."

"I believe it." Sweat beaded the barkeep's forehead the way condensation beaded the bottle. In his boiled shirt and black bow tie, he had to be hotter and more uncomfortable than Cincinnatus was.

Motion up near the ceiling caught Cincinnatus' eye. He glanced up. It was a strip of flypaper, black with the bodies of flies it had caught, twisting in the breeze from a nearby fan. That strip had been there since Cincinnatus started coming into the Brass Monkey, and probably for a long time before that. The dead flies couldn't be anything but dried-up husks. Plenty of live ones buzzed in the muggy air.

Two stools down from Cincinnatus, a very black man in dirty overalls waved to the bartender. "Gimme 'nother double," he slurred. By his voice and his potent whiskey breath, he'd had several doubles already. The bartender took his money and gave him what he asked for.

The drunk stared down into the glass as if the amber fluid inside held the meaning of life. Maybe, for him, it did. He gulped it down. When the glass was empty, the drunk set it on the bar and looked around. Whatever he saw, Cincinnatus didn't think it was in the Brass Monkey. During the last war, soldiers had called the glazed look in his eyes the thousand-yard stare. Too much combat and too much whiskey could both make a man look that way.

"What is we gonna do?" the drunk asked plaintively. Was he talking to Cincinnatus, to the bartender, to himself, or to God? No one answered. After half a minute of silence, the Negro brought out the question again, with even more anguish this time: "What *is* we gonna do?"

The barkeep ignored him, polishing the battered bar top with a none too clean rag. God ignored the drunk, too—but then, God had been ignoring Negroes in the CSA far longer than the Confederacy had been an independent country. If the man was talking to himself, would he have asked the same question twice? That left Cincinnatus. He thought about ignoring the drunk like the bartender, but he didn't have a polishing rag handy. Swallowing a sigh, he asked, "What are we gonna do about what?"

"Oh, Lordy!" Resignation and annoyance mixed in the bartender's voice. "Now you done got him started."

The drunk, lost in his own fog of alcohol and pain, might not have heard the barkeep. But Cincinnatus' words somehow penetrated. "What is we gonna do about what?" he echoed. "What is we gonna do about *us*?—dat's what."

He might have been pickled in sour mash. That didn't mean the question didn't matter. No, it didn't mean anything of the sort. Cincinnatus wished it did. "What *can* we do about us?" he asked in return.

"Damfino," the drunk said. "Yeah, damfino. But we gots to do *somethin'*, on account of they wants to kill us all. Kill us all, you hear me?"

His voice rose to a frightened, angry shout. Cincinnatus heard him, all right. So did about half the colored quarter of Covington, Kentucky. Even the bartender couldn't ignore him anymore. "Hush, there. Easy, easy," the man said, putting away the rag. He might have been trying to gentle a spooked horse. "Ain't nothin' *you* kin do about it, Hesiod."

Hesiod muttered and mumbled to himself. "Gots to be somethin' somebody kin do," he said. "*Gots* to be. If'n they ain't, we is all dead."

Before the barbed wire went up, Cincinnatus would have taken that for no more than a drunk's maunderings. He still took it for a drunk's maunderings—what else was it?—but not just for that, not any more. If Freedom Party goons wanted to reach into the quarter they'd cordoned off, take out some Negroes, and do away with them, they would. Who'd stop them? Who'd even know for certain what they'd done?

Hesiod slapped four bits on the bar. "Gimme 'nother double," he said, and then, as if still ordering the drink, "Gots to kill them ofays. Kill 'em, you hear me?"

"Here you is." The bartender set the drink in front of him. "Now you get outside o' this. When you ain't drinkin', shut your damn mouth. You gonna open it so wide, you falls in."

There was another home truth, even if the Brass Monkey was a long way from home. Somebody in the dive—maybe even the barkeep himself—was bound to be spying for the white man, spying for the government. Some blacks thought they could make deals with the devil, grab safety for themselves at the expense of their fellows, their friends, their families.

Cincinnatus didn't believe it, not for a minute. Like any wild beast, sooner or later the Freedom Party would bite the hand that fed it. Anyone who thought it would do anything else was bound to be a sucker. No, Jake Featherston had never bothered lying about what he aimed to do with and to Negroes, because that was exactly what so many whites in the CSA wanted to hear.

"Them ofays come in here, we gots to shoot 'em! *Shoot* 'em, hear me?" Hesiod said.

The only trouble with that was, the white men would shoot back. And they were the ones with the heavy weapons. Lucullus Wood had seen as much, and Lucullus knew more than anybody else about the guns the Negroes in Covington had. Lucullus, no doubt, had brought a lot of those guns into the colored part of town.

Expecting a drunk to know what Lucullus knew was bound to be blind optimism. Cincinnatus did say, "Anybody shoot at the ofays, everybody gonna be real sorry." He didn't want Hesiod grabbing a .22 and trying to blow out the brains of the first white cop he saw.

"Everybody real sorry already," Hesiod said, breathing more bourbon into Cincinnatus' face. "How you reckon things git worse?"

Before Cincinnatus could say anything to that, the bartender spoke up: "Things kin *always* git worse." He did not sound like a man who intended to let himself be contradicted.

And he did not impress Hesiod. "What they gonna do? Line us up an' shoot us?"

"Matter of fact, yes." This time, Cincinnatus spoke before the barkeep could. "They'd do that. They wouldn't lose a minute o' sleep, neither."

"But they's already doin' it. *Already,*" Hesiod said triumphantly. "They ship your ass to one o' them camps, you don't come out no more. They shoots you there, else they kills you some other kind o' way. Might as well shoot back at them ofay motherfuckers. They come after us, we gots nothin' to lose."

A considerable silence followed. Both Cincinnatus and the bartender wanted to tell Hesiod he was wrong. Both of them wanted to, but neither one could. He was too likely not to be wrong at all.

Cincinnatus finished his Jax, set the bottle on the bar, and walked out of the Brass Monkey. The tip of his cane tapped against the sawdust-strewn floor, and then against the battered sidewalk outside. He still carried the cane everywhere he went, but it wasn't a vital third limb for him the way it had been when he was first getting around after the car hit him. He wasn't as spry as his father, but he got around tolerably well these days.

Seneca Driver was listening to the wireless when Cincinnatus came back to the house where he'd grown up. The Confederates and the Yankees were jamming each other's stations extra hard these days, and most of what came out of the wireless set's speakers were hisses and unearthly whines.

"What you doin' home so quick, Son?" Seneca had been born a slave, and still spoke with the broad accent of a black man who'd never had a chance to get an education. "Reckoned you'd stay down at de saloon longer."

"No." Cincinnatus shook his head. "Can't get away from bad news anywhere." After so many years in Iowa, his own speech sounded half-Yankee, especially by comparison to what he heard around himself here. He laughed bitterly. And a whole fat lot of good not sounding ignorant was likely to do him!

"These is hard times," Seneca said. "We gots to be like turtles an' pull our heads into our shell an' not come out till things is better."

Most of the time, that would have been good advice. Cincinnatus was sure it had worked for his father many times before. But what were you supposed to do when those troubling you wanted to smash the turtle's shell to get at the meat inside? What then? Cincinnatus had no answers, and feared no one else did, either.

Somewhere up ahead, a machine gun started chattering. Armstrong Grimes threw himself flat. Bullets cracked past overhead. Any time you could hear bullets cracking, they came too damn close.

Armstrong shared a stretch of brick wall near the southern outskirts of Salt Lake City with Yossel Reisen. "Don't these Mormon maniacs ever give up?" he demanded—more of God, probably, than of the Congresswoman's nephew.

God had nothing to say. Yossel did: "Doesn't look like it. Long as they've got guns and people to shoot 'em, they're going to keep fighting."

"People." Armstrong made it into a swear word. Yossel was too right. Some of the Mormons who carried rifles, pistols, and grenades were women. Some of the Mormons who crewed mortars and machine guns were women, too. From everything Armstrong had seen, they fought just as hard and just as well as their male counterparts. He didn't know if that old saw about the female of the species' being more deadly than the male was true, but in Utah she sure wasn't any *less* deadly.

Mormon women usually fought to the death whenever they could. They had their reasons, most of them good. U.S. soldiers who captured women in arms were inclined to take a very basic revenge. That went against regulations. Officers lectured about how naughty it was. It went on happening anyway. Armstrong didn't see how to stop it. If he caught some gal who was trying to kill him . . . It was more interesting than thinking about shooting a guy the size of a defensive tackle, that was for sure.

Down in the Confederate States, some of the black guerrillas were of the female persuasion. The bastards in butternut who caught them served them the same way. U.S. propaganda said that only went to show what a bunch of cruel and miserable bastards the Confederates were. Armstrong didn't doubt the Confederates were cruel and miserable bastards; they'd come too close to killing him too many times for him to doubt it. But raping captives wasn't one of the reasons he didn't, not anymore. He understood the enemy in ways he hadn't before.

That sparked a new thought. He turned to Yossel Reisen and said,

"You ever get the idea we're more like the assholes on the other side of the line who're trying to kill us than we are like the fancy-pants fuckers back in Philly who give us orders?"

He realized he could have picked somebody better than the Jew to ask. Yossel's aunt was one of those fancy-pants folks. If he'd wanted to, he almost certainly could have got out of being conscripted. That he hadn't either spoke well for him or said he was a little bit nuts, depending.

But he nodded now. "Oh, hell, yes. I wonder how many guys in the War Department have ever had lice. Maybe a few in the last war, when they were lieutenants or something."

"Not many, I bet," Armstrong said. "People like that, they would've found cushy jobs back then, too."

"Wouldn't be surprised." Reisen took a pack of cigarettes out of a tunic pocket, stuck one in his mouth, and offered the pack to Armstrong. Once they were both smoking, he went on, "Did I ever tell you my Uncle David only has one leg?"

There weren't a whole lot of families in the USA that didn't have a wounded or mutilated male relative. Armstrong said, "Maybe you did. I think so, but I'm not sure."

"Aunt Flora could have kept him out of the Army if he'd wanted her to. Same with me," Yossel said, his voice matter-of-fact. "But you've got to do what you've got to do. Otherwise, how can you stand yourself?" After a moment, he added, "Did I ever tell you Uncle David's a fire-breathing Democrat?"

"Yeah, I think you did," Armstrong answered. Because Reisen seemed to expect him to, he asked, "How does your aunt like it?"

"She doesn't," Yossel said, as matter-of-factly as before. "They still get along with each other well enough, but they argue whenever they talk about politics."

Before Armstrong could say anything, a horrible screech filled the air. "Screaming meemies!" he yelled, and folded himself as small as he could, down there in the foxhole that was now suddenly, horribly, on the wrong side of the fence. Yossel Reisen did the same.

The spigot mortar burst with a roar like the end of the world. A lot of the rounds from the Mormons' weird makeshift artillery were duds. The ones that weren't packed a hell of a wallop. The ground shook under Armstrong. For a horrid moment, he thought the foxhole would collapse and bury him alive.

What if it did? The headline would be FORMER FIRST LADY'S NEPHEW KILLED IN COMBAT! Armstrong would make a one-sentence add-on to the story—*Another soldier also died*—if that.

When he could hear anything but the thunder of the explosion, he heard people screaming. There in the bottom of the hole, his eyes met Yossel Reisen's. He knew exactly what Yossel was thinking, because he was thinking the same thing himself. *Oh, hell,* or words to that effect.

He wanted to come out of the safety of the foxhole about as much as he wanted to dance naked in front of the Mormon Temple in Salt Lake City wagging his pecker at the gilded statue of the Angel Moroni. That might get him shot faster than this. On the other hand, it might not.

But you had to pick up your buddies. That had been drilled into him since day one of his abbreviated basic training. He'd seen the sense of it in the field, too, which wasn't true of a lot of the crap they'd fed him in basic. If you didn't help your buddies when they needed it most, they wouldn't help you if you did—and you were liable to.

"Come on, dammit." He and Yossel said the same thing at the same time, as if they were an old married couple. They'd both been around this particular block often enough, that was for damn sure.

Up they went, keeping their bellies rattlesnake-low on the ground. Rex Stowe was out there, too. The sergeant made no bones about disliking several of the new men in his section. He came to help them anyway. They were part of his job—and, again, he expected them to do the same for him.

That damned Mormon machine gunner opened up again after the spigot-mortar round went off. He knew there'd be wounded—and that there'd be guys trying to do what they could for them. Spray enough bullets around and you'd get some more wounded, maybe even some dead.

Armstrong and Sergeant Stowe reached the closest injured man at about the same time. They looked at him and then looked at each other. Armstrong was pretty sure his face wore the same horrified expression as Stowe's. That a man could make so much noise when so little of him was left . . . War was full of nasty surprises, and it had just pulled another one on Armstrong Grimes.

"Cavendish! Hey, Cavendish!" Stowe said. When he got a momentary lull in the screaming, he asked, "You want us to bring you in, or you want to get it over with right now? Your call."

Had that been Armstrong, he would have wanted it over and done with. He had no idea how Stowe knew the wounded man was Cavendish; there sure wasn't enough left of his face to tell by that, and one guy's shrieks sounded a lot like another's. But Cavendish seemed perfectly coherent when he said, "For the love of Mike, take me in." Then, hardly missing a beat, he went back to screaming again.

Stowe looked at Armstrong and shrugged. "He might live."

He didn't sound as if he believed it. Armstrong sure didn't. He looked at what was left of Cavendish. No, he wouldn't have wanted to go on if he looked like that. But if the other soldier did . . . "Gotta try, I guess."

They bandaged and tourniqueted Cavendish's wounds, stopping the worst of the bleeding. Stowe closed the one in the man's belly with a couple of safety pins. They weren't much, but they were better than nothing. Both Armstrong and Stowe gave him a shot of morphine. "Maybe he'll shut up," Armstrong said.

"Yeah, and if we gave him too much of the shit, maybe he'll shut up for good," Stowe said. "That's easier than going out the way he was." Armstrong grunted and nodded. His hands were all bloody. So were Stowe's. The sergeant asked, "You want to take him back, or shall I?"

No corpsmen were in sight. They did the best they could, but they couldn't be everywhere. Armstrong considered. Taking Cavendish back would get him out of the front line for a bit, but the Mormons might shoot him while he did it. He shrugged. "I'll take care of it if you want me to."

"Go on, then." Stowe could make the same calculation as Armstrong. "I'll get him on your back—you'll want to stay low."

"Fuckin'-A I will," Armstrong said fervently. He'd stayed as near horizontal as he could while working on Cavendish. So had Rex Stowe. They'd both spent a lot of time—too much time, as far as Armstrong was concerned—up at the front. They'd learned what tricks there were to know about staying alive and not getting hurt. The only trouble was, sometimes all the tricks in the world didn't do you a damn bit of good.

With what was left of Cavendish on top of him, Armstrong crawled away from the Mormon machine gun. At least the dreadfully wounded man wasn't wriggling so much. Maybe the morphine the two noncoms had given him was taking hold.

Even half a mile back of the line, they acted a lot more regulation.

A soldier in a clean new uniform stared at Armstrong and said, "What are you doing bringing a body back here? Leave him for Graves Registration."

"Fuck you, Jack," Armstrong said without heat. "For one thing, he ain't dead. For another thing, he's worth two of Graves Registration and four of you. Point me at the nearest aid station before I kick your worthless ass."

Armstrong wasn't small, but the other man was bigger. Fury wouldn't have worried him. Armstrong's complete indifference to consequences did. Maybe he thought Armstrong would just as soon kill him as look at him—and maybe he was right. He said, "There's a tent behind that pile of bricks. It shields 'em from small-arms fire."

"Thanks." Armstrong headed that way, carrying Cavendish now. The wounded man was a lot lighter than he had been before he got hurt. A corpsman came out before Armstrong got halfway there. "Hey!" he called. "Come give me a hand with this guy."

The corpsman trotted toward him. When he got close enough to take a good look at Cavendish, he stopped short, his boots kicking up dust. "Jesus!" he said.

"Tell me about it," Armstrong said. "You should've seen him before my sergeant and me patched him up. But he said he wanted to live if he could." He shrugged. "What are you gonna do when a guy says that?"

"Jesus." The corpsman looked green, and he'd seen some of the worst things war could do. "Well, I guess we've got to try. I'll help you get him to the tent."

"Thank you." Cavendish's voice was dreamy and far away. Armstrong had thought he'd long since passed out. The corpsman looked as if he'd just heard a ghost.

The surgeon in the tent did a double take when he saw Cavendish. Armstrong got out of there before the doc went to work. Watching would have made him sick. That was crazy, but it was true. He went back up to the front line. There, at least, death and mutilation came at random. You didn't know about them ahead of time. That made them, if not tolerable, at least possible to bear.

Jefferson Pinkard wondered why the hell the vice president of the Cyclone Chemical Company wasn't in the Army. Cullen Beauregard—

"Call me C.B."—Slattery couldn't have been more than thirty. He was obviously healthy, and just as obviously sharp.

"Oh, yes, sir," he said. "Anything alive, this'll shift. You don't need to worry about that at all."

"You make it for bugs, though."

"That's right." Slattery nodded.

"But it'll kill rats and mice," Jeff said. C.B. Slattery nodded again. Jeff went on, "And cats and dogs?" Another nod. "And people?"

"Yes, sir. It will absolutely kill people. That's why you've got to be careful when you use it," Slattery said. "Matter of fact, the chemical's the same one some Yankee states use to kill criminals."

"Really? Is that a fact?" Jeff said. One more nod from Slattery. He was one of the noddingest people Jeff had ever met. "If you wanted to, you could use it to kill a whole bunch of people, then?"

"Absolutely. You absolutely could." The chemical-company official didn't ask why Pinkard might want to use his product, made to get rid of roaches and other pests, to dispose of large numbers of people instead. What he did say was, "If you use large quantities, you'd be entitled to a bulk discount."

"That's nice. That's white of you, matter of fact," Jeff said. C.B. Slattery laughed uproariously. He didn't ask what color the people who might die were. Pretty plainly, he already knew.

Somewhere in Camp Determination, a work gang of Negroes chanted rhythmically as they carried or dug or did whatever the guards told them to do. Slattery smiled at that, too, the way he might have smiled at a bear playing with a medicine ball in a zoo.

The shape of his smile decided Jeff. This wasn't a man who would balk at what needed discussing here. "Let's get down to brass tacks, then," Jeff said. "Can your firm design us a facility, I guess you'd call it, that would let us reduce the camp population without leaving the niggers still here any the wiser about what was going on inside?" He'd talked about killing people when it was in the abstract. When it got down to something he might actually do, his own words turned abstract. Reducing population didn't seem to mean so much.

"My firm? No, sir. Sorry, but that's not what we do. We make insecticide," Slattery answered. Pinkard muttered under his breath; he hadn't expected a flat refusal. But when the bright young man continued, he discovered he hadn't got one, either: "But I can put you in touch with some design outfits that will help you along those lines. Just as a guess, I'd say you'd want to call it a delousing station or a bathhouse or something like that. Sound reasonable?"

"Sounds sensible. I was thinking along those lines myself, to tell you the truth," said Pinkard, who hadn't been. He picked up a pencil and wrote, *Delousing? Baths?* on a sheet of foolscap. Maybe Slattery saw through him, maybe not. He went on, "Now, these outfits you're talking about—they in Arkansas like you? If I have my druthers, I want to work with somebody local, you know what I mean?"

"I sure do, and I respect that," Slattery said quickly. Respecting it didn't mean agreeing with it, but did mean he'd go along if he wanted the Cyclone Chemical Company to get the business. When Jefferson Pinkard wanted his druthers these days, he damn well got them. He remembered wishing for them in the last war, wishing and not getting. A lot of things about growing older were damned unpleasant (his last visit to the dentist leaped to mind). But if you were halfway decent at what you did, you got your druthers a lot more often than you had when you were younger. As if to underscore that, C.B. Slattery continued, "Naturally, we work with people from Little Rock a lot of the time. But I do believe a couple of these outfits have branches in Texas— Dallas or Houston, I'm not quite sure which."

"Well, you can wire me the details when you get home," Jeff said, and it was Slattery's turn to write himself a note. "I'll do some checking on my own, too." If Slattery thought he could set up some sweetheart deal, maybe rig kickbacks for Cyclone Chemical, he could damn well think again.

He wasn't fool enough to let on that he'd had anything like that in mind. "You go right ahead, sir. I think you'll find out the firms I recommend are competitive in quality and in price." He paused to pull out a pack of cigarettes, offer one to Jeff, and then stick one in his own mouth. Once they both had lights, he remarked, "Something else occurs to me."

"What's that?"

"You might want to site this, ah, facility away from the main camp and take prisoners to it. You'd be less likely to spook the spooks that way, if you know what I mean." Slattery had a disarming grin.

He also had a point. Jeff scribbled some more on that sheet of foolscap. "Could be," he said. It applied the same principle as telling

Negroes they were going to another camp when they got into the trucks from which they would never get out. "We could move 'em right on through, just like a . . . factory."

The word that first crossed his mind, that caused the pause, was *slaughterhouse*. He didn't want to say that, any more than he wanted to talk about killing Negroes rather than reducing population. It made him think too openly about what this camp was for.

"You sure could." C.B. Slattery fairly radiated enthusiasm. "It'd be a privilege for my firm to be affiliated with such a patriotic enterprise. Freedom!"

"Freedom!" Jeff echoed automatically. "You'll be hearing from us. I expect some of those designers may, too, so get me that word quick as you can. Like I say, though, I'll check out some other outfits in these parts along with 'em."

"You know your business best." No, Slattery wasn't about to argue. No matter who built the places where the Negroes went in and didn't come out, the chemical that made sure they didn't come out would come from his company. He said, "Freedom!" one more time and hurried out of Pinkard's office. By the way he moved, his next appointment was just as urgent and just as important as this one. It wasn't likely to be, but treating it that way made him a good businessman.

Jeff got up and watched him leave the administrative center, then went back to his desk. He picked up the telephone and called Richmond. He wanted Ferdinand Koenig knowing what was going on every step of the way. The Attorney General heard him out—he did try to keep things short—and then said, "This all sounds pretty good. Only one thing bothers me a little."

"What's that?" Jeff asked. Whatever bothered Jake Featherston's right-hand man was guaranteed to be dead on arrival.

"This whole business of building the, uh, fumigator—whatever the hell you want to call it—away from the camp. That means we're using trucks again. I thought one of the big points of building the fumigator in the first place was getting away from the goddamn trucks."

"Well, yes, sir," Jeff said reluctantly. "Only problem I see with building it here is, the niggers won't take long to figure out this is the end of the line if we do. We'll have more trouble from 'em in that case. Camp's been pretty quiet so far, and I'd like to keep it that way."

"I understand that, but we've got to think about efficiency, too,"

Koenig said. "If we can give your trucks back to the Army—minus your exhaust hookup, of course"—he laughed, which meant Pinkard had to do the same—"that'll help the war effort a lot. We need all the transport we can get right now, what with the big push into Pennsylvania. And you've got a good solid perimeter around the camp, right? You've got guards who know what they're doing, right?"

"Well, yes, sir," Jeff repeated. He couldn't very well say the camp didn't have a solid perimeter, or that the guards didn't know what the hell they were doing. If he said that, he wouldn't stay camp commandant for another five minutes, and he wouldn't deserve to, either.

"All right, then," the Attorney General said. "Any trouble comes up, I reckon you'll be able to handle it. A few bursts from the guards' submachine guns should settle most troubles pretty damn quick. If they don't, well, the machine guns in the towers outside the barbed wire sure as hell will."

"Yes, sir," Pinkard said one more time. Everything Ferd Koenig said was true. If the Negroes caused trouble, the guards ought to be able to smash it.

"Good." Koenig sounded pleased. "You keep at it, Pinkard. I'm sure everything will work out fine. Freedom!"

"Freedom!" Jeff said, but he was talking to a dead line.

He hung up, swearing under his breath. Everything Koenig said was true, yeah, but what he said was only part of the story. Jeff remembered how things had been back at Camp Dependable in Louisiana when his guards were reducing population by taking niggers out to the swamps and shooting them. Not only had that put a strain on the white men, it had also made them stay on edge every minute of the day and night. The Negroes in the camp had known too well they had nothing to lose. If they tried to nail a guard, they'd get killed, sure. But if they didn't, they'd get killed anyhow. So why not try to take somebody with you when you went?

Camp Determination wasn't like that now. The blacks here believed this wasn't the last stop. They were wrong, but the belief itself mattered. It mattered a lot. Because they still believed they had a future, they were much more docile than they would have been otherwise.

Building the fumigator here would ruin all that. They'd figure out what was what. How could they help it? Everybody knew Negroes weren't as smart as white people, but they wouldn't have to be geniuses to figure this out. And guards would have to stay on their toes every second from then on.

But now Jeff had his orders. He wished he'd never called Richmond. He should have just gone ahead and built the fumigator where he wanted it and then told Ferd Koenig what he'd done. The Attorney General would have gone along with it. The way things worked out, Jeff was stuck.

He swore again, louder this time, sat down to look at a map of Camp Determination, and then swore some more. Pretty plainly, he'd have to build two fumigators, one for men, the other for women and pickaninnies. Otherwise, the sexes would meet on the way to getting eliminated, and that would cause all kinds of trouble—to say nothing of making inmates' attitudes even worse than they would be anyhow.

After another look at the map—and some more venting of his spleen—he decided how things would have to work. The fumigators could go at, or even next to, the present outer boundaries of the camp. That way, he could use the current perimeter to separate them from the areas where the Negroes lived. Maybe he could send people through on the pretext that they had to be deloused before going to a new camp. That would explain why they didn't come back.

How long could he keep them from learning that only bodies left Camp Determination? Not forever, he feared. But he could buy at least some time that way. The longer he didn't have to worry about uppity niggers, the better he liked it. And he would be following orders.

Irving Morrell got his first look at one of the new Confederate barrels just outside of Salem, Ohio. The town, east of Canton, called itself "Ohio's City of Friends." It had been founded by Quakers, and many still lived there. What was happening around Salem now had nothing to do with those peaceable people or their ideals.

A U.S. 105 firing over open sights had knocked out the barrel in question. The young lieutenant who gravely explained that to Morrell didn't see anything funny about it. He didn't associate it with Jake Featherston's ranting tract of the same name. Morrell wondered whether to explain why he was laughing. In the end, he didn't. Any joke you had to explain wasn't funny.

Neither was the new barrel. It stank of gasoline and cordite and burnt paint and rubber and burnt flesh. Morrell's nostrils tried to pinch in on themselves to hold out as much of that horrible smell as they could. His stomach lurched as soon as he recognized it. He'd smelled it too often before.

No barrel in the world could withstand a direct hit from a 105 at point-blank range. *Getting* hits with an artillery piece even at point-blank range was a much bigger problem, though. The best antibarrel weapon was still another barrel.

When Morrell walked around the charred corpse of this one, he got the feeling that the machines he commanded were like boys trying to stop men. The long gun with the big bore, the sloped armor, the low profile . . . This was what the USA should have had at the start of the war.

He turned to the lieutenant. "Can the inch-and-a-half guns on our barrels hurt these monsters at all?"

"They can penetrate the side armor, sir," the youngster answered. "That frontal plate—I'm afraid not. Our barrels' armor-piercing rounds mostly just bounce off."

"Happy day," Morrell muttered, and then, "We've *got* to upgun. That's all there is to it."

"Yes, sir," the lieutenant said. "But the turret ring on our present model won't let us mount a three-incher like these bastards have. Two and a fraction, that's it—and even then we need a new turret to hold the larger weapon."

"We've got to do it," Morrell said, more to himself than to his guide. "Building a whole new machine from the ground up—well, we should have started a long time ago. Since we didn't, we've just got to squeeze the most out of what we have for a while longer."

"Can we?" the lieutenant asked—a question Morrell wished he didn't have to contemplate.

After a moment's thought, he answered, "Of course we can, son— because we've got to. Now where's the map that shows our armored dispositions?"

"It's back in town, sir," the young lieutenant said. Morrell wished it were farther forward: one of a lot of things he wished that he wasn't going to get. Back to Salem they went. Refugees from farther west clogged the road. Some of them tried to take shelter in Salem, even as the people who lived there cleared out.

Once upon a time, before bombs and artillery started landing on it,

Salem had been a pleasant little city. It had held ten or twelve thousand people, and had boasted a flour mill, a dairy outfit, a couple of china factories, and some metalworks. It also boasted a monument to one Edwin Coppock, an abolitionist who'd raided Harpers Ferry with John Brown, and who'd been hanged with him. If the Confederates took Salem, they would blow that to hell and gone.

When Morrell actually got a look at the armored dispositions in northeastern Ohio, his own disposition soured, and his temper almost blew to hell and gone. "My God!" he burst out. "They've got them scattered all over the damned landscape!"

"They support the infantry, sir," the shavetail said.

"No, no, no, no, no!" Morrell didn't pound his head against the wall in the pleasant little clapboard house now doing duty for his head-quarters. Why he didn't, he couldn't have said. As far as he was concerned, that restraint should have been worth a medal. "We've been at war for more than a year now. Hasn't anybody learned anything about anything?"

"Sir?" The lieutenant, an earnest young man, realized he was out of his element.

Morrell didn't try to explain. It would have taken too long. But the officer he was replacing hadn't learned a thing from two wars' worth of barrel tactics. The one thing you needed to do to get the most out of your armor was to mass it, to use it as the spearhead to your attack. Putting some of it here, some of it there, and some more of it in a no-account town twenty miles away was asking—begging—to get de-feated in detail. And the Confederates—who, while they were manifest sons of bitches, were also capable sons of bitches when it came to han-dling armor—were only too happy to oblige.

The study Morrell went into was more nearly black than brown. "How the hell can I get my forces concentrated so I can *do* something with them?" he muttered.

"How can our infantry respond to the Confederates if they don't have barrels to stiffen them, sir?" the lieutenant asked.

The look Morrell gave him should have left him charred worse than the burnt-out C.S. barrel. "I don't want to respond to Feather-ston's fuckers," he ground out. The young lieutenant's eyes widened, perhaps at the obscenity but more likely at the heresy. Morrell pro-ceeded to spell it out: "I want to make Featherston's fuckers respond to *me*. I can't do that, can I, unless I can pull together enough barrels to get their attention?" It seemed obvious to him. Why didn't it seem obvious to anybody else in a green-gray uniform?

"But, sir, if the infantry isn't supported, the enemy will just slice through it, the way he has before." The lieutenant sounded like a man trying to reason with a dangerous lunatic.

"He's welcome to try," Morrell said, which made the shavetail's eyes get big all over again. "If I have a decent force of barrels of my own, though, I'll land on his flank and cut his supply line neat as you please. Let's see how much slicing he does without gasoline or ammo."

He waited. The lieutenant contemplated. "Do you really think you could do that, sir?" He was too polite and too far under military discipline to call Morrell a liar in so many words, but he didn't believe him, either.

"Would they have sent me here if they didn't think I could?" Morrell asked. "Or don't you think the War Department knows what it's doing?"

"Sir, if the War Department knew what it was doing, would we be in a quarter of the mess we're in?" the lieutenant replied.

Morrell stared at him as if he'd never seen him before. In a very real way, he hadn't. He stuck out his right hand. When the lieutenant hesitated, Morrell grabbed his hand and pumped it up and down. "Congratulations!" he said. "That's the first halfway smart thing I've heard out of you."

"Uh, sir?" He'd bewildered the lieutenant.

"Always distrust what the people too far from the front line to hear small-arms fire tell you," Morrell said. "*Always*. Most of what they think they know is going to be out of date or wrong some other way. It will have gone through too many mouths before it finally gets to them. And a lot of them won't *ever* have got close enough to the front to hear small-arms fire. Half the time, they won't understand what other people are trying to tell them even if it turns out to be the gospel truth. Sometimes it does—accidents will happen."

The young officer eyed him. "What about *you*, sir?"

"There. That's the second smart thing you've said." Morrell grinned. "All I can tell you is, I've got an oak-leaf cluster for my damn Purple Heart. Do I pass inspection?"

"Uh, yes, sir." The lieutenant blushed like a schoolgirl. A glance at the short row of fruit salad on his chest showed he'd never been wounded. He probably thought that made him less of a man. Morrell had had stupid notions like that till he got shot in the leg. Nothing like a wound infection to take the romance out of war.

He got down to business. "All right, then. How secure are the telephone lines out of this place?"

"Well, we do the best we can, sir, but I can't guarantee the bastards in butternut aren't tapping them," the lieutenant said. "Same with the telegraph."

"It would be," Morrell muttered. A war between two countries that spoke the same language was harder than other kinds just about every which way. You had to assume the enemy was listening to everything you did, and that he knew what you were up to as soon as you did. You'd give him too much credit some of the time, but you didn't dare give him too little.

You had to assume he was listening. You had to assume he knew what you were up to . . . "Do you know, Lieutenant, I hope he is. He's almost bound to be, isn't he?"

"Sir?" The blank look was back on the kid's baby face.

Morrell clapped him on the shoulder. "Never mind. Point me at a typewriter. We do have messengers we can rely on, right?" If the lieutenant told him no, he was up the well-known creek without even a canoe, much less a paddle.

But the young officer nodded. "Oh, yes, sir. They're very reliable, and they make sure to destroy what they're carrying if they run into trouble."

"That's what I wanted to hear," Morrell said. "Now where's that typewriter?"

For the next couple of hours, he pounded away at it. He was no secretary; he typed with his two forefingers. He wasn't fast, but he got the job done. A look at the messengers reassured him more than the lieutenant's praise did. They were a raffish lot, men who could be counted on to get where they were going. And if they liberated booze or smokes or a steak along the way . . . well, so much the better.

He gave them oral orders. Then he handed them the dispatches he'd written. Off they went, in command cars, on horseback, on bicycles, on shank's mare. Before long, one-word responses started coming in by telephone and telegraph. *Received*, Morrell heard, again and again and again. He marked the map, again and again and again.

When he was satisfied, he got on the telephone. He called officer after officer, delivered his orders, and hung up. Maybe this would work and maybe it wouldn't. It seemed worth a try, though.

One thing: U.S. reconnaissance was good. Most people who lived in Ohio, especially in this northern part of it, wanted nothing to do with the Confederates. They slipped through enemy lines, risking their necks to report on what Jake Featherston's men were up to. When Morrell heard the Confederates were assembling armor in Homeworth, a few miles west of Salem, he smiled to himself.

Their attack on Salem went in two days later. They came loaded for bear, convinced they had a big force of barrels in front of them. Morrell showed a few and shelled the Confederates heavily to slow them down. That only made them push harder. They'd just about reached Salem's outskirts . . . when the real U.S. barrel force, which had concentrated some miles to the north, roared down and struck them in the flank.

The Confederates still might have made a fight of it. They had at least as many machines as the USA did, and theirs hit harder. But they were rattled, as anybody hit from a direction he didn't expect would have been. They fell back in some disorder, and left a lot of barrels burning in front of Salem.

"That was amazing, sir!" Now the young lieutenant looked at Morrell with something not far from hero worship.

"That's what we're supposed to do, dammit," Morrell said, wondering how—and if—he could bring off the same sort of thing again.

Abner Dowling was the man who'd spotted the Confederates thinning their lines in Virginia so they could send more men into Ohio. He hadn't had the chance to attack them after he caught them doing that. Oh, no. His reward was thinning his own lines so the USA could try to smash through the Confederates' position at Fredericksburg, which hadn't worked at all. Now he was thinning them still further to send reinforcements to the West.

He took a half pint of whiskey out of his desk drawer and stared at it. Like most half pints, it was curved to fit the hand. He wasn't a man who drank to excess. He remembered General Custer. With whiskey as with women, Custer could resist everything except temptation. And Custer with a snootful was even more a bull in a china shop than he had been any other time.

No, Dowling wasn't like that—which didn't mean he was teetotal, either. Every once in a while, a nip was welcome. Sometimes you needed *not* to think about things for a little while, and whiskey was the best thought preventer this side of a blackjack. He undid the metal screw top, raised the bottle to his lips, and took a healthy slug.

His adjutant chose that moment to walk in the door.

Captain Angelo Toricelli had been with him since his unhappy stay as commandant in Salt Lake City—another one of the garden spots of the universe. Unlike some adjutants, Toricelli understood that he wasn't about to end up on Skid Row just because he drank now and again. It was embarrassing all the same.

Trying to cover that embarrassment, Dowling held out the bottle and asked, "Want some for yourself?"

"No, thank you, sir," Captain Toricelli answered—not primly, but not in a way that suggested he'd change his mind, either. "We have a message from General MacArthur inquiring how the pullback is going in this corps."

"Tell General MacArthur to—" Dowling broke off. If he went on in that vein, Toricelli would think it was the whiskey talking. That was nonsense. Dowling needed no booze to despise Daniel MacArthur. Still . . . "Tell General MacArthur to rest assured that we are complying with his orders and the War Department's."

"Yes, sir. Thank you, sir. That's well phrased." Toricelli's dark eyes glinted. He knew what Dowling had been on the point of saying. But Dowling hadn't said it. Neither he nor the half pint could get the blame. Toricelli saluted and left the room.

Dowling eyed the little bottle. It was almost as if the narrow escape gave him the license for another drink. He shook his head and put the bottle back in the desk drawer. It would be there when he really needed it. If he drank when he didn't really need it . . . That was how trouble started.

Off in the distance, somebody's artillery opened up. He thought those were U.S. guns. With fewer foot soldiers on the ground, artillery had to take up some of the slack. Of course, some of his artillery was getting pulled west to try to stop the Confederates, too.

After fifteen or twenty minutes, the guns fell silent. Dowling hoped that meant they'd smashed whatever they were aiming at. If not, some wireless man would rush in with news of a new disaster. And Dowling would have to try to put the pieces back together—and take the blame if Humpty Dumpty remained bits of eggshell.

His eyes went to the large-scale map of Virginia on the wall. He didn't like the way his right flank was vulnerable. He never had. General Patton, the Confederates' answer to Irving Morrell, had roared out of the mountains trying to roll him up. Patton hadn't managed it. Dowling took a certain amount of pride in the way he'd defended against the CSA's armored wizard, but they didn't pin medals on your chest for losing only a few square miles. Often that deserved a medal, but it never got one.

If Patton or some other Confederate hotshot tried charging out of the mountains again, could Dowling's corps hold the enemy again? He muttered unhappily. If the Confederates hit him as hard as they had the last time, he probably couldn't. But he brightened a little a moment later. He might not have the wherewithal to defend that he'd had before, but he was pretty damn sure the boys in butternut couldn't mount the same kind of attack as they had then. They seemed to be putting everything they had into the push through Ohio and into Pennsylvania.

He looked at the map again, then slowly nodded to himself. Ever since the war started, people had been saying that whoever could mount two big drives at once would likely win. So far, neither side had come close. Logic said the United States had the better chance. They had more men and more resources. They also had more problems. The Confederates had a smoldering Negro uprising to worry about; their response seemed to be massacre. The United States had to flabble about the Mormons, and now the Canadians, the Japanese in the Pacific, and the really mad naval struggle in the North Atlantic. With all the sideshows, they couldn't concentrate on the main event.

Captain Toricelli came in again. "Yes? What is it?" Dowling asked with a sinking feeling. His adjutant could bear bad tidings at least as well as a wireless operator.

But Toricelli only asked, "Sir, do you know a Miss Ophelia Clemens?"

"The reporter? I should say I do," Dowling answered. "I spoke with her outside General MacArthur's headquarters not more than a few weeks ago, as a matter of fact. Why?"

"Because she just pulled up in front of this building, sir," Toricelli said. "I doubt like the dickens she's here to talk to me."

"Send her in. Send her in," Dowling said. "How subversive do you think I can be?"

"I couldn't begin to guess." By Toricelli's expression, though, he feared for the worst.

When Ophelia Clemens marched into Dowling's office, she looked him in the eye and said, "General, I'd murder somebody for a drink."

"Not me, I hope." Dowling opened his desk drawer and, with the air of a vaudeville conjuror, produced the half pint. "Here you are, ma'am. At your service."

"God bless you," Ophelia Clemens said. "I hoped I could find a St. Bernard in all these Alps." After that rhetorical outburst, she unscrewed the cap and swigged like a man. She eyed the bottle in her hand with a certain amount of respect. "That's what they call panther piss, isn't it?"

"Something like that," Dowling allowed. "It sure isn't sipping whiskey."

She handed the half pint back to him. When he put it away without drinking, she said, "Keep it around just for poisoning visitors, do you?"

"By no means, ma'am. You misunderstand me. I'm about half an hour ahead of you, that's all. And what besides bartender duty can I do for you on this none too lovely day?"

"Well, I've got my own cigarettes," she replied, and lit one to prove it. "I don't suppose you could spare me some truth?"

Dowling snorted. "You don't ask for much, do you?"

"If you had it, I think you might give it to me," Ophelia Clemens told him. "That's more than I can say about most of the people in your line of work I know."

"You flatter me," he said. "Keep it up. I love it."

"I'll give you the reporter's ultimate flattery, then," she said. "How would you like to be 'a reliable source'?"

Dowling knew what that meant: somebody who shot off his mouth without getting called to account for it. At his age and station, such a chance tempted him more than a twenty-two-year-old virgin—more than a twenty-two-year-old professional, come to that. "Go ahead and ask," he said, "and we'll see how reliable I am."

"All right." Ophelia Clemens took out a spiral-bound notebook, opened it to a blank page, and poised a pencil above it. "How bad do things look in Ohio and Pennsylvania?"

"You just named Pennsylvania. Right there, that says we aren't doing as well as we ought to be." Dowling shook his head. "No, I take it back. That's not fair. I don't know what things are like on the ground over there. I have my own troubles, Lord knows. You can say things aren't going as well as we wish they were."

Her pencil scratched across the page. "Do you think Featherston's going after Pittsburgh?"

"Too early to be sure, but that's how it looks right now," Dowling said.

"Uh-*huh*." Ophelia Clemens wrote some more. "Do you know, they wouldn't give me a straight answer in the War Department? You never heard so many variations on 'No comment' in all your born days. Franz Liszt couldn't write variations like that."

"Heh," Dowling said doubtfully as the allusion flew over his head. Had he been up in the War Department, he would have played it cagey, too—he knew that. You could get in trouble for saying yes and being right, for saying yes and being wrong, and conversely with no as well. *No comment* looked pretty good under those circumstances.

"Can the Confederates take Pittsburgh?" Ophelia Clemens asked.

When Dowling got questions like that, being a "reliable source" looked a lot less enjoyable. "I hope not," he blurted.

Scritch, scritch, scritch went the pencil point. "Can we stay in the war if they do take Pittsburgh?"

No, this wasn't any fun at all. "I hope so," Dowling answered. "Losing it would hurt us. We make an awful lot of steel there. But it's not like Birmingham—it's not just about the only place where we make steel. As far as that goes, we can hold on and hold out. Even so . . ."

"Will the country stand for it?" she asked. "Cleveland was supposed to hold up the Confederates for a long time. It didn't, not for nearly long enough. It's gone. It's lost. If Pittsburgh goes the same way, won't we just say, 'Oh, no, we can't win this one,' and throw in the towel?"

"That's what Jake Featherston hopes we'll do, anyhow," Dowling said. "We've got elections coming up this fall. Now, I'm just a soldier. I'm not supposed to know anything about politics, and I mostly don't." Soldiers, even soldiers acting as reliable sources, had to say such things. Dowling—and, no doubt, Ophelia Clemens with him—knew he was being disingenuous, but he couldn't help it. He went on, "One thing I haven't seen is anybody from any party campaigning on a 'Peace Now!' platform."

Scritch, scritch, scritch. "Well, neither have I," the reporter said. "Why do you suppose that is?"

"Because everybody figures Featherston would kick us while we're down," Dowling answered at once. "Don't you? What else could it be? He's made it pretty damn clear that he tells lies whenever he opens his mouth. Or do you think I'm wrong?"

"Me?" She shook her head. "No, sir. Not even a little bit. You know the number of the beast, all right. I've been in this business for as long as you've been in the Army—longer, really, because I watched my father before I was old enough or good enough to do it myself. Jake Featherston scares the spit out of me. I've never seen anybody like him, not on this continent. Some of the people in *Action Française,* maybe, and that Mosley fellow in England, but nobody here comes close."

"We should have smashed him when we had the chance, just after he got power," Dowling said. But Featherston didn't look so dangerous then. And the USA was stuck in the economic collapse. And so . . . *Yes,* Dowling thought sourly. *And so . . .*

Hipolito Rodriguez sat on his cot in the guards' barracks at Camp Determination, methodically cleaning his submachine gun. He'd learned in the dirt and mud and dust of the trenches that a clean weapon could make the difference between life and death. The submachine gun had a more complicated apparatus than his old Tredegar, too.

Another guard, an Alabaman named Jonah Gurney, said, "Anybody'd reckon you was married to that gun." He carried his weapon when he walked through the camp and ignored it the rest of the time. He was a younger man, not a recruit from the Confederate Veterans' Brigades. He'd never seen combat, and it showed.

"Married? No." Rodriguez shook his head. "My wife screw me, I like that. This gun screw me, I don't like nothin' no more." He pushed an oily rag through the barrel with a cleaning rod.

The rest of the men in the barracks laughed. "He got you, Jonah," somebody said. "He got you good."

By the dull flush rising on Gurney's blunt features, he already knew that. He liked ragging on other people. Oh, sure—he liked that fine. It wasn't so much fun when somebody turned the tables on him. If Rodriguez had had a dime for everybody like that he'd met, he would have been one of the richest men in Sonora, certainly too rich to be a camp guard.

Scowling, Gurney said, "You're asshole buddies with the big cheese in the camp, ain't you?"

"We were in the war together," Rodriguez answered with a shrug. Because he'd practiced stripping and assembling the submachine gun so much, he could let his hands do it while he kept an eye on the other guard. "I dunno about asshole buddies. I don't think I like the sound of that too much." He did like the sound with which a full magazine went into place: a satisfying click.

Jonah Gurney didn't seem to notice. "No?" he said. "What you aim to do about it, greaser?"

One step up from niggers—that was how Sonorans and Chihuahuans seemed to a lot of whites in the CSA. Another, smaller, click from Rodriguez's gun: the safety coming off. Casually, calmly, Rodriguez said, "What do I aim to do? I aim to blow your fucking head off, *pendejo*." All at once, the barrel of the gun pointed straight at Gurney's nose. Rodriguez's finger twitched on the trigger.

That wasn't what shook the Alabaman. The smile on his face was. Gurney's own face went pale as a plate of grits. He tried a smile of his own. The only word that suited it was ghastly. "Hey," he said with lips and tongue that suddenly seemed numb, "I didn't mean nothin' by it, honest to God I didn't."

"Kiss my ass," Rodriguez said succinctly.

"Put down the piece, Rodriguez." That was Troop Leader Porter, the noncom in charge of Rodriguez's squad. "There ain't gonna be any killing here today."

"Thank you, Troop Leader," Jonah Gurney gabbled. "You see what that crazy Mexican fucker was gonna do to me? Ought to take him out and—"

"Shut up." Porter's voice was flat and hard. "Pack up your shit and get the hell out of here. You're reassigned, as of now. Maybe some other camp'll take you. I don't know. I don't care. But you're not gonna stay at Camp Determination another minute, and you can take that to the bank. You're a troublemaking son of a bitch, and we've got no need for people like you. Get out. Fuck off."

Gurney stared at him as if he couldn't believe his ears. "You're gonna back a goddamn dago against a white man?"

"I'm going to back a guard who pulls his weight against a slacker who does as little as he can to get by," Porter said. "I wouldn't have been real sorry to see you dead, Gurney, if it wasn't for the paperwork I'd have to fill out to make sure Rodriguez didn't end up in hot water over your worthless carcass."

Gurney plainly thought himself as much abandoned and thrown over the side for no good reason as the original Jonah. He gestured toward the rest of the guards in the barracks, a wave full of angry disbelief. "Come on, y'all!" he cried. "You gonna let him get away with that? You gonna let him screw over a white man for the sake of a goddamn *Mexican?*" Disbelief stretched his voice high and shrill.

For close to a minute, nobody said anything. Nobody seemed to want to look at Gurney, or at Rodriguez, or at Troop Leader Porter. For that matter, nobody seemed to want to look at anybody else. Finally, somebody behind Gurney said, "He's got the stripes, Jonah. Reckon that gives him the right."

"Like hell it does!" Jonah Gurney shouted furiously. "We're white men! That gives *us* the right. That's what this here country's all about, ain't it? That's what the Freedom Party's all about, ain't it?"

Again, silence stretched. This time, Porter broke it. "Go on, Jonah," he said, his voice surprisingly gentle. "Go on now, and don't get yourself any deeper in Dutch. I'm gonna make like I didn't hear any of what you said just now. A man's gotta blow off steam. I know that. But you don't want me to have to tell the commandant you were trying to make a mutiny, now do you?"

When Rodriguez was in the Army, they'd read out the Articles of War every so often. Making a mutiny was one of the things they could shoot you or hang you for. Even mentioning it put a chill in the hot, muggy air. Rodriguez didn't know if camp guards came under the same military law as soldiers, but he would have bet they did.

The ominous words seemed to get home to Gurney, too. "This ain't right, dammit," he muttered. "My Congressman's gonna hear about it, so help me God he is." But he might have shrunk, standing there in plain sight. He filled his gray canvas duffel bag, slung it over his shoulder, and trudged out of the barracks.

Rodriguez nodded to Porter. "Thank you," he said softly.

"I didn't do it for you," the noncom answered.

"Thank you anyway," Rodriguez said.

His gratitude only embarrassed the troop leader. "I didn't do it for you, dammit," he repeated. "I did it for all of us. When we're in there with the coons, we've got to know we can trust each other to guard our backs. Anybody who doesn't care to help another man who wears the same uniform no matter what, I don't want that son of a bitch here. I can't trust him. Nobody can trust him." He looked around the barracks. "We got anybody else who feels the way Gurney did? Anybody who does, clean out your footlocker and head out the door. I won't put a bad word on your fitness report—swear to Jesus I won't—but I want you doin' somethin' else. Anybody?"

No one moved. No one spoke.

"All right, then," Porter said. "Rodriguez isn't the only man from Sonora and Chihuahua we've got at this camp—not even close. Has anybody seen any sign that those people are falling down on the job? Anything at all?" Again, no one said a word. The noncom nodded. "I haven't, either. The government and the Party—*and the Party,* mind you—thought they could do it, or they wouldn't have recruited them in the first place, right? Y'all gonna tell Jake Featherston he doesn't know what he's doin'? You let me know where you want your body sent first."

That pretty much took care of that. White men were careful around Rodriguez from then on out. He wasn't sure whether they were afraid to say anything bad to him even if he had it coming or they were afraid he'd shoot them if they did say anything. Either way felt awkward. He wished they would just treat him the way they treated one another. Too much to hope for, he feared.

He wasn't a Mexican, a greaser, to the Negroes in the camp. Maybe that was because they knew most Sonorans and Chihuahuans had no more use for them than most whites did. More likely, he judged, it was because to them, in his gray uniform, he was a guard. The uniform took precedence over the face.

When he went over to the women's side of the camp, the prisoners always tried to soften him up. If he'd do something for them, they made it plain, they would do something for him. And some of them left nothing to the imagination. Taking up all the offers and come-ons and out-and-out propositions would have drained a man half his age dry in nothing flat.

Some of the guards took up as many as they could. In a way, Rodriguez understood that. They had to think, *Why not?* Sooner or later, whether she knew it or not, a woman was going out in a truck. Why not enjoy her while she was here? If she was enjoyable, why not fix it so she went out later, not sooner? In the end, what difference did it make?

Rodriguez took up an offer himself every now and then, but only every now and then. Most of the time, he remembered he was a married man. When three guards in quick succession got the clap, that made him more cautious than ever. Magdalena wouldn't thank him for bringing home a drippy faucet.

Troop Leader Porter was loudly disgusted when that happened. "Jesus fucking Christ!" he exclaimed. "And *fucking*'s about right, ain't it? We gonna have to set up a shortarm station around here? I knew we had some dumb pricks on this duty, but y'all have gone over the line. Next man who comes down venereal, he's gonna get a dishonorable discharge to go with his dishonorable discharge, you hear me?"

"Yes, Troop Leader!" the guards chorused. Sooner or later, somebody would. If it was later, the noncom might have forgotten about his threat. If it was sooner . . . Rodriguez resisted temptation till he got shifted to the men's side.

That was a different business. Walking through the men's side, inspecting barracks to make sure the prisoners weren't working on tunnels or any other nefarious schemes, was like walking through a cage full of wolves and cougars. Nothing was likely to happen to you if you were careful and if you stayed with your buddies. If you went off by yourself . . .

One guard got his head smashed in. His weapon disappeared. Everybody turned the men's half of the camp upside down and inside out. Rodriguez thought that submachine gun was gone for good, or till a *mallate* emptied the clip into more guards. But, by what had to be not far from a miracle, it got fished out of a latrine trench. It was wrapped in greasy rags and slathered with lard—not as good as Cosmoline, but enough to keep it in working order. No one ever found out who did in the guard. All the prisoners had their rations cut in punishment, but nobody squealed.

"Suh, what they buildin' out past the wire?" a man asked Rodriguez not long after the gun was recovered.

By chance, the black had picked a guard who knew. The answer would get Rodriguez a promotion as soon as the paperwork went through. But he just scowled at the scrawny prisoner and said, "You find out when the time comes."

"You don't got to be dat way, suh." The Negro's voice was a sheepish whine he'd no doubt used to talk his way out of trouble before. "I didn't mean no disrespect. I wasn't rude or crude or mean or nothin' like that. I just wants to know."

"You find out when the time comes," Rodriguez repeated, and glared at the prisoner. The fellow knew when to back off in a hurry. When the time came, when he found out, that wouldn't help him a bit.

XII

All ahead one-third," Sam Carsten called down to the engine room from the *Josephus Daniels'* bridge.

"All ahead one-third, sir, aye aye." The answer came back at once. The destroyer escort picked up a little speed.

Sam read the chart by the dim glow of a flashlight with red cellophane taped over the bulb. That didn't spoil his night vision and wouldn't be visible from any great distance. Getting out of Philadelphia Harbor and Delaware Bay was going to be even more fun than escaping Chesapeake Bay.

If the clouds overhead broke . . . If they did, moonlight would pour down on the U.S. warship while she was still sneaking through the minefields that protected the harbor. That, to put it mildly, wouldn't be good. Confederate subs lurked just outside, hungry for anything they could catch.

"I wish they would have given us a pilot who really knows these minefields," Pat Cooley said.

"Me, too," Sam told his exec. "I asked for one at the Navy yard. Hell, I screamed for one. They wouldn't give him to me. They said we'd have to stop and lower a boat to let him come back, and that that would make the mission even more dangerous. They said they didn't have enough pilots like that for us to just go on and take him with us."

"Well, I can sort of see their point," Cooley said reluctantly. "Sort of." In the light of that cellophane-covered flashlight, he looked like a pink, angry ghost. "If we were a battleship or a carrier, though, we would have got one."

"Now that you mention it, yes." Carsten gave the younger officer a crooked smile. "Didn't you figure out we were expendable the first time they gave us a shore-bombardment mission?"

"Sorry, sir. I guess I'm just naive," Cooley answered. "But I'll tell you something—I'm sure as hell convinced now."

"That's, uh, swell." Sam had almost said it was bully. To someone the executive officer's age, that would have smacked of the nineteenth century, if not the Middle Ages. Since Sam was only middle-aged himself—and not always reconciled to that—he didn't want Cooley to think of him as one with Nineveh and Tyre. Then he stopped flabbling about changing tastes in American slang and went back to worrying about getting blown out of the water if he screwed up. "Come left to 150. I say again, come left to 150."

"Coming left to one-five-oh: aye aye, sir." Cooley changed course without question or comment. He was still the best shiphandler on the *Josephus Daniels*. In a nasty spot like this, the best shiphandler belonged at the wheel. He had to make his course corrections on the basis of what Sam told him, and had to hope Sam was telling him the right thing. If that wasn't enough to give you an ulcer before you hit thirty, Sam didn't know what would be.

Even if I do everything right, we still may go sky-high, Sam thought unhappily. Not all Confederate submersibles carried torpedoes. Some laid mines. If they'd laid some that U.S. sweepers hadn't found yet, that could get—interesting. Or a moored mine might have come loose. If it drifted into their path . . . Sam would have done everything right, and a fat lot of good it would do him.

He gauged distances and times and speed and ordered other course corrections. Lieutenant Cooley coolly made them. "How am I doing?" the exec asked after a while.

"You're here to ask the question. You're standing on a nice, level deck. We're not burning. We're not sinking. You're doing fine. If you hit a mine, I'll have something to say to you. Till then, don't worry about it."

Cooley chuckled. "You've got a good way of looking at things, sir."

"Do I? I don't know," Sam said. "This whole business of being in

command is new to me. I'm making it up as I go along—and I probably shouldn't tell you a word of that. Well, too goddamn bad. It's not
like you and everybody else aboard don't already know it."

"Don't worry about it, sir. Everybody knows you're the Old Man,
and everybody feels good about it," Cooley said.

"Thanks," Sam said. On the *Josephus Daniels,* he was the old man
literally as well as figuratively. The destroyer escort had a couple of
grizzled chiefs with close to his mileage on them, but only a couple. He
was old enough to be father for most of the crew. If anything, that
might help his position of command. If somebody looked and sounded
like your dad, you were used to taking orders from him. Of course, if
you were eighteen you were probably convinced your dad was a jerk,
so maybe command authority didn't follow from age after all.

Like his early small worry, that one got submerged in the intricacy
and tension of what he was doing. He stayed at it till the gray light of
earliest morning grew brighter than the flashlight's red beam. Then he
stood up very straight and allowed himself to look away from the chart
and stretch.

"I think we're through it, Pat," he said.

"Good. That's hard work." The exec also stretched. "I think we
handled it about as well as we could."

"You did the hard part," Carsten said. "I just told you where to
go." He grinned. "I'm the only man on this ship who can."

"You're the only one who can *say* it," Cooley replied. "Everybody
else just thinks it." He turned to the bespectacled, extremely junior J.G.
in charge of the Y-range gear. "Isn't that right, Walters?"

"I don't know what you're talking about, sir," Thad Walters
replied, deadpan—which, in a perverse way, proved Cooley's point.

Sam took another look at the lightening sky. He didn't like what he
saw, not even a little bit. "Any sign of those damn Confederate maritime bombers?" he asked, knowing he sounded anxious. Any skipper
without air cover of his own—and even skippers with it—had the right
to sound anxious in this day and age.

Walters eyed the screen. So did Sam. *He* didn't see anything un-
toward, but would an expert? War was getting to be a business of gadget against gadget, not man against man. Well, that had been true when
battleships ruled the seas, too, but the gadgets were a lot subtler these
days.

"Looks all right for now," the young J.G. said.

"Keep an eye peeled," Sam told him. He spoke into a voice tube: "Anything on the hydrophone, Bevacqua?"

"No, sir," the petty officer's voice came back. "Everything's quiet."

"That's what I like to hear." *Another gadget,* Sam thought. They'd had hydrophones during the Great War, too. Back then, though, you'd had to stop to listen. If a sub *was* in the neighborhood, stopping wasn't the best thing you could do. In the last war, also, the hydrophone could give you a bearing on where a submersible prowled, but not a range.

The boys with the thick glasses and the slide rules had fancied up the device in the interwar years. These days, hydrophones could filter out a ship's own engine noise, though they still worked better in silence. They could also say just where in the water an enemy submarine hid. The way Vince Bevacqua explained it, new-model hydrophones used sound waves as Y-ranging gear used wireless waves: they bounced them off a target and picked up the reflections.

Technical details fascinated Sam. He knew he would never be able to repair, let alone improve, a Y-range set or a hydrophone. That didn't bother him. The better he understood how the gadgets worked, what they could and couldn't do, the better he'd be able to use them and the more he could count on what they told him.

"Keep listening," was all he said now.

"Who, me?" Bevacqua answered. Sam laughed. He knew how hard the petty officer concentrated with the earphones on his head.

Pat Cooley waved at the thick clouds overhead. "We've got a nice low ceiling this morning," he remarked. "We probably don't have to worry about the maritime bombers too much. Only thing that has any real chance of running across us is a flying boat out snooping."

"Yeah, those bastards fly low all the time," Sam agreed. "One of these days before too long, they'll have Y-range gear, too, and then everything'll be out to lunch. Makes you wonder what the Navy's coming to, doesn't it?" He wasn't worried, not as far as his own career went. A kid like Cooley would see a lot more change, though.

The exec didn't seem unduly worried. "If we're vulnerable to air power, we'll just have to bring our own air power with us, that's all. If our airplanes shoot down their airplanes before they can get at us, we win. That was the real lesson of the Pacific War."

Sam had been *in* the Pacific War. Cooley hadn't even been at Annapolis yet. That didn't mean he was wrong. "Carriers have a hard time operating against land-based air, though," he said. "Too many attackers can swamp you. We found that out at Charleston." He'd been there, too, when this war was new.

"Put enough carriers together and you'll swamp the land-based air." Cooley might have been right about that. Neither the United States nor Britain, the two major carrier powers in the Atlantic, had been able to prove it yet. Japan was trying its hardest to do so over and around the Sandwich Islands.

Since Sam couldn't prove anything one way or the other, he said, "Bring us around to course 090, Pat."

"Changing course to 090—aye aye, sir." Cooley swung the *Josephus Daniels* to port till she was steady on her new easterly course. "Steady on 090, sir."

"Thank you. Now we've got a clear track to Providence—except for subs and mines and raiders and those flying boats and other little details like that."

"Providence?" By the way the exec said it, he might have been talking about the Black Hole of Calcutta. He sighed noisily. "Well, it's better than staying stuck in Philadelphia would be . . . I suppose. What are we going to do there, deliver the *Daniels* so she can take over as a training ship for the swabbies there?"

Seamen learning their trade went out on the *Lamson,* a destroyer of Great War vintage. They learned to fire weapons aboard her. They formed the black gang that served her wheezy engines. They worked in the galleys. They cleaned heads. They learned what it was like to sleep in a hammock with another sailor's bad breath and backside only inches from their face.

"We're not quite spavined enough for that," Sam said. Cooley raised an eyebrow at an evidently unfamiliar word, but he figured out what it had to mean. Sam felt his years showing again. Back when people talked about horses all the time, you heard *spavined* every week if not every day. But the exec had grown up in an automotive age. If you talked about a spavined motorcar, you were making a joke, not describing anything real. Sam went on, "We're going to escort a convoy down the coast to New York City and then back to Philly."

"Should be exciting." The exec mimed an enormous yawn.

Sam laughed. "If you're on convoy-escort duty, you hope to Jesus it *isn't* exciting. Everything that could make it exciting is bad."

"I suppose so." Cooley grudged him a nod, then winked. "One

thing, Skipper—all that zigzagging will do wonders for you at the wheel."

"Yeah, I know," Sam answered seriously, which spoiled Cooley's joke, but the same thought had already occurred to him. And he wanted his shiphandling to get better. He wanted everything he did to get better. He'd got such a late start at being an officer, and still had so much catching up to do. . . .

Fremont Blaine Dalby stared at the ships coming into Pearl Harbor. The CPO shook his head. "If those aren't two of the ugliest sons of bitches I ever set eyes on, then you two guys are." He nodded to Fritz Gustafson and George Enos, Jr.

George said, "I dunno, Chief. They look pretty damn good to me."

"Yeah." Gustafson added a nod.

"Bullshit," Dalby said. The boss of the twin-40mm crew was a man of strong opinions. His being a Republican proved that. Some of his opinions were crackpot, too; as far as George was concerned, his being a Republican also proved that. He went on, "Don't get me wrong. I'm not saying we don't need 'em, on account of we do. But they're still as ugly as the guy sitting next to you on the head."

George grunted at that. Like any new sailor, he'd had to get used to doing his business in a facility without stalls. He hadn't thought about it for a while now, and wondered if he'd be stricken with constipation because he did. He admitted to himself—if not to Fremont Dalby—that the senior rating had a point of sorts. The *Trenton* and the *Chapultepec* didn't have the raked grace of a heavy cruiser. But the escort carriers brought something vital to the Sandwich Islands: hope.

They looked like what they were—freighters that had had their superstructures torn off and replaced with a flight deck. A tiny starboard island didn't begin to make up for what had been amputated. But they carried thirty airplanes apiece. They had dive bombers and torpedo-carriers, and fighters to protect the strike aircraft and the ships themselves. The two of them put together were worth about as much as one fleet carrier.

"What I want to know is, are there more of them out in the Pacific?" George said. "That's what really counts. If they can watch the gap where airplanes from the Sandwich Islands can't stay and the ones from the West Coast can't, either, then we really might hang on to this place."

"They didn't come by themselves, you know," Dalby reminded him. "Most of the freighters and tankers that came with 'em are un-loading in Honolulu, not here. But everybody'll have enough beans and gasoline for a while longer."

"Sure, Chief." Disagreeing with a CPO when you were only an able seaman took diplomacy. Picking his words with care, George went on, "But it's not waddayacallit—not economical, that's what I want to say—to send these ugly ducklings back and forth to Frisco or wherever for each new convoy."

"He's right," Gustafson said—another good-sized speech for him. He was a petty officer himself, though not an exalted chief. He could speak somewhat more freely to Dalby, but only somewhat. George was more than halfway convinced that CPOs really ran the Navy. They let officers think they did, but so many officers' orders were based on what they heard from CPOs. A lieutenant, J.G., who tried to buck one of the senior ratings didn't have a prayer. Even his own superiors wouldn't back him, and it wouldn't have helped if they did.

"Well, yeah," Fremont Dalby said, "but these babies ought to be good for more than defense. They ought to be able to play sixty min-utes. How many of 'em d'you figure we'd need to take Midway back from the Buddhaheads?"

Gustafson eyed the *Chapultepec,* which was closer. "Damn thing can't do more'n eighteen knots if you chuck her off a cliff," he opined—a veritable oration. He didn't bother to say what he already knew: that Japanese fleet carriers, like most self-respecting warships, could make better than thirty.

Dalby only shrugged. "Doesn't matter all that much. Airplanes are a hell of a lot faster than ships any which way."

That held some truth, but only some. Other things went into the mix. "Jap carriers can walk away from subs. These little guys won't be able to."

Another shrug from the gun chief. "That's why the *Townsend*'s in the Navy. If we can't keep submersibles off of carriers, what the hell good are we?"

George gave up. He wasn't about to change Dalby's mind. That was as plain as the nose on the CPO's face—which was saying some-thing, because Dalby had a formidable honker. In the end, changing

Dalby's mind didn't matter a dime's worth anyhow. Dalby wasn't the one who'd decide what to do with the escort carriers. He wasn't the one who'd decide what to do with the *Townsend,* either, though he often acted as if he were the skipper.

He said, "It'll be goddamn nice operating with real air cover for a change. Not even the brass'd be dumb enough to send us out naked anymore."

"Here's hoping." Fritz Gustafson packed a world of skepticism into two words.

This time, George thought Dalby had the right of it. There were plenty of land-based airplanes on Oahu. Why send carriers all the way to the Sandwich Islands if not to use them with the rest of the Navy?

When the *Townsend* put to sea a few days later, she did so without either the *Trenton* or the *Chapultepec.* Even though she did, George didn't flabble about it: she went out on an antisubmersible patrol to the east of Oahu. Japanese carrier-based aircraft were most unlikely to find her there.

After George remarked on that, Dalby looked at him—looked through him, really. "You'd sooner be torpedoed?"

"Got a better chance against a sub than we would against airplanes," George said stubbornly. Then he wondered if that was true. His father hadn't had any chance against a submarine. *But he got sucker-punched after the war was over. We'd be on our toes.*

Whenever George was on deck, he kept an eye peeled for periscopes. He also looked for the thin, pale exhaust from a submersible's diesel engine. What with the *Townsend*'s hydrophone gear, all that was probably wasted effort. He didn't care, not even a little bit. He did it anyhow. He noticed he was far from the only one who did.

He wasn't on deck when general quarters sounded. He was rinsing off in the shower. He threw on his skivvies and ran for his gun with the rest of his clothes, including his shoes, under his arm.

Nobody laughed, or not very much. Nobody who'd been in the Navy longer than a few weeks hadn't been caught the same way. He dressed at his post. His hair was still wet. It dripped in his face and down his back. He would have minded that much more in the North Atlantic in December than he did here.

"Now hear this!" The exec's voice crackled out of the loudspeakers. "We've found us a submarine, and we are going to prosecute the son of a bitch."

An excited buzz ran through the sailors. George looked enviously up toward the depth-charge launchers near the destroyer's bow. Their crews were the ones who'd have the fun of dropping things on the Japs' heads.

"Don't go to sleep, now," Fremont Dalby warned. "If those bastards surface, we're the ones who'll fill 'em full of holes." He set a hand on one of the 40mm's twin barrels. The quick-firing gun made an admirable can opener.

The *Townsend* swung to port. Down under the surface, a submersible was no doubt maneuvering, too. It could have been cat-and-mouse, but the mouse here had almost as good a chance as the cat. The *Townsend*'s advantage was speed, the sub's stealth. Where was that boat?

They must have thought they knew, for depth charges flew from the launchers and splashed into the Pacific. George waited, bracing himself. When the ashcans burst, it was like a kick in the ass from an elephant. The *Townsend*'s bow lifted, then slammed back down.

More charges arced through the air. Some would be set for a depth a little less than the hydrophone operator thought accurate, some for a little more. With luck, the submersible wouldn't get away. With luck . . .

"Oil! Oil!" somebody yelled. His voice cracked the second time he said it.

"Could be a trick," Fritz Gustafson said. George nodded. A canny sub skipper would deliberately release oil and air bubbles to try to fool his tormentors into thinking they'd smashed him. Then he could slink away or strike back as he got the chance.

Not this time, though. "Coming up!" screamed somebody near the bow. "Motherfucker's coming up!"

Like a breaching whale but far bigger, the Japanese submarine surfaced. She might not have been able to stay down anymore, but she still showed fight. Men tumbled out of her conning tower and ran for the deck guns. The odds against them were long—a destroyer vastly outgunned a submersible—but they had a chance. If they could hurt the *Townsend* badly enough, they might yet get away.

But the destroyer's guns were already manned and ready. George wasn't sure if his weapon was the very first to start blazing away, but it was among the first. Tracers walked across the water toward the sub less than a mile away. They were close enough to the target to let him see chunks of metal fly when shells slammed into the side of the boat and the conning tower. One of the shells hit a Japanese sailor amidships. He exploded into red mist. There were worse ways to go; he must have died before he knew it.

The Japs got off a few shots. One of them hit near the *Townsend*'s bow, just aft of the ashcan launchers. George heard shrieks through the din of gunfire. But the sub was in over its head. Its guns were out in the open and unprotected, and the American 40mms and machine guns picked off the crews in nothing flat. When the destroyer's main armament started taking bites out of the sub's hull, it quickly sank. It kept firing as long as it could. The crew had guts—no way around that.

A few men still bobbed in the water after the submersible went down. The *Townsend* steered toward them and threw lines and life rings into the water. The Japanese sailors stubbornly refused to take them. A couple of sailors deliberately sank when lines came near. Others shook defiant fists at the ship that had sunk their sub. They shouted what had to be insults in their own language.

"They're crazy," George said. "If that was me, I'd be up on this deck and down on my knees thanking God they'd rescued me instead of shooting me or leaving me for shark bait or just to drown."

"Japs aren't like that," Dalby said. "Bunch of crazy monkeys, if you want to know what I think."

"They figure being a POW is the worst thing in the world," Fritz Gustafson said. "Far as they're concerned, dying's better."

"Like I said—crazy," Dalby said.

"Nasty, too." Gustafson was, for him, in a talky mood. "Don't let 'em catch you. If you're a POW, they figure you're in disgrace. Anything goes, near enough."

"How do you know that?" George asked.

The loader shrugged. "You hear stuff, is all."

One of the last Japanese sailors afloat spat seawater up at the *Townsend*. He made gestures that probably meant the same as giving her the finger. The ship took the perfect revenge: she sailed away. The sailors whooped and cheered. "I think you're right, Chief," George said. "They *are* crazy."

"Told you so," Fremont Dalby said smugly. "I just wish they weren't so goddamn tough, that's all."

* * *

Jefferson Pinkard inspected his dress grays in the mirror. He looked pretty goddamn sharp, if he did say so himself. The three wreathed silver stars on either side of his collar gleamed and sparkled. The way he'd polished them, they couldn't very well do anything else. His silver belt buckle shone, too. So did the black leather of his belt and boots.

When he got married the first time, back before the Great War, he'd done it in a rented tailcoat. He'd thought he was hot stuff, then. Maybe he'd even been right. His belly hadn't bulged over his belt in those days, anyhow.

He scowled as the memory came back. Emily'd been hot stuff in those days, too. Too goddamn hot, it turned out. "Little whore," he growled. She hadn't wanted to wait till he got back from the trenches. She'd spread it around, starting with his best friend. He remembered walking in after he got a leave he hadn't told her about ahead of time, walking in and . . .

Angrily, he turned away from the mirror. Then, feeling foolish, he had to turn back to get his hat—almost a Stetson, but with a higher crown and a wider brim—cocked at just the right jaunty angle. Everything was going to be perfect, dammit, perfect, and he wasn't going to think about Emily even once.

A Birmingham painted in official butternut waited for him. "Take you into town, sir?" the driver said.

"If you don't, we ain't got a show," Jeff answered, and the fellow behind the wheel laughed. Jeff added, "Yeah, you might as well. I've come this far. I don't reckon I'll chicken out now." He slid into the back seat.

"Better not," the driver agreed. "That's where you get one of them waddayacallems—breeches of promise suits, that's it."

That wasn't exactly it, but came close enough. Jeff wondered if any lawyers were filing breach of promise suits these days, or if the Army had grabbed them all. Most, anyhow, he guessed. But a maiden spurned could probably still find a lawyer to be her knight in shining armor—at a suitable hourly rate, of course.

Edith Blades was no maiden. On the other hand, Jeff didn't aim to spurn her. "Long as I'm at the church, everything'll be just fine," he said.

A couple of buses sat in the church parking lot. They'd brought guards in from Camp Determination. Patrols would be thin there this afternoon and evening. Jeff hoped they wouldn't be *too* thin. He didn't think they would. He'd made the camp as hard to break out of as he could. It ought to get along just fine for a few hours with a skeleton crew.

Hip Rodriguez waited in the doorway and waved when Jeff got out of the Birmingham. Edith had squawked a little when Jeff asked a Mexican to be his best man, but he'd won the argument. "Wasn't for him, sweetheart," he'd said, "it's not real likely I'd be here to marry you." Edith hadn't found any answer for that. Pinkard hadn't figured she could.

"You look good, *Señor* Jeff," Rodriguez called.

"So do you," Pinkard said, which was true. His old Army buddy hadn't put on nearly so much weight as he had, and looked impressive as the devil in his guard's uniform. Whoever had designed those clothes knew how to intimidate.

"*Gracias.*" Rodriguez's smile was on the sheepish side. "You know something? This is the very first time I ever go inside a Protestant church."

Thinking about it, Jeff realized *he'd* never set foot inside a Catholic church. He remembered some of the things he'd heard about those places when he was growing up in Birmingham. Turning them on their head, he said, "Don't worry, Hip. I promise we don't keep the Devil down in the storm cellar."

By the way his pal started to cross himself, he must have been wondering something like that. Rodriguez broke off the gesture before completing it. "Of course not, *Señor* Jeff," he said, though his expression argued it was anything but *of course*.

Jeff went on into the vestibule or whatever they called the antechamber just inside the entrance. Edith's sister, who would be her maid of honor, stood guard at the door to the minister's little office. The bride waited in there, and the groom was not going to set eyes on her till the ceremony started.

Jeff liked Judy Smallwood just fine. If he hadn't got to know Edith first, he might have liked her sister better. Since Judy was going back to Alexandria right after the wedding, though, that wasn't likely to prove a problem. "You look mighty nice," he told her, and she did. Her dress was of glowing blue taffeta with short puffed sleeves that set off her figure and her fair skin, dark blond hair, and blue eyes.

By the way those eyes traveled him, she thought he cut a pretty fine figure himself in his fancy uniform. She said, "Kind of a shame you haven't got anybody coming out from Alabama for the day."

"My ma and pa been dead for years," Jeff answered with a shrug. "Don't have any brothers or sisters. My cousins . . ." He shrugged again. "I don't recollect the last time I talked to one of them. They heard from me now, they'd just reckon I was aiming to pry a wedding present out of 'em."

"Well, if it's like that, you shouldn't," Judy said. "It's too bad, though."

"Have I got time for a cigarette before we get going?" Jeff wondered. He'd just pulled the pack out of his pocket when the minister emerged from the office. Jeff made the cigarettes disappear again. A smoke would have calmed his nerves, but he could do without. Anyhow, the only real cure for prewedding jitters was about four stiff drinks, and that would make people talk. He touched the brim of his hat. "Howdy, Parson."

"Mr. Pinkard," the Reverend Luke Sutton said, bobbing his bald head in return. He sent Hip Rodriguez a slightly fishy stare. Rodriguez showed no sign of sprouting horns on his forehead or letting a barbed tail slither out past his trouser cuffs, so the minister looked away and started down the aisle.

Mrs. Sutton struck up the wedding march on a beat-up old upright piano against one wall. Some Baptist churches didn't approve of music at all; Jeff was glad the Suttons weren't quite so strict. As they'd rehearsed, he listened to her play it through once. Then he headed down the aisle himself. His best man followed.

Uniforms filled the folding chairs on one side. The other held Edith's relatives: ordinary-looking men and women in black suits and in dresses of a variety of colors and styles—some of them must have dated from just after the Great War, and they ran up to the present.

Edith's sons by Chick Blades were the ring bearers. Small, smothered chuckles rose as people got a look at the young boys. Jeff had to work to keep his own face straight. Edith had told him she would make sure Frank and Willie didn't have silly grins on their faces when they came down the aisle. She'd put the fear of God in them, all right, better than Reverend Sutton could have dreamt of doing. They looked serious past the point of solemnity—all the way to absurdity, in fact.

Edith's sister came next. She was grinning, but on her it looked good. And Edith herself followed a moment later. Her dress was identical in cut to Judy's, but of a taffeta somewhere between cream and beige: this wasn't her first marriage, so white wouldn't have been right. She'd had to do some searching to find a veil that matched, but she'd managed.

She stood beside Jeff. They faced the minister. He went through a wedding sermon he'd probably delivered a hundred times before. It wasn't fresh. It wasn't exciting. It wasn't even very interesting. Pinkard didn't care. It was official—that was all that mattered. Before too long, Sutton got down to business. They exchanged rings, taking them from the velvet pillows Edith's sons carried. "Do you, Jefferson Davis Pinkard, take this woman as your lawful wedded wife, to have and to hold, to love and to cherish, in sickness and in health, for richer, for poorer, for better, for worse, till death do you part?"

"I do," Jeff said.

Edith's vows were the same, except there was a *to obey* in them somewhere. Jeff hardly noticed it, and suspected Edith would hardly notice it, either. Her chin went up in pride as she also said, "I do."

"Then by the authority vested in me by the Confederate Baptist Convention and by the sovereign state of Texas, I now pronounce you man and wife," Luke Sutton declared. "You may kiss the bride."

Jeff lifted Edith's veil to do just that. He made the kiss thorough without, he hoped, making a spectacle of himself. Edith stayed relaxed in his arms, so he didn't think he overdid it.

The wedding march rang out again as the new couple and their attendants went up the aisle to the back of the church. Everybody else filed by to congratulate them. "Well, what do you think?" Jeff asked Hip Rodriguez after the last guards and cousins of Edith's slowly shuffled past.

"Very nice, *Señor* Jeff," Rodriguez answered, but he couldn't help adding, "I miss the priest's fancy robes and the incense and the Latin. This way, it hardly seems like you are in an *iglesia*—a church."

"Oh, it's a church, all right," Jeff said. He *had* seen priests in rich robes down in the Empire of Mexico. He hadn't seen a service there, though. It didn't seem as if those prelates and somebody like Reverend Sutton were talking about the same God.

The church boasted a little social hall next to the sanctuary. The reception was there. The punch and cider were teetotal; Reverend Sutton wouldn't have it any other way. Warned of this, Jeff had got the intelligence to the guards. A lot of them carried flasks with which to improve the liquid refreshment. They stayed reasonably discreet, and the minister stayed reasonably polite.

One of the guards made models for a hobby. Working with a tiny brush, he'd changed the clothes of the groom atop the wedding cake from white tie and tails to dress-gray uniform. The figure was still too slim to make a good image of Jeff Pinkard, but it looked a lot more like him than it had before. Edith stuffed gooey chocolate cake into his mouth, and he did the same for her.

He wasn't sorry not to dance on church property. He'd never been much for cutting a rug. At about ten o'clock, he and Edith went out to the Birmingham. People cheered and yelled bawdy advice and pelted them with rice. The driver took them back to Jeff's quarters. Edith squeaked when he picked her up to carry her over the threshold. Then, as he set her down, he said, "What's this?"

This was a bottle of champagne in a bucket of ice by the bed. A card in an envelope leaned against the bucket. When Jeff opened the envelope and took out the card, his eyes almost bugged out of his head. *Hope the two of you stay real happy together,* it read in a looping scrawl surely written by no secretary. The signature was in that same rough hand: *Jake Featherston.*

"Oh," Edith said, reading it with him. "Oh, Jeff."

"Yeah," Jeff said. "That's . . . somethin', all right." He picked up the champagne bottle. "Reckon the least we can do is drink some o' this before . . ." He stopped. Edith turned pink anyhow. He laughed. Wedding nights were for laughing, weren't they?

Champagne went down smoother than spiked punch had. Edith got pinker yet, not from embarrassment but from the sparkling wine. Jeff picked her up again. He was a big man, and she wasn't a very large woman. This time, he set her down on the bed.

She was no giggling maiden. She knew what was what, the same as Jeff did. That made it better, as far as he was concerned. When it was over, he stroked her, lazy in the afterglow. "Hello there, wife," he said.

"Hello . . . husband," Edith said, and started to cry. "I love you, Jeff." Even though she said it, even though he was sure she meant it, he knew she was remembering Chick, too. He didn't know what the hell he could do about it. Doing nothing seemed the smartest thing, so he did that.

* * *

Chester Martin's leg still didn't feel like carrying him around. Like it or not, though, the leg could do the job. The Army let wounded men heal, but only as long as it absolutely had to. Then it threw them back into the meat grinder to see if they could get chopped up again.

As Martin lit a cigarette in a replacement depot somewhere in western Pennsylvania, he wondered why the devil he'd joined up again. He'd known he could get hurt. Get hurt, hell—he could get killed. He'd done it anyhow. After a while, you forgot how bad it had been. That was the only thing he could think of. Women said the same thing happened when they had babies. If they'd truly remembered how bad labor was, none of them would have had more than one.

He couldn't imagine a lonelier place than this depot. He was still part of the Army, of course, but he wasn't exactly *in* it. He wasn't part of a unit. A soldier by himself was hardly a soldier at all. Whatever outfit he joined now, he'd be *the new guy* for a while—till enough other men got killed and maimed and enough other replacements took over for them to make him an old-timer again.

The way things were going these days, it wouldn't take long.

Men ranging in rank from private up to major sat on benches and folding chairs. Some of them smoked, some read newspapers or paperback adventures or mysteries, some just stared into space. Chester recognized that stare, because he'd worn it: the look of a man who'd seen too much of hell. You could help a buddy out when things got bad, or he could help you. Nobody here had a buddy. That was part of being in limbo, a bad part. You were stuck with yourself.

A fat technical sergeant who would never get any closer to the front than this called out three names, following each with a serial number. Two privates and a corporal shouldered the packs they'd had between their feet. They went up to the tech sergeant, signed some papers, and went out the door by which Chester had come in. They were fully part of the military machinery again.

Off in the distance, antiaircraft guns barked. Confederate dive bombers and strafing fighters were tearing up U.S. positions in these parts, softening them so C.S. barrels and foot soldiers could cut through them more easily. The boys in butternut had the bit between their teeth again, and they were running like hell.

Chester ground out the cigarette under his heel and lit another one.

He didn't have the wind he'd had the last time around, but who did? Smoking gave him something to do. It was as much fun as he was allowed to have here.

Out popped that tech sergeant again. Half a dozen privates got up and trudged off to whatever awaited them. Chester went on chainsmoking. Second lieutenants got killed in droves. First sergeants were a tougher, smarter—or at least more experienced—breed. Till one went down, he'd sit here twiddling his thumbs.

"Martin, Chester A.!" the tech sergeant yelled, and his pay number after it. The man also shouted several other names.

Speak of the devil, Martin thought. He rose, slung on his pack—which didn't make his sore leg rejoice—and went over to the other noncom. The men with him were all kids—a PFC and five or six newly minted privates. The technical sergeant paid more attention to him than to the rest of them put together. Chester signed off on his paperwork, then went outside.

He'd wondered if his new outfit would have sent another senior sergeant to collect men from the repple-depple. Instead, a shavetail second lieutenant awaited him. That was good news and bad: good because it showed his new CO had enough sense to pick somebody who wasn't needed in the field, bad because the youngster here was liable to know that and resent it.

By the sour expression on the lieutenant's rather rabbity features, he knew it too well. "Hello, Sergeant. I'm Jack Husak," he said. "You're my new nursemaid, aren't you?"

Yes, Chester thought as he saluted and gave his own name. But dealing with a superior with a chip on his shoulder was the last thing he wanted, so he said, "I'm sure that won't be necessary, sir."

"So am I," Husak said. "I've been in charge of my platoon for a good six weeks now, and I've got it running solid—*solid,* all right."

"I'm glad to hear it, sir." Chester wondered what the youngster's notions of solid were. He hadn't got shot in six weeks, but what did that prove? Not much, as Chester knew too well.

Second Lieutenant Husak didn't want to leave it alone. "Commanding a platoon is an important responsibility," he said, which only proved he didn't understand his place in the world. Lieutenants in charge of platoons had the company CO above them and a senior noncom below to fix things if they screwed up too badly. Doing all right meant you were training for a real role. *Not* doing all right probably

meant getting wounded or killed, and certainly meant you'd never see
another promotion. Husak went on, "What's the biggest command
you ever had, Sergeant?"

All right, sonny boy. You asked for it. "Sir, I led a company for a
while in the last war, over in northern Virginia."

"What?" Husak's voice went high and shrill. By the way he jerked,
he might have sat on a tack. "How could you do that?"

"Usual way, sir: all the officers were killed or wounded," Martin
answered stolidly. "This was 1917, sir, and we were almost as beaten
down and beat up as the Confederates were. Eventually they got
around to putting a lieutenant in the slot, so I got bumped back down
again, but I had it for a month or so."

"Oh." Husak looked as if he wanted to call him a liar, but he didn't
have the nerve. Chester's matter-of-fact account was impossible to contradict, especially for someone who'd been making messes in his drawers in 1917. The young lieutenant also looked as if he hated Chester
and as if he was scared to death of him, both at once. He jerked a
thumb towards a waiting truck. "Hop in. We'll see how you do in the
war we've got now."

"Yes, sir." As Chester did, he called himself seventeen different
kinds of idiot. For this sour little punk he'd walked away from his wife,
his son, and a pretty damn good slot in the construction business? What
had those bastards at the recruiting station put in his coffee? Whatever
it was, they should have used it against the Confederates instead. It
would have made them quit without a fight.

The other replacements got in after him. Husak did, too. He spent
a lot less time on them than he had on Chester. The PFC—Chester
thought his name was Fitzpatrick, though he looked more Italian than
Irish—sent him a sympathetic look, but with the lieutenant in the truck
with them that was all he could do.

"Move out," Husak called to the driver.

"Yes, sir." The man fired up the engine, put the truck in gear,
and started west. Chester sighed softly. *Back to the war, dammit,* he
thought.

Instead, the war came to him, and within ten minutes. The truck,
which had been rumbling along at a good clip, slowed and then stopped.
The driver leaned on his horn. Lieutenant Husak went up to the little window that separated the rear compartment from the driver's and
shouted, "What the hell?"

"Refugees." The driver's answer was equally laconic.

"Jesus Christ!" Husak clapped a hand to his forehead.

A few seconds later, Martin, who could only see where he'd been, not where he was going, got a look out the back of the truck at the detritus of war. By the time he'd got to Virginia, all the civilians who'd wanted to leave the combat zone were long gone. Here, a woman stared at him out of eyes as empty and exhausted as those of an overworked draft animal. Sweat plastered her hair to her head; her freckled skin was badly sunburned. She had a knapsack on her back and a crude harness rigged from bed sheets on her chest that let her carry a howling toddler there. A little girl of four or five clung to one hand, a boy a year or two older to the other.

Beside her stood a man in a battered straw hat pushing a wheelbarrow that held whatever he'd been able to distill of his life. He hadn't shaved for a week or so. His checked shirt was filthy, his dungarees were out at the knees, and his shoes out at the toes. He looked as weary and as beaten as the woman.

Except as an obstacle, they and the others like them ignored the truck. They flowed around it, flowed past it—and kept the men in it from getting to where they could do anything about stopping the Confederate advance that had set the refugees in motion in the first place.

A Model T that edged around the truck held—Chester counted carefully—fourteen people. He wouldn't have bet you could cram that many in as a stunt. This was no stunt; it was, literally, life and death. The ancient flivver ran, even if it sagged on its springs.

"Lord, what a fuckup," the PFC said softly. Chester nodded and lit yet another cigarette. That was about the size of it.

Lieutenant Husak, meanwhile, started throwing a fit. "We've got to clear these people!" he yelled. "How are we supposed to fight a war if civilians keep getting in the way?" Civilians getting in the way weren't an accidental consequence of Confederate attacks; Featherston's men knew they would, and took advantage of it. Husak turned to the soldiers with him. "You men! Fix bayonets and get these refugees off the road. If an Asskicker comes by, we're sitting ducks, and so are they."

He wasn't wrong. Chester hadn't used his bayonet for anything but a knife and a can opener since the Great War. He put it on the business end of his Springfield now. It was still good for intimidating civilians.

"Get out of the road!" he shouted as he hopped down from the truck. He did his best to sound like a traffic cop. "Come on, people— move it! You're blocking military traffic! You've got to get out of the way!"

Had the truck been full of soldiers, he would have got results faster. It wasn't so easy with only half a dozen men at his back. The civilians didn't want to listen. All they wanted was to get away from the Confederates. They returned to the highway as soon as Chester and his comrades went by.

And then a Confederate dive bomber *did* spot the column and the halted truck.

Chester knew what that scream in the sky was as soon as he heard it. "Hit the dirt!" he yelled, and took his own advice, scrambling away as fast as he could. The PFC dove for cover, too. The rest of the soldiers and the civilians were still mostly upright when the Mule machine-gunned them, dropped a bomb right in front of the truck, and roared back toward the west.

Screams. Shrieks. Raw terror. People running every which way. People down and bleeding—some writhing and howling, others lying still. Pieces of people flung improbably far. The truck going up like Vesuvius. Whatever problems Lieutenant Husak had with his temper, he'd never fix them now.

And now there was even more chaos and delay on the road than there had been before. Chester looked around. With the lieutenant dead, he was the highest-ranking man here. He wanted the responsibility about as much as he wanted a root canal. Want it or not, it had just landed in his lap. He got up and started doing what little he could to set things right.

Despite its quaint name, Tom Colleton found himself liking Beaver, Pennsylvania. The town sat in the middle of a mining and industrial belt near the border with Ohio, but was itself pleasant and tree-shrouded. He'd commandeered the ivy-covered Quay House, former home of a prominent Socialist politician, for his regimental headquarters.

The runner from division HQ, a few miles farther south, caught up with him there. After saluting, the corporal said, "Sir, I have a special order for you."

It must have been special, or his superiors would have sent it by wireless or field telephone, enciphering it if they thought they had to. Tom nodded. "Give it to me, then."

He expected the messenger to pull out a piece of paper for him to read and then destroy. Instead, it came orally. The powers that be really didn't want anything that had to do with it falling into U.S. hands. "Sir, you are ordered to allow a special unit to pass through your lines, and to make sure the troops under your command do nothing to interfere with this special unit in any way."

That said just enough to leave Lieutenant-Colonel Colleton scratching his head. "Of course I'll obey, but I'd like to know a little more about what I'm obeying," he said. "Why would my men want to interfere with this special unit, whatever it is? How can I tell them not to if I don't know why it'll cause trouble?"

"Sir, I was told you'd likely ask that question, and that I was allowed to answer it," the corporal said seriously. "The answer is, this special unit is made up of men who can talk like damnyankees. They wear Yankee uniforms and act like U.S. soldiers."

"*Son* of a bitch!" Colleton exclaimed. Whatever he'd expected, that wasn't it. After a moment, he wondered why not. Troops like that could raise merry hell behind enemy lines. Of course, they'd have a short life and not a merry one if they got captured. But that was their lookout, not his. He asked, "How will they get up here without having some overeager kid in butternut shoot their asses off?"

He won a smile from the runner. "They've come this far, sir," the corporal said. "They'll have escorts who look the way they're supposed to. And they'll move up at night, when they're less likely to be noticed."

"All right. Makes sense." Tom wondered if the special unit had come up from the CSA entirely by night, lying quiet and hidden by day. He couldn't think of any better way to keep his own side from trying to kill them. He asked, "Can you tell me anything about what they'll be doing?"

"No, sir," the messenger answered. "They didn't tell me, so I couldn't tell the damnyankees in case I got caught."

"Fair enough—that makes sense, too," Tom said. "What time can I expect 'em? My men will need some warning."

"They should get here about eleven o'clock," the messenger said.

"Please don't brief your men too soon. If they get captured, or if they just start bragging to damnyankee pickets . . ."

"I understand." What Tom understood was that he was between a rock and a hard place. His men *did* need warning, or they would do their best to murder the ersatz Yankees. If he had to hold off till the last minute for fear of breaching security, some of them might not get the word. "I'll do what needs doing."

"Yes, sir." The corporal saluted. "If you'll excuse me . . ." He headed back toward division HQ, presumably bearing word that the special unit could come ahead.

Tom shook his head in wonder. Then he got on the field telephone with his company commanders, trying to find out where U.S. lines in front of him were most porous. "What's cooking, sir?" one of his captains asked. "We going to sneak raiders through?"

"You might say so, Bobby Lee," Tom answered. "You've got the quiet sector, so you win the cigar. Alert your men that the infiltrators will have escorts, and that they are to follow the orders they get from those escorts. Got it?"

"Well enough to do what I'm told," the captain answered plaintively. "Something funny's going on, though, isn't it?"

"You don't know the half of it." Tom didn't want to go into detail on the telephone. The damnyankees were better than he wished they were at tapping telephone lines. He didn't know some U.S. noncom with earphones was listening to every word he said, but he didn't want to elaborate on what was going to happen, not when his own superiors had gone out of their way to keep from sending anything on the air or over the wires.

With his own curiosity aroused, he waited impatiently for nightfall. Somewhere off to the north, artillery rumbled. His own area stayed pretty quiet. He supposed his superiors wanted it that way. If the Confederate soldiers dressed as Yankees were going to cause the most trouble, they ought to go in where the real enemy wasn't keyed up and ready to start shooting at anything that moved.

Trucks rumbled into Beaver a few minutes past eleven. A Confederate major in proper uniform alighted from the first one and came looking for Tom. After being directed to the Quay House, he said, "Here we are, sir. You've been warned about us?"

"I sure have," Tom Colleton answered.

"Good," the major said. "Please bring some men with you to form a screen around the, ah, special soldiers as they go forward. We don't want to have any unfortunate accidents."

We don't want the ordinary soldiers shooting up the special men, he meant. Tom nodded. "I understand, Major. I agree one hundred percent."

Nobody had got out of the trucks a couple of blocks away. Tom rounded up a couple of squads' worth of clerks and technicians and other rear-echelon troops and had them surround the silent vehicles. "What's up, sir?" one of them asked, reasonably enough.

"Don't be surprised and don't start shooting when you see who gets out of these trucks," Tom answered. "No matter what these men look like, they aren't real damnyankees. They're infiltrators. They're going to cause trouble behind the enemy's lines. If this goes well, it'll make the advance on Pittsburgh a hell of a lot easier." He turned to the major. "All right?"

"Couldn't be better, sir. Thanks." The major raised his voice: "You can come out now, boys!"

Tom's men swore softly as the *faux* Yankees emerged. He couldn't blame them; he muttered under his breath, too. They looked much too much like the real thing. Their uniforms and helmets were the ones he'd been shooting at for more than a year. They wore U.S. shoes and carried U.S. weapons. And, when they spoke, they *sounded* like damnyankees, too. That really made the hair on his arms and at the back of his neck want to stand on end.

One of his men said, "Sir, you *sure* these bastards is on our side?"

"If I was a real Yankee, I'd shoot you for that, you son of a bitch," one of the men said. He wore a sergeant's uniform, and sounded like a cocky noncom . . . a cocky noncom from New York City. He could have taken his act to the stage. In fact, he was taking it to the stage— and a bad review would cost him his neck.

"Come on," Tom said. "I'll take you up to the line. One of my companies is facing a sector where the enemy doesn't really have much of a line in place against us—that's what happens sometimes when you push hard."

"Good," the major said. "Can you start a little firefight somewhere else to distract the Yankees some more?"

The request made sense, even if it would get some of his men wounded or killed. "I'll take care of it," he said, and sent the order over

the field telephone. A machine gun and some riflemen opened up off
to the right. The enemy returned fire. Springfields sounded very different from automatic Tredegars. Machine guns differed, too. The U.S.
weapons were closely related to their Great War ancestors. The C.S.
model was lighter, cooled by air rather than a clumsy water jacket, and
designed to put out absolutely as much lead as possible. It sounded
like nothing so much as a giant tearing up an enormous sheet of cloth:
the individual rounds going off blended into an almost continuous
roar.

"All right, Major," Tom told the officer in charge of the imitation
Yankees when they got to the perimeter. "I've done what I can do. The
rest is up to you and your boys. Good luck."

"Thank you kindly, sir." The major, at least, sounded like a proper
Confederate. He turned to the men in his charge. "Come on. Y'all
know the drill."

"Yeah." "Sure thing." "No problem." Those laconic grunts sounded
as if they came from the wrong side of the border. One of the men muttered, "Goddamn cowflop cigarettes from now on." Tom sympathized
with that. Everybody knew how eager Yankees were for Confederate
tobacco.

A few at a time, the Confederates in U.S. uniform slipped off into
the night. Tom waited tensely. If gunfire erupted right in front of him,
something had gone wrong up there. But everything stayed quiet. Could
they have the passwords for this sector? If the enemy had any brains,
he would change those every day. Tom knew his own side wasn't perfect at that. He supposed the Yankees also were unlikely to be.

Everything stayed quiet. However the infiltrators were doing it,
they were doing it. The company commander said, "If that doesn't buy
us a breakthrough, nothing will."

Even talking about breakthroughs made a Great War veteran nervous. "We'll see what happens, that's all, Bobby Lee," Tom answered.
"And I reckon we'd better tighten up our own procedures."

"What do you mean, sir?" Bobby Lee asked.

"What goes around comes around," Tom answered. "You don't
suppose the damnyankees have men who sound like they come from
the CSA? You don't suppose they can get their hands on our weapons
and uniforms? Like hell they can't. I think we came up with this one
first—I hope to God we did—but we're liable to be on the receiving end
one day."

"Son of a bitch," the young captain said. "My hat's off to you, sir." He took himself literally, doffing his helmet.

Tom snorted. "Never mind that. Just have our men ready to move fast if the order comes."

"Yes, sir. They will be, sir," Bobby Lee promised.

By the time Tom got back to Beaver, the buses that brought in the phony U.S. soldiers had gone. But Confederate barrels—with, he devoutly hoped, real Confederates inside them—were rumbling into town.

The storm broke the next afternoon. The barrels slammed into the shaky U.S. position, and it turned out to be even shakier than anybody would have expected. Enemy reinforcements showed up late, showed up in the wrong places, or didn't show up at all. Unlike a lot of people, Tom Colleton had a pretty good notion of why that was so. He wondered what it was costing the Confederates in U.S. green-gray. *We'd better make it worthwhile,* he thought, and pushed his own men forward without mercy.

Jonathan Moss mooched back toward the barracks at the Andersonville POW camp from the latrine trenches. Nick Cantarella was coming the other way. He gave Moss a sour nod. "They still have guys looking up your ass when you take a crap?" he asked.

"Just about," Moss answered. They both rolled their eyes. Ever since that downpour made part of the U.S. escape tunnel fall in on itself, the Confederates had been as jumpy as mice at a cat's wedding. Moss knew they had every reason to be. Knowing it didn't make him like it any better.

"Such fun," Cantarella said. The Confederates still didn't know who'd built the tunnel. That Cantarella kept on walking around proved as much. If the guards had had any idea what was what, he would have been in solitary confinement or manacles or leg irons or ball and chain or whatever else they thought up to keep POWs from absquatulating.

"I wonder if anyone has anything else going on," Moss remarked.

"You never can tell," said the captain from New York. "One of these days, the guards are liable to wake up and find out we've all flown the coop. What do they do then? Jump off a cliff? Here's hoping."

"Yeah. Here's hoping." Moss knew his own voice sounded hollow. He wanted *out.* He wanted *out* so bad he could taste it. He wasn't the only POW who did, of course. The guards knew as much, too. They'd known that even before the tunnel collapsed. Now, with their noses rubbed in it, they tried to keep an eye on everybody all the time.

Wrinkling his own nose, Captain Cantarella walked on toward the latrine trenches. Jonathan Moss ambled back to the barracks. Other POWs nodded to him as he went by. He was one of the boys by now, not a new fish who drew dubious glances wherever he went and whatever he did. Having the enemy suspicious of you was one thing. It came with being a prisoner of war. Having your own side suspicious of you felt a lot worse.

" 'Day, Major," First Lieutenant Hal Swinburne said.

"Hello, Hal." Moss hid a smile at his own thoughts of a moment before. Hal Swinburne hadn't been at Andersonville very long, but nobody suspected him of being a Confederate plant. For one thing, three officers already incarcerated vouched for him. For another, he was a Yankees' Yankee: he came from Maine, and spoke with such a thick down-East accent, half his fellow POWs had trouble following him. Moss couldn't imagine a Confederate plant talking like that.

"Hot today," Swinburne said mournfully.

"Hot yesterday. Hot tomorrow. Hot the day after, too." Moss kicked at the red dirt. Dust rose from under his foot. He pointed up into the sky, where big black birds circled. "See those?"

Swinburne looked, shielding his eyes with the palm of his hand. He was about six-one, on the skinny side, with dark blond hair and a thin little mustache that almost disappeared if you looked at it from the wrong angle. "Ravens?" he asked.

Did you see ravens soaring over the Maine woods? Moss wouldn't have been surprised. He wasn't sure he'd ever seen one, but he was no birdwatcher. He did know the birds he was watching now weren't ravens. "Vultures," he said solemnly. "Waiting for something to fall over dead from the sun so they can come down and have dinner."

"Vultures." The way Swinburne said it, it sounded like *vuhchaaz*. He nodded. "Ayuh. Seen 'em on the field, time or two. Nasty birds." He stretched out the *a* in *nasty* and swallowed the *r* in *birds*. After wiping his forehead with the back of his hand, he went on, "How do folks live in weather like this all the time, though?"

People wondered the same thing about Maine, of course, for opposite reasons. Moss said, "I'm from Chicago. I don't think there's any kind of weather in the world you don't see there."

"That's not so bad," Swinburne said. "That's variety, like. But this here every day?" He shuddered. "I'd cook."

There was a variation on this theme. When it wasn't hot and muggy and sunny, it was hot and muggy and pouring rain. Moss didn't bother pointing that out. He doubted the other POW would find it an improvement.

With another nod, Hal Swinburne went on his way. He didn't move any faster than he had to. In this heat and humidity, nobody moved any faster than he had to. Sweat coated Moss' skin, thick and heavy as grease. It welded his shirt and even his trousers to his body.

Coming into the shade inside the barracks hall was a small relief, but only a small one. "A little warm out there," Moss remarked.

That made even the men in the unending corner poker game look up. "Really?" one of them said.

"Never would have guessed," another added.

"Come on, Major," a third poker player put in. "You knew hell was supposed to be hot, right?"

Moss laughed. A moment later, he wondered why. If this wasn't hell, it had to be one of the nastier suburbs of purgatory. He went over to Colonel Summers. "Could I talk with you for a moment, sir?" he asked.

The senior U.S. officer in the camp nodded. "Certainly." He closed the beat-up paperbound mystery he'd been reading. "I already know who done it, anyhow." Moss knew who done it in that one, too. The camp library didn't hold enough books. Anyone who'd been here for a while and liked to read had probably gone through all of them at least once. Monty Summers got to his feet. "What's on your mind, Major?"

Till they walked outside again, Moss kept it to small talk. Summers didn't seem surprised or put out. When Moss was sure neither guards nor fellow prisoners could overhear, he asked, "Are we still working on an escape?"

"Officially, I don't know what you're talking about," Colonel Summers answered. "Officially, I had no idea there was a tunnel under these grounds till the rain showed it. I was shocked—shocked, I tell you— to learn that some men here were planning to break out. The Confederates couldn't prove any different, either. I'm glad they couldn't. It would have been troublesome if they could."

He wouldn't admit a damn thing. That was bound to be smart. The less he said, the less the Confederates could make him sorry for. The less Moss heard, the less the enemy could squeeze out of him. All the same . . . "I do believe I'm going to go smack out of my mind if I stay cooped up here much longer."

"Oh, I wouldn't," Summers said. "They'll put you in a straitjacket, and those things are uncomfortable as the devil, especially in this weather."

"Yes, sir," Moss said resignedly. He should have known he wouldn't get a straight answer. As a matter of fact, he had known it, or had a pretty good idea. That he'd squawked anyhow was a telling measure of how fed up and cooped up he was feeling.

Voice far drier than the dripping air they both breathed, Summers said, "Believe me, Major, you aren't the only one incompletely satisfied with the accommodations around here."

"No?" Moss' spirits revived, or tried to. "Is there anyone in particular I should talk to? Is anybody besides me *especially* unhappy about them?"

"If someone is, I'm sure he'll get in touch with you," Colonel Summers said, which again told Moss nothing. "Was anything else troubling you? As I say, you're not the only one who doesn't like it here. Remember that and you may keep from winning one of the guards a furlough."

"Bastards," Moss muttered. The POWs didn't know for a fact that their guards got time off for shooting a prisoner who'd set foot on the smoothed ground just inside the barbed wire—or, sometimes, for shooting a prisoner who looked as if he was about to do such a thing. They didn't know it, but they believed it the way a lot of them believed in the divinity of Jesus Christ.

"Of course they're bastards," Summers said. "They get paid to be bastards. You don't want to make things easy for them, do you?"

"Well, no, sir," Moss said.

"Good." Summers nodded in a businesslike way. "I should hope not." He waved to Lieutenant Swinburne, who was on his way back to the barracks. "What do you think of the guards, Lieutenant?"

"Me, sir? Pack of bastards," Swinburne answered at once. The word was *bahstuds* in his mouth, giving it only a vague resemblance to what Moss had called the guards.

"Thanks. I couldn't have put that better myself," Summers said. The officer from Maine touched his cap with a forefinger and went on his way. Colonel Summers turned back to Moss. "You see? You're not the only one who loves these people."

"I never said I was, sir." Moss scowled. "I've got more right to complain than he does. I've been here longer."

"Yes, but they interrogate him more. They've already squeezed everything out of you that they're going to get," Summers said. "He's new, so they still have hopes."

"If there's more than three Confederate officers between here and Richmond who don't know my name, rank, and pay number, I'd be amazed. And not a goddamn one of them knows anything but that." Moss spoke with a certain somber pride.

"They've grilled all of us, Major," Summers replied, wearily rolling his eyes as if to say, *Haven't they just!* "I know they get more out of some people than they do from others." He held up a hasty hand. "I'm not talking about you, and I'm not talking about Swinburne, either."

"I know, sir. I understood that. Some men will talk more than others, and they lean on some harder than others, depending on what they think the poor sons of bitches know." Moss sighed. "I can't even cuss 'em for that, or not real hard, because I know damn well we do the same thing."

Monty Summers shrugged. "It's war," he said: two words that covered a multitude of sins. "We all do the best we can."

"Yes, sir," Moss agreed mournfully. "And look what that's got us." His wave encompassed the camp. "God knows what would have happened if we tried to screw up."

"Heh," Colonel Summers said—a noise that sounded like a laugh but wasn't. "A hell of a lot of people who didn't do their best are dead right now."

"Oh, yes, sir," Moss agreed. "And some of them are back in Philadelphia with stars on their shoulder straps. They're drinking good booze and eating steaks and screwing their secretaries. For them, the war's a nuisance or an opportunity, depending on how you look at things."

Summers eyed him for a long moment before saying, "That holds on both sides of the border, you know."

"I sure hope so, sir," Moss said. "But what worries me is, the Confederates may have done a better job of sweeping away their deadwood than we have, and that's liable to cost us. It's liable to cost us a lot."

XIII

Dr. Leonard O'Doull wondered how many places he'd set up his aid station since returning to the war. A lot of them—that was all he knew for sure. After a while, they started blurring together. So did cases. What made that worse was, he never saw them again after they went back for more treatment. He never found out whether they got better or worse. They were just arms or legs or bellies or chests or heads—not that he or anybody else this side of God could do much for too many head wounds.

When he complained about that outside the aid tent one day, Granville McDougald said, "Well, Doc, remember the fellow who had the round burrow under his scalp and come out the back?"

"*Calisse!* I'm not likely to forget him," O'Doull said. That one would stay in his memory forever. "I haven't come that close to crapping myself since I was three years old. But most of the bullets don't go around. They go in."

McDougald grimaced. He crushed a cigarette under his foot. They'd set up in some woods north of Pittsburgh. Catbirds mewed and squawked in the trees. They made an ungodly racket, not all of it cat-like. You didn't see them all that often. They were gray with black caps and rusty brown under their tails—good camouflage colors—and stayed where leaves and bushes were thick. A cardinal scratching for seeds on the ground, on the other hand . . .

"I used to love those birds," O'Doull said sadly, pointing towards it. "Nowadays, though, the color just reminds me of blood."

"You *are* cheery this morning, aren't you?" McDougald studied the plump, crested cardinal. "I still like 'em."

"To each his own." O'Doull looked up at the leaves and branches overhead in a different way. "I wish we were a little more out in the open. A tree burst right above us would fill the aid tent with shrapnel."

"If we were out in the open, we'd get shrapnel from ground bursts that the tree trunks will stop," McDougald answered, which was also true. "Only way not to worry about artillery is not to have a war, and it's a little late for that now."

"Just a bit, yeah," O'Doull said. "And ain't it a shame?"

His head came up like a pointer's taking a scent. So did McDougald's. But they didn't smell anything. No, they heard heavy footsteps: the footsteps of stretcher bearers bringing back a casualty. "Doc!" Eddie yelled. "Hey, Doc! Here's a new model for you!"

"Back to work," O'Doull murmured, and Granville McDougald nodded. The doctor raised his voice: "Bring him to us, Eddie!" He went inside and washed his hands with soap and disinfectant, taking special care to clean under and around his nails. McDougald did the same. They slipped on surgical masks together. Sometimes O'Doull wondered how much good that did when wounds were often already filthy before they got back to him. He supposed you had to try.

Another groaning wounded man, this one shot in the leg. Except, as Eddie had said, he wasn't what O'Doull was used to seeing. He was short and swarthy and black-haired, and wore a uniform of cut and color—a khaki more nearly yellow than brown—different from either U.S. green-gray or C.S. butternut. When words broke through the animal noises of pain, they came in Spanish, not English.

"Heard there were Mexican troops in front of us," McDougald remarked.

"So did I." O'Doull nodded. "Poor devil came a long way just to let some nasty strangers put a hole in him."

McDougald shook his head. "He came to put holes in the nasty strangers himself. Suckers always do. They never figure the guys on the other side are gonna shoot back."

The Mexican soldier's moans eased. Eddie or one of the other corpsmen must have given him morphine. He said something. O'Doull couldn't figure out what it was. Spanish and French were related, sure, but not closely enough to let him understand one even if he knew the other.

He spoke in English: "You'll be all right." From what he could see of the wound, he thought that was true. The bullet looked to have blown off a chunk of flesh, but not to have shattered any bones. He turned to McDougald. "Put him under."

"Right you are, Doc." McDougald settled the ether cone over the wounded man's face. He and Eddie had to keep the soldier from yanking it off; a lot of men thought they were being gassed when they inhaled the anesthetic. After a few breaths, the Mexican's hands fell away and he went limp.

O'Doull cleaned out the wound and sewed it up. Had men from the soldier's own side brought him in, it would have been a hometowner: good for convalescent leave, but nothing that would keep him from coming back to the front. As things were, he'd sit out the rest of the war in a POW camp.

When the job was done, O'Doull nodded to Eddie. "You can take him back to the rear now. If they have anybody who speaks Spanish handy, they'll probably want to grill him."

"I suppose," Eddie said. "Like worrying about the Confederates wasn't bad enough. Now we've got the greasers jumping on us, too."

No matter what he called Mexicans, he handled this one with the same rough compassion he would have shown any wounded soldier, white, brown, black, or even green. He and the other stretcher bearers carried away the still-unconscious man.

"Interesting," Granville McDougald said. "Does this mean the Confederates are starting to run low on their own men?"

"Don't know," said O'Doull, who hadn't looked at it like that.

"Well, neither do I," McDougald allowed. "I don't think like Jake Featherston or Francisco José, thank God. I hope I'm not a son of a bitch or a moron." That startled a laugh out of O'Doull. The medic went on, "But even if I don't *know,* that's sure how it looks to me."

"It makes sense," O'Doull said. "We beat the CSA last time by hammering on them till they couldn't hammer back anymore. If we're going to win this war, we'll have to knock 'em flat again."

"Flatter," McDougald said. "Last time, we let 'em up again. If we beat 'em this time, we'd better not do that again. I don't know how long we'll have to sit on 'em, but we need to do it, however long it takes."

"I suppose so," O'Doull said mournfully. "But remember what Kentucky and Houston were supposed to be like before the plebiscite?"

"I'd better remember—I was *in* Houston for a while. Half of what went on never made the papers in the USA, let alone in Quebec, I bet." Granville McDougald paused. He looked very unhappy. "I don't want to think about how much trouble sitting on the whole Confederacy would be. Those people purely hate us, no two ways about it. But if we don't occupy them and control them, we'll have to fight 'em again in another twenty years, and I sure as hell don't want to do that, either."

"So what you're telling me is, we're in trouble no matter what happens," O'Doull said. "Thanks a lot, Granny."

"There's trouble, and then there's *trouble,*" McDougald said. "Trouble is us occupying the Confederate States. *Trouble* is the Confederates occupying us. If I've got a choice, I know which one I'd take."

"Yeah, me, too," O'Doull said. "Here's hoping we've got a choice."

"Now why would you say something like that?" McDougald inquired. "Haven't you got confidence in our brilliant leaders? Doesn't the fact that we're fighting in Pennsylvania mean victory's right around the corner?"

"That's what I'm afraid of," O'Doull answered. "The only trouble is, whose victory are you talking about?"

McDougald laughed, for all the world as if they were sitting in a saloon telling jokes. The fate of nations? Who could get excited about the fate of nations if the beer was cold and the joint had a halfway decent free-lunch spread? The medic said, "If we were a little farther back of the line and we talked like this, we'd catch hell for defeatism, you know?"

"Yeah, they'd yell at us," O'Doull agreed. "But that's all they'd do. If we talked like this on the Confederate side of the line, they'd probably shoot us."

"Y'all are damnyankee sympathizers." McDougald's Southern drawl wouldn't get him into espionage. "Y'all can have blindfolds. I ain't gonna waste good Confederate tobacco on you, though—that's for damn sure."

"A Kentucky colonel you're not," O'Doull said. But then he thought about the warning that had come in: Confederate soldiers in U.S. uniform were supposed to be operating behind U.S. lines. They were supposed to have good U.S. accents, too. O'Doull had no idea if that was true, or how you went about telling a disguised Confederate from an average screwup. He also wondered what to do if one of those Confederates in U.S. clothing came into the aid station. Then he wondered how the devil he'd know.

* * *

Scipio got more frightened every day. Nothing had changed in the Terry since the sweep that would have swept out his family and him. Nothing had changed, no, but trouble was in the air. Something new was stirring, and he didn't know what it was.

He came right out and asked Jerry Dover. The manager at the Huntsman's Lodge just shrugged and said, "I haven't heard anything."

"Do Jesus!" Scipio said. "Them Freedom Party stalwarts, they looks like they gwine kill all o' we, an' you ain't *heard* nothin'?"

"If I had, I'd tell you," Dover said. "This time, I think you're flabbling over nothing."

"Ain't you got no mo' errands fo' me to run? Ain't you got no errands fo' me an' my whole fambly to run?" Scipio paused, then switched dialects to the one he hardly ever used: "Mr. Dover, please understand me—I am a desperate man, sir." He had to be desperate to use his white man's voice.

It rocked Dover, the way it would have rocked any white in the CSA. Biting his lip, the restaurant manager muttered, "If I'd known you were that goddamn sharp, I never would've sent you to Savannah."

Scipio wanted to laugh, or possibly to scream. Jerry Dover had worked alongside him for more than twenty years. If that didn't give Dover the chance to figure out what kind of brains he had . . . Scipio knew what the trouble was, of course. All that time, he'd talked like a nigger, and an ignorant nigger at that. Perception clouded reality. Like so many whites, Dover had assumed anybody who sounded like an illiterate field hand had to be as ignorant and probably as stupid as a field hand.

Of course, there were holes in that line of thought. Dover had known all along that he could read and write and cipher. Set that against sounding like a buck from the Congaree swamps, though, and it suddenly became small potatoes.

"What *was* in that envelope I took there?" Scipio pressed his advantage. He didn't get one very often, and knew he had to make the most of it. "Something for the United States? Something for the Freedom Party? Something for a lady friend of yours, perhaps?" Even to himself, he sounded smarter when he talked like a white man. If that wasn't a measure of what living in the Confederate States his whole life had done to him, he didn't know what would be.

Jerry Dover turned red. "Whatever it was, it's none of your damn beeswax," he snapped. "The less you know about it, the better off we both are. Have you got that?"

He made sense, no matter how much Scipio wished he didn't. If they arrested Scipio instead of just hauling him off to a camp, he couldn't tell them what he didn't know. Of course, he could tell them Dover's name, at which point they'd start tearing into the restaurant manager. And how would *he* stand up to the third degree? Scipio almost looked forward to finding out. If Dover's ruin didn't so surely involve his own, he would have.

"Somethin' else you better keep in mind," Dover said. "Wasn't for me, you'd be dead. Wasn't for me, you'd be in wherever niggers go when they clean out part of the Terry. Instead, you're still walkin' around Augusta, and you don't seem any too goddamn grateful for it."

"If walking around Augusta involved anything even approaching freedom—lowercase *f*, mind you—I *would* be grateful," Scipio said. "But this is only a slightly more spacious prison. I don't ask for much, Mr. Dover. I could accept living as I did before the war began. It was imperfect, but I know it was as much as I could reasonably expect from this country. What I have now, sir—I do believe a preacher would call it hell."

He'd hoped his passion—and his accent—would impress the white man. Maybe they even did. But Dover said, "All I got to tell you is, you don't know what you're talking about. You go on about a preacher? You ought to get down on bended knee and thank God you don't know what you're talking about."

Where Scipio had rocked him before, now he shook the black man. He sounded as if he knew exactly what *he* was talking about. "Mr. Dover, if what you say is true, then my family and I have even more urgent reasons to leave Augusta immediately."

"Bullshit," Dover said. Scipio blinked as if he'd never heard the word before. "Bull*shit*," Dover repeated. "What the hell makes you think things are better anywhere else, for crying out loud?"

Scipio bit down on that like a man breaking a tooth on a cherry pit in his piece of pie. "Do Jesus!" he exclaimed, startled for a moment back into his usual way of talking. He'd always thought of Augusta as an aberration, a disaster. If it wasn't . . .

"Jesus ain't got nothin' to do with it," Jerry Dover said brutally. "Don't be dumber than you can help, all right? If you reckon you're the only one in the world with troubles, what does that make you? Besides a damn fool, I mean?"

"Do Jesus!" Scipio said again, softly this time. "What am I gonna do?"

He wasn't asking the question of the restaurant manager. He wasn't asking God, either. He was asking himself, and he had no more answers than either God or Dover did.

Dover thought he had one: "Get your ass out there, do your job, and keep your head down."

Had Scipio been alone in the world, that might even have sufficed. As things were, he shook his head. "I got a wife, Mistuh Dover. I got chilluns." He couldn't talk like a white man now; that would have hurt too much. "I wants dem chilluns to do better'n I ever done. How kin dey do dat? Likely tell, dey don't even git to grow up." Tears filled his eyes and his voice.

Dover looked down at his desk. "I don't know what you want me to do about it."

"He'p me!" Scipio burst out. "You gots to he'p me. Git me outa here."

"How? Where?" the restaurant manager demanded. "You reckon I got some magic carpet that'll fly you to Mexico or the USA? If you do, give me some of whatever you're drinking, on account of I want to get goofy, too."

Scipio looked wildly around him. The walls of Dover's office seemed to be closing in. Except it wasn't the office alone. . . . "You know somethin', Mistuh Dover?" he said. "This whole country—this whole goddamn country—ain't nothing but a prison camp fo' black folks."

"Yeah, well, I can't do nothin' about that, neither," Jerry Dover said. "All I can do is run this place here. And if you aren't out there waiting tables in five minutes, I start having trouble doing that."

"No, suh," Scipio said, and Dover blinked; whites in the CSA seldom met outright refusal from Negroes. Scipio went on, "Reckon you do more'n dat. Reckon you never woulda sent me to Savannah, you didn't do more'n dat." He still didn't know why the white man had sent him there. He didn't care, either. That he'd gone gave him a weapon. "You got to he'p me. You got to he'p my chilluns."

"I already have," Dover said quietly. Scipio grimaced. That was true. Dover went on, "You want me to do more than I can do. You want me to do more than anybody can do. I can't make you turn white. That's what you really want out of me, isn't it?"

He made Scipio grimace again. Even when times were relatively good for blacks in the CSA, skin lighteners and hair straighteners—a lot of them, especially the lighteners, only quack nostrums—sold briskly. The worse times got, the better they sold, too. These days, anyone who could possibly pass for white was doing it. Scipio's own skin was far too dark even to let him think about it. Bathsheba was lighter, but not light enough. Neither were Antoinette and Cassius. They were all irredeemably marked as what they were.

"Damn you, Mistuh Dover," Scipio said dully.

"I'm sorry. Hell, I *am* sorry. I didn't want things to turn out like this," Jerry Dover said. "I'm no goddamn Freedom Party goon. You know that. But I can't stick my neck out too far, either, not unless I want it chopped."

Scipio tried to hate him. Try as he would, he couldn't. Dover wasn't as big a man as he might have been. But plenty were smaller, too, and not all of them were white. Dover didn't even use his advantage in color and class to order Scipio out of his office. He just waited. Scipio could tell no hope was to be had here. He left by himself.

Taking orders in the restaurant, bringing them back to the kitchen, and carrying food out again felt strangely surreal. The prosperous white men and their sleek companions treated him as they always would have: like a servant. They talked as if he weren't there. Had he been a U.S. spy, he could have learned some interesting things about railroad repairs and industrial bottlenecks. He could have picked up some pointers on barrel deployment from an officer trying—the wrong way, in Scipio's view—to impress a really beautiful brunette.

He kept waiting to hear word about the Terry, about yet another cleanout. He'd been doing that ever since the night when the Angel of Death, thanks to Jerry Dover, passed over his family and him. But the whites in the Huntsman's Lodge never talked about things like that. Maybe they didn't want to think about them while they were eating venison or duck in orange sauce and drinking fancy French wine. Or maybe they weren't quite so oblivious to the colored staff as they let on.

It was probably some of each. Scipio wouldn't have wanted to think about sending people off to camps while he was enjoying a fine meal, either. And, while whites in the CSA often pretended to ignore

Negroes, they knew they couldn't really afford to do it very often. They would pay, and pay high, if they did.

He got through the evening. He clocked out of the Huntsman's Lodge and walked through Augusta's dark, silent streets—the city remained under blackout even if no Yankee bombers had ever appeared overhead—toward the Terry. It was like going back to jail—with the barbed wire all around, just like that.

"Halt!" called one of the policemen and stalwarts at the gate. "Advance and be recognized. Slow and easy, or you never get another chance."

They were jumpy tonight. Scipio didn't like that; it was too likely a harbinger of trouble. "Ain't nobody but me," he said. What would the ruffians have done if he'd used his white man's voice with them? Shot him, probably, for not being what they expected.

As things were, they laughed. "It's the old spook in the boiled shirt," one of them said. The gate creaked as they opened it. "Go on through." They didn't even ask for his passbook. Whatever the shape of the trouble they were flabbling about, it wasn't his.

The Terry's streets were even quieter than those of the white part of Augusta. Scipio imagined he heard ghosts moaning along them, but it was only the breeze . . . or was it? With more than half the Negroes scooped out of the place and carried off to a fate unknown but unlikely to be good, ghosts were bound to be wandering the streets where so many real people no longer went.

His apartment was dark. Bathsheba had got a couple of kerosene lamps after the electricity was cut off, but kerosene was hard to come by these days, too. They used it only when they had to. He navigated with the confidence of a man who knew where everything was whether he could see it or not. His wife had left his nightshirt out for him on a chair by the bed. He sighed with relief at escaping the tuxedo. Sleep dissolved night terrors.

Breakfast was bread and jam. Cassius and Antoinette were already up when Scipio rose. His son said, "Pa, we got to fight the ofays. We don't fight 'em, reckon they go an' kill us all."

"We do fight de buckra, reckon dey kills all o' we anyways," Scipio answered.

"Leastways we gets to hit back," Cassius said.

Yond Cassius has a lean and hungry look;/He thinks too much:

such men are dangerous. Having watched the brutal collapse of the Congaree Socialist Republic, Scipio knew black uprisings against whites in the CSA had no hope. He looked around. Was there hope anywhere else in the Terry? Not that he could see. All he said was, "Be careful, son. Be careful as you kin."

Cassius' face lit with a terrible joy, the joy of a man who had nothing left to lose.

Midnight was the traditional time for the knock on the door. Had the police come then, Cincinnatus Driver would have greeted them with the bolt-action Tredegar he'd hidden under a floorboard in the front room. But they caught up with him in the middle of the afternoon and found him on the street, armed only with a cane.

There were four of them. Three were older than Cincinnatus. The fourth, who must have been a cadet or a pup or whatever they called it, couldn't have been above sixteen. But he carried a .45, while the regular cops sported two submachine guns and a shotgun. They didn't come into the colored part of Covington without being ready for trouble.

They started to walk on past Cincinnatus. Then one of the geezers— he wore a bushy mustache that had been red once but was almost all white now—paused and said, "You're Cincinnatus Driver, ain't you?"

Cincinnatus thought hard about denying it. But if he did, they'd ask him for his passbook, and that would prove he'd lied. The truth seemed a better bet. "Yes, suh," he said, and waited to see what happened next.

"He's on the list!" the cadet exclaimed, his voice breaking.

"He sure as hell is," the cop with the mustache agreed. Cincinnatus didn't like the sound of that. As usual in the CSA, what a Negro liked or didn't like didn't matter. The cop gestured with his submachine gun. "You're gonna come along with us."

"What for?" Cincinnatus yelped. "I ain't done nothin'!" He didn't think he had done anything they could prove. Hadn't they grabbed him once and let him go?

The white-mustached cop chuckled. "Buddy, if I had a dime for every asshole I nabbed who hadn't done anything, I could've quit workin' a hell of a long time ago. Now you can come along quiet-like or you can come along some other way. But you're gonna come. So what'll it be?"

One cane against all that firepower made ridiculous odds. And the policemen were pros. The old-timers didn't come close enough to let Cincinnatus lash out even if he'd been crazy enough to do it. When the kid started to, one of them pulled him back and explained how he'd almost been a damn fool. "I'll come quiet," Cincinnatus said.

"Smart fellow," the mustachioed cop said. He turned to the cadet. "He's smarter'n you are, Newt. How's that make you feel?" By the look on Newt's face, it made him want to cry.

A blue jay scolded Cincinnatus and the policemen for having the nerve to walk under the oak tree where it perched. A little kid playing in his front yard stared at them, eyes enormous in his dark face. So did a drunk draped over a front porch. Cincinnatus happened to know the drunk reported to Lucullus Wood. He feared that wouldn't help him.

When the gate closed behind him and he passed out of the barbed-wire perimeter around the colored quarter, that small latch click had a dreadfully final sound. A police car waited just beyond the gate. The policeman with the mustache took Cincinnatus' cane away when he got into the back seat, then got in beside him. "I'll give it back when we get to the station," he said in the tones of a man just doing his job. "Don't want you trying anything silly, though."

"Know how to get what you want, I reckon," Cincinnatus said. The cop laughed.

When they got to the station, they didn't tell Cincinnatus what he was charged with. He feared that was a bad sign. They stuck him in a cell by himself. None of the other cells close by had anybody in it, so he had no one to talk to. He feared that was a bad sign, too.

But they let him keep the cane. Maybe they knew how much trouble he had getting around without it. Police, though, weren't in the habit of showing white prisoners consideration, let alone blacks. Sitting on the edge of the cot—the only place he could sit except for the concrete floor—he scratched his head.

A guard who must have been called back from retirement brought him supper on a tray: two cheese sandwiches on coarse, brownish bread and a big cup of water. Cincinnatus shoved the empty tray and cup out into the hall and went back to the cot.

The guard nodded when he came back to pick up the tray. "You know the drill, all right. Reckon you been in the joint before."

"Not for anything I did," Cincinnatus said.

"Likely tell. That's what they all say." Bending made the guard swear under his breath: "Goddamn rheumatism."

Cincinnatus had never expected to sympathize with a screw. But he had aches and pains, too. Whatever his thoughts, the guard never knew them. The white man would have taken sympathy as weakness. Show weakness in a place like this and you were . . . even worse off than you were already, which wasn't good.

He waited for them to come and start squeezing him for whatever they thought he knew. No matter what they did, he couldn't tell them much about Luther Bliss. He had no idea where the U.S. secret police-man was staying, or even if he was still in Covington. If they started asking him about Lucullus, though . . . He could do Lucullus a lot of harm. He didn't want to, but he knew the best will in the world wouldn't always stand up against enough pain.

They left him in there. They fed him. The food was a long way from good, but he didn't go hungry. They took out the honey bucket twice a day. It was just . . . jail. It didn't feel as if they were softening him up for anything drastic. They could easily have done much worse.

Maybe they thought they were lulling him. He didn't mind. He would take whatever he could get. Boredom wasn't much, but it beat the hell out of brutality. If he yawned, if he paced—well, so what? He could have bled. He could have spat out teeth. He'd heard of things they could do with a motorcar battery and some wires that made his stomach turn over. Compared to any of that, boredom was a walk in the park on a sunny spring day.

It had to end. And when it did, it was even worse than he'd feared. Police didn't come for him. Instead, the man at the head of three guards who carried submachine guns was a jackbooted Confederate major with a face like a clenched fist. "You're Cincinnatus Driver?" he barked.

"Yes, suh," Cincinnatus admitted apprehensively.

"Damnfool notion, letting niggers have last names," the officer muttered. Cincinnatus kept his mouth shut. It wouldn't do him any good—he was all too sure of that—but it wouldn't harm him, either. Anything he said might have. The major glowered at him. The man's mouth got even tighter. Cincinnatus hadn't thought it could. One of the guards had a key. He opened the cell door. "Come on," the major said. "Get out. Get moving."

Cincinnatus obeyed—what choice did he have? "Where you takin' me?" he asked. They couldn't get too angry at him for wanting to know.

That didn't mean they would tell him. "Shut up," the major said. "You're coming along with me." He looked as if he would sooner have scraped Cincinnatus off the soles of those highly polished boots than had anything more personal to do with him. Cincinnatus wasn't all that eager to have anything to do with the major, either. The white man, however, had a choice. As usual, Cincinnatus got none.

They marched him down the corridor to the front desk. The Confederate officer signed whatever paperwork he had to sign to take Cincinnatus farther than that. Then he and two of the guards took Cincinnatus out of the city jail altogether (the third one, the one with the key, stayed behind). They bundled him into a motorcar and took him up to the docks on the Ohio. Another auto pulled up beside his. To his surprise, his father got out of that one. Seneca Driver had his own contingent of guards. "What's goin' on, Son?" he asked.

"Beats me," Cincinnatus answered.

"Shut up, both of you," the major said. "Into the boat." He pointed. It was a smallish motorboat with, at the moment, a Red Cross flag draped across what had to be a machine-gun mount up near the bow. Awkwardly, Cincinnatus obeyed. Then he helped his father into the boat, though the older man was probably sprier than he was.

The engine roared to life. The motorboat arrowed across the river to the Cincinnati side. More guards waited at a pier there. One of them condescended to give Cincinnatus a hand as he struggled out of the boat. "Thank you, suh," he said softly.

"Shut up! No talking!" The major had strong opinions and what seemed to be a one-track mind. He pointed to a waiting motorcar painted C.S. butternut. "Get in."

Soldiers stood near the motorcar. The automatic rifles they carried made the submachine guns he'd seen before seem children's toys by comparison. Their expressions said they would just as soon shoot him as look at him. He got into the auto. One of them got in beside him. "Don't fuck with me, Sambo," the Confederate said casually, "or you'll never find out how the serial down at the Bijou turns out."

"I ain't done nothin'," Cincinnatus said. "I ain't gonna do nothin', neither." The soldier only grunted. He didn't believe a word of it. Another heavily armed man sat in the front seat next to the driver.

Away went the motorcar. Cincinnatus looked out the window. Cincinnati had taken more battle damage than Covington. The people on the streets looked shabby and unhappy. He never saw Confederate soldiers in parties smaller than four. That told him a lot about what the occupied thought of their occupiers.

"Can I look out the back window, suh, without you shootin' me?" he asked the soldier.

After considering, the man nodded. "Hand me your stick first," he said. "Move slow and careful. Don't get cute, or you'll be sorry—but not for long."

Cincinnatus obeyed in every particular. He saw what he'd hoped to see: another motorcar full of soldiers right behind this one. With any luck at all, that one also held his father. He swung around so he was sitting straight ahead again. "Thank you kindly, suh."

"Huh," the Confederate soldier said, and then, "Looks like we're here."

Here was the Cincinnati city jail. Cincinnatus wondered if he'd just traded one cell for another. Nobody told him to get out of the auto, though. In fact, three more motorcars joined the ones he and his father were in. The procession headed west and north through occupied Ohio.

Most of the countryside looked normal, as if war had never touched it. Here and there, usually around towns, were patches of devastation. You could see where U.S. soldiers had stood and fought and where they'd been outflanked, outmaneuvered, and forced from their positions.

The little convoy passed through checkpoint after checkpoint. At one of them, a soldier put something on the wireless aerial to Cincinnatus' auto. He couldn't see what it was. He asked permission to look back at the motorcar behind him again. The soldier with the automatic rifle looked disgusted but nodded. He didn't get any less alert. He also showed no sign of needing to take a leak, though they'd been traveling for quite a while. Cincinnatus didn't know how much longer *he* could go on before asking for a stop. He didn't know if he'd get one, though, even if he asked.

A white flag flew from the other auto's aerial. He supposed his motorcar carried the same flag of truce. But when he asked about it, the soldier stared through him and said, "Shut up." He didn't argue with an armed man.

Just before he had to ask for a stop—and just after they'd rolled through a small town called Oxford—the convoy halted on its own. "Where the hell are they?" the driver grumbled.

"They'll be here," said the other man in the front seat. "Ain't like we never done this before."

Sure enough, five minutes later another convoy of motorcars approached from the west. Those also had white flags on their wireless antennas. They were painted green-gray, not butternut. The soldier next to Cincinnatus nudged him with the muzzle of his rifle. "Get out." He obeyed. The soldier passed him his cane. His father left the auto behind him. Three skinny white men who needed shaves emerged from the other motorcars.

Along with U.S. soldiers, five whites got out of the green-gray autos. Cincinnatus' dour major went up to confer with a U.S. officer who might have been his long-lost twin. They signed some papers for each other. The C.S. major turned back. "You are exchanged!" he shouted to Cincinnatus and the others. "You're the damnyankees' worry now. Far as I'm concerned, they're welcome to you. Go on—git!"

"Do Jesus!" Cincinnatus whispered as he limped forward into U.S. custody. That cop in Covington hadn't lied to him after all. "Do Jesus!" He looked back to his father. "Come on, Pa. I think we're goin' home."

Sergeant Michael Pound had a new barrel. Considering what had happened to the old one, that was anything but a surprise. But this wasn't a new barrel of the same old style. U.S. engineers had rapidly figured out they needed to do something about the fearsome new machine the Confederates had introduced. Their answer was . . . not everything it might have been, but a damn sight better than no change at all.

The chassis hadn't changed much. The engine was of similar design to the old one, but put out an extra fifty horsepower. That was all to the good, because the new barrel was heavier, and needed the extra muscle to shove it around.

Almost all the weight gain came from the new turret. It was bigger than the old one. Its armor was thicker and better sloped. And it had been upgunned. Instead of a 37mm gun—an inch and a half to a gunner—it now carried a 60mm piece—a little less than two and a half inches. That still didn't match the three-inch monster the new Confederate barrels used, but it was big enough to make any enemy barrel say uncle, where you had to be damn good or damn lucky to hurt the new C.S. machine with the 37mm cannon.

And the 60mm gun was absolutely the biggest one that would fit on the turret ring of the old chassis. A new, improved body took a lot longer to turn out than a reworked turret. The Confederates must have been planning their Mark 2 while the Mark 1 was just starting production. The USA hadn't done that. And so, instead of a proper Mark 2, the United States had to make do with Mark 1.5, more or less.

"Ugly beast," Pound said, laying a hand on its armored flank. He didn't see how anybody could argue with that. The new turret went with the old chassis about the way a rhino's head went with a cow's body. Everything on the Confederates' new barrels fit together with everything else. They had a grim, functional beauty. The Mark 1.5 was just grim.

"Well, Sergeant, Featherston's fuckers will think it's ugly, too, especially after it bites them a few times." That was Cecil Bergman, Pound's new loader. He was a skinny little guy, which helped him do his job— even though the new turret was bigger on the outside, it had even less room within than the old one.

"That's a fact. The new gun will make them sit up and take notice. About time, too," Pound said. "Maybe we have a chance of holding them out of Pittsburgh now. Maybe." He sounded anything but convinced.

He sounded that way because he *was* unconvinced. The U.S. Army hadn't been able to stop the latest Confederate push, any more than it had been able to stop the Confederate drive up through Ohio the summer before. If you couldn't stop the enemy, how the devil were you supposed to win the war? Pound saw no way.

He could have elaborated on the many failings of the U.S. War Department, but Bergman hissed at him and jerked a thumb off to the left. "Here comes the lieutenant," he warned.

Second Lieutenant Don Griffiths was typical of the breed. He was young, he didn't know much, and one of the things he didn't know was how much he didn't know. He had blond hair and freckles and couldn't possibly have bought a drink without proving to the bartender that he was over twenty-one.

Sergeant Pound and PFC Bergman saluted him. He returned the gesture. "Men, we have our orders," he said.

He sounded full of enthusiasm. It was too early in the morning for Pound to feel enthusiasm or much of anything else except a deep longing for another cup of coffee. But Griffiths stood there waiting expectantly, so Pound did what he was supposed to do: he asked, "What are they, sir?"

"We are going to drive the enemy out of Pennsylvania," the lieutenant said grandly.

"What? All by ourselves?" Pound said.

Don Griffiths wagged a finger in his face. "I've heard about you, Sergeant—don't think I haven't," he said. "You haven't got the right attitude."

"Probably not, sir," Pound agreed politely. "I do object to being killed for no good reason."

"Don't get smart with me, either." Griffiths' voice didn't break the way the late Lieutenant Poffenberger's had, but he still sounded like a kid. "I'll bust you down to private faster than you can say Jack Robinson."

"Go ahead, sir," Pound answered, politely still. "I'll never get rich on Army pay no matter what my rank is, and if I'm a private again I'll get out from under you. Besides, how likely is either one of us to live through the war? Why should I get excited about whether my sleeve has stripes on it?"

Lieutenant Griffiths gaped at him. The gold bar Griffiths wore on each shoulder strap was the only thing he had going for him. He couldn't imagine anybody who didn't care about rank. In fact, Pound did, very much, but the best way to hang on to what he had and be able to mouth off the way he wanted to was to pretend indifference. "You are insubordinate," Griffiths spluttered.

"Not me, sir. Bergman is my witness," Pound said. "Have I been disrespectful? Have I been discourteous? Have I been disobedient?" He knew he hadn't. He could be much more annoying when he stayed within the rules.

Griffiths proved it by spinning on his heel and storming away. PFC Bergman chuckled nervously. "He's gonna get you in Dutch, Sarge," Bergman predicted.

"What can he do to me? Throw me in the stockade?" Pound laughed at the idea. "I hope he does. I'll be warm and safe in a nice cell back of the line, three square meals a day, while he's stuck up here with unfriendly strangers trying to shoot his ass off. The worst thing he could do to me is leave me right where I am."

Bergman shook his head. "Worst he could do is bust you *and* leave you where you're at."

Pound grunted. That, unfortunately, was true. He didn't think Lieutenant Griffiths had the imagination to see it; if he'd had that kind of imagination, he would have been a real officer, not a lowly shavetail. Pound proved right. The next time Griffiths had anything to do with him, the barrel commander pretended their last exchange hadn't happened. Pound played along. He watched the way Griffiths eyed him: like a man watching a bear that might or might not be ready to charge.

Their barrel moved out the next morning. Several platoons of the new machines rumbled north and west from the classically named town of Tarentum. Tarentum lay northeast of Pittsburgh; the barrels wanted to knock in the head of the Confederate column sweeping past the industrial center. Another enemy column was pushing up from the southwest. If they met, they would put Pittsburgh in a pocket. That had happened to Columbus the summer before. If the Confederates brought it off here, they could smash up the U.S. defenders in the pocket at their leisure.

Pittsburgh was the most important iron and steel town in the United States. If it fell, how could the country go on with the war? If it fell, would the country have the heart to go on with the war? Those were interesting questions. Michael Pound hoped he—and the USA— didn't find out the answers to them.

"This is pretty good barrel country, sir," he remarked to Lieutenant Griffiths after they'd been rolling along for a while.

"It is?" Griffiths sounded suspicious, as if he feared Pound was pulling his leg. "I thought you wanted wide-open spaces for barrels, not all these trees and houses and other obstructions."

Anyone who used a word like *obstructions* in a sentence was bound to have other things wrong with him, too. "You do, sir, if you're on the attack," Pound said patiently. "But if you want to defend, if the enemy's coming at you, having enough cover to shoot from ambush is nice."

"Oh." The lieutenant weighed that. "Yes, I see what you mean."

"I'm glad, sir." Now Pound sounded—and was—dead serious. "Because the point of the whole business is to kill the other guys and not get killed ourselves. That's the long and short of it."

Griffiths didn't disagree with him. The young officer opened the cupola and stood up in the turret to see what he could see. Pound just got glimpses through the gunsight—which was also improved from the one in the earlier turret. The Confederates hadn't got here yet, so the landscape wasn't too badly battered. That didn't mean he would have wanted to live here even if no one had ever heard of war. Coal mines, tailings from coal mines—he'd heard the locals call the stuff red dog— and factories dealing with coal and steel and aluminum dotted the landscape. Some of the factories belched white or gray or black or yellowish smoke into the sky even though the enemy was only a few miles away. They were going to keep operating till the Confederates overran them.

Michael Pound scowled. When they shut down, all the workers would try to get away at once. He'd seen that before. They'd clog the roads, U.S. troops would have trouble going around them or through them, and the Confederates would have a high old time bombing them and shooting them from the air.

Not five minutes after that thought crossed his mind, the barrel slowed and then stopped. Lieutenant Griffiths shouted from the cupola: "You people! Clear the road at once! At once, I tell you! You're impeding the war effort!" Pound wouldn't have moved for anybody who told him he was impeding anything. This crowd didn't, either.

And they paid for not moving. No Asskickers screamed down out of the sky to pummel them, but they were in range of Confederate artillery. So were the advancing U.S. barrels. That didn't worry Pound very much—except for the rare unlucky direct hit, long-range bombardment wouldn't hurt them. He did tug on Griffiths' trouser leg and call, "Better get down, sir. Fragments aren't healthy."

"Oh. Right." The lieutenant even remembered to close the cupola hatch after himself. He was faintly green, or more than faintly. "My God!" He gulped. "What shellfire does to civilians out in the open . . . It's a slaughterhouse out there."

"Yes, sir," Pound said, as gently as he could. "I've seen it before." He'd got glimpses through the gunsight here, too, and was glad he'd had no more than glimpses. Shrapnel clattered off the sides and front of the barrel. There were times when sitting in a thick armored box wasn't so bad, even if it was too damn hot and nobody in there with you had bathed anytime lately.

Griffiths spoke to the driver over the intercom: "If you can go forward without smashing people, do it." The barrel moved ahead in low gear. Pound didn't like to think about what it was running over, so he resolutely didn't. The lieutenant peered through the periscope: a far cry from sticking your head out and looking around, but nobody would have done that under this kind of shellfire. Well, maybe Irving Morrell would have, but officers like him didn't come along every day.

Suddenly, Griffiths let out an indignant squawk. "What is it, sir?" Pound asked.

"Our men," Griffiths answered. "Our soldiers—retreating!"

Pound got a brief look at them, too, and liked none of what he saw. "We'd better find an ambush position pretty quick, then, sir," he said. "We're going to have company."

Griffiths didn't get it right away. When he did, he nodded. A stone wall that hid the bottom half of the barrel wasn't perfect cover, but it was a lot better than nothing.

"Have an AP round ready," Pound told Bergman. The loader tapped him on the leg to show he'd heard.

"There's one!" Griffiths squeaked with excitement. "Uh, front, I mean!"

"Identified," Pound confirmed. "Range six hundred yards." He added, "Armor-piercing." Bergman slammed the round into the breech. With quick, fussy precision, Pound lined up the sights on the target: one of the new-model C.S. barrels. Now to see what this new gun could do. He nudged Lieutenant Griffiths. "Ready, sir."

"Fire!" Griffiths said, and the cannon spoke.

Here in the turret, the report wasn't too loud. The empty casing leaped from the breech and clattered down onto the deck. Cordite fumes made Pound cough. But he whooped at the same time, for fire spurted from the enemy barrel. "Hit!" he shouted, and Griffiths with him. The old gun wouldn't have pierced that armor at that range.

"Front!" Griffiths said again, more businesslike this time. "About ten o'clock."

"Identified," Pound replied. He scored another hit. Whatever the Confederates wanted today, they weren't going to buy it cheap.

Out of the line. Armstrong Grimes knew only one thing besides relief: resentment that he'd have to go back when his regiment's turn in reserve was up. For the time being, though, nobody would be shooting at him. He wouldn't be ducking screaming meemies. He wouldn't wonder if the stranger in a green-gray uniform was really a U.S. soldier, and worry that that unfamiliar face might belong to a Mormon intent on cutting his throat or stabbing him in the back and then sneaking away.

He turned to Sergeant Rex Stowe, who tramped along beside him down what had been a highway and was now mostly shell holes. "Ain't this fun?"

"Oh, yeah. Now tell me another one." Stowe needed a shave. His helmet was on crooked. A cigarette dangled from the corner of his mouth. He looked like most of the other U.S. soldiers trudging through the wreckage that had been Provo.

"Anybody figure this fight would take so long when it started?" Armstrong persisted. "We've been here forever, and we're still not in Salt Lake City." He was no lovelier than his sergeant, and had no doubt he smelled as bad, too.

"We're doing it on the cheap," Yossel Reisen complained. "We could end this mess in a hurry if we'd put enough men and barrels and bombers into it."

"Write your Congresswoman," Stowe said—a joke that had grown old in the company.

But Reisen answered, "I've done it. Aunt Flora says the Confederates and now Canada are taking away what we need."

Sergeant Stowe didn't seem to know what to say to that. Neither did Armstrong. They both outranked Yossel, but when it came to clout. . . . Armstrong had none, and as far as he knew Stowe didn't either. Yossel Reisen, on the other hand, had all the clout in the world—and didn't want to use any of it.

If he had wanted to use it, he would have been anywhere but here. Provo looked as if God had dropped a cigarette here and then ground it out with a hobnailed boot. The city had fallen weeks ago, but smoke still rose here and there. The smell of death lingered, too. By the urgent insistence it took on every now and then, some of the dead were a lot more recent than the fall of the town.

As Armstrong and his buddies slogged south, other soldiers came north. They were cleaner and better barbered, but their faded uniforms and hard, watchful faces said this wasn't the first time they were heading up to the front. "What's new?" one of them called in Armstrong's general direction.

"You know about the fucking spigot mortar?" he replied.

"Sure do." The soldier going the other way nodded. "Ka-*boom!* They had that the last time I went up."

"Yeah, but now they've started loading the screaming meemies with mustard gas. They can carry a lot of it, too."

"Well, shit," the other soldier said bitterly. "If it's not one god-damn thing, it's another. If I have to put on that rubber gear, the heat'll kill me."

It was probably somewhere in the upper nineties. That wasn't so dreadful as it would have been back in Washington or Philadelphia. As people from out West never got tired of saying, it was a dry heat. That didn't mean it wasn't hot, though. And when you wore full antigas gear, you cooked in your own juices. Who needed humidity then?

A little blond girl came out of the ruins to stare at Armstrong. She was about eight years old, and would have been pretty if she weren't scrawny and filthy and wearing what looked like a torn burlap bag for a dress. The stony hatred on her face didn't help, either.

"Jesus!" He wanted to make the sign of the cross to ward off that look, and he wasn't even Catholic. "She'll shoot at us in the next go-round, and her kid'll pick up a gun in the one after that."

"We oughta just shoot all of these bastards and start over here," Stowe said. "Treat 'em like the Confederates treat their niggers. Then we could do this place right."

"You think Featherston's fuckers really are doing that shit?" Armstrong said. "Seems hard to believe."

"You'd better believe it—it's true," Yossel Reisen said. "My aunt knows more about that stuff than she ever wanted to find out. They're filthy down there, really filthy."

His aunt was likely to know if anybody did. Armstrong said, "Still seems crazy to me. Why would anybody want to do that to somebody else just on account of what he looks like? I mean, I've got no use for niggers, God knows, but I don't want to kill 'em all." He had no idea how many oversimplifications and unexamined ideas he'd packed into that, and was probably lucky he didn't.

"People do it all the time," Yossel said. "You're not Jewish, that's for sure."

"Nope, not me." Armstrong might have had more to say on the subject of Jews, too, but not where his buddy could hear it. You didn't do things like that. Life at the front was tough enough as is. If you pissed off somebody who might save your ass one day soon, you only made it worse.

A sign led to the trucks that would take them back to the R and R center at Thistle. Before long, they'd have to leave again, but Armstrong looked forward to getting clean, getting deloused, and eating real food and sleeping on a real mattress.

As happened too often in the Army, somebody'd screwed up. There were far more soldiers than trucks to take them to Thistle or anywhere else. The men milled around, waiting for something to happen. A lot of Army life was like that. A captain climbed up on what was left of a brick wall and shouted that more trucks would be along in an hour or so. The cheers he drew were distinctly sarcastic. The catcalls, on the other hand, came from the heart. The captain turned red and got down in a hurry.

Armstrong didn't know what drew his eye to the woman who walked toward the crowd of soldiers. Maybe it was just that she *was* a woman. Most of the ones he'd seen lately wore dungarees and carried rifles and wanted to kill him. He returned the favor the best way he knew how.

This one had on a dress, a baggy dress that reached almost to her ankles. Her face was pinched and pale. Maybe that was what kept Armstrong's eye on her—not her good looks, though she wasn't half bad, but her absolute determination. An alarm bell went off in his mind. He nudged Rex Stowe. "Sergeant, something's wrong with that broad." He pointed.

"Yeah?" Stowe didn't see it for a second. Then he did. "Yeah." He took a step toward her, and started to take another one—

And the world exploded.

Next thing Armstrong knew, he was on his back. Something that stung ran into his eyes. He put up a hand and discovered it was blood. He was bleeding from the leg, too, and from one arm. He looked around. Yossel Reisen, somehow, was still on his feet and didn't seem to be scratched. Sergeant Stowe was down and moaning, both hands pressed to a swelling scarlet stain on his belly.

"She blew herself up!" The words seemed to come from a million miles away. Armstrong realized the bomb must have stunned his ears. He hoped they weren't ruined for good.

He scrambled to his feet. Closer to the woman—who wasn't there anymore, of course—the landscape was a surreal mess of bodies and body parts. How many had she killed? How many had she hurt? Armstrong watched a soldier pull a nail out of his arm. He realized the woman hadn't just carried explosives. She'd had shrapnel, too. She'd done what she'd done on purpose, and she'd made sure she did as much damage as she could when she did it.

"You all right?" Yossel's voice came from far, far away, too.

"If I'm not, I'll worry about it later," Armstrong said. "We've got to do what we can for these poor mothers."

He bent beside Rex Stowe and gave him a shot of morphine. He might have wasted it; Stowe was going gray. He put a dressing on the noncom's wound, but blood soaked through right away. "Corpsman!" Yossel Reisen shouted. But a dozen other soldiers were yelling the same thing, and no medics seemed close by. Who would have thought trouble might strike *here*?

Nobody would have. Nobody had. And that was probably *why* it had happened here. The men waiting for transport hadn't paid any attention to the Mormon woman . . . till too late.

Yossel Reisen slapped a bandage on Armstrong's forehead. "Thanks," he said.

"It's all right," Yossel said absently—he had other things on his mind. In disbelieving tones, he went on, "She blew herself up. She fucking blew herself up. She fucking blew herself up on purpose."

"She sure as shit did." Armstrong liked that no better than his buddy did. "How do you stop somebody who wants to make like a bomb?"

"I don't know. I have no idea, and I don't think anybody else does, either," Yossel said. "Who would have thought anybody could be that crazy?"

"Mormons," Armstrong said. The Mormons had caused so much trouble for the USA, and had notions so different from those of most Americans, that blaming things on them just because they *were* Mormons came easy. But even Armstrong, who was anything but reflective, realized more than that went into it. Despite the heat, he shivered. "A woman. She waited till she could hurt the most soldiers, and then—she did."

"They could pull shit like this anywhere," Yossel Reisen said, a new horror in his voice. "Anywhere at all. On a bus, in a subway, in a theater, at a football game—anywhere there's a crowd. If you hate enough and you want to hit back enough . . . you just do."

"Fuck." Armstrong meant the word more as prayer than as curse. He said the worst thing he could think of to follow it: "You're right."

Men with Red Cross armbands did rush up then. They got Rex

Stowe on a stretcher and carried him away. He was still breathing, but Armstrong didn't think he'd live. Even if he did, he'd be out of the war for months, probably for good.

Bodies and pieces of bodies remained after all the wounded were taken away. So did the butcher-shop stink of blood. Armstrong walked over to where the woman had been standing. He found a torn and charred shoe that wasn't Army issue. But for that, there was no sign she'd ever existed—except the carnage all around. "Fuck," he said again, no less reverently than before.

A dozen U.S. trucks painted Army green-gray rumbled up then. The drivers stared in disbelief at the blood-soaked scene. "What the hell happened here?" one of them said.

Somebody threw a piece of broken brick at his truck. It clanged off the hood. "You son of a bitch!" the soldier shouted. "If you'd got here on time, we wouldn't have been here when she did that!"

Another rock or brick banged off a different truck. For a moment, Armstrong wondered if the soldiers who'd survived the bomb would lynch the truck drivers. They might have if a burly first sergeant hadn't said, "She was gonna do it anyways. If it wasn't us, it woulda been the next poor bunch of bastards. What the fuck you gonna do?"

He was so obviously right—and so large—that he threw cold water on the lynching bee. An officer thought to set up a perimeter in case more Mormons decided to blow themselves to kingdom come for their cause. And then the unwounded and the walking wounded got on the trucks and headed down to Thistle after all. *What the fuck are you gonna do?* Armstrong thought. Like Yossel, he had no idea. He hoped somebody did.

Flora Blackford had never warmed to the Philadelphia cheese steak. The only way they could have made it more *treyf* was to add ham and oysters. She stuck with pastrami on rye. Robert Taft probably wouldn't have minded if they'd added ham and oysters to his cheese steak. Those weren't forbidden foods for him.

The Old Munich was near the damaged Congressional building. It had pretty good prices and air conditioning. Looking around, Flora didn't think she could assemble a quorum from the Representatives and Senators in the place, but she didn't think she would miss by much, either.

Taft raised a schooner of beer. "Here's to you—most of the time," he said, and sipped from it.

Flora had a gin and tonic: almost as good a cooler as the refrigerated air. "Same to you," she said. "We see eye to eye about the war, anyhow."

"Seems that way." Taft made a very unhappy face. "Maybe the President knew what he was doing when he tried to come to terms with the Mormons."

"Maybe." Flora sounded unhappy, too. Did Taft know that woman had almost blown up her nephew? Instead of asking, she went on, "Would you be comfortable making peace with people who do things like that?"

"It depends," Taft said judiciously. "If peace meant they weren't going to do them, I might. If every nut with a grievance is going to strap on some dynamite and start seeing how many honest people he can take with him, we've really got a problem." He drained the schooner. "The way things look now, we've really got a problem."

Flora remembered that she was about to answer. The explosion outside beat her to the punch. Women screamed. So did a couple of men. Flora didn't, quite. What came out instead—a soft, "Oh, dear God!"—was close to a sob of despair.

Taft jumped to his feet, the cheese steak forgotten. "We'd better see if we can do anything to help," he said, and hurried out of the Old Munich. Flora paused long enough to pay the check, then ran after him.

A bus halfway down the block sprawled sideways across the road. The crumpled shape was burning fiercely. Window glass glittered in the streets and on the sidewalk like out-of-season snow. Some people were still trapped on the bus. Their shrieks dinned in Flora's ears. One of them threw himself out a window. He was on fire. Passersby tried to beat on the flames with their hats and with their hands.

"He blew himself up!" shouted a man with blood rilling down his face. "The motherfucker blew himself up! He had a, a thing, and he pushed it, and he blew himself up." He paused, then spoke again in an amazingly calm voice: "Somebody get me a doctor." He folded up and passed out.

Plenty of others were wounded. Flora couldn't tell whether some had been on the bus or were just luckless passersby. Others, the burned, had obviously been passengers along with the man with the thing—

some sort of switch, Flora supposed. She tore her handkerchief in half and made two bandages with it. After that, she used the tissues in her handbag on smaller cuts.

Robert Taft sacrificed his handkerchief and his tie. Then he took off his shirt and his undershirt and used a pocket knife to cut them into strips of cloth. "Other people need them worse than I do," he said, and he wasn't the only bare-chested man around, either.

"Good for you," Flora told him. "Let me have some of those, too, please."

Ambulances roared up, sirens wailing. Philadelphia was good at responding to disasters. And so it should have been—it had had enough practice. "Somebody put a bomb on the bus?" asked a white-coated man from an ambulance.

"Somebody *was* a bomb on the bus," a woman answered. The man's answer was eloquent, heartfelt, and altogether unprintable.

"Well," Taft said, "looks like we have the answer to my question, and it's not the one I wish we had." He was splashed with blood past his elbows. His trousers were bloodstained, too, but Flora didn't think any of the gore was his.

She glanced down at herself. The cotton print dress she had on would never be the same. Blood also dappled her arms. "What are we supposed to do?" she asked, a question aimed more at the world at large than at Senator Taft. "How do we fight people who'll kill themselves to hurt us?"

"If we have to, we—" Taft broke off, as if really hearing what he'd been about to say. He shook his head. "Good Lord. I started to sound like Jake Featherston."

"Yes." Flora wanted to cry, or to scream. Here, for once, the USA faced a knottier problem than the CSA. Negroes looked like Negroes. Mormons? Mormons looked and talked just like anybody else. Anybody here could be a Mormon, and could have another bomb waiting. How would you know till it went off?

"Good Lord," Taft said again. "We're going to have to start searching people before we let them gather. Football games, films, trains, buses, department stores—for all I know, we'll have to check anybody who goes into the Old Munich."

"I was thinking how many members of Congress were in there," Flora said shakily. "If that bomber had walked inside instead of blowing up the bus . . ." Philadelphia was its usual hot, muggy summer self. That kind of weather wouldn't last much longer, but it was still here—sweat ran down Flora's face. She shivered anyhow.

"Auto bombs are bad enough," Taft said. "People bombs . . ." Like Flora, he seemed to run out of words. He spread his bloody hands. "What could be worse?"

What were they working on, out in western Washington? Something they thought might win the war. Whatever it was, that all but guaranteed it would be a horror worse than any they'd known up till now. Worse than poison gas? Worse than the camps where the Confederates were systematically doing away with their Negroes? She had trouble imagining such a thing. That didn't mean the people out in Washington State had any trouble, though.

While horror swelled inside her, rage seemed to fill Taft. "This is no fit way to fight," the Senator from Ohio ground out. "If they want to meet us like men, that's one thing. If they want to see how many innocent civilians they can blow up—"

"They used it against soldiers first," Flora said, remembering Yossel's narrow escape again. "And we drop bombs on civilians all over the CSA. It's just that . . . Who would have expected people to *be* weapons instead of using weapons?"

"Well, the genie's out of the bottle now," Taft said grimly. "Nobody in the world is safe from here on out. Nobody, do you hear me? There isn't a king or a president or a prime minister somebody doesn't hate. A man comes up to you in a reception line. Maybe you didn't appoint him postmaster. Maybe he just hears voices in his head. You reach out to shake his hand. Next thing you know, you're both dead, and a dozen people around you, too. How do you stop something like that?"

Flora only shrugged helplessly. For thousands of years, war had been based on the notion that you wanted to hurt the other side without getting hurt yourself. Now the rules had shifted under everybody's feet. How *could* you stop someone who embraced death instead of fleeing it?

Fresh dread filled her when she thought about how *useful* a weapon like this might be. Surely the United States could find men willing to die for their country. If you sent them after Jake Featherston and you got him, weren't you doing more to win the war than you would by smashing a division or two of ordinary soldiers?

But the Confederates would have targets of their own. *I might even be one,* Flora thought, and ice walked up her back again. Like it or not, it was true. Nobody in the USA had spoken out more ferociously than she had about what the Confederate States and the Freedom Party were doing to their Negroes.

"How many more of these bombs will we see in the next week? In the next month? In the next year?" Taft asked. "We've *never* known anything like this before. Never. That Canadian who kept blowing up American soldiers after the last war, the one who tried to blow up General Custer—he finally blew himself up, but he didn't want to. If he'd been like these Mormons, he could have gone to a rally and done even worse." He suddenly laughed, which made Flora stare.

"What could possibly be funny about this?" she demanded.

"I'd like to see Featherston's face when he hears about it," Robert Taft answered. "He knows how many people . . . mm, don't love him, shall we say? He's the one who'll really have reason to be shaking in his boots. *Sic semper tyrannis,* by God—*thus always to tyrants,* if your Latin's rusty."

It was; Flora hadn't even thought about those classes in close to forty years. At the time, she hadn't thought they were good for anything; it wasn't as if she were likely to train for the Catholic priesthood! Looking back, though, they'd probably improved her English. And, looking back, that had probably been the point. It sure hadn't occurred to her then.

What Taft said made a certain amount of sense. What he said often did. People who had or should have had bad consciences would worry more about men—or women—with bombs than others would. And yet . . . "The Mormons are using them against us," she said bleakly.

"Yes, but the Mormons are a pack of crazy fanatics," Taft said. But that wouldn't do, and he realized it wouldn't. "I see what you're saying. I wish I didn't. To them, *we* look like the tyrants."

"That's what I was thinking," Flora agreed. "A lot of it's like beauty—it's in the eye of the beholder."

"God help us," Taft said.

"*Omayn,*" Flora said, "or *amen,* if you'd rather."

"*That* doesn't matter to me one way or the other," Taft said. Flora believed him; whatever else he was, he was no anti-Semite. He sadly shook his head. "What *are* we going to do?"

"I can't begin to tell you, and I wish I could," Flora answered. "We might have a better chance now if we'd done something different a life-time ago, but it's a little late to worry about that now."

"Yes—just a little," Taft said. "We have this pack of people who hate us right there in the middle of the country, and the most we can hope for, as far as I can see, is that they do us as little harm as we can manage." Taft absently wiped his high forehead with the heel of his hand, and left a red streak on his skin.

"This has gone on for too long," Flora said. "If we don't settle it once and for all during the war, we have to try afterwards." That sounded good, but what did it mean? She listened to her own words with the same sick horror Taft had known before her. What could settling it once and for all during the war mean but killing all the Mormons? If the United States did that, they wouldn't have to worry about it afterwards—except when the country looked at itself in a mirror. Flora shuddered. All the carnage around her hadn't nauseated her the way that thought did. "Dear God in heaven," she whispered. "There's a little bit of Jake Featherston in *me,* too."

"A little bit of that bastard's in every one of us," Taft said. "The point of the exercise is not to let him out."

"Well, Senator, we've found one more thing we agree on." Flora held out her bloodstained hand. Taft clasped it in his.

XIV

The telephone on Clarence Potter's desk rang. He picked it up. "Potter here," he said crisply.

"Hello, Potter there," Jake Featherston rasped in his ear. "I need you to be Potter *here,* fast as you can, so get your ass on over right now."

"On my way, sir." Potter hung up. He grabbed his hat, closed and locked the office door behind him, and went upstairs to get a motorcar. From the War Department to the Gray House on Shockoe Hill shouldn't have taken more than five minutes. In fact, it took more like fifteen. The U.S. air raid the night before had cratered several streets on the most direct routes.

"Sorry, sir," the driver kept saying as he had to double back. Potter suspected the President would make *him* sorry, too, but he didn't take it out on the luckless young soldier behind the wheel. When he arrived, he hopped out of the Birmingham, showed his ID to the guards at the entrance to the battered Confederate Presidential residence, and was escorted below ground to the enormous bomb shelter in which Jake Featherston operated these days.

New York City had skyscrapers. Potter wondered how long it would be before men built twenty, thirty, even fifty stories underground to keep from getting blown up when bombers came overhead. He laughed. That wouldn't work in New Orleans, where the cemeteries were on top of the ground because of the high water table. Such details and anomalies aside, the picture seemed scarily probable.

Saul Goldman sat in the waiting room. Potter nodded to the director of communications. "Am I after you in line?" he asked.

"I don't think so, General," Goldman answered. "I think we go in together."

"Do we?" Potter kept his voice as neutral as he could. Goldman was good at making propaganda, but the Intelligence officer didn't want to be part of any propaganda, no matter how good. He'd had that argument with the President before. He hadn't completely lost it, which only went to show how good his case was.

Featherston's secretary stuck her head into the room. "Come with me, gentlemen." Goldman caught Potter's eye and nodded. Sure enough, they were an entry, like 3 and 3A at the racetrack.

When Potter came into the President's sanctum, Featherston fixed him with a fishy stare and barked, "Took you long enough. What did you do—walk?"

"Sorry, sir. Bomb damage." Potter had been braced for worse.

And Featherston let him off the hook after that, which also surprised him. "We need to get down to brass tacks," the President said. "You've both heard about these people bombs up in the USA—Mormons strapping on explosives and blowing themselves to hell and gone as soon as they can take a raft of damnyankees with 'em?"

"Yes, Mr. President," Saul Goldman said. Potter nodded. Goldman went on, "We've been working on ways to play them up—to show the Yankees are so low and evil, people will kill themselves before they live under them."

That sounded like a good line to take to Potter, but Jake Featherston shook his head. "I was afraid you were gonna do somethin' like that," he said heavily. "That's how come I called you in here—to tell you not to. No way, nohow. Not a word about 'em out of us, and jam the Yankees hard as you can when they talk about 'em. You got that?"

"I hear you, sir, but I don't understand." Goldman looked and sounded pained. Clarence Potter didn't blame him. Had he been in the communications director's shoes, he would have been pained, too.

But Featherston repeated, "Not a word, goddammit, and I'll tell you why." He went on, "I don't want the damn niggers to hear anything about people bombs, you hear me? Not one fucking word! Coons are enough trouble as is. You don't reckon some of those bastards'd blow themselves to the moon if they could take a raft of decent white folks with 'em? I sure do."

"But—" Saul Goldman began. Even starting the protest took nerve; not many people had the nerve to squawk to Featherston's face.

Here, though, Potter agreed with the President. "I'm sorry, Mr. Goldman, but I think he's right," he said. "We'd better keep the lid on that one for as long as we can, because the niggers will make us sorry if we don't."

"Damn straight," Featherston said.

The director of communications still looked unhappy. "Since you've made up your mind, sir, that's the way we'll do it." He plainly thought the President was wrong to have made up his mind that way.

Jake Featherston just as plainly didn't care. "Make sure you do. And pick up the jamming on the damnyankees, too. We will be sorry— we'll be sorry as hell—if we can't keep this quiet."

"I'll do my best, Mr. President. If you'll excuse me . . ." The little Jew left the President's office very abruptly.

As soon as the door clicked shut behind Goldman, Jake Featherston let out a long sigh. "I don't like making Saul do like I tell him instead of like he wants to. He's good—he's damn good. You need to give a man like that his head. This time, though, I just don't reckon I've got much choice."

Potter nodded. "I think you're right, Mr. President. I said so."

"Yeah, you did." Featherston eyed him. "You're not one to do something like that just to make me wag my tail, either."

Remembering the weight of the pistol in his pocket as he rode the train up to Richmond in 1936, Potter nodded again. "No, sir. Whatever else I am, I'm no yes-man."

"Son of a bitch. I never would've known if you hadn't told me." Maybe Jake Featherston was remembering that pistol, too. He drummed his fingers on top of his desk. "Got a question for you, Mr. Straight Answer."

"Go ahead," Potter said.

"Those fucking Mormon people bombs—did any of your men give 'em the idea, or did they come up with it all by themselves?"

"Mr. President, our people did not have thing one to do with that," Potter said positively. "Nobody in the CSA—no white man in the CSA, anyhow—is that crazy. The Mormons came up with it on their own."

"All right. I believe you. But if I ever find out you're lying to me about this one, I'll have your head," Featherston said. "People bombs hurt the damnyankees, yeah, but they can hurt us a lot worse. And you know as well as I do that Saul won't be able to clamp down on the news forever. One way or another, this kind of shit always comes out."

"I knew that, sir. I wasn't sure you did," Potter answered. People who weren't in the intelligence business often had an exaggerated notion of how easy keeping a secret was.

Jake Featherston laughed at him. "I never went to a fancy U.S. college, General, but I reckon I may know a thing or two anyways."

"That's not what I meant, Mr. President," Clarence Potter said stiffly.

Featherston laughed some more. "Yeah, likely tell." But amusement didn't live long on his face. It never did, not that Potter had seen. The President of the CSA always had to be angry at something or worried about something. And today he had something to be angry and worried about. "Damn niggers are gonna start blowin' themselves up, sure as hell they are. Damfino how much we can do about it, either."

"Massive reprisals," Potter suggested. "Kill ten coons for every white a people bomb blows up, or twenty, or a hundred."

"That won't stop 'em," Featherston predicted morosely. "There'll always be some bastards who think, *Who gives a damn what happens after I'm dead?* And the ones who go after us without counting the cost are the ones we've got to be afraid of."

He knew what he was talking about. The Freedom Party had always gone after its foes without counting the cost, whether those foes were Whigs and Radical Liberals, Negroes, or the United States. Potter said, "Yes, sir. You're right—we'll still have trouble even if we do that. But I think we'll have less. We'll make some niggers think twice before they turn into people bombs. And we'll make the niggers who don't want to blow themselves up think twice before they help or cover up for the ones who do. They'd better, anyhow, if they know they're going to get shot after a people bomb goes off."

"It could be." Featherston picked up a pencil and wrote himself a note. "It's a better scheme than anybody else has come up with, I'll say that. Whatever else you are, General, you aren't soft on niggers."

"I should hope not, sir," Potter said. "That's how we first met, remember. I was trying to head off the Red uprising before it got started. I was after that officer's body servant—"

"Pompey, his name was," Jake Featherston said at once. Potter wouldn't have remembered the Negro's name if they'd set him on fire.

Featherston had a truly marvelous memory for detail—and never forgot an enemy or a slight. He went on, "He was a mincing, prissy little bastard, thought his shit didn't stink. Just what you'd expect from a stinking blueblood like Jeb Stuart III to have for a servant." He looked as if he wanted to spit on the carpet, or possibly start chewing it.

And he wasn't wrong. During the Great War and even afterward, the Confederate States had had too many sons and grandsons and great-grandsons of founding fathers in positions of authority for no better reason than that their ancestors had done big things. It wasn't like that anymore, Nathan Bedford Forrest III notwithstanding. Forrest was there because of what he could do, not because of what great-grandpa the cavalry general had done. The Freedom Party had swept away most of the Juniors and IIIs and IVs. And that, Potter was willing to admit, needed doing.

Featherston let the pencil fall. "All right, General. That's about it, looks like. Main reason I wanted you here was to find out if those damn people bombs were your notion. But you gave me a good idea, and I reckon we'll try it out when the time comes—and it will, goddammit. I thank you for that."

Potter got to his feet. "You're welcome, Mr. President. We're on the same side in this fight."

"In this one, yeah. How about some of the others?" But Featherston waved that aside. "Never mind. Get out of here."

A man in a State Department uniform went in as Potter went out. Potter wondered what that was all about. He knew he could learn with a little poking and prodding. He also knew he'd catch merry hell if anybody found out he was doing it. You didn't try to find out what was none of your business. That was one of the rules in this game, too. There were often good reasons why it was none of your business.

After the air conditioning under the Gray House, ordinary Richmond late summer seemed twice as hot and muggy as usual. A haze of dust and smoke hung over the Confederate capital: a souvenir of Yankee bombing raids. The same sort of haze was said to hang over Philadelphia.

Will anything be left of either side when this war is over? Potter wondered. More and more, it reminded him of a duel of submachine guns at two paces. Both countries could strike better than they could defend.

He didn't know what to do about that. He didn't think anyone else did, either. Maybe taking Pittsburgh away from the damnyankees really would knock them out of the fight. It had a chance of doing that, anyway. Potter couldn't think of anything else that did.

A truck dumped gravel and asphalt on the street in front of the Gray House. A heavy mechanized roller started smashing it down into a more or less level surface. And it would stay level till the next time U.S. bombers visited Richmond, or the time after that, or perhaps the time after *that*.

The machine was more interesting to Clarence Potter than the job it was doing. Not long before, a swarm of Negroes with hand tools would have done work like that. No more. Machinery was much more common than it had been . . . and there weren't so many Negroes around. Potter nodded to himself. Both halves of that suited him fine.

Hipolito Rodriguez awkwardly sewed a sergeant's—no, a troop leader's—stripes onto the left sleeve of his gray tunic. The letter that came with his promotion notice said it was for "contributions valuable to the safety and security of the Confederate States of America." That left the guards at Camp Determination who hadn't been promoted both puzzled and jealous. It also gave the noncoms whose ranks he'd suddenly joined something new to think about.

Tom Porter, who'd been Rodriguez's squad leader till he got the promotion, added two and two and got four. "This has to do with those new buildings going up alongside the men's and women's half, doesn't it?" he said.

"I think maybe it does, *sí*," Rodriguez answered. He was still getting used to the luxury of the noncoms' quarters. He had a room of his own now, with a closet and a sink. No more cot in the middle of a barracks with a lot of other noisy, smelly guards. No more shoving everything he owned into a footlocker, either. He had more room to be a person as a troop leader; he wasn't just one more cog on a gear in a vast machine.

"I know you helped give the commandant the idea for those new buildings," Porter said. "If they work out as well as everybody hopes, I reckon you've earned your stripes."

Porter's acceptance helped ease the transition from ordinary guard to troop leader. It meant the other noncoms made it plain they would back Rodriguez if he ran into trouble. With that going for him, he didn't, or never more than he could handle by himself. And those buildings rapidly neared completion.

Nobody ever called them anything but that. If you talked about one of them, it was *that building*. The guards knew what they were for; they'd been briefed. They had to be, by the nature of things. But, also by the nature of things, they didn't call them by their right names. If you didn't name something, you didn't have to dwell on what it really was and really did. Not thinking about those things helped you sleep at night.

A few of the guards, men who'd come to Camp Determination as it went up, would sometimes talk about shooting Negroes in the swamps of Louisiana. They were mostly matter-of-fact, but they would also talk about comrades who couldn't stand the strain. "So-and-so ate his gun," they would say. That was how Rodriguez learned Jeff Pinkard's new wife was a dead guard's widow. He'd known she was married before; two boys made that obvious. The details . . .

"Poor son a bitch just couldn't take it," a guard said sympathetically.

"He shoot himself, too?" Rodriguez asked with a certain horrid fascination.

"Nope." The veteran guard shook his head. "Chick must've got sick of guns. He ran a hose from his auto exhaust into the passenger compartment and fired up the motor. Sure as hell wish we'd've had those trucks back then. You don't have to worry so much about what you're doing when you load one of them."

"The trucks, they came after this fellow kill himself?" Rodriguez said.

"That's right." The guard who was talking didn't see anything out of the ordinary about that. Maybe there was nothing out of the ordinary to see. To Rodriguez, the timing seemed . . . interesting, anyhow. *Señor* Jeff was good at getting ideas from things that happened around him.

Rodriguez almost remarked on that. Then he thought better of it. He couldn't prove a thing, after all—and he couldn't unsay something once he'd said it. Better to keep his mouth shut.

And keeping his mouth shut proved a good idea, as it usually did.

A few days later, an officer tapped him for special duty, saying, "The commandant tells me you won't screw this up no matter what. Is that a fact?" He sent Rodriguez a fishy stare.

"I hope so, sir," Rodriguez answered. He recognized that stare. He'd seen it before on white Confederates. They looked at him, saw a Mexican, and figured he wasn't good for much. He asked, "What do I got to do?"

"Well, we're going to test out one of those buildings," the officer answered. "We're going to pick about a hundred niggers and run 'em through it."

"Oh, yes, sir. I do that. Don't you worry," Rodriguez said.

His confidence seemed to relieve the officer. "All right," the man said. He drummed the fingers of his left hand against the side of his leg. His right sleeve was pinned up short, as his right arm ended just below the shoulder—he too came out of the Confederate Veterans' Brigade. He went on, "This has to go good, mind you. We got bigwigs from Richmond comin' out to watch the show."

Rodriguez shrugged. "Maybe it go good. Maybe it go wrong. I dunno. All I know is, it don't go wrong on account of me."

The other man considered that. He finally nodded. "Fair enough. Make sure all the ordinary guards you're in charge of feel the same way."

"*Sí, señor.* I do that," Rodriguez promised.

Because they were trying things out for the first time—and because bigwigs from Richmond were watching—they used far more guards than they normally would have to deal with a hundred black men. They got the Negroes formed up in a ten-by-ten square. The inmates carried whatever small chattels they intended to take away to the new camp where they thought they were going.

That was part of the plan. As long as they thought they were going somewhere else, they would stay docile. They wouldn't cause trouble unless they figured they were going on a one-way trip. The one-armed officer worked hard to keep them unsuspecting: "You men, we want y'all to be clean and tidy when we ship you out of Camp Determination. We're going to get you that way before you leave. You're gonna take baths. You're gonna be deloused. No horseplay, or we will make your black asses sorry. Y'all got that?"

"Yes, suh," the Negroes chorused. Black heads bobbed up and

down. The Negroes didn't think anything was wrong. They were dirty. Most if not all were lousy. They probably wanted to get clean, and they could see why the men who ran the camp would want them to be that way before they left. Oh, yes—everything made perfect sense to them. But it made a different kind of sense to the guards and their superiors.

"Come on, then," the one-armed officer said. "Keep in formation, now, or you'll catch it." The Negroes had no trouble obeying. They often marched here and there through the camp in formation.

Guards opened the barbed-wire gate separating the main camp from that building. In the Negroes went. Two guards waited in an antechamber. One of them said, "Strip naked and stow your stuff here. Everybody remember who put what where. You get in a fight over what belongs to who, you'll be sorry. You got that?" Again, the Negroes nodded.

So did Hipolito Rodriguez, watching as the black men shed their rags and set down their sorry bundles. This was a very nice touch. It convinced the prisoners they'd come back. The large contingent of guards was hardly necessary. A handful of men could have done the job. But Rodriguez understood why Jefferson Pinkard had assigned so many men to the prisoners. The more ready for trouble you were, the less likely you were to find it. And with visiting firemen watching, you couldn't afford it.

A sign on the wall above an onward-pointing arrow said DELOUS-ING AHEAD. The Negroes who could read went that way without hesitation. Most of the others followed. "Move along, move along," the guards said, and chivvied the rest of the men into the room at the end of the corridor.

It could hold a lot more than a hundred people—but this was, after all, only a test. Even here, the deception continued. A doorway was set into the far wall. A sign above it said TO THE BATHS.

At the officer's nod, Rodriguez shut the door through which the Negroes had gone in. That door didn't match the rest of the scene. It was thick and made of steel, and had rubber gasketing all around the edge to make an airtight seal. Rodriguez spun the wheel in the center of the door's back, making sure it fit snugly against the frame and locking it in place.

Above the wheel, a small window with rounded corners let him look into the chamber he'd just sealed off. More rubber gasketing, inside and out, made sure what was inside that chamber would stay there.

Other windows were set into the chamber's walls. They too were protected with rubber inside and out. Guards took their places at some of them. Higher-ranking camp officials and the delegation from Richmond already stood by the rest. They wanted to see how this building worked out.

Near the center of the chamber stood half a dozen steel columns, painted the same gray as the walls. The bottom two or three feet of them were not solid metal, but a grillwork too fine to poke a finger through. The naked Negroes in there milled about. Some of them went up to one column or another. A man rapped on a column with his knuckles. Rodriguez heard the dull clang.

He knew exactly when guards up above the ceiling poured the Cyclone into the columns. All the Negroes sprang away from them as if they'd become red-hot. Men started falling almost at once. Not all of them fell right away, though. Some ran for the doorway marked TO THE BATHS. They pounded on it, but—what a surprise!—it didn't open.

And some ran back to the door through which they'd come. Desperate, dying fists battered against the steel. An agonized face looked out at Rodriguez, with only glass and the gasketing between them. Startled, he took a step away from the door. The Negro shouted something. Rodriguez couldn't make out what he said. His words were drowned in the chorus of yells and screams that dinned inside the chamber.

As the insecticide took hold, the black man's face slid down and away from the window. The frantic pounding on the door eased. One by one, the shouts and screams faded and stopped. Rodriguez looked in again. A few of the huddled bodies in the chamber still moved feebly, but only a few. After fifteen or twenty minutes, they all lay still.

A bell rang. Several heavy ceiling fans came on; he could feel their vibration through his feet. They sucked the poisoned air out of the chamber. After about ten more minutes, another bell chimed. Now the door marked TO THE BATHS opened—from the outside. Guards went in and carried corpses out to the waiting trucks.

Rodriguez nodded to himself. This would work. Those hundred black men hadn't come close to filling the chamber. Of course, this was only a practice run. Now that they knew things really went about the way they'd expected, they could load in a lot more *mallates*. Load them in, take them out, load in the next batch . . . You could use ordinary trucks to haul away the bodies now, too, and you could pack them much tighter with dead men than you could with live ones. Yes, the scheme would definitely do what it was supposed to.

"Attention!" the one-armed officer called.

Automatically, Rodriguez stood stiff and straight. Here came Jefferson Pinkard with one of the men from Richmond: a burly fellow with a tough, square, jowly face. Rodriguez recognized him right way. It was the Attorney General, Don Fernando Koenig, the biggest man in the Freedom Party except for Jake Featherston himself! No wonder everything had to go just right today!

Pinkard and the Attorney General stopped. "Sir, this here's my buddy, Hip Rodriguez," the camp commandant said. "He helped give me the notion for this whole setup."

"Well, good for him, and good for you, too, Pinkard. This is all first-rate work, and I'll say so to the President." Koenig stuck out his hand in Rodriguez's direction. "Freedom!"

Dazedly, Rodriguez shook it. "Freedom, *señor*!"

Then Koenig clapped him on the back—man to man, not superior to inferior. "We're going to have freedom from these damn niggers, aren't we? And you've helped. You've helped a lot."

"Yes, sir," Rodriguez said. "Thank you, sir."

Koenig and Pinkard went on their way. The rest of the guards stared at Rodriguez in awe.

Jake Featherston had been in Pennsylvania before. During the Great War, the Army of Northern Virginia had pushed up almost to within shelling distance of Philadelphia. That *almost* counted for everything. If the de facto capital of the USA had fallen along with Washington, would the enemy have been able to go on with the fight? No way to know now, but a lot of people in the CSA doubted it. As things were, Jake had survived the grinding retreat through Pennsylvania and Maryland and back into Virginia. He'd survived defeat, and hoped for victory.

Now he was within shelling distance of Pittsburgh, in the western part of Pennsylvania. Confederate 105s boomed in their gun pits, sending shells south toward the Yankee defenders and the factories and steel mills they fought to hold. He wanted to take off his uniform shirt and serve one of those 105s himself. He'd done that before, too, over in Virginia.

His bodyguards were more nervous now than they had been then. "Sir, if we can shell the damnyankees from here, they can reach us here, too," one of them said. "What do we do then?"

"Reckon we jump in a hole, just like the gunners." Jake pointed to the foxholes a few feet away from each 105.

"Yes, but—" the bodyguard began.

"No, no buts," Featherston said firmly. "Chances are I'm safer here than I am back in Richmond, and that's the God's truth."

The guard looked at him as if he'd lost his mind. The man was young, brave, and good at what he did. He also had all the imagination of a cherrystone clam. Most of the time, the lack didn't affect the way he did his job even a dime's worth. Every once in a while . . . "Sir, you don't know what you're talking about." His voice couldn't have been any stiffer if he'd starched and ironed it.

"Hell I don't," Jake said. "Difference is, here I know where the enemy's at. I know what he can do, and I know what I can do about it." He pointed to the foxholes again. "In Richmond, any goddamn son of a bitch could be kitted out with explosives. If he's got the balls to blow himself up along with me, how you gonna stop him?"

All his bodyguards looked very unhappy. Featherston didn't blame them. He was very unhappy about people bombs himself. A man willing—no, eager—to die so he could also kill made a very nasty foe. War and bodyguarding both assumed the enemy wanted to live just as much as you did. If he didn't give a damn . . .

If he didn't give a damn, then what would stop a rational soldier or assassin wouldn't matter a hill of beans to him. That seemed more obvious to the President of the CSA than it did to his guards. They didn't want to admit, even to themselves, that the rules had changed.

This one said, "Mr. President, there's no evidence anyone in the CSA has thought of doing anything like that."

Jake Featherston laughed in his face. "Evidence? First evidence'll be when somebody damn well does blow himself up. It's coming. Sure as shit, it's coming. I wish like hell we could stop it, but I don't see how. We can't jam all the U.S. wireless stations—too many of 'em. And they can't hardly talk about anything else. Fucking Mormons." He shook his head in disgust.

"Good thing there aren't hardly any of them in our country," the bodyguard said, proving he'd missed the point.

If he were smarter, if he were able to think straighter, he probably wouldn't want to be a bodyguard. You couldn't get all hot and bothered because people weren't the way you wanted them to be. Oh, you could, but a whole fat lot of good it would do you. Taking them as they were worked better. *Will this fellow see it if I spell it out in small, simple words?* Jake wondered.

The decision got made for him. He knew what that rumbling, rushing sound in the air was. "Incoming!" he shouted, and was proud his yell came only a split second after the first artilleryman's.

He sprang for the foxholes, and was down in one before the first shells landed. The men who fought the 105s were just as fast, or even faster. Some of his bodyguards, though, remained above ground and upright when shells burst not far away. They didn't know any better— they weren't combat troops. Here, ignorance was expensive.

"Get in a hole, goddammit!" he yelled. Some of the artillerymen were shouting the same thing. And the bodyguards who hadn't been hit did dive for cover, only a few seconds slower than they should have. But a barrage was a time when seconds mattered.

Till things let up, Jake couldn't do anything. If he came out of his foxhole, he was asking to get torn up himself. He wasn't afraid. He'd proved that beyond any possible doubt in the last war. But he knew too well the CSA needed him. That kept him where he was till the U.S. bombardment moved elsewhere.

That bombardment wasn't anything that warned of an attack. It was just harassing fire, to make the Confederates keep their heads down and to wound a few men. During the Great War, Jake had fired plenty of shells with the same thing in mind.

If he wasn't the first one out of a foxhole when the shelling eased, he couldn't have been later than the third. "Fuck," he said softly. You forgot what artillery could do to a man till you saw it with your own eyes. One of his guards lay there, gutted and beheaded—except the reality, which included smell, was a hundred times worse and only a tenth as neat as the words suggested.

Another bodyguard lay hunched over on his side, clutching his ankle with both hands. He had no foot; he was doing his best to keep from bleeding to death. Jake bent beside him. "Hang on, Beau," he said, far more gently than he usually spoke. "I'll make you a tourniquet." His boots—the same sort he'd worn in the field in the last war—had strong rawhide laces. He pulled one out, fast as he could. "Easy there. I got to move your hands so I can tie this son of a bitch."

"Thank you, sir." Beau sounded preternaturally calm. Some wounded men didn't really feel it for a little while. He seemed to be one of the lucky ones, though he hissed when the President of the CSA tightened the tourniquet around his ragged stump. Jake used a stick to twist it so the stream of blood slowed to the tiniest trickle. He'd tended to battlefield wounds before; his hands still remembered how, as long as he didn't think about it too much.

"Morphine!" he yelled. "Somebody give this poor bastard a shot! And where the hell are the medics?"

The men with Red Cross smocks were already there, taking charge of other injured guards. One of them knelt by Beau. The medic injected the bodyguard, then blinked to find himself face to face with Jake Featherston. "You did good, uh, sir," he said. "He ought to make it if everything heals up all right."

"Hear that, Beau?" Jake said. "He says you're gonna be fine." The medic hadn't quite said that, but Jake didn't care. He wanted to make the bodyguard as happy as he could.

"Fine," Beau said vaguely. Maybe that was shock, or maybe it was the morphine hitting him. The medics got him onto a stretcher and carried him away. Jake wondered what kind of job he could do that didn't require moving around. The President shrugged. Beau would be a while getting better, if he did.

The head of the bodyguard contingent came up with fire in his eye. He'd got his trousers muddy; Jake judged that accounted for at least part of his bad temper. When the man spoke, he did his best to stay restrained: "Sir, can we please move to a safer location? You see what almost happened to you here."

Jake shook his head. "Not to me, by God. I know what to do when shells start coming down. I'm sorry as hell some of your men didn't."

"And if a shell had landed in your hole, Mr. President?" the bodyguard asked.

"It didn't, dammit," Jake said. The guard chief just looked at him. Jake swore under his breath. The man was right, and he knew it. Admitting somebody else was right and he himself wrong was the hardest thing in the world for him. He didn't do it now, not in so many words.

He just scowled at the bodyguard. "I reckon I've seen what I came to see."

"Thank you, sir." The man saluted. He called to the other guards who hadn't been hurt: "We can get him away now!"

They all showed as much relief as a drummer who finds out his latest lady friend isn't in a family way after all. And they hustled Jake back from the gun pit with Olympic speed. He thought it was funny. The guards thought it was anything but. One of them scolded him: "Sir, did you *want* to get yourself killed?"

If he'd asked whether Jake wanted to get the guards killed, the President would have gone up in smoke. But that wasn't what he'd wanted to know, and so Jake Featherston only sighed. "No. I wanted to watch the damnyankees catch it."

"Well, you've done that, and now you've seen we can catch it, too," the bodyguard said. "Will you kindly leave well enough alone?"

"Sure," Featherston said, and all the bodyguards brightened. Then he added, "Till the next time it needs doing." Their shoulders slumped.

"We really shouldn't be anywhere close to the line," the guards' leader said. "Damnyankee airplanes are liable to drop bombs on our heads. Even less we can do about that than we can about artillery, dammit."

Jake laughed raucously. "Jesus H. Christ, don't the damnyankees come over Richmond about every other night and drop everything but the fucking kitchen sink on our heads? Bastards'd drop that, too, if they reckoned it'd blow up."

Some of the bodyguards smiled. Their chief remained severe. "Sir, you've got a proper shelter there, not a, a—hole in the ground." He slapped at the knees of his trousers. Not much mud came away. He fumed. He didn't like to get dirty.

"Hell of a lot of good a proper shelter did Al Smith," Jake said. That made all the guards unhappy again. They didn't like remembering all the things that could go wrong. Jake didn't like remembering those things, either, but he would do it if he could score points off men who liked it even less.

The guard chief changed the subject, at least a little: "Sir, couldn't you just stay somewhere safe and follow the war with reports and things?"

"No way in hell," Jake replied at once. "No place'd stay safe for long. Soon as the Yankees found out where I was at, they'd send bombers after me. I don't care if I went to Habana—they'd still send 'em. But that's beside the point. Point is, you can't trust reports all the goddamn time. Sometimes you've got to, yeah. You can't keep up with everything by your lonesome. But if you don't get your ass out there and see for yourself every so often, people'll start lying to you. You won't know any better, either, 'cause you haven't been out to look. And then you're screwed. Got it?"

"Yes, sir," the bodyguard said mournfully. He knew what that meant. It meant he and his men would have to keep worrying, because Jake would go on sticking his nose where the damnyankees could shoot it off.

Airplanes droned by overhead. Jake looked for the closest hole in the ground. So did most of the guards. They weren't combat troops, no, but a trip to the field taught lessons in a hurry. The airplanes flew from west to east. They had familiar silhouettes. Jake relaxed—they were on his side.

None of the bodyguards relaxed. They weren't supposed to, not while they were on duty. Their leader said, "Mr. President, can we please take you someplace where you're not in quite so *much* danger?"

"Gonna fly me to the Empire of Brazil?" Jake quipped. A few guards gave him another round of dutiful smiles. Most stayed somber. He supposed that was just as well. Like sheep dogs, they had to be serious about protecting him. Trouble was, he made a piss-poor sheep.

Sometimes Sam Carsten thought the Navy didn't know what to do with the *Josephus Daniels*. Other times he was sure of it. After the destroyer escort had threaded its way out through the minefields in Delaware Bay once more, he turned to Pete Cooley and said, "I swear to God they're trying to sink us. I really do."

"I think we'll be all right, sir," the exec said. "We will as long as Confederate airplanes don't spot us, anyhow."

"Yeah," Sam said. "As long as." His ship was ordered to strike at the CSA. U.S. flying boats and other aircraft constantly patrolled the United States' coastal waters. If there was intelligence to say the Confederates didn't do the same thing, he hadn't seen it.

"Mission seems simple enough," Cooley said. "We start heading in as soon as night falls, land the raiders, pick 'em up, and get the hell out of there." He sounded elaborately unconcerned.

Sam snorted. "One of these days, Pat, somebody needs to explain the difference between 'simple' and 'easy' to you."

"I know the difference," Cooley said with a grin. "An easy girl puts out right away. A simple girl's just dumb, so you've got to snow her before she puts out."

"All right, dammit." In spite of himself, Sam laughed. The exec *wouldn't* take things seriously. Maybe that was as well, too. "Just so we don't get spotted. And our navigation better be spot-on, too."

"I'll get us there, sir," Cooley promised.

As with shiphandling, Sam was learning to use sextant and chronometer to know where the ship was and where it was going. He thought it was the hardest thing he'd ever tried to pick up. The Navy had tables that made it a lot easier than it was in the days of iron men and wooden ships, but *easier* and *easy* didn't mean the same thing, either. Sorrowfully, Sam said, "This is the first time in a million years I wish I'd paid more attention in school."

"You're doing real well, sir, for a—" Two words too late, Pat Cooley broke off. He tried again: "You're doing real well."

For a mustang. He hadn't quite swallowed enough of that. Or maybe it had been *for a dumb mustang.* Taking sun-sights and then trying to convert them to positions sure as hell made Sam feel like a dumb mustang. He painfully remembered the time when he'd screwed up his longitude six ways from Sunday and put the *Josephus Daniels* halfway between Philadelphia and Pittsburgh.

The only thing the exec said then was, "Well, the infantry could use the fire support." Sam thought that showed commendable restraint.

For now, he swung the destroyer escort well out into the North Atlantic before steaming south. He figured that was his best chance to get where he was going undetected. He didn't know that it was a good chance, but *good* and *best* also weren't always synonyms. The ocean wasn't nearly so rough as it would be when winter clapped down, but it wasn't smooth, either. Sailors and Marine raiders spent a lot of time at the rail.

Sam might not have been much of a navigator. He might not have been the shiphandler he wished he were. He might—he would—burn if the sun looked at him sideways. But by God he had a sailor's stomach. Some of the youngsters in the officers' mess and some of the Marine officers who dined with them looked distinctly green. Sam tore into the roast beef with fine appetite.

"Be thankful the chow's as good as it is," he said. "When we're on a long patrol or going around the Horn, it's all canned stuff and beans after a while."

"Excuse me, sir," Lieutenant Thad Walters said. The Y-range operator bolted from the mess with a hand clapped over his mouth. Carsten hoped the J.G. got to a head before he wasted the cooks' best efforts.

Lieutenant Cooley brought the *Josephus Daniels* about 125 miles off the North Carolina coast just as the sun was sinking in flames in the direction of the Confederacy. "We're as ready as we'll ever be, sir," the exec said.

"Fair enough." Sam nodded. "All ahead full, then. Course 270."

"All ahead full. Course 270," Cooley echoed. "Aye aye, sir." He called the order for full power down to the engine room. The ship picked up speed till she was going flat out. Sam wished for the extra ten knots she could have put on if she were a real destroyer. Of course, they never would have dropped a mustang on his first command into a real destroyer. He knew damn well he was lucky to get anything fancier than a garbage scow.

Lieutenant Walters seemed to have got rid of what ailed him. The Y-range operator was still a little pale, but kept close watch on his set. If the ship could spot an enemy airplane before the enemy spotted her, she would have a better chance of getting away. The darker it got, the happier Sam grew. He didn't think the Confederates had aircraft with Y-ranging gear. He sure hoped they didn't.

"Keep an eye peeled for any sign of torpedo boats, too," he warned. "A fish we're not expecting will screw us as bad as a bomb."

"Yes, sir," Walters said, and then, "Aye aye, sir." *We're doing everything we know how to do,* Sam thought. *Now—is it enough?*

The *Josephus Daniels* ran on through the night. Listening to her engines pound, Sam felt she was yelling, *Here I am!* to the world. If she was, the world stayed deaf and blind. Every so often, Lieutenant Walters looked over at him and shrugged or gave a thumbs-up. CPO Bevacqua on the hydrophone kept hearing nothing, too.

Shortly before 2300, the commander of the Marine detachment came onto the bridge. "About an hour away, eh, Captain?" he said.

"That's right, Major," Sam answered. Mike Murphy outranked him—except that nobody on a ship outranked her skipper. Murphy understood that, fortunately. He was a black Irishman with eyes as blue as a Siamese cat's—bluer than Sam's, which took doing. Carsten went on, "Your men are ready?"

"Ready as they'll ever be." Murphy pointed into the darkness. "They're by the boats, and they'll be in 'em in nothing flat." He snapped his fingers.

"Good enough," Sam said, and hoped it would be.

Not quite an hour later, the shape of the western horizon changed. It had been as smooth and flat there as in any other direction. No more. That deeper blackness was land: the coast of the Confederate States of America. "Here we are, sir," Pat Cooley said. "If that's not Ocracoke Island dead ahead, my career just hit a mine and sank."

So did mine, Sam thought. The Navy Department might blame an exec who'd been conning a ship for botched navigation. The Navy Department would without the tiniest fragment of doubt blame that ship's skipper. And so it should. The destroyer escort was *his* ship. This was *his* responsibility. Nothing on God's green earth this side of death or disabling injury could take it off his shoulders.

"Send a petty officer forward with a lead and a sounding line," Sam said, an order more often heard in the riverboat Navy than on the Atlantic. But he didn't want the *Josephus Daniels* running aground, and she drew a lot more water than any river monitor. She needed some water under her keel. Cooley nodded and obeyed.

Feet thudded on the deck. "Sir, we've spotted a light about half a mile south of here!" a sailor exclaimed. "Looks like it's what we want!"

It wouldn't be the Ocracoke lighthouse at the southwestern tip of the island; that had gone dark at the beginning of the war. If you didn't already know where you were in these waters, the Confederates didn't want you here. Major Murphy quivered like a hunting hound. "I'd best join my men, I think," he said, and left the bridge.

"Very pretty navigation, Pat," Sam said. "Bring us in a little closer and we'll lower the boats and turn the Marines loose."

"Aye aye, sir," Cooley said, and then, to the engine room, "All ahead one third." The *Josephus Daniels* crept southwest.

After a breathless little while, Sam said, "All stop." The executive officer relayed the order. The ship bobbed in the water. Sam sent a sailor to Major Murphy to let him know everything was ready. Murphy had no doubt figured that out for himself, but the forms needed to be observed.

Lines creaking in the davits, the boats went down to the ocean. For this raid, they'd been fitted with motors. One by one, they chugged toward the shore that was only a low, darker line in the night. North Carolina barrier islands were nothing but glorified sandbanks. Every time a hurricane tore through, it rearranged the landscape pretty drastically. Sometimes, after a hurricane tore through, not much landscape—or land—was left in its path.

"Confederates at that station are going to think a hurricane hit 'em," Sam murmured.

He didn't know he'd spoken aloud till Pat Cooley nodded and said, "Hell, yes—uh, sir."

Grinning, Sam set a hand on his shoulder. "Don't worry about it, Pat. We're on the same page."

Gunfire crackled across the water. Sam tensed. If something had gone wrong, if the bastards in butternut somehow knew the Marines were coming . . . In that case, the destroyer escort's guns would have to do some talking of their own. The wireless operator looked up. "Sir, Major Murphy says everything's under control."

Sure enough, the gunfire died away. Sam had nothing to do but wait. He drummed his fingers on the metalwork in front of him. Waiting was always a big part of military life. Right this minute, it was also a hard part.

"There we go!" Pat Cooley pointed. Fire rose from the station.

"Yeah, there we go, all right," Sam agreed. "Other question is, did the Confederates get off an alarm call before we finished overrunning the place?" He shrugged. "Well, we'll find out."

Not very much later, sailors peering over the starboard rail called, "Boats coming back!" Sam almost said something like, *Stand by to repel boarders!* He wondered when the skipper of a ship this size last issued an order like that. But these boarders were on his side—or they'd damned well better be.

Raising boats was harder than lowering them. He had nets out against the sides of the ship for the Marines and their prisoners—he hoped they'd have prisoners—to climb if the crew couldn't do it. But they managed. He went down to the deck and met Major Murphy there. "Everything go well?" he asked.

"Well enough, Captain," the Marine officer answered. "We lost one man dead, and we have several wounded we brought back." The groans on deck would have told Sam that if Murphy hadn't. The Marine went on, "But we destroyed that station, and we've brought back prisoners to question and samples of Confederate Y-ranging gear for the fellows with thick glasses and slide rules to look at. What they do with the stuff is up to them, but we got it. We did our job."

"Sounds good," Sam said. "Now my job is to make sure we deliver the goods. Is everybody back aboard ship?"

"I think so," Major Murphy said.

An indignant Confederate came up to them. "Are you the captain of this vessel?" he demanded of Sam. "I must protest this—this act of piracy!" He sounded like an angry rabbit.

"Go ahead and protest all you please, pal," Sam said genially. "And you can call me Long John Silver, too." Major Murphy and several nearby Marines spluttered. Sam went to the rail to make sure no boats or Marines were unaccounted for. Satisfied, he hurried back up to the bridge.

"Are we ready to leave town, sir?" Pat Cooley asked.

"And then some," Sam said. "Make our course 135. All ahead full."

"All ahead full," Cooley echoed, and passed the order to the engine room. "Course is . . . 135." He sounded slightly questioning, to let Sam change his mind without losing face if he wanted to.

But Sam didn't want to. "Yes, 135, Pat," he said. "I really do want to head southeast, because that's the last direction the Confederates will look for us. Once we get away, we can swing wide and come back. But I figure most of the search'll be to the north, and I want to get away from land-based air the best way I know how. So—135."

Cooley nodded. "Aye aye, sir—135 it is." The *Josephus Daniels* steamed away from the North Carolina coast at her sedate top speed.

Brigadier General Irving Morrell did not like getting pushed around by the Confederates. They'd done it in Ohio, and now they were doing it in Pennsylvania. They had the machines they needed to go forward. He didn't have as many machines as he needed to stop them. It was as simple as that.

Men . . . Well, how much did men count in this new mechanized age? The United States had more of them than the Confederate States did. The question was, so what?

A nervous-looking POW stood in front of Morrell. In the other man's beat-up boots, Morrell would have been nervous, too. He said, "Name, rank, and pay number."

An interpreter turned the question into Spanish. A torrent of that language came back. The interpreter said, "His name is José María Castillo. He is a senior private—we would say a PFC. His pay number is 6492711."

"Thanks." Morrell studied Senior Private Castillo. The prisoner from the Empire of Mexico was medium-sized, skinny, swarthy, with mournful black eyes and a big, bushy mustache like the ones a lot of Confederate soldiers had worn during the Great War. His mustard-yellow uniform would have given good camouflage in the deserts on Mexico's northern border. Here in western Pennsylvania, it stood out much more. Morrell said, "Ask him what unit he's in and what their orders were."

More Spanish. The POW didn't have to answer that. Did he know he didn't have to? Morrell wasn't about to tell him. And he answered willingly enough. "He says he's with the Veracruz Division, sir," the interpreter reported. "He says that's the best one Mexico has. Their orders are to take places the Confederates haven't been able to capture."

"Are they?" Morrell carefully didn't smile at that. He suspected any number of Confederate officers would have had apoplexy if they heard the Mexican prisoner. If the Veracruz Division was the best one Francisco José had, the Emperor of Mexico would have been well advised not to take on anything tougher than a belligerent chipmunk. The men all had rifles, but they were woefully short on machine guns, artillery, barrels, and motorized transport. The soldiers seemed brave enough, but sending them up against a modern army wouldn't have been far from murder—if that modern army hadn't been so busy in so many other places.

The prisoner spoke without being asked anything. He sounded anxious. He sounded, frankly, scared out of his wits. Morrell had a hard time blaming him. Surrender was a chancy enough business even when two sides used the same language, as U.S. and C.S. soldiers did. Would-be POWs sometimes turned into casualties when their captors either wanted revenge for something that had happened to them or just lacked the time to deal with prisoners. If a captive knew no English . . . *He likely thinks we'll eat him for supper,* Morrell thought, not without sympathy.

Sure enough, the interpreter said, "He wants to know what we're going to do with him, sir."

"Tell him nobody's going to hurt him," Morrell said. The interpreter did. José Castillo crossed himself and gabbled out what had to be thanks. Every once in a while, war made Morrell remember what a filthy business it was. That a man should be grateful for not getting killed out of hand . . . Roughly, Morrell went on, "Tell him he'll be taken away from the fighting. Tell him he'll be fed. If he needs a doctor, he'll get one. Tell him we follow Geneva Convention rules, if that means anything to him."

The prisoner seized his hand and kissed it. That horrified him. Getting captured had, in essence, turned a man into a dog. He gestured. The interpreter led José Castillo away. Morrell wiped his hand on his trouser leg.

"Don't blame you, sir," one of his guards said. "God only knows what kind of germs that damn spic's got."

Germs were the last thing on Morrell's mind. He just wanted to wipe away the touch of the desperate man's lips. If he couldn't feel them anymore, maybe he could forget them. He needed to forget them if he was going to do his job. "He's out of the fighting now," he said. "He's luckier than a lot of people I can think of."

"Well, yeah, sir, since you put it that way," the guard said. "He's luckier'n me, for instance." He grinned to show Morrell not to take him too seriously, but Morrell knew he was kidding on the square. Only a few hard cases really *liked* war; most men endured it and tried to come through in one piece.

From everything Morrell had heard, Jake Featherston was part of the small minority who'd enjoyed himself in the field. Morrell couldn't have sworn that was so, but he wouldn't have been surprised. Who but a man who enjoyed war would have loosed another one on a country— two countries—that didn't?

That guard shifted his feet, trying to draw Morrell's attention. Morrell nodded to him. The soldier asked, "Sir, is it true that the Confederates are inside Pittsburgh?"

"I think so, Wally," Morrell answered. "That's what it sounds like from the situation reports I've been getting, anyhow."

"Son of a bitch," Wally said.

"It isn't what we had in mind when this whole mess started," Morrell allowed. What the USA had had in mind was a victory parade through the ruined streets of Richmond, preferably with Jake Featherston's head on a platter carried along at the front. Richmond was close to the border, which didn't mean the United States had got there. They hadn't in the War of Secession or the Great War, either.

"So what are we gonna do?" Wally asked—a thoroughly reasonable question. "How come we don't just pitch into 'em?"

"Because if we do, we'd probably lose right now," Morrell said unhappily. "We don't have enough men or matériel yet. We're getting there, though." *I hope.*

As a matter of fact, things could have been worse. The Confederates had been planning to surround Pittsburgh instead of swarming into it, but U.S. counterattacks hadn't let them do that. Now they had to clear the Americans from a big city house by house and factory by factory. That wouldn't come easy or cheap. Again, Morrell hoped it wouldn't, anyhow.

He'd been screaming at every superior in Pennsylvania to let him concentrate before he counterattacked. He'd been screaming at Philadelphia to get him enough barrels so he'd have a legitimate chance of getting somewhere when he finally did. He was sure he'd made himself vastly unpopular. He couldn't have cared less. What could they do to him? Dismiss him from the Army? If they did, he would thank them, take off the uniform, and go back to Agnes and Mildred outside of Fort Leavenworth. Whatever happened to the country after that . . . happened. Whatever it was, it wouldn't be his fault.

Before long, he discovered they could do something worse than dismissing him. They could ignore him. They could, and they did. His requests for more barrels and more artillery fell on deaf ears. Since they wouldn't dismiss him, he sent a telegram of resignation to the War Department and waited to see what came of that.

He didn't want them to accept it. He thought he could hit the Confederates harder than anyone they could put in his slot. But if they thought otherwise, he wasn't going to beg them to let him stay. Maybe they would give his replacement the tools they were denying him. If someone else got the weapons he wasn't getting, that made him less indispensable than he thought himself now.

No answering telegram came back. Instead, less than twenty-four hours later, Colonel John Abell showed up on his doorstep. No, Brigadier General Abell: he had stars on his shoulder straps now. "Congratulations," Morrell told the General Staff officer, more or less sincerely.

"Thank you," Abell answered. "For some reason, I'm considered an expert on the care and feeding of one Irving Morrell. And so—here I am."

"Here you are," Morrell agreed in friendly tones. "Nice weather we're having, isn't it?"

"As a matter of fact, it looks like rain," Abell said—and it did. He gave Morrell a severe look. It was like being haunted by the ghost of an overstrict schoolteacher. "See here, General—how dare you threaten to resign when the country is in crisis?"

"After all these years we've been banging heads, you still don't know how I work." Morrell wasn't friendly anymore. "How can you care for me and feed me if you don't know where I live or what I eat? I wasn't threatening anything or anybody. I've just had enough of being asked to do the impossible. If you put someone else here, maybe you'll support him the way you should."

"You are the recognized expert on barrel tactics—recognized by the Confederates as well as your own side." Abell spoke the words as if they tasted bad. To him, they probably did. He said them anyhow. He did have a certain chilly integrity.

"Confederate recognition I could do without," Morrell said. As if in sympathy, his shoulder twinged. The enemy wanted him dead—him personally. That was why he tolerated Wally and the other bodyguards he didn't want. He knew too well the Confederates might try again. Anger rising in his voice, he went on, "And if the War Department thinks I'm so goddamn wonderful and brilliant and all that, why do I have to send a letter of resignation to get it to remember I'm alive?"

"That is not the case, I assure you," John Abell said stiffly.

"Yeah, and then you wake up," Morrell jeered. "Now tell me another one, one I'll believe."

"We are trying to meet your needs, General." If Abell was angry, he didn't show it. He was very good at not showing what he thought. "Please remember, though, this is not the only area where we are having difficulties."

"Difficulties, my ass. The Confederates are in Pittsburgh. They're going to tear hell out of it whether they keep it or not. That's not a difficulty—that's a fucking calamity. Tell me I'm wrong. I dare you. I double-dare you." Morrell felt like an eight-year-old trying to pick a fight.

"If we destroy the Confederate Army causing the devastation in Pittsburgh, that devastation may become worthwhile," Abell said.

Morrell clapped a hand to his forehead. If he was going to be melodramatic, he'd do it in spades. "Christ on His cross, Abell, what do you think I'm trying to do?" he howled. "Why won't Philadelphia let me?"

"You will agree the cost of failure is high," Abell said.

"You make sure I fail if you don't support me," Morrell said. "Is that what you've got in mind?"

"No. Of course not. If we didn't want you here, we would have put someone else in this place," Abell said. "We had someone else in this place before you recovered from your wound, if you'll remember."

"Oh, yes. You sure did." Morrell rolled his eyes. "And my illustrious predecessor scattered barrels all over the landscape, too. He aimed to support the infantry with them. Perfect War Department tactics from 1916."

John Abell turned red. In the last war, the War Department had thought of barrels as nothing more than infantry-support weapons. George Custer and Morrell had had to go behind Philadelphia's back to mass them. The War Department would have stripped Custer of his barrels if it found out what he was up to—till he proved his way worked much better than its.

"That's not fair," Abell said once his blush subsided. "We did put you here to set things right, and you can't say we didn't."

"All right. Fine." Morrell took a deep breath. "If that's what you want, I'll try to give it to you. Let me have the tools I need to do my job. Stand back and get out of my way and let me do it, too."

"And if you don't?" Now Abell's voice was silky with menace.

Morrell laughed at him. "That's obvious, isn't it? If I make a hash of it, you've got a scapegoat. 'Things went wrong because General Morrell fucked up, that no-good, bungling son of a bitch.' Tell every paper in the country it's my fault. I won't say boo. If I have what I need here and I can't do what needs doing, I deserve it."

"You'll get what's coming to you," the General Staff officer said. "And if you don't deliver once you get it, you'll *really* get what's coming to you. I'm glad you think it seems fair, because it will happen whether you think so or not."

"Deal." Morrell stuck out his hand. John Abell looked surprised, but he shook it.

The other sailor tossed five bucks into the pot. "Call," he said.

"Ten-high straight." George Enos, Jr., laid down his cards.

"Oh, for Christ's sake!" The other sailor couldn't have sounded more disgusted if he tried for a week. George understood when he threw down his own hand: he held an eight-high straight.

"Got him by a cunt hair, George," Fremont Dalby said as George scooped up the cash. It was a nice chunk of change; they'd gone back and forth several times before the call. Losing would have hurt. It wouldn't have left George broke or anything—he had better sense than to gamble that hard—but it would have hurt. Dalby scooped up the cards and started to shuffle. "My deal, I think."

"Yeah." George wiped sweat from his forehead with his sleeve. The compartment where they played was hot and airless. A bare bulb in an iron cage overhead gave the only light. The door said STORES on the outside, but the chamber was empty. The sailors sat on the gray-painted deck and redistributed the wealth.

Fremont Dalby passed George the cards. "Here. Cut." George took some cards from the middle of the deck and stuck them on the bottom. Dalby laughed. "Whorehouse cut, eh? All right, you bastard. I had my royal flush all stacked and ready to deal, and now you went and fucked me. Some pal you are."

"Sorry," George said in tones suggesting he was anything but. As the CPO dealt, George asked, "Ever see a real royal flush in an honest game?"

"Nope, and I've been playing poker for a hell of a long time," Dalby answered. "I saw a jack-high straight flush once. That was a hum-dinger of a hand, too, on account of it beat four queens. But I knew the people, and they weren't dealing off the bottom of the deck or anything."

Nobody else in the game admitted to seeing a royal flush, either. George looked at his cards. None of them appeared to have been intro-duced to any of the others. This wasn't a jack-high straight flush; it was jack-high garbage. He almost threw it away, but he'd won the last hand, so he stayed in and asked for four cards.

That left him with a pair of jacks. When Dalby called for jacks or better to open, he put in a dollar. The hand got raised twice before it came back to him. He tossed it in with no regret except for the vanished dollar. Fremont Dalby ended up taking it with three kings.

George had just started to shuffle when the klaxons called men to battle stations. Everyone paused just long enough to scoop up the money in front of him. "To be continued," somebody said as the poker game broke up. And so, no doubt, it would be; it seemed as unending as any movie serial.

His feet clanged on the deck as he ran for the nearest stairway. Dalby was older and rounder, but stayed with him all the way. They got to their antiaircraft gun at the same time. Along with the *Townsend,* three other destroyers surrounded the *Trenton.* The escort carrier's fighters buzzed high overhead. Kauai lay somewhere to the southeast. They were out tweaking the Japs again, much as Francis Drake had singed the beard of the King of Spain. Like King Philip, the Japs were liable to singe back.

"Is this real or a drill, Enos?" Dalby said. "I got five bucks says it's a drill."

The odds favored him. They had many more drills than real alerts. Still, in these waters . . . "You're on," George said. They shook to seal the bet.

"Now hear this! Now hear this!" the intercom blared. "Aircraft from the *Trenton* are attacking a Japanese carrier. The Japs are sure to try to return the favor if they can. Be ready. It is expected that the *Trenton* will be their main target, but we want to remind them that we love them, too."

"There's a fin you owe me," George said happily. "That'll buy one of the boys some shoes."

"My ass," Fremont Dalby said, his voice sour. "It'll buy you a couple of shots and a blowjob from a Chinese whore on Hotel Street when we get back to Pearl."

Since he was probably right, George didn't argue with him. He just said, "Well, that's a damn sight better than nothing, too." The gun crew laughed. Even the CPO's lips twitched.

They waited. Before too long, the executive officer said, "Y-ranging gear reports inbound aircraft. They aren't ours. We're going to have company in about fifteen minutes. Roll out the welcome mat for our guests, boys." Five minutes later, he came back on the loudspeakers:

"*Trenton*'s aircraft report that that Jap carrier is on fire and dead in the water. Score one for the good guys."

Cheers rang out up and down the *Townsend*'s main deck, and probably everywhere else on the ship, too. The crew had faced savage air attacks more than once. Getting their own back felt wonderful.

"Those Jap pilots are liable to know they can't go home again," Dalby warned. "That means they'll give it everything they've got when they hit us. Knock 'em down as quick as you can so they don't crash into the ship or something."

Knocking down airplanes was hard enough without any extra pressure to do it fast. George just shrugged. Unless somebody got hurt, all he had to do was make sure the gun had enough ammo to keep shooting. What happened after that was Dalby's responsibility, not his.

The Y-range antenna swung round and round. George and everybody else up on deck peered northwest, the direction from which trouble had so often come before. The *Townsend* picked up speed. She would want to do as much dodging as she could. George glanced over toward the *Trenton*. The carrier couldn't pick up a lot of speed. Her engines wouldn't let her.

"There they are!" somebody yelled.

George swore softly. Those were Jap airplanes, all right. Their silhouettes might have been more familiar to him than those of U.S. aircraft. The half dozen fighters in combat air patrol over the little U.S. fleet streaked toward the enemy. Japanese escort fighters were bound to outnumber them. Their pilots would want to take out as many enemy strike aircraft as they could before the enemy shot them down. A pilot's life wasn't always glamorous. George wouldn't have traded places with anybody up there.

An airplane tumbled out of the sky, leaving a comet's trail of fire and smoke all the way down to the Pacific. "That's a Jap!" someone shouted. George hoped he knew what he was talking about.

This wasn't like the last few times the *Townsend* had ventured out in the direction of Midway. The main attack wasn't aimed at the destroyer. The Japs wanted the *Trenton*. A carrier was really dangerous to them, as aircraft from the converted freighter had just proved. Destroyers? Destroyers were nuisances, annoyances, worth noticing now only because they tried to keep enemy aircraft away from the *Trenton*.

That made the 40mm crews' jobs easier. They were less rattled, less hurried, than they had been when enemy dive bombers singled the *Townsend* out for attention. George fed his gun shells. Fritz Gustafson loaded them into the breeches. At Fremont Dalby's command, two other sailors shifted the antiaircraft gun in altitude and azimuth. Empty shell casings clattered down onto the deck by the gun crews' feet. Every so often, George or Gustafson would kick them out of the way so nobody tripped over them.

The *Townsend*'s five-inch guns blasted away at the Japs. Their shells could reach a lot farther and packed much more punch, but they couldn't fire nearly so fast. Their roar, on top of the thunder from all the smaller weapons, hammered the ears. George wondered whether he'd be able to hear at all by the time the war ended.

And the big guns' blast shook and jarred loose damn near everything on the deck. The last time they'd cut loose, a sailor George knew ended up spitting a filling out into the palm of his hand. He'd been lucky, too, even if he didn't think so when the pharmacist's mate played dentist on him. Stray too close to a five-incher's muzzle when it went off and blast could kill, even if it didn't leave a mark on your body. George didn't aspire to be a corpse, unmarked or otherwise.

"Hit!" The whole gun crew shouted at the same time when a Japanese dive bomber they'd been shooting at suddenly wavered in the air and started trailing smoke. "We *got* the son of a bitch!" George added exultantly.

That pilot must have known he had nowhere to go. With his own carrier in flames, he wouldn't have had anywhere to go even if his engine were running perfectly. Taking a hit must have rubbed his nose in it. He dove for the *Trenton*. Instead of releasing his bomb and trying to pull up, he seemed intent on using his airplane as an extra weapon.

A hail of antiaircraft fire from the escort carrier said its gunners realized the same thing. They scored more hits on the dive bomber, but didn't deflect it from its course. The ship swung to starboard—slowly, so slowly. A carrier built from the keel up as a warship would have had a much better chance of getting away.

But that turn, small as it was, saved the *Trenton*. Maybe the enemy pilot was dead in the cockpit, or maybe the heavy fire severed the cables to his rudder and ailerons so he couldn't swerve no matter how much he wanted to. He splashed into the Pacific a hundred yards to port of the carrier. His bomb went off then, sending up a great plume of white water. A near miss like that would damage the *Trenton* with fragments, and might make her leak from sprung seams. But it wouldn't turn her into a torch and send her to the bottom.

"Fucker had balls," Fritz Gustafson said with grudging respect. As grudgingly, George nodded. Trying to get in a last lick at your foe when you knew you were a goner took nerve.

Not so many Japanese airplanes were left in the sky now. U.S. fighters and ferocious AA had knocked down a lot of them. Then George watched something that chilled him to the bone. A Jap fighter pilot heeled his undamaged airplane into a dive and swooped on the *Trenton* like a hunting falcon. He didn't try to save himself—all he wanted to do was damage that carrier the only way he had left. That he would die if he succeeded couldn't have mattered to him. He wasn't going home anyway.

The *Trenton* shot him down. His fighter broke up and fell in flaming pieces into the sea. But he'd given the other Japs an idea—or maybe he'd told them over the wireless what he aimed to do. One after another, they all dove on the American ships below them. Dead men themselves, they didn't want to die alone.

George's gun put as many rounds as it could into a fighter. The Japanese didn't make their aircraft as sturdy as Americans did—not that a U.S. fighter would have survived a pasting like that. But the Jap wasn't trying to survive, only to take Americans with him. He didn't quite make it. His burning airplane crashed into the ocean off the *Townsend*'s starboard bow.

One fighter did crash on the *Trenton*'s flight deck—and then skidded off into the sea, trailing flames. It scraped eight or ten sailors off the ship with it. Fires lingered on the flight deck after the Jap was gone. Damage-control parties beat them down with high-pressure seawater. By the time the escort carrier's strike aircraft got back, she was ready to land them. "By God, we did it," George said. In the waters off the Sandwich Islands, Americans hadn't said anything like that for a while, but they'd earned the right today. George said it again, with feeling.

XV

Brigadier General Abner Dowling's guards now enforced a wider perimeter around the house he was using than they had before. He wondered if they joked that he had a wide perimeter, too. He wouldn't have been surprised. The perimeter around the place, though, was no laughing matter. It came by direct order from the War Department.

"People bombs," Dowling said as he showed his adjutant the order. "Not just auto bombs anymore, but people bombs, too. What on God's green earth are we coming to? That's all I want to know."

Captain Angelo Toricelli studied the order. "The Mormons have done this in the USA," he said. "Negroes have done it in the CSA. It doesn't say white Confederates have started doing it anywhere."

"If they haven't, it's only a matter of time till they do," Dowling said gloomily. "If you think the Freedom Party doesn't have people who'd martyr themselves for St. Featherston, you're out of your tree. Plenty of fanatics who'd thank him for the chance to blow up a damnyankee or three. Go ahead. Tell me I'm wrong. I dare you."

"I wish I could, sir." Toricelli sounded mournful, too. He went on, "I don't think the world is ever going to be the same. From now on, if you're in a big city or if you're in politics or the military, you won't be able to go down to the corner diner for a cup of coffee or a ham on rye without wondering whether the quiet fellow in the next booth is going to blow himself to hell and gone—and you along with him."

"You're in a cheerful mood today, aren't you?" But Dowling feared the younger officer was right—dead right. "One thing consoles me, anyhow."

"What's that, sir?"

"Bound to be more people who want to blow up Jake Featherston than ones who want to see me dead bad enough to kill themselves to get me."

"Sir, I believe they call that a dubious distinction."

"And I believe you're right." Dowling laughed, but on a note not far from despair. "What *is* the world coming to, Captain? Just before the war started, I listened to a fellow named Litvinoff going on and on about nerve agents—he wouldn't call them gases. He was happy as a clam in chowder, you know what I mean?"

"Oh, yes, sir." Toricelli nodded. "I've met people like that. It's their toy, and they don't care what it does, as long as it does what it's supposed to."

"That's right. That's exactly right." Dowling nodded, too. "And now this. Is there *anything* we won't do to each other?"

Toricelli considered that. "I don't know, sir. I'm not sure I'm the right person to ask," he said. "Don't you think you ought to talk to one of the Negroes in a Freedom Party camp instead? But ask fast, while there are still some left."

"Ouch!" Abner Dowling winced. "Well, you got me there. Maybe I ought to put it a different way: aren't there some things we *shouldn't* do to each other?"

"We've got the Geneva Convention," Toricelli said.

"It doesn't talk about people bombs," Dowling said. "It doesn't talk about those camps, either. It doesn't talk about gas, come to that. Nobody wanted to talk about gas when they were hammering it out, because everybody figured he might need it again one of these days."

Now Toricelli eyed Dowling with a certain bemusement. "You're just about as cheerful as I am, aren't you, sir?"

"I'm as cheerful as I ought to be," Dowling answered. He looked out the window. An auto painted U.S. green-gray was coming up to his headquarters. The guards stopped it before it got too close. Anybody could paint a motorcar. Who was inside mattered far more than what color it was.

But the driver seemed to satisfy the guards. He got out of the Chevrolet and hurried toward the building. "I'll see what he wants, sir," Captain Toricelli said.

"Thanks," Dowling told him.

His adjutant returned a few minutes later with the man from the auto—a sergeant. "He's from the War Department, sir," Toricelli said. "Says he's got orders for you from Philadelphia."

"Well, then, he'd better give them to me, eh?" Dowling did his best not to show worry. Orders from Philadelphia could blow up in his face almost as nastily as a people bomb. He could be cashiered. He could be summoned before the Joint Committee on the Conduct of the War again—and wasn't even once cruel and unusual punishment? He could be ordered back to the War Department to do something useless again. The possibilities were endless. The *good* possibilities seemed much more sharply limited.

"Here you are, sir," the sergeant said.

Dowling opened the orders and put on his reading glasses. If this noncom had orders to report on how he took bad news, he was damned if he'd give the man any satisfaction. Wounded soldiers bit back screams for the same reason.

He skimmed through the orders, blinked, and read them again more slowly. "Well, well," he said when he'd finished.

"May I ask, sir?" Captain Toricelli was sensitive to everything that might go wrong. What hurt Dowling's career could hurt his, too.

"I've been relieved of this command. I've been transferred," Dowling said.

Toricelli nodded. Like Dowling, he didn't want to show a stranger his wounds hurt. "Transferred where, sir?" he asked, trying to find out how badly he was hit.

"To Clovis, New Mexico, which is, I gather, near the Texas border," Dowling answered. He couldn't keep the amazement out of his voice as he went on, "They've appointed me commander of the Eleventh Army there. They want somebody to remind the Confederates there's a war on in those parts. And—"

"Yes, sir?" Toricelli broke in, eyes glowing. He might have been a soldier who'd discovered a bullet had punched a hole in his tunic without punching a hole in him.

"And they've given me a second star, Major Toricelli," Major General Abner Dowling said. He and Toricelli shook hands.

"Congratulations, sir," the sergeant from the War Department said to Dowling. The man turned to Toricelli. "Congratulations to you, too, sir."

"Thank you," Dowling said, at the same time as Toricelli was saying, "Thank you very much." Dowling went back to his desk and pulled out the half pint. He eyed how much was left in the bottle. "About enough for three good slugs," he said as he undid the cap. He raised the little bottle. "Here's to Clovis, by God, New Mexico." He drank and passed it to Angelo Toricelli.

"To Clovis!" Toricelli also drank, and passed it to the sergeant. "Here you go, pal. Kill it."

"Don't mind if I do," the noncom said. "To Clovis!" He tilted his head back. His Adam's apple worked. "Ah! That hits the spot, all right. Much obliged to you both." He would still have a story to tell when he got back to the War Department, but it wouldn't be one of frustration and rage and despair. Sergeants didn't drink with generals—or even majors—every day.

One swig of whiskey didn't turn him into a drunk. He drove off toward Philadelphia. That left Dowling and his adjutant in a pleasant sort of limbo. "What the deuce is going on in New Mexico?" Toricelli asked.

"All I know is what I read in the newspapers, and you don't read much about New Mexico there." Dowling figured he was heading to Clovis to fix that, or try. "Only thing I can really recall is that bombing raid on Fort Worth and Dallas a few months ago."

"Probably a good idea to find out before we get there," Toricelli said.

"Probably," Dowling agreed. He was sure that never would have occurred to George Custer. Custer would have charged right in and started slugging with the enemy, regardless of what was going on beforehand. Nine times out of ten, he and everyone around him would soon have regretted it. The tenth time . . . The tenth time, he would have ended up a national hero. Dowling didn't make nearly so many blunders as his former boss. He feared he would never become a national hero, though. His sense of caution was too well developed.

"I'm sure we'll stop in Philadelphia on our way to Clovis," his adjutant said. "The War Department can brief us there." Captain—no, Major—Toricelli had a well-developed sense of caution, too.

Not even the stars on his shoulder straps kept Dowling from being searched before he got into the War Department. "Sorry, sir," said the noncom who did the job. "Complain to the Chief of Staff if you want to. Rule is, no exceptions."

Dowling didn't intend to complain. As far as he could see, the rule made good sense. "How many people bombs have you had?" he asked.

"Inside here? None," the sergeant answered. "In Philadelphia? I think the count is five right now."

"Jesus!" Dowling said. The man who was patting him down nodded sadly.

He felt like saying *Jesus!* again when he got a look at the situation map for the Texas–New Mexico border. The so-called Eleventh Army had a division and a half—an understrength corps—to cover hundreds of miles of frontier. The bombers that had plastered Dallas and Fort Worth had long since been withdrawn to more active fronts.

Only one thing relieved his gloom: the Confederates he was facing were just as bad off as he was. Where he had a division and a half under his command, his counterpart in butternut commanded a scratch division, and somebody had been scratching at it pretty hard. Dowling thought he could drive the enemy a long way.

After studying the map, he wondered why he ought to bother. If he advanced fifty miles into Texas, even a hundred miles into Texas—well, so what? What had he won except fifty or a hundred empty, dusty miles? All those wide-open spaces were the best shield the Confederacy had. Advance fifty or a hundred miles into Virginia and the CSA staggered. Advance fifty or a hundred miles into Kentucky and you cut the enemy off from the Ohio River and took both farming and factory country. Texas wasn't like that. There was a lot of it, and nobody had done much with a lot of what there was.

"Are you sending me out there to do things myself, or just to keep the Confederates from doing things?" he asked a General Staff officer.

That worthy also studied the map. "For now, the first thing is to make sure the Confederates don't do anything," he replied. "If they take Las Cruces, people will talk. If they go crazy and take Santa Fe and Albuquerque, I'd say your head would roll."

"They'd need a devil of a lot of reinforcements to do that," Dowling said, and the colonel with the gold-and-black arm-of-service colors didn't deny it. Dowling went on, "They'd have to be nuts, too, because even taking Albuquerque won't do a damn thing about winning them the war."

"Looks that way to me, too," the colonel said.

"All right, then—we're on the same page, anyhow," Dowling said.

"Now, the next obvious question is, who do I have to kill to get reinforcements of my own?"

"Well, sir, till we settle the mess in Pennsylvania, you could murder everybody here and everybody in Congress and you still wouldn't get any," the General Staff officer said gravely. That struck Dowling as a reasonable assessment, too. The colonel added, "I hope you'll be able to hold on to the force you've got. I don't promise, but I hope so."

"All right. You seem honest, anyhow. I'll do what I can," Dowling said.

When he headed to the Broad Street Station for the roundabout journey west, he discovered fall had ousted summer while he wasn't looking. The temperature had dropped ten or twelve degrees while he was visiting the War Department. The breeze was fresh, and came from the northwest. Gray clouds scudded along on it. No red and gold leaves on trees, no brown leaves blowing, not yet, but that breeze said they were on their way.

Home. Cincinnatus Driver had never imagined a more wonderful word. While he lived in it, the apartment in Des Moines had seemed ordinary—just another place, one where he could hang his hat. After almost two years away, after being stuck in a country that hated his— and hated him, too—that apartment seemed the most wonderful place in the world.

The apartment and the neighborhood seemed even more amazing to his father. "Do Jesus!" Seneca Driver said. "It's like I ain't a nigger no more. Don't hardly know how to act when the ofay down at the corner store treat me like I's a man."

Cincinnatus smiled. "It's like that here. I tried to tell you, but you didn't want to believe me." Of course one reason it was like that was that Des Moines didn't have very many Negroes: not enough for whites to flabble about. The United States as a whole didn't have very many. Cincinnatus' smile slipped. The USA didn't want many Negroes, either. That left most of them stuck in the CSA, and at the tender mercy of Jake Featherston and the Freedom Party.

No such gloom troubled his father. "Bought me a pack of cigarettes, an' I give the clerk half a dollar. An' he give me my change, an' he say to me, 'Here you is, sir.' Sir! Ain't nobody never call me 'sir' in all my born days, but he do it. Sir!" He might have been walking on air. Then something else occurred to him. "That clerk, he call a Chinaman 'sir,' too?"

"Reckon so," Cincinnatus answered. "What color you are don't matter—so much—here. Achilles and Amanda, they both graduated from high school. You reckon that happen in Kentucky? And you got yourself two grandbabies that are half Chinese, and another one on the way. You reckon *that* happen in Kentucky?"

"Not likely!" His father snorted at the idea. "I seen Chinamen in the moving pictures before, but I don't reckon I ever seen one in the flesh in Covington. Now I ain't just seen 'em—I got 'em in the family!" He thought himself a man of the world because of that.

"They've got you in the family, too," Cincinnatus said. Achilles' wife, the former Grace Chang, really seemed to like Cincinnatus' father, and to be glad Cincinnatus himself was home. Her parents had much less trouble curbing their enthusiasm. They weren't thrilled about being tied to Achilles or Cincinnatus or Seneca. The funny thing was, they would have been just about as dismayed if the Drivers were white. What bothered them was that their daughter had married somebody who wasn't Chinese.

"They is welcome in my family, long as they make that good beer," Seneca Driver said. Cincinnatus nodded. Homebrew mattered in Iowa, a thoroughly dry state. He first got to know Joey Chang because of the beer his upstairs neighbor brewed. Achilles and Grace got to know each other in school. The rest? Well, the rest just happened.

Cincinnatus wondered how the Freedom Party would look at that marriage. Who was miscegenating with whom? He didn't have to worry about that here. He didn't have to worry about all kinds of things here, things that would have been matters of life and death in the Confederate States. He could look at a white woman without fearing he might get lynched. He didn't much want to—he'd always been happy with Elizabeth—but he could. He could testify in court on equal terms with whites—and with Chinese, for that matter. And . . .

"You're a U.S. citizen, Pa," he said suddenly. "Once you've lived in Iowa long enough to be a resident, you can vote."

His father was less delighted than he'd expected. "Done did that once in Kentucky," Seneca Driver replied. "There was that plebiscite thing, remember? I done voted, but they went ahead an' gave her back to the CSA anyways." He plainly thought that, since he'd voted, things should have gone the way he wanted them. Cincinnatus wished the world worked like that.

Elizabeth came out of the kitchen and into the front room. "You two hungry?" she asked. "Got some fried chicken in the icebox I can bring you." She thought Cincinnatus and his father were nothing but skin and bones. Since they'd eaten too much of their own cooking down in Covington, she might have been right.

"I would like that. Thank you kindly," Seneca said. Cincinnatus nodded, but he was less happy than his father sounded. To Seneca Driver, his son's family seemed rich. Compared to anything the older man had had in Kentucky, they were. But Cincinnatus knew money didn't grow on trees, and neither did chickens. Elizabeth had done cooking and cleaning to make ends meet while he was stuck in Covington. Achilles had helped out, too. All the same . . .

Cincinnatus knew his hauling business was dead. His wife had sold the Ford truck he'd been so proud of. He didn't blame her for that; if she couldn't pay the rent, the landlord would have thrown her out onto the street. But he didn't have enough money to buy another one. He wasn't going to be his own boss anymore. He would have to work for somebody else, and he hadn't done that since the end of the Great War. He hated the idea, but he didn't know what he could do about it.

Were there jobs for a middle-aged black man with a bad leg and a none too good shoulder? There, for once, Cincinnatus wasn't so worried. With the war sucking able-bodied men out of the workforce, there were jobs for all the people who wanted them. He'd seen how many factories and shops had NOW HIRING signs out where folks could see them. Women were doing jobs that had been a man's preserve before the war. He figured he could find something.

Elizabeth came back with a drumstick for his father, a thigh for him, and two more glasses of beer. "You holler if you want anything else," she said. She swung her hips as she walked off. In some ways, Cincinnatus was glad to discover, he wasn't crippled at all. His homecoming had been everything he hoped it would be along those lines.

"Sure is good," his father said, taking a big bite out of the chicken leg and washing it down with a sip of Mr. Chang's homebrew. "They always said folks in the USA had it good. I see they was right."

All he had to do was enjoy it. He didn't have to worry about where it came from. For the past couple of years, Elizabeth had done that. Cincinnatus was sure she'd done a lot of worrying, too. But she'd managed. Now that Cincinnatus was finally home, the worrying fell on his shoulders again.

He'd hoped the government would help him out. No such luck. To those people, he'd been in Kentucky on his own affairs, and never mind that the plebiscite and its aftermath were what had stuck him there.

Amanda came into the apartment. She'd found work at a fabric plant, and her paycheck was helping with the bills now, too. She smiled at Cincinnatus and Seneca. "Hello, Dad! Hello, Grandpa!" she said, and kissed them both on the cheek. She'd always got on better with Cincinnatus than Achilles had. There was none of that young goat bumping up against old goat rivalry that sometimes soured things between Cincinnatus and his son.

"How are you, sweetheart?" he asked her.

She made a face. "Tired. Long shift."

Seneca laughed. "Welcome to the world, dear heart. You better git used to it, on account o' it gonna be like dat till God call you to heaven."

"I suppose." Amanda sighed. "I wish I could have gone on to college. I'd be able to get a really good job with a college degree."

"Lawd!" The mere idea startled Cincinnatus' father. "A child o' my child in college? That woulda been somethin', all right."

"Even if you had started college, hon, reckon you would've gone to work anyways with things like they were," Cincinnatus said. "Sometimes you just can't help doin' what you got to do."

"I suppose," his daughter said again. She went into the kitchen to say hello to Elizabeth. When she came back, she had a glass of beer in her hand.

Cincinnatus raised an eyebrow when she sipped from it. "When did you start drinking beer?" he asked.

"I knew you were going to say that!" Amanda stuck out her tongue at him. "I *knew* it! I started about a year ago. I needed a while to get used to it, but I like it now."

Cincinnatus smiled, remembering how sour beer had tasted to him the first few times he tasted it. "All right, sweetheart," he said mildly. "I ain't gonna flabble about it. You're big enough. You can drink beer if you want to. But when I went away, you didn't." He didn't want to get upset about anything, not here, not now. He was so glad to see his daughter, he wouldn't worry about anything past that.

She looked relieved. "I was afraid you'd get all upset, say it wasn't ladylike or something."

"Not me." He shook his head. "How could I do that when your mama's been drinkin' beer a whole lot longer'n you've been alive?"

"You could have," Amanda said darkly. "Some people think what's fine for older folks isn't so fine for younger ones."

So there, Cincinnatus thought. "Yeah, some people do that," he admitted. "But I ain't one of them." He listened to the way his words sounded compared to those of the people around him. After so many years in Iowa, he'd seemed more than half a Yankee whenever he opened his mouth in Covington. But Amanda and Achilles had taken on much more of the flat Midwestern accent of Des Moines than he had. Next to them, he sounded like . . . a Negro who'd just escaped from the Confederate States. *Well, I damn well am.*

"When I was jus' a li'l pickaninny—this here was back in slavery days—my pa give me my first sip o' beer," his father said in an accent far thicker and less educated than his own. He screwed up his face at the memory. "I axed him, 'Am I pizened?' An' he tol' me no, an' he was right, but I done pizened myself with beer a time or two since. Yes, suh, a time or two."

"Oh, yeah." Cincinnatus remembered times when he'd poisoned himself, too, some of them not so long ago. He wondered how the Brass Monkey and the dedicated drinkers—and checker-players—who made it a home away from home were doing. Already, the time when he was stuck in Covington was starting to seem like a bad dream. He remembered waking up in the hospital. If only that were a bad dream! The pain in his leg and shoulder and the headaches he still sometimes got reminded him it was all too real.

He still didn't remember the motorcar hitting him. The doctors had told him he never would. They seemed to be right. From what they said, lots of folks didn't remember what happened when they had a bad accident. If his were any worse, they would have planted him with a lily on his chest.

"Glad you're home, Dad," Amanda said. *Dad.* There it was again. Down in Covington, she would surely have called him *Pa.* She had called him *Pa* for years. When had she changed to this Yankee usage? Whenever it was, he hadn't particularly noticed—till he went away and came back and got his nose rubbed in it.

"I'm glad I'm home, too," Cincinnatus said. When you got right down to it, he didn't much care what she called him. As long as she could call him anything and he was there to hear it, nothing else mattered.

He thought about the Brass Monkey again, and about Lucullus Wood's barbecue place, and about his father and mother's house, now empty and, for all he knew, standing open to the wind and the rain. And he thought about the barbed wire and the guards around Covington's colored quarter. Autumn was coming to Des Moines, but winter lived in his heart when he remembered that barbed wire.

Allegheny. Monongahela. Beautiful names for rivers. Even Ohio wasn't a bad name for a river. When you put the three of them together, though, they added up to Pittsburgh. Pittsburgh hadn't been beautiful for a long time. The way things looked to Tom Colleton, it would never be beautiful again.

The damnyankees were not going to give up this town without a fight. They poured men into it to battle block by block, house by house. Crossing a street could be and often was worth a man's life. Barrels came in and knocked houses flat and machine-gunned the men who fled from the ruins. Then some damnyankee they hadn't machine-gunned threw a Featherston Fizz through an open hatch and turned a barrel into an iron coffin for the men inside. And *then* a counterattack went in and threw the Confederates back six blocks.

Somebody not far away started banging on a shell casing with a wrench or a hammer or whatever he had handy. "Oh, for Christ's sake!" Tom said, and grabbed for his gas mask. The weather seemed to have broken; it wasn't so hot and sticky as it had been. But the gas mask was never any fun. If U.S. artillery was throwing in nerve gas, he'd have to put on the full rubber suit. He'd be sweating rivers in that even in a blizzard.

Confederate shells crashed down on the factories and steel mills ahead. The bursts sent up smoke that joined the horrid stuff belching from the tall stacks. Air in Pittsburgh was already poisonous even without phosgene and mustard gas and the nerve agents. They called the thick brown eye-stinging mix smog, jamming together smoke and fog. What they got was more noxious than the made-up word suggested, though.

Tom wouldn't have wanted to work in one of those places with shells bursting all around. But the factories kept operating till they burned or till the Confederates overran them. Trucks and trains took steel and metalware of all kinds east. Barges took them up the Allegheny, too. Confederate artillery and dive bombers made the Yankees pay a heavy price for what came out of the mills and factories. Some of it got through, though, and they must have thought that was worthwhile.

Barrels painted butternut ground forward. Telling streets from blocks of houses wasn't so easy anymore. Confederate-occupied Pittsburgh was nothing but a rubble field these days. The whole town would look like that by the time Tom's countrymen finished driving out the damnyankees . . . if they ever did.

A machine gun fired at the barrels from the cover of a ruined clothing store. Bullets clanged off the snorting machines' armor. Tom didn't know why machine gunners banged away at barrels; they couldn't hurt them. Bang away they did, though. He wasn't sorry. The more bullets they aimed at the barrels, the fewer they'd shoot at his foot soldiers, whom they really could hurt.

Traversing turrets had a ponderous grace. Three swung together, till their big guns bore on that malevolently winking eye of fire. The cannons spoke together, too. More of the battered shop fell in on itself. But the machine gun opened up again, like a small boy yelling, *Nyah! Nyah! You missed me!* when bigger kids chucked rocks at him. The crew had nerve.

All they got for their courage was another volley, and then another. After that, the gun stayed quiet. Had the barrels put it out of action, or was it playing possum? Tom hoped his men wouldn't find out the hard way.

And then, for a moment, he forgot all about the machine gun, something an infantry officer hardly ever did. But a round from a U.S. barrel he hadn't seen slammed into the side of one of the butternut behemoths. The Confederate barrel started to burn. Hatches popped open. Men dashed for cover. The U.S. barrel was smart. It didn't machine-gun them and reveal its position. It just waited.

The other two C.S. barrels turned in the general direction from which that enemy round had come. If the U.S. barrel was one of the old models, their sloped front armor would defeat its gun even at point-blank range. But it wasn't. It was one of the new ones with the big, homely turret that housed a bigger, nastier cannon. And when that gun roared again, another Confederate barrel died. This time, several soldiers pointed toward the muzzle flash. By the time the last C.S. barrel in the neighborhood brought its gun to bear, though, the damnyankee machine had pulled back. Tom Colleton got glimpses of it as it retreated, but only glimpses. The butternut barrel didn't have a clear shot at it, and held fire.

He sent men forward to keep the enemy from bringing barrels into that spot again. He was only half surprised when the machine gun in the ruined store opened up again. His men were quick to take cover, too. He didn't think the machine gun got any of them. He hoped not, anyway.

The Confederate barrel sent several more rounds into the haberdashery. The machine gun stayed quiet. Ever so cautious, soldiers in butternut inched closer. One of them tossed in a grenade and went in after it. Tom wished he had a man with a flamethrower handy. The last fellow who'd carried one had got incinerated along with his rig a few days earlier, though. No replacement for him had come forward yet.

Not enough replacements of any kind were coming forward. Little by little, the regiment was melting away. Tom didn't know what to do about that, except hope it got pulled out of the line for rest and refit before too long. However much he hoped, he didn't expect that would happen soon. The Confederates needed Pittsburgh. They'd already put just about everybody available up at the front.

After a minute or so, the soldier came out of the wreckage with his thumb up. There was one damnyankee machine gun that wouldn't murder anybody else. Now—how many hundreds, how many thousands, more waited in Pittsburgh? The answer was too depressing to think about, so Tom didn't.

One thing he hadn't seen in Pittsburgh: yellowish khaki Mexican uniforms. The Mexicans hadn't done badly in Ohio and Pennsylvania, but they weren't the first team, and everybody knew it. They held the flanks once the Confederates went through and cleared out the Yankees. They were plenty good enough for that, and it let the Confederates pile more of their own troops into the big fight.

A rifle shot rang out. A bullet struck sparks from the bricks just behind the head of the soldier who'd thrown the grenade. He hit the dirt. Three other Confederates pointed in three different directions, which meant nobody'd seen where the shot came from. The machine gun might be gone, but the Yankees hadn't given up the fight for this block. It didn't seem as if they would till they were all dead.

Down in the CSA, some people—mostly those who hadn't been through the Great War—still believed U.S. soldiers were nothing but a pack of cowards. Tom laughed as he ducked down into a shell hole to shed his mask and smoke a cigarette—he didn't turn blue and keel over, so it was safe enough. And much better not to let the match or the coal give the damnyankee sniper a target. He just wished Confederate propaganda were true. Pittsburgh would have fallen long since.

A runner came skittering back to him, calling his name. "Here I am!" he shouted, not raising his head. "What's up?"

"Sir, there's a Yankee with a flag of truce right up at the front," the runner replied. "Wants to know if he can come back and dicker a truce for the wounded."

The last time a U.S. officer proposed something like that, he'd scouted out the C.S. positions as he moved with his white flag. The damnyankees kept the truce, but they knew just where to strike after it ended. Tom threw down the half-finished smoke. "I'll meet the son of a bitch at the line," he growled.

He made his own flag of truce from a stick and a pillowcase, then went up with the runner. The truce already seemed to be informally under way. Firing had stopped. Confederates were swapping packs of cigarettes for U.S. ration cans. Both sides deplored that. Neither could do anything about it. Commerce trumped orders. The Yankees had better canned goods and worse tobacco, the Confederates the opposite.

A U.S. captain in a dirty uniform waited for Tom. "I could have come to you," the man remarked.

Colleton smiled a crooked smile. "I bet you could," he said, and explained why he didn't want the Yankee back of his lines.

"I wouldn't do a thing like that," the U.S. officer said, much too innocently. "And I'm sure you wouldn't, either."

"Who, me?" Tom said with another smile like the first. The U.S. captain matched it. They'd been through the mill, all right. Tom got down to business: "Is an hour long enough, or do you want two?"

"Split the difference?" the damnyankee suggested, and Tom nodded. The captain looked at his watch. "All right, Lieutenant-Colonel. Truce till 1315, then?"

"Agreed." Tom stuck out his hand. The U.S. captain shook it. They both turned back to their own men and shouted out the news. Corpsmen from both sides came forward. Ordinary soldiers did some more trading. Somebody had a football. C.S. and U.S. soldiers tossed it back and forth. Tom remembered the 1914 Christmas truce, when the Great War almost unraveled. He knew that wouldn't happen here. Both sides meant it now.

Corpsmen poked around through rubble. They called outside of smashed houses. Sometimes they got answers from smashed people trapped inside. Soldiers helped move wreckage so the medics could do their job. When U.S. corpsmen found wounded C.S. soldiers, they gave them back to the Confederates. Corpsmen in butternut returned the favor for the Yankees.

Tom and the officer in green-gray—his name was Julian Nesmith—hadn't agreed to that, but neither of them tried to stop it. "Won't change how things end up one way or the other," Nesmith remarked.

"I was thinking the same thing about smokes and grub a little while ago," Tom agreed. He'd handed Captain Nesmith a couple of packs of Raleighs, and was now the proud possessor of two cans of deviled ham, a delicacy esteemed on both sides of the front. His mouth watered. If he could scrounge up some eggs . . . Even if he couldn't, the ham would be a treat.

"We might as well be comfortable as we can while we slaughter each other," Nesmith said.

"We're enemies," Tom said simply. "You won't make me believe the United States wants to do anything but to squash my country, and I don't expect I can persuade you the Confederate States aren't full of villains."

"It wouldn't matter if you did," Nesmith answered. "As long as you've got villains at the top, all they have to do is shout loud enough to make everybody else go along."

That came close to hitting below the belt. Tom hadn't much cared to listen to Jake Featherston on the wireless at all hours of the day and night. But Jake Featherston had got Kentucky and Houston back into the CSA after the damnyankees stole them at gunpoint in 1917. The Whigs hadn't come close to managing that. Featherston was doing something about the Negroes in the Confederate States, too. The Whigs hadn't known what to do. And so . . .

"Who's a villain and who isn't depends on how you look at things," Tom said.

"Sometimes," Julian Nesmith replied.

They shook hands again when the truce ended. Corpsmen disappeared. Men got back under cover. Almost ceremoniously, a U.S. soldier fired a Springfield to warn anybody who hadn't got the word. In that same spirit, a Confederate soldier answered with one round from a Tredegar.

Then another Confederate squeezed off a burst from his automatic rifle. A U.S. machine gun opened up. Tom sighed. The little peace had been nice while it lasted.

Salt Lake City wasn't hell, but you could see it from there. Armstrong Grimes peered toward the rubble of the Mormon Temple—twice built and now twice destroyed. He peered very cautiously. All the Mormons still fighting were veterans. Some of them were veterans of two uprisings. Show any body part, and they'd put a bullet through it faster than you could say Jack Robinson.

Armstrong wondered who the hell Jack Robinson was. He also wondered how life would change now that he was a sergeant instead of a corporal. He'd hesitated before sewing the new stripes onto his sleeve. The Mormons' snipers liked to pick off officers and noncoms.

Yossel Reisen had two stripes now. He wore them, too. Their promotions both came through while the regiment was in reserve in Thistle. Somebody must have thought they were on the ball when that woman blew herself up in Provo. All Armstrong knew was that the two of them hadn't got badly hurt when the people bomb went off, and afterward he'd done what anybody else would have. That must have been enough to impress one officer or another.

He turned to Reisen, who crouched behind a stone fence not far away. "You hear the skinny last night?" he said. "They figure Sergeant Stowe's gonna make it."

"Yeah, somebody told me." Yossel nodded. "I would've thought he was a goner for sure. He looked like hell."

"Boy, didn't he?" Armstrong said.

"He's lucky."

"Hunh-unh." Now Armstrong shook his head. "*We're* lucky. We didn't catch shrapnel. We aren't in the hospital with our guts all messed up. If Stowe was lucky, he'd still be here, same as we are. Instead, he's in a bed somewhere, and they probably have to shoot morphine into him all the goddamn time. Belly wounds are supposed to hurt like anything."

His vehemence surprised him. It must have surprised Yossel Reisen, too. Armstrong didn't usually argue with him. Yossel was older and more experienced, even if he didn't care about rank. Here, though, Armstrong couldn't keep quiet. And after a few seconds, Yossel nodded. "Well, you're right," he said. "He's alive, and that's good, but he still isn't lucky."

"There you go," Armstrong said. "That's how it looks to me, too."

"Sarge! Hey, Sarge!" somebody yelled.

Armstrong needed a moment to remember that meant him. "Yeah? What is it?" he said, a beat slower than he should have.

"Mormon coming up with a flag of truce."

Firing had died away. Armstrong hadn't noticed that, either. He felt as far down on sleep as he had before his regiment got R and R. Cautiously, he stuck his head up again. Sure as hell, here came a Mormon in what the rebels used for a uniform: chambray shirt, dungarees, and boots. "Hold it right there, buddy, or you'll never know how your favorite serial comes out on the wireless!" Armstrong yelled.

The Mormon waved the white flag. "I want to talk to an officer. I mean no harm."

"Yeah, now tell me another one," Armstrong said. "How do I know you're not a goddamn people bomb waiting to go off?"

"Because I say I am not," the rebel answered. "I am a major in the Army of the State of Deseret." Armstrong could hear the capital letters thud into place.

Capital letters didn't impress him. "And I'm the Queen of the May," he said. "You want to come forward?" He waited for the Mormon to nod, then made a peremptory gesture. "Strip. Show me you're not loaded with fucking TNT."

If looks could kill . . . But they couldn't, and TNT might. Fuming, the Mormon major shed his boots, his jeans, and his shirt. He even took off his Stetson. That left him in a peculiar-looking undershirt and longish drawers. It was getting toward long-underwear time—nights were downright chilly—but it hadn't got there yet. The strange getup didn't particularly bother Armstrong; he'd seen it on other Mormons. Some sort of religious rule said they had to wear it.

That didn't mean he had to trust it. "Lift up the shirt," he called.

"The drawers are snug enough—don't bother with those." The Mormon did, showing a hard belly covered with hair a shade darker than the blond hair on his head. Armstrong waved to him. "Now turn around." After the rebel did, Armstrong reluctantly nodded. "All right. Looks like you're clean. Put your stuff back on and come ahead."

As the Mormon major dressed, he said, "I ought to complain to your officers."

"Go ahead, buddy," Armstrong said. "You think they'll come down on me? *I* think they'll pat me on the back. They don't trust you people any further than I do, and I don't trust you at all."

"Believe me, we feel the same way about you," the Mormon said, bending to tie his bootlaces. "If you would only leave us alone—"

"If you hadn't risen up, I'd be back east somewhere with Confederates trying to shoot me," Armstrong said. "And you'd be here in Utah, happy as a goddamn clam. They didn't even conscript you people."

"We want to be free. We want to be independent," the Mormon said as he picked up his white flag. "What's so wicked about that?" He came toward the U.S. lines.

Armstrong laughed a dirty laugh. "You want to have lots of wives. Are they all in the same bed when you screw 'em? Does one lick your balls while another one gets on top?"

The Mormon's jaw set. "It's a good thing I don't know your name, Sergeant." He walked past Armstrong as if he didn't exist. Armstrong called for a couple of privates to take him back toward the rear.

"He's going to put you on a list even if he doesn't know your name," Yossel said. "You'll be the sergeant in so-and-so sector, and those bastards will be gunning for you."

"Big fucking deal." Armstrong laughed again. "Easy enough to get shot around here even when the bastards aren't gunning for you. Won't make a whole hell of a lot of difference one way or the other."

"You better hope it won't." Yossel seemed willing to look on the gloomy side of life.

"Screw it. Nobody's even shooting right now." Armstrong lived for, and in, the moment. The less you thought about all the horrible things that had happened, the horrible things that would happen, and the horrible things that might happen, the better off you were.

After a bit, Captain Lloyd Deevers came over and got down in the hole with him. Armstrong liked Deevers a lot better than Lieutenant

Streczyk, who ran the platoon. Deevers actually had a pretty good idea of what he was doing. He nodded to Armstrong now and said, "I don't think that Mormon likes you."

"Now ask me if I care, sir," Armstrong answered. "I don't like him, either."

Deevers chuckled. "All right. I'm not going to flabble about it—except if you want to transfer to some other outfit on the line, I won't say no."

"No, thanks, sir. I already told Reisen I can stop one as easy somewhere else as I can here," Armstrong said. Captain Deevers grinned and slapped him on the back. Armstrong asked, "Did that Mormon say why he wanted the truce?"

"Not to me," Deevers answered. "He wanted to talk to the high mucky-mucks. I passed him back to Division HQ, and we'll see what they do with him. If I had to guess, I'd say he wants to dicker a surrender that isn't really a surrender, if you know what I mean. But that's only a guess."

"Good fucking luck, uh, sir," Armstrong said. Lloyd Deevers laughed.

"He would have had a better chance before they started blowing themselves up," Yossel said. "If we let 'em off the hook now, it's like they screwed it out of us. And if they want something else, they'll think all they have to do is use a few more people bombs to make us give in."

"That's how it looks to me, too, especially since we've almost got 'em licked," Armstrong said.

"Well, boys, I won't argue with either one of you, 'cause I think you're dead right," Deevers said. "But it isn't up to me, any more than it's up to you. We'll see what the fellows with the stars on their shoulders have to say—and maybe the fellows in the cutaway coats, too."

"They'll screw it up," Armstrong predicted. "They always do." He waved a hand at the devastation all around. The wreckage and the smell of corpses might not prove his point, but they didn't come out and call him a liar, either.

Captain Deevers just shrugged. "Like I told you, I can't do anything about it, either. I suppose what they decide to do here depends a lot on how things look in Pennsylvania and up in Canada."

That made sense. Armstrong might have been happier if it didn't. Soldiers in Utah didn't hear much news from Pennsylvania. Not hearing news was a bad sign all by itself. When things went right, nobody on the wireless would shut up about it. That same ominous quiet came out of Canada. For all Armstrong knew, hordes of pissed-off Canucks were swarming over the border toward Minneapolis and Seattle.

"We're off in the back of beyond," Yossel said. "Nobody tells us anything."

"Wonder how much news about us gets out," Captain Deevers said musingly.

"You ought to ask your aunt," Armstrong told Yossel. He kept an eye on the company CO as he spoke. Deevers didn't blink. He was fairly new to the unit, but he knew it had a VIP's nephew.

Yossel said, "She doesn't tell me a whole lot—nothing I'm not supposed to know. She's got to worry about security like anybody else."

"Too bad," Armstrong said. "What's the point of being related to a big shot if you don't get anything out of it?"

"People always say that," Yossel Reisen answered. "But if somebody important gives you a hand all the time, how do you know what you're good for by yourself?"

He had a point. Armstrong could see it. His family, though, had no fancy connections. He thought not having to worry about money or a good job or the right college would be awfully nice. No doors had opened for him because he was so-and-so's nephew. His family had plenty of so-and-sos in it, but not that kind.

Somebody called a question across the line to the Mormons: "How long is this truce supposed to last?"

"Till the major comes back," a rebel answered. "Then we give you thieving wretches more of what you deserve."

Thieving wretches. Armstrong smiled in spite of himself. The Mormons seldom came right out and cussed. Some of the insults they used instead sounded pretty funny.

Men on both sides walked around and stretched, showing their faces without fear of taking a bullet if they did. The Mormons were scrupulous about honoring truces. U.S. soldiers smoked. Some of them probably had something better than water in their canteens. The Mormons weren't supposed to use tobacco or alcohol, and most of them didn't. Armstrong figured that meant screwing was the only way they could have a good time. They sure did that. They'd raised up a big new generation of rebels after getting one killed off in their uprising during the Great War.

In midafternoon U.S. soldiers passed the Mormon officer back through the lines to his own side. His face was a thunderstorm of fury. He hardly even had an extra glare for Armstrong as he went by. The Mormons fired a warning shot into the air. A U.S. soldier answered it. A couple of minutes later, a screaming meemie came down on Armstrong's company, and then another one. All things considered, maybe he would rather have stayed anonymous.

Leonard O'Doull had worked in a hospital before. He'd met his wife working in one outside of Rivière-du-Loup during the last war. If the authorities hadn't decided Lucien Galtier was an unreliable nuisance and confiscated his land for the building, Nicole never would have come to work there. O'Doull knew he wouldn't have settled in the Republic of Quebec if he hadn't made family ties. Sometimes very strange things could twist a man's fate.

He was in a fancier hospital now. The University of Pittsburgh had had one of the best medical schools in the USA, and a large hospital where staff members trained residents, interns, medical students, and nurses. Now the hospital was full of wounded and gassed soldiers. Along with the people in training—those who hadn't put on the uniform—the staff were getting trained themselves, by experts like Leonard O'Doull and Granville McDougald.

"Speed," McDougald told a surgeon with an old-fashioned, upturned Kaiser Bill mustache. "The faster we can get to 'em, the better they do. If we're operating less than an hour after they get hit, they'll probably make it. Every minute after that hurts their chances."

The white-mustached healer nodded. "I've also seen this in motorcar accidents," he said.

"It's even more critical with gunshot and shrapnel wounds, because the trauma's usually worse," McDougald said. The surgeon nodded again, thoughtfully, and walked down the corridor. McDougald looked over at Leonard O'Doull and grinned. "Look at me, Doc, going on just like I know what I'm talking about."

"Don't sandbag, Granny," O'Doull answered. "When it comes to wounds, who's seen more than you?"

"Nobody this side of the guy who cuts up steers in a Chicago slaughterhouse," McDougald said. "But he always sees the same ones. Not like that in our line of work, is it?"

"Always something new," O'Doull agreed. "People keep coming

up with new ways to maim their fellow man. I don't know why I don't despair of the human race."

"Somebody once said people were the missing link between apes and human beings," McDougald said wistfully. "Damned if he didn't hit that one on the button."

"Didn't he just?" O'Doull listened to the artillery outside. "If the Confederates get over the Allegheny, we're going to be even busier than we are already."

"So will they," McDougald said. "They'll be busier than a one-armed paper hanger with the hives. They may take this place away from us, but Christ!—they're paying through the nose."

Leonard O'Doull nodded. It looked that way to him, too. The dashing C.S. barrels weren't dashing, not in Pittsburgh. They had to fight their way forward house by house, and a lot of them ended up as burnt-out hulks. Confederate infantry had trouble advancing without the barrels, too. Local U.S. counterattacks meant the hospital held a good many wounded Confederates along with U.S. soldiers. That might have been for the best—the more of their own men in this place, the less inclined the Confederates would be to hit it "by accident."

"Wouldn't put it past 'em," McDougald said when O'Doull remarked on that. "They fought as clean as we did the last time around. Here? Now?" He made a sour face. "I think they cheat when they use the Red Cross, and I think they think we cheat, too. Makes them more likely to hit our aid stations and hospitals and ambulances. Featherston's fuckers, sure as hell."

"I hope that isn't true." O'Doull let it go there. The bad news seemed more likely to be true with each unfolding day. There were even rumors Featherston himself traveled in an ambulance to keep U.S. fighters from shooting him up.

"Well, Doc, if you want some consolation, the bastards in butternut aren't as bad as they could be," Granville McDougald said. "It sounds like the *Action Française* boys really abuse the Red Cross."

"Yeah. I've heard that, too," O'Doull said. "There's another war as big as this one going on over there—"

"Bigger," the medic said.

"Bigger, all right." O'Doull accepted the correction. "But it's like noises in another room to us. Oh, we're working with the German High Seas Fleet where we can, but mostly we've got our troubles, and Germany and Austria-Hungary have theirs."

"Austria-Hungary's got more troubles than you can shake a stick at," McDougald observed. "All the uprisings in the Balkans make what's going on in Utah and Canada look like pretty small potatoes." He grinned crookedly at O'Doull. "Might as well be Ireland, matter of fact."

"Heh," O'Doull said sourly—something that sounded like a laugh but really wasn't. With U.S. help, Ireland had thrown off the English yoke after the Great War. The first thing Winston Churchill's government did when the new round of fighting flared was send in barrels and bombers and battleships. The Union Jack flew again in Belfast and Dublin and Cork—and the island heaved with rebellion. "I wonder how long it'll be before Irish people bombs start going off in London."

McDougald winced. "Those damned Mormons let the genie out of the bottle with that one," he said. "How do you stop somebody who's already decided to die?" By the evidence available so far, you *couldn't* stop somebody like that, not often enough. McDougald added, "They'll feel it in Vienna and Budapest, too." Serbs and Romanians and Bosnians and God only knew how many others from the Balkan patchwork quilt of peoples and competing nationalisms bushwhacked the King-Emperor's soldiers where and as they could. Russia encouraged them and sent them arms and ammunition, the way the British helped the Canucks, and the Confederates armed the Mormons.

Of course, the USA armed Negroes in the CSA. (O'Doull didn't even think about U.S. support for the Republic of Quebec, which would still have been a Canadian province absent the Great War.) Germany played those games with Finns and Jews and Chechens and Azerbaijanis inside the Tsar's empire. And both sides helped their own sets of guerrillas inside the Ukraine, which was, in technical terms, a mess.

An orderly trotted up to O'Doull and McDougald. "We've got a man with a leg wound in OR Seven," he said.

"We should do something about that," McDougald said, and O'Doull nodded. They hurried toward the OR. Working in an actual operating room was an unaccustomed luxury for O'Doull. It beat the hell out of doing his job under canvas. He had a real operating table, surgical lights he could aim wherever he wanted, and all the other amenities he'd almost forgotten in the field.

And he had a nasty case waiting on the table for him. *A leg wound* hardly did the injury justice. "Get him under fast, Granny," O'Doull said after one glance at the shattered appendage.

"Right," McDougald said, and not much else till the soldier was mercifully unconscious. Then he asked, "You're not going to try and keep that on, are you?"

"Good God, no," O'Doull answered. "Above the knee, too, poor bastard." He picked up a bone saw and got to work.

Like most amputations, it was bloody but fast. The wounded soldier was young and strong and healthy. O'Doull thought he would do well—or as well as you could do after you'd been maimed. How many men on both sides of the border were short an arm or a leg? Too many, that was for sure.

As he closed up the stump, O'Doull asked, "Ever see a real basket case, Granny?"

"No arms, no legs?" McDougald asked, and O'Doull nodded. The medic shook his head. "No, not me. You always hear about 'em, but I've never seen one. You get wounded like that, most of the time they take your pieces back to Graves Registration, not to an aid station. How about you?"

"The same," O'Doull answered. "You hear about 'em all the time. Hell, people talk about basket cases when they mean somebody who's just all messed up. But I've never seen the real McCoy, either."

"I suppose there really are some," McDougald said. "Would we have the name if we didn't have the thing?"

"Beats me," O'Doull said. "We have names for truth and justice and liberty, too. How often do you really see the things those names point at?"

"Touché, Doc." Granville McDougald gave him another sour laugh. "And then we've got 'Freedom!' too." By the way he said the word, he might have been a stalwart in white shirt and butternut trousers getting ready to go out there and break some heads.

"God damn Jake Featherston up one side and down the other," O'Doull said wearily as he went to the sink and washed the now one-legged soldier's blood from his hands. How much blood did Featherston have on *his* hands? But he didn't care about washing it off. He reveled in it.

McDougald stood beside him and scrubbed down, too. "I've been wishing that very same thing," he said, holding out his arms in front of him with the wrists up so water would flow down from his hands and carry germs away with it. "I've been wishing for it since before the war started, matter of fact, and God hasn't done thing one. Far as I can tell,

He's at a football game—probably standing in line to get Himself a couple of franks and a beer."

That was blasphemous, which didn't mean it didn't hold a lot of truth. "I don't know how anybody's going to be able to believe in anything by the time this damn war is done," O'Doull said.

"I don't know how anybody believed anything after the last one," McDougald said. "But you're right. This one's worse. The poison gas is more poisonous. We're better at dropping bombs on the Confederates' cities, and they're better at dropping them on ours. 'O brave new world, that has such people in't!'" He quoted Shakespeare with malice aforethought.

"You forgot one," O'Doull said. McDougald raised a questioning eyebrow. The doctor explained: "We didn't slaughter people just because of who they were the last time around."

"Oh, yeah? Tell it to the Armenians. And the Turks were on our side," McDougald said. O'Doull winced. He'd forgotten about the Armenian massacres. He was sure most people in the USA had. McDougald went on, "But you're right—*we* didn't, not on this continent. And Jake Featherston probably noticed nothing much ever happened to the Turks, and he must have figured nothing much would happen to him if we went after his spooks. And you know what else? Looks like he's right."

"It does, doesn't it?" O'Doull said unhappily.

"I don't think a whole lot of people in the USA like smokes a whole hell of a lot," McDougald said. "I'd be lying if I said I liked 'em a whole hell of a lot myself. Don't know very many. Don't know any very well—aren't that many here *to* know, and that suits me fine. What I do know . . . Well, you can keep 'em, far as I'm concerned. But there's a lot of difference between saying that and wanting to see 'em dead."

"I'm with you," O'Doull said. "I don't think I saw a Negro all the time I was up in Rivière-du-Loup, and I didn't much miss 'em, either. Lots and lots of 'em in the CSA, so the Confederates can't pretend they aren't there, the way we can. But making so they really *aren't* there— that's filthy."

"Yeah, we're on the same page again, Doc," Granville McDougald said. "And you know what else?" O'Doull raised an interrogative eyebrow. The medic went on, "It won't do those poor sons of bitches one damn bit of good." Leonard O'Doull sadly nodded, because that was much too likely to be true.

* * *

Coming back to the Lower East Side of New York City always felt strange to Flora Blackford. It was only a couple of hours by fast train from Philadelphia, but it was a different world. As she made a campaign visit just before the 1942 Presidential elections, she found it different in some new ways.

Confederate bombers hadn't hit her hometown nearly so hard as they'd hit Philadelphia. Those extra 90 miles—180 round trip—meant more fuel and fewer bombs aboard. They also meant U.S. fighters had all that extra time to try to shoot the Confederates down. And most of the bombs that had fallen in New York City had fallen on Wall Street and the publishing district, and on and around the factories in the Bronx and Brooklyn. The neighborhood where she'd grown up was— oh, not untouched by war, but not badly damaged, either.

She spoke in a theater where she'd debated her Democratic opponent during the Great War. This time, the Democrats were running a lawyer named Sheldon Vogelman. He stood well to the right of Robert Taft, and only a little to the left of Attila the Hun. He was the sort of man who, if he weren't Jewish, probably would have been a raving anti-Semite. Instead, he raved about plowing up the Confederates' cities and sowing them with salt so nothing ever grew there again. He also wanted to plow up anybody in the USA who presumed to disagree with him.

"My opponent," Flora said, "would ship salt from the Great Salt Flats in Utah especially for the purpose. Digging up the salt and bringing it east for his purposes would create jobs. I'm afraid that's his entire definition of a full-employment policy."

She got a laugh and a hand. The Democrats could nominate a right-wing lunatic in this district because they weren't going to win no matter whom they nominated. Vogelman blew off steam for their party. He was loud and obnoxious and, for all practical purposes, harmless.

"We made mistakes," Flora said. "I'm not going to try to tell you anything else. We should have been tougher on Jake Featherston as soon as he made it plain he was building up a new war machine. But Herbert Hoover was President of the United States from 1933 to 1937, and he and the Democrats didn't do anything about Jake Featherston then, either."

"That's right!" somebody in the audience shouted. A few hecklers

booed. But there weren't many. Sheldon Vogelman was not only a reactionary nut, he was an ineffective reactionary nut. *Best kind,* Flora
thought. The best—or worst—example of the other kind was Featherston.

She and Vogelman agreed on one thing: the war had to be fought
to a finish. They had different reasons, but they agreed. She didn't
know of any Socialists, Democrats, or even Republicans running on a
peace-at-any-price platform. Jake Featherston had been effective at
uniting the United States against him, too.

"When this war is over—when we have won this war—" Flora
began, and had to stop for a flood of fierce applause. "When we have
won, I say, Featherston and his fellow criminals will face the bar of justice for their aggression against the United States"—more ferocious
cheers—"and for their cold-blooded murder of tens of thousands of
their own people."

She got cheers for that, too, but not so many, even if she didn't call
a spade a spade. The painful truth was that not even her mostly Jewish
audience could get excited about the fate of Negroes in the CSA. Flora
had been banging her head against that truth ever since she started
speaking out about Jake Featherston's persecutions.

"Don't you see?" she said. "Pogroms are *wrong.* How many of
your ancestors—how many of *you,* ladies and gentlemen—came to the
United States because of the Tsar's pogroms? Come on—I know it's
more than that."

All over the hall, hands went up. People raised them reluctantly
and lowered them as soon as they could. If they'd had their druthers,
they wouldn't have raised them at all. They didn't want to think about
why they'd come to America. They especially didn't want to compare
their past to the Confederate Negroes' present.

Flora wanted to make sure they remembered. She wanted that even
if it cost her votes. Against a candidate like Sheldon Vogelman, losing
a few didn't much matter. If the Democrats had run someone stronger,
she hoped she would have done the same thing.

"If you turn your back on other people when they're in trouble,
who'll look out for you when you are?" she asked. "Don't you see? If
we don't look out for the Negroes in the CSA, in an important way we
don't look out for ourselves, either."

"We don't want those people here!" somebody shouted. Several
people clapped their hands. They weren't all hecklers. She knew where

the hecklers were sitting. Listening to them hurt more because they weren't.

"The Democrats are the party for people who only care about themselves," Flora said. "If your fellow man matters to you, you'll vote Socialist next week. I hope he does. I hope you do. Thank you!"

She got a good hand as she stepped away from the lectern. She could have been caught pulling hundred-dollar bills out of a contractor's pocket with her teeth, and she still would have won here this time around.

For lunch the next day, she faced a more critical audience. David Hamburger had come out of the Great War with one leg and with politics not far from Vogelman's. He and Flora still got on well when they stayed away from political matters. When they didn't—and they couldn't all the time—sparks flew.

They met at Kaplan's, a delicatessen that had been around at least as long as Flora had. David was waiting for her when she came in. That was probably just as well; she didn't have to watch the rolling gait required by an artificial leg that started above the knee.

"Hello, there," he said as she joined him. "So how does it feel to be slumming in your old stomping grounds?"

"Kaplan's isn't slumming," Flora said. "Don't be silly. Not a place in Philadelphia comes close to it." The waiter was bald and had a gray mustache. Flora ordered corned beef on rye. Her brother chose pastrami. They both ordered beer. The waiter nodded and hurried away. "How have you been?" Flora asked.

"Not too bad—middle-class, or somewhere close." David shrugged. "My son's too little to conscript in this war, so that's good."

"Yes," Flora said tonelessly. Her own son was heading toward eighteen, and Joshua wouldn't hear of her doing anything to keep him out of the conscription pool. Having a nephew in harm's way was bad enough. Having a son on the front lines would be ten thousand times worse.

The food and the beers came quickly. Flora took a long pull at hers. David drank more slowly. He pulled a dill pickle from the jar on the table and nibbled it with his sandwich and his beer. After a bit, he said, "Looks like you'll be away for another couple of years."

"Well, I hope so," Flora said.

"You've done a good job, and Vogelman's *meshuggeh*," David said. "Between the two, that ought to do the job. If it doesn't, this district is even more *verkakte* than I give it credit for—and I didn't think it could be."

Hearing the Yiddish made Flora smile. Like her brothers and sisters, she'd grown up speaking it more often than English at home. Now, though, she never heard it, never spoke it, unless she came back to the district. No one she knew in Philadelphia used it. Her husband, a gentile from Dakota, had learned a few phrases from her, but that was all. Joshua knew a few phrases, too. He couldn't begin to speak it. Flora wasn't so sure she could speak it herself anymore.

She thought, and then did bring out a Yiddish sentence: "What's going to happen to this language in a couple of generations?"

"I don't know," David answered, also in Yiddish. He dropped back into English to go on, "And I won't lose much sleep over it, either. We brought Yiddish from the old country. Now we're Americans. They speak English here. So, fine—I'll speak English."

"I suppose so," Flora said. "Joshua doesn't seem much interested in learning it, anyhow. But I can't help wondering whether my grandchildren or great-grandchildren won't think they missed out on something special because they didn't get the chance to learn it."

"Well, if they do, there's always night school," David said, and Flora nodded. How many immigrants had learned all sorts of different things in night school? Hundreds of thousands, surely. Some were accountants, some were lawyers, because of the courses they'd taken in hours snatched from sleep and rest. Still . . .

"It won't be the same," she said. "What you learn in school isn't like what you pick up around the house."

"I can't do anything about it." David pulled another pickle spear out of the jar and aimed it at her like a bayonet. "I can't—but *you* can. You can pass the Preservation of Yiddish Act and make it a crime for all the *alter kackers*"—he tacked the English plural onto the Yiddish word—"who can still yatter away in the old language to use English instead. And you can make it another crime for anybody Jewish not to listen to them and talk back in Yiddish."

Flora laughed so hard, she almost choked on her sandwich. "You," she said severely, "are ridiculous."

"Thank you," her brother answered, which only made her laugh harder. "And while you're at it, you can have them make the Lower East Side a national park. Buffalo have Yellowstone. Why shouldn't people who speak Yiddish have their own game preserve, too? And if we get too crowded, you could issue hunting licenses to anti-Semites, and they'd come in here and thin us out. Only difference between us and the buffalo is, we might shoot back."

"You—" Flora stopped. She had to reach into her purse for a hand-kerchief to wipe her streaming eyes. She tried again: "You ought to sell that routine to the Engels Brothers. If they wouldn't pay you for it, I'm a Chinaman."

"You could do the same thing for Chinamen, here and in San Fran-cisco," David said, warming to his theme. "And think of the chances Jake Featherston's missing. If he charged fees to get into the hunting preserves for *shvartzers,* he could probably cut taxes in half."

That killed Flora's laughter. "It isn't hunting down there," she said. "It's slaughter, nothing else but."

"They might as well be Mormons, eh?" David insisted on being difficult.

"It's worse," Flora insisted. "We're fighting the Mormons, but we aren't murdering the ones in the land we've taken. The Confederates are emptying out one town after another, taking the Negroes off to camps and killing them once they get there. It's . . . about as bad as it can be down there."

"And it's just pretty bad up here," David said. "Well, nice to know we've still got room for improvement."

That wasn't funny, either—or, if it was, only in the blackest way. When Flora laughed this time, it was only to keep from sobbing.

XVI

Some lovely rubble lay between Sergeant Michael Pound's barrel and the advancing Confederate armor. Once upon a time, the rubble had been homes and shops and people's hopes. All things considered, Pound liked it better as rubble. If you knocked a wall down in a neighborhood that hadn't been trampled, the enemy would notice right away. If you rearranged what was already wreckage, though, so what?

Not many Pittsburgh neighborhoods had gone untrampled. The United States were making a stand here, defying the Confederates to drive them out. Jake Featherston seemed willing, even eager, to try. He keep feeding men and barrels and artillery and airplanes into the fight. No matter who held Pittsburgh by the time the battle here was done, one thing was clear: it wouldn't be worth holding.

Pound tapped Lieutenant Don Griffiths on the leg. "Sir, do you think we could crawl inside that ruined—garage, I guess it used to be— over there? We've got a nice field of fire where the window was, and the shadows inside'll keep the bastards in butternut from spotting us."

The barrel commander stuck his head out of the cupola for a good look. He had nerve; nobody could say he didn't. And he seemed to own more in the way of sense than the late Lieutenant Poffenberger, anyway. When he ducked back down again, he said, "Good idea, Sergeant," and spoke to the driver by intercom. Jouncing over shattered brickwork, the barrel took its new position.

Another reason Pound liked the ruined garage was that he'd seen U.S. infantrymen huddled in the ruins not far away. Your own foot soldiers were the best insurance policy you had in a barrel. They kept the other side's foot soldiers away. No sneaky bastard could plant a magnetic mine on your side, chuck a grenade through an open hatch, or throw a Featherston Fizz at your engine compartment so the flaming gasoline dripped down through the louvers and set you on fire, not if you had pals around.

He spotted motion up ahead through the gunsight. Not the dinosaurian shape of a Confederate barrel rumbling into position, but . . . "Sir, they're moving infantry up."

"Yes, I saw them, too," Griffiths answered. "Hold fire for now. Let our own infantry deal with them if they can. We've got this good position. I don't want to give it away for something as small as a few soldiers on foot."

"Yes, sir." Pound surprised himself by smiling at the lieutenant. What Griffiths said made perfectly good sense. Pound wouldn't have thought the junior officer had it in him.

Confederate Asskickers screamed down out of the sky to bomb and machine-gun U.S. positions. What seemed like every antiaircraft gun in the world opened up on them. So many guns blazed away, Pound wondered if some of them hadn't kept quiet before to lure the Confederate dive bombers into a trap. Three or four Mules didn't pull up from their dives, but went straight into the ground. The explosions made the ground shake under his barrel. He saw one funeral pyre through the hole that had held the garage window.

"Good riddance," he muttered.

"Amen," Cecil Bergman said. The loader added, "See anything out there that needs killing, Sarge?"

"Quiet right now," Pound answered.

"Good," Bergman said—not a bloodthirsty attitude, but a sensible one. Nobody in his right mind was eager for combat. You had a job to do, you did it, and you tried not to think about it. When you had to think about it, you thought about targets and barrels. You didn't think about men. Because those sons of bitches on the other side had a job to do, too, and theirs was turning you into a target. If that also meant turning you into raw hamburger or burnt hamburger, they would try not to think about it.

"Somebody coming over to us," Griffiths said, and then, "He's in our uniform."

"Right," Pound said, and pulled the .45 on his belt out of its holster. Confederates in U.S. uniform, Confederates who talked like U.S. soldiers, had caused a lot of grief in Pennsylvania. "Make sure he's got the right countersign before you let him get close."

"I intend to, Sergeant." Griffiths sounded like a small boy reproving his mother. The barrel commander popped out of the cupola. "Foxx!" he said.

"Greenberg," the soldier answered. Michael Pound relaxed—mostly. That was the right countersign. The Confederates had their own football heroes. They were unlikely to know the names of a couple of U.S. running backs. Of course, they might have captured a prisoner and torn the countersign out of him. Pound didn't relax all the way.

He was glad to see Lieutenant Griffiths didn't, either. "That's close enough, soldier. I don't know you," Griffiths said. Pound grinned, down there where nobody but Cecil Bergman could see him. Maybe the lieutenant wasn't *such* a little boy after all.

"Yes, sir," the man in green-gray said. "Just wanted to let you know Featherston's fuckers have armor coming forward. One of our artillery-spotting airplanes saw the barrels."

"All right—thanks," Griffiths said. The soldier sketched a salute and left. Griffiths ducked down into the turret. "What do you think, Sergeant?"

Pound had enormous respect for artillery spotters. They flew low and slow, and often got shot down. But that had only so much to do with the lieutenant's question. "Well, sir, if he's legit we'll find out pretty soon," Pound said.

"Yes," Griffiths said. "But that kind of message can't hurt us, so he must be the real thing, right?"

"Well, no, sir, not quite," Pound answered patiently. "He could have had a harmless message just waiting in case we were on our toes. If he did, he's out there looking for somebody else to screw."

"Oh," Griffiths said in a hangdog voice. "I didn't think of that." A moment later, softly and to himself, he added, "Dammit!"

"Don't worry about it, sir," Pound said. "You did what you were supposed to do. Nobody could ask for anything more."

"I'm supposed to see more than you do, though." The barrel commander sounded fretful. "If I don't, then you ought to be the officer."

"I don't want to be an officer, sir," Pound said for what had to be the hundredth time in his career. Senior enlisted men were supposed to curb junior officers' enthusiasms. That was at least as important a part of their job as anything else. Most junior officers didn't know it. Pound didn't know how to say it without offending the lieutenant. If he didn't say anything, Griffiths couldn't get his ass in a sling. He kept quiet.

A few minutes later, the Confederates laid on an artillery barrage. Griffiths kept the hatch up on the cupola as long as he could. When gas rounds started gurgling in, though, he clanged it shut. "Button up!" he yelled over the intercom to the driver and bow gunner. Then he put on his gas mask. Resignedly, Pound did the same. With autumn here, wearing it wasn't so awful as it had been during the summer. Even so, it cut down his vision, and it was awkward to use with a gunsight. Lieutenant Griffiths had an even harder time seeing out the cupola periscopes through his mask's portholes.

Shrapnel clanged off the barrel's chassis. A barrage like this wasn't dangerous to armor except in case of an unlucky direct hit. Pound traversed the turret so the big gun—the pretty big gun, anyway—bore on the approach route he would use if he were a Confederate barrel commander. Griffiths set a hand on his shoulder to say he understood and approved.

Not much later, the barrel commander sang out: "Front!"

"Identified," Pound answered—he saw the ugly beast, too. "Range 350."

"You lined up on him so nicely, Sergeant," Griffiths said. "Go ahead and do the honors."

"Yes, sir," Pound said, and then, to Bergman, "Armor-piercing."

"Armor-piercing," the loader echoed, and slammed a round in the breech.

Pound adjusted the main armament's elevation just a little. The C.S. barrel came on, sure nothing nasty was in the neighborhood. Pound wouldn't have been that confident. The enemy machine was one of the new models. Maybe that made the commander feel invulnerable. Infantrymen in butternut loped alongside, automatic rifles at the ready.

The U.S. barrel's gun spoke. Pound's mask kept out the cordite fumes. The shell casing clanged on the fighting compartment floor. "Hit!" Lieutenant Griffiths yelled. "That's a hit!"

Smoke and fire spurted from the stricken C.S. barrel. The U.S. bow gunner opened up on the Confederate foot soldiers. One of them spun, his rifle flying out of his hands. He crumpled, right out there in the open. Other Confederate soldiers went down, too. They were more likely diving for cover than hit. Nobody came out of the barrel. Flames and a cloud of smoke burst from the cupola hatch. *Five men dead,* Pound thought, and then, *Well, they wanted to kill me. I like it better this way.*

He tapped Lieutenant Griffiths. "Sir, shouldn't we move out of here and find another firing position? Next enemy barrel that comes this way is going to know where we're at. Most ambushes only work once."

"Good point," the barrel commander said, and then, over the intercom to the driver, "Back us out, Mancatelli. Shift us over behind that pile of bricks to the left."

He hadn't been ready to move quite soon enough, but he'd had a backup firing position in mind when he did. It was a pretty good one, too; Michael Pound would have suggested it if Griffiths hadn't seen it himself. But he had. No, he wasn't such a helpless puppy after all.

After the barrel backed out of the garage, Mancatelli stayed in reverse long enough to move forward toward the secondary position. That kept the front glacis plate and the front of the turret facing the direction from which the barrel was likeliest to take fire. It avoided exposing the machine's thinner side armor. Those who served in barrels knew their weaknesses best—except, maybe, for those who tried to destroy them.

Peering out through the gunsight, Pound saw soldiers in butternut pointing to where the barrel had been. That probably meant they were warning it was still there. Nobody pointed toward the wreckage behind which it now hunkered down. If a machine weighing upwards of twenty tons could be sneaky, this one had just done the trick.

And here came a pair of Confederate barrels. "Front!" Griffiths sang out. "The one on the right, Sergeant."

"Identified," Pound acknowledged. "Bergman, we're going to have to do this fast as hell, because that other bastard will start shooting at us as soon as we nail his pal." He assumed he *would* nail the first barrel; he had all the arrogance a good gunner should. As he traversed the turret, he added, "So give me two rounds of armor-piercing, fast as you can, when I say, 'Now.' . . . *Now!*"

The first round clanged home. Pound fired. He got his hit, on the enemy barrel's turret. The second round was in the breech well before he'd brought the gun to bear on the second Confederate barrel—and the new turret had a hydraulic traverse, too, a feature he adored. His gun and the enemy's belched fire at the same instant. The C.S. barrel burst into flames. The Confederate's round slammed into the rubble, slammed through the rubble, but slowed enough so that it clanged off the U.S. barrel's glacis plate instead of penetrating.

"Two hits! Two!" Griffiths yelled. He pounded Pound on the back. Cecil Bergman thumped him on the leg, which was the only part of him the loader could reach. They both told him what a wonderful fellow he was.

"Thank you, sir," he said to Griffiths. Then he added, "I'd like to go on being wonderful a while longer, too, so could we please find another firing position?"

Griffiths laughed, but the barrel moved. That was all that really mattered.

Night came earlier now. As autumn deepened, U.S. bombers could spend more time above Richmond and other Confederate cities. Jake Featherston hated that as much as he loved C.S. bombers' being able to spend more time over cities in the United States.

Except for that, night and day meant little to him in the shelter under what was left of the Gray House. He slept in odd chunks, a couple of hours here, three there, and stayed awake in equally odd chunks between the stretches of sleep.

Everyone around him had to adapt to that. If Jake was awake at four in the morning and needed to talk to Nathan Bedford Forrest III, Forrest could damn well get his ass over to the Gray House at four in the morning. The same went for Ferd Koenig and Clarence Potter and Saul Goldman and Lulu and the rest of his inner circle. He seemed to thrive on his erratic sleep schedule. No one else did.

Lulu stuck her head into his underground office. She was paler than she should have been. She didn't get up into the sun and fresh air as often as she should these days. Jake suspected he was paler than he should have been, too. He didn't like being stuck down here, but he didn't like getting blown up, either.

"General Forrest is here to see you, Mr. President," she said.

"Well, send him on in," Jake replied. "Did he tell you what it was all about?" Forrest had asked for this meeting; Jake hadn't summoned him. The chief of the General Staff had been coy about saying just what was on his mind, too.

But Featherston's secretary shook her head. "No, sir."

"All right. Never mind. I'll find out," Jake said.

Nathan Bedford Forrest III strode into the office and saluted. "Mr. President," he said, and then, "Freedom!" and then, "May I shut the door?"

"Go ahead," Featherston answered. Forrest had a pistol in his holster. He was one of the handful of men allowed to bear arms in Jake's presence. Jake didn't think Forrest had come here to plug him. If Forrest had, he wouldn't waste time with the door. He'd just go ahead and do it. Jake waved him to a chair and asked, "What's up?"

"Mr. President, it seems to me we've done a pretty good job of making Pittsburgh useless to the damnyankees," Forrest said. "We've smashed it up so the steel production there's gone straight to hell. Most of what the mills do make, the USA can't get out of the city. Do we really need to hold the ground?"

"Damn straight we do," Jake said without even a heartbeat's hesitation. "We need to show those bastards we can beat 'em anywhere we please. And besides, the second we ease up, that town'll come back to life like a monster in a horror flick. You know it as well as I do, too."

Forrest looked unhappy. "Sir, what I know is, the damnyankees are chewing up men and barrels and airplanes we can't afford to lose. They've got more people than we do, dammit, and that's what they're using. Between us, we and the Yankees've knocked Pittsburgh cockeyed. They squat in the ruins and potshoot us."

"We'll lick 'em," Jake declared. "That's why every infantryman's got an automatic weapon. Put enough lead in the air and the other guys fall over dead."

"Sir, it's not that simple," Nathan Bedford Forrest III said. "Fighting like that, there are no good targets. They make us come to them, and then they make us pay for coming. We've got crack regiments knocked down to the size of a couple of companies. Units just aren't the same when you have to rebuild 'em after losses like that. It's the same way with barrels. They pick a spot, they wait, and then they shoot first. Their new models aren't as good as ours, but getting the first shot off counts for a hell of a lot, especially at short range. We're losing barrels as fast as we can build 'em. And we're losing veteran crews, too. That just isn't good terrain for armor to attack in."

"Whatever we're losing, they're losing worse," Jake said.

Forrest nodded, which didn't mean he agreed. "Yes, sir. They are," he said. "But they can afford it better. This is how we got in trouble in the last war."

He hadn't been old enough to fight in the last war. Jake had been in it from first day to last. That a pup should have the nerve to tell him what had happened and what hadn't . . . "We are going to take Pittsburgh," Featherston said in a voice like iron. "We *are*. We'll take it, and we'll hold it, and if the damnyankees want it back they'll have to kiss our ass. That's the way it's gonna be, General. Have you got it?"

"Yes, sir." Nathan Bedford Forrest III got to his feet. He stood at stiff attention. He saluted with machinelike precision. He did a smart about-turn and marched out of the President's office. He didn't slam the door. He closed it silently, which was even more sarcastic.

"I haven't convinced that man," Jake muttered. But Forrest would follow orders when he got them. That was what soldiers were for. And Pittsburgh *would* fall. And when it did, the United States would have to make peace. They couldn't very well fight a war if they didn't have anything to fight with, could they?

Sometimes the fellows in the fancy uniforms started flabbling over nothing. Forrest hadn't been one to do that, but he was doing it now. Jake had no doubts. He hardly ever had doubts. That was why he'd got where he was, why the Freedom Party had got where it was. People with doubts stopped before they ought to. If you just kept going, you'd get there. And he was going to get Pittsburgh.

Lulu came in. "Mr. President, Mr. Goldman is here to see you. He says it's urgent."

"Well, then, I'd better find out what he wants, eh?" Jake wondered what had gone wrong. Something must have, or Saul wouldn't come to his office uninvited.

The director of communications gave him the news in three bald words: "Another people bombing."

"Son of a bitch!" Jake said. "Where? How bad?"

"Jackson, Mississippi, sir," Goldman answered. "A waiter at a restaurant there last night. It was crowded—some kind of ladies' club function. Eleven known dead, at least forty hurt."

"Plus the nigger, of course," Featherston said.

"Yes, sir. Plus him. Two other waiters were also injured." Goldman paused. "How do you want to treat this, Mr. President? I hate to say it, but keeping quiet about what the Mormons are doing in the USA hasn't worked."

Jake knew why he hated to say it: saying it meant saying Jake Featherston was wrong. But Goldman *had* said it, and Jake couldn't very well claim not talking about people bombs had kept them from scarring the CSA. He made a discontented noise down deep in his throat. He wanted to say exactly that. But he had to deal with the truth, no matter how little he liked it.

He thought for a few seconds, then nodded to himself. "All right. Here's how we'll play it. You can splash this one all over the papers, Saul. A ladies' club, you say? Make it an atrocity story to end all atrocity stories, then. Nigger murders Confederate white women! That'll make people's blood boil. And you can let folks know all the coons'll pay for what that one bastard went and did."

Goldman didn't always show everything he thought. By the way he brightened now, that was what he'd wanted to hear, and he'd wanted very much to hear it. "Yes, sir, Mr. President!" he said, enthusiasm bubbling in his voice. "That sounds like just the right line to take. I'll handle everything. Don't you worry about it."

"I don't," Jake said simply. "If I worried about the way you did your job, Saul, somebody else would be doing it, and you can take that to the bank."

"Uh, yes, sir," Goldman said. Jake didn't want him scared, so he made himself smile. That did the trick. Goldman got to his feet and said, "I'll get right on it. If you'll excuse me . . . ?"

"Go on, go on," Featherston said indulgently. The director of communications hurried away. Jake got on the telephone. "Ferd? . . . You heard about the shit that happened in Jackson? . . . Yeah, Saul told me just now. Eleven dead plus the nigger! Jesus Christ! . . . How fast can you get the Party mobilized to help the cops and soldiers? . . . That quick? Good! . . . By this time Thursday, then, I don't want one nigger left in Jackson—not one, you hear me? And when they get where they're going, I don't want 'em hanging around, either . . . You see to it, that's all. 'Bye." He hung up—he slammed down the telephone, as a matter of fact.

He wasted a few seconds swearing at the Mormons. Those damned fanatics had come up with a weapon other fanatics could use. Mississippi and Alabama had been in revolt since he took office, and they hadn't been what anybody would call calm even before that. Too damn many coons, that was all there was to it. Well, he aimed to thin 'em out. And what he aimed at, he got.

He wondered whom Lulu would announce when she came in again. Instead of announcing anybody, she asked, "When was the last time you ate something, Mr. President?"

"Why—" Before Jake could finish talking, his stomach let out a rumble you could hear across the room. "Been a while, I guess," he said sheepishly.

"I'll get the kitchens to send you something." She wagged a finger at him. "You've got to take care of yourself, you know."

"Right," Jake said. "I have been busy, you know." He was amazed at how defensive he sounded. He could ream out the chief of the General Staff and stop him in his tracks. His own secretary? That was a whole different story. What made the difference? Lulu was right, and Nathan Bedford Forrest III damn well wasn't. So he told himself, anyhow.

Not ten minutes later, Lulu came back with a tray with two thick roast-beef sandwiches, potato salad, and a bottle of beer. Jake got outside the food in nothing flat. He did feel better afterwards. He wasn't about to admit it to her. On the other hand, he didn't have to—she would already know.

His restless energy burned off what he ate and left him with the same lanky frame he'd had half a lifetime before. He knew he wasn't as strong as he had been then, though. He wasn't fat, but his muscles had gone soft and slack. He didn't get the exercise he once had. Manhandling a field gun was a lot tougher physically than being President of the CSA and running things from behind a desk.

"I ought to put in time every day at . . . something hard, anyway," he muttered to himself. "Something, dammit." When you got past fifty, you had to take care of yourself the way you took care of a motorcar. You'd break down if you didn't, and replacement parts for your carcass were mighty hard to come by.

But he had no idea what to do to keep fit. He couldn't imagine himself playing golf or riding a bicycle or anything like that. Plain old calisthenics, like the ones from his Army days, were too boring to stand without a drill sergeant making you do them. And where would he find the time, anyway? He didn't have time to do everything he needed to do now.

He muttered again, this time blasphemously. He knew what would happen. He *wouldn't* find the time, and then six months or a year from now he'd be even angrier and more disgusted with himself, because he'd be that much further out of shape. He didn't have any good answers, though. The only way he could find the time to exercise was to stop being President. He wasn't about to do that.

Some of his pilots took pep pills to stay awake when they needed to fly mission after mission after mission. He'd always stayed away from those. Coffee and his own drive kept him going. But if coffee and his own drive flagged . . .

He shrugged. It was something to think about, anyway. He didn't have to make up his mind once and for all right this minute. If he ever decided he needed those pills, he could get 'em.

Richmond. Capitol Square. A cool, gray, fall day, with the smell of burning leaves in the air—along with other, less pleasant, smells of burning and death. Clarence Potter sat on a bench in the bomb-cratered square and looked at the enormous pyramids of sandbags surrounding the great statues of George Washington and Albert Sidney Johnston. The Egyptians wouldn't have been ashamed of pyramids like those. So far, they'd done their job. Despite all the damnyankee bombing raids, both statues remained more or less intact.

The Confederate Capitol couldn't be sandbagged. It looked more like a ruin from the days of Greece and Rome than a place where important things happened. And important things didn't happen there anymore. Congress met somewhere else these days—exactly where was classified. Potter wasn't sure why. What difference did it make? Even if the USA blew Congress clean off the map, what difference would it make? Jake Featherston and the Freedom Party ran the CSA these days; Congress was a rubber stamp and a sounding board, and that was about it.

Potter lit a cigarette, adding more smoke to the air that had already made him cough twice. He looked at his watch. The man he was supposed to meet here was late, and he shouldn't have been. Had something gone wrong?

But when he looked up, Nathan Bedford Forrest III was picking his way across the battered ground. Forrest already had a cigarette going, the coal furiously red. He sat down next to Potter and smoked in angry silence for a minute or so. Then he said, "I do thank you kindly for coming."

"I should get out and about more often," Potter answered. "Keeps me fresh. What's on your mind?"

Instead of answering right away, Forrest lit another cigarette. He smoked it halfway down, blowing out an almost continuous stream of smoke. At last, he asked, "Do you . . . think Jake Featherston's got all his oars in the water?"

Whatever Potter had expected, that wasn't it. He looked around again to make sure nobody was paying extra attention to a couple of officers sitting on a park bench. Seeing nothing and no one out of the ordinary, he said, "Well, I haven't always been in love with the man"— which was a bigger understatement than Nathan Bedford Forrest III might realize—"but I never thought he was ready for the straitjacket, either. How come you do?"

Forrest hesitated again. Potter had no trouble figuring out why—if he went telling tales to the President, the chief of the General Staff was a dead man. But Forrest must have known that before he asked to meet with Potter. The Intelligence officer gestured impatiently, as if to say, *Piss or get off the pot.* Unhappily, Forrest said, "Well, things aren't going as well as we wish they were in Pittsburgh."

"That makes me unhappy, but it doesn't make Jake Featherston a candidate for the booby hatch." Potter's voice was desert-dry.

"No, of course not." Nathan Bedford Forrest III looked down at the ground between his feet. He bent and picked up something: a little chunk of shrapnel from a bomb casing. With a grimace, he tossed it away. "But a few days ago I went and asked him if maybe we wouldn't do better just wrecking Pittsburgh than throwing away more men and matériel than we can afford."

"And?" Potter asked. "There's always an 'and' to a story like that."

"Oh, there is," Forrest said. "And he damn near threw me out of his office—damn near threw me through the door, matter of fact. We're going to take Pittsburgh, take it away from the damnyankees, come hell or high water, no matter how many soldiers or barrels or airplanes we lose. He . . . just wouldn't listen to me. It was like he *couldn't* listen to me. His mind was made up, and nothing anybody could say would change it."

"And so?" Potter said. "The President's never been what you'd call good at listening to other people or changing his mind. I don't suppose he'd be President if he were, because he would have quit trying a long time ago." Not liking Jake Featherston didn't mean you could ignore his furious, driving, almost demonic energy.

"This wasn't like a stubborn man talking," Forrest said—stubbornly. "This was like—like a crazy man talking." He looked relieved at finally getting that out. "By God, Potter, it really was."

"All right. Let's say it was." Potter knew he sounded as if he might be humoring a lunatic himself. "If it was, what do you propose to do about it? Bear in mind that we're in the middle of a small disagreement with our neighbors right now." His wave encompassed the sandbagged statues, the cratered square, the ruins of the Confederate Capitol.

Nathan Bedford Forrest III's eyes followed his hand. Forrest grimaced again, as if he hadn't noticed how things were till then. Maybe he hadn't—maybe he hadn't let himself. "Jesus Christ, if we followed a nut into this war—"

"You didn't reckon he was a nut as long as things went our way," Potter said brutally. Forrest flinched. Potter went on, "Do you really think this is the time to start plotting a *coup d'état*? That's what it would have to be, you know. You'd have to take him down. He'd never leave or change on his own."

"I do understand that," Forrest said. "That's why I wanted to talk to you. You were a red-hot Whig even after it wasn't safe to be a Whig anymore." He did know a fair bit about Potter's past, then. "If anybody could see the need for putting our house in order, I reckoned you'd be the man. For God's sake, Potter, we can't afford to lose another war. It would ruin us for good."

"This one's a long way from lost. We may get Pittsburgh yet." Part of Potter wanted to leap at any chance to cast down Jake Featherston. That made him even more careful about what he said than he would have been otherwise. He didn't *think* Forrest was trying to entrap him—the other officer sounded too upset for that—but he wasn't a hundred percent sure. *When three men plot, one is a fool and two are government spies.* What about two men?

I'm already a spy, Potter thought. He laughed inside, though he held his face straight. But he was a spy for the Confederate States. He wasn't a spy for Jake Featherston and the Freedom Party, and he was damned if he'd turn into one. And if he did ever turn into such a debased creature, he doubtless *would* be damned.

"So we may." Forrest spoke cautiously, too. "But how likely do you think that is, what with the way things look now?"

"I don't know," Potter said: the exact and literal truth. He thought about Henderson FitzBelmont over at Washington University. He thought about 235 and 238, and the trouble FitzBelmont and his fellow physicists were having in separating the one from the other. He had no idea whether Forrest knew about FitzBelmont's project. He couldn't ask, either, for fear the chief of the General Staff didn't.

If the physicists could build their bomb, the CSA would win the war. Drop one of those on Pittsburgh, and it wouldn't cause problems anymore. Drop one on Philadelphia, one on New York City, one on Boston, one on Pontiac . . . That would knock the United States flat and kick them in the teeth while they were down.

Then Potter thought about the U.S. project in Washington State. He thought about bombs blowing Richmond and Atlanta and Louisville and Birmingham and New Orleans and Dallas off the map. It was a race, a race into the unknown. Whoever first played Prometheus and stole fire from the gods would drop that fire on his enemies' heads.

He tried to imagine fighting a war where both sides had bombs like that. His mind recoiled like a horse shying at a snake. That wouldn't be submachine guns at two paces. It would be flamethrowers at two paces.

And what sort of weapons would you use in the war after *that* one? To his surprise, the answer formed almost as soon as the question did.

You would fight that next war with rocks.

"We're on the tiger's back right now, and we've got hold of his ears," he said, not knowing and not much caring whether he was talking about Featherston or about the war. "If you tell me that's not where we want to be, I won't argue with you. But if you say we'd do better letting go and jumping off, I have to say I think you're out of your mind—sir. Do you want Don Partridge trying to run things?" He supposed he'd been talking about Jake after all.

Nathan Bedford Forrest III hissed like a wounded snake himself. "Damn you, Potter, you don't fight fair."

"I didn't know that was part of the requirement," Potter said. "I thought the only thing you had to do was win."

"That's it," Forrest agreed. "And that's what I wanted to ask you. Do you think we can win the war with Jake Featherston in charge of things?"

"Do you think we can win without him?" Potter asked in return. "Do you think we can even get out of the war without him?" He didn't ask about getting out of the war with Featherston still in the Gray House. That wouldn't happen. Period. Exclamation point, even.

Forrest sat on the bench with a faraway look in his eyes. Potter suspected his own face bore a similar expression. How would the Confederate States do if they had to fight on without that pillar of fire at their heart? No, he didn't love Featherston—far from it. He did, reluctantly, respect him.

Slowly, the chief of the General Staff got to his feet. "Maybe we'll talk about this another time," he said. "I hope we don't, but maybe we will." He tipped his hat and walked away.

A starling perched in a shattered tree not far from where Potter sat. It chirped metallically. The shimmering summer gloss was off its feathers; it wore a duller autumn plumage. Potter swore under his breath. The gloss was off the war, too. He thought of one question he hadn't asked himself before. Could the CSA win even *with* Jake Featherston at the helm?

Potter had thought so when the barrels charged from the Ohio up to Lake Erie. He hadn't believed he was guilty of the old Confederate error of underestimating how tough the damnyankees were. He hadn't believed it, but evidently he was, because the United States refused to fold up. Would even the fall of Pittsburgh knock them out of the fight? Again, he just didn't know.

And did Nathan Bedford Forrest III know what he was talking about? Was the President of the Confederate States of America nuttier than a five-dollar fruitcake? Potter shook his head. That was the wrong question. If Featherston *was* nuttier than a five-dollar fruitcake, what about it? Being out of your tree didn't necessarily disqualify you from holding office. Some people said only a crazy man would want to be President of the CSA. Potter wasn't one of them, but he could see their point.

Was Featherston crazy enough to be unfit to lead during wartime? That was what it came down to. Potter would have loved to believe it. He wouldn't have been sorry for an excuse to throw Jake Featherston out on his ear—no, to kill him, because he wouldn't go without a fight, and he'd fight hard. He always did. Forrest said he'd seemed crazy when he refused to pull back from Pittsburgh.

Maybe the chief of the General Staff was right. But Potter wasn't ready to upset the Confederate applecart on a maybe. Featherston was at least as likely to be crazy like a fox. He'd proved that time and again. Taking Pittsburgh might prove it once more.

"Better to wait," Potter murmured. Acting was irrevocable, and he didn't think the time ripe. If going into Pittsburgh proved a fiasco . . . Well, so what? Did that mean Featherston had gone around the bend, or just that he'd made a mistake?

Did it matter? If Pittsburgh proved a fiasco, the Confederate States were in trouble either way. Somebody would have to take the blame. Who else but Jake Featherston then?

Nodding to himself, Potter got to his feet with one more thing to worry about. If Pittsburgh proved a fiasco, who took the blame might not matter, either.

To say Jefferson Pinkard was not a happy man failed to use the full power of language. Somebody in Richmond got a brainstorm. Who got to make that brainstorm real? Pinkard did. Some damnfool Negro in Jackson blew himself up, and a bunch of white women with him? Yeah, all right, he was a dirty, stinking son of a bitch. But get rid of all the Negroes in Jackson on account of him? At once? That was lunacy. That was also what Jeff had orders to do.

When the telegram came in, he telephoned Ferdinand Koenig and asked, "How many niggers are we talking about here?"

"Hell, I don't know off the top of my head," the Attorney General answered, which did not fill Jeff with confidence. Koenig said, "I'll get back to you this afternoon. You want to know what you're getting into, do you?"

"You might say so," Pinkard said tightly. "Yeah, you just might."

Ferdinand Koenig was as good as his word. Just after Jeff's lunch, he got another telegram. TWENTY-FIVE OR THIRTY THOUSAND. F.K., it said. What Pinkard said when he saw that had an *f* and a *k* in it, too, with a couple of other letters in between. He said several other things right afterwards, most of them even hotter than what he'd started with.

Once his spleen was well and truly vented—once it had blown off about three counties' worth of steam—he called Vern Green into his office and gave the guard chief the news. "Well, Jesus Christ!" Green said. "We got to get rid o' these niggers? We don't just try and stuff 'em on in here?"

"That's what the orders are," Jeff said grimly.

"How soon they gonna start coming?" Green asked.

"I don't exactly know—not exactly," Pinkard answered. "But it won't be long—I sure as hell know that. Fast as they can throw 'em on trains and ship 'em out here. A few days—a week, tops."

"You figuring on using the bathhouses *and* the trucks?"

Jeff nodded. "Don't see how we've got even a prayer of doing it if we don't. You get the 'dozer crews out to the other place, too, and have 'em dig lots of new trenches. If we're doing all of Jackson, that'll take up some room." He didn't talk about mass graves, not in so many words.

The guard chief followed him even so. "I'll see to it," he promised. "We're gonna be busy as shit, ain't we?"

"No," Jeff answered. Green looked at him in surprise. He condescended to explain: "We'll be a hell of a lot busier than that."

"Oh. Yeah," Green said. "Wish to God I could tell you you were wrong, but that's how it's gonna be, all right." He scowled. "We'll have a fuck of a time keeping the rest of the niggers from figuring out what's goin' on, too."

"Uh-huh. That already crossed my mind," Pinkard said. "Don't know what we can do about it. We got orders on this—orders right from the top." Ferdinand Koenig wasn't *the* top, of course, but he was only one short step down. And he'd made it real clear the President of the CSA wanted every black from Jackson wiped off the face of the earth. What Jake Featherston wanted, Jake Featherston got.

Green sighed. "Well, we'll just have to take care of that when it turns into a problem, that's all. In the meantime . . . In the meantime, I'll let the boys know a big pile of shit's rolling down the hill, and we're on the bottom." He got to his feet. "Freedom!"

"Freedom!" Jeff echoed. The guard chief left his office. Jeff pulled his copy of *Over Open Sights* off the shelf by his desk. He knew just the passage he was looking for: the one where Featherston talked about how killing off a few thousand Negroes before the Great War would have saved a lot of trouble during and after. Jeff nodded to himself. That was true, every word of it. When he read the words, he could hear Jake Featherston's hot, angry voice.

Even so, after a while he scratched his head and put down the book. This didn't seem the same as that. People on the outside would know Jackson's blacks had been sent away to camps, but that was all they would know. Even the Negroes already in the camps weren't supposed to know they'd never come out alive. So what, exactly, was the point?

But that did have an answer. The point was to get rid of as many spooks as the Freedom Party and the Confederate government could arrange to get rid of. Jeff didn't see anything wrong with what the Party wanted—just the opposite. But doing it in such a big lump made things work less smoothly than they might have, less smoothly than they should. Camp Determination's profile was going to look like a boa constrictor that had swallowed a big old pig. You'd be able to see the lump the pig made as it worked its way from one end of the snake to the other.

Both sides of the camp, men's and women's, were on edge even before the first trains rolled in out of the east. The Negroes knew something was going on, even if they didn't know what. They must have got that from the guards. Pinkard thought about reaming Vern Green out about it, but he didn't. The guards wouldn't have been human if they didn't pass on the feeling that something was cooking. They hadn't said what, for which Jeff was duly grateful.

He went out to watch his crews at work when the first train from Jackson came in. He was proud of them. They had a routine, and they stuck to it as much as they could. They hauled the luckless blacks off the train and separated them, men to the left, women and children off to the right. Then they went through the train and pulled out any Negroes who'd tried to get cute and hide. Then more blacks—men as close to trusties as Camp Determination held—removed the bodies of those who'd died on the way.

There were more of those than usual. The survivors moaned about how they'd been packed like sardines, about how they hadn't had anything to eat or drink. Most of them moaned about how they hadn't even been able to pack a carpetbag.

The guards did their best to soothe them. "Don't y'all worry 'bout a thing," a troop leader called reassuringly, smooth and confident as a preacher in the pulpit. "We're gonna ship some of you out to other camps right away, and we're gonna let the rest of you get cleaned up before we move you. You do what people tell you, and you'll be just fine."

"This way!" guards yelled. "This way!" The Negroes obeyed. They were too dazed and battered not to—and the guards had automatic weapons to make sure they didn't get out of line. Most of them didn't even try.

One man did ask, "How come we gonna git shipped somewheres else when we only just got here?" Nobody answered him, and he didn't ask twice.

"Listen up, y'all!" an officer shouted. "You're gonna be in two groups. One group goes on to a camp by Lubbock, the other one goes down by El Paso." There were camps in both places, small ones. They were there mainly to keep Negroes from panicking when they heard something like that. The officer went on, "Those of you bound for the Lubbock camp, we're gonna bathe and delouse y'all right here, on account of we got bigger bathhouses than they do at that camp. Y'all goin' to El Paso, they'll take care of that when you get there."

Pinkard and his top officers had hammered out the story in the time before the trains started coming in. He didn't like it; it had holes you could throw a dog through. But it gave some kind of explanation, anyway, and the Negroes wouldn't have much time to wonder and worry.

Guards started going along the lines of Negroes. They would say, "Lubbock," to some and, "El Paso," to others. Every so often, they would add, "Remember where you're supposed to go, or you'll catch hell!"

When everybody had an assignment, officers yelled, "El Paso, this way!" and, "Lubbock, *this* way!" Two columns of men and two of women and children formed. "Now get moving!" the officers shouted.

A fat black woman let out a screech: "My husband goin' to de one place, an' I is goin' to de other one!" The baby she held in her arms wailed.

"Can't do anything about it now," a troop leader told her. "When you get where you're goin', you talk to the people there. They'll do the paperwork and transfer you."

She still grumbled, but she seemed happier. Pinkard craned his neck to see who that troop leader was. Hobart Martin, that was his name. He'd won himself a commendation letter, sure as hell. That kind of complaint could have caused real trouble, maybe even a riot. It was something the guards hadn't thought of, and they should have. Of course separating families made people jump and shout. But Martin had calmed the woman down, and his words kept other men and women from raising a stink. As long as they thought everything would be taken care of . . .

Pinkard nodded to himself. Everything would be taken care of, all right.

He went with the men who believed they were bound for El Paso. They had to march—or rather, shamble—all the way through the camp to get to the bathhouse that wasn't. He'd posted guards with automatic rifles on both sides of their route. He didn't think they would try to break away, but he worried that the present inmates might try to rescue them. A show of force ahead of time was the best thing he could think of to keep that from happening.

"Move along! Move along!" guards shouted. "Don't hold up the line, or you're in trouble!" They were already in the worst trouble they could find, but they didn't know it. This whole charade was to keep them—and the present inmates—from finding out.

Hipolito Rodriguez stood there with a rifle at the ready. Like most men from the Confederate Veterans' Brigades, Hip liked a submachine gun better because it was lighter and smaller. But Jeff wanted the guards to have weapons with real stopping power today. He nodded to Rodriguez. The Sonoran nodded back. Then he looked away, scanning the inmates for any sign of trouble. He knew how things worked. The more you showed that you were ready for anything, the less likely you were to run into trouble.

Jeff nodded to himself when the last black man passed through the gateway separating the main camp from the bathhouse. Getting the line through the camp was the hardest, most worrisome part. Already, trucks were taking away the first Negroes who thought they were heading for El Paso. Their true journey would be a lot shorter—and a good thing, too, because Jeff would need those trucks again pretty damn quick to handle more blacks.

He nodded again when the door to the bathhouse closed behind the last Negro man in the queue. Wasn't there some poem that went, *All hope abandon, ye who enter here?* Once that door closed, those Negroes lost their last hope. They'd get herded into the big room that wasn't a delousing chamber, and that would be that.

When was the next train coming? Would the camp be able to handle it? Could the crew get the corpses out of the alleged bathhouse, could the trucks get back from the mass grave, fast enough? They could. They did. By the time the next trainload of Negroes from Jackson stopped on the spur between the men's and women's camps, the guards were ready.

The next week was the busiest time Jeff remembered. He and his crew ran on sleep snatched in the intervals between trains and on endless cigarettes and cups of coffee. Every storage facility in the camp overflowed, even if relatively few of the Negroes had brought baggage with them. Where those Negroes went, they didn't need baggage.

And at the end of it, Jefferson Pinkard looked at Vern Green and said, "By God, we reduced that population."

"Sure as hell did," the guard chief agreed. Jeff pulled a pint of whiskey out of his desk drawer. He took a snort, then passed the pint to Green. The number two man at Camp Determination also drank. After what they'd just been through, they'd damn well earned the booze.

Black clouds boiled up over Andersonville, Georgia. Where the sky wasn't black, it was an ugly yellow, the color of a fading bruise. The rising wind blew a lock of Jonathan Moss' hair into his eyes. He tossed his head. The wind got stronger. A raindrop hit him in the nose.

He looked around the prison-camp grounds. POWs were heading into the barracks as fast as they could. That looked like a hell of a good idea. The wind tugged at his clothes as he hurried toward shelter.

"Well, I'll be damned," one of the other prisoners said when he walked in. "Moss *does* have the sense to come in out of the rain."

POWs laughed. Hell, Moss laughed himself. In Andersonville, fun was where you found it, and you didn't have a lot of places to look. But Captain Nick Cantarella, who'd come in just ahead of Moss, said, "Noah would find someplace to hide from this. It looks like a bastard and a half out there."

"Worse than that storm this summer?" somebody said.

"I think maybe," Cantarella answered, and Moss found himself nodding. That had been a cloudburst to end all cloudbursts, yeah. It had also been a cloudburst to end all escape plans, at least for the time being. But whatever was building out there now looked downright vicious. The light was weird, almost flickering; it might have come from the trick-photography department of a bad horror film.

Somebody sitting close by a window said, "Son of a bitch!" Several people asked him what was going on. He pointed. "The guards are coming down from their towers and running like hell!"

"Jesus!" Moss said, which was one of the milder comments in the barracks. The gray-uniformed guards never left the towers unmanned. Never. They always wanted to be able to rake the camp with machine-gun fire. If they were bailing out now . . .

"Oh, fuck!" said the man by the window. Then he said something even worse: "Tornado!"

Somebody with a flat Indiana accent said, "Open the doors, quick! It'll try and suck all the air out of any building it comes close to. If the air can't get out, the buildings'll blow up." Moss, who'd shut the door behind him, quickly opened it again. The Midwesterner sounded like a man who knew what he was talking about.

POWs crowded toward windows to watch the twister. Moss didn't. He didn't want to be anywhere near glass that was liable to splinter and fly as if a bomb went off close by. "Godalmightydamn, will you look at that motherfucker!" somebody said, more reverently than otherwise.

"Wish to hell we had a storm cellar," somebody else put in. That made good sense. Moss wished for one, too. What they had were bar-racks built as flimsily as the Geneva Convention allowed, or maybe a little cheaper than that. If the tornado plowed into them, it wouldn't even notice. Everybody unlucky enough to be inside sure would, though.

He could hear it now, and feel it, too. It sounded like the world's biggest freight train heading straight for him. That wasn't really fair to the tornado. If it ran into a train, it would scatter railroad cars like jackstraws. "The Lord is my shepherd—" somebody began.

The Twenty-third Psalm seemed right. "The Battle Hymn of the Republic" might have fit even better, because the Lord was doing some serious trampling out there. Wind tugged at Moss, trying to pull him out the open door. The officer who'd suggested opening it knew what was what. That air would have escaped anyway. With the doors open, it could get out without forcing itself out.

Moss stepped away from the door. The flow wasn't strong enough to keep him from doing that. He looked over his shoulder and got a glimpse of the onrushing funnel cloud. That made him do a little pray-ing of his own. He'd known one or two tornadoes when he lived near Chicago, but only one or two. They visited downstate Illinois more often.

And they visited the CSA.

"Looks like it's not gonna hit us," somebody said—shouted, actually, because that was the only way anyone could make himself heard through the roar and scream of the wind.

Maybe the man who'd yelled was a bombardier. Whoever he was, he seemed able to gauge what that horrid funnel would do. Instead of blowing the barracks to hell and gone, it walked along a couple of hundred yards away. A few windows blew out, but that was all the damage they took. The twister snarled away toward the east.

"Lord!" a POW said, which summed things up pretty damn well.

Nick Cantarella looked outside. He said, "My God," too, but in an altogether different tone of voice. The captain from New York City pointed. "That fucker just blew half the wire around the camp all the way to the moon."

Prisoners rushed to the windows, those that still had glass and those that didn't. Cantarella wasn't wrong. The tornado cared no more about barbed wire and guard towers than it did about anything else in its path. Three men had the same thought at the same time: "Let's get out of here!"

That sounded good to Jonathan Moss. He even had some brown Confederate bills—no, they called them banknotes down here—in his pocket. The CSA played by the rules of war, and paid captive officers at the same rate as their own men of equivalent grade. Why not? In camp, the notes were only paper, good for poker games but not much else.

"If they catch you, they can punish you," Colonel Summers warned. The senior U.S. officer went on, "We're a long way from the border. Odds of making it back to the USA aren't good. You might be smarter just sitting this one out."

Summers had to say something like that. Moss understood as much. Someone needed to be careful and responsible and adult. Captain Cantarella put the other side of things in perspective: "Anybody who's gonna go better get his ass in gear right now. Those Confederate bastards won't waste a hell of a lot of time hunkered down wherever they're at. They'll come out, and they'll have guns."

That made up Moss' mind for him. He wasn't the first one out the door, but he was only a couple of steps behind the guy who was. Cantarella was hard on his heels. "How did the escape committee sign up a tornado?" Moss asked him.

Cantarella's grin was swarthy and stubbly and full of exhilaration. "Hey, Mother Nature owed us one after the way that thunderstorm fucked us over. Every once in a while, I think maybe there's a God."

Moss had thought so, too, till that Canuck's bomb robbed him of Laura and Dorothy. Believing in anything but revenge came hard after that. He said, "You want to stick together? Two heads may be better than one."

"Long as we can, anyway," Cantarella answered. "We may have to split up somewhere down the line, but I'm with you till then." He stuck out his hand. Moss shook it.

Out past the wire they went, out past the wreckage of the guard towers. A machine gun stuck up from a clump of bushes. "Wish it was a rifle," Moss said. "Piece like that, though, it's too heavy to lug."

"Yeah," Cantarella said. "What we gotta do now is, we gotta make tracks. Somethin' tells me we don't have a whole lotta time." His clotted accent was about as far from a C.S. drawl as it could be.

The something that told him was no doubt common sense. "You think we have a better chance heading north, or east toward the ocean?" Moss asked.

"Depends," the other U.S. officer said. "If you figure our Navy's got boats or ships or whatever the hell out in the Atlantic, we haul ass that way. God knows it's closer. But if we gotta sail up the coast, fuhgeddaboutit, unless you're a hell of a lot better sailor than I am."

"John Paul Jones I'm not," Moss answered, and Cantarella laughed. What the Italian said made an unfortunate amount of sense. Moss faced the general direction of Atlanta. "North, then."

"Right. Maybe we can steal some clothes so we look like a coupla ordinary Confederate assholes, buy train tickets, and get up to Richmond or somewheres in style," Cantarella said.

They carried no papers. They wore elderly U.S. uniforms (Cantarella did remember that). They had the wrong accent. They probably didn't have enough money for train tickets. But for those minor details, it struck Moss as a terrific plan. He didn't criticize, not out loud. He liked the idea of hoofing it across Georgia, the Carolinas, and Virginia no better than Cantarella did.

They hadn't got very far into the pine woods north of Andersonville before gunshots rang out behind them. "Ahhh, shit," Cantarella said, which summed up Moss' feelings, too. The guards had noticed prisoners escaping, then.

Without Nick Cantarella, Moss figured he would have been recaptured in short order. The younger man was an infantry officer, and actually knew what he was doing as he clumped along on the ground. He and Moss splashed along creeks to throw hounds off the scent. "Didn't they do this in *Uncle Tom's Cabin*?" Moss said.

"Beats me," Cantarella answered. "All I know is, this shit works."

Maybe it did. Moss heard several more bursts of gunfire, but he didn't see any C.S. prison guards or soldiers. He did get tired. His feet got sore. He knew he was slowing Cantarella down. "If you want to go on without me, it's all right," he said.

"Nah." Cantarella shook his head. "Like you said, two heads are better than one. 'Sides, you can come closer to talking like these assholes than I can."

"I wonder," Moss said. Midwest overlain by Canadian didn't sound much more Confederate than strong New York City. He figured he'd worry about that when he had to, not before. He had other things to worry about now: not only his feet but also the growing emptiness in his belly. If this were a planned escape, he would have brought food along. Now, he and Cantarella would be raiding henhouses before long. That would leave a trail a blind idiot, or even a Confederate guard, could follow.

They came out of the woods into cotton country. Moss had always pictured swarms of darkies in the fields with hoes. It wasn't like that. Except for a cultivator chugging along in the distance, the countryside was eerily empty. Cantarella had the same thought. "Where'd all the smokes go?" he said.

"Beats me." Moss had trouble believing the atrocity stories he'd heard. Seeing that landscape without people, though, he had less trouble than before.

He and Nick went on up a poorly paved road till nightfall. Then they lay down by the roadside. All they had to cover themselves with were cotton plants. That would help give them away, too. But it got chilly after the sun went down. The plants weren't good blankets, but they were better than nothing. Moss wasn't sure he could fall asleep on bare ground. Five minutes later, he was snoring.

Morning twilight turned the eastern sky gray when he woke. But the growing light wasn't what roused him. Those voices weren't just part of his dreams. He saw three men silhouetted against the sky. They all carried rifles.

He nudged Nick, who'd stayed asleep. "Wake up!" he hissed. "We're caught!"

One of the armed men came up to them. In a low voice, he asked, "You some o' the Yankees what got outa Andersonville?"

"That's right." Suddenly hope flared in Moss. "Are you . . . fighting against the Confederate government?"

"Bet your ass, ofay," the rifle-toting Negro answered. "How you like to he'p us?"

Moss looked toward Nick Cantarella. Cantarella was looking back at him. Moss didn't think it was the sort of invitation they could refuse, not if they wanted to keep breathing. He got to his feet, ignoring creaks and crunches. "I think we just joined the underground," he said. Nick Cantarella nodded.

"Should auld acquaintance be forgot,
And never brought to mind?
Should auld acquaintance be forgot,
And days o' auld lang syne!"

Scipio didn't think he'd ever heard "Auld Lang Syne" sung when it wasn't New Year's Eve. He didn't think he'd ever heard it sung in such a variety of accents, either—none of them the least bit Scots.

Jerry Dover grinned at the cooks and waiters and busboys and dishwashers he'd bossed for so long. "I'd like to tell y'all one thing," he said. They waited expectantly. His grin got wider. "Fuck you, you sons of bitches!"

They laughed like loons. Scipio laughed as loud as anybody, but his mirth had a bitter edge. With Jerry Dover gone, all the Negroes who worked for the Huntsman's Lodge were liable to get fucked. Who could say what the new manager would be like? Would he take care of his people the way Dover had? Scipio supposed it wasn't impossible. He also knew only too well it wasn't likely.

"You go kill them damnyankees, Mistuh Dover! Shoot 'em down like the yellow dogs they is!" a cook shouted. He swigged from a bottle of champagne. Jerry Dover's sendoff was going to put a dent in the restaurant's liquor stock.

"If I have to pick up a gun, this country's in deeper shit than anybody ever figured," Dover said, and got another laugh. "It's the Quarter-master Corps for me."

That actually made good sense. The Confederate Army was doing it anyway. Jerry Dover knew everything there was to know about feeding people. Feeding them in the Army was different from doing it in a restaurant, but not all that different. He'd help the CSA more doing that than he would in the infantry, and somebody must have realized as much.

Scipio had an almost-empty glass in his hand. A moment later, as if by magic, it wasn't empty anymore. He sipped. He had had bourbon in there. This was Scotch. He'd feel like hell in the morning. Right now, morning felt a million miles away.

"T'ank you, *Señor* Dover. You give us work." That was José, one of the dishwashers from the Empire of Mexico. He'd taken a job from a black man. Scipio wanted to hate him because of that—wanted to and found he couldn't. José was only trying to make a living for himself, and he worked like a man with a gun to his head. How could you hate somebody like that?

"For he's a jolly good fellow!" The staff at the Huntsman's Lodge started singing again, louder and more raucously than ever. In some ways, blacks and whites in the CSA understood one another and got along with one another pretty well . . . or they would have, if the Freedom Party hadn't got in the way.

Jerry Dover hoisted his own glass. He'd been drinking as hard as his help. "You bastards are good," he said. "Sometimes I don't reckon y'all know how good you are. I'm gonna have to whip some new folks into shape, and I don't figure they'll be a patch on you."

"Take us with you!" somebody behind Scipio shouted. In an instant, everyone was yelling it: "Take us with you! Take us with you!"

"Hell, I would if I could," Dover said. "I don't think that'll happen, though."

The clamor went on all the same. Scipio understood why: if these black men were busy cooking for soldiers and serving them, they'd be less likely to go to a camp. Anything—anything at all—seemed better than going to a camp.

"I don't want anybody to get in trouble for being out too late," Dover said after a while. The response to that was angry and profane. This was a night of license, and would have been even if not fueled by booze. Whatever the restaurant staff did short of burning the place down, he would let them get away with it.

Aurelius tapped Scipio on the arm. "How you like bein' an old man at a young men's fling?" the other veteran waiter asked.

"Long as I's here," Scipio answered. "Long as I's anywhere."

"Amen," Aurelius said.

Scipio beckoned him off to one side. Once the two old men had put a little distance between themselves and the rest of the staff, Scipio said, "Tell you what I was afeared of. I was afeared of a people bomb. I done been through two auto bombs. Don't reckon I'd las' if somethin' else blow up around me."

"Auto bombs is nasty business," Aurelius said. "People bombs . . . People bombs is worse." He shuddered. "How you walk in somewhere, knowin' you got 'splosives strapped on you? All you got to do is click the switch or whatever the hell—and then you is splattered all over the walls."

"Way things is nowadays, lotta niggers reckon they gots nothin' to lose," Scipio said.

Aurelius nodded. "I know that. I don't like it. If it ain't a judgment on the Confederate States of America, I dunno what would be. But still, no matter how bad things is, is they ever bad enough to blow your ownself up?"

"Dat nigger in Jackson done thought so," Scipio said. "Damn nigger was a waiter, too. My tips ain't been the same since he done it."

"Your tips ain't all that's hurtin'," Aurelius reminded him. "They put all the niggers in Jackson on trains an' ship 'em off to camps. All of 'em, jus' like that." He snapped his fingers. "An' the Freedom Party don't try to hide it or nothin'. Hell, the Freedom Party braggin' to beat the band."

"Not too long after de Great War end, I's in de park takin' de air, an' who should come make a speech but Jake Featherston?" Scipio shuddered at the memory, even if it was almost a quarter of a century old. "Everybody reckon he nothin' but a crazy man. I reckon de same thing back then. But he scare de piss outa me even so."

Aurelius looked around to see if anyone was listening to them. Once he was satisfied, he said, "That Featherston, he *ain't* nothin' but a crazy man."

"No." Regretfully, Scipio shook his head. "He a crazy man, sho', but he ain't nothin' *but* a crazy man. You hear what I's sayin'? Nobody who's nothin' but a crazy man kin do as much harm as Jake Featherston."

Aurelius considered that. He also considered his glass, which was empty. When he too shook his head, Scipio wasn't sure whether he mourned the empty glass or the Freedom Party's devastation. Then he said, "Well, you is right, an' I wish you wasn't." He could do something about getting more whiskey. Nobody on the North American continent had had much luck doing anything about Jake Featherston.

Scipio and Aurelius reeled back to the Terry together. No explosions marred the night. No automobiles going up in fireballs threw jagged metal and blazing gasoline in all directions. No desperate Negroes threw nails and chunks of themselves every which way. Except for a whip-poor-will's mournful call, everything was peaceful and quiet.

"You damn coons are late," grumbled the cop who opened the gate for them. "Even for y'all, you're late."

"Sorry, suh," Scipio slurred. "We was sayin' good-bye to our boss. He goin' into de Army."

The cop's left hand had only the thumb and index finger. You didn't notice straight off, probably because he kept that hand in his pocket whenever he could. "Good luck to him," he said. "You spooks don't know when you're well off. You don't got to worry about shit like that."

Was he right? Scipio didn't think so. If Negroes had the same privileges and rights as whites, wouldn't they be glad to pick up rifles to help defend the Confederacy? It looked that way to him. But if they had all those privileges and rights, the Confederacy they were defending would be a very different place. Just for openers, it would be a place where Jake Featherston could never get elected, and neither could anyone like him.

Well, it wasn't like that, and it never would be. The thump of the gate behind Scipio and Aurelius proved as much, and proved it all too well.

He did have a headache when he got up. Cassius scowled at him. "How can you have a good time sayin' so long to a damn ofay?" his son demanded.

With a sigh, Scipio answered, "It ain't as simple as you think it is."

"Oh, yeah," Cassius said scornfully—he'd got to the point where he would quarrel with anything Scipio said just because Scipio said it. "How come?"

"On account of I be dead if Jerry Dover don't want me alive an' workin' there," Scipio said. "On account of you an' your sister an' your mama go to a camp—or else you jus' end up dead, too."

"Jerry Dover still a damn ofay," Cassius said.

"Fine." Scipio didn't feel like arguing with him, especially not with a head pounding like a drop forge. He took a couple of aspirins. They made his stomach sour, but after a while his headache receded.

He hated walking through the cleaned-out parts of the Terry on his way to work that afternoon. Lawns grew tall and untended and full of weeds. Lots of houses had broken windows. Quite a few had doors standing open. A skinny dog trotted out of one of them and gave Scipio a hard stare. If it were a little bigger, it might have gone for him. Stray dogs scrounged whatever they could. So did stray people. The cleanouts hadn't missed many. If not for Jerry Dover, they wouldn't have missed Scipio and his family.

And now Dover was in the Army. Scipio shook his head, dreading what would come next. He'd got to the age where he feared any kind of change. It was too likely to be change for the worse.

A white man waited just inside the kitchen entrance to the Huntsman's Lodge. "Are you Xerxes or Aurelius?" he asked.

"I is Xerxes, suh," Scipio answered. The new manager was younger than he'd expected—in his early forties. He had a thin, sharp, clever face and cold blue eyes. Scipio didn't wonder why he wasn't in the Army: he sat in a wheelchair, his legs thin and useless inside his trousers.

"My name's Willard Sloan," he said, and tapped the arms of the chair with his own arms, which seemed fine. A moment later, he explained why: "Stopped a damnyankee bullet with my back in 1917. I used to be a hell of a football player, you know? So much for that." His mouth twisted. Then he went on, "Jerry Dover says you've been here since dirt. If I need to know anything special, I'm supposed to ask you."

"I tells you anything I knows, suh." Scipio meant it. He didn't expect the white man to like him. It might end up happening, but he didn't expect it. If Sloan found him useful, that would do almost as well.

"All right. If I have to pick your brains, I'll holler. For now, you just go on about your business the way you always have. I'll keep an eye on things, cipher out how they are, before I decide what works good and what needs tinkering."

"Fair enough, suh. Dis place been de bes' in town a long time. Sure enough want to keep it dat way," Scipio said. He and the rest of the staff would be judging Willard Sloan as he judged them. The only trouble was, his judgment carried more weight than theirs.

He did start well. When the cooks were unhappy with some of the beef they got, he used the telephone like a deadly weapon. "You bastard, you reckon you can screw me over on account of I ain't Dover?" he screamed at the butcher. "You reckon I don't know Chet Byers? You reckon I won't do business with him from here on out if you *ever* pull this shit on me again? Make it right in fifteen minutes, or I blacken your name all over town." New beef—of the proper quality—got there in twelve minutes flat. Jerry Dover couldn't have done better, and there was no higher praise than that.

XVII

Autumn was when the leaves turned red and gold and then fell off the trees. It was when the weather got crisp, so your cheeks also turned red and tingled after you'd stayed outside a while. If you were a fisherman on the North Atlantic, it was when the ocean started tossing you around, not knowing—or caring—your boat was out there.

George Enos, Jr., was used to the rhythms of the changing year. A Massachusetts man had to be. In the Sandwich Islands, the year didn't change much. The sun still rode high in the sky, if not quite so high. Days remained warm. Everything stayed green.

Bigger swells did start rolling in out of the north. The *Townsend* would slide up over a crest and then down into a trough. That didn't seem enough to get excited about.

When George said so out loud, Fremont Dalby laughed at him. "Christ, Enos, haven't you had enough excitement for a while?" the gun chief said. "Far as I'm concerned, I can stay at my station and gather dust for a while, because that'll mean nobody's trying to strafe the ship or drop a bomb on her or stick a torpedo up our ass."

"Japs are out there somewhere," George said.

"I know, I know. You don't got to remind me," Dalby said. "But I don't like thinking about it every goddamn minute, you know what I mean?"

"Sure, Chief." George didn't want to get the CPO ticked off at him. Getting any CPO ticked off at you was a bad idea. When the man in question happened to be your boss, it was four times as bad.

They kept station with three other destroyers and with the *Trenton*. The escort carrier hadn't taken too much damage in her last brush with the Japanese. Her airplanes had given out more than she'd got. That was the first real naval victory the USA had had in the islands around the Sandwich Islands for quite a while.

U.S. fighters buzzed overhead. They flew a dawn-to-dusk combat air patrol. The *Townsend*'s Y-ranging antenna went round and round. Y-ranging gear could spot incoming enemy aircraft while they were still well out to sea. The other destroyers and the carrier all had sets, too. Whatever else happened, the Japs wouldn't be able to get in a sucker punch at the little flotilla. The *Trenton* would be able to scramble all her fighters. The destroyers would start throwing up as much anti-aircraft as they could. And after that, what could you do but pucker your asshole and hope?

Fritz Gustafson pointed off to starboard. The loader didn't bother with words when one finger would do. Fremont Dalby wasn't shy about words, though. "Dolphins!" he said with a smile. "They're supposed to be good luck. Here's hoping, anyway."

George enjoyed the dolphins for their own sake. They were swift and graceful and, as always, they looked as if they were having a good time out there. "I wonder what they make of us," he said. "Till we got ships like this, they were some of the biggest, toughest things in the ocean."

"They figure we're good for a handout, anyway," Dalby said, which was true. They would follow ships for scraps and garbage. Sometimes, though, they would track ships for what looked like nothing more than the hell of it. Were they skylarking? Did they really have the brains to play? More to the point, did they have the brains not to want to work? For their sake, George hoped so.

Four hours on, four hours off. When the other crew for the twin 40mm mount replaced Dalby's, George went below, grabbed himself a couple of sandwiches and some coffee, and then found his hammock. He laughed as he climbed up into it. "What's so funny?" asked another sailor about to grab some shut-eye.

"Used to be I couldn't sleep for beans in one of these goddamn things," George answered. "Used to be I couldn't hardly get into one without falling out on my ear. But now I don't even think about it."

"That's 'cause you're a real Navy guy now," the other sailor said, getting up into his hammock as nimbly as a chimp might have. "You know how to do shit. You aren't a little lost civilian anymore, looking for somebody to hold your hand and tell you what to do."

Was I really that green? George wondered, wiggling to get comfortable. He supposed he had been. He knew the sea from his fisherman days, but knowing the sea and knowing the Navy weren't the same thing—not even close. He settled his cap over his eyes. Two minutes later, he was snoring.

Standing watch and watch wore on a man. He felt groggy, almost underwater, when he slid out of the hammock and down to the deck again. He got rid of some of the coffee he'd drunk just after he came off the last watch, then went back to the galley for more. It might help keep him conscious, anyway.

Fremont Dalby was at the gun when he got there. The CPO looked fresh and fit. Maybe Dalby didn't need to sleep. George yawned. *He* damn well did, and he hadn't done enough of it. "All quiet?" he asked.

"Yeah," Dalby answered. "We're getting up toward Midway, too."

"Uh-huh." George looked north and west, as if he expected the atoll to come over the horizon any minute now. He didn't; they weren't *that* close, not by three or four hundred miles. "Anything from the Y-range?"

"Quiet as a mouse, far as I know," Dalby said. "Way it looks to me is, the Japs haven't got a carrier operating south of the island."

"Makes sense," George agreed. "If they did, they would've figured out we're around by now. Hell, we're almost close enough for land-based air from Midway to spot us."

"*Almost* is the word," the gun chief said. "And if they don't have a carrier operating south of Midway, we really have made them pull in their horns. Us coming up here is a lot better than them bombing the crap out of Oahu."

"You better believe it," George said. "It'd be good if we could push 'em off Midway, too. Where would they go then?"

"Wake," Fremont Dalby replied at once. "It's another pissant little bird turd of an island southwest of Midway. But I'll be damned if I'd want to hop from island to island across the whole stinking Pacific toward Japan."

"Oh, good God, no!" George shuddered at the very idea. "You'd have to be crazy to try something like that. You'd have to be crazy to want to. As long as they get out of the Sandwich Islands and stay away, that's plenty. This is a big goddamn ocean. There's room enough for us and them."

"That's how it looks to me, too," Dalby said. "Of course, how it looks to Philadelphia is anybody's guess. The big brains back there can screw up anything if they put their minds to it. Minds!" He rolled his eyes. "If they had any, we'd all be better off."

"Treason," Fritz Gustafson said. "Off with your head."

Dalby suggested that the loader lose some other organ important for happiness, if not absolutely necessary for personal survival. Gustafson didn't say another word. He'd got his lick in, and he was content.

George's watch passed quietly. No warning shouts of approaching Japanese airplanes came from the loudspeakers. The hydrophones didn't pick up telltale noises from lurking Japanese submersibles. No torpedoes from lurking submersibles the hydrophone hadn't picked up arrowed through the water toward the *Townsend*.

When the other crew took over the gun, George went down to the galley for more sandwiches and coffee. He felt as if he'd done the same thing just a few hours earlier. Of course, he *had* done the same thing, so no wonder he felt that way. These sandwiches were ham on wheat, not corned beef on rye. Other than that, he might have been running the film over again. Standing watch and watch made time blur. George tried to come up with the name of the artist who'd painted the pocket watch sagging and melting as if it were left out in the rain. It was something foreign, that was all he could remember.

Yawning, he headed for his hammock. "Here we go again," he said as he climbed up into it.

The sailor he'd talked with the last time he sacked out laughed. "We gotta stop meeting like this," he said. "People will get suspicious."

George laughed, too, a little nervously. Was that just a joke, or did something faggoty hide underneath it? Aboard ship, you always wondered. The *Townsend* went back to Oahu often enough to let the crew get their ashes hauled on Hotel Street, but you wondered anyway. Some guys were flat-out queers, no two ways about it, and they couldn't have cared less about the floozies on Hotel Street.

But you couldn't call somebody on what was probably nothing but a harmless joke. If the other guy didn't make another like it, George figured he would forget about this one. If he did . . . *I'll worry about that later.* With another yawn, an enormous one, George decided to worry about everything later, and went to sleep.

Night had fallen when he came back up on deck with another mug of coffee. It was cool and quiet: no CAP after dark. Fremont Dalby got to the 40mm mount with a mug of his own. He nodded to George and said, "We've got to stop meeting like this."

Him, too? "Uh, yeah," George said. He could imagine a lot of things, but the gun chief as a homo? Never in a million years.

"Should be a little easier this time through," Dalby said. "We don't have airplanes coming at us with bombs or torpedoes during the night."

"Or trying to crash into us, either," George put in.

"Yeah, that was fun, wasn't it?" Dalby said. *Fun* wasn't the word George would have used. He didn't know which one he *would* have used, but it wasn't one he would see in any family newspaper.

"All we gotta worry about now is submarines," Fritz Gustafson said. As usual, the loader didn't talk much. Also as usual, he got a lot of mileage out of what he did say.

Fremont Dalby's suggestion about what submarines could do was illegal, immoral, and impossible. George stared out over the black waters of the Pacific. Starlight glittered off the sea, but the moon was down. A dozen submersibles could have been playing ring around the rosy half a mile from the *Townsend* and he never would have known it. Out in the tropical Atlantic, a Confederate boat had sneaked up on his father's destroyer and sunk it in the middle of the night. The same thing could happen to him. At times like this, he knew it much too well.

Then Dalby said, "Those bastards have as much trouble finding us at night as we do finding them."

That was true enough, and reassuring to boot. Besides, what would a Jap sub be doing out here in the middle of the night? George wished he hadn't asked the question, because he saw an obvious answer: looking for American ships. If a submersible could, it would probably go after the *Trenton* ahead of the *Townsend*, but it might take whatever it could get.

He kept his nerves to himself. He didn't want his buddies to know he'd got the wind up. Odds were he was flabbling over nothing. He understood that, which didn't make not doing it any easier.

The watch passed quietly. No airplanes. No submarines. No nothing. Just the wide Pacific and, somewhere not far away, the rest of the flotilla. The other crew took over the gun. George went below for food and coffee and sleep. Coffee had trouble keeping him awake through watch and watch.

He came back on at four in the morning, and watched the sun rise out of the sea. The flotilla turned away from Midway during his watch, and started back towards Oahu. Now the United States were doing the poking. He hoped Japan liked getting poked.

"Hey, Mistuh Guard, suh."

Hipolito Rodriguez swung the muzzle of his submachine gun toward the Negro who'd spoken to him. The motion was automatic and not particularly hostile. He just didn't believe in taking chances. "What you want?" he asked.

"What I want?" The skinny black man laughed. "Mistuh Guard, suh, I got me a list long as your arm, but gettin' let outa here do the job all by its ownself." Rodriguez waited stonily. That wouldn't happen, and the Negro had to know it. He did; the laughter leaked out of his face as he went on, "What I wants to ask you, suh, is where them niggers from Jackson is at now. They come through here, but they don't hardly stop for nothin'."

"Some go to Lubbock," Rodriguez answered. "Some go to El Paso." He was stubborn about sticking to the story the guards told the Negroes in Camp Determination. Not all the *mallates* believed it. But they weren't sure what really had happened, which was all to the good.

This prisoner looked sly. "That a really fo'-true fac', suh?"

"Of course it is." Rodriguez lied without hesitation. He had as much of an interest in keeping the Negroes quiet as Jefferson Pinkard did himself.

"Ain't how I hear it," the fellow said.

"What you hear, then?" Rodriguez asked. "Tell me what you hear. Tell me who you hear it from, too."

"Well . . ." The Negro suddenly realized he might have talked more than was good for him. "I ain't so sure I recollects now."

"No, eh?" Now the muzzle of Rodriguez's submachine gun pointed toward the man's midsection in a businesslike way. "Maybe we take you back. Maybe we ask some questions. We find out who telling lies here, *sí?*"

The black man couldn't turn pale. If he could have, he would have. If he could have, he would have disappeared. Since he couldn't, he said, "You don' need to do nothin' like that, Mistuh Guard, suh. My memory, it's much better all sudden-like."

"*Bueno.* Glad to hear it," Rodriguez said dryly. "Tell me, then—what you hear?"

"Well . . ." the Negro repeated. He licked his lips. "I don't say this or nothin'—not me. I jus' hear it." Rodriguez gestured impatiently with the submachine gun. A weapon that could cut a man in half in the blink of an eye made a hell of a persuader. The black man spoke up in a hurry: "Some folks say them niggers didn't go nowheres. Some folks say they was kilt."

Some folks were right—dead right. "Who say stupid things like this?" Rodriguez asked. The Negro hesitated. He didn't want to squeal on his friends, even with the threat from the submachine gun. Rodriguez asked a different question, one that seemed safer on the outside: "What barracks you live in?"

"I's in Barracks Twenty-seven, suh," the Negro said.

"Twenty-seven." Rodriguez turned to the guards with him. "Remember that."

"Will do, Troop Leader," the three of them said as if they were one man. Rodriguez had discovered he liked wearing three stripes on his sleeve. He gave more orders than he took these days. In orders as in many other things, it was better to give than to receive.

He turned back to the Negro. "I find you lie to me about where you at, *mallate,* this camp ain't big enough for you to hide. You understand?"

"I ain't lyin', Mistuh Guard, suh." The prisoner practically radiated innocence—and no doubt would keep doing it till Rodriguez looked away or turned his back. "If I's lyin', I's flyin'."

"If you lyin', you dyin'." Rodriguez capped the black man's rhyme with one of his own. He gestured with the muzzle of the submachine gun once more, this time in dismissal. The prisoner scurried away, glad to be out of the dread eye of officialdom.

"Troop Leader, how come we got to remember that barracks number?" asked one of the guards.

Rodriguez swallowed a sigh. Some of these people had no business looking down their noses at Negroes for stupidity. Patiently, he answered, "Because, Pruitt, we got to do something about Barracks Twenty-seven."

"Like what, Troop Leader?" Pruitt radiated innocence, too. The trouble was, his was real.

"Ain't gonna talk about it here." Rodriguez gestured once more, this time with his left hand. There were four of them in their gray uniforms. All around them were Negroes, thousands of Negroes. Even though the men in gray all carried submachine guns, Rodriguez found himself sweating despite the cooler weather. The Negroes could rush them. Other guards would come try to save them. The machine gunners in the guard towers outside the barbed-wire perimeter would fire till their gun barrels glowed cherry red. They would massacre the blacks. Rodriguez doubted that would do him much good.

But no attack came. He and his companions finished their patrol. When they got back to the guards' quarters, he reported to an officer what the Negro had told him. "Hmm," said the chief assault leader— the equivalent of a captain in the Freedom Party guards. "What do you reckon we ought to do?"

"Clean out Barracks Twenty-seven, sir," Rodriguez answered at once. "Tell them we ship them somewhere else because they talk too much. Then put them in trucks or send them to the bathhouse."

"Hmm," the chief assault leader said again. "I can't decide that. I'll have to pass it on up the line."

"Yes, sir," Rodriguez said resignedly. He'd seen this sort of thing in the Great War. Some officers knew what needed doing, then went and did it. Others knew what needed doing, then waited till somebody over them told them to do it. They weren't so useful as the first kind, but they weren't hopeless. The ones who didn't know what needed doing . . . those were the officers who got their men killed.

Barracks Twenty-seven got cleaned out four days later than it should have, but it did get cleaned out. Rodriguez was part of the crew that took care of it. He wasn't sorry; he wanted to see the job done. He also wanted to see it done right. "Gotta make sure we don't spook the spooks," another guard said. That summed things up, though Rodriguez's smile was more dutiful than amused: he'd heard that joke, or ones too much like it, too many times before.

A different chief assault leader was in charge of the cleanout. Rodriguez wouldn't have entrusted it to the man with whom he'd spoken, either. This fellow—his name was Higbe—handled it with aplomb. "We are too goddamn crowded here," he told the black men lined up in front of the barracks, "so we're shippin' your asses down to El Paso. Y'all go back in the barracks and get whatever you need. Much as you can keep on your lap in a truck." He looked at his watch. "You got ten minutes. Get movin'!"

That was a nice touch. Nothing too bad could happen to a man if he could bring his handful of miserable possessions with him . . . could it? One Negro hung back. Rodriguez recognized the black who'd spoken to him before at the same time as the *mallate* recognized him. Instead of hurrying into the barracks, the black man came over to him and said, "Mistuh Guard, suh, I don't want to go to no El Paso."

He knows what's coming, all right, Rodriguez thought. "I think we fix it so you don't got to," he said aloud. He didn't want the Negro kicking up a fuss. The less fuss, the better for everybody—except the prisoners, and they didn't count. He went on, "Let me talk to my officer. We take care of it. You stay here. Don't go nowhere."

"Lawd bless you, suh," the Negro said.

Rodriguez spoke briefly with Chief Assault Leader Higbe. Unlike the other officer, Higbe didn't hesitate. He just nodded. "That sounds good to me, Troop Leader. You take care of it like you said."

"Yes, sir." Rodriguez saluted and went back to the Negro, who was nervously shifting from foot to foot. He nodded to the black man. "You come with me."

"Where you takin' me, suh?"

"Guards' quarters. Got some questions to ask you."

"Oh, yes, suh." The Negro almost capered with glee. "I sings like a canary, long as you don't put me on no truck."

"You don't want to go, you don't go," Rodriguez said. "What's your name?"

"I's Demetrius, suh," the Negro answered.

Another fancy name, Rodriguez thought scornfully. The more raggedy the *mallate,* the fancier the handle he seemed to come with. "*Bueno,* Demetrius." His words gave no clue to what lay in his mind. "You come along."

Demetrius came, all smiles and relief. None of the other prisoners took any special notice; guards pulled blacks out of camp for one reason or another all the time. "What you need to know, suh?" Demetrius asked as they got near the barbed wire that segregated prisoners and guards. "Don't matter what, not hardly. I tell you."

"*Bueno,*" Rodriguez said once more. He waved to the gate crew. They opened up for him and Demetrius. Rodriguez urged the Negro on ahead of him. As soon as buildings hid them from the prisoners' view, he fired a shot into the back of Demetrius' head. He waited to see if he would need give him another one to finish him off, but he didn't. The black man probably died before he finished crumpling to the ground.

"What's up, Troop Leader?" another guard asked, as casually as if they were talking about the weather.

"Troublemaker," Rodriguez answered: a response that could bury any black man. "We got to get rid of the body quiet-like."

"Niggers'll know he came in here. They'll know he didn't come out," the trooper said.

Rodriguez shrugged. "And so? We say we catch him dealing in contraband, they think he deserve what he get."

That overstated things a little. The prisoners admired people who could smuggle forbidden things into Camp Determination. But they knew the guards came down hard on the smugglers they caught. Dealers in contraband usually bribed guards to get stuff for them and look the other way. Guards got fired for doing things like that. The Negroes got fired, too: fired on.

"Get the body out of here," Rodriguez told the man who'd questioned him.

He had stripes on his sleeve. The other guard didn't. "Yes, Troop Leader," he said, and took the late, unlamented Demetrius by the feet.

"I want to congratulate Troop Leader Rodriguez for a fine piece of work," Jefferson Pinkard said at a guards' meeting a few days later. "He spotted trouble, he reported it, and we dealt with it. Nobody in Barracks Twenty-seven is going to spread rumors anymore, by God. Chief Assault Leader Higbe deserves commendation for making the cleanout run so smooth. A letter will go in his file."

He didn't talk about a letter going into Rodriguez's file, even if they were friends. Rodriguez might get rockers under his stripes, but that was it. All the commendation letters in the world wouldn't make him anything more than a top kick. The Confederate States were more likely to name a Sonoran peasant an officer than they were to appoint a Negro Secretary of State, but only a little. Rodriguez didn't worry about it. He knew he'd done a good job, too. He'd saved everybody in camp—except the Negroes—some trouble. That was plenty.

Major General Abner Dowling could see the Confederate States of America from his new headquarters in Clovis, New Mexico. His only major trouble was, at the moment he couldn't see much of the Eleventh Army, with which he was supposed to go after the enemy. He had a lot of territory to cover and not a lot of men with which to cover it. The war out here by Texas' western border seemed very much an afterthought.

Back in the lost and distant days of peace, Clovis was a minor trade center on the U.S.–C.S. frontier. The town was founded in the early years of the century with the unromantic handle of Riley's Switch; a railroad official's daughter suggested renaming it for the first Christian King of France. Cattle from the West Texas prairie paused at its feed lots before going on to supply the meat markets of California. It had flourished when western Texas, under the name of Houston, joined the USA: those same cattle kept coming west, only now without a customs barrier. Houston's return to Texas and to the CSA sent Clovis into a tailspin from which it had yet to recover.

Men in green-gray weren't cattle, even if they were often treated in ways that would have made a rancher blush or turn pale. Feeding them and separating them from the little money the U.S. government doled out to them had produced a small upturn, but the Clovis Chamber of Commerce still sighed for the days when the longhorn ruled the local economy.

The Chamber of Commerce's sighs were not Dowling's worry, except when the local greasy spoons all jacked up their prices to gouge soldiers at the same time. He growled then. When growling didn't work, he threatened to move his headquarters and place Clovis permanently off-limits to all military personnel. A threat to the pocketbook got people's attention. Prices promptly came back down.

Up till now, that was the biggest victory Dowling had won. Both his side and his Confederate counterparts patrolled the border on horseback. Even command cars were hard to come by in these parts, and some of the terrain was too rugged for anything with wheels. Every so often, cavalrymen in green-gray and those in butternut would shoot at one another. Their occasional casualties convinced both sides they were being aggressive enough.

Dowling was plowing through paperwork and patting himself on the back for getting out from under Daniel MacArthur when his adjutant stuck his head into the office. "Sir, there's an officer from the War Department here to see you," Major Angelo Toricelli said.

"There is?" Dowling blinked. "Why, in God's name?"

"Beats me, sir. He didn't say," Toricelli answered cheerfully. "All he said was that his name is Major Levitt and he's got something he's supposed to hand-deliver to you." Toricelli paused. "I had him searched. Whatever it is, it's not a people bomb."

"Thank you, Major," Dowling said. "Maybe you'd better show him in."

Major Levitt was skinny, sandy-haired, and not particularly memorable. After Toricelli ducked out of the office, he said, "Your adjutant is, ah, a diligent young man."

"Well, yes," Dowling said. In a low-key way, Levitt had style. Dowling knew his features would have been much more ruffled if he'd just been frisked. "What can I do for you today, Major?"

"I have this for you, sir." Levitt set a sealed envelope on Dowling's desk. "Major Toricelli didn't find anything obviously lethal about it."

"I'm so relieved," Dowling murmured, not about to let the officer from Philadelphia show more sangfroid than he did himself. Levitt smiled. When he did, his whole face lit up. He looked like a human being, and a nice one, instead of a cog in the military machine. Dowling opened the envelope, unfolded the papers inside, and began to read. He suddenly looked up. "Jesus Christ!" he said, and then, "You know what's in these orders?"

"Yes, sir," Levitt said. "You're allowed to discuss them with me."

"Oh, joy." Dowling went on reading. When he finished, he looked up again. "I understand what I'm supposed to do. But why on earth am I supposed to concentrate my forces and launch an attack? There's nothing in West Texas worth having."

"I know." Major Levitt smiled another of his charming smiles. "I served there for a while between the wars, when it was Houston."

"These"—Dowling tapped the orders with the nail of his index finger—"are very strange. When I was sent here, they told me that as long as the Confederates didn't steal Albuquerque and Santa Fe while we weren't looking, I'd be doing my job. And now this. What's going on?"

Levitt told him exactly what was going on, in about half a dozen sentences. "Any questions, sir?" he finished.

"No," Dowling said. "You're absolutely right. I can see the need. Just the same, though, Major, and no offense to you, I'm going to keep you here for a while, till Philadelphia confirms that it really did send these orders. They look authentic—but then, they would if they were phony, too. Featherston's bound to have some good forgers in Richmond, same as we're bound to be forging Confederate papers."

"No offense taken, sir," Levitt said. "As long as your force gets rolling by that date, what happens beforehand doesn't matter."

"Ha!" Dowling muttered. Major Levitt was a General Staff officer. To them, logistics was an abstract science like calculus. They didn't have to worry about moving actual men and guns and munitions and fuel and food. Abner Dowling did, and knew his supply train was as flimsy as the rest of the alleged Eleventh Army. "Major Toricelli!" he called. "Can I see you for a moment?"

"Yes, sir?" Toricelli was in the office in nothing flat, sending Levitt a suspicious look. "What is it?"

Dowling handed him the orders. "Please get confirmation of these from Philadelphia. Until we have it, Major Levitt is not to leave this building."

"Yes, sir!" Toricelli gave Levitt a real glare this time.

"Highest security," Dowling added. "Don't compromise the orders to verify them." Toricelli saluted and hurried away. Dowling nodded to Levitt. "Care for a cigarette?"

"No, thank you, sir. I never got the habit. I ran track at West Point, and they're bad for your wind."

"Ah. I was a football man myself—a tackle," Dowling said. "Even back in those days, I was built more like a brick than a greyhound." He lit up. He wasn't running anywhere.

Not quite half an hour later, the telephone on his desk rang. He picked it up. "Dowling here."

"Hello, sir. This is John Abell. Do you recognize my voice?"

Even across two-thirds of the country and an indifferent connection, Dowling did. "Yes, indeed, General," he said.

"Good. That makes things easier," the General Staff officer said. "I can confirm those orders for you. We did send Major Levitt west with them. Please follow them precisely."

"I'll do it," Dowling promised. "Anything else?"

"No, sir. That covers it," Abell answered. The line went dead.

Dowling nodded to Levitt. "All right, Major. You are what you say you are, and these"—he tapped the orders again—"are what they say they are. I'll carry them out."

"Thank you, sir." Levitt grinned. "Would you be kind enough to let your adjutant know I don't have horns and fangs and a spiked tail?"

Dowling smiled, too. "If he frisked you, he should already know that." But he did get up and let Major Toricelli know the courier was neither a devil nor, worse, a Confederate.

"I didn't *think* he was, sir, but you never can tell," his adjutant said. "I wondered if he was a Mormon in disguise, too, to tell you the truth."

"Gark," said Dowling, who hadn't thought of that. "No wonder you checked to see if he was loaded with explosives."

"It's a rum old world, sir," Toricelli said.

"Ain't it the truth?" Dowling agreed. "And we're going to be the busiest people in it the next few days. The Eleventh Army is strung out from the border with Chihuahua to the border with Sequoyah. I want to concentrate here, but I want to leave enough of a screen behind so the Confederates don't notice we're concentrating till we go over the border."

"That would be easier if we had more men," Major Toricelli said.

"Of course it would. And if pigs had wings we'd all carry umbrellas," Dowling said, which made his adjutant send him a quizzical look. He ignored it and went on, "Let's go to the map room and see what we can work out."

The more he studied the situation, the less happy he got. Major Toricelli had it right: if he left enough men behind to fool the foe, he wouldn't be able to mount the kind of attack the War Department had in mind. He grumbled and fumed, thinking about bricks without straw. His adjutant seemed sunk as deep in gloom—till Toricelli suddenly started to laugh.

Now Dowling had the quizzical stare. "What's so funny, Major? Nice to think something is."

"Sir, I don't think we need the screening force," Toricelli said. "If the Confederates see what we're doing and attack us somewhere else along the line—well, so what? Aren't they doing exactly what we want them to do?"

Dowling eyed the map a little while longer. Then he laughed, too. "Damned if they aren't, Major," he said. "Damned if they aren't, by God. All right. We'll keep it just secret enough so Featherston's fuckers think we're trying to but we aren't very good at it. We can't be too open, or they'll start wondering what's up."

Toricelli nodded. "Got you, sir. I like that."

"So do I," Dowling said. "Let's start drafting orders, then."

The orders went out. The U.S. Eleventh Army started concentrating on Clovis. U.S. air strength in New Mexico started concentrating on Clovis, too. The fighters would help keep the Confederates from breaking up the concentration with bombers when they noticed it. They didn't take long. Urgent signals started heading east from the C.S. Army of West Texas. Dowling's cryptographers couldn't make sense of all of them, but what they could read suggested the enemy was alarmed.

"If I were in West Texas, I'd be alarmed, too," Dowling told Angelo Toricelli. "I'd think the U.S. general on the other side of the border had gone clear around the bend. Why stir things up here?"

"Because the USA can fart and chew gum at the same time?" his adjutant suggested.

"That's what we're doing, all right." Dowling had to stop, because he was laughing too hard to go on. "If we had a real army here . . ." He shrugged. "But we don't, so we do the best we can with what we've got."

He was ready on the appointed day. He was less than an hour away from issuing the order to start the opening barrage when he got another phone call from John Abell. "Please hold up for three days, sir," Abell said. *Please* made the order more polite, but no less an order.

"All right, General. I can still do that—just barely," Dowling said, and shouted for Major Toricelli to put the brakes on things. Toricelli swore, then started making calls of his own. Dowling asked Abell, "Can you tell me why?"

"Not on a line that isn't secure," the General Staff officer replied. Dowling found himself nodding. The Confederates had a couple of thousand miles of wire on which to be listening in. And, after a little thought, he had a pretty fair notion of the answer anyway.

November in the North Atlantic wasn't so bad as, say, January in the North Atlantic. Nobody would ever have mistaken it for July off the Sandwich Islands, though. The *Josephus Daniels* climbed over swells, slid into troughs, bounced all the time, and generally behaved like a toy boat in a bathtub with a rambunctious four-year-old.

Sam Carsten took it all in stride. He'd rounded the Horn more than once, facing seas that made the North Atlantic at its worst seem tame by comparison. But he wasn't surprised when the destroyer escort's passageways began to stink of vomit. A lot of men were seasick. He ordered cleaning parties increased. Smelling the result of other men's nausea helped make sailors sick. The reek diminished, but didn't go away. He hadn't expected anything different.

"You're a good sailor, sir," Pat Cooley said, watching Sam tear into a roast beef sandwich on the bridge. The exec hadn't been sick, not so far as Sam knew, but he did look a little green.

"Not too bad," Sam allowed, and took another bite. "I've had plenty of practice, that's for damn sure." He looked up at the cloud-filled sky. "Weather's right for people like us, anyhow."

The fair, auburn-haired exec eyed the even fairer blond skipper. "Well, that's true," Cooley said. "But everything comes with a price, doesn't it?" Yes, he *was* green.

"It does." Sam finished the sandwich and wiped crumbs off his hands. "When we're up and down so much, and when all this damn spray's in the air, the Y-ranging set doesn't give us as much as it would in softer weather."

Cooley gulped. "I wasn't thinking of the Y-ranging set, sir." Sam thought he would have to leave the bridge in a hurry, but he fought down what might have been about to come up. Sam admired that. Carrying on in spite of what bothered you was a lot tougher than not being bothered, which he himself wasn't.

"I know, Pat," he said now, more gently than he was in the habit of speaking. "But it also means we have to patrol the hard way, and it means we can't see as far. I hope it doesn't mean something slips past us."

Along with several other destroyer escorts and destroyers, the *Josephus Daniels* sailed east of Newfoundland. Their goal was simple: to stop the British from sneaking men and arms into Canada to keep the rebellion there sizzling. As with most goals, setting it was easier than meeting it.

The U.S. Navy had bigger fish to fry, or it would have committed more ships to the job. Fortunately, the Royal Navy did, too. If it didn't keep the USA away from the convoys from South America and South Africa that fed the United Kingdom, Britain would start to starve. Losing that fight had made the U.K. throw in the sponge in the Great War. Under Churchill and Mosley, the limeys were doing their best to make sure it didn't happen again. They didn't treat supporting the Canuck rebels as job number one.

But the British had one big advantage: the North Atlantic was vast, and the ships in it relatively tiny. A lot of what they sent got through. And as for what didn't—well, if it didn't, what did they lose? A rusty freighter, some munitions, and a few sailors captured or killed. Cheap enough, for a country fighting a war.

Meanwhile, the United States had to pull ships away from attacking Britain's supply convoys for this thankless job. Carsten didn't love convoy-hunting; he'd done too much of it the last time around. But it seemed like a trip to Coney Island next to this.

Up to the crest of a wave. As the *Josephus Daniels* started to slide down into the trough, the Y-range operator stirred in his seat. "Something?" Sam asked.

"I'm—not sure, sir," the young officer answered. "I thought so for a second, but then we lost the target."

"What bearing?" Sam tried not to sound excited. He *wanted* to go after something.

"About 315, sir," said Lieutenant, J.G., Thad Walters.

"Mr. Cooley." Now Sam's voice was sharp and crisp. "Change course to 315. All ahead full. And sound general quarters, if you please."

"Changing course to 3-1-5: aye aye, sir," Cooley said. He called, "All ahead full," down to the engine room. His finger stabbed a button near the wheel. Klaxons hooted. Sailors dashed to their battle stations.

Sam stared northwest. *You bastard—you almost snuck past us,* he thought. He knew he might be thinking unkind thoughts at a figment of the electronics' imagination. That was a chance he took. He spoke to the wireless operator on the bridge: "Signal the other ships in the patrol that we are changing course to pursue a possible enemy ship."

"Aye aye, sir." The rating at the Morse key reached for the book to find the proper code groups.

Lieutenant Walters watched his set like a cat keeping an eye on a mousehole. He didn't say anything the first time the *Josephus Daniels* climbed to the top of a crest. The next time, though, he jerked as if he'd stuck his finger in a light socket. "It's there, sir!" he exclaimed. "Bearing 310, speed . . . eleven knots."

"Change course to 310, Mr. Cooley," Sam said, and then, to the Y-range operator, "Mr. Walters, give me a range as soon as you can." Eleven knots. That sure sounded like a lumbering British freighter. He couldn't think of any other kind of ship likely to be in these waters right now.

After a couple of more climbs to the crest, Walters said, "Sir, range is about six miles."

"Thank you," Sam answered. In good weather, the target would have been easily visible. Of course, for the limeys to bet that the weather off Newfoundland in November would be lousy gave odds a hell of a lot better than putting chips down on double-zero at the roulette table.

Before too long, the freighter did come into sight: a big, lumbering tub not much different from what Sam had expected. At his order, the wireless operator sent more code groups.

"Come up alongside, Mr. Cooley," Sam said. "I think we'll need to put a prize crew aboard."

The *Josephus Daniels* was a tub herself, but she seemed all sharklike grace alongside the freighter. Sam handled the blinker himself, signaling, WHAT SHIP ARE YOU? HEAVE TO FOR BOARDING AND INSPECTION.

WE ARE THE *KARLSKRONA*. WE ARE SWEDISH. WE ARE NEUTRAL, came the reply.

"Fat chance," Sam said. He signaled, HEAVE TO FOR BOARDING AND CONTRABAND INSPECTION. He called to the forward gun turret: "Put one across her bow if she doesn't stop."

She didn't. The shot rang out. LAST WARNING, Sam signaled. Sailors ran across the *Karlskrona*'s deck. For a couple of seconds, Sam thought it was panic. Then, suddenly, he didn't: it was too well organized, too well drilled.

"Sink that ship!" he shouted at the same time as Pat Cooley yelled, "She's got guns!"

Ever since taking over the *Josephus Daniels,* Sam had concentrated on gunnery. His men hadn't been the best then. They were now. He would have matched them against the gunners from any other destroyer escort in the Navy.

And they needed to be. He and Pat Cooley both exclaimed in horror when the armed freighter opened fire. The size of the spout that miss kicked up . . . "She's got six-inchers!" Cooley yelped.

"Uh-huh," Sam said grimly. The enemy outgunned his ship, and they weren't far from point-blank range. A couple of hits could sink the *Josephus Daniels.* "Flank speed and zigzag, Mr. Cooley. Let's not make it easy for them."

"Aye aye, sir." Cooley swung the wheel hard to port, then just as hard to starboard. Another great gout of water rose, this one closer to the destroyer escort. The limeys were getting the range.

But the *Josephus Daniels*' gunners already had it. Both turrets were firing, and the ship's violent maneuvers fazed them not a bit. "Hit!" Sam yelled, and then, "Hit!" again. He whooped after the second one— it was near the bow, where the freighter carried one of her guns. The destroyer escort's twin 40mms opened up, too—they were close enough for them to reach the foe. He felt as if he'd fallen back in time to the War of 1812, when ships went toe to toe at short range and slugged away at each other till one surrendered or sank.

One of those big shells—the damn freighter had a light cruiser's firepower—burst much too close to the *Josephus Daniels*' stern. Shrapnel howled through the air. That one would cause casualties even if it was a miss. If the burst was close enough, it might spring hull plates, too, and make the destroyer escort's seams leak. But it wouldn't hurt her badly.

And she was chewing up the freighter. Her four-inch guns threw shells that weighed only a third as much as the enemy's, but she fired much faster and she fired much straighter. "She's on fire!" Pat Cooley yelled, and then, half a minute later, "She's struck her colors!"

Sure enough, the freighter's ensign came down, and a white flag of surrender went up to replace it. "Cease fire!" Sam ordered. The turrets stopped at once; the men at the antiaircraft guns needed a few seconds to get the word—or maybe they just didn't want to hear it. That went against the rules, but not against human nature. "Approach to pick up survivors, Mr. Cooley," Sam said. He told the men at the gun turrets what the destroyer escort was doing, and added, "If you see anybody going near her guns, open up again."

But the freighter—Sam didn't suppose she was really the *Karlskrona*—had no more fight in her. Her men were taking to the boats—which, in the North Atlantic, was no joke. Sam ordered nets lowered to let the British sailors come up the *Josephus Daniels*' side. His own crew, armed with a couple of submachine guns, rifles, pistols, axes, and even some big wrenches, looked like a nineteenth-century boarding party as they took charge of the prisoners. The pharmacist's mate had groaning wounded men to deal with.

Sam went down to the deck for a closer look at the vanquished enemy. The British skipper, a weary and bedraggled man with a horsy face and bad teeth, recognized him for the destroyer escort's captain at once. "Well fought, sir," the limey said, saluting. "Thought we might surprise you, but you maneuvered well—and those bloody guns! Damn me if I think you missed even once."

"You gave us a nasty start," Sam said. "You were loaded for bear, all right." That probably made him sound like Daniel Boone to the Englishman, but he didn't care. If the freighter's gunners were better . . . But the best gun crews were bound to be in the Royal Navy. Little jaunts like this would have to take whoever was left, and whoever was left hadn't been good enough.

"Kind of you to take us aboard, all things considered," his opposite number said.

"If you'd fired after the white flag went up, I'd've sunk you," Sam said matter-of-factly. "Short of that, though, I wouldn't leave a ship's cat in an open boat on the North Atlantic. I've been in the Navy better than thirty years. I've seen a few things I'd rather not see again, or think about, either."

"I believe you, sir. I'm grateful all the same," the Englishman said.

"Gratitude is worth its weight in gold," Sam said, and the limey flinched. Sam went on, "You and your men are POWs now. We'll take you back to the USA. When the war's over, you can go home. For now . . ." *For now,* he thought, *you didn't blow me to hell and gone. I'll take that.*

Irving Morrell looked up into the western sky. A snowflake hit him right between the eyes. "By God, the bastards weren't lying," he breathed, and his breath smoked as if he had a cigarette in his mouth. Just this minute, he didn't, though a pack sat in his pocket.

For once, the weathermen had hit things right on the button. They'd said this early snowstorm would get here now, and they were right. He'd gambled and held up his attack three days to wait for it, and his gamble looked as if it would pay off.

Meadville, Pennsylvania, lay in the foothills of the Alleghenies. Morrell stood on the grounds of Allegheny College. The Georgian and Greek Revival architecture told of timeless elegance and dedication to scholarship. But Confederate bombs and artillery had turned some of the buildings to ruins—not that the Greeks hadn't wrecked masterpieces in their own wars. And the barrels snorting on the yellowing lawn were not in perfect keeping with an academic atmosphere.

Only a few blocks away stood the world's biggest zipper factory. Morrell wondered if button manufacturers cursed Meadville whenever they thought of it. That wasn't his worry, though. He aimed his curses at Jake Featherston, and before long he'd aim them through the barrel of a gun.

He scrambled up into the closest barrel, which was his to command. When the fighting started, he intended to lead from the front. Generals who stayed in back of the line soon lost track of what was really going on. Generals who didn't stay back of the line often got killed, but Morrell refused to worry about that.

"We just about ready, sir?" asked his gunner, a dark, and darkly clever, corporal named Al Bergeron. He was a good soldier and a good gunner; Morrell missed Michael Pound all the same, and hoped the veteran underofficer was safe. Wherever Pound was, he'd be acting as if he wore three stars, not three stripes.

But Morrell would have to worry about him later, too. "Just about, Frenchy," he answered. During the Great War, more than a few people with French names changed them to German-sounding ones so their neighbors wouldn't suspect them. That kind of hysteria hadn't come again. The Confederate States were the only enemies people flabbled hard about now.

Morrell put on his earphones. This barrel had a fancier wireless setup than any of the rest. He could link up not only to other barrels but also to artillery, infantry, and aviation circuits. He wondered whether being able to talk to so many people at once was part of the privilege of his rank or part of the price of it.

He connected to the artillery web. "Ready at 0730?" he asked. If he got a no, somebody's head would roll—H-hour was only fifteen minutes away.

But the answer came back at once: "Ready, sir." The officer who replied sounded young and excited. Morrell wondered if he'd seen action before. Whether he had or not, he would now.

Those fifteen minutes, like the last fifteen minutes before every attack, seemed to crawl by on their bellies. Corporal Bergeron said, "Almost seems a shame to do this to those damn greasers."

"Almost—but not quite," Morrell said dryly. The gunner chuckled. Morrell's mouth stretched in a grin of savage anticipation. No, he didn't think it was a shame, not even slightly. If Jake Featherston was stretched so thin that he needed to use second-grade troops from the

Empire of Mexico to hold part of his line, he had only himself to blame if the USA tried to stomp the stuffing out of them.

No sooner had that thought crossed Morrell's mind than the artillery opened up. Even here inside the turret, the thunder was cataclysmic. He'd been hoarding guns as hard as he'd been hoarding barrels. The Mexicans would like things even less.

The barrage went on for a precise hour and a half. As soon as the guns let up, Morrell spoke into the intercom to the driver and then over the webs connecting him to the rest of the barrels and to the infantry. He said the same thing every time: "Let's go!"

Engine roaring, his barrel rumbled forward. Morrell stuck his head out of the cupola so he could see better. That was a splendid way to get shot. He knew as much. It was the chance he took. If he got another oak-leaf cluster for his Purple Heart, then he did, that was all. He needed to see what was going on, as much as he could. And if he stopped one with his face . . . Well, a general officer's pension would leave Agnes and Mildred without many worries about money.

Along with the rest of the barrels, his pushed southwest out of Meadville. Some foot soldiers loped along among the big, noisy machines. Others rode in trucks or in lightly armored carriers to keep up more easily. A few infantrymen clambered up onto barrels and let them do the work. That was highly unofficial. Doctrine handed down from on high—which is to say, from Philadelphia—frowned on it. Riding barrels left soldiers vulnerable to the fire they inevitably drew. But it also got them where they were going faster and fresher than marching would have done. No matter what doctrine the War Department laid down, Morrell liked that.

He knew just when they broke into the Mexicans' lines. The U.S. barrage had come down right on the button. Only a few soldiers in that yellowish khaki were in any shape to fight. Scattered rifle fire and a handful of machine guns greeted the advancing U.S. forces, but that was all. Francisco José's soldiers didn't carry the automatic rifles that made C.S. infantrymen so formidable. They had bolt-action Tredegars, pieces much like U.S. Springfields.

They didn't have barrels. They didn't have much artillery. They didn't have armored personnel carriers. And they didn't have a chance. Morrell had loaded up with a rock in his fist. Now he swung it with all his might.

Here and there, the Mexicans fought bravely. Knots of them held up Morrell's forces wherever they could. Stubborn men who would die before they yielded a position were an asset to any army, and the Empire of Mexico's had its share. But the Mexicans didn't have enough men like that, and the ones they did have couldn't do what they might have done with better equipment. More often than not, the U.S. advance flowed past those stubborn knots to either side. They could be cleaned up at leisure. Meanwhile, the push went on.

"Keep moving!" Whenever Morrell ducked down into the turret, he spread his gospel over the wireless. "Always keep moving. Once we get in among 'em, once we get behind 'em, they'll go to pieces. And then we'll be able to move even faster."

And he had the pleasure of watching his prophecy come true. Till the early afternoon, the enemy soldiers in front of his barrels and infantry did everything they could to stop them and even to throw them back. After that . . . After that, it was like watching ice melt when spring came to a northern river. Once the rot started, it spread fast. By that first nightfall, he was seeing the enemy's backs.

He didn't want to stop for the darkness. He kept going till his driver couldn't see any farther. He sent infantry ahead even after that. And he had the barrels moving again as soon as the first gray showed in the east.

The Mexicans kept trying to fight back early in the second day. But when they saw barrels coming at them out of the swirling snow, a lot of them lost their nerve. Morrell would have lost his nerve, too, trying to stand up against barrels with no more than rifles. Some of the men in the yellowish khaki ran away. Others dropped their rifles and raised their hands. A lot of them looked miserably cold. They didn't have greatcoats, and probably didn't have long johns, either. Down in the Empire of Mexico, they wouldn't have needed them. They were a long way from home.

By the end of that second day, Morrell's barrels had smashed through the crust of enemy resistance. Behind it lay . . . not much. Morrell had a gruesomely good time shooting up a Confederate truck convoy. The big butternut trucks rolled right up to his barrel, sure it had to be on their side even if it was the wrong color.

They found out how wrong they were in a hurry. At Morrell's orders, Frenchy Bergeron wrecked the first truck in the convoy with a well-aimed cannon shell. The second truck tried to go around it. Bergron blasted that one, too, effectively blocking the road. Then he and the bow gunner used their machine guns to shoot up the rest of the trucks. More U.S. barrels came up and joined the fun.

It wasn't much fun for the poor bastards on the receiving end. Soldiers spilled out of some of the trucks and tried to find shelter from the storm of bullets wherever they could. Other trucks carried munitions, not men. When they burned, they sent tracers flying every which way. Standing up in the cupola again, Morrell whooped. Corporal Bergeron got the view through his gunsight. He pounded Morrell gently on the leg, which also amounted to a whoop.

Desperate to escape the trap, some of the trucks went off the road and into the fields on either side. Like their U.S. counterparts, they had four-wheel drive. That gave them some traction on the wet ground, but only some. Great gouts of mud flew from their tires as they struggled forward. While they did, the green-gray barrels went right on shooting at them, and they couldn't shoot back. Without antibarrel cannon, the only weapons foot soldiers had against armor were grenades through the hatches and Featherston Fizzes. They couldn't get close enough to use anything like that here.

Once he'd smashed the column of trucks, Morrell got on the wireless circuit to the barrels closest to his: "Let's get rolling again. We've got to keep moving." He popped up again and cast a wary eye at the sky. So far, the promised storm was still rolling through. When the weather got better, the Confederates were going to throw anything that could fly at his armored forces. From what he could see, air strikes had the best chance of slowing him down—if anything could. Now that he'd broken through the C.S. line, he saw nothing in the rear that had much chance of doing the job.

As his armored column pushed south and west from Meadville, another, slightly smaller, U.S. force was driving north from Parkersburg, West Virginia. If everything went according to plan, Morrell's men and the troops advancing from West Virginia would clasp hands somewhere in eastern Ohio. And if they did, the Confederate Army infesting Pittsburgh would find itself in a very embarrassing position indeed.

Surrounded. Cut off from reinforcements, except perhaps by air. Cut off from resupply, with the same possible exception. Could Featherston's men fly in enough fuel and ammo to keep a modern army functioning? Morrell didn't know, but this whole two-pronged attack was based on the assumption that it was damned unlikely. And even if the

Confederates could at first, would they be able to build transports as fast as U.S. fighters shot them down? He didn't think so.

What *would* he do if he were Jake Featherston? Try to pull out of Pittsburgh and save what he could? Try to break the ring around the city from the outside? Try to do both at once? Did the CSA have the men and machines to do both at once? With every mile his barrels advanced, Irving Morrell doubted that more and more. At the front, Confederate armies remained formidable, even fearsome. But they were like an alligator that went, "I've been sick," in an animated cartoon: all mouth, with no strength anywhere else. If you concentrated on the puny little legs and tail instead of the big end that chomped . . . "Well, let's see how Jake likes this," Morrell murmured, and he rolled on.

During the Great War, Chester Martin would never have imagined hitching a ride on a barrel. For one thing, there hadn't been so many of the lumbering monstrosities in the last fight. For another, a Great War barrel going flat out was faster than a man, but not by a whole hell of a lot.

Here at the end of 1942, though, things had changed. Most of Chester's new platoon had attached itself to a platoon of barrels. They rumbled through Pennsylvania—or maybe they were in Ohio by now. One state didn't look a whole lot different from another, especially when you were crashing along at fifteen or twenty miles an hour.

Every once in a while, the platoon had to fight. Sometimes the men would drop down from the barrels and shoot at startled Confederates. Sometimes they wouldn't bother descending. A PFC from Chicago carried a captured Confederate submachine gun and sprayed bullets around from the back of a barrel. Chester kept thinking he should have been called Vito or something like that, but he was a big blond Pole named Joe Jakimiuk.

What really amazed Chester was the speed of the U.S. advance. "It wasn't like this in the Great War, I'll tell you," he said as he sat by a campfire the second night and ate something alleged to be beef stew out of a can. It bore as much resemblance to what Rita called beef stew as boiled inner tube in motor-oil gravy, but it filled him up. "Back then, even in a breakthrough we only made a few miles a day, and nobody figured out how to do even that much till 1917."

"Better barrels and better trucks now." That was Second Lieutenant Delbert Wheat, the platoon commander. He spoke with the flat vowels and harsh consonants of Kansas. Odds were he hadn't been born in 1917. Even so, he wasn't an obnoxious twerp like the other shavetails Chester had met since reenlisting. He actually seemed to have some idea of what he was doing—and when he wasn't sure, he didn't act as if asking questions would cost him a couple of inches off his cock. If he lived and didn't get maimed, he wouldn't stay a second lieutenant long. Chester could see a big future ahead of him.

For now, Wheat paused and lit a cigarette. Chester's nostrils twitched at the fragrant smoke. "You lifted a pack off of one of Featherston's fuckers, sir," he said. "The smokes we get with our rations don't smell that good."

"Right the first time, Sergeant." Wheat grinned. His looks were as corn-fed as his accent: he was a husky blond guy, good-sized but not quite so big as Joe Jakimiuk, with a narrower face and sharper features than the PFC's. He held out the pack to Chester. "Want one?"

"Sure. Thanks a lot, sir," Chester answered. A lot of lieutenants would have gone right on smoking the good stuff themselves without a thought for their noncoms. Some officers acted as if they were a superior breed of man just because of their metal rank badges. Wheat didn't have that kind of arrogance—another sign he'd do well for himself if he stayed healthy.

"Sentries all around our position tonight," he told Chester. "No telling which way the Confederates will come at us. We're really and truly in their rear, so they could come from any direction at all."

"Yes, sir," Chester said. "I'll take care of it." In the enemy rear! He didn't think that had ever happened in the Great War: not to him, anyway. You could beat back the Confederates, but get behind them? Retreating troops had always been able to fall back faster than advancing troops could pursue them through the wreckage of war. Now . . . Now this armored thrust had pierced the zone of devastation and found nothing much behind it.

"You men will want to sleep while you can," Lieutenant Wheat told his soldiers. "I don't know how much we're going to get from here on out."

"Listen to him, guys," Chester said. "He knows what he's talking about."

He curled up in his own bedroll not long after he stubbed out the mild, flavorful Confederate cigarette. Exhaustion blackjacked him moments later. He forgot the chilly air and the hard, damp ground and everything else. He wished he could have slept for a week. What was hard on the young guys was a hell of a lot harder for somebody of his vintage.

Instead of a week, he got till the end of the wee small hours. Jakimiuk shook him awake, saying, "Sorry, Sarge, but we're gonna move out."

"Coffee," Chester croaked, like a man in the desert wishing for water. The instant coffee that came with rations was nasty, but it did help pry his eyelids open. And it was hot, which was also welcome.

Ham and eggs out of a tin can made the beef stew from the night before seem delicious by comparison. Chester shrugged. The ration would keep him going another few hours. Maybe he'd eat something better then. The really scary thing was, the soldiers who wore butternut had it worse.

As the sky grayed toward dawn, the barrels the platoon had been riding roared to life. Chester clambered aboard the one he'd ridden the past two days. The barrel's commander popped out of his cupola like a jack-in-the-box. He was a sergeant, too, though a younger man than Chester. "We going to give them another boot in the balls today?" he asked cheerfully.

"Here's hoping, anyway." Chester wasn't about to commit the sin of optimism. Justifiably or not, he feared it would jinx everything.

No one would see the sun even when it rose. Clouds filled the sky. They couldn't seem to make up their mind whether to give rain or snow or sleet. Since they couldn't decide, they spat out a little of each at random. Even when nothing was coming down, the wind out of the northwest had knives in it. Chester would have disliked the weather much more than he did if it hadn't kept C.S. Asskickers from diving on him.

"Here we go!" Lieutenant Wheat shouted when the barrels moved out. He might have been a kid on a Ferris wheel at a county fair. Chester suspected he wouldn't take long to lose that boyish enthusiasm. Once you'd been through a few fights, once you'd seen a few horrors, you might be ready to go on with the war, but you weren't likely to be eager anymore.

A train ahead chugged east. *On its way to Pittsburgh?* Chester

wondered. He couldn't think of any other reason why an engine pulling a lot of passenger cars should be on its way through what had been
territory firmly under the Confederate thumb.

The barrel commander evidently decided the same thing. The
big, snorting machine stopped. The turret—one of the massive new
models, with a bigger gun—slewed to the left, till it bore on the locomotive. When the cannon fired, the noise was like the clap of doom.
Hearing it, a man with a hangover might have his head fall off—and if
he didn't, he might wish he did. The shot was perfect. It went right
through the boiler. Great clouds of steam rose from the engine. Only
momentum kept it moving after that; it wasn't going anywhere under
its own power.

Other barrels started shelling and shooting up the passenger cars.
Chester had an abstract sympathy for the soldiers in butternut who
tumbled out like so many ants when their hill was kicked. The Confederates had been going toward battle, yes. They'd been thinking about
it, worrying about it, no doubt. But they hadn't expected it, not yet.
Too bad for them. Life was what you got, not what you expected.

"Come on, boys," Chester said to the men on the barrel with him.
"Let's make them even happier than they are already."

They got down and started shooting at the dismayed Confederates
from behind the barrels and whatever other cover they could find. The
machine guns in the turret and at the bow of each barrel raked the scat-
tering soldiers in butternut, too. Every so often, for variety's sake, a
cannon would lob a high-explosive shell or two into the Confederates.

A few bullets came back at the U.S. barrels and foot soldiers, but
only a few. A lot of the Confederates probably hadn't even been able to
grab their weapons before they spilled from the train. Some of the ones
who had were bound to be casualties. And others, instead of returning fire, were doing their best to disappear, keeping the battered railroad cars between themselves and their tormentors as they ran for the
woods.

Chester wasn't so sure he wouldn't have done the same thing.
Sometimes going forward, or even staying where you were, was asking
to be killed. He'd retreated more than once in the Great War, and by
Fredericksburg not so long ago. He wouldn't have been surprised if he
did it again before too long.

Now, though, he was going forward. That was better. He didn't
suppose even the Confederates could disagree with him. They'd done

more advancing than retreating in this war. He hoped they enjoyed going the other way.

The sergeant in charge of the barrel he rode popped out of the cupola again. "We've got orders to get moving," the other noncom said. "Faster we put a ring around Pittsburgh, faster we can pound Featherston's fuckers inside to pieces."

Somebody was driving the U.S. forces as if a pack of wolves ran right behind them. Chester didn't mind. They probably needed driving. If they weren't driven, they wouldn't do what needed doing. Even if they were, they might not.

On they went. Every so often, Confederate soldiers would shoot at them. That caused a few casualties, but only slight delays. Machine-gun and small-arms fire didn't make the barrels slow down. They had somewhere important to go, and they wanted to get there in a hurry. More foot soldiers would be coming along behind them, and artillery-men, too. People like that could deal with the odd set of holdouts.

From everything Chester heard, Featherston's men and barrels fought that way when they stormed through Ohio to Lake Erie, and then again this summer when they smashed east to Pittsburgh. He didn't think the United States had ever done anything like this before. He wondered why not.

The barrels and the men who rode them and the men who tried to keep up with them did have to slow down when they passed through towns. That usually wasn't because Confederate soldiers made stands there. Most towns held hardly any Confederates. But the people who hadn't fled ahead of the advancing Confederate tide came out in droves to welcome the U.S. Army's return.

Chester got handed eggs, an apple pie, a chunk of home-cured ham, and a pouch of pipe tobacco. He got snorts of booze ranging from good Scotch to raw corn liquor. He got his hand shook and his back slapped. Several pretty girls kissed him. What Rita didn't know wouldn't hurt her. If he could have stayed in any one place for a little while . . . But the speed of the advance helped hold him to the straight and narrow.

Locals hauled down the Stars and Bars and burned it. Up went the Stars and Stripes in its place. Chester hoped the CSA didn't retake any of these towns. People would catch it if the Confederates did. They didn't seem to care. "Them bastards would just as soon shoot you as look at you," an old man said. "My pa, he fought 'em in the War of Secession. He always said they fought fair then. No more. They hanged one poor son of a bitch for thumbing his nose at 'em when they rode down the street. Hanged him from a lamppost, like he was a nigger."

In the field, the Confederates played by the rules most of the time. Up till now, Chester hadn't seen what they did behind the lines. It didn't make him like them any better. It did make him think the atrocity stories he heard were more likely to be true.

Lafayette, Ohio, was a little town notable only for the red-brick tavern in the middle of it—the place looked older than God. As Chester's barrel paused in the village square, more green-gray machines rumbled up from the south. Barrel crews and the infantrymen with them exchanged backslaps and cigarettes. "Lafayette," Chester said happily. "Here we are!" They'd encircled the Confederates. Now—would the ring hold?

XVIII

Mr. President, sir, we have got to break out from Pittsburgh," Nathan Bedford Forrest III said. "We have got to do it right now, right this minute, the sooner the better, while the machines still have enough gas to go at least partway."

Jake Featherston scowled at the head of the Confederate General Staff. "We're doing all right in there," he said.

"We are *now*, Mr. President," Forrest said. "We've still got ammo. We've still got fuel. When we start running low . . ." He shook his head. "And it won't be long, either. They've cut the supply routes, same as we cut the USA in half last summer."

"If we can't get the shit in by road or railroad, we'll damn well fly it in," Jake said. "That'll keep the men fighting."

"Sir, we've got a whole army in there," Forrest replied, shaking his head. "No offense, sir, but no way in hell we can bring in enough by air to keep that many men going."

"That isn't what the flyboys tell me," Jake said. "I've talked with 'em. They say they're up for the job."

"They're lying through their teeth, Mr. President, on account of they're scared to tell you you truth," Nathan Bedford Forrest III declared. "You tell me who you talked to, and I'll personally go punch the son of a bitch in the nose."

"You'll do no such thing. They had diagrams and everything— showed just what they could do," Featherston said. "Long as they can do it, the boys up there can keep fighting, right? And you can work out some kind of way to break through to 'em. How many damnyankees can there be in that ring, anyhow?"

"Too many," Forrest said morosely. "They hit us where we were weakest and punched on through."

"Goddamn Mexicans. I ought to have Francisco José's guts for garters. If he had any guts, by God, I would, too." Jake was not only furious, he wanted to blame someone—anyone—else for what was going on in Pennsylvania and Ohio. That way, the blame wouldn't come down on his own head.

The chief of the General Staff didn't seem interested in casting blame: a blessing and an annoyance at the same time. "Sir, we just didn't have enough of our own people to go around. That's the trouble with fighting a country bigger than we are," he said. "That's why we've got to get as many of our men in and around Pittsburgh out as we can. If we lose them all—"

"They'll take plenty of damnyankees with 'em," Jake broke in.

"Yes, sir." Forrest sounded patient. He also sounded worried. "But if we trade men one for one with the USA, we lose, on account of they've got more men than we do. Pretty soon we just run dry, and they keep going. That's the point of everything we've done up till now: to make them pay more than we do. If that whole big army's stuck inside of Pittsburgh, it can't play that game anymore."

Jake Featherston grunted. However little he wanted to see that, Forrest's picture left him little choice. But trying to break out of Pittsburgh would be a disastrous admission of defeat. "What can we get together in Ohio?" he asked. "What can we use to break through the ring and get those people out?"

Forrest frowned. "It won't be easy, Mr. President. We put the best of what we had into the attacking force. That's what you're supposed to do, sir: make the *Schwerpunkt* as strong as you can."

"Yeah, yeah. Don't you go spouting German at me," Jake said. "Goddamn Kaiser's got troubles of his own. You'd better believe he does. If we can break in far enough for the men in Pittsburgh to break out and link up, that'll be all right." He shook his head. "It won't be all right, but we can take it. There's politics in this damn war, too, don't forget."

"All right, sir. If that's all I can get from you, that's all I can get," Nathan Bedford Forrest III said. "I'll . . . see what we can put together.

And the air resupply will do the best job it can. If you'll excuse me . . ." He saluted and hurried away.

"Fuck," Featherston muttered. He scowled at the map on the wall of his underground and armored office. He would have been tougher on Forrest if he hadn't seen at once that the head of the General Staff wasn't alibiing—he was telling the truth. Where the devil *could* they scrape up enough men to relieve Pittsburgh? Wherever it was, they had to do it pretty damn quick.

He turned his head to the bigger map on the far wall, the one that showed the whole frontier from Sonora to Virginia. He could yank some soldiers from. . . .

"Fuck," he said again, louder this time. The damnyankees were mounting an attack on Lubbock. He didn't think it would get there, but the town had to be held. They were kicking up their heels in Sequoyah. A column from Missouri was pushing down into Arkansas. It wasn't a real big column, but it was big enough to keep him from taking men out of the state. General MacArthur was getting uppity just a little north of Richmond, too. The Confederates had already pulled men from the Army of Northern Virginia to load up farther west. They couldn't very well pull more.

Featherston repeated the obscenity yet again. Early in the war, somebody'd said that whoever could keep two big campaigns going at once would probably win. Both sides seemed to have taken that as gospel. Now, suddenly and painfully, Jake saw it wasn't necessarily so.

The damnyankees had done one big thing. They were also doing a bunch of little things. By itself, not one of those little things mattered. Added together, though, they kept the Confederates from properly countering the big thrust. It was like being gnawed by rats instead of eaten by a bear. It was ignominious. It was humiliating.

You ended up just as dead either way. That was the point, and he'd taken too damn long to see it. Something, somewhere, would have to give. That was all there was to it. While Jake eyed the map with the big picture, he also scowled at the red pins stuck into the interior of the CSA: from South Carolina all the way west to Louisiana, and some in the mountains of Cuba, too. They marked spots where Negro guerrillas were kicking up their heels.

He swore so foully, he took a hasty look toward the door to make sure Nathan Bedford Forrest III had closed it behind him. He didn't want Lulu hearing and wagging a finger at him. That was pretty funny when you got right down to it: the most powerful man the Confederate States had ever known, afraid of his own secretary. But Featherston wasn't laughing at all.

If the blacks in the country had just stayed quiet, he would have had several more divisions to throw at the damnyankees. He wouldn't be jumping up and down now about where to find men to try to bail out the force trapped in Pittsburgh.

"Those bastards'll pay," he growled. "Oh, Lord, how they'll pay." He got on the telephone and called Ferdinand Koenig. Ferd had a new secretary, one with a hell of a sultry voice. Jake wondered if the rest of her lived up to it. If it did, Koenig might be finding after-hours work for her, too.

"Office of the Attorney General," she purred, as if she'd just got out of bed.

Featherston didn't have time for that, though. "This is the President," he said. "Get Ferd on the line right this second, you hear?"

"Y—Yes, sir." Most of that sexy lilt disappeared—most, but not all.

"Ferd Koenig." The Attorney General's deep, gruff voice sounded the way it always did. Jake tried to imagine Koenig talking in soft, throaty tones. He couldn't do it.

"Listen, we have got to get rid of more niggers faster," he said without preamble. "The damn guerrillas are a running sore. We've got to get rid of it, or it's going to screw us for the rest of the war."

"Camps are running pretty close to capacity," Koenig said dubiously.

"Bump it up," Jake said. "Build more bathhouses. Build more trucks. Hell, build more camps. Whatever it takes, but bump it up. And fast."

"All right, sir. I'll handle that," Koenig said, and he was a man who did what he said he would do. He was an old Party buddy, one of the last ones Jake had, but he was also damn good at his work. He went on, "The more we step it up against the coons, the more they're liable to try and fight back, you know. That'll cost us men who could be at the front."

He was thinking along with Jake, but Jake was a little bit ahead of him. Jake hoped he was, anyhow. "You handle your end of it, Ferd," he said. "I'll take care of the other—or if I don't, somebody's gonna be mighty goddamn sorry, and it won't be me or you."

"I'll do everything I can. The camps will do everything they can," Koenig promised.

"Good. That's what I need to hear. Freedom!" Featherston hung up. His next call was to the Secretary of State. He talked with Herbert Walker much less often than with Ferdinand Koenig. The Secretary of State was a real diplomat, and always looked uncomfortable wearing a Freedom Party uniform instead of striped pants and cutaway coat.

Walker knew better than to keep Jake waiting, though. "Yes, Mr. President? What can I do for you today, sir?"

Again, Featherston came straight to the point: "I need another five divisions of Mexicans from Francisco José, and I need 'em yesterday."

"Mr. President!" The Secretary of State sounded horrified. "After what's happened to the men he sent you before, you'll be lucky to get the time of day out of him, let alone anything more."

"Tell him I won't use them against the damnyankees. Promise him on a stack of Bibles—it's the truth," Jake said. "Tell him I want 'em for . . . for internal security. That's what it is, all right. I'm gonna sic 'em on the damn uppity niggers, free up our own men to fight against the USA. That's what I should've done with the last batch of Mexicans, only I didn't think of it then. Sometimes you're smarter the second time around."

"Well, I'll try, sir," Walker said. "On that basis, I will try. Even so, I don't know what the answer will be."

"We've got Mexicans coming up here to get work now, lots of 'em," Jake said. "Tell Francisco José that if he doesn't want to give us a hand, we won't just seal the border—we'll ship the ones who are already here back to Mexico."

"The way things are, that's liable to hurt us worse than the Mexicans," Walker said.

Jake understood what he meant: the Mexicans were doing the scut-work Negroes had done in the CSA for generations. They were also filling more and more factory slots white men would have taken if they weren't off fighting a war. Even so, he said, "Tell him anyway, by God. If we don't have Mexicans giving us some help with the work, it's a pain in the ass. If Francisco José's got a pile of Mexicans who can't get *any* work sitting around, it's a civil war waiting to happen. You reckon he doesn't know it? He's dumb, but he's not that dumb."

"All right, sir. I'll tell him. Internal security. It's a good phrase," the Secretary of State said.

"He damn well better say yes," Jake said. A small gasp came from the other end of the line. Hastily, he added, "It'll be his hard luck if he doesn't, not yours. I didn't mean that."

"Thank you, Mr. President. I'm glad you didn't. And now I'd better get on with it." When Jake didn't say no, Walker hung up. Jake chuckled harshly. He could still make people afraid of him, an essential part of the business of ruling.

But the chuckle cut off as he looked from one situation map to the other. How was he supposed to make the damnyankees afraid of him? He'd hurt them badly. He'd stopped their first big counterattack. Now, though, they were running with the ball, and he was going to have a devil of a time tackling them.

Abner Dowling had spent too long either retreating before the Confederates or banging his head into a stone wall. Now, for the first time since gaining a command of his own, he was going forward—and he was enjoying it, too. So what if the force he had consisted mostly of what nobody else in the USA wanted? The force trying to stop him consisted mostly of what nobody else in the CSA wanted. By the way it had performed so far, it was even more raggedy than his own.

His new headquarters lay in the grand metropolis—say, a thousand people—of Sudan, Texas. He'd been disappointed when one of the locals told him it was named for the kind of grass that fed the local cattle, not for the place in Africa. He supposed the grass was named for the place in Africa, but it didn't seem the same.

Sudan grass didn't cover everything. Not far away, a brownish-yellow ridge line ran east and west. It was called, bluntly, the Sand Hills. People from the north side of the hills were supposed to vote differently from those to the south, and each group was supposed to have its own little social sets. Dowling lost not a moment's sleep about that. People on both sides of the Sand Hills were Confederates, which was everything he needed to know about them.

His line stood about four miles farther down C.S. Highway 84, halfway between Sudan and Amherst, a town of about the same size. Another eight or ten miles down the road was Littlefield, which was the next size up. Lubbock lay thirty-five miles southeast of Littlefield, and Lubbock, with more than 20,000 people, was a real city. If he could take it, people as far away as Richmond would jump and shout and swear.

And if he couldn't . . . "News from Pennsylvania and Ohio's better than what we've heard before," he said to Major Toricelli.

"Yes, sir," his adjutant agreed. "Now we get to see how tough the enemy is when things don't go his way."

Dowling coughed. He wished the younger man hadn't put it that way. He'd seen the Confederates in adversity during the last war, and they'd fought like sons of bitches. They *were* sons of bitches, as far as he was concerned, but that didn't mean they weren't brave and tough and stubborn.

"We're playing some little part in what's going on there, too," he said. "I like that."

"Yes, sir. Me, too," Angelo Toricelli said. "Wherever they get reinforcements from, they won't get 'em from here. We're keeping 'em too busy for that."

"We may even grab Lubbock," Dowling said. "I didn't think we could when we got started, but you know what?"

"The Confederates around here are even more screwed up than we are?" Toricelli suggested.

"That's just exactly what I was going to say." Dowling raised an eyebrow. "By now, you've signed my name with 'by direction' after it so many times, you really are starting to think like me. No offense, of course."

"Did I say anything like that, sir?" Toricelli looked and sounded so innocent, Dowling wouldn't have been surprised to see a halo suddenly start glowing above his head. The general commanding Eleventh Army chuckled under his breath. If his adjutant had started thinking like him, he could also start thinking like his adjutant. He'd been an adjutant for years, while Toricelli would have to wait for the next war against the Confederates for his turn as a CO.

The next war against the Confederates . . . The noises Dowling made under his breath when that thought crossed his mind weren't nearly so amused. When the Great War ended, he'd hoped the USA would never have to worry about the CSA again. He'd been too optimistic once. He would be a fool to make the same mistake twice. Nothing kept a man from making a fool of himself now and again. Dowling did try not to make a fool of himself that way too often.

Half a dozen artillery rounds came down a few hundred yards short of Sudan. "They're probably after you, sir," Major Toricelli said.

"They're a pack of idiots if they are," Dowling replied. "This attack doesn't need Julius Caesar or Napoleon at the top. As long as I keep the boys in butternut too busy to head east, I'm a hero."

"A regular Robert E. Lee," Toricelli said with malice aforethought. Dowling scowled, his severity more or less real. If his Confederate opposite number talked about officers to emulate, Lee's name would likely be the first one in his mouth. Why not? Lee trounced every U.S. general he faced in the War of Secession.

When the War of Secession was new, just as Virginia was going from the USA to the CSA, Abe Lincoln offered Lee command of U.S. forces. Had Lee said yes, the USA might well be one country now. Lincoln might not share with James G. Blaine the dubious distinction of being the only Republican Presidents. They also shared the even more dubious distinction of starting wars—and losing them.

Dowling tried to remember. Wasn't it during Blaine's term that Lincoln had pulled out of the Republican Party and gone over to the Socialists? He thought so. The Republicans had never been the same since. Now Dowling, a thoroughgoing Democrat, had to hope the Socialists hadn't started a war they were going to lose. He had to do whatever he could to help make sure they didn't lose it, too.

More shells crashed down southeast of Sudan. These were closer. Dowling and Major Toricelli both raised eyebrows. Toricelli said, "Sir, I move we adjourn to the storm cellar. You may not think you're important, but it looks like they do."

"Damn nuisance," Dowling grumbled, but he didn't say no. An unlit kerosene lantern hung on the wall by the trap door to the cellar. Tornadoes tore across the West Texas prairie every now and again. Most houses in these parts—and on the U.S. side of the line in New Mexico, too—had shelters that could save lives . . . if you were lucky enough or quick enough to get into them fast enough.

Toricelli ceremoniously lifted the trap door. "After you, sir." A couple of the wooden stairs creaked under Dowling's weight, but they held. Toricelli followed him down and closed the door behind them. "I've got a match, sir," he said, and lit one.

Dowling hadn't checked to see if the lamp held fuel. "Just my luck if it's dry," he said. But it wasn't. Buttery light pushed back shadows. It wasn't very bright, but it would do. Four milking stools comprised the cellar's furniture. He set the lamp on one and perched himself on another. It also creaked.

"We've done what we can do, sir," Major Toricelli said. One more set of booms came in, some of them very loud and close. "I'm glad we did, too," he added.

"Well, now that you mention it, so am I," Dowling allowed. His adjutant smiled. Dowling didn't think of himself as particularly brave. General Custer, now, had been as brave a man as any ever born, even up into his seventies and eighties. Dowling admired that without being convinced it made Custer a better commander. It might have made him a worse one: since he didn't worry about his own safety, he also didn't worry much about his men's. Daniel MacArthur also had as much courage as any four ordinary people needed, which didn't make him any less a vain blowhard or any more a commanding general in command of himself. If you weren't a hopeless coward—more to the point, if the soldiers you led didn't know you were a hopeless coward—you could function as a commanding officer.

More shells crashed down in Sudan. "I hope the sentries outside the house are all right," Toricelli said. "They've got foxholes, but even so . . ."

"Yes, even so," Dowling said. "We ought to be going after the Confederates' guns. They must have pushed them well forward to land shells this far back of the line. Our own artillery should be able to pound on them."

"Here's hoping," his adjutant said. "Do you want me to go up and get on the telephone with our batteries?"

"No, no, no." Dowling shook his head. "If the people in charge of them can't figure that out for themselves, they don't deserve to have their jobs."

"That's always a possibility, too." Toricelli had seen enough incompetents in shoulder straps to know what a real possibility it was.

So had Abner Dowling. "If they just sit around and waste the chance, that will tell us what we need to know about them," he said. "And if they do just sit around, we'll have some new officers in those slots by this time tomorrow, by God."

"What do we do with the clodhoppers, then?" Toricelli asked. "Not always simple or neat to court-martial a man for moving slower than he should."

"You're right—a lot of the time, it's more trouble than it's worth,"

Dowling agreed. "But somebody who can't do what he needs to when the chips are down shouldn't be face-to-face with the enemy. We damn well can transfer people like that out of here. As long as they're in charge of the coast-defense batteries of Montana, they don't do much harm."

"The—" Major Toricelli broke off and sent him a reproachful stare. "Every so often, the devil inside you comes out, doesn't he?"

"Who, me?" Dowling said, innocent as a mustachioed baby. His adjutant laughed out loud.

About ten minutes later, the Confederate shelling suddenly stopped. "Maybe some of our people had a rush of brains to the head," Toricelli said.

"Here's hoping." Dowling's devil must still have been loose, for he went on, "'Hmm. They're shooting at us. What should I do? Why, I'll—I'll shoot back!'" He snapped his fingers as if that were a brilliant idea arrived at after weeks or maybe months of research. In tones more like the ones he usually used, he went on, "If we need to send people to West Point or Harvard to figure that out, Lord help us."

"No, sir," Toricelli said. "If we sent people to West Point or Harvard and they *can't* figure that out, Lord help us. And some of them can't. That's probably why we've got coast-defense batteries in Montana."

"Wouldn't be a bit surprised." Dowling picked up the lantern and started up the stairs. "Let's see if they've blown Sudan to hell and gone. I don't suppose many people will miss it if they have."

No shells had landed on the house. When Dowling went outside, he found the sentries just coming out of their holes in the ground. They saluted him and then went back to brushing themselves off.

An irate local shouted at him: "You damnyankee son of a bitch, you trying to get me killed?"

"I don't know why you're blaming me. I didn't shoot at you. Jake Featherston's men did," Dowling answered.

"The hell you say!" The Texan wouldn't believe a word of it. "We used to have to belong to the USA when y'all called this place Houston. Jake Featherston done gave us back our freedom." The last word wasn't quite the Party howl, but it came close.

"Watch how you talk to the general, buddy," one of the sentries warned, swinging his Springfield toward the local.

"It's all right, Hopkins," Dowling said. By the look on the sentry's face, it wasn't even close to all right. Dowling turned back to the Texan. "Jake Featherston gave you *this*—all of it. If he was as tough and smart as he said he was, it never could have happened, right? Since it *has* happened, he's not so tough and he's not so smart, right?"

Somehow, that didn't make the unhappy civilian any happier. Somehow, Abner Dowling hadn't thought it would. And somehow, he couldn't have cared less.

About one day in three, the skies above central Ohio cleared. Those were the days when Confederate dive bombers and fighters struck savagely at the U.S. soldiers in and around Lafayette. Chester Martin liked being strafed and bombed no better than anyone else in his right mind.

But the U.S. position was a lot stronger than it had been when troops moving southwest out of Pennsylvania joined hands with men coming up from West Virginia. Antiaircraft guns followed close on the heels of barrels and hard-driving soldiers. They weren't much use against Hound Dogs; the C.S. fighters more often than not struck and then vanished. But Asskickers, slower and clumsier, paid a high price for screaming down on U.S. entrenchments.

And fighters with the U.S. eagle in front of crossed swords came overhead as often as their C.S. counterparts did. They were a match for Hound Dogs and more than a match for Asskickers. Confederate aircraft hurt the men in green-gray down on the ground, but the Confederates hurt themselves, too, and badly.

"How many airplanes can they throw away to soften us up?" Chester asked, scooping hash out of a ration can with a spoon. He sat by a campfire with several other men from the platoon. Banks of earth shielded the fire from any lurking C.S. snipers.

"That's only part of the question." Lieutenant Delbert Wheat lit a cigarette. It smelled good, which meant it was Confederate. After taking a drag, he went on, "The other part is, when do they counterattack on the ground? That's got to be what they're softening us up for."

Chester nodded. He'd been thinking the same thing ever since the linkup here. "I would have looked for them to try it already, sir," he said. "I wonder why they haven't."

"Only one answer I can think of," Lieutenant Wheat said. "They aren't strong enough to bring it off."

"They'll be sorry if they wait around much longer," Chester said.

"They may be getting stronger, but so are we." Not far away from the fire lay the wreckage of a downed Asskicker, the crumpled tail pointing pathetically toward the sky.

Del Wheat's smile made his mouth crooked. "And you're sorry for this because . . . ?"

Chester laughed. "Not me, sir. Not even a little bit. But this is the first time I've seen 'em where it doesn't look like they know what they want to do. Makes me suspicious—know what I mean?" He'd seen in the last war that the Confederates could be beaten, that their plans didn't always work. But to find them without any plans . . . That struck him as a more typical U.S. failing.

"They were taking a chance when they struck at Pittsburgh," Wheat said. "Taking it away or even wrecking it hurts the USA. Maybe they've gone and wrecked themselves, too, though."

"Here's hoping," Chester said.

Rain and a little sleet came in the next morning. That meant the Mules and the Asskickers would stay away till the weather got better. It didn't mean the throb of airplane engines left the sky. Up above the clouds, Confederate transports were doing what they could to keep Jake Featherston's surrounded army supplied.

The antiaircraft guns near Lafayette boomed, firing by what one gunner called earsight. It would take a lot of luck to knock down any airplanes that way. As long as the guns had plenty of ammo, though, why not put it in the air? Shoot off enough and you were bound to hit something sooner or later.

Besides, the ring around the Confederates trapped in Pittsburgh was getting thicker as the USA rushed more troops through the gaps the men and barrels in green-gray had torn in the C.S. flank defenses. These weren't the only antiaircraft guns that would be shooting at the cargo planes on their way to Pennsylvania—far from it. If they didn't go down in flames here, they might yet farther east.

And U.S. fighters also prowled above the clouds. Transports weren't made to go fast and be nimble, any more than buses were. If fighters attacked them, their best hope lay in how much damage they could take before they fell out of the sky.

Sometimes the Confederate transports had Hound Dogs of their own to escort them to the target and drive off U.S. Wright fighters. Sometimes they didn't. When they didn't, they paid for it.

"Why don't the Confederates send escorts along all the time?"

Chester asked when a burning transport crashed less than half a mile from his foxhole.

"Well, I don't know for sure, but I think I can make a pretty fair guess," Lieutenant Wheat answered.

"Sir?" Chester said. He'd served under a couple of platoon commanders whose opinions he didn't want, but who insisted on giving them anyhow. Del Wheat wasn't like that. Some of the things he had to say were worth hearing, but he didn't make a big deal out of them. Those other guys seemed to think they were the Pope speaking *ex cathedra.*

"Well, my guess is that the Confederate States don't have enough airplanes—or maybe enough pilots—to be able to do all the things they'd like to do," Wheat said. "Now they can do this, now they can do that—but it doesn't look like they can do this *and* that at the same time."

Chester thought about it. After a moment, he nodded. "That does make sense, yes, sir." He paused again, then resumed: "Getting that cargo into Pittsburgh is pretty important for them right now. If they can't take care of that because of everything else they've got going on, maybe they bit off more than they can chew."

"That's true. Sergeant. Maybe they did." Lieutenant Wheat looked like a cat contemplating a saucer of cream.

Civilians came from C.S.-occupied territory farther west. They claimed the Confederates there were building up for an attack on the U.S. ring. Lieutenant Wheat listened to them and sent them on to Intelligence officers back at division HQ. "You're not flabbling much about this," Chester remarked.

"Nope, not me," the platoon commander said. "If the enemy does try to come through here, we'll do our damnedest to stop him. That's all we can do. But what do you want to bet that some of those so-called civilians are really Confederate plants, and they're trying to make us jump at shadows?"

"Ah," Chester said. "Well, sir, since you put it that way, I wouldn't be a bit surprised."

"Neither would I," Delbert Wheat said. "So I'll worry when my superiors tell me to, but not till then."

Chester did notice that some of the ammunition coming in for the antiaircraft guns had the black-painted tips of armor-piercing rounds. The Confederates used their antiaircraft guns against barrels with vicious effect. Imitation was the sincerest, and most deadly, kind of flattery.

Not long before Christmas, word came down from on high that the Confederates would be coming soon. The United States had taken advantage of the weather to break through in November. A new snowstorm might give the Confederates the same sort of extra concealment.

The C.S. bombardment had gas shells in it. They were less deadly in cold weather, and gas masks more nearly tolerable—unless your mask froze up. That didn't mean Chester wanted to put on his mask. Want it or not, he did. He'd seen gas casualties in the Great War, and a few this time, too. Getting shot was bad enough. He knew just how bad it was from twofold experience. By everything he knew except that direct experience, getting gassed was worse.

As soon as the shelling let up, Lieutenant Wheat shouted, "Be ready!" Up and down the U.S. line, that same cry rang out. The troops in green-gray had the advantage of standing behind the Tuscarawas River. Chester hoped that would mean something. The Confederates had more practice crossing in the face of resistance than any Great War army had.

Where Chester's platoon was stationed, the river, which ran mostly north and south, took an east-west bend. Instead of pressing down on that east-west length, the soldiers in butternut trundled past it to hit the next north-south stretch. "They're giving us their flank!" Wheat exclaimed in amazement.

True, the Confederates did stay out of effective rifle range of the men on the south bank of the Tuscarawas. But several of their barrels trundled along only a few hundred yards from the antiaircraft guns that could also fire against ground targets. When the gunners got targets that artillerymen mostly only dreamt of, they made the most of them. Four or five barrels went up in flames in a few minutes' time. U.S. machine guns and riflemen harried the crewmen bailing out of the machines. They were shooting at long range, but with enough bullets in the air some probably struck home.

Some barrels paused, presented their glacis plates to their tormentors, and fired back. Others scooted farther north, so the U.S. guns wouldn't bear on them any more. Artillery fire fell around those antiaircraft guns. Sometimes it fell on them. Had the weather been better, Asskickers would have gone after them one by one. With clouds huddling low, though, dive bombers were liable to fly straight into the ground instead of pulling up in time.

When yet another Confederate barrel brewed up because it incautiously came too close to the U.S. antiaircraft guns, Chester yelled and pounded the dirt at the front of his foxhole. "Those butternut bastards aren't buying anything cheap today!" he yelled.

But he could see only his little corner of the fight. Early in the afternoon, orders came to fall back to the east. "Why?" somebody said indignantly. "We're pounding the crap out of 'em here!"

"Here, yes," Lieutenant Wheat said. "But Featherston's fuckers are over the Tuscarawas south of Coshocton—south and west of here. If we don't give up some ground, they'll hit us in the flank and enfilade us."

Taking enfilading fire was like getting your T crossed in a naval battle: all the enemy's firepower bore on you, but most of yours wouldn't bear on him. It was, in other words, a damn good recipe for getting killed.

"Have we got positions farther east that face west instead of north?" Chester asked.

"Good question, Sergeant," Del Wheat said. "We'll both find out at the same time." He paused. "I hope we do. We must have known this was coming. If we *didn't* get ready for it, then we've got the same old muddle up at the top."

When they came to zigzag trenches hastily dug and bulldozed out of fields, Chester felt like cheering. Somebody with stars on his shoulder straps could actually see a step or two ahead. That made Chester think things might go better than he'd expected.

The Confederates who came up against those trenches went to earth in a hurry when a fierce blast of fire met them. More than a few U.S. soldiers carried captured C.S. automatic rifles for extra firepower. They had to get ammunition from dead enemy soldiers, but there'd been a lot of them around.

Before long, Chester and his comrades needed to fall back again. Again, though, they fell back into prepared positions. In spite of retreating, he felt more confident. The Confederates could overrun any one position, but each one cost them. How many could they overrun before they started running out of men to do it?

* * *

Not far from Ellaville, Georgia, ran a stretch of highway locally called the Memorial Mile. Marble stelae stood by the side of the road. Brass plaques mounted on the marble commemorated Sumter County soldiers who'd served in the Great War. WIA by a name meant the soldier had been wounded in action; KIA by a name meant he'd been killed.

The Negro guerrillas who'd attached Jonathan Moss and Nick Cantarella to their number hated the Memorial Mile with a fierce and terrible passion. "How many names you reckon they be if they put up all the niggers from here they done killed?" asked their chief, who went by the name of Spartacus. Moss suspected that was a *nom de guerre;* it was, as far as he was concerned, a damn good one.

"If you're gonna keep on playing this game, you'll put some more crackers' names on some kinda stones," Nick Cantarella said. His clotted New York vowels and Spartacus' lazy-sounding drawl hardly seemed to belong to the same language. Sometimes they had to pause so each could figure out what the other was saying. But they had something in common: they both wanted to cause the Confederates as much grief as they could.

A convoy of trucks rumbled along the road from Ellaville towards Americus. Command cars with machine guns shepherded the trucks along. Opening up on them would have invited massive retaliation. "One advantage you've got with these pine woods," Moss said.

"What's that?" Spartacus asked.

"They don't lose their leaves this time of year," Moss replied. "Easier to hide here than it would be in a forest full of bare-branched trees."

"Not gonna be much snow on the ground, neither," Cantarella said. "It's really a bitch, tryin' to cover your tracks in the snow."

Spartacus pursed his lips, then slowly nodded. He was about forty-five, just going gray at the temples, with a scar that looked like a bullet crease on his right forearm. If he hadn't been black, he would have put Moss in mind of a career noncom—he had that air of rough, nononsense competence about him. Suddenly, Moss asked, "Did *you* fight for the CSA the last time around?"

"Sure enough did," Spartacus answered. "Got shot fo' mah country—reckoned it *was* mah country in them days. Case you wonderin', ain't no niggers' names on them goddamn memorials, neither. I even vote once—they let me do it in '21, on account of they was afeared that Featherston fucker was gonna win then. But he los', an' I never seen the inside o' no votin' booth since. Ain't seen nothin' but trouble since the Freedom Party come in."

A boxy, old-fashioned Birmingham with a white-haired white man at the wheel drove by. "You could nail somebody like him easy enough, make the Confederates try and go after you here, then hit somewhere else," Cantarella said.

"Don't want to shoot that there ofay," Spartacus said. "That there's Doc Thomason, an' he been settin' bones an' deliverin' babies for buckra and niggers for damn near fifty years. If you can only pay him a chicken, he take your chicken. If you can't pay him nothin', he set your arm anyways. Ain't all white folks bad—jus' too many of 'em."

"All right. Fine. We don't shoot the doc. He ain't gonna be the only guy on the road, though," Cantarella said. "Shoot somebody else. Maybe even hang around to shoot at the first fuckers who come to see what you went and did. Then when they're all flabbling about that, kick 'em in the nuts some other place. Make them react to you."

"We done some o' that," Spartacus said. "We done a couple of people bombs, too, over by Americus. Them Freedom Party assholes, they don't like people bombs none." He spoke with a certain grim satisfaction.

Moss looked at Cantarella. The Army captain was looking back at him. Moss didn't need to be able to read minds to know what Cantarella was thinking. They didn't like people bombs, either. But as weapons the weak could use against the strong, they were hard to match.

"How do you get people to volunteer to blow themselves up?" Moss asked carefully, not sure if the question would offend Spartacus.

But the guerrilla leader looked at him—looked through him, really—and answered, "Don't gotta drug 'em none or get 'em drunk. Don't gotta say we's gonna kill their wives an' chillun, neither. Dat's what you mean, ain't it?" Moss gave back an unhappy nod. Spartacus went on, "See—you is a white man, even if you comes from the US of A. You is happy most o' the time, an' you reckons everybody else happy most o' the time. Ain't like dat if you is a nigger in these here Confederate States. Somebody blow hisself up here, he a lucky man. Do Jesus!—he mighty lucky. He go out quick—it don't hurt none. He make the ofays pay. And he don't go to no goddamn camp where they let him in but he don't come out no mo'. I got mo' people wants to be people bombs'n I got 'splosives an' chances to use 'em."

"Shit," Nick Cantarella said softly. His comment was at least as reverent as Spartacus'. He added, "That explains the Mormons up in the USA, too—to hell with me if it doesn't."

"We is powerful jealous o' them Mormons," Spartacus said.

"Because they thought of people bombs and you didn't?" Moss asked.

"No, no." Spartacus waved that aside. "On account o' they is white, jus' like the rest o' you damnyankees. Can't tell who a Mormon is jus' by lookin'. He go where he please before he press the button. Nobody worry about him none till too late."

Moss and Cantarella looked at each other again. The Negro wasn't wrong. And he understood the difference between deaths and effective deaths. A lot of Great War generals hadn't—their method for smothering fires was burying them in bodies. Some officers in this war had the same disease; Daniel MacArthur's name sprang to mind. Had Spartacus worn stars on his shoulder straps instead of a collarless shirt with rolled-up sleeves and dungarees out at the knees, he might have made a formidable officer, not just a sergeant.

But the United States didn't let Negroes enlist in the Army as privates, let alone send them to West Point to learn the art of command and the fine points of soldiering. In a troubled voice, Moss said, "You make me wonder about my own country, Spartacus, not just yours."

"Good," the black man rumbled. "Wonderin's good. Ain't nothin' gonna change till you wonder if it oughta."

A band of his raiders slipped south from Ellaville toward Plains, a small town west of Americus. Moss and Cantarella went along with them, bolt-action Tredegars in their hands. They were moving south and west from Andersonville: deeper into the Confederacy. In a way, that was good—the camp guards and county sheriffs and whoever else went after escaped POWs were less likely to look for them there. But they had to move cautiously. Negroes walking through peanut fields could be sharecroppers looking for work, but whites doing the same thing were bound to rouse suspicion.

Burnt cork, the staple of minstrel shows for generations, solved the problem. Up close, Cantarella and especially the fairer Moss made unsatisfactory Negroes, but they passed muster at a distance.

"What do we do when we get there?" Moss asked Spartacus.

"Much as we kin," Spartacus replied. "Burn, kill, and then git." That seemed to cover everything that needed covering, as far as he was concerned.

Real sharecroppers and farm laborers put the guerrillas up for the night. The way the other blacks accepted them said everything that needed saying, as far as Moss was concerned. Not all the Negroes in the CSA would fight against the Freedom Party. That took more spirit than some people owned. He couldn't imagine a black betraying those who would fight to the authorities, though.

Negroes raised eyebrows at him and Cantarella, but relaxed when they heard the white men were escaped U.S. POWs. "Damnyankees is all right," said an old man with only a few teeth. He didn't seem to know any other name for people from the United States. Sowbelly, fatback, hominy, sweet potatoes, harsh moonshine—the locals fed them what they had.

"Gots to make the ofay pay." Moss heard that again and again.

The band that approached Plains numbered about fifty—a platoon's worth of men. Moss worried as he trudged through the night toward the little town. If the Confederates had a real garrison there, they could slaughter the raiders. "Don't flabble about it," Nick Cantarella said when he worried out loud. "First thing is, the smokes around here would know if they were layin' for us. Second thing is, they don't have enough guys to garrison every little pissant burg, not if they want to fight a war with us, too."

Logic said he was right. Sometimes logic let you down with a thud, but. . . . "Sounds good," Moss said.

Sentries did patrol the peanut fields around Plains. With almost contemptuous ease, the Negroes disposed of the one who might have discovered them. The gray-haired man died almost before he knew someone was drawing a knife across his throat. Only a small, startled sigh escaped him. A guerrilla threw aside his own squirrel gun and appropriated the sentry's Tredegar. "Too good a piece to waste on a damn fool," he said.

"Let's go," Spartacus said.

They trotted silently into Plains. The silence didn't last long. They started firing into some houses and tossing Featherston Fizzes into others. Fires roared to life. Alarm bells started ringing. Volunteer firemen emerged from their houses to fight the flames. The raiders picked them off one after another.

"Niggers!" somebody shouted. "Holy Jesus, there's niggers loose in Plains!"

"Phone wires cut?" Cantarella demanded of Spartacus.

"We done took care of it," the guerrilla leader said with a savage grin. "Don't want no help comin' from nowhere else."

Here and there, townsfolk fired from windows with rifles or shotguns. Those houses got volleys of fire from the Negroes, as well as gasoline bombs to kill the resisters or drive them out in the open where they made easier prey. Moss also heard women's screams that sounded more outraged than terrified. "You won't find any fighting force in the world where that shit doesn't happen," Cantarella said. Moss nodded, which didn't mean he liked it any better.

Somebody in Plains organized defenders who fought as a group, not as so many individuals. "Over here, Jimmy!" a woman called. "We got trouble over here!"

"Be there real quick, Miss Lillian!" a man answered. Moss got a glimpse of him in the firelight: a kid with a mouthful of teeth, wearing a dark gray C.S. Navy tunic over pajama bottoms. Home on leave? Whatever the reason he was here, he was tough and smart and brave, and he'd make real trouble if he got even half a chance.

He didn't. Moss made sure of that. The Tredegar's stock didn't fit his shoulder quite the same way as the U.S. Army Springfield he'd trained with, but the difference didn't matter. He pulled the trigger gently—he didn't squeeze it. The rifle bucked. Jimmy, the Navy man here in the middle of Georgia, spun and crumpled.

"Good shot!" Spartacus yelled.

Without a commander who sounded as if he knew what he was doing, the defenders went back to fighting every man for himself. Spartacus' raiders weren't well disciplined, but they had a better notion of what they were doing than their foes. They killed as many whites as they could, started fires all over town, and faded back into the countryside. "Well," Moss said, "we yanked their tails pretty good."

"Sure did," Nick Cantarella agreed. "Now we see how hard they yank back."

Clarence Potter had been going at a dead run ever since he put on the Confederate uniform again. He'd been going even harder than that since the war started. And he was going harder still these past few weeks, since things started turning against the CSA.

To make matters worse, he and Nathan Bedford Forrest III flinched whenever they saw each other even if they were just getting bad fried chicken in the War Department cafeteria. He wished Forrest had kept his mouth shut. Now the chief of the General Staff had him thinking— always a dangerous thing to do.

What if Jake Featherston wasn't crazy like a fox? What if he was just plain crazy, period? Around the bend? Nutty as a fruitcake? Two cylinders short of a motor?

"Well, what then?" Potter muttered. He wouldn't have been surprised if there were microphones in his subterranean office. The President of the CSA wouldn't need to be crazy to mistrust him, not after everything that had happened between them over the past twenty-five years. Featherston wouldn't need to be crazy to mistrust his spymasters, either, no matter who they were. But that handful of words seemed safe enough; Potter could have been wondering about any number of things.

He laughed, as people will laugh when the other choice is crying their eyes out. The rescue drive toward Pittsburgh was moving forward. The map on his wall showed that. But it wasn't moving forward fast enough. And the cargo airplanes that were supposed to supply the Confederates trapped in the Pittsburgh pocket were taking an ungodly beating. Potter didn't know what the officers who'd promised transports could do the job had been smoking. Whatever it was, he wished he had some now. Reality needed some blurring.

And Featherston still wouldn't let the men in the pocket fight their way west to meet their would-be rescuers, either. "What we have, we hold!" he said, over and over again. Clarence Potter didn't know what he'd been smoking, either.

Just to make matters more delightful, Lubbock was liable to fall. Some of the nuisance drives the USA had launched to keep the Confederates from strengthening themselves for the rescue effort in Ohio and Pennsylvania were turning into bigger nuisances than even the generals who'd launched them probably expected.

The Attorney General's office, of all things, was having conniptions about this one. Somewhere southeast of Lubbock was something called Camp Determination. Clarence Potter didn't know what that was, not in any official way. He didn't *want* to know, not in any official way. He had a pretty good unofficial idea.

He also saw the need for places like that. Negro raiders were getting more and more annoying. That Navy man in that little Georgia town, shot down in front of his mother . . . Half the town was wrecked, too, and it wasn't the only one guerrillas had hit. Two people bombs in Augusta, one in Savannah, another in Charleston . . .

Potter whistled tunelessly between his teeth. The really alarming part was, things could have been worse. The USA did only a halfhearted job of supplying black guerrillas. Whites up there didn't love them, either. If the damnyankees had gone all-out, they could have caused even more trouble than they did.

One bit of good news—Mexican troops would take some of the spook-fighting off the CSA's hands. Potter didn't know what Jake Featherston said to Maximilian. Whatever it was, it got the Emperor of Mexico moving. It probably scared the living bejesus out of him, too. Jake Featherston was not a subtle man.

Someone knocked on Potter's door. He paused to put a couple of papers into drawers before he said, "Come in."

"Here you are, sir." A lieutenant handed him a manila envelope.

"Thanks," Potter said. "Do I need to sign for it?"

"No, sir," the junior officer answered, which surprised him.

"All right, then." The lieutenant saluted and disappeared. When Potter opened the envelope, he understood. It was a progress report from Henderson V. FitzBelmont. That project was so secret, it didn't have a paper trail. This way, no Yankee spy filing sign-off sheets would wonder about it. Better safe.

He quickly read through the report. It was, for the most part, an account of technical difficulties. Uranium hexafluoride was poisonous and savagely corrosive. FitzBelmont and his people were still working out techniques for handling it. Till they did, separating U-235 from U-238 couldn't even start.

Do you have any idea how the U.S. project is proceeding? FitzBelmont wrote. Potter didn't. He wished he did. He didn't think anyone in the Confederate States did. If someone did, the report would have come through him . . . wouldn't it? If it didn't, it would have gone only one place: straight to Jake Featherston. The President knew Potter was loyal to the CSA—otherwise, he wouldn't have got involved in this uranium business in the first place. So everyone else in the country was probably as ignorant as he was about Yankee progress, if any.

Featherston didn't seem to have found out he and Nathan Bedford Forrest III had met, there in Capitol Square. If the President did know, neither man would still be free. Potter's first thought was that neither would still be alive. After a moment, he realized that wasn't necessarily so. Some of the people Ferd Koenig bossed could keep a man alive and hurting for a long, long time before they finally gave him peace—or maybe just made a mistake and hit him too hard or once too often.

Potter rolled a sheet of paper into the typewriter on his desk and started an answer to Professor FitzBelmont. If he worked on something important, he wouldn't have to think about some of the people who took the Attorney General's orders. *Dear Professor,* he typed, *I hope you and your fmaily are well.* The error in the first sentence assured FitzBelmont the letter really came from him: a simple code, but an effective one. *Thank you for your recent letter, which I have just received. I wish I were more familiar with the Japanese project you mention, but I am afraid I cannot tell you how close they are to invading the Sandwich Islands.*

That, of course, was also code. It might be obvious to anyone who intercepted the letter that Potter wasn't talking about Japan. What he was talking about wouldn't be so obvious, though. He wondered if the Japanese were working on nuclear fission. They weren't white men, but they'd proved they could play the white man's game. He shrugged. That wasn't his worry. It was probably the USA's nightmare. If one bomb could wreck Pearl Harbor or Honolulu, how did you defend them?

Back to what was his problem. He clacked away at the big upright machine. It had a stiff action, but that didn't matter; he was a two-fingered typist with a touch like a tap-dancing rhinoceros. *You did not state when we could expect success from your own work. Its early completion could result in a major increase in efficiency. Hoping to hear from you soon on this point, I have the honor to remain. . . .* He finished the flowery closing phrases on automatic pilot, took out the sheet of paper, and signed the squiggle that might have been his name.

He put the letter in an envelope, sealed it, and wrote Professor Fitz-Belmont's name and *Washington University* on the outside. Then he took it down the hall to the couriers' office, first carefully locking the door to his own office behind him. He nodded to the major in charge of the War Department's secret couriers. "Morning, Dick," he said. "I need one of your boys to take this out of the city."

"Yes, sir. We can do that." The dispatching officer took the envelope, glanced at the address, and nodded. "Do you want someone who's been there before, or a new man?" That was the only question he asked. Who Henderson V. FitzBelmont was and what the professor was working on were none of his business, and he knew it.

"Either way will do," Potter answered. FitzBelmont might recognize a courier he'd seen before. Then again, he might not. He wasn't quite the absentminded professor people made jokes about, but he wasn't far removed, either. Potter got the feeling subatomic particles and differential equations were more real to him than most of the human race.

"We'll take care of it, then," the major said. "You'll want the courier to report delivery, I expect?"

"Orally, when he gets back here," Potter said.

The major raised an eyebrow. Potter looked back as if across a poker table. He held the high cards, and he knew it. So did the major. "Whatever you say, sir."

"Thanks, Dick." Potter went back to his own office. *Whatever you say, sir.* He liked the sound of that. As a general, he heard it a lot. The more he heard it, the more he liked it.

How long had it been since Jake Featherston heard anything but, *Whatever you say, sir?* Since he took the oath of office in 1934, certainly. In most things, nobody'd tried arguing with him for years before that. And he was a man who'd liked getting his own way even when he was only an artillery sergeant.

If somebody had tried telling the President more often, the country might be in better shape right now. Or it might not—Featherston might just have ordered naysayers shot or sent to camps. He'd done a lot of that.

Potter lit a cigarette and blew a meditative cloud of smoke up toward the ceiling. Two questions: was Jake Featherston leading the Confederate States to ruin, and could anybody else do a better job if Featherston came down with a sudden case of loss of life?

With the building disaster in Pittsburgh, with Featherston's stubborn refusal to cut his losses and pull out (which looked worse now than it had when Nathan Bedford Forrest III and Potter sat on the park bench), the answer to the first had gone from *unlikely* through *maybe* and on toward *probably,* even if it hadn't got there yet.

As for the second . . . Potter blew out more smoke. That wasn't nearly so obvious. Nobody could wear Jake Featherston's shoes. The Vice President? Don Partridge was a cipher, a placeholder, somebody to fill a slot because the Confederate Constitution said you needed to fill it. His only virtue was knowing he was a lightweight. Ferdinand Koenig? The Attorney General would have the Freedom Party behind him if the long knives came out. He was able enough, in a gray, bureaucratic way, but about as inspiring as a mudflat. As a leader . . . ? Potter shuddered. Ferd Koenig was one of those people who made a terrific number two but a terrible number one. Unlike some of them, he had the sense to realize it.

Which left—who? Congress was a Freedom Party rubber stamp. Potter couldn't think of any governor worth a pitcher of warm spit. Besides, most people outside a governor's home state had never heard of him.

What about Forrest? Clarence Potter blinked, there in the privacy of his office. He was surprised the idea had taken so long to occur to him. He laughed at himself. "You old Whig, you," he murmured. If the armed forces were going to overthrow the President—and it wouldn't happen any other way—who better to take over the government than the chief of the General Staff? The Freedom Party had danced on the spirit of the Constitution while holding on to most of the letter. Throwing it out the window altogether seemed not just unnatural but wicked. But Forrest just might do.

Losing the war is wicked. Anything else? Next to losing this war to the USA, anything else looks good. Anything at all. Potter nodded decisively. About that, he had no doubts at all. The United States had forced a harsh peace on the Confederate States in 1917, but hadn't kept it going for very long. Terms would be even worse this time, and the United States would make sure the Confederates never got off their knees again.

The next time Potter saw Nathan Bedford Forrest III in the cafeteria, he nodded casually and said, "Something I'd like to talk to you about when we have the chance."

"Really?" Forrest said, as casually. "Can we do it here?"

Potter shook his head. "No, sir," he answered. "Needs privacy." From one general to another, that wasn't a surprising thing to say. For a split second, Forrest's eyes widened. Then he nodded and put some silverware on his tray.

Michael Pound grinned as his barrel rumbled forward, jouncing over rubble and grinding a lot of the big chunks into smaller ones. "Advancing feels good, doesn't it, sir?" he said.

Lieutenant Don Griffiths nodded. "You'd better believe it, Sergeant. We've done too much falling back."

"Yes, sir." Pound wouldn't have argued with that for a moment. "Looks to me like the Confederates are starting to feel the pinch."

"Here's hoping," Griffiths said. "I wouldn't want to try reinforcing and supplying an army the size of theirs by air, I'll tell you that. And I don't think they've got an airstrip left that our artillery can't reach."

"My heart bleeds—but not as much as they're going to bleed before long," Pound said. "I wonder why they haven't tried to break out to the west. Somebody in their high command must have his head wedged. Too bad for them." He had no respect for his own superiors. Finding out some dunderheads wore butternut was reassuring.

A rifle bullet pinged off the barrel's armored side. *That* wouldn't do the Confederates any good. As if to prove it wouldn't, the bow machine gun chattered. Pound peered through his own gunsight, but he couldn't see what the bow gunner was shooting at—if he was shooting at anything. It hardly mattered sometimes.

Off to the left, something on the Confederate side of the line blew up with a roar loud enough to penetrate the barrel's thick skin. "That sounded good," Pound said. "Wonder what it was."

"Want me to stick my head out and look around?" Lieutenant Griffiths asked.

"Not important enough, sir," Pound answered. "Who knows if our machine gun took out whoever was shooting at us?" Barrel commander was a dangerous job. Now that Pound had finally found an officer with some notion of what he was doing, he didn't want to lose him for no good reason. There were too many times when a barrel commander had perfectly good reasons for exposing himself to enemy fire.

Something else blew up, even louder. Griffiths put a hand to his earphones. He often did that when he was getting a wireless message. Sergeant Pound had no idea whether it helped or how it could, but he'd never said anything about it to the officer. It couldn't hurt.

Lieutenant Griffiths leaned forward to use the speaking tube to the driver's position: "Forward again, and a little to the left, but slowly," he said. He turned to Pound. "That was an ammunition dump. They won't be able to shell us so well for a while."

"We hope," said Pound, ever willing to see the cloud next to the silver lining.

"Well, yes. We hope. There's always that," Griffiths agreed. "But we've got infantry moving up with us. With luck, they'll keep the short-range trouble away from us. As for the other side's barrels and anti-barrel guns—we've done all right so far. Of course, we've got a pretty good gunner."

"So we do." Pound knew his own talents too well to be modest about them. Half a second later than he should have, he added, "You're not bad at spotting trouble before it spots us. Best way to get rid of it that I know."

No sooner had he said that than something clanged against the front of the turret with force enough to shake the whole barrel. *I'm dead,* Pound thought. Only a moment later did he realize he would have been too dead to think if that round had got through. *Thank God for the upgraded armor on the new turret. If this beast hadn't been retrofitted, I'd be burnt meat right now.*

Without waiting for orders, the driver roared forward, looking for cover behind the nearest pile of rubble. Then, abruptly, he slammed on the brakes. "Did you see it, sir?" Pound asked.

"No, goddammit." Griffiths sounded angry at himself. "That son of a bitch knows where we're at, and I didn't spot the muzzle flash. Wherever he is, he's hidden good."

"Not sporting," Pound agreed. He'd been more than happy enough to ambush C.S. barrels from an empty garage, but having them turn the tables on him wasn't playing fair. Someone with a more objective view might not have found that unfair, but so what? It wasn't the impartial observer's neck. It was his.

He traversed the turret, staring through the gunsight as he did. The hatch opened. Lieutenant Griffiths stood up to get a better look than he could through the periscopes in the cupola. This was one of *those* times. Griffiths might get shot, but he also might get a better look at the hidden cannon or barrel that had just come within inches of incinerating him.

It didn't fire again, which argued that the rubble in front of Pound's barrel gave pretty good protection. A rifle bullet snapped past; as always, the sound seemed hatefully malicious. Lieutenant Griffiths ducked a little—you did that without thinking—but he didn't come back inside the steel shell. He had balls. Pound nodded approvingly.

Probably not somewhere close, the gunner thought, looking for straight lines that broke the irregular pattern of the ruins of Pittsburgh. If the enemy were close, he would have a better shot at the U.S. barrel. And, if he were close, his round likely would have penetrated in spite of the improved turret. A cannon made a damned effective door knocker.

There! Or Pound thought so, anyhow. "Armor-piercing!" he snapped.

"Armor-piercing," Cecil Bergman answered. The loader slammed a black-tipped cartridge into the breech. Pound worked the elevation handwheel. Fifteen hundred yards *was* a long shot. As near as he could tell, he fired at the same time as the C.S. gunner. The enemy's shot snarled past, a few feet high. Pound's struck home. The enemy barrel started to burn.

"Hit!" Lieutenant Griffiths shouted. "How on earth did you make that shot?"

"Twenty-odd years of practice, sir," Pound answered. The Confederate gunner hadn't had so much—though he'd hit Pound's barrel before Pound even knew he was there. He wouldn't get another chance now. A great cloud of black smoke was rising, almost a mile away.

The shot ricocheting inside the barrel would have killed or maimed some of the crew. The fire would be searing the rest. By the way the smoke billowed out, that barrel was a total loss. Odds were the crew was, too. Pound had bailed out of a crippled barrel, but then only the engine compartment was burning. Could anyone get out here? He didn't think so.

I just killed five men. Most of the time, he didn't worry about that. When he watched a barrel brew up, it was only a machine that died. But he'd just had his own brush with death, and it reminded him of the soldiers inside the barrels. He knew what they were going through; he'd come close to going through it himself. If he'd met them in a bar, he could have drunk the night away talking shop with them.

But they'd just done their best to kill him, and their best was hideously close to good enough. *They're dead and I'm alive and that's how I want it to be.*

"We can move up a little more now, sir," he said.

Griffiths thought about it, then nodded. He called up to the driver. The barrel came out from behind the pile of wreckage and clattered towards another one. Pound tensed when it came out into the open. If the Confederates had drawn a bead on them . . . But no hardened-steel projectile tore into the machine's vitals. He breathed again as a pile of tumbled bricks came between his machine and the people who wanted to do unto it as he'd done unto theirs.

U.S. foot soldiers ran forward with the barrels. A Confederate machine gunner opened up on them. "Front!" Lieutenant Griffiths shouted.

"Identified!" Pound answered. He turned his head and shouted to the loader: "HE!"

"HE," Bergman said. A white-tipped high-explosive round went into the breech. Pound lined up the sights on the C.S. machine gun's winking muzzle. He jerked the lanyard. The cannon bellowed. The shell casing clanked on the floor of the fighting compartment.

A 2.4-inch shell didn't have room for a whole lot of explosive. A three-incher from one of the Confederate barrels would have held almost twice as much. Sandbags and rubble flew from in front of the C.S. gun, but it kept shooting. Tracers drew fiery lines through the air.

Pound abstractly admired the enemy gunners' nerve. If a round burst right in front of him, he would have got the hell out of there. They kept doing what they'd been trained to do. "Another round," he said. In went the shell. He swung the cannon's muzzle a gnat's hair to the left and fired again.

Another hit, but the enemy gun went on firing. He needed two more rounds before it fell silent. The stink of cordite was thick in the turret. "Stubborn bastards," Lieutenant Griffiths said.

"Yes, sir," Pound agreed, coughing. "They're the ones you've especially got to get rid of."

With the machine gun knocked out, U.S. infantry moved up some more. They took casualties. With automatic rifles and submachine guns, the Confederate soldiers could outshoot them. But how long could the Confederates keep outshooting them if more ammunition didn't come into Pittsburgh?

The Confederates couldn't use captured U.S. ammo unless they also used captured Springfields. They'd chosen different calibers on purpose, to make it harder for U.S. soldiers to turn captured automatic rifles against them. It must have seemed a good idea at the time. It probably was. But it cut both ways.

Off to the left, a U.S. barrel got hit and started burning. Nothing in Pittsburgh came cheap. Nothing came easy. The Confederates weren't going to quit, and they fell back only when they had no choice. How long could they keep it up?

He shrugged. That wasn't his worry. People with shoulder straps and metal ornaments on them had to fret about such things. All he had to do was shoot whatever he and Lieutenant Griffiths spotted in front of their barrel and hope like hell nobody shot him. He nodded. That would do nicely.

Shells started bursting around them. The bursts weren't the ordinary kind; they sounded wrong, and even through the gunsight he saw the crawling mist that spread from them. "Gas!" he yelled.

Griffiths clanged down the hatch on top of the cupola. "I saw it," he said. "I was hoping those fuckers were running short. No such luck, I guess."

"No, sir," Pound said as he put on his mask. Out in the open, U.S. infantrymen paused to do the same. Pound went on, "Now we'll throw some at the Confederates, just to make sure they have to wear masks, too. As long as both sides have it, it doesn't change anything."

"I'm not saying you're wrong," Griffiths answered. He had his mask on, too. "But I am saying it's out there." Pound couldn't very well quarrel with that. The barrel commander started to wave to emphasize his point. He choked off the gesture before it was well begun. The inside of a turret was a crowded place.

Michael Pound made a good prophet, as he often did. A U.S. gas barrage followed in short order. It was heavier than the one the enemy had laid down. Infantrymen advanced in short rushes. The barrel moved up to the next decent firing position. Another block of Pittsburgh, cleared of Confederates.

XIX

New Year's Eve. One more day till 1943. Flora Blackford was back in her Philadelphia apartment. She hadn't expected to be anywhere else. Even if she hadn't campaigned at all, she thought she would have beaten Sheldon Vogelman. People in her district were used to reelecting her. She nodded to herself. It was a nice habit for them to have.

Joshua was out with friends. "I'll be back next year," he'd said. How long had people been making that joke? Probably as long as people had divided time into years. He was liable to come back drunk, too, even if he was underage. Well, if he did, the hangover the next morning ought to teach him not to do it again for a while. She could hope so, anyhow.

"Underage," she muttered, and clicked her tongue between her teeth. He would turn eighteen in 1943. Old enough to be conscripted. And conscripted he probably would be. He was healthy. He didn't have flat feet, a punctured eardrum, or bad eyes. Nothing could keep him out of the war—except being a Congresswoman's son.

And he was as stubborn and as stupid as her brother had been in the last war. He didn't want her to do anything to keep him out. Not even Uncle David's artificial leg could make him change his mind. He didn't believe anything like that would happen to him. No one ever believed anything would happen to him—till it did.

The telephone rang. It made her start. She hurried towards it, more relieved than anything else. If she was talking to somebody, she wouldn't have to worry about Joshua . . . so much. "Hello?"

"Flora?" That cheerful baritone could belong to only one man.

"Hello, Franklin," she said. "What can I do for you?" Roosevelt had never called her at the apartment before.

"How would you like to ring in the New Year with me at the War Department?"

She hesitated only a moment. "I'll be over as soon as I can get a cab."

"See you in a little while, then." He hung up.

She didn't think the USA's military planners had a fancy party waiting for her. But the Assistant Secretary of War wasn't going to go into detail about why he wanted to see her, not over the telephone. She called the cab company. They started to tell her she would have to wait half an hour. "It's our busiest day of the year, lady. Sorry." The dispatcher didn't sound the least bit sorry.

"This is Congresswoman Blackford." Flora didn't tell him he would be sorry if she didn't get a cab sooner than that, but she didn't need to, either. He got the message, loud and clear.

A cab sat waiting when she got to the street. An ordinary person wouldn't have been able to summon one so fast. Remembering that chafed at her Socialist sense of equality. She consoled herself by thinking she carried more responsibility than an ordinary person. *From each according to his abilities; to each according to his needs.* Right now, she needed to get to the War Department in a hurry.

The cabby hopped out and held the door open for her. "Where to, ma'am?" he asked. She told him as she got in. He nodded. "Fast as I can," he promised; the dispatcher must have let him know who she was.

He kept his word, but he couldn't go very fast. Confederate bombers had been over the night before, so some of the roads had fresh craters, while sawhorses and red tape closed off others so specialists could try to defuse time bombs. Flora had heard their life expectancy was measured in weeks. That information was secret from the public, but she feared the specialists knew it.

Not far from downtown, the wreckage of a downed C.S. airplane further snarled traffic. "Nice to see we nail one every once in a while," the taxi driver said. "Those . . . people need to pay for what they do." The little pause said he'd remembered just in time that he carried someone important.

"Yes." Flora almost spoke more strongly herself. There wasn't enough plywood and cardboard in Philadelphia—there probably wasn't enough in the world—to cover up all the windows the Confederates had blown out. So many buildings had pieces bitten from them, or were only charred ruins. Ordinary bombs could start fires, and the Confederates dropped incendiaries, too. One popular propaganda poster showed a long, skinny incendiary bomb with Jake Featherston's bony face at one end clamped in a pair of tongs and about to go into a bucket of water. Underneath the sizzling Confederate President were three words: COOL HIM OFF!

"Here you go, ma'am." The driver pulled up in front of the War Department. It had taken plenty of damage, too, even if it was built from the best reinforced concrete taxpayer dollars could buy. Most of its business went on underground these days. Flora didn't know how far underground the tunnels ran. She didn't need to know. Not many people did.

She paid the cabby. Her breath smoked as she went up the battered steps. She showed the sentries her identity papers. "I'm here to see Assistant Secretary Roosevelt," she said.

"Hold on for a minute, ma'am." One of them picked up a telephone and spoke into it. After not much longer than the promised wait, he hung up and nodded to her. "You can go ahead, ma'am. You're legit, all right. Willie, take her to Mr. Roosevelt's office."

Willie looked younger than her own Joshua. He led her down endless flights of stairs. All she knew when he walked her along a corridor was that at least one more level lay below the one she was on. He stopped at a door with ASSISTANT SECRETARY OF WAR neatly painted on the frosted-glass window. "Here you are, ma'am. When you need to come up, call the front desk and somebody will come down to guide you."

Don't go wandering around on your own, he meant. "All right," Flora answered. Willie looked relieved.

She opened the door. "Hello, Flora! Come in," Franklin D. Roosevelt said. Sitting at his desk, a cigarette holder in his mouth at a jaunty angle, he looked strong and virile. But he sat in a wheelchair, and went on, "You'll have to excuse my not rising, I'm afraid." A shrug of his broad shoulders might have added, *What can you do?*

"Of course," Flora said quickly, and then, "Happy New Year." She couldn't go wrong with that.

"Same to you," Roosevelt answered. "And I hope it will be a

Happy New Year for the country, too. We're in better shape now than we were when 1942 started, anyhow. I don't think the Confederates will be able to get out of the noose around Pittsburgh, and that will cost them. That will cost them plenty."

"Good," Flora said. "Lord knows they've cost us plenty. Is that what you wanted to talk about tonight?"

"As a matter of fact, no. I wanted to tell you Columbus has discovered America."

Flora didn't know how to take that. With a smile seemed the best way. "I thought he might have," she agreed. "Otherwise we'd be doing this somewhere else and speaking a different language—a couple of different languages, I expect."

Roosevelt's big, booming laugh filled the office. "Well, when you're right, you're right. But that's the message we got back from Washington State—Hanford, the name of the town is—the other day. It means they've done the first big part of what they set out to do."

"And what is that, Franklin?" she asked. "I've sat on the secret for so long, don't you think I'm entitled to find out?"

"*That's* what I wanted to talk about tonight," he answered. "I have clearance from the President to tell you what's what." He cocked his head and gave her a coy, even an arch, smile. "So you want to know, eh?"

"Maybe a little," Flora said, and Roosevelt laughed again.

"Tell me everything you know about uranium," he said.

Flora sat silent for perhaps half a minute. "There," she said. "I just did."

This time, Roosevelt positively chortled. "Well, that's what I said when this whole thing started—my exact words, to tell you the truth. Now I'm going to tell you what the professors with the slide rules told me."

And he did. He was a lively, well-organized speaker. He could have lectured at any college in the country. Flora's head soon started spinning even so. Uranium-235, U-238, uranium hexafluoride, centrifuges, gaseous diffusion, thermal diffusion . . . It all seemed diffuse to her, and quite a bit of it seemed gaseous.

"What have they done out there now?" she asked.

"They've enriched enough uranium to have a self-sustaining reaction," Roosevelt replied. Enriched, Flora had learned, meant getting a mix with more U-235—the kind that could explode—and less U-238, which couldn't. A sustained reaction wasn't an explosion, but she gathered it was a long step on the way towards one.

"If everything goes right and we get the weapon soon enough, this could win us the war, couldn't it?" Flora said.

"Well, nobody knows for sure," Roosevelt answered, "but the professors seem to think so."

"The Germans are working on it, too?" she asked.

"Yes. No doubt about it. They're the ones who found fission in the first place," he said.

"All right. What about the Confederates?" Flora asked.

"We think they have something going on," the Assistant Secretary of War said carefully. "We don't know as much about it as we wish we did. We're trying to find out more."

"That sounds like a good idea." Flora's own calm meant she would have started screaming at him if he'd told her anything else. "How much do they know about what we're doing?"

"That *is* the question." Maybe Roosevelt was quoting *Hamlet,* maybe just answering her. "The truth is, we're not sure. Counterintelligence hasn't picked up whatever intelligence they've gathered on us."

"I hope you're trying everything under the sun," Flora said, again in lieu of yelling.

"Oh, yes," Roosevelt said. "So far, we've only figured out one defense against these atomic explosions."

"Really? That's one more than I'd imagined," Flora said. "What is it?"

"To be somewhere else when they go off."

"Oh." Flora laughed. But Franklin Roosevelt wasn't laughing now. He meant it. Another thing she hadn't imagined was a race where the winners won everything and the losers were probably ruined forever. "How long between the, uh, sustained reaction and a real bomb we can use?"

Roosevelt spread his hands. "That's what we're trying to find out. The physicists say anywhere between six months and ten years, depending on how fast they can solve the engineering problems."

"That's no good!" Flora said. "If it's ten years for us and six months for the CSA, we'll never get the chance to finish."

"They tell me it's more likely to be the other way around," Roosevelt said. "For one thing, we do seem to have started before the Confederates did. For another, we've got three times as many physicists and engineers and such as they do."

"Serves them right for not educating their Negroes." Flora stopped and grimaced. These days, the Confederates were doing worse with their Negroes than not educating them. Thinking of what they were doing made her say, "We'd better win this race."

"I think we will." Franklin Roosevelt sounded confident—but then, he usually did. "Whether we'll win it in time to use one of those bombs in this war . . . That I don't know, and I'd be lying if I said I did."

"What about Germany and England and France? What about Japan?" Flora asked.

"As I said, we have to guess the Kaiser is somewhere ahead of us. How far, I don't know," Roosevelt said. "The others? I don't know that, either. If we have intelligence about what they're doing, it doesn't come through me." Flora thought it should have, but that wasn't her province. She decided she had done the right thing by not making a fuss about the budget entry she'd found. If this worked, it *would* win the war.

And if it didn't, how many hundreds of millions of dollars would they have thrown down a rathole? As 1942 passed into 1943, she tried not to think about that.

Armstrong Grimes had charge of a platoon. In the middle of Salt Lake City in the middle of winter, he could have done without the honor. But Lieutenant Streczyk was somewhere far back of the line, his left leg gone below the knee. He'd been unlucky or incautious enough to step on a mine.

One of these days, they might send another junior officer out to the front to take charge of things. But the Utah campaign got what other fronts didn't want or need, and these days didn't get a whole lot of that. Till some luckless and probably brainless lieutenant showed up, Armstrong had the job.

Yossel Reisen commanded the squad that had been his. "If this shit keeps up, we'll be majors by the time we got out of here," Armstrong said.

"I don't even care if I'm a corporal when I get out of here," Yossel answered. "As long as I get out, that's all that matters."

"Well, yeah. I'm not gonna tell you you're wrong, on account of you're not," Armstrong said. "Wish to God the Mormons would pack it in and quit. They gotta know ain't no way in hell they can win."

"I don't think they care. I think all they've got left is going down swinging." Yossel paused to light a cigarette. He and Armstrong sprawled behind a stone wall that protected them from snipers. If Armstrong stuck his head up, he could see the rebuilt and rewrecked Mormon Temple ahead. He didn't—if he were so foolish, a Mormon rifleman would put a round in his ear. After a drag, Yossel went on, "Jews were like that once upon a time. They rose up against the Romans whenever they saw the chance . . . and the Romans handed them their heads every damn time."

Palestine, these days, was a sleepy Ottoman province. It had lots of Arabs, some Jews, and just enough Turks to garrison the towns and collect taxes. No matter how holy it was, nothing much ever happened there. Odds were nothing ever would.

Something erupted from behind the Mormon lines. "Screaming meemie!" Armstrong yelled.

The spigot-mortar bomb came down a few hundred yards away. Even that was close enough to shake him with the blast. "They really do love you," Yossel Reisen said. "Ever since you had that Mormon strip, we've got more little presents like that than anybody else."

"Oh, shut up," Armstrong said, not because Reisen was wrong but because he was right. Armstrong wished he hadn't given the Mormon a hard time, too. Fighting these maniacs was hard enough when you were just one enemy among many. When they were trying to kill you in particular . . . The most Armstrong could say was that they hadn't done it yet.

U.S. artillery woke up about ten minutes later. Shells screamed into the area from which the screaming meemie had come. But then, the launcher was bound to be long gone.

"How far do you think it is to the Temple?" Armstrong asked. His voice sounded strange because he was talking through his gas mask. Some of the crap the Army threw at the Mormons was liable to blow back into the U.S. positions. And the Mormons still had gas of their own, which they fired from mortars whenever the artillery used it against them. Armstrong didn't know whether they got it from the CSA or cooked it up in a basement in Ogden. He didn't care, either. He did know it was a major pain in the rear.

Yossel Reisen also looked like a pig-snouted Martian monster in a bad serial. "Couple miles," he answered, sounding almost as unearthly as he looked.

"Yeah, about what I figured," Armstrong agreed. "How long you think we'll need to get there? How hard will those Mormon fuckers fight to hang on to it?"

"Too long, and even harder than they've fought already," Yossel said.

That wasn't scientific, but it matched what Armstrong was thinking much too well. He said, "What do you think the odds are we'll live through it?"

This time, Reisen didn't answer right away. When he did, he said, "Well, we're still here so far."

Armstrong almost asked him what the odds of that were. The only reason he didn't was, he already knew the answer. The odds were damn slim. He wouldn't have been leading a squad if that people bomb hadn't got Sergeant Stowe. He wouldn't have had the platoon if that mine hadn't nailed Lieutenant Streczyk. Either or both of those disasters could have happened to him just as easily. So could a thousand others. The same went for Yossel. But they were both still here, neither of them much more than scratched.

In the next few days, Armstrong really started wondering how long he would last. More and more barrels came forward. Most were the waddling monsters kept in storage since the Great War, but some more modern machines went into the mix. None, though, had the stouter turrets and bigger guns that marked the latest models. Every time one of those rolled off the assembly line, it headed straight for the closest Confederate concentration.

More artillery came in, too. And when the weather cleared enough for bombers and fighters to fly, there were more of them, and less antiquated machines, than usual. He knew the signs. The United States were gearing up for another big push.

All the support would help. When the balloon went up, though, it would still be man against man, rifle against rifle, machine gun against machine gun, land mine against dumb luck. Armstrong had a wholesome respect for the men he faced. Nobody who'd been in the line more than a few days had anything but respect for the men of what they called the Republic of Deseret.

Armstrong respected them so much, he wished he didn't have to go after them one more time. Such wishes usually mattered not at all. This time, his fairy godmother must have been listening. The high command pulled his battered regiment out of the line and stuck in a fresh one that was at full strength.

"Breaks my heart," Armstrong said as he trudged away from what was bound to be a bloody mess.

"Yeah, I can tell," Yossel Reisen agreed. "I'm pretty goddamn disappointed myself, if anybody wants to know the truth." They both laughed the giddy laughs of men who'd just got reprieves from the governor.

The rest of the soldiers heading back into reserve were every bit as relieved. They were dirty and skinny and unshaven. Their uniforms were faded and torn and spotted. A lot of them wore ordinary denim jackets and canvas topcoats liberated from the ruins instead of Army-issue warm clothing. Their eyes were far away.

By contrast, the men replacing them might have stepped out of a recruiting film. They were clean. Their uniforms were clean. Their greatcoats were the same green-gray as everything else. Armstrong was younger than most of the rookies, but felt twenty years older. These fellows hadn't been through hell—yet.

"Does your mama know you're here?" he called to a natty private moving up.

By the private's expression, he wanted to say something about Armstrong's mother, too. He didn't have the nerve. It wasn't just that Armstrong outranked him, either. The kid probably hadn't seen action yet. Armstrong's grubby clothes, his dirt, and his whiskers said he had. He'd earned the right to pop off. Before long, the youngster would enjoy it, too—if that was the word, and if he lived.

"Look at all these men." Yossel nodded toward the troops marching past. "Remember when our regiment was this big?"

"Been a while." Armstrong tried to work out just how long it had been. He needed some thought. "Shit, I think we'd taken enough casualties after the first time we ran into the Confederates in Ohio to be smaller than that outfit."

"I think you're right," Yossel said. "And they never send enough replacements to get us back up to strength, either."

"Nope." Armstrong pulled out a pack of cigarettes, stuck one in his mouth, and offered them to Yossel. The other noncom took one. He lit it. Armstrong leaned close to get his started, then went on, "The ones we do get aren't worth much, either."

"If they live long enough, they mostly learn," Yossel said. "Those first few days in the line, though . . ."

"Yeah." Armstrong knew he'd lived through his opening brushes with combat as much by dumb luck as for any other reason. After that, he'd started to have a better idea of what went into staying alive when Featherston's fuckers or Mormon fanatics tried to do him in. That gave him no guarantee of living through the war, something he knew but tried not to think about. But it did improve his chances.

Replacements got killed and wounded in large numbers, just because they didn't know how not to. They didn't dig in fast enough. They didn't recognize cover when they saw it. They didn't know when to stay down and when to jump up. They couldn't gauge whether incoming artillery bursts were close enough to be dangerous. And that wasn't the worst of it. The worst was that they got veterans killed, too, because they gave things away without even knowing they were doing it.

Most veterans tried to stay away from them those first couple of weeks. That wasn't fair. It meant even more replacements became casualties than might have been otherwise. But it saved veterans' lives—and it saved the pain of getting to know somebody who wasn't likely to stick around long anyway.

A swarm of soldiers waited at the makeshift bus depot to go from the line back to some of the comforts of civilization: hot showers, hot food, clean clothes, real beds. Armstrong surveyed the swarm with a jaundiced eye. "Something's fucked up somewhere," he predicted.

"Bet your ass, Sarge." That was one of the men already milling around. "Goddamn Mormons snuck a machine gun somewhere down the highway. They shot up a bus like you wouldn't believe. Now everybody's trying to hunt 'em down."

"Christ, I hope so," Armstrong said. "That'd be what everybody needs, wouldn't it?—getting your goddamn head blown off when you're on your way to R and R?"

"Sooner we kill all the Mormons, happier I'll be," the other soldier said. "Then we can get on with the real war. Finally starting to go our way a little, maybe."

"Maybe, yeah. Depends on how much you believe of what they tell you." Armstrong knew damn well the wireless didn't tell the truth all the time. When he was in Ohio, it had gone on and on about U.S. victories and advances while the Army got bundled back and back and back again. He couldn't prove it wasn't doing the same thing about what was going on in Ohio and Pennsylvania now.

The other soldier spat a stream of brown tobacco juice. "There is that," he allowed. Armstrong had thought about chewing tobacco himself. You could do it where the sight of a match or a glowing coal or even the smell of cigarette smoke would get you killed.

An officer called, "The route south has been resecured. Boarding will commence in five minutes."

Do I want R and R enough to risk getting shot on the way? Armstrong wondered. He must have, because he got on the bus when his turn came.

When Cincinnatus Driver walked into the Des Moines Army recruiting station, the sergeant behind the desk looked up in surprise from his paperwork. Cincinnatus eyed him the same way: the sergeant held his pen between the claws of a steel hook.

"What can I do for you?" the sergeant asked.

"I want to join up," Cincinnatus answered.

"Sorry, pal. We don't use colored soldiers," the sergeant said. "Navy takes colored cooks and stewards. If you want to, you can talk to them. You don't mind my saying so, though, you're a tad overage. That cane won't do you any good, either."

"You got a uniform on even though you got a hook," Cincinnatus said.

"I was in the last one," the recruiting sergeant said. "That's where I got it. I'm no damn good at the front, but I can do this."

"Well, I was in the last one, too," Cincinnatus said. "Drove a truck haulin' men an' supplies in Kentucky and Tennessee. Been drivin' a truck more'n thirty years now. Sure as hell can do it some more. Put me in a deuce-and-a-half and you got one more white boy can pick up a rifle and shoot at Featherston's fuckers."

"Ah." The sergeant looked more interested. "So you want to be a civilian auxiliary, do you?"

"If that's what you call it these days," Cincinnatus answered. "Last time around, I was just a truck driver." He eyed the man behind the desk. "They pay any better on account of the fancy name?"

"Oh, yeah, pal—and then you wake up," the sergeant said. Cincinnatus chuckled; he hadn't expected anything different. The veteran reached into his desk drawer and pulled out a fresh form. He did that with his left hand, which was still flesh and blood. Then he poised the pen over the blank form. "Name?"

"Cincinnatus Driver."

After the sergeant wrote it down, he glanced over at Cincinnatus. "Heard of you, I think. Didn't you get exchanged from the Confederates not so long ago?"

"Yes, suh, that's right," Cincinnatus said.

"You don't call me 'sir.' You call me 'Sergeant.'" The noncom scribbled a note. He handled the pen very well. As he wrote, he went on, "Just so you know, they're gonna check you seven ways from Sunday on account of you were in the CSA."

"They can do that," Cincinnatus agreed. "They reckon a colored man'd help Jake Featherston, though, they're pretty goddamn stupid."

"Yeah, you'd think so, wouldn't you? But it all depends," the sergeant said. "Maybe they got your wife an' kids down there, and they'll feed 'em to the alligators unless you play along."

"My wife an' kids are right here in Des Moines," Cincinnatus said.

"Good for you. Good for them," the sergeant said. "You know what I mean, though. They'll check. Now—you say you drove an Army truck in the Great War? What was your base? Who commanded your unit?"

"I drove out of Covington, Kentucky, where I come from," Cincinnatus replied. "Fella who ran things was a lieutenant name of Straubing."

The sergeant raised his right eyebrow. "Think he'd remember you?"

Straubing had shot a Confederate diehard dead on Cincinnatus' front porch. With a jerky nod, Cincinnatus said, "Reckon he would. He still in the Army?"

"Oh, you might say so." The sergeant wrote another note. "There's a Straubing who's a brigadier general in logistics these days. Might not be the same man, but you don't hear the name every day, and the specialization's right. You know what logistics is?"

Are you a dumb nigger? he meant. But Cincinnatus did know the answer to that one: "Gettin' men and stuff where they're supposed to go when they're supposed to get there."

"Right the first time." The sergeant nodded. "Bet you did drive a truck in the last war. Where else would you have heard the word?"

"I done said I did." Cincinnatus paused. "But I bet you hear a lot o' lies, sittin' where you're sittin'."

"Oh, you might say so," the sergeant repeated, deadpan. "You sure you want to go through with this, Mr. Driver?"

"Yes, suh—uh, Sergeant—an' I tell you why," Cincinnatus answered. The sergeant raised a polite eyebrow. Cincinnatus went on, "You just called me *Mistuh*. Ain't no white man anywhere in the whole CSA call a colored man *Mistuh*. Call him *boy*, call him *uncle* if his hair's goin' gray like mine is. *Mistuh?* Never in a thousand years. An' if you don't respect a man, you don't have no trouble killin' him off."

"Uh-*huh*." The sergeant wrote something else on Cincinnatus' papers. Cincinnatus tried to read what it was, but he couldn't, not upside down. The man with the hook looked across the desk at the man with the cane. "Thanks for coming in, Mr. Driver. Like I told you, we're going to have to look at you harder because the Confederates turned you loose. You have a telephone?"

"No, suh," Cincinnatus answered.

"All right. We'll send you a letter, then," the sergeant said. "Probably be ten days, two weeks, something like that. We'll see what General Straubing has to say about you."

"Thank you, Sergeant." Cincinnatus did it right this time. "When he was in Covington, he always treated the colored fellows who drove for him like they was men. Reckon he was the first white man I ever knew who did."

Cincinnatus went home, not so happy as he'd hoped but not so disappointed as he might have been. He felt as if he were cluttering up the apartment. That was another reason he'd visited the recruiting station. But his urge to get even with the Confederates counted for more.

"Don't want to jus' sit here playin' with my grandbabies," he told Elizabeth. "I love my grandbabies, but I got some doin' in me yet."

"I didn't say nothin', dear," his wife answered.

"I love you, too," Cincinnatus said, mostly because she hadn't said anything. They'd been married a long time. Despite the separations they'd gone through, she knew him better than anybody.

The letter from the recruiting station came eight days later. That was sooner than the sergeant had said. Cincinnatus didn't know whether the quick answer meant good news or bad. He opened the letter—and still didn't know. It just told him to come back to the station two days hence.

"Why couldn't that blamed man say one way or the other?" he asked when he took it upstairs.

"You find out then, that's all," Elizabeth said. She was calmer than he was—and she wasn't trying to find out what she'd be doing for the rest of the war.

Cincinnatus took a trolley to the recruiting station bright and early on the appointed day. He got there before it opened, and went across the street to a diner to get out of the cold. The guy behind the counter who served him a cup of coffee gave him a fishy look, but took his five cents without saying anything.

The one-handed sergeant got to the station when Cincinnatus was about halfway through the cup. He left it on the counter and limped over to find out what was what. The sergeant was getting his own pot of coffee going on a hot plate. He looked up without much surprise when the bell above the door jingled.

"Good morning, Mr. Driver," he said. "You didn't waste any time, did you?"

"No, suh—uh, no, Sergeant," Cincinnatus said, and the noncom smiled at the self-correction. Cincinnatus wished he'd got it right the first time. He went on, "You gonna let me drive a truck, or shall I see what I can do in a war plant? Gotta do my bit some kind o' way."

Reaching into the top desk drawer, the recruiting sergeant pulled a sheet of Army stationery. "Here's what Brigadier General Straubing has to say about you, Mr. Driver." He set a pair of reading glasses on his nose. "'I remember Cincinnatus well. He was a solid driver, clever and brave and resourceful. I have no doubts as to his loyalty or devotion to the United States.' How's that?"

"That's—mighty fine, Sergeant. Mighty fine," Cincinnatus said. "So you let me drive again?"

"We'll let you drive," the sergeant answered. "You said it yourself—if you go behind the wheel, a younger man gets to pick up a Springfield."

"Ain't quite what I said." Cincinnatus knew he ought to leave it there, but he couldn't. "What I said was, a white man gets to pick up a

Springfield. I still don't reckon that's fair. Do Jesus, in the last war the Confederates let some o' their colored men carry guns."

"Yeah, and they've been regretting it ever since," the sergeant said dryly. He held up his hook. "You can say it wouldn't be like that here. You can say it, and I wouldn't give you any grief about it, Mr. Driver, 'cause I think you're likely right. But I don't make the rules, and neither do you. The War Department says we'll play the game like this, so we will. Do you want to do it, or don't you? If you do, you've got about a million forms to fill out. If you don't, well, thanks for stopping by."

He had no give in him. He didn't need to; the government backed him straight down the line. Cincinnatus sighed. "Let me have the damn forms. You ain't what you oughta be, but you're a damn sight better'n Jake Featherston."

The sergeant had to go back to a filing cabinet to get the papers. "You're a sensible man, Mr. Driver. The difference between bad and worse is a lot bigger than the difference between good and better."

Cincinnatus started to answer, then stopped before he said anything. That would give him something to think about when he had the time. Now . . . paperwork. The recruiting sergeant had exaggerated, but not by much. Cincinnatus filled out forms till he got writer's cramp—not an ailment he worried about very often.

Officially, he wasn't joining the Army. Officially, he was becoming a civilian employee of the U.S. government. *The undersigned agrees, acknowledges, and accepts that his duties may require him to enter areas not definitively known to be safe.* He wasn't sure what *definitively* meant, but he signed anyway. He knew he wasn't going to be driving from Idaho to Minnesota.

For purposes of self-protection, employees hired for the aforementioned duty may be permitted to carry firearms, another form told him. He looked at the recruiting sergeant. "The Confederates catch me with a gun, they gonna shoot my ass," he said.

"Don't worry about it," the sergeant answered. "If they catch you without a gun, they'll shoot your ass anyway." Since Cincinnatus couldn't very well argue with that, he signed again.

At last, only one sheet of paper was left: a loyalty oath. Cincinnatus signed that, too, then set down the pen and shook his hand back and forth to work out the kinks. "Lot o' paper to go through," he said. "What do I do next?"

"Go home," the sergeant told him, which caught him by surprise. "Bring a suitcase—a *small* suitcase—with you Monday morning. You report to the State Capitol, room . . . 378. After that, you do what they tell you."

"All right. Thank you kindly, Sergeant," Cincinnatus said.

"Thank *you,* Mr. Driver. You said it—you're doing your bit." The sergeant looked down at his hook for a moment, then up at Cincinnatus again. "And if you have to use a gun, make it count."

"I do that, Sergeant," Cincinnatus promised. "Yes, suh. I do that."

A clear predawn morning in mid-January. When Irving Morrell looked west, he saw red flares in the sky—Confederate recognition signals. When he looked east, he saw more red flares. The Confederates to the east and west could probably see each other's flares, too. Only twenty or thirty miles separated them, twenty or thirty miles and the force Morrell commanded.

So far, the C.S. rescue force pushing east hadn't been able to reach the men trapped in and around Pittsburgh. Morrell didn't intend that they should, either. He turned to his wireless man. "Send 'Rosebud' to Philadelphia, Jenkins," he said.

"'Rosebud.' Yes, sir." The wireless operator didn't know what the code phrase meant. He sent it anyway. A moment later, he nodded to Morrell. "Received, sir."

"Good," Morrell said. "Now we see how they like that."

"Yes, sir," Jenkins repeated. "Uh, what's it all about, sir?"

Morrell didn't think the wireless man could be a Confederate plant. He didn't think so, but he didn't take any chances, either. "It means Featherston's fuckers are going to have some tough sledding, that's what," he said. That seemed safe enough—the younger man still didn't know where or how.

He could have meant sledding literally. Snow blanketed eastern Ohio and western Pennsylvania. Everywhere he looked, everything was white—except for the soot smears that marked burnt-out barrels, wrecked strongpoints, and other works of man.

Artillery boomed, off to the north. Those were U.S. guns, throwing death at the Confederates pushing in from the west. The men in butternut who hung on around Pittsburgh hadn't pushed west to try to join them. Maybe they were too short of fuel to move. By now, Featherston's transport aircraft had taken a devil of a beating. And they were flying in from farther and farther away, too, as U.S. bombers plastered their fields.

Had Morrell been running the Confederates' show, he would have ordered the C.S. troops in Pittsburgh to break out no matter what. Yes, they would have given up the city. Yes, they would have taken losses. But if they'd done it soon enough, they would have saved most of their men and some—maybe a lot—of their equipment. Now they were in real trouble.

That didn't break Morrell's heart. For the first year of the war, everything Jake Featherston tried seemed golden. He'd jumped on the United States with both feet. He'd held the USA down, too, even though he ran a smaller country. That had really alarmed Morrell. Featherston didn't just intend to lick the United States. He intended to conquer them. Morrell wouldn't have believed it was possible—till the Confederates cut the USA in half.

After that, it was hang on tight and try to survive. Looking back on things, the U.S. counteroffensive in Virginia was ill-conceived. Sure, charge right into the teeth of the enemy's defenses. Featherston had known the United States were coming, and he'd baked a cake—a reinforced-concrete cake. Fredericksburg? The Wilderness? Nobody in his right mind would want to attack in places like those.

That didn't stop Daniel MacArthur, of course. He attacked, and paid for it, and attacked again, and got another bloody nose. He hurt the CSA, too, but not in proportion.

"Sir, there's enemy pressure near Cambridge," Jenkins reported.

"Is there?" Morrell said. The men and barrels in butternut would be coming along the east-west highway that went through the manufacturing town. A north-south road also ran through Cambridge. Morrell and the couple of dozen barrels he personally commanded were in bivouac along it, a few miles south of the place. Charging to the attack was a major's job, not a one-star general's. All at once, Morrell didn't care. "Then let's hit them, shall we?"

Within twenty minutes, his barrels were rolling north. The sun came up as they got moving. Infantrymen accompanied them, some riding barrels, some in trucks, some in half-tracked troop carriers that could cross ground where even a four-wheel-drive truck bogged down. When the fighting started, the foot soldiers would jump out and go to work.

The Confederates had stalled just outside of Cambridge. Morrell could see why: it was a tough nut to crack. It sat on a rise, and dominated the ground on which Featherston's men had to approach. Several butternut barrels burned. But there was already fighting just outside the town. The chatter of automatic weapons made Morrell grind his teeth. The Confederates had plenty of firepower.

Still, he was hitting them in the flank when all their attention was focused ahead of them. "Front!" he called to his gunner.

"Identified!" Frenchy Bergeron answered, a quarter of a heartbeat slower than he should have. Maybe Morrell was overcritical; maybe Michael Pound had spoiled him for other gunners. Morrell yelled to the driver. The barrel stopped. The gun slewed a few degrees to the left. It roared.

"That's a hit!" Morrell whooped with glee as the C.S. barrel caught fire. A pair of crewmen got out and ran for the closest trees. They didn't make it. Morrell picked another target. "Front!—the one next to the upside-down auto."

"Identified!" Bergeron sang out. The turret traversed again. The cannon shouted. The Confederate barrel went up in flames. Morrell whooped again.

For two or three minutes, the U.S. machines had it all their own way. Their enemies didn't seem to realize where the devastating fire was coming from. Then the Confederates rallied. Most of their barrels were new models, with the well-sloped armor and the big gun. When they turned toward the U.S. barrels on their flank, they suddenly became much harder to knock out. And those three-inch guns began taking a toll on the barrels Morrell led.

But in confronting Morrell's barrels, the Confederates left themselves vulnerable to the U.S. defenders holed up in Cambridge. The force in the town didn't seem to have many barrels, but did have plenty of antibarrel cannons. Those began picking off the C.S. barrels that turned to expose their thinner side armor to them.

A clear day had disadvantages as well as advantages. Confederate Asskickers screamed down out of the sky to bomb the antibarrel cannons. The dive bombers put several guns out of action in the space of a few minutes. Asskickers were hideously vulnerable to U.S. fighters, but no U.S. fighters seemed to be in the neighborhood. They were probably out chasing Pittsburgh-bound transports.

Morrell swore under this breath, and then over it. No matter how you tried, the pieces didn't all fit together the way you wanted them to.

If everything worked the way you hoped it would, you'd win the war in a couple of weeks, and you'd hardly take any casualties. If . . .

Fortunately, the Fuckup Fairy visited both sides. Considering all the Confederates trapped in the Pittsburgh pocket, she'd sprinkled more of her magic dust on Jake Featherston lately than she had on the U.S. General Staff. And if that wasn't a miracle of rare device, Morrell had never seen one.

He ducked down into the turret to use his fancy wireless set. "Close with them!" he called to his crews. "Front to front, they can hurt us from farther away than we can hurt them. If we get in close, it evens out."

What had Horatio Nelson said? *No captain can do very wrong if he places his ship alongside that of the enemy,* that was it. Nelson had a better turn of phrase than Irving Morrell. They both thought the same way, though.

Engine growling, Morrell's barrel raced forward. His driver had got the order along with the others. A couple of bullets clanked off the machine's steel hull. Bullets didn't matter. Confederate foot soldiers could shoot at the barrel till the cows came home. A three-inch armor-piercing round, unfortunately, was another story.

It was a wild melee, there on the snow-covered fields. The two barrel forces got within point-blank range of each other. Whoever shot first won. U.S. barrel turrets had hydraulic traverse. The Confederates had to crank theirs around by hand. It gave the green-gray barrels a small edge on the ones painted butternut.

And the antibarrel fire from Cambridge didn't stop. After as wild a half hour as Morrell had known, the Confederates sullenly drew back. They'd lost fifteen or twenty barrels, and taken out about half as many U.S. machines. "We smashed 'em, sir!" Bergeron exclaimed.

"Maybe," Morrell said. "I hope so. But maybe they're just waiting till reinforcements come forward. If they are, we've got some problems." He smiled. That was putting it mildly. He didn't know where he would find reinforcements. The Confederates had stretched him about as thin as they'd stretched themselves. If what he had here and what was in Cambridge couldn't stop Featherston's men, they might link up with their trapped comrades after all.

That wouldn't be good. Not even slightly.

He drew back to the outskirts of the town. He had more cover for his remaining barrels there. The Confederates had got themselves mired in a big house-to-house fight in Pittsburgh. If they tried coming this way again, he aimed to give them a smaller one in Cambridge.

Time crawled by. The Confederates didn't return to the attack. Maybe they couldn't scrape together any more reinforcements after all. Morrell hoped not. They'd already put in a stronger attack from the west than he'd expected. They were bastards—no doubt about that. But they were formidable bastards—no doubt about that, either.

After the Confederates left him alone for a couple of hours, he sent foot soldiers down the west-facing slope to reoccupy the open ground where his force and theirs had clashed. When another hour went by with everything still quiet, he sent three or four barrels down there, too. They took up positions behind the burnt-out hulks of dead machines.

"Not like those assholes to stay quiet so long," Bergeron remarked.

"No, not usually," Morrell said. "I hope I know why they're doing it, but I'm not sure yet." The longer the Confederates held off, the higher his hopes rose.

The officer in charge of the infantry down below showed initiative. He ordered scouts west to see what the enemy was up to. When he got on the wireless to Morrell, he sounded as if he could hardly believe what the men told him. "Sir, they're pulling back," he said. "Looks like almost all of 'em are heading west as fast as they can go."

"Are they?" Morrell breathed. That was as far as his hopes had gone, and maybe a couple of furlongs further.

"Yes, sir," the infantry officer said. "I've got four independent reports, and they all tell me the same thing. They're leaving a screen behind to slow us down if we come after them, but most of their force is going like nobody's business."

"Thank you, Major. Thank you very much," Morrell said. "Out." After he broke the connection, he murmured, "Son of a bitch—it worked."

"Sir?" Bergeron asked.

"Rosebud." Morrell could talk about the code name now. "We took what we could piece together in northern Indiana and the northwestern corner of Ohio and threw it east against the Confederates from there. And they don't have anything around those parts that can stop it. They stripped themselves naked to mount this push toward Pittsburgh. The only prayer they've got of holding the corridor up to Lake

Erie is breaking off the attack and using their men from this force to defend instead."

"But if they do that, their guys inside Pittsburgh are screwed." The gunner saw the key point in a hurry.

"They sure are," Morrell said. This still wasn't the two big simultaneous attacks planners on both sides dreamt of. It was about one and a half. It might be enough. Maybe the Confederates' position in Ohio would unravel even if they did go over to the defensive. Morrell aimed to make it unravel if he could. He got on the all-hands wireless circuit. "The enemy is retreating. We're going after him."

Jefferson Pinkard stood outside the house in Snyder, Texas, where his wife and two stepsons lived. He kept staring northwest, toward Lubbock and toward the damnyankees not far outside the town. He couldn't hear the artillery—it was too far away. But it was close enough to let him imagine he could when he was feeling gloomy. He felt plenty gloomy this morning.

Edith came out with him in spite of the raw wind blowing down from the north. He'd never seen such a place for wind as the West Texas prairie. No matter what direction it came from, it had plenty of room to get a good running start. "What's the matter?" she asked him.

"Wondering what the devil we're gonna do if Lubbock falls," he answered. "If Lubbock falls, there's not a . . . heck of a lot between the Yankees and here. Just miles." He didn't worry that much about Snyder itself. The locals could always evacuate to the east. But Camp Determination . . . Camp Determination was a different story.

"They can't expect you to take all the niggers out of that place." Edith knew he worried about the camp, not the town.

"No, don't reckon they can." Jeff let it go at that. But the bathhouses that weren't bathhouses, the trucks with the sealed passenger compartments, the mass graves—all those would be worth millions to damnyankee propaganda. Richmond wouldn't want such secrets getting out. How could he do anything to stop that, though?

You could drive the trucks away. You could, he supposed, blow up the bathhouses. That would make Camp Determination look like an ordinary concentration camp . . . till the damnyankees found the mass graves. How many tens, how many hundreds, of thousands of corpses lay in them? Pinkard didn't know, though he could have figured it out from camp records.

He did know the graves were too big to hide. Even if he bulldozed the ground flat, the bodies and bones remained below. And somebody was bound to blab. Somebody always blabbed. Some secrets you couldn't keep, and that was one of them.

"Records," he said to himself.

"Records?" Edith said. "The kind you listen to? The kind you dance to?"

Jeff didn't answer. Those weren't the records he had in mind. Just like any other big operation, the camp generated lots of paperwork. If the U.S. Army got close, that paperwork would have to disappear, too. Right this minute, he didn't know where all of it was. He did know it wasn't all in the same place, and he couldn't get rid of all of it in a hurry. And he realized he would have to fix that as soon as he could.

The things you never reckon you'll have to worry about, he thought. But that was foolish. He'd fought not too far from here a generation before. The Yankees had pushed east from New Mexico then. Why shouldn't they be able to do it again?

Because we were going to lick 'em this time. Because Jake Featherston promised we'd lick 'em this time. Jeff believed what Jake Featherston said. He'd believed him ever since first hearing him in Birmingham not long after the end of the last war. He didn't want to think—he hardly dared think—the President of the CSA might be wrong.

He muttered again, this time without words. Whether he wanted to or not, he had to be ready to do what he could in case the Confederates didn't come out so well in this particular part of the war. (Putting it like that meant he didn't have to dwell on how things were going across the length and breadth of the North American continent.)

When Edith looked northwest, she had other things on her mind. "Jeff . . ." she said.

"What is it?"

"Will . . . Will the boys be all right? The war's not as far away as I wish it was."

"Things aren't bad now. I don't reckon they'll turn bad real quick. If the damnyankees get into Lubbock, or if they get past Lubbock, maybe you and the boys ought to go east for a bit."

His wife nodded. "I've got some stuff packed up in case we have to leave in a hurry."

"Good. That's good, babe," Jeff said. "Should be easy enough to get away. Nothing around here is what you'd call a great big target."

"What about the camp?" Edith asked.

"Nah." He shook his head. "Don't you worry none about that. What's in the camp? Niggers. Who gives a . . . darn about niggers?" To anyone else, he would have said, *Who gives a rat's ass?* or something like that. But he tried to watch his language around Edith. He answered his own question: "Nobody does, not on either side of the border."

She nodded again, reassured. "Well, you're right about that, Lord knows. They're nothing but our misfortune."

Jeff kissed her. "That's just what they are, all right." Not even Saul Goldman and the other fancy-pants slogan-makers for the Freedom Party had ever put it any better. He went on, "They're not going to be such a big misfortune after a while, though; that's for sure."

He didn't talk in any detail about what Camp Determination did, not even to Edith, not even if she'd been married to a guard at Camp Dependable in Louisiana before she said her I do's with him. Nobody who didn't wear the uniform needed to know the details. He felt a certain lonely pride in the knowledge of what he did to serve the Confederate States. He was part of the war, just as much as if he commanded a division of troops.

Edith didn't ask for details, either. She just said, "All right," and let it go at that.

When Jeff got back to Camp Determination, he summoned the camp's chief engineer, a dour assault band leader—the Party equivalent of a major—named Lyle Schoonover, and told him what he needed. One of the reasons Schoonover was dour, and that he held a Party rank and not one in the regular Army, was that he'd lost his right leg below the knee. He heard Pinkard out, nodded, and said, "I'll take care of it."

"Not just the bathhouses, mind," Jeff said. "Set something up where we can get rid of the records in a hurry, too."

"I said I'd take care of it." Schoonover sounded impatient. "I meant all of it."

"You meant all of it . . ." Jefferson Pinkard tapped the three wreathed stars on the left side of his collar.

The engineer had only one star on each side of his collar, and no wreath. He gave Jeff a dirty look, but said what he had to say: "Sir."

"That's more like it," Jeff said. "I'm in charge here, dammit, for better and for worse. Now that things don't look so good, we've got to ride it out the best way we know how."

Schoonover's expression changed. There was respect on his narrow features now—reluctant respect, maybe, but respect all the same. Jeff smiled, down inside where it didn't show. Educated people often started out looking down their noses at him. He hadn't finished high school. Before he wound up running prison camps, he was a steel-worker and a soldier of fortune. But he had a good eye for what needed doing. He'd always had it, and it let him get and stay ahead of a lot of people who thought they were more clever than he was.

"You're not running from trouble, anyway—sir," Schoonover said.

"Trouble's like a dog. You run from it, it'll chase you and bite you in the ass," Pinkard said. A startled grunt of laughter escaped Schoonover. Jeff went on, "You go at it, though, sometimes you can make it run instead."

"Wish we could make the damnyankees run," the assault band leader said.

"That ain't the point." Educated or not, Jeff knew enough to say *isn't*. He used *ain't* with malice aforethought. "The damnyankees are the Army's trouble. Them finding out about what all we're doin' here—that's our trouble. That's what we can take care of on our own."

"Some of it, anyhow," Schoonover said. "Those graves won't dis-appear all by themselves."

"Well, you're right. I already figured that out myself, too," Jeff said. "But since we can't do anything about 'em, no point to flabbling about 'em, either. We got to take care of what we can take care of, that's all."

Lyle Schoonover got to his feet. He moved well, as long as he didn't have to get anywhere in a tearing hurry. "Fair enough, sir. That's a sensible attitude." His salute didn't seem too grudging. He left Pink-ard's office. If you didn't know he'd been maimed in the Great War, his gait wouldn't give it away.

He hadn't been gone more than ten minutes before the telephone on Jeff's desk jangled. Jeff picked it up. "Pinkard here." He wondered what had gone wrong now. Telephone calls while he was at work were rarely good news.

"Hello, Pinkard. This is Ferd Koenig."

"What can I do for you, sir?" Jeff tried to stay cool. Calls from the Attorney General were never good news.

"You've got the damnyankees a little closer to you than we thought you might," Koenig said.

"Yes, sir. That's a fact." Jeff began to suspect he knew why Koenig was calling. "We're doing what we can to get ready, just in case."

"Are you?" the Attorney General said. "Like what?"

With the conversation with the camp engineer fresh in his mind, Pinkard went into detail—maybe more detail than Ferdinand Koenig wanted to hear. He finished, "Nothin' we can do about the graves, sir. Except for them, though, we can have this place looking like an ordinary concentration camp mighty quick."

"All right," Koenig said when he got done. The Attorney General sounded more that a little stunned. Yes, Jeff had told him more than he wanted to know. *Serves you right,* Jeff thought. After a moment to gather himself, Koenig continued, "Sounds like you've done everything you could."

"You come up with anything else, sir, you just tell me, and I'll take care of it," Pinkard promised. He didn't believe Koenig could. If he'd thought the man back in Richmond would have orders for him, he would have kept his mouth shut.

"I'll do that." By the Attorney General's tone, he didn't want to talk to anybody from Camp Determination for quite a while. That suited Jeff fine; he didn't want to talk to Ferd Koenig, either. Koenig added, "I'll tell the President how thorough you've been out there. He'll be glad to have the good news."

"Thank you kindly, sir." Jeff might not be an educated man, but he could read between the lines. He heard what Koenig didn't say: that Jake Featherston hadn't had much good news lately. "Things aren't going so good up in Yankeeland, are they?"

"They could be better." By the Attorney General's heavy sigh, they could be a lot better. Koenig went on, "But with any luck at all, the Army will do its job up there by Lubbock, and everything you're doing will be like putting a storm cellar into a house—it'll be nice to have, but you won't really need it."

"Here's hoping, sir," Pinkard said.

"Yeah, here's hoping. Freedom!" Ferdinand Koenig hung up.

"Freedom!" Jeff echoed, but he was talking to a dead line. He put the handset back in its cradle. How much freedom could the CSA enjoy if the USA came down and took it away? The Negroes in his domain? Their freedom? They never entered his mind.

*   *   *

January in the North Atlantic was about as bad as it got. Waves threw the *Josephus Daniels* this way and that. The destroyer escort had a course she was supposed to follow. Keeping to it—keeping anywhere close to it—was a long way from easy. Even knowing exactly where the ship lay was a long way from easy.

Sam Carsten had only one thing going for him: he didn't get seasick no matter what. Pat Cooley was a good sailor, but the exec looked a little green. A lot of the men seemed even less happy with their own insides than they had when they whipped the British auxiliary cruiser a couple of months earlier.

Cleaning crews with mops and buckets kept patrolling the heads and passageways. The faint reek of vomit persisted all the same. Too many sailors were too sick to hold in what they ate. More often than not, they couldn't use the rail, either. To try would have asked to get washed overboard.

Waves and spray made the Y-ranging gear much less reliable than it would have been in better weather and calmer seas. Thad Walters looked up from his screens and put the best face on things he could: "Well, sir, the damn limeys'll have just as much fun finding us as the other way round."

"Oh, boy," Sam said in hollow tones. "They'll find Newfoundland. They'll find the Maritimes. They'll find trouble for the USA—find it or make it."

"That's the name of the game for them, sir," Lieutenant Cooley said.

"I know. But the name of the game for me is stopping them if I can," Sam answered.

"Sir, with that gunship to our credit we're still a long way ahead," the exec answered.

"No." Sam shook his head. "That's ancient history. Anything that happened yesterday is ancient history. What we do today matters. What we're going to do tomorrow matters. Forget the old stuff. We've still got a big job ahead of us."

The Y-ranging officer and the exec exchanged glances. "Sir, I'm sorry you didn't go to Annapolis," Cooley said. "To hell with me if you wouldn't have flag rank. You've got more killer instinct than anybody else I know."

"What I haven't got is the brains to make an admiral," Sam said. "You know it, I know it, and the Navy Department sure as hell knows it. I'm damn proud I've come as far as I have."

"You've got plenty of brains, sir. You've got as many as any officer I've served under," Cooley said. "It's just too bad you had to start late."

"Well, thank you very much, Pat. That's white of you," Carsten answered. He knew the exec meant it; whatever else the younger man was, he was no brown-noser.

A wave crashed over the *Josephus Daniels*' bow. White water cascaded back. No sailors manned the ship's antiaircraft guns. They would have gone overboard in a hurry if they'd tried. No carrier-based aircraft could fly or hope to land in weather like this, either, so things evened out.

"Boy, this is fun," Lieutenant, J.G., Walters said, raising his eyes from the electronic display for a moment.

"This time of year, the weather's a worse enemy than the limeys and the frogs and the damn Confederates all rolled together," Sam said. "When spring finally comes around, we'll all get serious about the war again."

"Sub drivers are always serious," Cooley said.

"That's a fact. And they've got it easy once they submerge—that's another fact," Sam agreed. "But God have mercy, I wouldn't want to be a submersible skipper here and now, not even a little bit. They have to get into position on the surface, remember. They're way too slow underwater to do it there. I'll tell you one thing—*I* wouldn't like to be a sub captain trying to stay up with us here."

"Wouldn't be a whole lot of fun, would it?" the exec allowed after a moment's contemplation.

"Not hardly." Sam thought about the wave his ship had shrugged off. He thought about the captain of a submarine standing on top of the conning tower when a wave like that washed over his boat. He thought about that skipper either washed out to sea or, if held in place by a line, doing his best imitation of a drowned puppy. He thought about Lord only knew how many gallons of the North Atlantic going down the hatch and into the submersible. He was glad to be thinking about such things as the captain of a destroyer escort. They couldn't happen to him. They sure could to a sub driver.

Somewhere out in the North Atlantic, such things probably were happening to several submarines from both sides right this minute. Sam hoped no enemy boats were within a hundred miles. Then he hoped no U.S. boats were within a hundred miles, either. You were just as dead if your own side sank you as you were any other way. And in weather like this, mistakes were too simple.

Things only got worse. Snow and sleet blew down out of the north, coating the *Josephus Daniels'* deck and lines and railings with ice. Sam ordered everyone who had to go up on deck to wear a lifeline. Ice made slipping even easier than it had been before.

After leaving the bridge, Sam went down to the wireless shack. One of the yeomen there was telling the other a dirty story. He broke off when his pal hissed. Both ratings sprang to attention.

"As you were," Sam said. "You can finish that joke if you want to, Hrolfson. Don't mind me if I don't laugh real hard—I've heard it."

"It's all right, sir," Petty Officer Hrolfson said, not relaxing from his stiff brace. "It'll keep. What can we do for you, sir?"

"What's the last weather forecast?" Sam asked.

"Ours or theirs?" Hrolfson said. The USA and the UK both sent predictions to their ships. The United States had broken the British weather code. The limeys had likely broken the American code, too; it wasn't a tough cipher. Both sides had weather stations in Greenland and Newfoundland and Labrador and Baffin Island to keep an eye on conditions as they developed. Sam had heard quiet, deadly warfare went on up there in the northernmost reaches of the world.

"Whatever you've got," he said now.

"Well, sir, the limeys figure the storm's good for about another three days. Our guys figure it'll blow out sooner than that," Hrolfson said.

Sam grunted. "I'd bet on the Englishmen." He usually did when their reports disagreed with the ones from the Navy Department. And the blow he was in now felt strong enough to last a long time.

"We've got more stations up there than they do," Hrolfson said. "How come their forecasts are better than ours?"

"More experience, I guess," Sam answered. "They've been doing this a long time, and we didn't get serious about it till the war." The ship plunged down into a trough. He steadied himself without even knowing he'd done it. "What else have we got besides the weather reports?"

"Well, the BBC says England won a big battle against the Germans in the North Sea," Hrolfson told him. "The Kaiser's English-language news station says Churchill's full of shit."

Sam sighed. "That figures, I guess. Nobody who wasn't there will really know what's what—and the people who were there won't be sure, either. I still couldn't tell you who won the Battle of the Three Navies."

"You were there, sir?" said the other yeoman, whose name was Lopatinsky. "My uncle was there, too. He used to say the same thing. He was in the *Dakota* when the hits jammed her steering and she made that circle through the fleet."

"Son of a—gun!" Sam said. "I was in the *Dakota*, too. What's your uncle's name?"

"Kruk, sir," Lopatinsky answered. "Jerzy Kruk—people call him Jerry most of the time."

"Son of a bitch!" This time, Sam didn't sanitize it. "I knew him. Kind of a big gut, eyes green like a cat's, ears that stuck out, and a go-to-hell grin. He fought one of the one-pounders topside, right?"

"That's him," Lopatinsky said. "His gut's even bigger nowadays, but he's still got that damn grin."

"What's he doing these days?" Carsten asked.

"Coal miner. We're a family of miners, down in West Virginia," Lopatinsky said. "I went down below myself for a couple of years, but I figured there's got to be a better way to make a living."

"That's how I got off the farm," Sam said. "Take it all together and I expect I was right."

"I feel the same way, sir," the yeoman said. "Yeah, we get shot at, but so what? At least we can shoot back. The roof comes down or the mine floods, what can you do about it? Not much."

"Here's something, sir." Hrolfson had been listening intently to whatever was coming in through his earphones. "Our wireless says we've sent the Confederates in Pittsburgh a messenger under flag of truce. He's asking for their surrender."

"That *is* good news," Sam said. "What are the Confederates doing?"

Hrolfson listened for a little while longer before shrugging. "They don't say anything about that, sir."

"Ha!" Lopatinsky said. "That means the Confederates told 'em to fold it till it was all corners." Carsten nodded. That was his guess, too. If you listened to the wireless much these days, you had to learn to sift through the crap to get at the few nuggets of truth the broadcasters were, as likely as not, trying to hide.

"If they don't give up pretty soon, we'll kill all of them." Hrolfson sounded as if he looked forward to it.

So did Sam. Even so, he said, "Depends on how many of our guys they can take out before they go down. If they hurt us bad enough, then it's not a bad bargain for them even if they do buy a plot."

"Think they can do that, sir?" Lopatinsky asked anxiously.

"I hope not, and that's the best answer I can give you." Sam tapped the two broad gold stripes on his sleeve. He was proud he'd got them. He hadn't dreamt of coming so far when he scrambled up the hawse hole into officers' country. "I know a little something about what we do on the water. Land fighting—the only thing I know is, I'm glad I'm not in it. It's a nasty, bloody business. When we go into action here, it's usually over in a hurry, anyhow."

"Yes, sir," Lopatinsky said. "How long did we need to knock that limey out?"

"I didn't look at my watch, but it wasn't long." Sam let it go at that. If one of the *Karlskrona*'s big shells had hit the *Josephus Daniels,* the fight might have been over even quicker, with the wrong side winning. That bastard carried big guns, even if she had no armor and only a freighter's engines.

"Could she have sunk us if she hit us?" Hrolfson asked, proving ignorance could be bliss.

"You bet your sweet ass she could," Sam blurted. Hrolfson and Lopatinsky both stared at him. He laughed self-consciously. "You wanted a straight answer. You got one."

"You usually give 'em, Skipper. That's good," Lopatinsky said. Hrolfson nodded. They made Sam almost as proud as knocking out the *Karlskrona* had done.

XX

On the women's side again. In a way, Hipolito Rodriguez had to be more careful there than he did on the other side of Camp Determination. He knew in his gut that the black men were dangerous. With the women, he and the other men in gray could let down their guard. They could regret it if they did, too.

The women tried to make the men set over them let down their guard. They dressed provocatively, and acted provocative. And it wasn't just an act—a lot of them would deliver. They wanted more food, better food, better quarters. They wanted to stay out of the bathhouses. They hadn't needed long to realize those were news as bad as it got. The trucks, by contrast, nobody seemed to mind. The *mallates* knew they would be leaving Camp Determination in them, so didn't worry about climbing aboard. That the trips had no destination, they hadn't figured out.

"Hello, Mistuh Sergeant, suh." The black woman who spoke to Rodriguez was falling out of her blouse. "You takes care o' me, I takes care o' you. I takes care o' you real good." She had only her body to get what she wanted. She used what she had, striking a pose that would have got her arrested on any street corner in the CSA.

Rodriguez just kept walking. He'd found that worked best. If you stopped to talk it over and argue with every colored woman who made advances, you'd never go anywhere and you'd never get anything done all day.

Sometimes nothing worked. "You lousy fairy!" the woman snarled at his back. He ignored her. If he turned around, he could get her into whatever kind of trouble he wanted, up to and including a trip to the bathhouse.

He kept walking anyhow. With or without his help, she'd get hers soon enough any which way. Even if she latched on to some other guard as a protector, she'd get hers before long. Either he'd get bored with her or he'd find somebody else or he'd be off duty when she got picked in a cleanout. He might even be sorry afterwards. She wouldn't be, not for long.

Another woman came up to him. "Mistuh Sergeant, suh?" None of them ever called him *Troop Leader*. They knew about Army ranks. The ranks Freedom Party guards used might have been in some foreign language for them. Since Rodriguez felt the same way about those ranks, he couldn't blame the women—not for that, anyhow.

"What you want?" he asked. Unlike most, this one wasn't trying to act like a slut. The novelty intrigued him. Because it did, he answered her instead of pretending she wasn't there.

"Mistuh Sergeant, suh, my little boy, he powerful hungry. He only five year old. You got chilluns your ownself, suh?"

"I got children," Rodriguez said. "I'm sorry, but I can't do nothin'." Children died fast in the camp. Their mothers often died with them, from trying to share rations that weren't enough for one.

The Negro woman sighed. "You find him some extra food, Mistuh Sergeant, suh, I do anything you want. Reckon you know what I mean. I don't want nothin' for me. But he too little to die like dat. He ain't done nothin' to nobody."

"I don't want nothing like that. I got a wife, too." Rodriguez occasionally forgot about Magdalena—temptation would get the better of him. But he didn't forget more than occasionally.

"You sound like you is a Christian man." The colored woman sounded surprised.

Almost all *mallates* were Protestants. To Rodriguez, that meant they hardly counted as Christians themselves. He didn't want to argue with the woman. The less he had to do with the prisoners, the less he had to think of them as people. The job went better when they were just—things—to him. So all he said was, "I try," and he started to go on with his rounds.

"If you is a Christian man, suh, an' if you loves Jesus Christ, what you doin' here?" the woman asked.

He knew what he was doing: reducing population. As far as he was concerned, that needed doing. If it weren't for the Negroes, the Confederate States wouldn't have had so many troubles. He'd got his first taste of combat not against the USA but stamping out a Negro Socialist Republic in Georgia. Were blacks any more loyal to the Stars and Bars than they had been a generation earlier? If they were, would the country need camps now?

"Reckon I ax somebody else, then," the woman said with another sigh. "You seemed like you was a decent fella, but I gots to do what I gots to do to keep my Septimius alive."

Another raggedy-ass pickaninny with a ten-dollar name. Rodriguez almost asked the woman why she couldn't have called him Joe or Fred or Pete or something sensible. In the end, he held his tongue. That little kid had nothing left but his fancy name. Why not let him make the most of it for whatever small span of days he had here?

When Rodriguez walked on, the woman didn't try to stop him. He wondered what her chances of hooking up with some other guard were. She wasn't anything special to look at. With so many women throwing themselves at the men in gray, it was a buyers' market. The Freedom Party guards could pick and choose. Ordinary girls got left behind.

Off to the northwest, something that might have been distant thunder muttered. But it wasn't thunder, not on a day that was fine and bright if chilly. It was artillery. Rodriguez knew the sound—he knew it at much closer range than this. Just the other side of Lubbock, Confederate and damnyankee gunners were doing their best to blow each other to hell and gone.

If the men in green-gray broke through, if they started down the highway toward Snyder and toward Camp Determination . . . That wouldn't be so good. The guards had orders to get rid of as many Negroes as they could, and then to blow up the bathhouses and escape themselves.

More mutters in the distance. Would the prisoners know what those sounds meant? Some of the men would; Rodriguez was sure of that. Either they'd fought for the C.S. government or against it—maybe both. Any which way, they would know what artillery was. That could mean trouble.

Rodriguez glanced at the young men with submachine guns who accompanied him. They showed no signs of recognizing the far-off rumble. That only proved they'd never seen combat.

Why aren't you in the real Army? Rodriguez wondered. The answer wasn't hard to figure out—they'd pulled strings. This was bound to be a safer duty than facing soldiers in green-gray. The *mallates* here might be troublesome, but they didn't shoot back. And they definitely didn't have artillery.

An airplane buzzed over the camp. It was a Confederate Hound Dog; Rodriguez could make out the C.S. battle flags painted under the wings. U.S. warplanes had made appearances, too. If they wanted to bomb or strafe, they could. Camp Determination wasn't set up to defend against air attack; nobody had ever thought it would have to.

So far, the U.S. aircraft had left the place alone. Maybe the fliers didn't know what this place was. Or maybe they knew and didn't care. It wasn't as if people in the USA loved Negroes, either. They complained about what the Confederates were doing to them, but that struck Rodriguez as nothing but propaganda. If the United States really cared about Negroes, they would have opened their borders to them. They hadn't. They weren't about to, either.

Two women got into a catfight. They screeched and scratched and wrestled and swore. Rodriguez and his comrades hurried toward the squabble. The women were shrieking about somebody named Adrian. Was he a guard? Rodriguez couldn't think of any guards named Adrian, but he might have missed somebody. Was he a black man in the other half of the prison? Or was he somebody they'd known back where they came from?

Whoever he was, he wasn't worth disturbing the peace for. "Enough!" Rodriguez yelled. "Break it up!"

The women ignored him. They were too intent on maiming each other to care what a guard said. "You whore!" one of them shouted.

"I ain't no whore!" The second woman pulled the first one's hair, which produced a shrill scream. "*You* the whore!"

"Break it up!" Rodriguez yelled again. "Punishment cell for both of you!"

Life at Camp Determination was hard anyway. It was harder in a punishment cell. They didn't give prisoners room to stand up or sit down. They had no stoves—you froze in the winter. In the summer, you baked, but everybody in the camp baked in the summer. You got starvation rations, even skimpier and nastier than the cooks doled out to anybody else.

But the two women really meant this brawl. They wouldn't stop no matter what a man in uniform said. That was unusual. Rodriguez nodded to the junior guards with him. "Take care of it," he said.

They did, using the butt ends of their submachine guns. Some of the models that went up to the front were of all-metal construction, so cheap they'd fall to pieces if you dropped them on the sidewalk. But the guards got better-made weapons with real wooden stocks. One reason they did was for times like this. Even if you didn't want to shoot somebody, you sometimes had to knock sense into an empty head.

Now the women shrieked on a different note. Back when they first got half the camp to themselves, some of the guards were reluctant to clout them. No more. Familiarity had bred contempt.

"Didn't you hear the troop leader yell for you to break it up?" one of the guards panted. "He tells you to do something, you cut the crap and you do it, you hear?"

If Rodriguez hadn't had three stripes on his sleeve, he likely would have been nothing but a damn Mexican to the guard. Of course, even a damn Mexican stood higher on the Confederate ladder than a nigger (unless you were a white Texan from down near the Rio Grande). And a troop leader stood infinitely higher than a prisoner in an extermination camp.

One of the women had an eye swollen shut. The other one had blood running down the side of her head. They pointed at each other. At exactly the same time, they both said, "She started it."

"Nobody cares who start it," Rodriguez said. "You don't stop when I say to stop. I say twice, you still don't stop. Now you pay." He turned to the guards. "To the punishment cells. They start this shit again, you shoot. You hear?"

"Yes, Troop Leader!" they chorused, their timing almost as good as the women's.

Rodriguez wondered if the Negroes thought he was joking. If they did, it was the last mistake they'd ever make. Nobody in the Confederate States—nobody who mattered, anyway—would care whether a couple of colored women died a little sooner than they would have otherwise. Far away in the distance, artillery rumbled again. As long as it didn't get much closer, everything was all right. Rodriguez hoped everything would go on being all right, too.

*   *   *

Willard Sloan was not a nice man. Scipio listened to him screaming on the telephone: "You call that lettuce? Holy Jesus, only thing it was good for was wiping my ass! What do I mean? I'll tell you what I mean. It was limper than an old man's dick, that's what, and it looked like the bugs ate as much as you sold me. Nobody pulls that kind of shit on me twice, you hear?" *Bang!* Down went the receiver.

Sloan might have been nice before the Yankee bullet paralyzed him from the waist down. Or he might have been a son of a bitch from the start. If he'd ever heard the old saying about catching more flies with honey than with vinegar, he didn't believe it. Maybe he just didn't like flies.

Most restaurant managers worth their pay had some son of a bitch in them. Jerry Dover sure did. But the new man at the Huntsman's Lodge took it to extremes. When something made him unhappy, you heard about it, loudly and profanely. Sloan operated on the theory that the squeaky wheel got the grease. He didn't just squeak—he screeched.

He cussed Scipio out when the black man made mistakes. Scipio did make some—with all the things that went on in a busy restaurant, he couldn't help it. But he didn't make many, and Willard Sloan noticed. "Well, looks like Dover knew what he was talking about," he said one day. "You do know what the fuck you're doin'."

"I thanks you, suh," Scipio said. "You do somethin', you likes to do it good."

"Ha!" Sloan said. "Most people"—he didn't say *most niggers,* for which Scipio gave him credit—"only want to do enough to get by. You show up every day, and you work like a bastard."

"I does my job bes' way I knows how," Scipio said.

"Well, that's what you're supposed to do," the manager said. "Doesn't happen as often as it ought to, though. I can hire a hundred people who could wait tables kinda half-assed, you know what I mean? Good enough to get by, but not really good. One of you is worth all of them put together. You're the kind of waiter a place like this is supposed to have. You're the kind of waiter who makes the Huntsman's Lodge the kind of place it is."

"Thank you, suh. Don't reckon I hear many finer compliments." Scipio meant it. Willard Sloan didn't have to waste praise on him. If Sloan did it, he meant it. Maybe hearing that praise made Scipio rash, for he went on, "How much it matter, though, when they kin ship me off to a camp whenever they please?"

As soon as the words were gone, he wished he had them back. Whining to a white man never did a Negro any good. Willard Sloan didn't answer for a while. Then he said, "When I got shot, I was out in no-man's-land, between our lines and the damnyankees'. A nigger soldier brought me back, or maybe I would've died out there."

"What happen to him afterwards?" Scipio asked.

Sloan sighed. "Xerxes, I don't know. I just don't know. I don't know where he's from. I don't know his name. I don't know if he got himself killed next day or next week or next month. I can't tell you, that's all. I wasn't an officer leading colored troops or anything—their sector was next to ours, that's all. I don't even know if he was out there already or if he came out to get me. I was in the hospital a hell of a long time after that. I never had the chance to find out."

"All right, suh." Thus encouraged, Scipio felt bold enough to add, "If he still 'live now, reckon he either in a camp or worried about goin' in. Don't hardly seem fair."

Sloan sighed again. He spread his hands. "Ain't much I can do about it. Who pays attention to a guy in a wheelchair who runs a restaurant? Maybe I can help my own people some. I hear tell Dover did. Things are getting tougher all the time. I don't know if it'll still work. I aim to try, anyhow."

"Can't ask for no more'n dat," Scipio said. So a human being did lurk under that acid-tongued exterior. Worth knowing, maybe.

Human being or not, Sloan didn't put up with slackness, any more than Jerry Dover had. When a cook came in late three times in two weeks, he was gone. The Mexican who took his place spoke next to no English, but showed up early every day. He picked up the language in a hurry, especially the obscenities that laced the conversation of the rest of the kitchen staff.

How many Mexicans were in Augusta these days? How many Mexicans were in towns and fields all over the Confederacy, doing what had been nigger work till blacks started getting cordoned off by barbed wire and disappearing into camps? Not so many as the Negroes they replaced, surely. But enough to keep crops coming in, wheels turning, meals cooked and served, hair cut.

They can get along without us. The idea terrified Scipio. He hadn't thought the Freedom Party could strike at Negroes in any really important way. He hadn't thought the CSA could do without the hard, unglamorous labor colored men and women provided. He hadn't thought so, but maybe he was wrong.

One good thing about a busy shift: it left him no time to brood. He was always hopping, taking orders, bringing food out from the kitchen, barking at the busboys, trying to hear the gossip at his tables without letting the whites know he was listening.

Everybody talked about Pittsburgh. The more that people knew, the gloomier they sounded. Some of them sounded very gloomy indeed. "We're going to lose that whole army," a colonel home on leave told his banker friend. "We're going to lose a big piece of Ohio, too. It's just a mess—a mess, I tell you."

"What can we do?" the banker asked.

"Hold on tight everywhere else and hope we can ride it out," the officer answered. "Don't know what else there is *to* do. Give up? Not while we've still got bullets in the gun. You reckon the last peace was bad? It'd be a walk in the park next to what we'd get from the damn-yankees this time around."

Scipio wished for the destruction of the Freedom Party with all his heart. He had mixed feelings about the Confederate States of America. Every man needed a country, and the Confederate States, for better and often for worse, were his. He'd had no trouble getting along before Jake Featherston took power. Things hadn't been perfect or even very good, but they hadn't been so bad, either. He'd known where he fit.

But Negroes didn't fit anywhere in Featherston's CSA. And enough whites agreed with Featherston to bring him and his followers into places where they could do something about their ideas. And so . . .

And so, when Scipio went home that night, he passed the barbed-wire perimeter around the Terry. No street lights inside kept him from tripping. Power had been off for a long time. He stepped slowly and carefully. Falling would be bad, not just because he was an old man and getting brittle but because he might tear his trousers. That would be a real disaster.

He made it back to the apartment undamaged. It was chilly in there. No buildings in the Terry had heat anymore. The handful of people left here used makeshift wood-burning stoves for cooking and heating. One of these days, maybe, a fire would get loose. Scipio dreaded that, but didn't know what he could do about it.

Bathsheba stirred when he came to bed. "Sorry," he said. "Didn't mean to bother you none."

"'S all right," his wife answered sleepily. "Sunday tomorrow. We kin go to church."

"All right." Scipio didn't argue. He thought God had long since stopped listening to the Confederacy's Negroes, but Bathsheba still believed. Going along was easier than quarreling.

He thought so, anyway. In the morning, Cassius said, "I ain't goin'. I got to see some people about some business."

"What kind of business?" Scipio asked.

His son just looked at him—looked through him, really. Cassius didn't answer. Some kind of resistance business, then. Scipio sighed but didn't insist. Bathsheba tried to. It didn't work. Cassius was going to go his own way. Seeing what things were like these days, Scipio had a harder time thinking him wrong than he would have a couple of years earlier.

The church was as rundown as everything else in the Terry. The preacher's coat and trousers were shiny with age. The reverend preached a careful sermon, praying for peace and for justice and for an end to misery and oppression. He made a point of not saying that the members of his congregation should rise up against oppression. Somebody was bound to be listening for the authorities. If the government or the Freedom Party—assuming there was any difference between the two— didn't like what he said, he would vanish off the face of the earth as if he'd never been born.

He might have preached fire and brimstone. He might have preached revolt and revolution. It wouldn't have mattered. He was just finishing his sermon when somebody at the back of the church exclaimed, "Lord have mercy, dey is out dere!"

Nobody wondered who *they* were. With gasps of horror, people sprang up from their rickety seats and hurried out of the church, hoping to get away before it was too late. "God be with you, brothers and sisters!" the preacher called after them. He didn't try to get them to stay. Maybe he had his own escape route planned.

Scipio and Bathsheba and Antoinette scurried away with the rest of the congregation. *Like rats,* he thought. Any kind of hiding place would do now.

But there were no hiding places. Augusta policemen and Freedom

Party stalwarts and guards waited out in the street. They had smiles on their faces and rifles and submachine guns in their hands. One of them shifted a wad of tobacco into his cheek so he could talk more clearly: "Y'all can come along with us quiet-like, or y'all can get shot right here. Don't matter none to us. Which'll it be?"

One young man, only a little older than Cassius, ran for it. A submachine gun spat fire. The young man fell and writhed on the cracked pavement. The stalwart who'd cut him down ambled over and put a bullet through his head. The Negro groaned and lay still.

"Anybody else?" asked the cop with the chaw. No one moved. No one spoke.

Cassius. Thank God Cassius isn't here. Someone may get away, Scipio thought. He glanced over at his wife. She nodded when their eyes met. She had to be thinking along with him.

The policeman spat a brown stream of tobacco juice in the dead man's direction. "All right," he said. "Get moving."

Away the Negroes went. The congregation was only part of the cleanout. Some men tried to offer money to get away. Some women tried to offer themselves. The white men only laughed at them.

Out of the Terry they went. A lot of white Augustans were worshiping and praying at this hour of the day. Maybe God listened to them. He sure hadn't paid any attention to the colored preacher. The whites who weren't at church stared at the Negroes herded along like cattle. Some just stared. Some jeered. No one called out a word of protest.

Confederate Station was by Eighth and Walker, right next to St. Patrick's Catholic Church. Did God listen harder if you called on Him in Latin? Scipio wouldn't have bet on it. The station wasn't far from the Terry. The captured Negroes were lucky in that, because he was sure they would have had to walk no matter how far it was.

And then all their luck ran out. Everything happened so fast, neither Willard Sloan nor anyone else had the slightest chance to do anything. "In! Get in, God damn you!" shouted the white men with guns. They stuffed cars tighter than should have been humanly possible. By the way the boxcar Scipio and his family went into smelled, it had hauled cattle the last time. The whites packed it till no one could sit down, then slammed the door shut. That cut off almost all of the air. Scipio resigned himself to dying before he got wherever the train was going. With a jerk and a lurch, it began to roll.

* * *

Dr. Leonard O'Doull sometimes thought he was trapped in one of the nastier suburbs of hell. One bleeding, mangled, screaming man after another, from the time he gulped coffee to wake up to the moment he lay down for a stolen bit of sleep. Some of the soldiers wore green-gray, others butternut. He'd almost stopped noticing which color uniform he had to cut away to get at the latest mutilation.

"When will this end?" he groaned to Granville McDougald after amputating a shattered arm.

"You're asking the wrong guy," the medic answered. "Only one who can tell you is the Confederate CO."

"He should have quit three weeks ago," O'Doull said.

McDougald shrugged. "He's got orders to hold to as long as he can, and he's got ammo for his guns. Featherston would probably send a people bomb after him if he did throw in the towel. As soon as we smash him flat, that frees up all of our men here to roll west and knock the Confederates out of Ohio. So he's holding down a lot more men than he's still got left himself."

"You spent all these years as a medic, right?" O'Doull asked. McDougald nodded. The doctor went on, "So how come you talk like you come from the General Staff?"

"Me?" Granville McDougald laughed. "I'm just picking up stuff I hear from the wounded. We've got enough of 'em."

"Well, God knows you're right about that," O'Doull said. The University of Pittsburgh hospital held U.S. wounded ranging in rank from private to brigadier general—and Confederates ranging from private to full colonel. It was always stuffed. Men lay on gurneys in the hallway, sometimes on mattresses on the floor, sometimes—when things were at their worst—on blankets on the floor.

The Confederates never had made it over the Allegheny River. They never had tried to break out of Pittsburgh to the west, either. They'd waited till the relieving column could link up with them—but it never did. Now, outside the pocket, there were no Confederate soldiers for miles and miles. The men who'd tried to relieve Pittsburgh had turned west themselves, to try to stem the U.S. advance out of northwestern Ohio and Indiana.

"One thing," O'Doull said. McDougald raised an eyebrow.

O'Doull went on, "I bet the poor bastards stuck here don't think Jake Featherston is always right anymore."

"That doesn't matter," McDougald said. "What matters is the people down in the CSA. When they figure out Featherston's led 'em down the primrose path, that's when things get interesting."

"Maybe—but maybe not," O'Doull said. "Yeah, some of them may hate Featherston after things go wrong. But won't they go on hating us even worse? They really do, you know." He'd listened to wounded men, too, and some of the captured Confederates were alarmingly frank.

"I don't care if they hate us. I hate them, too." Granville McDougald was so matter-of-fact, he might have been talking about the weather. "What I want 'em to remember is, if they mess with us, we're going to pound the kapok out of 'em, and they better get used to the idea."

"*Oderint dum metuant,*" O'Doull murmured. McDougald made a questioning noise. Half embarrassed, O'Doull explained: "I did a lot of Latin when I was an undergrad—in those days, you had to when you went to college. It's helped with the medical terms, I will say. But the Emperor Caligula said that."

"Caligula? The crazy one?"

"That's him. He was nuttier than Jake Featherston, to hell with me if he wasn't. But it means, 'Let them hate, as long as they fear.'"

"Three words," McDougald said admiringly. "Boy, that packs more into three words than anything this side of 'I love you.' There I was, yakking about how I feel about the Confederates, and that old son of a bitch got it into three words."

"He wasn't an old son of a bitch. He was a young son of a bitch," O'Doull said. "I think he was twenty-seven when they murdered him."

"Well, he's been dead long enough that he seems old," McDougald said. O'Doull nodded; he was right about that. It was something over 1,900 years now.

He didn't get the chance to cudgel his brains over exactly how many years it was, because the PA system brayed, "Major O'Doull! Sergeant McDougald! Report at once to OR Three! Major O'Doull! Sergeant McDougald! Report at—"

"No rest for the wicked," McDougald said.

"I thought that was 'weary,'" O'Doull said.

"Works both ways, don't you think?" McDougald was right about that, too.

They hastily scrubbed in and gowned and masked. Then they found what they were dealing with: a soldier who'd stepped on a mine. That was an even worse misfortune than it might have been, because the Confederates, or possibly the Devil, had come up with a new model. Instead of just exploding and blowing off a man's foot or his leg, it bounced up to waist height and then burst . . . with the results they had in front of them.

The kid on the table was shrieking in spite of surely having had a morphine shot. He held his hands in front of his crotch like a maiden surprised, and wouldn't move them no matter what. "My nuts!" he moaned. "It got my nuts!"

"You're gonna be all right, son." O'Doull feared he was lying through his teeth. He turned to McDougald and spoke in a quick, low voice: "Get him under."

"Right, Doc." In one swift, practiced motion, McDougald put the ether cone over the soldier's face and turned the valve on the gas cylinder. The wounded man choked on the pungent fumes, but didn't try to yank off the mask the way a lot of people did. His hands stayed right where they were till the ether got him and he went limp.

"Let's see how bad it is," O'Doull said grimly. Now he could move those blood-dripping hands. When he did, he wished he hadn't. What he saw made him want to cover himself up the same way.

"How bad?" McDougald asked.

"Well, he won't need to worry about getting a girl in trouble anymore—that's for damn sure," O'Doull answered. "I'll see if I can put his dick back together well enough for him to piss through it. And he's got some nasty belly wounds, too."

"Remember we were talking about the Geneva Convention a while ago?" McDougald said as O'Doull, his mouth a tight line behind the mask, got to work.

"Yeah," he answered absently, trimming mangled tissue as conservatively as he could. "What about it?"

"Nobody'd thought of Popping Paula back when they were hammering it out," McDougald said. "Otherwise, it'd be on the list for sure."

"It's filthy, all right," O'Doull agreed. "And you know what's even worse? I bet you anything the engineer who came up with it got a bonus."

"I won't touch that," McDougald said. "If you look at it the right way—or the wrong way, depending—it's almost the perfect weapon. Who'd want to maybe trade his family jewels for a hundred-yard advance?"

"I'm just glad they don't have many of those little toys here," O'Doull said. "And we've got all their airstrips under our guns now, so they won't be bringing in more."

"Always parachute drops," McDougald said helpfully. But there weren't many of those anymore. Pittsburgh had cost the CSA a godawful lot of transports. No more than a handful tried to make the trip these days; U.S. Wright fighters ruled the skies above western Pennsylvania.

Outside the hospital, the thunder of U.S. guns went on around the clock. O'Doull hardly noticed it. He might have looked up in surprise if it stopped. Incoming rounds were growing scarcer. That Confederate Army might have got into Pittsburgh. It didn't look as if it would get out.

"How are you doing there?" McDougald asked after a while.

"Oh, he'll live. I'm not so sure he'll think that's doing him a favor, though," O'Doull said. "I *think* he'll have a penis that works, even if he won't get much fun out of it. I sure hope it works—otherwise, it's catheter time."

"Ouch." McDougald winced. "Don't even want to think about that."

"It's a bitch." O'Doull used the smallest needles and finest catgut for his sutures. He couldn't remember the last time he'd done such delicate work. He wished he could have done more for the wounded soldier, but the essential parts were gone.

At last, the job was done. McDougald surveyed the site. "Well, I think you did about as much as anybody would have been able to," he said.

"Yeah." O'Doull gave back a somber nod. "I wish I could say more. I wish I had a drink, too."

"Don't blame you a bit. Why don't you, once you get out of the OR?"

"When I come off, maybe I will," O'Doull said. "Don't want to do it now—odds are I'll be operating again before long."

"There is that," McDougald allowed. "I'll tell you something, though—I've known plenty of docs that wouldn't have stopped for a second, let alone a minute. Some of the old-timers in the last war, the guys who'd been in the Army since 1880—hoo-boy!" He rolled his eyes.

"Yeah, I ran into some of those fellows, too," O'Doull said. "This one surgeon named Schnitzler—I don't think he drew a sober breath all the time I knew him. But put a wounded man in front of him and a scalpel in his hand and he'd do as good a job as anybody you'd ever want to meet. He could operate in his sleep. I think he did sometimes."

"That's the kind I mean," McDougald said. "There's the drunk who goes and drinks till he passes out. And then there's the other kind, the guy who gets a buzz in the morning and stays buzzed all day long, and as long as he is, he's fine."

"Till his liver craps out on him, anyway," O'Doull said.

"Oh, sure." By the way McDougald said that, he took it for granted. "Of course, there are some of the first kind, too. Part of the way I learned surgery was when one of the docs who should have been doing it got too toasted to see, let alone operate. If I didn't cut, this soldier was ruined for sure. If I did, maybe he had a chance. So I did, and he made it—and I thought, *Son of a bitch! I can do this shit!* I was hooked."

"It grows on you, all right," O'Doull agreed. "What happened to the drunken doctor?"

"He kept at it whenever he was sober enough to work," McDougald answered. "After a while, people said I was doing better work than he was. I don't know about that. He had the training, after all, and I was amateur city. But I sure was doing *more* work than he was, 'cause he got loaded more and more often."

"They should have discharged the fool." Though a Catholic, O'Doull had more than a little New England Puritan sternness in him.

Granville McDougald shook his head. "It was a war, Doc. If he was only a quarter of what he should have been, that was still a quarter of a surgeon more than they would have had if they canned him. Hell, he may be in the Army yet. He may be in the OR next door, for all I know."

"He probably killed patients he should have saved," O'Doull said.

"So have I," McDougald said. He didn't ask if O'Doull had. That was generous of him. Like any doctor, O'Doull had buried some of his mistakes. It came with being human. The most important thing was trying not to make the same mistake twice.

* * *

Hotel Street in Honolulu was a raucous, drunken place twenty-four hours a day, seven days a week. Sailors who had liberty got drunk and got laid, caring about nothing but the moment. George Enos, Jr., knew exactly how they felt. He should have—he was one of them.

He'd drunk enough to make the sidewalk seem to sway and twist under his feet like the *Townsend*'s deck in a heavy sea. But the pavement wasn't listing—he was.

"Where do we go now?" he asked Fremont Dalby. He'd pretty much given up thinking on his own. If the gun chief could manage it, George would follow along.

Dalby made a production out of pondering. He'd taken plenty of antifreeze on board, too. "Well, do we want to drink some more, or do we want to screw?" he asked.

George frowned. He didn't want to decide anything. He wasn't sure he could decide anything. Fritz Gustafson settled things by walking through the next open door they passed.

If it had been a brothel, they would have done their best there. But it was another gin mill. The air smelled of cigarette smoke and spilled beer and vomit. A record player was cranking out Hawaiian music much too loud. George's head started to ache, and he wasn't even hung over yet. That would come tomorrow morning, and tomorrow morning might as well be ten years away.

He and his buddies from the *Townsend* elbowed their way up to the bar. A couple of the men they muscled by gave them sour stares, but nobody threw a punch. "What'll you have, gents?" the barkeep asked.

"Whiskey," Fremont Dalby said. George nodded. So did Fritz Gustafson. The man behind the bar poured the booze into three glasses, added ice, and waited till he saw money before sliding the drinks across the bar. Dalby gulped his. So did Gustafson. George went a little slower. By himself, he would have stuck with beer. He liked it better. But when he was out with friends, whiskey got him drunk faster. On a forty-eight-hour liberty, speed mattered.

He wasn't sorry this had turned out to be a bar, not a cathouse. He always felt bad about being unfaithful to Connie. Oh, not while he was in the act—it felt wonderful then. It always did. How could it not, even with a bored Chinese floozy who chewed gum while you pounded away? But he never failed to feel guilty afterwards.

"Drink up, George," Dalby said. "The night is young, and you are—hell, I ain't drunk enough to think you're beautiful."

George laughed. He knocked back his drink, then coughed two or three times. The rotgut in the glass was smooth as sandpaper. Gustafson pounded him on the back. "Thanks," he wheezed.

"Sure," the loader said. Even pretty well lit up, he spent words as if he paid for them out of his own pocket.

"Another round," Dalby told the the bartender.

"Coming up." The man's gray hair said he'd been around a while. So did his faint British accent. The Sandwich Islands had belonged to the limeys before the USA took them away in 1914. A lot of the old-timers had been here since the Union Jack flew alongside the flag of the Sandwich Islands, which joined it to the Stars and Stripes in what had been the old Kingdom of Hawaii's doomed effort to keep everybody happy.

George would have loved to spend the rest of his life in the Sandwich Islands. He didn't suppose many people who came here didn't want to stay. After the winter he'd just been through, he would never look at January in Boston the same way again. He wouldn't look at the North Atlantic in January the same way again, either. Oh, they had swells here. But nothing he'd seen came within miles of the Nantucket sleighride. And you'd never have to worry about working on deck in the middle of an ice storm.

Again, Dalby and Gustafson poured down their drinks in nothing flat. Again, they waited not too patiently for him to finish his. He was about to go bottoms up when a brawl broke out behind him.

He never knew what started it. An argument over a barmaid? Two sailors from the same ship who didn't like each other? Sailors from two ships that didn't like each other? The roll of the dice at a corner table?

Whatever got it going, it was everywhere fifteen seconds later. Nobody tried to stop it; everyone just joined in. If that didn't prove there were a lot of drunks in the place, nothing ever would have.

Somebody swung at George: a big, burly machinist's mate. The haymaker would have knocked him into the middle of next week had it landed, but it missed by at least a foot. George threw what was left of his drink in the other sailor's face. The man roared and rubbed frantically at his eyes. George hit him in the belly. He folded up with an explosive, "Oof!"

Oh, shit! The bartender was probably yelling it, but George had to read his lips to understand it. Everybody in the joint was shouting at the top of his lungs. The noise of things breaking didn't help.

Somebody took a swing at Fremont Dalby. The gun chief ducked so the punch caught him on top of the head. That hurt the puncher much more than it hurt Dalby. One of the things you learned in a hurry was not to punch bony places. By the way the sailor clutched his wounded hand, he'd probably broken a knuckle or two. A heartbeat later, he had other things to worry about. Dalby, a barroom veteran, didn't waste time fighting fair. He kneed the sailor in the crotch. The man howled like a wolf.

George stopped a punch with his forehead. He saw stars. It probably hurt the other guy worse than it hurt him, but that didn't mean he enjoyed it. Plenty of sailors got into fights for the fun of it. George didn't understand that. Watching a fight was fun. Getting punched and kicked and elbowed? That wasn't what he called a good time.

He hit the other guy in the ribs. He'd aimed for the sailor's solar plexus. If he'd hit it, that would have taken the SOB out of the brawl till his motor started working again.

But a shot to the ribs just pissed the sailor off. He gave George a punch identical to the one he'd just taken. George grunted and swore. That would leave a bruise, and he'd probably be sore whenever he breathed for the next week.

Nobody in a barroom brawl played much defense. George slugged the guy in front of him again. Then Fritz Gustafson hauled off and belted the sailor in the chops. The man went down like a felled tree. With a small smile, Gustafson displayed a set of brass knucks. He would have made a hell of a Boy Scout. He was prepared for anything.

Halfway down the bar, somebody who didn't have brass knuckles improvised. He picked up a long-legged stool and swung it like a flail, felling whoever he could reach. Maybe the rising and falling screech that burst from him was intended for a Rebel yell. Maybe it just meant he was enjoying himself.

Whatever it meant, the screech abruptly cut off. Someone cold-cocked the stool swinger from behind with a beer bottle. The bar stool crashed to the floor. So did the sailor, bleeding from a scalp wound.

A fighting knife gleamed in the hand of a Marine in a forest-green uniform. George didn't see the leatherneck stick anybody. All the same, he decided he was up way past his bedtime.

Getting out of a brawl without getting a name for running away from brawls wasn't so easy, though. George didn't want to skip out on his buddies. And so he stayed there and took some punches and dealt out a few more. Dalby and Gustafson both seemed happy enough where they were.

Then somebody yelled, "Shore patrol!" That sent everybody surging toward the door. George hoped the bartender had shouted out the warning to get the sailors to quit tearing his place to pieces. No such luck. The Navy equivalent of MPs waded into the fray, nightsticks swinging.

George counted himself lucky—he didn't get hit in the head. He did get hit in the ribs, which made the punch he'd taken there seem a love pat by comparison. Fremont Dalby got a bloody stripe over one eye. Fritz Gustafson knocked a shore patrolman ass over teakettle with his knuckleduster. That could have won him a pounding to end all poundings, but none of the shore patrolman's pals saw him do it. Some people had all the luck.

Gustafson's luck didn't keep him—and George, and most of the rest of the people in the bar, including the barkeep—from getting grabbed and tossed into one of the paddy wagons that pulled up outside.

The SPs had a brig set up a couple of blocks away. It had probably been there for years, but George hadn't known about it. They found out he and Dalby and Gustafson had legitimate liberty papers, and they found out the three men from the *Townsend* hadn't started the fight. When they discovered Gustafson's persuader, they took it away from him. He looked aggrieved, but he didn't say anything. Under the circumstances, that was bound to be smart. Of course, Gustafson never had much to say.

Another paddy wagon delivered them to their ship and two more men to the destroyer tied up next to her. The officer of the deck eyed them as if he'd found them in his apple. "Well, well," he said. "What have we got here?"

"Drunk and disorderly, sir," a shore patrolman answered. "Tavern brawl on Hotel Street."

"All right. We'll take care of them," the OOD said.

And they did. No one got very excited about it. Captain's mast was something that happened now and again. George had never come up in front of one before. He might have been more worried if he were less hung over. That made him think more about internal miseries than any the *Townsend*'s skipper would inflict.

By their expressions, Dalby and Gustafson also had a bad case of the morning afters. Lieutenant Commander Brian McClintock glowered at each of them in turn. "Anything to say for yourselves?" he growled.

"No, sir," Dalby said. George and Fritz Gustafson shook their heads. George wished he hadn't. It only made the throbbing behind his eyes worse.

"Why the devil didn't you get out of there before the SPs came? Now I have to notice this." McClintock sighed. "Three days in the brig, bread and water."

The brig was tiny and cramped. Through most of the first day, George didn't want anything resembling food. He drank lots of water. It helped the hangover a little. By the time he got out, he was sick of piss and punk: Navy slang for the punishment rations. Making him sick of them so he didn't want to do it again was part of the point of the sentence, but that didn't occur to him.

Ordinary chow on the *Townsend* was no better than it had to be. It tasted like manna from heaven when they turned him loose. Greasy fried chicken? Lumpy mashed potatoes? Coffee like battery acid? He made a pig of himself.

"Didn't figure you for a brawler, Enos," somebody said.

"Yeah, well . . ." George shrugged and let the well-gnawed bone from his drumstick fall to the plate in front of him. He had a few bruises to show he'd been in a fight, and delivered the classic line with as much conviction as if no one had ever said it before: "You ought to see the other guy."

Some British poet talked about ending the world with a whimper, not a bang. Tom Colleton figured that meant the limey had missed out on the Great War. It sure as hell proved he'd never set foot in one of the two or three Confederate pockets left in Pittsburgh.

That Tom didn't know how many positions his countrymen still held spoke volumes about how bad things were. He was hungry. He was cold. He was lousy—he itched all the time. The regiment he commanded might have had a company's worth of effectives, which made it one of the stronger units in this pocket. They were desperately low on ammo for their automatic weapons. Most of them carried captured U.S. Springfields instead. They had no trouble scrounging cartridges for them.

Only a couple of hundred yards from the edge of the pocket, the Allegheny rolled south towards its junction with the Monongahela. Tom Colleton felt a certain somber pride at being where he was. His regiment had pushed as far east as any Confederate outfit. They'd done everything flesh and blood could do.

They'd done it, and it hadn't been enough.

Confederate commanders had already refused two U.S. surrender demands. Tom didn't know who was in charge over the twitching, dying C.S. positions in Pittsburgh. A light airplane had sneaked into the city and taken out General Patton at the direct order of Jake Featherston. Patton might be useful somewhere else later on. Nobody could do much about what was going on here.

The wind picked up. Snow started to swirl. Crouched in the ruins of what had been a secondhand book shop, Tom lit a cigarette. He muttered something foul under his breath. It was U.S. tobacco, and tasted like straw. He'd taken the pack from a dead Yankee. No way to get the good stuff from home, not anymore.

U.S. barrels rattled forward. Before long, the damnyankees would take another shot at overrunning this pocket, and they just might bring it off. Few Confederate barrels were still in working order. Even fewer had fuel. Fighting enemy armor with grenades and Featherston Fizzes was a losing game.

"Give it up!" a U.S. soldier shouted across the narrow strip of no-man's-land. "You're dead meat if you stick it out. We play fair with prisoners."

Tom knew some of his men had thrown down their rifles and saved their skins. They had orders to hold out, but blaming them for surrendering wasn't easy. Still, what would happen if—no, when—the Yankees didn't have to worry about the Confederates in Pittsburgh anymore? How many U.S. soldiers and barrels and guns and airplanes would that free up? How much would C.S. forces elsewhere have to pay?

All those things mattered. Living mattered more to a lot of people. Tom was too hungry and weary to care anymore one way or the other. And he thought like a soldier. As long as he still had bullets in his rifle, he wanted to shoot them at the damnyankees.

He wasn't a professional. He hadn't gone to VMI or the Citadel or one of the other schools that turned out the Confederacy's professional officer corps. But he'd made it through the Great War and through more than a year and a half of this one. He knew what he was doing.

He hadn't had any experience when they gave him a captain's uniform in 1914. But he'd come from a plantation-owning family. In those innocent days, they didn't think he needed anything else. He was innocent himself back then. He was sure he would come home, the Yankees whipped, in time for the cotton harvest.

Innocence died fast on the Roanoke front. So did soldiers, in both butternut and green-gray. The dashing war he'd imagined turned into a brutal slog of trenches and barbed wire and machine guns and gas and always, always, the stench of death.

He'd lived. He hadn't even been badly hurt. And he'd liked spending the next twenty-odd years as a civilian. He'd gone into this second war with his eyes open. This time, he'd known from the start the Yankees would be tough.

And everything went just the way Jake Featherston said it would. Tom was part of the lightning thrust that carried Confederate troops all the way to Lake Erie. No one could have imagined the operation would go so well.

And no one could have imagined having it go well could mean so little. *Maybe my eyes weren't so wide open after all,* Tom thought unhappily. He didn't know one single Confederate who hadn't been sure the United States would fold up once they got cut in half. But the USA—again!—proved tougher than the CSA figured.

Pittsburgh, then. Taking Pittsburgh would surely knock the damnyankees out of the fight and give the Confederates the victory they deserved. Except they didn't take it. And if they were getting what they deserved . . . In that case, God had a nastier sense of humor than even Tom had imagined.

Pittsburgh then and Pittsburgh now. Pittsburgh now was cold and smoke and blood and fear. Pittsburgh now was that Yankee yelling, "Awright, then, you ast for it!" Most of the time, letting your enemy know you were going to hit him would be stupid—idiotic, even. If you already held all the aces, though, what difference did it make?

Artillery and mortar fire came first. Dive bombers followed a few minutes later. The U.S. airplanes didn't scream in a dive like Confederate Mules. They didn't have an impressive nickname like Asskickers; nobody ever called them anything but Boeing 17s. The damnyankees made war as romantically as a bunch of insurance salesmen. But their uninteresting bombers did a fine job of blowing holes in the landscape where they needed them most.

"Barrels!" somebody yelled.

U.S. barrels weren't as good as their C.S. counterparts. They had more of them than the Confederates did, though. In this pocket of Pittsburgh, that was all too painfully true. And after a while, quantity took on a quality of its own.

The leading U.S. barrel commander rode with his head and shoulders out of the cupola. He was brave and smart. He wanted to see more of what was going on than he could all buttoned up.

He didn't see Tom draw a bead on him and fire two quick shots. He crumpled as if made from paper when they both struck home. Tom had long since forgotten about his sidearm. He carried a captured Springfield himself. In a battlefield full of artillery and machine guns, even a rifle seemed pitifully inadequate.

Tom worked the bolt and chambered a new round. Springfields didn't measure up to automatic Tredegars, either. But they were good enough, or more than good enough. Despite losing its commander, the barrel still came on. Tom hadn't expected anything else. The gunner would run the behemoth now. But it wouldn't fight so well as it had with a full crew.

A machine next to it hit a mine and threw a track. That barrel slewed sideways and stopped. The five men inside stayed where they were. They could still use the turret and the bow gun, but they weren't going forward anymore. The barrel's steel skin protected them from small-arms fire. If a cannon started shooting at the crippled machine, they were in trouble. The Confederates in the Pittsburgh pocket were as short on guns and shells as they were on everything else, though. The Yankees in there might make it.

There weren't enough mines to stop the rest of the barrels, either. The U.S. machines really were ugly compared to the sleek, elegant Confederate new models. It wasn't a beauty contest, though. The damnyankees could do the job, which was the only thing that mattered.

If they kept coming, they would tear a hole in the C.S. line. Tom knew only too well what lay behind it: not much. He didn't know what anybody in the line could do about it.

Some men were ready to give up their lives to try to stop them. Two soldiers ran out with Featherston Fizzes, wicks alight. A Yankee foot soldier cut down one of the Confederates before he got close enough to throw his. As he fell, the burning gasoline gave him his own pyre. Tom hoped he was already dead; if he wasn't, that was a hard way to go.

But the other soldier flung his Fizz. Fire spread across a barrel's turret and dripped down into the engine compartment. Paint and grease made barrels vulnerable to fire anyway. When the engine started to burn, too . . .

Hatches popped open as the crew bailed out. Tom Colleton wasn't the only man who fired at them. One barrelman might have reached the shelter of a pile of bricks. The rest lay dead.

But all that only put off the inevitable. The Yankees had the firepower, and the Confederates didn't. The Yankees threw reinforcements into the battle. The Confederates didn't have enough men to begin with. Fight as the men in filthy butternut would, the pocket shrank.

Tom stumbled back to the next line of trenches and foxholes. If he hadn't fallen back, the damnyankees would have flanked him out and killed him. Oh, maybe he could have surrendered, but maybe not, too. U.S. soldiers treated prisoners all right—when they took them. They didn't always. Sometimes they were too busy to be bothered. Then would-be POWs ended up dead. It wasn't anything the Confederates didn't do, just . . . part of the game.

Another weary, unshaven Confederate soldier—a corporal— crouched in a hole a few feet from Tom's. The noncom managed a smile. "Ain't this fun?" he said.

"As a matter of fact," Tom said, "no."

"Reckon we'll win the war anyways?" the corporal asked.

"I stopped worrying about it a while ago," Tom answered after a moment's thought. "Whatever happens in the rest of it, I think it'll happen without me." He popped up and snapped off a shot at what might have been motion. It stopped. Maybe he'd cut down a damnyankee. Maybe he'd fired at nothing.

"Freedom!" the corporal said. "That's what it's all about, ain't it? Fighting so the Confederate States can be what they want and do whatever they please?"

"I never thought about it much," said Tom, who avoided Jake Featherston's slogan whenever he could. "All I know is, I never liked the damnyankees. They gassed my brother and they bombed my sister, and I owe 'em plenty. I've paid back a lot, but I want to get some more."

Mortar rounds started falling. Tom pulled in his head like a turtle, and wished he had his own hard shell. Machine-gun bullets snarled overhead. Yes, this was going to be a big push. "Here they come!" the corporal yelled. "Freedom!" He fired—once, twice, three times.

Tom fired, too, at the Yankees coming from the front. But more were slipping around the right flank. He turned and got off a couple of quick shots at them. Then he had to slap a fresh clip into the Springfield. An automatic Tredegar took a twenty-round magazine, not a five-round box. Of course, you could empty it faster, too.

If he and the corporal didn't fall back again, they were dead. The men in green-gray would surround them and hunt them down. "I'll cover you," Tom said. The corporal ran for a hole deeper in the pocket. He made it, then waved for Tom to follow him.

Up. Run like hell. Hunch over to make yourself a smaller target. How many times had Tom done it before?

This was once too often. The bullet caught him in the back. He spun and toppled. His chin hit the snowy, rubble-strewn ground. His legs didn't want to work. He reached for the Springfield. One more shot. "Oh, no, you don't," a Yankee said. He fired from no more than ten feet away. And Tom Colleton didn't.

A wan early-February sun shone on the snowy, soot-streaked disaster that had been Pittsburgh. The last Confederate pocket on the North Side had surrendered, or was supposed to have surrendered, an hour earlier. Sergeant Michael Pound hadn't made it this far by being trusting. He had a round of HE in the barrel's cannon. If any of the men going into captivity felt like getting cute, he would do his damnedest to make sure they couldn't.

Lieutenant Griffiths stood up in the cupola. He had a much broader view of the devastation than Pound did. He said something in a language that wasn't English. "What was that, sir?" Pound asked.

The barrel commander laughed self-consciously. "Latin, Sergeant.

From Tacitus, the Roman historian. 'They make a desert and they call it peace.'"

"Oh." Pound weighed that. He approved of the sentiment, taken all in all. But he was not the sort of man to resist discordant details: "It's sure as hell a desert out there, sir, but we don't have peace."

"Not everywhere," Griffiths agreed. "But nobody's shooting at anybody in Pittsburgh anymore."

After another moment of judicious consideration, Michael Pound nodded. "Well, no, sir. Nobody's shooting right here." And if anybody in butternut tried shooting right here, Pound intended to shoot first.

"Here they come!" Griffiths squeaked in excitement.

Pound peered through the gunsight, his reticulated window on the world while he was in the barrel. The Confederates were a sorry-looking lot. Out they came, a long, draggling column of them, from the last few square blocks of Pittsburgh they'd held. Their breath smoked in the chilly air. None of them was smoking a cigarette, though. The U.S. infantrymen guarding them had no doubt already relieved them of their tobacco. *Lucky bastards,* Pound thought without rancor.

The Confederates were skinny and dirty and hairy. They'd been living mostly on hope the past few weeks. Pound had heard of raids with the sole aim of stealing U.S. rations. If that wasn't desperation, he didn't know what was. When you were empty, any food looked good.

A lot of the Confederates looked miserably cold. Their issue great-coats were thinner than U.S. models. Some of the men were all lumpy and bumpy, because they'd stuffed crumpled newspapers under the greatcoats for a little extra warmth. Others wore a variety of captured civilian coats on top of or instead of their greatcoats. They didn't have good winter boots, either. Those needed to be oversized, to allow for extra padding. They needed to be, but the Confederates' weren't.

"There they are," Lieutenant Griffiths said. "Jake Featherston's supermen. They don't look so tough, do they?"

"Sir, if they aren't tough, what have we been doing here since November?" Pound asked. Griffiths didn't answer.

A newsreel crew cranked away, filming the enemy soldiers' trudge into captivity. Maybe the Confederates would look like beaten men on the Bijou screen in St. Paul. Well, they *were* beaten men—now. If Michael Pound knew the way propagandists' minds worked, the newsreels would make the Confederates out to be weaklings and cowards. If they were, though, how had they fought their way into Pittsburgh in the first place? The newsreels wouldn't talk about that. And most people, unless Pound was wildly wrong, would never think to ask.

"I wonder where we'll go from here," Griffiths said.

"Wherever it is, I don't think it'll be as tough as this," Pound answered. *It had better not be, or there's no way in hell I'll live through it.*

How many Confederates were holed up in that pocket? More than he'd figured. Some of them helped wounded men along. Others carried stretchers. How many unburied dead lay in the pocket?

"Good thing we fought through the winter," Griffiths said, thinking along with him. "Can you imagine what this battlefield would be like in August?"

"Yes, sir, I can," Pound answered. That probably wasn't what the barrel commander expected to hear. But Pound had gone through the Great War. The stench of those fields soaked into your clothes, soaked into your lungs, soaked into your skin. You thought you'd never be rid of it. Pound still sometimes smelled it in his nightmares, so maybe he wasn't even now.

The young barrel commander sighed. "I sometimes forget you're on your second go-round."

"Wish I could, sir," Pound said. Was that strictly true? A lot of what he'd learned the last time around helped keep him alive here. Some of it helped keep Lieutenant Griffiths alive, too, whether Griffiths knew it or not. That wasn't the main thing on the gunner's mind, though. "Those damned foot soldiers will plunder the bodies. We won't get a crack at 'em, and we'll have to pay through the nose for good tobacco and whatever else they've got."

"Won't be much of that stuff left," Griffiths said. "They weren't quite eating their boots when they gave up, but they weren't far from it, either."

Michael Pound grunted, more in annoyance than anything else. The shavetail saw something he'd missed. It was supposed to be the other way around. Most of the time, it was—most of the time, but not always. "Well, sir, you're right," Pound said.

"You're a strange man, Sergeant," Griffiths said.

"Me, sir? How come?" Pound thought himself normal enough, or as normal as anyone could be after close to thirty years in the Army.

"Well, for starters, you just say, 'Well, you're right,'" Griffiths answered. "Most people would want to argue and fuss."

"What's the point?" Pound said, genuinely puzzled. "You *are* right.

I said something silly, and you called me on it. You should have. If I tried to tell you it wasn't silly, I'd just make a bigger fool of myself." Clinging to a position that was bound to fall seemed as senseless to him as Jake Featherston's failure to pull his troops out of Pittsburgh while he still had the chance. Being stubborn just cost you more in the long run.

At last, the stream of Confederates slowed up. There were bound to be stragglers heading west and south, hoping to link up with other units in butternut or simply to get away. But for them, though, Pennsylvania was clear of Confederates. And if half of what people said on the wireless was true, Confederate control in Ohio was crumbling, too.

"He's not going to win, not anymore," Pound said, thinking aloud.

"I'm sorry, Sergeant," Lieutenant Griffiths said. "What was that?"

"Jake Featherston," Pound answered. "He's not going to win the war. I don't see how he can now. Only question left is, can he still get a draw?"

"Nice to know you've got it all worked out," Griffiths said dryly. "Takes a lot of the strain off Philadelphia."

Pound laughed. "Good shot, sir. But I still think it's true."

"Well, I hope you're right," the barrel commander said. "With this damn war, though, you never can tell. They've done some awfully surprising things. And so have we, now. The move that pinched off Pittsburgh was as pretty as you'd ever want to see."

"General Morrell knows what's what," Pound said.

Griffiths started to rise to that, then caught himself. "No, wait. You were his personal gunner for a while. How did that stop?"

"He got wounded, sir," Michael Pound answered, remembering Morrell's weight on his back when he carried the armor commander general to cover after a Confederate sniper hit him. "They didn't think I deserved that long a vacation."

"And so now you're stuck with me," Griffiths said, his voice still dry.

"You've got a pretty good idea of what you're doing, sir." From Michael Pound, that was highest praise. By the barrel commander's quiet snort, he realized as much. Pound went on, "I hope we get a vacation after this. We're way, way overdue for rest and refit."

"I know," Griffiths said. "I haven't got any more say over that than you do, though. We'll go where they tell us to go and we'll do what they tell us to do."

"Anybody would think we were in the Army or something," Pound said.

"Wonder why that is." Lieutenant Griffiths grew intense. "Here come their big shots."

Pound peered through the gunsight. A few days earlier, he would have loved to put a couple of rounds of HE—or, better yet, shrapnel—on that group of eight or ten Confederate officers. All the men had three stars on the collar tabs of their greatcoats. All but two or three had those stars enclosed in wreaths, which meant they were generals, not colonels. They all looked to be in their late thirties or early forties, younger than most U.S. officers of similar grade.

And they all looked as if they'd just watched a bulldozer run over their kitten. "They really didn't think this could happen to them," Pound said. "They've been whipping us for a year and a half. They figured it would go on forever."

"Too damn bad," Griffiths said.

One of the U.S. soldiers guarding the high-ranking Confederate officers carried an automatic Tredegar rifle, another a captured C.S. submachine gun. Pound wondered whether the colonels and generals in butternut appreciated the compliment. He was inclined to doubt it.

"They get off easy," Griffiths said. "They stay in a camp away from the fighting for the rest of the war, and the U.S. government pays their salary. The rest of us still have to go on out here."

Some of the C.S. officers looked as if they would rather be dead. If they were smart, though, they wouldn't say anything about that to the men in green-gray who herded them along. The U.S. soldiers might oblige them.

"If we get a refit, where do you suppose we'll go next?" Pound asked.

Lieutenant Griffiths ducked down into the turret to favor him with a wry grin. "I said that before, Sergeant. I thought you'd have a better idea than I did."

"Not me, not now." Pound shook his head. "General Morrell would tell me what was up sometimes. Far as everybody else is concerned, I'm just a damn noncom." He spoke without heat.

"Can't imagine why that would be," Griffiths said, and Pound chuckled. The young lieutenant went on, "Well, all I can tell you is, we'll go wherever they need us most once we get our refit—if we get our refit."

"Sounds about right." Pound pictured a map. He pictured what was likely to happen over the next few weeks. "Virginia or Ohio," he said. "Whichever heats up fastest, I guess."

"I wouldn't bet against either one of them," Lieutenant Griffiths said. "I hope it's Ohio, to tell you the truth."

"Me, too—we have a better chance of hurting them bad there, I think," Pound said. "But wherever it is, by God, we'll get the job done."

About the Author

HARRY TURTLEDOVE is a Hugo Award–winning and critically acclaimed writer of science fiction, fantasy, and alternate history. His novels include *The Guns of the South; How Few Remain* (winner of the Sidewise Award for Best Novel); the Great War epics *American Front, Walk in Hell,* and *Breakthroughs;* the World War series: *In the Balance, Tilting the Balance, Upsetting the Balance,* and *Striking the Balance;* the Colonization books: *Second Contact, Down to Earth,* and *Aftershocks;* the American Empire novels *Blood & Iron, The Center Cannot Hold,* and *Victorious Opposition; Settling Accounts: Return Engagement; Homeward Bound; Ruled Britannia* (also a Sidewise winner), and many others. He is married to fellow novelist Laura Frankos. They have three daughters: Alison, Rachel, and Rebecca.

About the Type

This book was set in Sabon, a typeface designed by the well-known German typographer Jan Tschichold (1902–74). Sabon's design is based on the original letterforms of Claude Garamond and was created specifically to be used for three sources: foundry type for hand composition, Linotype, and Monotype. Tschichold named his typeface for the famous Frankfurt typefounder Jacques Sabon, who died in 1580.